Saint Francis of Assisi

THE *Passionate Troubadour*

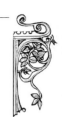

Cross of San Damiano

THE *Passionate Troubadour*

THE *Passionate Troubadour*

A Medieval Novel about

FRANCIS OF ASSISI
by
EDWARD HAYS

Forest of Peace
from Ave Maria Press, Inc.
Notre Dame, IN
www.avemariapress.com

www.forestofpeace.com

International Standard Book Number: 0-939516-69-1

Cover and interior art by Edward M. Hays

Cover and text design by Katherine Robinson Coleman

Printed and bound in the United States of America.

Library of Congress Cataloging-in-Publication Data

Hays, Edward M.
  The passionate troubadour : a medieval novel about Francis of Assisi / Edward Hays.
     p. cm.
  ISBN 0-939516-69-1 (pbk.)
  1. Francis, of Assisi, Saint, 1182-1226—Fiction. 2. Italy—History—476-1268—Fiction. 3. Christian saints—Fiction. 4. Assisi (Italy)—Fiction. I. Title.
PS3558.A867P37 2004
813'.54—dc22
                                            2004008818

Introduction

"If the Vatican Council needed a patron saint,
Francis of Assisi would be the one chosen."

CATHERINE DE HUECK DOHERTY

*C*atherine Doherty, a holy laywoman of the twentieth century who was the founder of Madonna House Lay Community in Combermere, Canada, called Francis of Assisi an authentic inspiration for our age. She wrote, "He would not allow us to rationalize away the Gospel. He would cut through all the red tape, all hypocrisy, all verbiage, whatever its name, and lead directly to the heart of the master."

The famous Francesco of Assisi, whom she praised for his radical love, today has too often been relegated to being the serene patron saint of birdbaths rather than the patron of extremist lovers. Francesco is also the patron saint of the laity, those nonclerical, nonprofessed religious lovers of God, whose baptismal priesthood, dignity, and vocation to live the gospel in their daily world was proclaimed by the Second Vatican Council.

The thirteenth century stories of Francesco and Clare of Assisi continue in this twenty-first century to be magnetically enchanting and challenging, for those who long to live the gospel radically. Imagine the religious and social earthquake-like impact on the world if only a handful of men and women could live with such great love and joy. On his deathbed, Vladimir Lenin, the architect of the Russian Revolution to liberate the poor, lamented to a former classmate, who was a Hungarian priest, his sadness over the bloody massacres of the Revolution. Lenin said, "To save our Russia, what we needed (but it is

too late now) was ten Francises of Assisi. Ten Francises of Assisi, and we should have saved Russia."

The author's intention here is not to create *another* story to be added to the already oversaturated library of books about Francis. Rather, it is to arouse, even if in a few of his readers' hearts, the spark of fiery desire. Saints continue to possess the enchanting power to inspire us today and to be instigators of personal revolutions. Francis is a dynamic example of one who challenges us to fulfill our God-given destinies by daring to live out fully our personal uniqueness. He throws down the gauntlet at our feet to allow the Spirit to do in us what that Sacred Muse and Force did in him. While customarily seen as a patron saint of poverty, Assisi's little man in rags is more the patron of passion. He is a holy pyromaniac, eager to set our hearts madly ablaze with love for God, Christ, all humanity, and all creation.

"Future Christianity is generating itself from the lives of those who have fled to the margins." This quote by the contemporary English television art critic, Sister Wendy Beckett, speaks to the secondary purpose of this book. The author's wish is that this story of Francesco the Passionate Troubadour will encourage those holy seekers living on the margins of society and the church. They are the nameless ones quietly involved in the great renaissance of spirituality that was birthed on the threshold of a new millennium during the last thirty-some years of the twentieth century.

This book was written as well for those anonymous explorers of inner space, the attic experimenters in the sacred chemistry of transfiguration who are never invited to speak at prestigious conferences or lecture to theological institutes. May this story of the conversion and transformation of Francis of Assisi, truly a holy man of the margins, encourage and confirm them to become living generators of the Spirit's electric energy to illuminate a future Christianity. Like Francis, their influences will also touch those of other religions to live in joy and hope in an inclusive, global spirituality.

"Piss on the Pope!" Pietro Bernadone bellowed out like an angry bull. "And piss on Duke Conrad of Assisi!" Turning around in his saddle and pointing to the eastern horizon with a gloved hand, he added, "Gentlemen, it's sunrise. A brand new day is dawning. But alas, for the Church and for the nobility, the sun only rises on *yesterday!*" Pietro Bernadone, the master of the Cloth Guild of Assisi had a barrel-like chest and stood a head-and-a-half taller than the other cloth merchants traveling to France to attend the Great Fair at Chambery.

"Pietro, lower your voice lest our servants and apprentices hear you speaking so disrespectfully of the Holy Father and our Lord Duke," moaned white-haired Filippo Villani, the oldest of the merchants, who nervously glanced back toward the men following them.

"Filippo, my dear old friend, is not travel educational? Let them hear—and learn. Perhaps on this adventure they'll have their young eyes opened to reality as well as to all the wonderful possibilities of this new thirteenth century."

"Pietro, you're always in a hurry! This is only the beginning of May in the year of our Lord 1197. The thirteenth century is still. . . ."

"Congratulations!" Pietro interrupted him. "Comrades, let us applaud our wise elder and brother merchant Filippo, for he knows what time it is! That puts him centuries ahead of the Pope in Rome and his Vatican cronies. They and their black hordes of priests continue to connive to keep us prisoners of the past. The world is not the Mass, endlessly unchanging—and so always boringly the same! An earthquake is rumbling across all of Europe—do you feel it? It's like the tremors we've felt back in Umbria, only this one is so powerful that it

will bring down all the old social structures, crumbling to the ground our long-outdated feudal system."

When several of the merchants chuckled in approval, Pietro felt encouraged. So, like an uncorked bottle, he gushed forth, "Everywhere the people are on the move. Villagers are abandoning their small towns. Peasants by the thousands are hungering for a better life; they're leaving the farms for the cities. Are not travelers arriving at our city gates daily, carrying tales of new inventions? They've brought new fabrics, from fine silk to the new cloth they call cotton. The old days of barter as the form of exchange are gone! The new master of the marketplace is money!" Dropping his reins into his saddle, Pietro clapped his hands loudly. "Money! Money! That silver magician, my dear brother guild members, is rapidly transforming us merchants into the new nobility. Let those old titled nobles, along with the Pope and his holy henchmen, try their damnedest, but I assure you, they will never reverse the great upheaval of this new age and this new century bursting upon us, even if, my dear Filippo, this is only early May of 1197."

Pietro spoke to the eyes, not just to the ears of those traveling on the road. He was dressed like a prince: bedecked in a cloak of deep forest-green wool with a board collar of Russian fur, boots of the finest Florentine leather, and riding gloves that covered his ring-adorned fingers. Master Bernadone prided himself on being a stunning icon of the new wealthy merchant class.

The small caravan of merchants had departed from the base camp before sunrise and was proceeding westward toward France along what had once been the old, narrow Roman military road. At least a thousand years ago the road had been carved out of the stone ledges of the rugged Alpine mountains that tumbled down end over end into the surging surf of the Mediterranean Sea. Usually confined to the walled city of Assisi, these merchants were now intoxicated by the adventure of travel as they inhaled this new spring day's fresh morning air saturated with the salty aromas of fish and sea. The hoofs of their horses resounded off the ancient road, blending with the melody of birdsongs welcoming the dawn, accompanied by the rhythmic chorus of chanting waves crashing loudly against the rocks far below.

Directly behind the senior merchants rode four of their sons, the youngest being Francesco Giovanni Bernadone, the fifteen-year-old son of Pietro. Unlike his father, he was short and slight of stature, and the olive complexion of his oval face was crowned with ringlets of

ebony black hair. While not impressive in his physical stature, he possessed large brown eyes of extraordinary beauty. On this fresh early May morning Francesco was devouring the previously uncharted sights of this grand adventure. This was his first time accompanying his father outside the gates of Assisi, and here he was on his way to one of the greatest fairs in France! Only the year before, on his fourteenth birthday, he had been formally inducted into the Guild of Cloth Merchants—and he had just begun to shave!

"Gentlemen," Pietro announced, "chastise your sons, for as the Bible teaches, 'The father who loves his son chastises him often, that he may be his joy when he grows up.'"

"Your favorite quotation, Pietro," chimed in Albertino Compagni. "And to it the holy book adds, 'At his father's death, he will not seem dead, since he leaves after him one like himself.'"

"Ah, the ancient wisdom of how to make men out of boys," added Guittone d'Acsoli. "'Bend him to the yoke when he is young; thrash his sides while he is still small.' We men know how that has worked wonders with our sons."

Leonardo, the twenty-year-old son of Guittone, tilted his head, throwing a knowing glance toward his fellow rider, Cino, Compagni's son, who was Leonardo's senior by only a year. Francesco's buttocks ached, but the source of his discomfort wasn't the stiff saddle; it was the memory of his entrance into the world of men. His father would thrash his young backside, always repeating the same words, "The father who loves his son chastises him often."

"Let's see," he thought, "I couldn't have been twelve years old when I first began working in my father's shop. I remember the day I was sent on an errand to deliver some cloth to a customer and on my way home stopped to play a game with some friends. When I finally returned to the shop, my father grabbed me by the arm, led me to the rear of the shop and thrashed me without mercy with his thick leather belt." Francesco thought he could still feel that painful lesson and the critically important one that followed it—never to cry or whimper when you experience pain. "Men do not cry, Son. Repeat after me: Men do not cry." Ever since, those four words that have defined manhood for many had echoed in his mind.

"Discipline, gentlemen," Pietro continued, rupturing his son's thoughts, "is the primary tool by which men are made out of boys. It

 has always been the best instrument; it remains so today, and it will always be the great teacher of manhood."

"So, Pietro," chided the aged Filippo, "are we to understand that you are not eager to see *all* of our old ways abandoned by the arrival of your new century?"

"Ah, yes, my friend," the Master of the Cloth Guild said after a long pause. "Ways change, but traditions are what made us who we are. Traditions are essential, especially in an age of great change."

As the merchants rode in silence, pondering the wisdom of those last words, Francesco was riding through a land of memories, recalling his boyhood in Umbria. He reflected on how he, like almost all boys in his native Italy, from his birth until he was placed under the exclusive authority of his father, had been in his mother's care. Mothers were the primary teachers and caregivers in Italy, and they delighted in lavishing love and affection upon their sons. Some boys, Francesco had heard, were nursed at their mothers' breast for as long as three years. He mused on how he was one of the fortunate few who after age seven or eight had the opportunity to spend part of the day being instructed in basic studies by the priests. Yet even in this schooling period, he continued to associate primarily with his mother and with other women and girls. He recalled once overhearing a merchant say, "An Italian boy never leaves home." While the other men had laughed in agreement, he had wondered what it meant. Ah, but how his life had changed when he reached the age of twelve. Then his father was in complete charge of him—just as his friends were under the wings of their fathers. From that day onward he had begun to fear his father's wrath and to crave his love and affection.

He looked ahead to where his father was riding, and his heart ached to hear him say, "Francesco, I love you." Perhaps, he thought, when he was truly a man he would not have this great hunger for his father's approval, but when would that happen? Wandering through memory land, he recalled the time when he was walking with his father and accidentally tripped over a stone. He fell to the street, badly bruising his knee. As he cried out from the pain, his father grabbed him by the arm and jerked him to his feet, saying, "Stop that whimpering. When are you going to grow up and be a man?" Francesco was fifteen now, but not nearly as tall as his father. Moreover, he was the same height and weight as he was a year ago. "O God," he thought to himself, "I hope I haven't stopped growing." At the same time as he formed this

prayer, his father's voice echoed in his heart like the chanting of monks, "When, when, when are you going to grow up?" It was like a tug of war inside Francesco: On one end of the rope was his passionate longing to be a man—strong, rough and tough, capable of fighting, and beating, others. On the other end, he felt pulled back into the pampered, gentle, always loving world of his mother and the other women—that land where competition is unknown, where play and fantasy are the law.

He knew his father loved him, even if he had never said so in words. Didn't his mother tell him—at least he thought she once did—that Pietro by his nature wasn't a man who easily expressed affections. "Did he not express his love by attiring me in the most expensive of clothes? The clothes my father provided were more costly than those worn by other merchants' sons, and even sons of noblemen were not dressed as splendidly as I." Francesco glanced down and gently stroked the rich material of his opulent tunic. It was his favorite color, scarlet, and had slits in the sleeves that revealed folds of sky-blue fabric. The tunic was covered by a rich chestnut-brown cloak fastened with an ornate silver clasp. Like the other merchants, he wore a stylish broad-brimmed riding hat, and on his belt he wore a sword, which was not only dashing but by imperial law was also required raiment for all traveling merchants. There was no cold wind blowing that May morning, yet the magnificently attired Francesco shivered, and he knew why: Despite being richly dressed, he felt naked of his father's warm approval, unadorned by lavish affection.

He turned in his saddle and looked behind him at those on foot: the merchants' young apprentices, the servants, and the muleteers, whose pack mules would carry back to Assisi the bundles of new cloth and other goods purchased at the fair. Escorting their convoy were mounted armed guards, two of which rode in front of Pietro and the other merchants to ward off beggars and to clear a path for their caravan along the crowded highway. Francesco admired the sturdy build of these guards. Their physical appearance spoke infallibly of their aptness as mercenaries who offered their services in the endless feuds and small wars between Italian city-states. They were tough, muscular men, some missing fingers, an ear, or an eye, all of them wearing the ugly scars of vicious hand-to-hand combat. As he turned forward in the saddle, he felt himself transported from this common merchant's caravan bound for the Great Fair at Chambery to riding in the company of crusader knights dressed in shining armor on their way

to rescue the Holy City of Jerusalem from the infidels. As the knights traveled along a dusty Oriental desert road, the desert wind suddenly surged, snapping with a crack the crusaders' lily-white flag emblazoned with a large red cross. . . .

"Stop the caravan!" Pietro Bernadone suddenly exclaimed as they came to a turn in the road. "Gentlemen, let us pause to pray at this wayside shrine dedicated to the Three Wise Men." As the merchants, who remained seated in their saddles, turned toward the small stone roadside shrine, their apprentices and the muleteers circled the shrine's faded fresco painting of the three Magi.

"Saints Melchior, Caspar, and Balthasar," prayed Pietro, "you three holy kings of the Orient, patron saints of travelers, protect us from sickness and harm, and bless us richly with prosperity."

"Amen," everyone shouted.

"And may this holy relic of Saint Leonard," Pietro continued, holding high above his head a small oblong silver relic case, "the patron saint protector against attacks by highway robbers, safeguard and protect us and our goods. May the divine power of this holy relic of good Saint Leonard bring all of us safely home again."

"Amen," everyone shouted even louder as they hastily traced the sign of the cross upon themselves.

Francesco mused on how his father never traveled anywhere without carrying with him that relic bone from St. Leonard's body. Francesco's mother, Pica, who loved the stories of saints, had taught him about this holy French hermit of long ago who was the patron protector of travelers and also the patron saint of prisoners of war. She told him stories of how after their release from the infidel prisons, the victorious returning crusader knights had come to St. Leonard's shrine to give thanks to him for obtaining their freedom. "Maybe," he thought, "someday I will also do that."

As he lowered his hand from his right shoulder after completing the sign of the cross, Francesco touched the spot on his chest where a protective amulet was pinned to cover his heart. A flood of emotions filled him as he returned to a scene on the morning of his departure, shortly before the merchants had departed on their expedition. His mother had sewn onto to his new cotton inner tunic a cloth packet containing a cross made from a yellowed blessed palm. He recalled how beautiful she looked to him as she stitched the fine seams with great care. Unlike the other women in Assisi, his mother was French. She had

a more refined and noble air, and she was as lovely as she was warm and gracious. Her deep blue eyes were accented by flowing chestnut-colored hair. She sang like a songbird, and her delicately fresh voice and graceful bearing were eternally etched on Francesco's soul. To him she would always be the gorgeous Signora Lady Pica.

When his mother had finished sewing the last stitch securing the packet to his tunic, she embraced him so warmly that he could inhale the sensual scent of her soul as well as the fragrance of her body. Holding him close, she prayed, "Dearest Giovanni, my beloved son, may this blessed palm cross protect you from all evil, guarding you day and night from the wiles of the devil and his evil demon spirits." Then placing her hand firmly on the amulet, she added, "and may this holy palm cross keep you safe from all sin."

Francesco reflected on how the sweetness of that moment was squelched by a call from the street: "Hurry up, Francesco! We are ready to depart—everyone is waiting on you. What's keeping you?" His father's voice came thundering through the narrow opened doorway, seeming to amplify the force of the command. Francesco quickly slipped on his outer tunic and riding cloak, as his mother kissed him good-bye and traced the sign of the cross on his forehead. He could still feel the touch of her fingers when she took his hand in hers, and could still sense the "do not leave" plea when her eyes met his.

"Francesco, the *men* are waiting!" He still felt the razor-sharp edge of that verbal arrow hissing through the air, aimed for his heart, "all the *men,* the *men,* the *men,* are waiting." As it plunged deep into its destination, Francesco quickly turned and walked away, forcing himself not to glance back at his mother as he marched out the door of his home to begin this first great adventure of his manhood.

Now, as his fingers traced the outline of the amulet sewn into his inner cotton tunic, the very thought of that new cloth catapulted him back to his father riding up ahead of him. Cotton was not only a brand-new but also a very expensive cloth, and his excessively generous father had given him this so soft-to-the-skin cotton tunic as well as all his other fine clothes. Surely, didn't all of this loudly assert that his father loved him? Were not such lavish gifts signs of his love? Yet he longed for his father to love him as his mother did. That very thought again transported him back to the hilltop city of Assisi and his mother Pica.

He knew that she had been born in the district of Provence, in southwest France, and that his father had met her years ago when on a

journey to a French fair. They had quickly fallen in love and married, and with great pride Pietro brought her back to Assisi. In his mind Francesco again pictured her in detail: She was about his height, fair of complexion, with beautiful long brown hair. He could see her walking with dignity and grace when as a boy he would accompany her to daily Mass. He could picture her teaching him his prayers as a small child and telling him spellbinding stories of the lives of the saints. From what seemed an inexhaustible storehouse of stories, she would hold him enthralled with tales of diabolic possessions of people, stories of witches and sorcerers who had sold their souls to vile demons, and accounts of the various dark ways one could be cursed by the evil eye. She had been the spirit guide escorting him into a world where at every turn there were angels or demons, protecting saints, or diabolically evil spirits, telling him that these spirits were the source of all kinds of afflictions— from madness, to pestilence, to rotting teeth. "Giovanni," he could hear her say, "cross yourself whenever you feel the evil spirits are near, for the holy cross will banish those demons of hell."

Francesco smiled to himself at how she always called him Giovanni—that, indeed, was the name she had given him at his baptism. Because he was born while his father was away from Assisi on a buying trip in France, his dear mother had him baptized before his father's return, fearful lest he die in original sin. And as he was baptized, she told the priest to name him Giovanni. Upon his return, Pietro immediately renamed him Francesco, for France, which he loved so much, boasting that it was the most charming and exciting land in the entire world.

"Mother, what is hell?" Francesco recalled asking, as in his imagination he became part of a vivid fresco of a morning when he was about seven years old after he and his mother had returned home from attending Mass together. He could even now feel his little feet resting on the highest rung of a stool as he sat in the kitchen. He could practically hear the pasta bubbling away in the hissing hot water in the iron pot on the stove. His nose was pleasantly assaulted by the mix of the aromatic smoke of wood burning in the stove and the zesty smell of the Parmesan goat cheese that his mother was grating for the pasta. As his young nostrils inhaled the ambience of his mother's kitchen, he listened to her response.

"Hell is horrible, Giovanni"—his mother always called him by his baptismal name whenever his father was not at home. "It's that ghastly

place of torment deep down in the bowels of the earth where God casts all sinners."

"For how long?"

"Forever, Giovanni! Hell is never-ending punishment. So we must never commit a sin; we must always be good, say our prayers, and never offend God."

"But Mother, what makes hell so horrible?"

"Giovanni, come here and I'll show you."

He climbed down carefully from the stool as she was opening the stove to reveal its blazing belly of raging red and yellow flames.

"Come over here, my son." Then, taking his little hand, she moved it close to the fire, saying, "My beloved son, do you feel the searing heat of that fire?"

"Yes, Mother," he said in a shaking voice.

"Hell is fire! Unlike our kitchen stove, the roaring, searing flames in hell never die out. Those scorching fires of damnation never cease, never ever. Yet by a miracle they never consume the flesh of the poor sinners being punished in them. O, my beloved Giovanni, you must never, ever commit a sin. Promise me you will never sin! Promise me that you will always be a good boy and never fail to keep all of God's commandments and all the laws of Holy Mother Church. Promise me."

"I promise I will, Mother. I promise you. I'll always be a good boy."

"Giovanni, you are good. You are a very good boy. How could any mother not be proud of such a good boy as you, so gentle and caring, so loving. Yes, perhaps someday you might become a priest! Wouldn't that be wonderful? Think of it, my son; how beautiful it would be if you were a priest, for then every day you could say holy Mass and pray for me. And by all your prayers and Masses, my son, you could release your poor mother from the terrible pains of purgatory. I cannot think of anything better for you to become when you grow up than to be a holy priest of God. Of course, only if that is God's holy will for you."

"Caravan, forward!" The shout of his father shattered that childhood memory, and Francesco found himself seated in his saddle in front of the small roadside shrine. While it seemed to Francesco that his childhood recollection had lasted a long time, it actually had been less than the passage of a few grains of sand in an hourglass. As the muleteers began prodding the caravan forward, he gazed back at the roadside shrine with its chipped, fading fresco of the three holy Magi

of Epiphany. Mounted on their horses and dressed as kings, they were pointing toward a blazing star in the East. "The East!" he thought. "Yes, the Orient, the mystic Orient—that's where I wish some holy star were leading me."

Francesco glanced up at the sun that by now had journeyed toward the peak of the sky. The old Roman road that had wandered northward away from the seacoast was now a broad and noisy river of humanity. Flowing along it in both directions was a living mural of medieval society: wealthy merchant travelers; peddlers hawking their goods to other travelers; elegantly attired noble families with their armed escorts; farmers with their barking dogs herding cows, pigs and sheep to market; black-cassocked priests accompanying their brilliantly dressed bishops on their way to Rome; ragged, dirty peasants off in search of a better life; black-hooded monks on their way to a neighboring abbey; blind and lame beggars loudly shouting for alms over the songs of pious bands of pilgrims tramping on pilgrimage to some shrine.

So vivid was Francesco's imagination that he now heard none of the clamor, for once again he was envisioning himself as a crusader knight victoriously riding toward the Holy City of Jerusalem. The hot, dry desert wind was briskly flapping Francesco's imaginary brightly colored banners as his heart pounded excitedly in rhythm with the rolling beat of marching drums and the piercing blare of war trumpets. Behind him, the young merchant apprentices had been magically transformed into rugged foot soldiers, bold men-at-arms eagerly marching behind him into battle against the despised infidels. Gripping the handle of his sword, he envisioned himself single-handedly slashing his way through hordes of fierce Muslim enemies to liberate the Savior's Holy Sepulcher. As a bold knight warrior, he would be able to prove his manhood—a thought that reminded him of how he had recently begun to feel his manhood rising in his groin. This new and different physical sensation was both strangely fascinating and excitingly pleasurable, yet it was equally disturbing, for he worried that if it was pleasurable it might also be sinful.

"Changes, Gentlemen! Changes unlike anything any of one of us has ever seen before are even now at our very doorstep." His father's voice had again jerked him back into reality. "Indeed, in years past, merchants like ourselves were forced to carry heavy bags of silver with which to purchase their new cloth at the fairs. When we were youths—

no older than the age of our sons who accompany us today—we can recall how our fathers spent sleepless nights and fearful days worrying about being attacked by robbers. Now, we have our *letters of exchange!*" He held up a scroll tied with a red cord and waved it triumphantly back and forth. "These letters allow us to engage in broader—yes, truly international—trade. We can exchange these mandates from our bank in Florence as payment for any cloth we desire to purchase at the fair in Chambery—but to robbers they are worthless! Nor do we have need of those greedy moneychangers, for these new *letters of exchange* are all we need to conduct our business with any French, English, German or Flemish merchants. Absolutely marvelous, isn't it?"

"Indeed, it is as you say, Pietro. You speak truly," affirmed Guittone d'Acsoli. "Just as my son is doing today, as a youth I accompanied my father on a trip to a French fair to purchase cloth. I recall his great fear of being robbed of his money. Yes, Pietro, this commercial upheaval already begun that will radically change our lives, those of our sons, and even the future of all Christendom."

"I hope they'll not change our lives too much," Filippo spoke softly. "I'm getting too old for change. I hate to see the good old ways disappear. The old ways have been tested and found worthy, but, ah, these new. . . ."

"Progress, my good Filippo," Pietro declared with all the fervor of a preacher, "like growth in all of nature, requires change. Boys do not become men without changing; is that not right? The church and the nobility, on the other hand, do not want progress and, indeed, react violently against any change, treating it like the plague." Reaching inside his traveling wallet, which hung from his belt, he withdrew a small leather folder. "And now I have one of these—perhaps the great symbol of this wondrous new era—a Florentine bank account!"

"A bank account," the others echoed from one to another, their words gilded in admiration that one of their fellow merchants from Assisi would have such a status symbol. Perhaps the great merchants in Rome or Florence might have a bank account, but a cloth merchant of Assisi?

"I can use this to borrow any monies I might need in advance for my various transactions. After I have completed my sales, I can pay back my loans. And, if I wish, I can also lend out my money to make money, charging an interest rate just as my bank does."

"But Pietro, Holy Mother Church forbids the lending money at interest. It is sinful—the sin of usury!" moaned old Filippo, shaking his head.

"Dear Filippo, the bankers of Venice and Florence have found small loopholes in Holy Mother's sturdy sin-wall, allowing them to slip through the Church's laws. They consider it only as profit on an investment, a return they ultimately give back to depositors. Does not God permit profit on an investment? As for the Church, let her mind her own business, which is saving souls and preaching about that other world, the kingdom of heaven. The kingdom of earth is our responsibility! Yes, and the Church should keep her long, pious nose out of our business, which," he laughed, "*is* business! And, Brothers of the Guild, business, as I have said before, is rapidly changing and is carrying with it all of society, as our new world explodes outward with countless new and previously unseen things."

"Duke Conrad says," Filippo answered, "that the Holy Bible teaches, 'What is, will be. There is nothing new under the sun.' Isn't the Duke right? I mean, since God has declared there is nothing new under the sun, then how can. . . ?"

"Filippo, your eyes have grown old with age, but even you can see better than Duke Conrad, for although he's years younger than you, he is blind! As for the Bible, God says many things that I find impossible to believe; so let Duke Conrad quote from the Bible or even the Qur'an. . . ."

Even over the noise rising from the crowded highway, a gasp of shock could be heard from Filippo and the others at Pietro's boldness.

"Gentlemen, very soon the great authority and wealth of the Duke and that of the other nobles will shrink faster than open space on this crowded road." Spurring his horse forward, he continued, "Forget about Duke Conrad. We merchants will replace him as the new nobility in the new world that is being birthed this very day. We already eat and dress better than many nobles, and our homes are more comfortable than those dreary stone castles of the nobility. Indeed, I assure you, Gentlemen of the Cloth, we merchants will soon be the new nobility, an aristocracy determined not by bloodlines but by the bottom lines of our bank accounts! Oh, we may lack their noble blood and their divinely high-sounding aristocratic titles. And even if they and the Church considered our parents to have been *minores*, insignificant lowly people, we are the burgeoning superior class of

tomorrow's society! I solemnly assure you, some day we will surpass even the Church and the nobility in wealth and power."

"Pope Pietro II, the infallible Bernadone, has spoken, "joked the portly Albertino Compagni. "As Augustine said, *'Roma locuta est; causa finita est*—Rome has spoken; the case is closed'!"

Francesco smiled broadly at Albertino's humorous comparison of his father to the Pope. Yet despite the edge of satire in Albertino's quip, it was with enormous respect that Francesco gazed up ahead at his father, who was indeed dressed more magnificently than many a nobleman. He took pride that his father was not only a physically strong man, but quite likely the most powerful man among Assisi's various merchant guilds. Whenever his father spoke, regardless of the subject, he always did so with energetic conviction and almost papal authority. He was not merely clever, he was highly creative at making money, having personally built up his father's small shop into one of the most prosperous cloth businesses in all of Umbria. As Francesco stroked his beautiful riding cloak, he once again beamed with gratification at all the fashionable clothing his father had given him, along with whatever money he needed to entertain his friends.

"Francesco, my son!" Pietro's penetrating voice smashed the silky spiderweb of his thoughts. "Come up here and ride with me, for we are about to cross over into the country for which you were named."

Digging his heels into his mount, Francesco spurred his horse forward, eager to ride alongside his father. As he rode up close, his father leaned over from his saddle and placed a large, muscular arm around his son's shoulders. His father's strong embrace felt wonderful: It was what he had long dreamed of, a sign in front of the other men of his father's love and approval, an acknowledgment of his manhood.

"My son, as you and all these fine gentlemen know, you were born while I was away on business in France. Your good and pious mother, fearful that you might die a heathen before I had returned, had you baptized at once. She instructed the priest to name you Giovanni. Alas, such an ordinary name: In Italy I'd wager there are thousands of men named Giovanni. It was intolerable for my son to have such a common name, so I renamed you Francesco, for this wondrous land of France that you see up ahead of us!"

"I'm so glad you did, Father. No one else I know has my name. It makes me feel unique and special."

 "Francesco, you are very special!" With his gloved left hand he made a broad sweeping arc across the green timbered landscape of France. "You were named for this colorful country of beautiful women and exquisite music, of the finest wines and enchanting poetry, of awe-inspiring landscapes and the soul-stirring songs of the troubadours. Unlike our homeland of Italy, this country of France does not fear to think new thoughts, to live in fresh, novel ways and to experiment with whatever is original and enterprising." Then, speaking loud enough to ensure that everyone in the caravan could hear, Pietro went on: "And why is this so, men of Assisi? Is it not because she is far enough away from Rome to be able to breathe the fresh air of freedom?" Spurred on by their laughter, the patriarch continued, "Italy needs more French blood to give her life. My son, your father wishes that you would become as French as your first name, yet as robustly virile as our Italian wines and as Umbrian-clever as the distinguished ancestors of your Bernadone family. Ah, if you could do that, what a gift that would be to me, to our beloved Assisi, and, who knows, Son, someday perhaps even to those beyond the borders of Umbria. Eh?"

Francesco's mind raced wildly at his words, "beyond the borders of Umbria"! How could that ever be possible, he thought. Yet the idea of traveling beyond the tall brown stone walls of Assisi, out beyond the rolling fields of yellow sunflowers and groves of green olive trees on the slopes below her—ah, yes, that was an intoxicating idea.

"To prepare you, Francesco, to take my place and someday become the wealthiest merchant in Umbria, I have sent you to school with the priests at our own San Giorgio's. I told them to teach you all you would need to know to become Assisi's most outstanding merchant: some Latin, it being the universal language; some arithmetic to be able to manage our family business; some geography to know the trade routes in our expanding world . . . but as little religion as possible," he added with a laugh. "One of the priests there spoke French, and while your mother had begun teaching you French, I instructed him to teach you how to speak the language properly so as to buy and sell in France when you come here to trade for cloth. . . ." Then, with a broad, sensual grin, he added, ". . . and also so you could make love to women in the language of the angels."

After pausing for his companion merchants' laughter, he continued, "The priests reported that you were no great scholar, but I took pride when they said that you were at the head of your class in the

skill of memorizing. I'm proud of you, Son, but don't waste that skill of memory to rattle off the Psalms or verses of pious scripture. Instead, use it to remember our places of business, the names of other merchants and of our customers. People are impressed when you remember their names. Don't forget that."

"Thank you, Father. I already know by heart the words and melodies of many songs as well as some poetry, but I promise I will begin at once to commit to memory the names of each one of our customers."

As his father firmly gripped his son's shoulder with affection, Francesco's face sparkled like a sunrise, and he savored the rare gift of being able to accompany his father on this journey. He felt his heart swelling with pride that now, at long last, he was considered man enough to travel this far away from Assisi with his father on a dangerous trip to France. He had just once before traveled beyond the sight of Assisi, a year ago, shortly after he turned fourteen. He had journeyed with his best friend, Emiliano Giacosa, to Montepulciano in neighboring Tuscany. Emiliano's father, Signore Giacosa, was the main wine merchant of Assisi, and for the first time was taking his young son along on a journey to purchase some of Tuscany's great wines. Emiliano had pleaded with his father to allow Francesco, who was the same age as he, to accompany them, and the two fathers readily agreed.

"Soon, my beloved Son," again, the familiar voice abruptly shattered the fragile jug containing Francesco's memories of his trip with Emiliano to Tuscany, "you'll soon see my purpose in having you learn French. Someday you will be the master of our family cloth business, and having French as your second tongue will give you great advantage in dealing with other merchants at the Great Fair of Chambery and the other French fairs."

Habitually concerned about his shortness of stature, Francesco felt he now had grown a full foot taller as he rode proudly beside his father. He mused that if only Emiliano could be riding alongside him as they went to Chambery, it would be perfect. Of all his friends back in Assisi, Emiliano was his *caro mio*, his dear friend, with whom he had shared his secret thoughts and dreams. The tumbling, green timbered landscape of France rinsed in the clear midday sunlight faded from his view as his imagination winged him back to the hilltop Tuscany village of Montepulciano. He could almost run his fingers along one particular memory, as if it had been chiseled in stone. He could clearly visualize

the night in Montepulciano when they had slept together in a hayloft over the stable that sheltered Signore Giacosa's horses and mules. The two boys had eagerly volunteered to sleep in the hayloft to guard the horses and pack mules. Emiliano's father smiled as he agreed to their brave offer, fully aware that his horses and mules were in no danger of being stolen. He understood that his son and his son's young friend were away from their homes and parents for the first time and so wanted the adventure of a night alone in the barn loft.

Francesco could still inhale the dusty smell of the dry hay that was their bed that night, as well as the musty odor of the aged stone and wood of the barn and the heady blend of animal manure and the sweat of the mules and horses. The boys had stayed awake most of the night talking, the only light in the blackened loft coming from the silver shafts of blue moonlight cutting slashes through the cracks in the old roof.

"Do you think we should say our night prayers?" asked Francesco.

"You mean the ones that the priests at school taught us to pray—their night prayers of compline?" asked Emiliano. "'Be watchful! For your adversary the devil, like a roaring lion, goes about seeking someone to devour. . . .'"

"Growl, growl," Francesco howled humorously.

"Like you, my friend," Emiliano continued, "I've never met any lions in my bed. Shall you or I say the rest of prayer, the part about the ghostly foe?"

Let me, I know it by heart:

'From all ill dreams defend our eyes,

from nightly fears and fantasies.

Tread under foot our ghostly foe,

that no pollution we may know.'

After a brief pause, Francesco mused, "As little boys we had to memorize those night prayers, and back then I didn't even know what was meant by a nightly fantasy or pollution. Have you been visited by them?"

"You mean the kind of ill dreams that cause the ghostly foe to rise up? Yes, Francesco, but whenever I am, I just pray as the priests taught us."

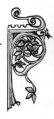

"Does that help you?"

"Sometimes, if I'm awake. Otherwise, I wake up to find myself soaked in pollution and guilt."

"The same with me, Emiliano. Do you think it is sinful when one is visited by the ghostly foe? I've never asked anyone before about that, only you tonight."

"I don't know; I'm no priest. But in order for anything to be sin, don't you have to do it on purpose?"

The two lay there in silence in the loft listening to the horses snort and paw below them. After a while Francesco asked, "Emiliano, have you thought about what you want to do when you grow up and become a man?"

"All the time, Francesco. I see myself following in my father's footsteps, but I dream of going beyond Assisi. I'm going to become the largest and most prosperous wine merchant in all of Umbria. I shall go on journeys farther than just here to Montepulciano. I shall travel to the famous Piedmont vineyards in northern Italy and even over into France. I may even travel all the way to Sicily and purchase their fine wines to bring them back to Assisi's famous Giacosa wine cellars."

"Emiliano, how exciting to travel to all those far-distant places. Yes, I can easily see you extending your father's world." Then, after a pause, Francesco said, "Let me tell you a secret tonight, Emiliano. I dream of *not* following my father to become a wealthiest cloth merchant of Assisi!" In the moonlight he could see the surprise in his friend's eyes, "My dreams are larger than Assisi. I dream of being a manly hero, a gallant knight going into battle against dragons and evil. As a noble champion of the Church, I would go to fight in the Holy Land and boldly rescue the holy places. Then having fulfilled my Christian duty, I would return home to Italy to become the most famous of all the troubadours, traveling the open roads to faraway places singing about love and romance."

"Crusaders! Crusaders, make way for the crusaders." The loud shouts yanked Francesco out of Montepulciano and back into the present as their caravan's horses and pack mules began moving off to the side of the road. The horde of travelers, peddlers and pilgrims likewise began parting left and right to make way for an approaching band of twenty or thirty French knights. Each knight had a large red crusader's cross emblazoned in the center of the white tunic worn over his chest armor. Walking behind the mounted troop were the knights'

France

Italy

Genoa

Italy

Gulf of Genoa

Pisa

Florence

Perugia

Siena

Corsica

Assisi

Montepulciano

Spello

Spoleto

Rome

GAUDEAMUS IGITUR

The Road to Chambery

men-at-arms and servants leading packhorses piled high with their masters' belongings and tents.

"God's blessings on you, noble knights of the Church," Francesco shouted over the clanking of armor and jangling of harnesses as they rode past him. "May all the saints of heaven make you victorious in your battles against the infidels." His cries were joined to others, who exclaimed, "God bless you," or "Safe journey," or "God grant you a blessed return home."

"Where are you headed to this day?" Francesco shouted to one of the young servants walking behind the men-at-arms.

"We are eastward bound for the port of Genoa, sir, " answered the lad years younger than he. "There we shall board ships to depart for the Holy Land." Then the lad reached up, grabbing Francesco's leg, and pleaded, "Young sir, please pray for me, for I am afraid!"

"My prayers go with you, as do my body and spirit long to join you." Francesco watched over his shoulder as the serving boy disappeared into the tide of animals and people eagerly surging back onto the road as the troop passed. The caravan of Assisi merchants continued westward for Marseilles, but young, idealistic Francesco was only with them in body. In his heart, he had turned around to ride back with the French crusaders on their way to Genoa to board a ship for the Holy Land.

The Assisi merchants' conversation bubbled over with anticipation about the Great Fair of Chambery as they followed the highway that swung northward from the seaport of Marseilles to join with the main road leading toward Avignon. After passing Montelimar and taking the road eastward toward Grenoble, they began sharing the road with other merchant caravans. As a great rainstorm causes a river to rise quickly and overflow, so the narrow highway to Chambery surged by the hour with increasing numbers of merchants. Also joining the influx of those bound for the fair were brightly attired jugglers, troubadours, musician entertainers, relic peddlers, wine merchants and colorfully painted enclosed wagons, from whose windows beautiful, full-breasted women waved at the merchants.

The Great Fair of Chambery had become like an enormous luxurious lake into which merchant caravans flowed from Europe and Asia like exotic rivers. The roads leading to the fair were brimming over with fabled spices, soft wools and silken cloths, expertly crafted swords, silver engraved weapons, musical instruments made of elegant wood

inlaid with pearl, stunningly brilliant works of art, exquisitely tooled leather goods, precious jewels and gems the size of hen's eggs, along with every luxury item one could imagine. Overnight, the quiet, pastoral fields surrounding the drab gray-walled city of Chambery had sprung up into a sprawling city of rainbow-colored tents used for selling the merchants' goods, for their living quarters and for their nightly entertainment of drinking, gambling, and pleasures of the flesh. The counts of the district of Champagne, eager for profit, had royally decreed special protection along the roads for those coming to and from the fair, as well as assuring the personal security of those attending. Even the Church had suspended its usual laws against usury for the days of the fair, allowing the merchants to charge the maximum rates of interest.

His Lordship the Bishop of Chambery officially opened the fair with a long prayer asking God's blessings. He concluded his prayer by extending a blessing onto the massive crowd, tracing over them the sign of the cross with a jewel-encased relic of the True Cross. A shimmering sparkle of sunlight reflecting off the jewels on the reliquary, and the echo of great Amen lingered for a brief moment. Then, the vast tent city erupted in thunderous jubilant sounds of selling and buying.

The Chambery Fair was renowned as one of the most cosmopolitan of all markets, for there one could find beautiful Russian soft furs, the newest Flemish cloth and the very finest wool from England, along with sinfully exotic, delicate silks from the Orient. These and many other goods were being sold and exchanged along with the most recent news.

All the business of the fair ended at sunset with the ringing of the vesper bells from the Cathedral of Chambery. The merchants secured their goods, posted their private guards against thieves, and retired to their tents for the evening meal. Then would begin the evening's amusements that made attending the fair such an extraordinary delight. The merchants and their servants would visit the gambling and drinking taverns and could also avail themselves of other notorious delights offered in the tents reserved for the sensual pleasures of life. In the center of the large encampment of pavilions was a large wooden platform where each night minstrels and troubadours performed by the light of blazing pitch torches.

For the young, first-time-away-from-home Francesco, the carnival nightlife of the Fair of Chambery was a fabled new world in which he

went about gaping open-mouthed. He marveled at all the wondrous new things, the ever-changing sea of faces from various races and the exotic forms of dress from those of foreign lands. He was surprised by the large number of monks who were peddling relics. He wondered if perhaps they were wayward monks or even thieves dressed as monks. Like flies they pestered him to buy relics of Holy Mother Mary's breast milk in small glass vials or bone relics of saints whom he had never heard of before. One fat peddler in a dirty, tattered monk's robe forced him to look at a bunch of yellowed parchment documents, which he said bore the signature of the Pope in Rome attesting to the authenticity of the saints' relics he offered to sell him.

"This relic, my young man," the monk whispered, leaning close, his breath heavy with garlic, "is a bone of the Celtic Saint Guignole, who was purported to be the most virile of all the saints of heaven. Both old and young men find it a most potent aid to, ah . . . as they say, help them 'rise to the occasion.' Lad, from the looks of you, this holy relic of St. Guignole is just what you need to be a real man the next time you're with a young maiden. I assure you, this potent relic will do the trick, and it's yours for only the small sum of. . . ."

Blushing, Francesco pulled himself away from the monk and slipped into the crowd. Surely, he thought, that horrible man couldn't have been a real monk if he were peddling such a wicked relic. Then he came face-to-face with two of his traveling companions, Leonardo Compagni and Cino d'Acsoli, both of whom were in their early twenties.

"Francesco, come join up with us. We're on our way to the Pavilion of Paradise to have a little fun," Leonardo said, winking at him.

"We both saw you gawking at their delicious merchandise," added Cino Compagni, playfully wagging his index finger at him. "You know, when their whore wagons passed us on our way here, eh, Bernadone?"

He did, indeed, remember, since as one wagon passed him a young woman wearing a low-cut blouse was leaning over the ledge of the wagon's window so that her large breasts were fully exposed, a sight that he had never seen before. "I would like to, but. . . ."

"You're not afraid, are you, Bernadone?" snickered Leonardo.

"Some of these whores, we're told, are from Paris. And your father boasted on the journey here about how you can speak French, calling it the angelic language of lovers. Well, Bernadone, these French whores would be in heaven if you were to make love to them while speaking

French. They lie to us Italians, saying that Italian is the most romantic language, just to get our money. So, why this delay—you're a man aren't you? Come on and join us!"

"I can't tonight, I'm sorry, but I . . ." he stammered, "promised the young apprentice of Filippo Villani I would join him at the minstrel's stage to watch the dancing Russian bear. Perhaps another night . . . I've promised. . . ." As he turned away to leave, he called back to the two, "Have fun!"

"And you *boys* have fun!" Cino replied, laughing, as the two young men were enveloped into the crowd. Cino's five-word dagger was wedged deeply in Francesco's heart. Moreover, he burned with shame. Inside, he was a bright shade of pink, first, because he had lied. He'd made up the story about the dancing bear to avoid having to deal with his fears of having to perform sexually. He was also ashamed about his fear of appearing sexually inexperienced and his fear of having to compete in the presence of other men who might be there. He dreaded like the plague appearing awkward when confronted with the unknown, and while he knew what took place inside those infamous tents, he didn't know how it was actually done. Although he was popular and a leader among friends his own age, he felt intimidated and overwhelmed by this strange new world. He turned and plunged deeper into the crowd, attempting to drown his feelings of failure to be a "real" man, trying to deafen the piercing laughter of Cino and Leonardo that continued to echo in his ears.

Wandering up and down the narrow alleyways of the tent city, he finally came upon the performers' stage that was brightly lit by flaming torches. He was immediately absorbed as he watched the stunning performances of the troupes of minstrels and acrobats, magicians and troubadours. While the agility of the tumblers and the mind-binding tricks of the magicians fascinated him, the most spellbinding was the enchanting music of the colorfully, flamboyantly attired troubadours. One particular handsome, young troubadour soon became his favorite. The troubadour had sable-black hair, a narrow chin-clinging dark beard and appeared to be only a few years older than Francesco.

After sitting captivated by the performance for what seemed like hours, he introduced himself during a short break. "I am Francesco Bernadone of Assisi, Italy," he said, tossing a handful of coins into the troubadour's hat. "You're wonderful; I could listen all night to your playing and singing."

"Thank you for your contribution to . . . er . . . the arts. I'm glad you enjoyed my music. You have a strange name for an Italian; it's one I've never heard before. My friends call me Tourdion," he said as he took a soft cloth and carefully wiped his lute, a half-pear-shaped instrument with a bent neck, a fretted fingerboard, and pegs. "I'm called Tourdion, but that's not my real name. My brother minstrels use it because I play my lute at such a quick pace. Tourdion is French for a dance done in triple-time."

"You play your instrument with great facility, Tourdion. You are able to make the very strings themselves seem to sing. I wish I could play as beautifully. May I ask the name of your instrument?"

"Don't they have these in Italy?"

"Yours is unique in my part of the world. What is it called?"

"We French call it a *mandoline*," he said with a smile. "Perhaps elsewhere it's called a lute. We've borrowed its design from the Arabs, who, I understand, originally adopted it from Persian instruments."

"Persia! That far away?"

"Yes, and perhaps from even greater distances. Some, at least, claim it originated in far-off India, or even in that most distant land on the edge of the world called China. Yet while its origin may be exotic, playing the strings is really quite simple. You just draw a quill or a piece of shell across them. So, Frenchie, if that's what your name means in Italian, would you like to try your hand at it?"

"I'd love to! May I please?" Francesco carefully took the lute into his hands and began strumming the strings with the quill.

"The Arabs also play them by using a bow that is drawn across the strings. When played that way, it's called a *rebab*. Here, let me show you." Taking back his lute, he said, "This is how it's played with a bow." As he effortlessly moved the bow across the strings, he began slightly swaying to the music. It seemed to Francesco that the lute became a living instrument of the soul, whose magical rising and falling melody deeply moved him.

When he finished, he handed the lute to Francesco, saying, "Now, my young Italian friend, you try it." After playing with it for only a short time, he knew, without any doubt, that this had to be what it feels like to be in love.

He skipped and danced as he left that night, whirling around and around as he returned to his tent. As he danced among the darkened tents, he pretended he was caressing an invisible bow across an

imaginary lute tucked under his chin and, like a little child, he hummed an improvised song.

Daily in the Bernadone cloth tent, working alongside his father and their apprentice, Francesco suppressed a bursting-at-the-seams desire to tell his father about his new love. Night after night following supper, when the others went off to the tavern tents or the Paradise Pavilions, he was in the front row at the stage, memorizing the words of the songs and the steps of the dances performed by the troubadours and minstrels. When Tourdion finished his act, he would allow Francesco to play his lute. To Francesco's surprise he discovered he had hidden musical gifts. He quickly picked up melodies and techniques for playing the lute, and he was able to learn by heart many of the troubadour songs.

"Lad, for an Italian, you learn quickly," Tourdion laughed, "and for a beginner, you play very well! Why don't you get your own lute? They sell them here at the fair." Then, laughing so generously that he revealed all his sparkling white teeth, he added, "In fact they sell everything—*everything* any man's heart would desire."

"Where can I find a lute?"

"You surely know where the Pavilion of Paradise is. Well, the merchant who I believe sells the finest musical instruments at the fair has his tent just a short distance beyond it—next to the German leather dealer's tent."

"Yes, I've seen both of those tents, but somehow I missed the one selling musical instruments. I'm afraid to ask, but are lutes expensive?"

"Of course, Francesco! It takes much time and great skill to make a lute such as mine. But it takes more than time and labor to invest a piece of wood with a soul so it can sing. For that, the craftsman must be a great artist, if not a magician learned in the secrets of enchantment. Ah, but my young Italian friend, when a master craftsman has finished crafting a lute that possesses a soul—ah, it's divine, truly an instrument descended from heaven." Now, for the first time in his young life, Francesco knew lust—for he passionately craved a lute.

Francesco sweated secretly for several anxious days as he practiced endless variations of little speeches he might give to his father. Finally, one day he gathered enough courage to say, "Father, I can never thank you enough for allowing me to come along with you on this trip to the marvelous fair here at Chambery. It has been wonderful, beyond all my

wildest dreams. You have been so good to me; you've given me my beautiful clothes, my education—everything. You're such a generous father, I don't how I can I ever thank you enough. . . ."

"Son! Enough of your honeyed praise!" Pietro chuckled, folding his large arms across his broad chest. "Don't plaster your old father with flattery; tell me straight out what you want from me!"

"O Father, I promise I'll never ask you for anything else in my whole life, but I want you to buy me a lute to take home with me, please Father." His overly anxious words tumbled out so rapidly they wedged themselves together in a string of confused babble.

"Slow down, slow down, Francesco! In the midst of that deluge of mishmash, did I hear the word 'lute'? Are you asking me to buy you one of those goad-shaped musical instruments?"

"Yes, yes, Father. Back home in Assisi they don't have anything like the ones they have here at the fair. And while we've been here at Chambery, I've even learned how to play one!"

"Now I know where you've gone off to each night. Not seeing you join Leonardo and Cino, I wondered. So, you've been attending those shows performed by the jugglers and troubadours. No harm in that; if a man's worked hard all the day long, he should have a bit of fun at night, especially when he's here at the fair."

Then, breaking into a broad smile, he beamed, "I'm proud of you, Son. You have a quick mind. I'm not surprised that you learned quickly how to play the lute—are you not a Bernadone? I only wish you could just as quickly learn the business of selling cloth. But as for buying you one of those instruments, we must be practical, for are we not businessmen? I'd wager they're quite expensive."

Francesco held his breath as his father paused and slowly rubbed his smooth-shaven chin. "Well, why not? You're the son of the richest merchant in Umbria. Are you not my young prince heir? So, yes, I'll provide the money for your lute."

"Oh, thank you, Father!"

"While I did have another gift in mind for you, a very special gift here at the fair, I guess I can give you both of them."

Francesco threw his arms around his father's neck, wanting to kiss him but afraid to do so. His father stiffened, flushed, and quickly escaped their embrace. "Customers are waiting, Son. No time for this sort of thing. I've got to go back to work, or how shall I pay for that

lute of yours? It's back to business for me, but you go and find whatever instrument you like; then I'll come and buy it for you."

Francesco was engulfed in a strange excitement, a combination of joyful anticipation and nervous apprehension, causing him to shutter momentarily as he entered the tent of musical instruments. He gasped as he beheld the array of instruments. On velvet cloth-covered tables lay lutes, harps, lyres, and several stringed instruments the likes of which he had never seen before. There were also long brass horns, curved trumpets, wooden flutes and pipes, cymbals, bells, castanets, and drums of all sizes.

"If you've only come in here to gawk, know that we also charge for that, lad," snapped the fiery, fat, red-haired merchant who had one eye covered by a black leather patch. "Also, lad, don't you even think about touching any of these expensive instruments without my permission. I've only got one good eye, but it's watching you like a Cyclops." While the tent was crowded with instruments, Francesco was glad the tent was vacant of customers, who might have observed his embarrassment at the merchant's rude remarks and at being addressed as "lad."

"I've come for more than mere looking, sir," he said with as much authority as a fifteen year old could muster. "And once I've selected a lute that is to my liking, my wealthy father will come and buy it from you."

"Ah, then, young sir," the shopkeeper said with a bow and a broad sweep of his hand, "be my guest. Everything in this tent is for sale—to the highest bidder."

"Not everything," came a soft-as-a-feather, aged voice from behind a curtain hanging across the rear of the tent.

"What kind of instrument do you desire?" asked the fat merchant, ignoring the voice as he rubbed his hands together.

"I have come to buy a lute, a rather special one. I desire a lute that has . . . a . . . soul."

"All the lutes you see laid out here before you are true works of art, created by the finest craftsman in all of France. Each is excellently crafted from only the finest of wood, with strings made of. . . ."

"I wish to purchase a lute with a soul! Do you have such an instrument?"

"Lad . . . I mean . . . young sir, with your permission allow me to educate you on the art of lute-making. The quality of the sound a good lute provides is totally dependent upon the quality of wood from which it is crafted. Only the finest wood that has also been properly aged makes for a superior lute. As for having a soul, such a thing is given to any instrument by the manner by which it is played by a great artist and master musician."

"I'm sure that you're correct, sir. However, I was told by a master artist only to purchase a lute with. . . ."

"Henri," again the aged voice spoke softly from behind the curtain, "bring the young man back here."

"But, Father, you never. . . ."

"Henri!"

"Yes, Father," replied the red-haired merchant, gesturing with his hand for Francesco to follow him to the rear of the tent. He raised the flap of the blue silken curtain to a darkened interior. Henri stood to one side, and out of that darkness came an exotic wave of perfumed incense that engulfed Francesco almost to the point of overwhelming his senses. The scent wasn't the same as the incense used at Mass in Assisi; this was a mysterious, extraordinarily exotic fragrance. As Francesco stepped through the parted curtain, Henri silently dropped the flap behind him. Swallowed by the darkness, Francesco focused on a tiny flickering yellow orb created by a small oil lamp. As his eyes adjusted to the halo of light, he could make out in the center of the circle of light the pale, wrinkled face of an old man. Below his wild, dancing, bushy eyebrows were two piercing blue eyes. The way they glistened caused Francesco to wonder if they were somehow being illuminated by hidden fiery lamps. Francesco was captivated by those eyes shining like precious stones.

"Sit, sit down, young sir," the old man said, nodding toward a small stool that had only now become faintly visible in the darkness. As he sat down, he saw in the lap of the ancient man a lute upon which he had apparently been sanding. Next to his chair was a table covered like an altar with a heavy brocade fabric luxuriously woven with fascinating oriental designs. Francesco judged that the cloth must have been very expensive. On the top of the table was a small glowing oil lamp surrounded by a variety of woodworking tools, small metal knives, spirals of string, balls of wax, and several rolled-up manuscript scrolls. Near the oil lamp was a small brass dish, in the middle of which was a narrow stick whose tip glowed bright red and from which spiraled up a thin ribbon of blue-white aromatic smoke.

"My name is . . . not important," said the old man smiling so generously that a wave of wrinkles rippled across his aged face. "Ah, but you're a handsome young sapling of a man for whom a name is important, since it bestows upon you an identity . . . and . . . ," once again the waves of wrinkles rippled out from a smile, ". . . a destiny. By what name are you called?"

"Francesco Bernadone of Assisi."

"Your accent being Italian, I suppose that Assisi is to be found in the land of Italy. But, Francesco—that's not an Italian name, is it?"

"No, sir, you are correct. I was named after this beautiful country of France for which my father has such great love—and where he found a most beautiful bride, my mother."

"Ah, how sumptuous is the music that harmonizes into a song of life rising from the duet of French and Italian blood. No wonder you're interested in having a lute with a soul.

"But I feel uncomfortable with you addressing me as sir, as if I was some great lord or titled nobleman. How shall you address me?" The old man mused for a moment and then said, "Properly, I am known as Claude of Lyons, for the city where I was born. But why don't you call me Claude de Lune. My friends often use that playful twist on *Clair de Lune*, French for 'the light of the moon.' They say that name reflects the quality of my music." He paused, deeply inhaling the incense. Then he began chanting over and over, ever more softly, *Claude de Lune . . . Claude de Lune . . .* until it became only a wisp of sound, thin as the thread of incense spiraling upwards into the darkness of the tent. Then his voice disappeared into silence. For some time they sat in a stillness that made young Francesco a bit uncomfortable, until out of the deep well of a long silence, Claude's crystal clear voice slowly arose, "Now, as to your request. There are three types of musicians: If you know what kind you desire to become, then I can readily suggest the right lute for you."

Francesco's youthful face filled with surprise, and then concern, at the old man's sage utterance. He listened intently as the master craftsman continued, "First, there are those musicians who perform only to entertain others. The better of these are cleverly skillful in the use of their instruments and even more clever to play only the type of music that satisfies the tastes of the crowd. Naturally, such musicians as these have no need of an instrument with a soul."

Francesco wondered if the troubadours whom he had heard at the fair belonged to this first group. If so, surely his new friend, Tourdion, had to belong to another group, for he had spoken with understanding about Francesco's need to obtain a lute with a soul.

"The second type is comprised of those who could be called court musicians. They are very skilled and disciplined, well-versed in the vast range and control of their instruments, as well as knowledgeable about the kind of music that delights the minds of scholars and the nobility. Yet neither do the musicians in this second group have need for an instrument that possesses a soul—but only those capable of great elegance."

Francesco's attention now was completely fixed on the old man who had aroused his curiosity and anticipation, for he could think of no other kind of musician than those described in the first two groups.

"Rare, my young Italian friend, are the musicians who belong to the last group. They are often spiritual recluses and hermits who only play their instrument in solitude. They make their music for the trees and flowers, for the birds and wild beasts. And if they do play for others . . ." he paused and looked not so much at Francesco as directly into him, asking, "Do you pray?"

"Yes, of course, I pray. Doesn't everyone pray? I pray when I go to church, before I eat and sleep and always when I am in danger."

"I didn't ask if you recited prayers. I asked, 'Do you pray?' One only needs a lute with a soul if one truly knows how to pray. For it makes the same kind of music that monks create with only their voices as they sing Gregorian chant. It makes that hypnotic, opulent music produced by the night orchestra of stars, or the music of cascading waterfalls or mountain streams as their waters leap joyfully over boulders and rocks. It is the music that comes from a lute played by poets and mystics, who in the midst of playing forget who they are and so become the very melody. And, ah, if they play with enough passion, they are consumed by the same music that moves the sun and the stars. Indeed, Francesco, it is not the bow or the fingers that create this rare angelic music; it flows only from a holy communion of two souls— yours and the lute's. If you learn to play like that, then you will become an instrument that spins the enchantingly mysterious music that can seduce those who hear it into the clutches of the same God that has possessed you. Do you understand what I've said? Now, my young friend, what type musician do you wish to become?"

"I think I understand what you've said, Claude." Francesco fell silent as he struggled with the deeper meaning of the old man's challenge. He had heard Gregorian chant several years ago when he went to pray vespers with his mother at the Benedictine monastery near Assisi, and he recalled how beautifully soul-stirring was the monk's chanting. Yet he didn't grasp what "being possessed by God" meant, since he had only heard the priests and his mother speak of being possessed by the devil. Nor had he ever thought of the stars or waterfalls as making music. He also wondered how an instrument could get a soul, since only God created souls. While his lap was full of these mysterious unknowns, he did know without any doubt that he passionately wanted to have a lute that somehow was invested with a soul. As he slowly pondered these things, old Claude patiently sat in silence, totally absorbed in watching the thread of incense smoke floating upward.

"I don't just think," Francesco finally said, "I *know* that I want to become that third type of musician—or, rather, I desire it with all my heart. So, Claude de Lune, do you have a lute with a soul that I can purchase?"

"Ah, very good, my young friend." His smiling eyes danced over Francesco's face. "You may have this very lute which I've just now completed." Caressing the lute as if it were a small child, he asked, "Would you like it?"

"May I ask a question first, since I am only a beginner at playing lutes? Your son, Henri, told me that for a lute to be of the highest quality, it is supremely important that it be made from an excellent wood. May I ask, what was the source of the wood in that beautiful lute on your lap?"

"I will tell you a secret, but you must promise never to reveal it."

Francesco quickly nodded in agreement, his eyes large with anticipation. Claude leaned very close to Francesco and softly said, "In springtime, when my soul whispers to me that the time is right, I take my sharpest saw and go up into the deep forests in the mountains east of Chambery near Germany. Then I wait for a thunderstorm. As the dark rainstorm is almost upon me, I begin running along with the rain, watching the skies, waiting for a lightning flash. When I see one, and hear the great rumble of thunder that follows it, I run like the wind to find the tree that has been struck. Sometimes when I arrive, it is still smoking—a very good sign. Then, with the greatest care, I saw away the wood I'll need to make my most extraordinary instruments. When that wood has been slowly dried, and after prayerful meditation, I lovingly begin to fashion from it a lute. So, you have the answer to the source of the wood in this lute on my lap." Then reverently stroking it, he said, "Francesco, it still retains the fire from heaven that scorched a soul inside of it. It is one of my finest pieces."

"I would love the one you've offered me, but my father told me he would buy any instrument. Do you have an even more wondrous lute than the gorgeous one in your lap?"

"Yes, I do have one, but that lute is only suited for a truly great master. It will produce the most marvelous, awe-inspiring music—but only in the hands of an exceptional artist. And you, my son, as you yourself said, are only a beginner."

"Please, Claude de Lune, even if I am not a master musician, may I at least look upon this amazing lute?"

Claude slowly reached beneath the heavy brocaded cloth draped over the table and gradually lifted up a stunning, ancient-looking lute. With the same great reverence and affection he would have used to handle a relic of the True Cross, he held it up before the aspiring musician. It felt to Francesco like his tongue was glued to the roof of his mouth. He was awestruck by its dazzling beauty, speechless in astonishment. Yet he was confused as well, for the lute lacked a bridge, strings and even the pegs at the end of the neck used to tighten the strings.

"Thank you, Claude de Lune," Francesco stammered out, still bewildered, because he couldn't understand how a lute without strings could play awe-inspiring music. "How fortunate I feel to be given the opportunity to see such a marvelous lute, as well as to meet you and hear all the wise and marvelous things you have shared with me. I will go at once and fetch my father, Pietro Bernadone, and, God willing, he will purchase for me that newly finished lute in your lap. Thank you, and God's blessings be upon you for your special kindness."

Francesco hurried out through the curtain and past the tables loaded with instruments. He ran, almost leaping with joy, out of the tent. Old Claude nodded his head slowly, softy stroking the stringless lute. "Some day, my young Italian friend, you'll understand the mystery of my precious lute without strings. But before you gain that knowledge, you'll learn quickly that it will not be you, Francesco, who owns this lute: It will own you, and become your teacher!"

"Henri."

"Yes, Father."

"When that young Italian lad and his father return, reduce the price of this new lute by half! I wish it to be old Claude's gift to Italy —and perhaps, who knows, to lands far, far beyond it." As he carefully returned the ancient stringless lute to its place beneath the table, he mused to himself, "Ah, yes, old Claude of the Moonlight senses in that passionate young man a certain rare genius of soul that someday will enable him to play this Lute of Ecstasy."

As Tourdion strummed his young friend's new lute, he exclaimed, "Francesco, what a magnificent lute! It must have cost a fortune. You're a fortunate young man to have a father who is willing to buy you such an instrument as this."

"Yes, he loves me greatly, and I am so grateful to him. But I am also grateful to you, Tourdion, for you first taught me how to play the lute, and have introduced me to an entire new world. If it had not been for you, I would not have met Claude de Lyons. He is perhaps the most unusual man I have ever met in my life. He told me many wondrous things about music and life, but I confess that I couldn't understand some things he said and showed me. How lucky I am that by chance, Tourdion, I have met both you and old Claude here at the fair."

"By *chance*, my young Italian friend? Musical notes do not by chance find their way into the melody of a song, and the same is true in each song of life. When the time is right," he said as he smiled, "we meet not by accident those notes that are intended—dare I say *destined*—to impact the melody of our personal life songs. Blessed are those who are not tone deaf."

As the twelve days of the Chambery Fair drew to a close, they seemed to Francesco to race one another to the finish line. Tomorrow morning the merchants would pack up their tents, purchases, and belongings and begin the return journey to Assisi. On the last night, at the campfire after supper, Francesco sat sharing the fire's circle with some of the young cloth merchants' apprentices. Cino and Leonardo and the older merchants, including Pietro, had gone off, leaving Francesco and his lute to entertain the youths gathered around the crackling fire. As he sang, his sparkling, melodic voice harmonized with the dancing flames that sent glowing sparks swirling skyward into the dark night sky.

When he had concluded all the songs he knew, he laid his lute beside him, and the young men began sharing their various adventures at the fair. As one apprentice was engaging them with his wild story, Francesco felt a soft tap on his shoulder. Turning, he saw the face of a young girl faintly illuminated by the fire. She appeared to be only about two or three years older than he, yet her eyes were those of a woman twice his age.

"You must be Francesco Bernadone. I surmise that by the lute laying beside you. I was told you would be a handsome young man with a lute." As he looked up somewhat suspiciously at her, she continued, "Your father sent me to you, and I'm to show you something that you've never seen before. A surprise."

"Really!" He beamed as he stood up. "Here at the fair, I've already seen so many new and unbelievable things, and you mean to tell me that there is even more?"

"Oh, yes, young sir," she whispered, stepping back away from the light of the fire into the shadows. "There are more things indeed. Now put your lute in your tent, and come and follow me."

The young men at the fire were so absorbed in the apprentice's outrageous tale that they barely noticed Francesco stepping back into the darkness. Dashing off to his tent, he safely placed his lute inside and then returned to the waiting girl. She led him through a maze of twisted lanes between the clusters of darkened tents and blazing campfires, from which came the laughter and voices of merchants celebrating their last night at the fair. He continued following her beyond the last pavilions of the tent city, leaving behind its luminous yellow dome created by all the campfires flaming up into the darkness. As they walked, he delighted in how the full moon of May was artistically painting the darkened fields in shimmering silver, yet delight was not the only emotion he felt. His heart was like a tumbler juggling joy, curiosity, and apprehension. The farther they went, the more he felt something wasn't right. Nervous doubts began to gnaw rat-like at his heart. Did his father really send her to him? If he had, wouldn't he have told him about it? Was he being tricked, led away from the security of the camp only to be robbed? He had heard tragic stories of stupid merchants who had been lured outside of the tent city only to be beaten near to death by thieves. His very life could be at risk. Then an inner judge began to speak, "How could you be so stupid!" It was the voice of his father: "How could you fall for such a hoax? Francesco, when are you going to grow up?"

"Miss, what is this new thing you're going to show me? We've been gone for some time now, and I think that perhaps I should be getting back to my companions at the fair, for tomorrow we. . . ."

"We're almost there, Francesco. Soon I will show you something magical. You're an adventurous young man, I can tell. Surely you don't want to miss seeing the magic?"

"Something magical?" Hesitating, he cast a brief glance over his shoulder at the glow of the tent city on the horizon. Then he said, "I'm fascinated by magic and feats of enchantment."

At the far side of the field they were crossing he could see a large grove of trees silhouetted in silver by the moonlight. They walked a short distance into the dark woods until they arrived in a grassy, moonlit clearing on the banks of a small creek that ambled through clusters of dark, voiceless trees. Their intertwining branches formed a

dome of dark lacework overhead, with openings that allowed showers of pale moonlight to fall mutely upon the two young people. Francesco was awash in the awesome beauty of the place, particularly the playful moonbeams dancing on the water of the rippling stream that jubilantly tumbled over a large stone ledge and into a waiting pool, before secretively flowing away into the blackness of the night.

"This *is* magical! Never have I seen such enchantment. We have nothing to compare to this back home in Assisi."

"Yes, it is wonderful, isn't it? This is my secret place, where I come whenever I need to be alone. I've named it *chateau d'eau*, which means, 'water castle.' It is my very own precious Chambery water castle. You are the first person, the only one with whom I have ever shared it."

"Really? This place is magical. Why am I the first?"

"Your eyes. When I first met you back there at the campfire, I looked into those large, deep, brown eyes of yours and saw something I've never seen in another man's eyes. I knew at once that you would be one who could relish my *chateau d'eau*.

"Thank you. It's fantastic!" he said as he slowly turned around and around, drinking in all the beauty.

"But there's more magic than you see here," she said softly.

"There is? What could be more magical than this?"

Without a word, but with only a moonlit smile, she tenderly placed her arms around him and gracefully guided the two of them down onto the rain-softened grass, now caressed by the subtle white moonlight. His breath taken away, Francesco lay on his back looking upward in wonder at the full, round moon and sighed, "How stunningly beautiful and awesome is this place; the moon seems to be. . . ." He suddenly swallowed his words, for she had slowly slid her hand underneath his tunic and was caressing the newly appeared, dark, curly hairs in the center of his chest. As her moist lips began to trace a seductive path across his neck toward his left earlobe, he quickly forgot about the full moon and about seeing something magical. His heart wildly throbbed in fascination and apprehension of the unknown.

"Now, my young Italian prince of merchants, I'll show you the most ancient of all magic in the world." With skillful fingers she quickly undid any obstructive clothing and gracefully rolled him over on top of her. As his chest pressed against her full breasts, she artfully arched and lowered her young firm body under him as he choked in panic.

Pierced by the stiletto-like thought of his mother's last counsels to him, and almost strangled by the presence of her blessed palm cross on his cotton tunic now bunched around his neck, he prayed silently, "Holy Mother of God, protect me; save me from sin." His head was burning with a fiery fever caused by vivid images of the raging crimson hellfires of his mother's kitchen stove.

As the young woman's body rhythmically rose and fell beneath him, he was seized by an eruption of blazing fire rising in him, a fiercely passionate feeling he had never felt before in his life, a feeling that quickly eclipsed the images of the fires of hell. It felt like passionate and exotic fingers of those primordial flames had come spiraling up out of the dark netherworld of the fertile earth and now totally engulfed him. Never had he felt such desire, such a sense of being overwhelmingly possessed. He forgot his blessed palm cross; he forgot his mother's talk of hellfires, and he forgot everything of his present world as he was magically transported back into the Garden of Paradise.

It was over. Francesco lay on his back staring up at the moon, feeling like an explorer who had discovered a new land. "How strange," he thought. "I found something and I lost something, for at the peak of what happened, I was catapulted out of myself. The clay jug that had held the fluid of myself was shattered, and it merged me not just with this maiden, but with the moon, the earth, the trees—with everything!" Yet as quickly as it had happened, now it had disappeared! "It feels," he thought, "like I'm in an eerie garden, on one hand, crowded with perfumed flowers of sensuous exotic delight and, on the other, with ugly purple bramble bushes filled with piercing thorns of guilt." Then, without warning, the painful prickling thorn bushes vanished, and he was once again in that exotic garden overflowing only with the most fragrant passionflowers, for suddenly the earth beneath him erupted up through his body in a violent explosion of primal fire.

As the silent, nonjudgmental moon gazed down on the two of them laying side by side, the young maiden leaned over and whispered in his ear, "I was only paid for one time! But you're such a passionate man, and that one was free."

He lay next to her on that springtime bed of silken grass, absorbed in the slowly releasing embrace of intense pleasure, watching the moon on its leisurely westward night journey. He felt strangely caught in a contradiction: At the height of both times he had felt intimately united with God. Then, he felt his mind wandering. He could no longer focus

on the contradiction as his thoughts drifted aimlessly, before his eyelids closed in sleep.

The moon sagged and was now low in the western sky. Francesco awoke startled. He realized he was alone; the young girl was nowhere to be seen. He quickly pulled on his clothing and began racing across the fields toward the still-sleeping tent city of Chambery. He could see the eastern sky beginning to paint herself in delicate shades of blue-green at the first glimmer of dawn, and he could hear the first chirping of birds awakening. He was running as fast as he ever had, yet each step was full of excruciating agony. It felt like the skin under his tight leggings was being pierced by a thousand needles of stinging shame, each a stabbing reminder that he was guilty of grievous mortal sin.

As the sun stood two hours high over the tent city, those who had attended the Chambery Fair were now gathered at the platform used for the minstrels' nightly entertainment to celebrate the Solemn High Mass of thanksgiving that would conclude the fair. The Bishop of Chambery, wearing golden, heavy brocade vestments and surrounded by scores of clergy, officiated at this closing Mass. For Francesco the ageless Latin prayers and chants of his childhood faith that usually inspired and comforted him, on this morning, were guilt-edged instruments of torture. While the custom was not to go to confession until on one's deathbed, on this morning after, many were availing themselves of the sacrament. There were rows of priests sitting on stools off near the edge of the crowd hearing the confessions of pious merchants who were afraid to travel in the state of mortal sin. His heart pulled at him to go and confess to one of the priests, but his legs refused. His heart pleaded with him lest he be consigned to the fires of hell, but his mind screamed back that it would be much too embarrassing to speak of the horrible, disgraceful things he had done. Smelling victory, his mind cleverly applied more pressure: "Don't forget what your young friends back in Assisi told you, those stories of men who had confessed their sexual sins to priests and were then given severe penances, often public ones. No imagination is required to guess what kind of sins merit those harsh penitential acts. It won't just be the priest—everyone will know by your outward penance the terrible things you did with that girl last night!" At the end of the Mass, along with all the others, he knelt for the bishop's solemn blessing for travelers. "Not for me," he mumbled. "That blessing of God will fly

over my head like the wind, leaving not a trace behind. God will not bless me, for I am cursed by my sin."

After the Mass, the tent city of Chambery was folded up with amazing speed. Apprentices and servants loaded pack animals with merchandise as merchants exchanged farewells. The roads leading away from Chambery were jammed with homeward-bound merchants, while in the opposite direction came hoards of the poorest peasants. These rag-picking scavengers were racing one another to the abandoned tent grounds to grab up anything the merchants had left behind. The caravan from Assisi, with its pack mules loaded down with English and Flemish wool, fine cloth and Russian furs, moved southward with other groups of merchants on the road toward Valence.

Francesco, riding with the other sons just behind the older merchants, was surprised when his father turned his horse around and cantered back to him. "Francesco," he asked with sly grin, "how was last night?"

"Purgatory," he mumbled, unprepared for his father's question.

"What was that, Son?" he asked with a furrowed brow. "It's so noisy on this road, I thought I heard you say 'purgatory'!"

"I said 'paradise,' Father," he lied, faking a smile. "Last night was pure paradise—an experience I shall never forget."

"Wonderful! I'm proud of you, my son. Regardless of what those damn priests say, it's the next best thing to heaven, eh? In fact, it just might *be* heaven! That was the surprise gift I spoke about when you asked me to buy you a lute. Some gift, wasn't it? Francesco, you're no longer a boy. You are now a real man!" The smile on his father's face was as expansively brilliant as any sunrise. He then spurred his horse, wheeled around and galloped forward like a conquering general to join the older merchants at the head of the caravan.

"Why did I say it was like purgatory?" he mumbled. "Why did I call it that?" Then he recalled the answer his mother gave him when he was a child about the pains of purgatory. He had a vivid picture of himself as a small child seated on her lap and listening to her response:

"Son, God's holy priests tell us that purgatory is a place of terrible torment created by our all-loving God to purify us of our sins so we can enter into heaven. Every sin, my dear Giovanni, requires a complete repayment in pain and suffering."

"You mean, even after we've confessed them?"

The Way
to the
Chambery
Fair

"Yes, confessing and absolution don't remove the punishment due for our sins. So our God has lovingly created a place called purgatory that is located halfway between heaven and hell. The saddest of souls, those who die in mortal sin, go directly to hell, and those souls on their way to heaven must first pass through purgatory. Only those who have repented, have confessed their sins before they die and have been given absolution, can go to purgatory to suffer the cleansing fires and pains that will remove their sins."

"What are the pains of purgatory?"

"The good priests tell us that the poor souls in purgatory suffer the grotesque tortures of fully experiencing the sensual delights of their sins while at the same time suffering the purifying fires of God's justice."

"Of course," he now thought; "that's why I answered Father by saying 'purgatory.' I feel like I've been plunged into a kind of little hell where I am suffering the excruciating tortures of shame and guilt for sinning against God, yet at the same time tasting again the sensual delights of my body mingling with hers. Delight—yes, never before have I felt my whole body exploding with pleasure; never have I felt so alive as I did last night! But, O God, how terrible is the cost of having tasted such bliss. The memory of his mother momentarily liberated him from the remorseful agony he felt sitting in his saddle—the memory taking him back to sitting as a child in her lap. "And Giovanni," he heard her telling him, "those poor souls in purgatory must suffer endlessly—endlessly, Son—until all the sweetness of their sinning has turned sour. And that can take years and years of cleansing torture. But, remember, God is all-loving! So while we're still here in this life, our Lord sends us penances like burning fevers, deadly sicknesses, and various other sufferings as ways by which we can begin to pay the debt for our sins. We can also reduce the punishments of purgatory by obtaining indulgences from the Church, by giving alms to the poor, by wearing itchy hair shirts or placing rough pebbles in our shoes as hidden penances while we walk—and, of course, by harsh fasting."

"Mother, what if I would do penance not just during Lent and on other fasting days? Could I then escape the punishment of purgatory?"

"I don't know, Giovanni. I doubt it, for sins so offend God. Yet, perhaps. Only God knows. As for fasting, do you remember, my son, those beautiful stories of the saints that I've told you? Consider those holy hermits who spent their entire lives in misery and pain so as to please God and escape the fate of purgatory. Some of them also spent

their lives enduring great penances for the sake of others, both living and dead. But the less you sin in life, the less will be the recompense you will have to make. So, my dear son, you must try never, ever to sin!"

Well, he'd failed her, he thought as he sat in his saddle again on the road to Valence—he had sinned gravely. He never recalled sharing with her his confusion about why a God who so greatly loves us would also send us awful pains and unbearable sufferings. Or why an all-loving God, who forgave all our sins, wouldn't also forgive the punishments for them.

"Please, noble sir," cried a voice, erasing Francesco's revisiting of his childhood memories. Looking down, he saw a ragged, dirty beggar clutching at the hem of his cloak. "Please, young sir, you have a kind face. For the love of Christ, can't you spare a few coins for a hungry man?" Those closest in the surging human river on the road were looking with expectation at Francesco when a loud snap of a whip intruded upon the scene. A mounted guard from the merchant's caravan had urged his horse forward with his whip. Reaching Francesco's side, the guard used his whip again, lashing the beggar away from him. Francesco raised his hand to halt the guard, thinking, "Charity, yes, if I give a fist full of alms to this poor beggar, some of my punishment in purgatory will be removed." His hand hung limp in the air, however, an impotent gesture, for he feared being questioned by his companions about why he was giving money to a beggar on a road that was full of them. One of his father's many dogmas echoed in his ears: "Never give alms to a beggar, for more than twenty of his wretched, filthy fellow beggars will pounce on you like fleas."

At that moment, coming up toward him on the crowded roadway was a black-cassocked priest leading a small band of pilgrims on its way to some shrine. He heard a new commanding voice that was not his father's: "Francesco, stop that priest; beg him to hear your confession. He can't refuse. He'll take you over there along the roadside and free you from your sin!" Fearful of what his father and the other merchants would say if they saw him doing such a thing, he began shaking his head, trying to dislodge this voice. This was the first time he remembered of hearing a voice without benefit of his ears. As he pondered that weird experience, the priest and his company of pilgrims swiftly swept past him and down the road.

How perfectly, he thought again, had his mother's indelibly imprinted words about purgatory described what he was feeling.

Vividly reliving the sensual pleasures of his delicious sin with the maiden while simultaneously being painfully scourged by the sting of shame and guilt seemed to him a uniquely cruel torture. As the rest of the caravan was enjoying the warm spring beauty of the French countryside, Francesco rode shivering in the bitter icy cold of winter. Never before had he felt the freezing guilt of being dead in mortal sin, and he thought it paradoxical that his present frozen condition should make him an applicant for the raging fires of hell—if, indeed, he were to die without first receiving absolution from a priest or some saintly hermit.

He clung to his saddle, fearing that he might be dislodged by the fierce winds of these powerful besieging emotions. Then, without warning, a new passion shattered his frozen state. He could almost hear the splintering sound of his icy heart being cracked open by a fiery surge of anger toward his father for stealing his youthful romantic ideals about love and knightly courtship. "I didn't even learn her name," he fumed, "and I never had an opportunity to court her by reciting poetry and singing passionate love songs." He felt his soul groan that there were no exchanges of love tokens, no ardent anticipations of secret rendezvous, no "until death do us part" pledges of lifelong fidelity. In short, there was no love.

"I'm not guilty," he muttered. "My father is completely to blame. He, not I, is the one who actually sinned. I was only an innocent victim of his scheming to force me into manhood." His rage, however, failed to offer more than momentary relief, and he had to resist the urge to scratch himself, for he again felt the anguish of his entire body being infested with the crawling lice of shame and guilt.

Once more, the winds of emotion shifted, and a new wave of ruminations rolled through his mind: "No, it wasn't just my father! She's was also to blame. It must have been her *malocchio,* her evil eye, that ensnared me into committing sin with her. Yes, she got money for sinning, but she was no ordinary whore. I'll bet she was a young witch who had sold her soul to the demons of hell, and it was they who invested her with diabolic powers to seduce me into committing a grave sin. Yes, yes, it was she who. . . ." Just as suddenly as these thoughts had appeared, a firm, clear voice now broke in: "No! This guilt belongs to you alone, Francesco. You are fully responsible for these sins of the flesh, not your father, not that girl. You, and you alone, are to blame, for you did not try to escape from those passionate fires within you that erupted from deep down in the earth.

"And not once," he mumbled in agony, "but, O my God, I did it twice!" Twice . . . twice . . . twice. . . . The word ricocheted in his head as his soul pleaded to be given a voice. Spontaneously, from his boyhood school lessons at San Giorgio's, a psalm-prayer arose in his heart:

> Have mercy on me, O God, according to thy great mercy;
>
> according to thy great clemency, blot out my iniquity.
>
> Wash me completely from my guilt,
>
> and cleanse me of my sin.
>
> For I acknowledge my iniquity,
>
> and my sins are always before me.
>
> Against thee only have I sinned;
>
> I have done what is evil in thy sight.

Instead of comforting his soul, his unspoken prayer only intensified the stabbing pains of guilt, causing his breakfast to rise up out of his stomach and fill his throat. The possibility of vomiting again gave rise to the fear of what his father and the other men would say. Would they be able to guess why?

This ever intensifying experience of purgatory was the first time he ever recalled being so physically affected by his emotions that they were alternately able to bring him great bodily joy and extreme physical pain. Did others have this capacity, or was he unique? Was it a gift or a curse, he wondered, to have one's emotions so enfleshed in one's body. And did being a truly a passionate person mean feeling *everything* so intensely?

As his rising guilt and shame pushed his stomach upward into his throat, he remembered a prayer ritual for relief that his mother had taught him as a child. Touching his tongue with his forefinger, he wet it, leaned down from the saddle and made three signs of the cross on the toe of his boot, saying softly, "Crosses three we make to ease us, two for the thieves, and one for Christ Jesus." Then he leaned back up in his saddle, breathed deeply several times and touched the place on his tunic where his mother had pinned the blessed palm cross, praying the continuation of the psalm quietly:

Turn away thy face from my sins,

and blot out all my guilt.

Create a clean heart for me, O God,

and renew in me a steadfast spirit.

Pausing, and again deeply inhaling the morning air, he added to the psalm verse, "Yes, blot out all my guilt." He remembered something else his mother had told him: "Giovanni, our Lord Jesus promised us if we asked for anything in his name, and did so with great faith, it would be granted to us! So, my son, whatever you need, ask God for it with great faith." As when the bright sun bursts through a dreary, gray, overcast winter sky, his heart lit up with hope, and he prayed with all the faith he could muster, "In the name of Jesus Christ, I ask that you blot out all my guilt and forgive my sin." Almost immediately he smiled and felt better. Once again it was springtime, and he was riding under the beautiful, blue French sky. Briefly, another dark cloud drifted across his heart: "Wasn't it essential for forgiveness to confess your sexual sins to a priest?" But he brushed away that question with a self-affirming thought: "The Lord Jesus wants me to trust in the goodness of God's mercy and also in the power of prayer." And didn't his father Pietro always say, "Leave the past to graveyards. Engage your mind and hands fully in today, for it is the only place where you can make a difference."

He smiled again, for now the sun was shining both inside as well as outside of him, and once more he enjoyed riding with his companions through this stunningly beautiful countryside. He reached down, fondly touching the reinforced leather saddlebag that held his wondrous new lute. He was now eager for evening when they would set up camp and he could again play his beloved souvenir from the Fair of Chambery.

The merchants' caravan, now homeward bound for Assisi with its heavily loaded mules, had traveled southwest from Chambery until the road joined with the larger highway at Valence. At that junction was a wooden post with two signs, one pointing south toward Montellimar and one pointing north to Lyons.

"Lyons! O beware, brother merchants," cried Albertino Compagni in mock horror, "Don't forget what happened to that good merchant Peter

Waldo of Lyons. Even now, twenty-five years later, we who share his vocation must practice the greatest caution lest we also become infected with his disease. Hold your noses, companions." At this he tilted his head back, playfully sniffing the air. "Yes, do you not smell it? The stench of his plague, now rotten ripe, is riding upon the wind from the north."

Filippo Villani piously traced the sign of the cross upon himself as Guittone said, "It is easy to avoid the plague, Albertino, but we don't have to hold our noses to be spared Waldo's fate. All we need to do is never take the Gospels seriously! What I always say is, leave the Gospels in church, for that's where they belong. That's what stupid Peter Waldo failed to do. Alas, that once prosperous merchant foolishly sold all of his possessions and gave the money to the poor!"

"Gentlemen, beware, as good Albertino has warned us," chimed in Pietro, playfully covering his nose with his gloved hand. "Waldo's madness is indeed contagious! His pious plague quickly spread across France, infecting those with soft brains who eagerly began to follow his example and became the Poor Men of Lyons! Ordinary laymen just like us fell under his spell, selling all they owned and going barefoot about the countryside preaching the Gospel. And not in the proper way—in Latin, mind you—but in French!"

"I heard that at first the Pope didn't object to their poverty. Well, how could he," joked Albertino, "unless he was going to rewrite the Gospels? Indeed, didn't Jesus tell his disciples to give away all their property and follow him? Waldo's big blunder was that he and his little barefoot band went about preaching the Gospel. Unfortunately, those who preach for their living got angry as hell!" Then, he comically intoned in a solemn voice, "Unreverend Brothers of the Guild, that mistake sealed his doom, for the bishops and priests have a more tightly controlled association than any guild we poor merchants could ever dream of creating. After all, they have no competition!"

"You're right about that being Peter's big mistake," added Filippo. "I heard the Pope sent him a letter telling him, 'Live the Gospel; don't preach it!' To pacify the French bishops and others in Rome, the Holy Father then ordered Waldo to stop preaching and submit to the Church, but sadly for his immortal soul, he refused."

Guittone joined in, "The pious but bold Peter sent a letter back to the Pope saying that he was bound to obey only God, not some pope in Rome who was only a man. None were surprised after such an audacious deed when the Pope sent back a decree of excommunication

for Peter and his followers. Ah, but that piece of parchment from Rome didn't stop the Poor Men of Lyons from preaching. They claimed that they, not the Church, had the truth, and that one can only find the truth in the Bible."

Intrigued by the bits and pieces of what he could overhear, Francesco urged his horse closer so he could better take in the conversation.

"The French bishops were delighted," Albertino continued, "that Rome silenced those heretics of Lyons, but that wasn't the end of it, for the Poor Men only went underground, meeting secretly. I tell you, comrades, nothing ensures the growth of any religious sect or idea, as does persecution. Sadly, you would think the Church, of all organizations, would know that. Well, to escape being imprisoned or, worse, being turned into ashes at the stake, some of his heretic disciples fled to the high Alpine valleys of Savory and called themselves Waldensians."

"Religion," Pietro Bernadone declared pontifically, "is only for Sundays and feast days, baptisms and weddings, death beds and funerals. Period! Religion fits women and children like a glove, but it fits a man like a cage. A wise man should keep a safe distance downwind from filthy, diseased lepers and should stay even a hundred times farther away from religion!"

After joining the others who were laughing over Pietro's comparison of religion with leprosy, Albertino said, "From what I've heard, the heretical Lyons disease has spread into southern France, where an offshoot is called the Cathars, meaning 'the Pure.' These 'Pure Ones' believe in the eternal war between good and evil. They also preach that sex was created by the devil, that all fleshy things are evil and that marriage is only legalized sin."

"Those Cathars aren't only in southern France," added Filippo, sadly shaking his head. "My parish priest says there are some in northern Italy! Fearful of being reported to Rome, they meet secretly while cleverly keeping their true religious beliefs hidden. They even go to Mass. Perhaps there could be heretic followers of Peter Waldo even in our own Assisi." Placing his index finger across his lips as he glanced at those around him and then back toward the apprentices, he continued, "Who knows? Even among us there might be a secret Cathar!"

"I ask you," demanded Pietro, turning around in his saddle as he scanned those who were riding with him, "is there any man here among us who's opposed to sex? Is there a man among us who rejects the juicy joys of the flesh?"

"No man in this caravan!" shouted Leonardo Compagni as the rest crowed loudly with laughter—everyone, that is, except Francesco, who only pretended to laugh.

"*Magnifico!*" roared Pietro. "Just as I thought! Now, Gentlemen of the Cloth, let us enjoy the beauties of France and breathe in its fresh, clear breeze, for all too soon we shall be back home in stinking Assisi."

"Stinking?" echoed a shocked Filippo. "Pietro, you call our beautiful ancient city on the crest of Mount Subasio *stinking?*"

"My dear old friend, not only have your eyes grown dim, your nose must also have stopped working. Assisi does stink! Even a cloth soaked in French perfume when held to one's nose won't hinder the stench of Assisi's rotting garbage, animal dung, and human waste. Assisi lacks an organized system for the removal of her waste—we all know that. It is the duty of each household to carry away its own waste outside the walls of the city. But who cleans up the crap off her streets and alleys? No one—is that not correct? Not only do our streets reek to the high heavens, but they're dangerous, gentlemen. They breed the plague!"

"Perhaps, then," Filippo replied, "we should petition Duke Conrad to. . . ?"

"Asking any help from his elevated eminence Duke Conrad of Lutzen, my dear Filippo, would be utterly useless. He cares not a mouse's tit for what happens to those who inhabit our fair city. He lives high up on the summit of Mount Subasio in his old palace citadel of Rocca Maggiore, where he sniffs only the fresh Umbrian air."

"And Conrad is a lackey of the Pope," Albertino added.

"You're right," agreed Pietro, "In Umbria we're trapped between the devil to the north and the Pope to the south, both seeking sovereignty over Assisi. Since the days of old Otto the Great, those northern German princes, or their emperors, have lusted to possess as much of Italy as possible as part of their so-called Holy Roman Empire. The Holy Roman Empire—what a laugh! Unlike the original Roman Empire, it now encompasses only Germany and a few other lands its greedy fingers have grabbed."

"Like the Germans, Duke Conrad is only interested in collecting taxes," Albertino replied, "and I think it's time we governed ourselves, even if we need to give a nod now and then to the Pope."

"Surely there must be a peaceful way," suggested Filippo. "Perhaps if a delegation of our guild and other citizens of Assisi went to see the duke, he might. . . ."

"No!" exclaimed Pietro. "What Assisi needs is an uprising! Yes, we her citizens should arise and overthrow the citadel of Rocca Maggiore and everything that it represents. The time is long overdue for our beloved Assisi to be governed by a public commune composed of her citizens and merchants—as has happened, and is still happening— elsewhere in Italy.

"An uprising?" a wide-eyed Filippo replied. "Perhaps war with Perugia, but, Pietro, surely not war with our own Duke Conrad and the ageless authority of the noble families of Assisi? Only madmen make war against their own city. And if we were ever so foolhardy as to attempt such a thing, where would we find citizens willing to mount an armed attack upon. . . ."

"Gentlemen—and we are gentlemen, not serfs or peasants," snapped Pietro, interrupting his senior compatriot in mid-sentence, "I assure you that our Assisi is at a crossroads. Gone forever are the days of the old ways; is not the old being overthrown by the new? Yes, I assure you, a public commune is the only answer to the numerous problems of our city, and at the top of that list I would place the critical task of organizing some public system for the removal of our filth and garbage. A commune would also have the authority to order new gates by breaking open our city walls. Such new gates would allow for greater trade to enter our city. And, my good Filippo, to your question about where we would find the necessary men to join an armed struggle to tumble down the duke's fortress, that hated symbol of our domination, I would say: Assisi abounds in good men, and many are those who would be willing to fight for her honor. Yes, brave, strong young men such as my son, Francesco."

"*C*urious," commented Pietro. "Comrades, what do you make of it?" It was odd during this the growing season, when peasants would usually be hard at work in the fields, that ever-growing numbers of them were flowing onto the road. As they approached Montellimar and noontide drew near, the road became even more congested with

crowds of people entering from the side roads. Above distant treetops Francesco could see the gray stone spire of the Cathedral of Montellimar rising fingerlike into the sky. He could also faintly discern the distant sound of its bells. A most unusual occurrence, this noontime tolling caused him to shudder with an ominous foreboding. Lacking any logical reason for this premonition of evil, the thought vanished in the midst of the growing sea of humanity surging around him.

Just outside Montellimar, Pietro leaned over from his saddle to question a shabbily dressed man in the swelling crowd tramping alongside him on the dusty road, "Friend, may I ask: What is the occasion for this large crowd headed for Montellimar? Is today a special local feast day or, perhaps, a local fair?"

"No, sir," the man replied respectfully, removing his hat in deference to the richly-clothed, mounted merchant. "'Tis far better than any holy feast day. Today in the town square in front of the cathedral there's to be a burning of a heretic. Everyone's a'coming from the nearby villages. Even farmers are leaving their fields to see it."

"A heretic!" responded Pietro. "To what heretical sect does the man belong?"

"Not a man, sir. The heretic is a woman!" the peasant shouted in order to be heard over the rising roar along the crowded road. "She's one of those damned Cat'tar heretics. The story I've heard is that some priest tried to make love with her, but she rejected him, saying, 'Never, priest! I would suffer everlasting damnation by having sex with you or with any man!' Well sir, at once the good priest realized she must be one of those damned heretical Pure Ones that's been rising up in this part of southern France. So he did his duty straight away and reported her to the authorities. At her heresy trial, they say she boldly declared that the Church rulers had no authority from God to judge her. She then brazenly proceeded to speak to the reverend fathers about her cult's heretical beliefs, such as women being equal to men—in all things, mind you! Despite their many attempts to sway her back to the truth, she stubbornly refused to recant her false religion and return to Holy Mother Church. So today she'll be burned at noon. Blessed be the Lord."

The powerful forward-rushing waves of men, women and children began sweeping the caravan along with it off the main road and down toward the looming city gates. "Heresy, indeed!" Pietro shouted over the noise to his companions. "Women being equal to men: Now that's what I call real heresy—truly madness! God has ordained that men are

 superior to women. He gave us greater strength of body and of mind to rule our families. Women are subjected to the authority of their fathers or their husbands. Submission, not equality, is God's will." As they reached the shadows of Montellimar's city gates, the mournful peeling of the cathedral bells ceased. Pietro took command of the situation, shouting to his armed guards, "We're going into the city, but you fight yourselves free from this mob and return to the main road. And, you servants, take our loaded pack mules and join up with them there. If necessary, don't hesitate to use your weapons to clear a path through this mob to insure the safety of our goods until we return."

Then, along with the other merchants and their sons, he was swept along with the human flood pouring through the gates toward the center of the town. As that river of witnesses emptied into the cathedral square at the end of the street, Pietro shouted to his companions, "Guide your horses off to the side, allow the mob to move up and then fall in behind the last of them."

They now sat mounted at the back edge of the crowd where they could still easily see over the heads of the peasants that filled up the cathedral square as a single tower bell began tolling the hour. Just in front of the cathedral a large wooden platform had been erected, upon which sat the bishop, robed clergy, and other dignitaries. Directly in front of the platform, closed in upon by the mob, a young woman was chained to a tall post and surrounded with logs and branches piled as high as her breasts. The restless mob slowly grew quiet as a single large church bell tolled the twelfth hour of high noon.

Silence followed the fading echo of the twelfth and final bell. A stillness settled upon the crowd like a shroud, as a hooded, black-robed monk from the Cluny Abbey began to descend the steps of the platform. He walked solemnly toward the young woman chained to the post, stopping only when he stood directly in front of her.

"Repent! Save your soul from the claws of the Devil and his undying fires of hell," he shouted, holding up a crucifix before her face. "In the name of our blessed Lord Jesus Christ and the generous mercy of Holy Mother Church, you are this day given one final chance to renounce your false beliefs. Do you, accursed maiden, submit to the Church of Rome and know that by doing so you will save your soul?"

Holding its breath, the crowd, as one body, leaned forward, eager to hear her response, while secretly hoping she wouldn't repent of her heresy. The monk held his large crucifix even higher above her and

repeated his plea for her to renounce her heresy, but the young woman remained as mute as the aged gray stones of the cathedral.

"Burn the witch!" came an angry cry from the crowd to the right, and then from the left someone shouted, "Burn, Satan's bitch!" As when flaming torches are thrown on piles of dry straw, so now the chants began, "Burn Witch . . . Burn Bitch . . . Burn Witch . . . Burn Bitch. . . ." The raging ire leapt quickly across the mob, consuming it until the screams of fury fused into the thunderous roar of a single voice.

Mounted next to Francesco, Albertino shouted to him over the roar, "This crowd has come to Montellimar for a holiday away from the endless dawn-to-dark drudgery of their drab lives. They're starving for a savage spectacle, hungry for this most hideous of all human punishments, and none of them wants to be disappointed by her denouncing her beliefs!"

"Fool! You've sealed your eternal fate," the monk cried out over the chanting. "May God have mercy on you, for this very day you have sent yourself to hell." Then, whirling around, he motioned to a soldier with a flaming torch in his hand. At that signal, the man ran forward, tossed the torch onto the stacks of dry branches and logs and then jumped back. Mounted on horseback, Francesco watched everything. He gasped in horror as the dry logs quickly erupted into a spiraling tower of hungry flames leaping skyward. As red and yellow fingers of the fire and clouds of swirling white smoke encircled her body, the young woman neither wept nor cried out. Soon the square was saturated with the stench of burning human flesh only slightly softened by the aroma of burning wood. It was something that Francesco had never smelled before; it was a sickening experience he knew he would never forget. He also felt sure that he would always remember the sight of this poor woman's hideous death as she was engulfed in roaring flames so intense that the onlookers in the front rows held their hands over their faces to shield themselves from the searing heat. Searching far and wide over the faces of the crowd, he hoped he might see some sign of pity or sympathy. Yet even in the countenances of children, he saw only an eerie fascination, even glee, as they watched her painfully die."

Francesco felt himself becoming nauseous as his head and stomach were spinning from the horror of the inferno and the stench of the burning flesh. So he was greatly relieved when his father shouted an order for them to return to the road and the rest of their caravan.

After the merchants' caravan rode some distance in silence, Pietro opened the issue: "A necessary lesson. Harsh, but necessary. For the Church must be like a good father, who in certain circumstances chastises his son—or, in this case, daughter. The most serious errors demand the most severe discipline. Was not the Patriarch Abraham willing to slaughter his only son out of obedience to God's command? God requires a stable society on this earth. The Church must be a stern patriarch as was Abraham, and the burning of that heretic woman was not just a necessary lesson for her but, more importantly, for all those ignorant peasants. Even though they can't read or write, they clearly understood today's lesson: Obey the Church and don't stray from it, or *this* will be your fate! What happened to her can just as easily happen to any one of you! I ask you, gentlemen, must not the Church act unflinchingly to crush this claptrap of seeing women as equal to men, of ignorant laymen making themselves equal to the clergy, of bands of unemployed, pious poverty-addicted men and women wandering the countryside waiting for God to feed and cloth them as if they were the lilies of the field. Jobless, mind you, unproductive for society! They're nothing more than religious beggars who roam the roads prattling on about the kingdom of God! As businessmen our fortunes depend upon a social order that guards against the dire consequences of such deviant ideas. Gentlemen, what happened back there, while it may seem harsh, was clearly necessary, for God compels the Church to cleanse society thoroughly of every poisonous infection."

No one in the caravan challenged Pietro's remarks or even commented on how unusual it was for him to be speaking favorably of the Church. Francesco, deeply submerged in thought, hadn't really listened to his father. "What unbelievable silent courage," he pondered, "and what an enormous cost she paid for her unshakable religious conviction. Could I, Francesco of Assisi, be as unwavering in my beliefs as that heroic heretic maid of Montellimar? Could I steadfastly endure the same intense suffering and torture without crying out in pain?"

The entire caravan let out a joyful cry at the first distant sighting of Assisi's orange-brown walls and stone houses topped with red tile roofs. As they stair-stepped up the steep side of Mount Subasio, Francesco removed his lute from its protective leather bag and began strumming it, softly singing to himself:

My beloved Assisi, I'm coming home again.

I left a naive lad, but return, I hope, a man.

My soul is churning with life's turbulent foam,

disquieted by escapades and events in a far-off land.

O Assisi, will you be a home or prison for me?

For this son of yours has grown restless to roam.

My journey to the Chambery Fair has set me free,

yet it's imprisoned me in chains of guilt and doubt.

I've felt great joy and excitement, shame and fear,

seen worldly wonders and the horrors of hell.

I've encountered the wise and the wicked

And learned to make music that can cast a spell.

O beloved lute, let your soul sing free.

As heaven's lightning seared your wood,

may your strings release a divine energy,

awakening my soul to full manhood.

As the waters of the large fountain in the central piazza of Assisi were gushing up and bubbling over, so were the greetings of Francesco's friends. Gathered at their usual place in front of the old Roman temple of Minerva, they cried out, "Francesco, Francesco, tell us everything!" Tell us all that happened at the Chambery Fair!"

Animated by his recent creative surge as well as his well-exercised storytelling gift, Francesco proceeded to embellish with copious and colorful exaggeration the various events and sights of his journey to France and back home. He loved imitating his father, and so spoke to them with bravado about the new age that was dawning and how it would introduce new ways of life and conducting business, creative possibilities that would produce fresh ways of thinking and great new inventions.

"That's just talk, Francesco," said one of his friends. "I haven't seen any new inventions here in Assisi."

"Did you see any in France?" asked another.

"Well, not actually myself, but I did speak to men at the fair who had, and they even showed me a picture of a wondrous invention called

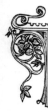

a windmill. Windmills are being used everywhere now in the Lowlands and in France to. . . ."

"Windmills? We've had watermills here in Italy ever since the Romans, but mills run by the wind? Come on, Francesco, you're making a joke."

"No, they really exist! They're as high as fortress towers, only at the top they have four large arms that look like spokes on a wheel. These long wooden arms have struts to which are tied large pieces of cloth, much like the sails of a ship. When the wind blows, it fills these cloth sails and makes them rotate. This causes a series of wheels and cogs inside the tower to move machinery that grinds grain. My father hails them as one of the signs of this new age, for unlike watermills, which require a river, these new mills can be set up anywhere the wind blows, and they will soon revolutionize. . . ."

"Francesco, your windmills are interesting," Emiliano interrupted, "but we'd rather hear about something more to our tastes—like the French women! Is it true that they are more beautiful than our native Umbrian maidens?" Of all his friends gathered around the fountain, Francesco was most overjoyed to see his dear friend Emiliano. He was muscularly built and stood a head and a half taller than his wiry friend. He often joked that he was more muscular because he was the son of a wine merchant and daily had to carry heavy wine barrels and cases of wine. Emiliano was as handsome as he was strong, possessing thick black hair, fair skin and classical Roman features. However, what attracted Francesco most about Emiliano as a friend was his vitality, sense of humor, and a luminous inner quality that surpassed his physical presence.

"Yes, yes, Francesco," chuckled the chorus of friends, wagging their fingers at him. "Tell us all about those French whores at the fair! Our older friends who have traveled there have told us all kinds of stories. So, what about you? Did you. . . ? Come on, Francesco, tell us the truth."

"Well, am I not a man? What do you think happened?" he said with a wink toward Emiliano. "Use your imaginations, my friends. I would not want to lead you into the mortal sin of impure thoughts with a detailed retelling of my lusty adventures with those French beauties. But I will show you one beauty with whom I fell in love. Like my father, who brought many treasures back to Assisi, I did not return simply with memories, my young comrades." Removing his lute from its leather bag, he continued, "This is the real treasure I brought home from my trip. Allow me to reveal her great beauty."

From the moment he began strumming his lute, his friends were captivated by the enchanting beauty of the music he played. He could see the change in their eyes. While he knew how his flamboyant personality could magically draw friends, as he now strummed his lute and sang the lusty songs of the troubadours, he saw how his charm was greatly enhanced. Spontaneously, he jumped up on the stone rim of the fountain and began strolling around it, singing and accompanying himself with his new French lute. Townfolk passing through the piazza and merchants whose shops lined the square paused to listen, commenting to one another about how truly gifted was the son of Pietro Bernadone.

Emiliano was beaming, proud of his friend's unusual ability to attract all kinds of people, a talent that he sensed sprung from his unique sense of freedom and his fountain-like, bubbling enthusiasm. He reflected on how Francesco seemed to have been born with the enthusiasm and zest for life of ten average men. Watching his friend singing as he strolled around the rim of the fountain, he thought, "Bernadone, you're a born entertainer; you're fully alive when you're performing in front of others." Then, like a town herald, he cried out, "Hail, Francesco, the passionate troubadour of Assisi."

As his young companions clapped and shouted agreement with Emiliano's declaration, Assisi's church bells began peeling their announcement of the noon hour, and merchants dutifully started to close their shops. Francesco slipped his lute back into its leather bag, saying, "Dear friends, it's great being back with you. After we've had our dinner and the old folks are taking their midday naps, the streets will be empty. So, let's play some football! I'll bring a ball, and we can meet up at the other end of town at the Piazza San Giorgio."

After Pica's usual large noon meal, Pietro took his customary long nap before returning to work at his shop. Francesco hurried out of his

home and up the empty, quiet streets to the piazza, glad for this brief time away from assisting his father in their cloth shop. While shorter and slighter in stature than his good friend Emiliano and his other friends, he made up for anything he lacked in physical stature by being extremely agile and a fast runner. That day, as usual, he zestfully outraced his friends from one end of Assisi to the other while kicking a leather bag filled with beans—otherwise known as a football. Cheering and hollering in their youthful exuberance, they chased him down the narrow, twisting streets, eager to get their feet on the ball. On this afternoon, Signore Guittone d'Acsoli returned early to his shop, just at the moment Francesco and his friends came racing down the narrow street leaping over stalls in front of the merchants' shops, dodging carts and people.

Shortly after Pietro returned from his nap, an angry Guittone, accompanied by several other merchants, stomped into the Bernadone cloth shop. Shaking his finger at Pietro, he snapped, "This afternoon, your son, Francesco, along with his gang of reckless youths, nearly frightened to death some of my best customers, who had just come at the end of their afternoon naps to purchase some cloth. Pietro, this is not the first time! They recklessly play their wild game in our streets even after the nap time has ended, and they have disturbed the business of these brother merchants as well. We have finally agreed on the need to speak to you, Pietro. You must. . . ."

"Gentlemen, welcome to my shop. Alas, I was taking my nap and so was unaware of the commotion. So, pray tell me, Guittone, my friend, in these games who wins?"

"Your son, naturally. He always wins!"

"Ah, good! That's all that counts, isn't it? This game is good training for business—to play football harder than any of the others, to compete heartily. I want my son to be a winner." Smiling, Pietro shrugged his large shoulders and said, "And, gentleman, I ask you to be patient, for he's still young enough to need a bit of play."

"He's fifteen!" Guittone fired back. "Surely, Bernadone, isn't it time for him to put aside play for serious work, time to look toward getting married and settling down? My own son, Cino, is soon to be married— in a few months when his bride-to-be will turn sixteen. They have been betrothed since he was fifteen and she eleven. I have completed, I might say proudly, a most beneficially arranged marriage, one in which the joining of our two families will be of great profit, especially to my

family. And my Cino, naturally, is eager to be married, as are all virile young men. Is your son Francesco betrothed yet?"

"Signore Guittone, and you other distinguished gentlemen," Pietro said, stretching out his arms as if attempting to place them around all their shoulders, "know how truly I regret the disturbance today at your stalls. I promise to speak to my son as soon as he returns to the shop. As a merchant's son, he especially must be respectful of each of you and your businesses—and, of course, your customers as well." His grandiose and gracious reply artfully avoided the question about his son's betrothal. Then he extended his right hand, escorting them to the rear of his shop, saying, "Please, spare me some of your precious time, for I have something of importance to say to you." When they had gathered at the far end of his shop, he spoke in a low voice, "What I have to say, gentlemen, is most secret, as confidential as if spoken in a confessional. Is that understood? I am entrusting you with the good news that the birth of our long-awaited commune is finally near! In a few days, preparations will be completed in our plan to storm and lay siege to the fortress of Rocca Maggiore and depose Duke Conrad!"

"I'm an old man, Pietro," sighed one of the merchants patting his large belly. "I can't climb up that peak. I'm too old and fat to fight, as are most of the others," he said as he widened his arms to include the other gray-haired merchants in the shop.

"No, my good friends. We're not asking that any of you go to war or bear arms. All that we need is your support and backing. We've secretly gathered enough men to mount an attack upon that old fortress, which upon careful examination is very vulnerable. What is needed if we are to establish Assisi's commune is the support of our leading merchants. If you are with us, then like docile sheep the rest of the citizens will follow. Friends, I remind you that we're living at a critical moment in history. A new age is dawning that will witness the emergence of a new wealth, and it will surpass the old order of wealth and noble privilege." They continued to discuss the various benefits that an uprising would have for them and the city, such as a solution to Assisi's garbage problems, new gates for trade and a power base from which to greatly expand their business interests. When they were finished, the merchants gathered in Pietro's shop voiced their wholehearted approval of the plan. While Pietro never precisely identified the "we" in his military plan, these men understood only too well the need for secrecy in such a dangerous affair. After carefully detailing their involvement, they promised that when the day of the attack came, they would fully support the violent overthrow of Duke Conrad.

*F*rancesco knew how his father relished the power and influence of his position as one of the city's leading merchants, but even at age fifteen that prestige didn't appeal to him. Moreover, he found selling cloth to be boring. "I desire something," he would say, talking to himself as he folded cloth in the shop, "more than a dull merchant's life. I lust for something much more adventuresome. I even dread the idea of marriage, for it means I will be imprisoned for the rest of this life in some prearranged marriage to someone I don't love—especially to a woman I don't even know."

"Who is it that you don't you know, Francesco?" his father asked from the front of the shop.

"Sorry, Father. I was talking to myself. I was wondering what kind of customer might purchase this fine cloth that I'm folding."

As he refolded the cloth, he thought, silently this time, "I'm nearly sixteen now, and while I'm not interested in marriage, I am having increasing sexual stirrings. At the same time—though it doesn't make sense—I feel the arousal of powerful spiritual feelings. I wonder if that's normal? And the voices—they're back again. The other day after a church bell finished peeling out the hour, I heard them again. This time, I swear they—or it—said, "Come to me." He shook his head at the thought. Even stranger to him was the notion that sexual and spiritual stirrings seemed to go hand in hand. "Spiritual—or, at least, religious—isn't how I would describe myself—not since my boyhood, anyhow." Ignoring his recent Herculean struggle with his conscience on the return trip from Chambery, he thought to himself, "I know it disappoints my mother, but I'm becoming more like my father with regard to the Church. Like my friends and the other young men of Assisi, about all I do is accompany my mother to Mass at the Cathedral of San Rufino on Sundays and feast days." He had to smile at that thought; for most of Francesco's young friends, the primary reason for going to Sunday Mass wasn't to pray but to gape at the young women of Assisi—and to be seen by them.

The next Sunday morning as he dressed in his favorite scarlet tunic for Mass, he thought, "Were it not for church times, when would I and the other merchants' sons have an opportunity to parade before the young women in our finest clothing and newest styles?"

"More modest attire, young men, please," snarled the old priest after Mass at the cathedral doors. Shaking his finger at Emiliano and Francesco as they left church, he added, "Positively immodest, shameful, shameful." The two friends, along with their companions who dressed in the latest fashion, delighted in calling themselves *La Compagna della Calza,* the Company of the Hose. They wore plumed hats, short jackets with skintight hose, with each leg's hose being a different color. Their toe-to-waist tights revealed every contour of their legs, buttocks and crotch. The two friends nodded solemnly at the frowning old priest as they passed him. Then they ran out into the warm sunlight that bathed the piazza in brilliant canary yellow.

"'More modest attire, young men . . .'" Francesco perfectly imitated the sour voice of the priest. "'Positively immodest, and shameful. . . .' Ah, dear Emiliano, the priests want us to dress as they do—in dull, lifeless black—positively modest and positively boring, as boring as a funeral."

The members of the Company of the Hose stood around exchanging comments about the young women they had seen at Mass: which ones had the largest breasts or the most beautiful hair, or who would bring the largest wedding dowry. Then, one by one, they departed for home and their large Sunday dinners. As he and Emiliano walked arm in arm away from the piazza, Francesco was especially aware of how in the past year Emiliano had grown taller, more muscular and handsomer.

"Friend, did you see her this morning in church?" Emiliano asked eagerly.

"Who, pray tell, Emiliano, can you be speaking of?"

"You know very well who I mean, Francesco—Angela, Signore Fibonacci's oldest daughter! She's so beautiful. And her father is so rich. What a combination, eh, *caro mio?* And I, for one, am ready for marriage to such a beautiful woman as her." Tightly squeezing Francesco's shoulder, he added, "I can feel the wedding song playing in my loins. What about you, comrade?"

"Oh, yes, we're like twins. I've heard that same wedding song in my loins, and I'm more than ready. In fact, I've kept it secret until now, but my marriage has been arranged and the documents between my father and the father of my bride-to-be are now signed. I've been eagerly waiting to ask you, Emiliano: Will you be my best man?"

"Of course, my friend, but truly you surprise me with that announcement. Yes, yes, I'd be honored. So, tell me, now that the secret is out, whom are you marrying?"

"I'm marrying the divinely beautiful Angela Fibonacci!"

"Yeeee die, thief!" snarled Emiliano, as he playfully began choking his friend's neck with his muscular left arm. "I'll not be your best man, I'll be your pallbearer!"

The two friends continued their conversation until reaching the intersection, where they parted to return to their respective homes. "Alas, Emiliano," Francesco thought to himself as he walked alone. "I did keep secret from you that the strange stirring I've been feeling isn't in my loins. I would like to talk to you about it if I could, but it's so mysterious. I've tried to drown it in drink and partying, but that strange gnawing away in my soul won't go away. "

THIEF-LIKE, FRANCESCO SNEAKED ALONG, HUGGING THE
old stone-wall buildings that lined the street leading to the small
piazza of Santa Maria Maggiore. Although it was near the end of the
afternoon nap period and the streets were still deserted, he constantly
kept glancing over his shoulder to ensure that none of his young
companions was anywhere in sight. He was relieved at his good fortune
to find an empty piazza in front of the old Santa Maria Maggiore, the
original cathedral of Assisi. After days of anguish he had mustered up
the courage to go and speak to someone about all the strange stirrings
in his heart. Entering the dark, old Romanesque church, he scanned
the stout yellowish stone walls and then stood gazing up at its dark
ceiling of massive wooden beams spanning the nave. As he lowered his
eyes from the ceiling, he saw a priest standing near the altar in the front
of the church. Seized with panic, he whirled around and started toward
the front doors.

"Young man, don't leave!" the priest called out in a loud voice.
"Can I be of help? Do you wish to go to confession?"

"No, Father, I don't. It's nothing . . ." he stammered, his heart
throbbing like that of a rabbit snared in a trap. If there was one thing
he definitely had not come for, he thought, it was going to confession.
In the midst of that thought, he suppressed a surge of guilt that over
these past several weeks often haunted him about Chambery. It was
another of those moments when he realized that his lingering guilt
could seemingly sleep for long periods and then awaken without
warning.

"My son, come up here, please. Surely you've come for some
reason. Perhaps I can be of help."

"Thank you, Father. Yes, if you have time, I do have something I would like to . . . talk about."

"Good. Follow me; we can speak privately in the sacristy." The priest led him into the sacristy, which was located just off the altar area. Francesco had never been inside a sacristy before and found a certain fascination with this pious pantry of holy things used for the rituals of the sacraments, processions, and Mass. Three walls of the room were lined from floor to ceiling with dark wooden cabinets whose open shelves held bronze candlesticks of various sizes, gold chalices, large silver, jeweled reliquaries, and long-chained bronze censors used for incensing. Along the other wall were racks of processional banners bearing various gold-threaded images of the saints and the Madonna holding the Christ Child.

"I'm Padre Giuseppe," the priest said as he seated himself in a chair and began smoothing out the folds in his cassock. Gesturing toward a chair opposite his, he said, "Please be seated, my son. Now, tell me what brought you here."

Clearing his throat, Francesco drew in a deep breath and began, "I'm Francesco Bernadone, and my father is Pietro."

"Yes, I know who you are. Your mother, the devout Pica, frequently comes to daily Mass. She is a woman of deep prayer and holiness. And you, Francesco, what can I do for you today?"

"I'm confused, Padre, by the different voices I hear . . . well, they're not really voices in the way that we are speaking to each other; they're . . . er . . . more like voices one hears in one's heart. But they're as real to me as your voice is today. I hear several voices: One calls me to be a troubadour—I hear it when I see how my singing and playing the lute brings joy to people. Another voice sounds like my father's and tells me to obey my father and become a merchant. A third voice, a bold one, calls me to become a warrior, to seek knighthood. These three voices are understandable, I guess, but recently I've begun hearing . . . er . . . other, more disconcerting voices. I hear them in the stillness after church bells have rung or when I'm alone and watching a sunset or, most strangely, when I'm with my friends for an evening of drinking in the tavern."

"These voices, my son, what do they say to you?"

"'Come to me'—or something like that." Inwardly he breathed an enormous sigh of relief that he had withheld from the *padre* his fear that the voices were somehow connected to God.

"'Come to me,' you say? Well, Francesco Bernadone, it is clear that you have a vocation!" Spreading out wide his soft, pale white hands, he said, "Those voices you hear belong to God, who is calling you to the priesthood, or perhaps to join the monastery."

"No, I couldn't be a monk! For me that would be like being buried alive! And as for the priesthood. . . ."

"Oh, my son, don't misunderstand me. I don't mean being some simple, peasant parish priest serving in a remote Umbrian village. Indeed, while I know from the priests up at San Giorgio that your Latin isn't the best and that your education in the classics is limited, they have told me about your amazing memory. Padre Raniero says you know much of Holy Scripture and the Psalms by heart; that, of course, is a real asset! With that gift you can easily learn all the Latin prayers and master all the rituals of Holy Mother Church. Ah, but what is of much greater advantage is that the Bernadone family is wealthy! With your father's wealth and influence here in Assisi, you could rise quickly in the Church. You know, my son, the Holy Spirit, heaven's anointing dove, hearkens to the sound of silver." He giggled, wagging a finger near his ear, "Jingle, jingle, jingle. It's quite possible that you could become a bishop when you make connections and find the right patron."

Francesco's eyes had been downcast, as if studying the pavement stones in the room, but they now focused on his finely crafted, fashionable leather shoes. Though they were his favorite pair, at this moment they failed to give him any pride; instead, they began to pain him, as if his feet had been placed in a carpenter's vice that was tightly squeezing them. And it was not just his feet that felt cramped. He began to feel strangled by a strange swelling in his throat. It also seemed the sacristy's walls, with their tall, dark cabinets, were beginning to close in upon him, while the ceiling seemed to be slowly descending, intending to crush him. Overwhelmed with a need to move and almost gasping for air, he struggled to appear calm as he sat facing the pale-faced, black-cassocked priest, whose white, floating, effeminate hands again smoothed out the folds in his cassock. The room's rancid odor of incense, stale candle wax and musty smelling, ornate Mass vestments made him feel like he was suffocating.

"Padre Giuseppe," he said, nearly leaping out of his chair as if it was on fire, "Thank you for your counsel. Yes, I will think about. . . ."

"My son, don't you mean *pray* about it? You do pray, don't you?"

The City of Assisi

to Mount Subasio

to L'Eremo
the hermitage

1. Bernadone Cloth Shop & Home
2. Piazza del Commune
3. Temple of Minerva
4. Giacosa Wine Shop & Home
5. House of Angela Fibonacci
6. The Cathedral of San Ruffino
7. House of Clare Scifi
8. Fortress of Rocca Maggiore
9. San Maria Maggiore
   & the Bishop's House
10. Church of San Giorgio
11. Chapel of San Damiano
12. Dung Gate
13. The Collis Infernus
14. Portiuncula - Santa Maria
    of the Angels

"Of course, *pray*. Ah, yes, Padre," he nodded in agreement, backing out of the sacristy, "Yes, that's what I will do: I'll pray about these things. Thank you, Padre, for taking time to visit with me today." Standing in the doorway of the sacristy, he summoned up all his strength to restrain his urge to run. "I'm sorry that I must leave so quickly. The napping hour is nearly over, and I must return to my work at my father's shop. God bless you, Padre." As he rapidly walked down the long, empty nave, the sound of his fleeing footsteps echoed off the ancient stone walls. Reaching the large doors, he partially opened one and peeked outside into the piazza. Cautiously looking to the left and the right, he made sure none of his friends might see him leaving the church.

"Pray about it," he mumbled as he quickly walked up the cobblestone street toward the main piazza of Assisi. Why on earth, he wondered, did he ever go to see that priest? And as for prayer, except for brief prayers before going to bed and those he said at Sunday Mass with his mother, he had pretty much lost touch with that boyhood practice. Oh, he might mumble short prayers when he encountered a leper or deformed cripple asking to be spared their terrible affliction. Even now, he could hear his father's voice saying that prayer is the business of monks and priests—and perhaps of pious folk on Sunday morning. Then, like a mouse scampering across the floor, a recollection from the Chambery Fair streaked quickly in a diagonal path across his mind. Hadn't old Claude de Lune, the lute maker, also asked him if he prayed?

He was shaken out of his musings by the voices of his companions coming from the piazza. Before he had turned the corner to enter the piazza, their voices grew louder, and he could make out their taunting: "Signore Strapazzate, tell us, tell us, won't you, please: What is God's revelation for us on this warm afternoon?" He had no need to see the actual scene to know that his friends were unmercifully teasing one of the Assisi's wandering beggars. As Francesco entered the piazza, he saw the man, a deranged hunchback, short in stature with wild eyes that darted out from an unwashed, bearded face that was surrounded by snakelike, tangled black hair. He was filthy from head to toe and dressed in lice-invested rags. The fashionably attired youths had nicknamed him Signore Strapazzate as a play on *vova strapazzate*, "scrambled eggs," since they joked that his brains were scrambled. To

this ridiculing designation they added the ridiculously grand title of Signore.

Francesco's friends were gathered on the worn-smooth steps of the old Roman temple of Minerva. They were poking fun at the ragged old hunchback, engaged in their usual mockery of shouting his name as they simultaneously whirled one hand around over the top of their heads as if they were scrambling eggs. At the same time, they would give voice to taunts like, "Signore Strapazzate, oh please share with us even a small scrap of heaven's most recent revelation."

As Francesco approached, one of the youths knelt before the dirty hunchbacked beggar, and begged, "Signore Seer of Assisi, reveal to us your most recent vision."

Another chimed in, "O holy visionary with a pregnant back, what divine message have those saints and angels painted on the church walls delivered to you this day?"

Strapazzate raised his right hand high in the air and began moving it across the space to the left of his head as if it was outlining some invisible writing that hung suspended over the piazza. As he traced the message, he chanted:

"The Lord says, marry no woman, that you will leave no orphans.

Weeping mothers will cradle their shattered sons in their laps, and the agonizing wailing of Assisi will be heard in Perugia.

Kyrie eleison—Lord, have mercy—cry the seeping clouds. *Dominus vobiscum, doloroso Donna,* and donkeys. . . ."

Abruptly his jumbled prophecy ended as he began whirling round and round, flapping his arms like an angry rooster's wings. Saliva dribbled from his lips, and his eyes glowed like fiery embers. Then, just as quickly as he had begun, he stopped spinning and began chanting again, *"Dominus vobiscum,* you stupid children."

"Et cum spirit-two-two- to you, stupid Strapazzate."

"Repent, lecherous lads, gash yourselves and lament; War, riding a bony skeleton steed, even now is at Assisi's gates.
Your stinking corpses will be food for the birds of the air.

Beasts of the field will feast upon your fair arms and legs.
Evil brews up a dark summer storm over hunchbacked
Subasio, for even now your fathers are sowing the seeds of
disaster among the yellow sunflowers and the green olives
trees. Like Assisi's olive trees, your sad mothers will weep oily
tears. . . .
Alms, alms, forget not God's poor. Alms, alms for the poor."

Then he dropped to his knees, and laying his head flat onto the
stone payment of the piazza, said, "Listen! Don't you hear it?
Rumbling, tumbling, fumbling, jumbling—the earth is quaking."
Then, leaping to his feet he fearfully began glancing in all directions.
"Beware, stupid children: Everything, all of this, is about to be upside-
downed, overturned, and all will. . . ." Mid-sentence, he was thrown
into a seizure and began rolling and spinning around like a top on the
payment stones at the base of the fountain.

"Ah, the Gospel According to Santo Strapazzate," shouted one of
the youths, and they all made a small sign of the cross on their
foreheads, lips, and hearts, whirling their right hands around and
around over the top of their heads in their scrambling-eggs salute.

Francesco and Emiliano had not joined their friends in their
ridicule of this beggar, for they only felt great pity for tormented
Tommaso of Spello, which some said was his real name. They knew
that the women of Assisi fed him with scraps of leftover food and asked
him to pray for their needs. Francesco and Emiliano were also aware
that many held the folk belief that those who are physically deformed,
mentally deranged, or who suffer from seizures are often God's
messengers, calling them "the Children of Providence."

The dirty, disheveled hunchback slowly came to a stop and lay still
on the pavement. Then, with some effort, he stood up and hobbled
over toward Francesco and Emiliano. Nearly overwhelmed by the
stench of Strapazzate's unwashed body, Francesco feared he would
vomit. As the stinking beggar stood facing them unsteadily, he leaned
over closer to Francesco and stared into his eyes, saying, "You are not
like the others. *Deo gratias!*" Then, as his head began rocking back and
forth, he spoke in a whisper, "Francesco Bernadone, the Spirit of the
Lord is upon you . . . to proclaim glad tidings to the poor and to bring
joy to. . . ."

The loud clanging of the Santa Maria Maggiore bells announcing the top of the hour drowned out the rest of his words. The bells signaled to Francesco and Emiliano that it was time for them to return to their fathers' shops. As they left the piazza, Emiliano asked, "Good friend, what did you think of Strapazzate's prophecy?"

"Emiliano, look and see how bright the sun shrines; this day is as fair as heaven. I see no bony skeleton steed of death at our gates; I hear no blaring trumpets or rattling drums of battle. We're at peace with Perugia, at least for the moment."

"*Caro mio*, I did not mean his ramblings about death and war. I meant his final words: Even as soft as they were, I heard what he said about God's Spirit being upon you."

Francesco only smiled at him and began whirling his right hand around over the top of his head.

*A*s usual, Francesco's father was taking his nap after their large noon meal while his mother was cleaning the pots and dishes. Since he wasn't required to be at the family cloth shop until later in the afternoon, Francesco decided to go for a walk outside the city walls to feed his recent and growing hunger for solitude. He proceeded down a twisting path that led from the city to the groves of olive trees below and passed by the old, tumbled-down church of San Damiano. As he walked, he thought, "What I need is a quiet place where I can resolve these tensions. I feel like I'm being dragged in opposite directions by wild horses. One drags me along the way of my father into the life of being a cloth merchant. Another horse pulls me in the direction of being a traveling troubadour. Now, along with these two, a third horse has been harnessed to me and is pulling me with strange but strong spiritual feelings. Merchant, troubadour, and priest—well, forget that last one!"

Halfway down the path to the abandoned chapel, he changed his mind, thinking, "I'd rather walk up in the forest." Retracing his steps to the top of the hill, he began climbing up into the ridges of Mount Subasio. In the warm heat of the day he climbed higher, following deer and other animal paths. Upon coming to the crest of a high ridge, he sat down on a rock to rest and to gaze eastward out across the broad fertile green valley below now bathed in golden sunlight. From the west, dark gray rain clouds began moving upward into the sky above the ridge. In the distance over the treetops he could see Assisi's red tile

rooftops and her stately stone church towers. From this high point, how small and insignificant Assisi looked.

"Where do I belong," he said aloud. "Back there in Assisi as a merchant? On the road, wandering? Or should I be somewhere else? Who am I? Which shall I become in life: a troubadour or a businessman, a minstrel or a married man? Ah, Francesco, do not forget your other dream of being a knight and going off to fight in the Crusades! How difficult it is to choose."

A low rumble of thunder from behind caught his attention. He turned to see an approaching rainstorm for which he was quite unprepared. He was equally surprised by another rainstorm brewing within him. A tiny stream of tears began tricking down his cheeks at the seeming hopelessness of choosing his path. "Stop it," he snapped. "Men don't cry! If my father saw me crying like this, he would be so ashamed—for only women and children cry. Why am I even in this melancholic mood? My heart is grayer than those storm clouds gathering overhead. I know—I'll try singing, for at the fair Tourdion told me that singing cures melancholia." As if he were sitting with his lute back at the fair, he began to sing:

O Lord of the high heavens,
my partying comrades call me
'Assisi's noble Prince of Feasts,'
yet look at my sad state now.
O Lord of life's highs and lows,
look upon your poor servant,
for my happy heart has been stolen,
my soul is sunk in black despair.
O Lord, help your poor servant.
O God, who has breathed life into all things,
restore my old joyful heart.
May your Holy Wind blow strongly
upon my stuck weather vane.
Point me in the way I should go:
Am I to be knight or a priest?
A merchant or a troubadour?
A husband or a minstrel?
O God, answer my sad plea:

What is your holy will for me?

"Why must you choose?" spoke a voice that almost seemed to come from within him but actually came from directly behind him. "Why not be all of them—all at the same time?"

Turning around, Francesco saw a man wearing what appeared to be a monk's habit, only it was gray. Lean and taller even than Francesco's father, he had a gray beard, interlaced with streaks of white, that flowed down to the middle of his chest. In his right hand he held a tall, gnarled wooden staff.

"I am Francesco Bernadone of Assisi," he said leaping to his feet and using his sleeve to wipe away his tears, "and I was. . . ."

"Praying, I believe," replied the old man, smiling. His aged face seemed illuminated from within in a way that made it appear surprisingly youthful for a man of his years. "Allow me to introduce myself: I'm Padre Antonio, a priest monk of the nearby Benedictine Abbey of Mount Subasio who now is living, by the goodness of God— and my abbot—as a hermit . . . ," Swinging his staff in a wide arc, he added, "up here in these stunningly beautiful hills."

Seeing Francesco's quizzical look, the old man said, "You may question if I'm really a monk, since I have let my clerical tonsure grow out and have a full head of hair. Living up here alone with God, who knows well enough that I am a cleric of the Church, why should I continue to keep shaving that symbolic circle on the top of my head as do my brother monks?" Then he playfully began shaking his full head of hair, making his long gray locks flip-flop as if they were dancing about his head. A louder and closer rumble of thunder caused him to chuckle. "Young man, it appears we're about to be visited by an Umbrian rainstorm. Best that you and I quickly find cover. Would you care to be my guest at my hermitage? It's not far from here."

"Thank you, Padre," Francesco replied, almost grateful for the storm and the opportunity it gave him to spend time with this aged but playful hermit. He was instantly drawn to the old man, whose hazel eyes were as gentle as any deer's yet always seemed to be dancing, almost leaping with joyful excitement. As the first large, warm drops of rain began falling, Francesco said, "I'd be happy to visit your hermitage—especially if it provides a dry place from this storm."

"As I said, it's not far, but we'll have to run for it, if we don't want to get soaked."

After the rainstorm slowly drifted past the mountain and out across the valley, the afternoon sun reappeared and worked its magic of casting long, slender blue shadows from the tall cedars over the two men seated under a thatched porch roof at the entrance to the hermit's cave.

"I built this roof over the opening of my cave so I could sit outside on afternoons like this to enjoy the mountain breezes." The pungent aroma of the onions and garlic hanging on cords from the rafter branches accented the fresh, clean scent of rain-soaked creation as the two men, seated on two old tree stumps, listened to the gentle sound of the last raindrops dripping from the roof poles.

"Padre, before you came here to live as a hermit, what did you do in the monastery?"

"Like all monks, a little of this and a little of that, but I fear the list is too long and would only bore you."

"No, please tell me, I'm curious."

"Well, let's see, I served as guestmaster, taught theology and Scripture to the junior monks, and was the infirmarian for the sick monks. I also served as confessor and spiritual guide to the younger monks, and even was given permission by the abbot to serve some time outside the abbey when I went on . . . ah. . . ." Waving his hand, he said, "Enough, enough, about this old man. Did you not introduce yourself to me as Francesco? A most unusual name—not a Christian one. What's your baptismal name?"

"You're right, Padre, my mother had me baptized Giovanni shortly after I was born while my father was away. But upon his return he renamed me Francesco, after France, a country for which he has great affection. It is an unusual name, true, but it makes me feel unique, and it's a reminder of his great fondness for me."

"Well, well," the old monk interjected, "look who has decided to join us—Frater Nicoletto!" A beautiful pure-black cat had jumped up into his lap and was gently stretching. "Most unusual, Giovanni, I'm a hermit who rarely has visitors, but whenever anyone does drop by, good Brother Nicoletto usually hides in the back of my cave." Nicoletto jumped off Antonio's lap and began rubbing up against Francesco's leg. As he reached down and began stroking Nicoletto, the cat rolled over on his back with his paws up in the air.

"Remarkable, Giovanni, you've made a friend! Cats only do that when they trust you, since in that position they expose themselves to

being injured, and they have a sixth sense that tells them who they can trust. You must have a pet cat."

"No, my mother doesn't like them. She believes in the old saying that cats are creatures of the devil and that witches use them as agents of their dark magic. She'd never allow one inside our home. Like most merchants, my father has kept them in his shop to kill mice, but he never gives them names, and, as far as I can remember, has never showed them any affection. In fact, he yelled at me one day when I cradled one of the cats in our shop and was petting it. He said, 'Grow up, Francesco and be a man! Stop acting like a woman, petting that cat. A man might have a dog for a pet, but for God's sake, Son, not a cat!' So I've never had a pet, even a dog, since my father would say, 'We're merchants, not hunters, so what need do we have for a dog?'"

"Interesting."

"Do you keep a cat here to ward off mice or, being a hermit, for company?"

"Actually, I keep him for luck! Black cats are good luck! Alongside your mother's folklore that black cats are agents of the devil, there's another belief that if a stray black cat appears at your door, good fortune will soon visit your house. So I decided to keep him."

Breaking out in a grin again, the old hermit said, "I'm only joking about me *keeping* the cat, for it was Nicoletto who decided to keep me! One day a year or so ago, he just showed up here at my cave and has never left. Such visitations must be reverenced. I believe God finds unusual ways to gift us with what we need, even when we don't know that we need it. He was a homeless, skinny, hungry cat, so I began feeding him, and before the next full moon, I had a companion hermit."

"You call him brother. Is that because at the abbey the monks call each other by that title?"

"Kind of. The Rule of St. Benedict requires that we receive all guests as Christ. Now, since the Holy Rule says, 'all,' you could say I welcomed Nicoletto as my brother in Christ." Opening his arms wide, he added, "As, indeed, all of God's creatures are our sisters and brothers. Is that not one of the implications of the Scripture that says, 'and the Word was made flesh'?" Then, spreading his arms even wider, he said, "God has a very large family, one that includes much more than us humans—cats, dogs, birds, squirrels, horses, sheep, donkeys, and even wolves are our brothers and sisters."

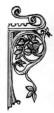

Francesco was a little taken aback by Antonio's strange words about animals being members of God's family. He had always thought the Word made flesh referred only to Christ, not to anyone else, especially not to Nicoletto and other dumb creatures. But not wanting to question the statement, his reply went down a different path: "Brother Nicoletto surely found good fortune when he came to your door and was adopted. He might easily still be a starving stray."

"Yes, you're right when you say he was fortunate, but are you not also fortunate? You've a good home, a caring father, and as with most Italian lads, I suspect, an adoring mother. You are most blessed in being a rich merchant's son, who has every reason to be happy. Yet earlier this afternoon as I came upon you, I couldn't help but overhear your prayer . . . or, should I say, your song—it expressed great sorrow. And as you turned around and saw me, your eyes were full of tears. It takes no great insight to see that you're not only an unhappy man but also a *hunted* one!"

"Hunted, Padre? I think your intuition misleads you: I'm no bandit or escaped prisoner!"

Tapping his forehead, the old hermit replied, "Giovanni, my mind knows you're no escaped prisoner or hunted criminal. " Then, as he tapped his chest, he added, "Ah, but this old heart tells me you're attempting to escape from one who is hunting you."

"Who would be hunting me, Padre?"

"God!"

Antonio's answer stung like the lash of a whip, confirming his worst fears about his mysterious voices. Eager, now, to change the subject, he asked, "Padre Antonio, you appear to be a wise man. May I ask you a couple of questions?"

"Of course, what do you wish to know?" he graciously replied, reverencing his guest's avoidance of something difficult.

"First, no one in Assisi, except my mother, calls me Giovanni, and she does so only when we are alone. Why have you been using my baptismal name when everyone else calls me Francesco? And secondly, when we met out on the ridge, you surprised me when you said something about my not having to choose between the various professions in life. What did you mean by that? How can one follow several ways at the same time?"

"Well Giovanni, let me address your second question first. But before I do, tell me more about your confusion in choosing a lifework.

Such questioning about career choices is very rare for young Italian men. As the son of Assisi's wealthiest cloth merchant, would not ancient custom dictate that you follow in his trade?"

"That's true, but unlike most of my friends, who desire only to follow in their father's footsteps, I do not. It's not that there isn't a tremendous pull into my father's profession—not only because of my father's strong will and even stronger expectations for me, but also because of the pull of power and affluence, and the new possibilities of trade and travel in the emerging social order. But my heart yearns to do other things, and I've recently come to hate the thought of being imprisoned in the drab life of a cloth merchant. When my friends and I play football, I enjoy kicking the leather ball down the streets—but now I'm beginning to feel just like that leather bag full of beans. It feels like others are kicking me where they want me to go instead of where I want to go. The tension of that pull in opposite directions is painful, and I guess that's the reason why I was so miserable when you came upon me this afternoon, even to the point of tears. I'm sorry I lost control and began to cry. It was particularly embarrassing to have someone see me—for men aren't supposed to cry!"

"Why is that? Why be ashamed of crying? Isn't it as natural as laughing? And men aren't afraid to laugh!"

"My father wouldn't agree. But even if crying is natural, I must confess to you something that isn't: I hear voices!"

"You hear voices?"

"Well, not really. I mean, they're not real voices in the same way that we're talking. Maybe they're only strong inclinations or feelings, but they seem to speak to me in . . . uh . . . unspoken words. It's difficult to explain to others, but to me they're very real. And recently, they've been more frequent and more insistent."

"I think I understand. Your soul has a tongue that speaks unlike any human tongue. Do not be afraid of your voices, Giovanni. Those who have souls with destinies hear stronger voices, and such voices express our deepest dreams."

"One voice calls me to become a warrior knight and to ride to glory fighting in the crusades."

"A noble aspiration, my young friend. And the other voices?"

"One of the strongest voices lures me to the open road singing love songs along the highways and across the countryside. I'm inspired by the wandering minstrels who bring such joy to others. I can play the

lute rather well, and listeners have old me that my music is beautiful, even enchanting."

"Indeed it is! Even with your sad words, I found your singing today most delightful!"

"Thank you, Padre. Right now I feel like I'm bursting with music, yet I'm afraid that this gift will dry up—or even die—when I am married and housebound and workbound. I can't imagine it surviving when I listen to the voice of my father, whom I love greatly and who has been so good to me. His voice shouts at me to grow up and become a man, and that means settling down, getting married, having a family, and following in his footsteps as the most successful cloth merchant in Assisi."

Brother Nicoletto jumped back up into Antonio's lap. As the old hermit gently stroked his cat's sable-black hair, he asked, "Do you not desire to share your bed with a loving wife, to have children and a home?"

"Sure, I have a real attraction to marriage—or at least to girls—but I don't know if that's really what I desire or if it's only the desire that as a man I'm supposed to have. While I'm confused about some desires, what I know for sure is that I desire *adventure*! And a family, wife, and home don't seem very adventuresome."

"Don't be too quick, Giovanni; perhaps they can be. Also, you've not yet mentioned the other voice that I feel quite certain you've been hearing. There is another voice, isn't there?" In the silence that followed Antonio's question only Brother Nicoletto's soft purring could be heard.

Finally, Francesco said, "I fear this will sound crazy, Padre, but I think I'm also beginning to hear the voice—or voices—of God, at least that's what my parish priest called them. These voices come to me at the strangest times. I've heard them in the ringing of church bells and even—and this may sound like madness—even in the midst of singing lusty ballads in Assisi's taverns."

"And this voice—what does it say?"

"I'm still mystified as to what it means, but it says, 'Come to me.'"

"Clearly, Giovanni, you're an unusual young man, and as you have many gifts, perhaps you also have many choices in life. Moreover, these desires may not be as conflicting as they first appear. So, as I asked earlier this afternoon, why choose?"

"That seems impossible! How can I not choose—my choices seem so opposite one another?"

"Giovanni, never say 'impossible'! Remember what the angel said to our Holy Mother Mary, 'With God all things are possible.' Our most generous Lord has given you many talents—and desires that you not bury a single one of them! The worst sin we can commit in life is to fail to become that special person God has destined us to be and not to develop the gifts with which we have been entrusted."

"That's the greatest sin?"

"I believe the sin that truly grieves God is for you not fully to become Giovanni Francesco!

"But, enough talking. I can see bewilderment scribbled across your face. So why don't the two of us just sit quietly for a short while."

It seemed to Francesco that the silence was infinitely long. He began to wonder if perhaps he was supposed to speak first, and then Padre Antonio cleared his throat and said, "As a pool of muddy water becomes clear only after it has remained calm for a time, perhaps now our hearts have become clear enough for us to see to the bottom of things."

"Good, I'm ready."

"Now, why don't we return to your first question of why I call you by your baptismal name of Giovanni. First of all, it's a beautiful name, a name shared by many saints. Was not Giovanni the most intimate friend of Jesus among all his apostles? At the Last Supper Giovanni rested his head on the Lord's breast—ah, a most intimate act. The eyes of my soul see you, Giovanni Francesco, as another such intimate lover of our Lord."

"My mother had me baptized with the name of Giovanni, but I'm not sure for which saint she named me. I hate to think it was after John the Baptist. You can always recognize him in the frescoes painted in churches: He's depicted as a skinny, wild-eyed prophet dressed in a rough camel's hair tunic and standing next to some desert palm tree. I remember all too well from the stories my mother told me about the saints how from the moment of his birth he fasted from wine, rich foods, soft clothing, and all the pleasures of life! Padre, I'm not anything like him—not in the least!"

"Maybe so, but think of it, my young friend. While seemingly worlds apart, those two holy men named Giovanni might someday, in

the right person at the right time, be fused together into the same person. And what if, just what if, you could be that person?"

"An impossible wedding," Francesco laughed. "At least for me it would be like a marriage of cats and dogs. You see, I love drinking wine, feasting, partying, and dancing far too much. And as for being an intimate companion of the Lord, that's even more impossible because I'm a sinner standing right on the edge of the fires of hell!"

"I'm hopelessly confused; I don't know which way to turn. You're a monk and a priest and a wise man, Padre Antonio; can you please tell me what I should do in life?"

A long silence followed; the only sounds were the larks singing their vesper chant. Then, to their evening song was added the far-distant tolling of Assisi's church bells announcing the end of the day.

"Padre, I didn't realize we've been visiting so long! Those are the vespers bells! My father will be furious that I failed to come to work this afternoon. Please excuse me, for I must hurry home at once."

The two stood up, and Brother Nicoletto scampered back into the cave as Antonio gently placed his arm around Francesco's shoulders, saying, "You asked me a direct question about what path to take in life. I will give a direct answer, my young friend: Walk the path that unfolds before you each day. Walk it as would a blind man. Sense your way; feel your way, and listen for your voices."

"Like a blind man?"

"Yes, for you are blind, at least in regards to the future. So you must be patient with yourself, especially when you stumble, make mistakes, or take the wrong turns in the darkness of your unfolding path. Speaking of darkness, my young friend, you are right. Soon night will be creeping over this mountain. It's time for you to return home and for me to turn to my evening prayers. If you wish, Giovanni, you may come back to visit to me. You're always welcome here. Now, be on your way, and may God's peace go with you."

After thanking him, Francesco quickly retraced his steps down the mountain and then began running toward Assisi so he could arrive before the closing of the town gates at sunset. While anxious about how he would explain his absence to his father, his heart was joyfully pounding. For the first time in months he felt peace, a strange new kind of peace, the tranquil yet restless excitement of anticipating a magnificent new dawn. "I was so fortunate," he thought, "to have met Padre Antonio. I will certainly accept his offer to visit him again. I've

never met a man so gentle—even in the way he was with his cat. And the tender way he pronounced my name reminded me of how my mother says it. Yet, he surely has a strong spirit to be able to live alone up here in these mountain forests filled with wild animals and robbers." But perhaps the greatest gift for Francesco was to be affirmed and encouraged by an older man.

"Mother, I hope I haven't caused you to worry," Francesco said breathlessly as he ran through the door where his mother was stewing more than their evening meal. "I went walking up in the hills, and I guess I got lost. Then that rainstorm came up, and I found shelter in a cave." Turning to his father, who sat with his large arms folded across his chest, he added, "Please, Father, forgive me for failing to assist you this afternoon at the shop. I know I've caused you to worry, and I ask your pardon. I was lost, but I found my way." He thought to himself that, indeed, he had begun to find his way.

"A new Pope! A new Pope!" Everyone was shouting in concert with the loud peeling chorus of Assisi's church bells jubilantly announcing the election of a new pontiff. Old and sickly Celestine III had died, and the cardinals surprisingly had elected a youthful, thirty-seven-year-old man who had taken the name of Innocent III. The people gathered in the main piazza of Assisi, eagerly sharing stories of Lotario di Segni, the new Pope, who was almost a neighbor, for his home had been in nearby Spoleto. They talked about how brilliant and learned he was, that he had studied law and theology under the greatest scholars in Paris and Bologna.

The news that Duke Conrad was leaving for Rome with his entire household raced across Assisi like fire in the stubble of a wheat field. The story was that Duke Conrad had departed for Rome to place himself and all his lands under the control of the new Pope. He was confident that once his domain was directly under Pope Innocent III's protection his own rule over Assisi would be untouchable. Upon hearing this news, Pietro jumped up clapping his hands.

"Glorious news, Francesco! Come with me to the back of the shop." Placing his apprentice in charge of their stall on the street, he led Francesco to the back of the shop, where he grabbed him by the shoulders and said, "Son, the hour has arrived! Our tyrant Conrad has left his mountain fortress of Subasio to go to Rome to kiss the Pope's foot. At long last the freedom of Assisi is at hand. Would you like to be

one of the brave soldiers who will fight to win your city's liberation and independence?"

"Yes, Father, yes, of course, I would. You know of my longing to be a knight. How long before the battle will begin? How many weeks before we are ready?"

"Not weeks, Francesco—we are ready now! All has been secretly arranged: We will storm the fortress as soon as we can gather together our troops. You're sixteen now, and because you are a man, I knew you would want to share in this great adventure." Then he added, "I'm so proud of you!" tightly squeezing Francesco's shoulders. "I've already purchased a full set of armor and a sword for you; it's here hidden beneath some bales of cloth in our storage room." Francesco was stunned at the news, and, magnetized, he followed his father, who opened the storage room and shared the plans of the citizen's committee that until now had been kept a guarded secret lest the Duke learn of them.

As Francesco stared in wonder at his new shining armor and weapons of war, he recalled the words of Strapazzate, wondering if, indeed, they were prophetic. Would the bodies of Assisi's youth be scattered like dung on the fields? As he picked up his sword, he recalled a time when he was only about four years old and was playing with a stuffed toy lamb his mother had made for him. He loved the little stuffed lamb and carried it with him everywhere he went, until that day when he found himself at the feet of his father, who stood towering over him. His father swiftly reached down and grabbed his toy lamb, saying, "Boys don't play with dolls!" When young Francesco began bawling, he shouted, "And boys don't cry!" Handing him a small wooden toy sword, he added, "Here's something for a real boy. From this day onward, I only want to see you playing men's games—like war."

The next day these childhood memories had vanished as he proudly strapped on his new armor in front of his weeping mother. There was also sorrow and fear elsewhere in peaceful Assisi. As Pietro's plan became known, the aristocratic and wealthy families of the city, fearful of mob violence in the uprising against Duke Conrad, were tearfully packing in great haste to flee for safety. Among the families escaping was the wealthy family of Signore Fovorina Scifi. He and his wife, along with their sons and two daughters, one of whom was the beautiful six-year-old Clare, were among the first who decided to flee

 into exile to nearby Perugia. The protection and security of Perugia was easily affordable for the wealthy Signore Scifi. While their household servants were busily loading as many of the family possessions as would fit on their wagons, the merchant leaders of the uprising tried unsuccessfully to dissuade Signore Scifi and his household. They attempted to ensure them and the other fearful aristocrats that their retreat wasn't necessary, that none of their homes or property would be disturbed in this civil uprising.

The capture of the almost-deserted fortress of Rocca Maggiore was accomplished swiftly without bloodshed and with unexpected colorful pageantry. A great surge of shouting men and boys carrying a variety of Assisi's local banners began flowing out of the city toward Duke Conrad's fortress on Mount Subasio. Francesco and Emiliano rode side by side along with other mounted warriors, including most of their young friends. As the soldiers of Assisi strode out of the city to assault the fortress, they were surrounded by a boisterous crowd of sword-waving citizens shouting for freedom, as well as barking dogs and throngs of peasants armed with wood-chopping axes, clubs, pitchforks and shovels. As they surged out of the city, on the top of the old tumbled-down Roman wall that ran along the northern edge of the Assisi was old hunchbacked Strapazzate. Whirling his right hand round and round over his head, he shrieked loudly,

> You're crazy—mad men, one and all,
>
> *Vova Strapazzat, Vova Strapazzat,*
>
> scrambled are your souls, scrambled
>
> on the red-hot, scorching skillet of hell!
>
> Bless your enemies, and your onions.
>
> Peace on earth, and a piece for me.
>
> Angels are a'singing; don't you hear them?
>
> *Pax et bonum,* peace wedded to good,
>
> not bloody war wedded to hell's evils.
>
> Save your souls, save 'em for a rainy day. . . .

The mob, drunk on the vintage of hell that gave them permission to engage in violence, had their courage fortified by being faceless in a large crowd. As they swept past the muddled fool of a beggar, they splattered him with insults and ridicule. Some opted for tangible weapons, hurling stones at him. However, old Strapazzate only danced wildly along the top of the wall, dodging the stones as he continued chanting,

> Doomed, yes, doomed are your efforts,
>
> for those who sit on thrones
>
> have glue on their seats—you're stuck with them;
>
> so don't be fools; turn around.
>
> Save your souls, abandon your swords,
>
> they're the arms of Satan himself.
>
> Those who use them perish by them.

Even those who weren't part of the mob dismissed his rambling words, particularly the wealthier and older citizens of Assisi, who stood at secure distance from the conflict outside the walls of the city. They enjoyed watching the storming of Conrad's empty fortress, seeing it more as a pageant than a battle. The Duke had left only a few guards and servants behind, and the attacking mob allowed this token resistance to flee unharmed from the castle as they began destroying the hated citadel.

That night Assisi erupted in rowdy celebrations as the injury-free warriors returned to the city as victorious heroes. The first act of the new city commune was to rename the piazza containing Assisi's landmark fountain, calling it the *Piazza Del Commune*. After this had been declared, Pietro Bernadone stood up to urge his fellow members to begin the city's long-needed reforms. "To prevent sickness and the plague, we must first of all organize a system for the removal of all garbage and filth from our city—as well as the animal dung from our streets. I propose that we hire a group of collectors whose duty it will be to travel certain routes gathering into their handcarts all the city's dung and trash. They will take their carts of refuse outside the city walls to dump it in a place to be determined by our commune."

"Signore Bernadone," asked one of the new commune members, "in heaven's name, where will we find workers willing to be dung-pickers? And more importantly, where will we get the money to pay them?"

"Our city has recently seen a great influx of poor peasants from the countryside. They know no trade and are eager for work. As with other cities, Assisi has its share of the poorest of the poor, those who survive only as day laborers. Many of these can be hired to do the kind of work others would find unthinkable. And as for the paying these 'dung-pickers,'" he added as he bowed to the previous speaker, "to use my esteemed colleague's title for them, we can use part of the tribute our city had previously paid to our tyrant duke. And if any other funds are needed," he said, pausing briefly for effect, "they will be supplied as a gift of charity to the city by the Guild of Assisi Cloth Merchants." The entire commune applauded loudly at this expression of generosity by the cloth guild, and all voted unanimously to begin at once the collection of the city's garbage.

The commune instituted numerous other reforms, including the breaking open of the city walls for the purpose of creating new gates that would allow for an influx of new customers and trade. However, change, especially rapid change, always contributes to unrest and confusion. So while all the population applauded the removal of the garbage and stinking animal manure, many were strongly opposed to chopping holes in the walls for new gates. Dissenters argued strongly against such new gates, claiming they endangered the security their old feudal structure provided. Some resisted the greater exposure to the influences of the outside world and its new, revolutionary ideas. Leading this opposition were the clergy, who feared any change in the established feudal order. They began inserting into their sermons dire warnings about the plague of radical ideas that threatened the peace and serenity of Assisi. The priests also privately opposed the overthrow of the ancient authority of Duke Conrad, as it placed in peril their own authority and that of Holy Mother Church.

Francesco wasn't immune to the social turmoil now disturbing once-peaceful Assisi and all of Umbria. Indeed, the seventeen-year-old son of Pietro Bernadone was suffering his own unrest. Yet he hid his painful turmoil, his wrestling with his conflicting voices, behind a joking façade. He was a good actor, and his pretending fooled most of his friends, even Emiliano. While engaged in hand-to-hand combat with these internal warring forces, he found escape from the struggle by being the city's fun-loving minstrel. Playing his lute and singing bawdy songs as the prince of Assisi's partying and drinking life, he was maintaining a lifestyle that appeared completely irresponsible.

Meanwhile, Pietro was plotting an arranged marriage for his son that would insure the financial fortune of the Bernadone family. However, he dragged his feet on completing the betrothal. He feared that if his son settled down and became a responsible married man he might take over the business too soon. Pietro still felt vibrantly alive and wasn't ready to step into the background as a kindly old grandfather and patriarch of the Bernadone family.

"Emiliano," Francesco said one night as he and his friend sat visiting in the flickering light of an oil lamp, "I love this spot in the back of your old stone wine cellar where you and I can talk privately apart from the others. It reminds me of an old catacomb—which is fitting, since it is the resting place for your father's sleeping wine!"

"Well, I say we should awaken another bottle from its slumber and taste some of its liquid sunlight!" Emiliano uncorked a bottle and filled two cups, handing one to Francesco. "A toast—to friendship and freedom." They both raised their cups in a salute and drank.

"This amber, sun-drenched wine is truly delicious, Emiliano. It fires my soul as it warms my heart.

"I liked your toast, my friend. I'm glad you included *freedom* in it." Peering into the dark red pool inside his cup, he added, "I confess that I dread being imprisoned for life."

"Imprisoned?"

"Yes, in some loveless marriage, chained down by the domestic life. *Caro mio*, you know how my heart desires to be a knight, a champion. I dream of being a glorious hero who proves his manhood and returns home victorious after battle with the infidels."

"A noble dream, my friend—as noble as this excellent wine, a Perugian Rubesco di Torgiano. Allow me to refill your cup." As Emiliano generously filled Francesco's cup full to overflowing, he added, "If only our blood was as noble red as this Torgiano—ah, we could both become knights."

"Even though I lack noble blood, Emiliano, in these new times I could well become a gentleman knight. My father is rich and can easily afford to outfit me in the finest armor in all of Umbria."

"You're fortunate to have such a wealthy father."

"Unfortunately, I lack one thing money and influence can't buy," he said, glancing over the rim of his cup at his friend, "a strong and muscular body. Unlike you, Emiliano, I lack the physical stature to be

a great warrior knight. I'm better suited for my other dream of being a troubadour, which only requires musical talent. Sometimes I prefer the thought of being a minstrel anyway, since I could live a life of adventure freely wandering across the countryside singing of love and enchantment."

"A toast, then, to my gifted friend, the Troubadour of Assisi! Forget your physical build, Francesco. God gave it to you, but God also gave you so many other gifts. You can easily become anything you desire to be. You're blessed with a soul of great passion, and with that you can overcome any difficulty. I toast the future of my richly talented and dearest friend."

"And I toast you and your bright future, Emiliano—and your engagement with lovely Angela. May great passion and love, as fierce as the great fire of the sun, wildly blaze in your heart."

"Thank you, Francesco. It's been a rich evening of conversation, but we've talked so long that we're almost to the bottom of our second bottle of that rich red Perugian wine. By now, it must be close to the nine o'clock curfew, when all fires must be out and all citizens indoors. The new commune regulations are very strict about keeping the curfew. So, Francesco, hurry home, for if the guards catch you. . . ."

"Yes, dear friend, sadly the time has disappeared faster than the wine. Indeed, I must be on my way."

When they reached the street level door of the wine cellar, the two friends exchanged a strong embrace. As it ended, Francesco kissed Emiliano on the lips and, turning, ran quickly down the narrow, dark street. Racing homeward in the dark, he savored that farewell kiss, which tasted better than the finest wine.

*S*till troubled over the uncertainty of his future, Francesco remembered Padre Antonio's invitation to visit him any time and so set off into the mountains. That afternoon the two sat in the quiet serenity that hung about the entrance of Antonio's hermitage, within view of the monk's small vegetable garden.

"Padre, I'm still confused," he lamented, stroking the fur of Brother Nicoletto, who was curled up in his lap. "I'm no closer to knowing what to do with my life. Deep in my bones I know the answer isn't following my father to become a cloth merchant, even if that's what everyone expects of me. Must I live out their expectations?

The old hermit smiled and gently shook his head.

"Then, there are my friends—some of whom are married and the rest of whom are betrothed—who tease me about when I'm going to settle down. And the other day on the street, the parish priest stopped me and again asked me about my becoming a priest. With all these questions swirling around, where do I find the right answer for me?"

"Giovanni, don't seek answers! Seek questions!"

"Seek questions? I have too many of them already!"

"One can never have too many questions. They lead us deeper into *the Mystery*, the Divine Mystery." Francesco was struck by the awe with which the old hermit had pronounced the word *Mystery*. Never had he heard anyone speak of God as a mystery—or invest that sense of God with such intense wonder.

"Padre Antonio, living in the city is so filled with the temptations of drinking, gambling, and every other sort of vice, including prostitution. Perhaps I should become a hermit!"

"Giovanni, there are just as many temptations here as there are in any city. In fact, far more evil temptations lurk in these seemingly innocent woods."

"How is that possible? What temptations are more sinister and sinful than those of the flesh?"

"Selfishness, for one! A hermit's life of quiet solitude can easily be visited by that insidious temptation that is disguised as a pious desire to live apart so as to live a life of complete prayer. A diabolic spirit wearing a saintly mask comes visiting the hermit's cell and weaves a spell over the solitary soul, ensuring him or her that by completely rejecting the world and the flesh, the hermit's heart will be better able to entertain God's presence. Diabolically clever, it has fooled many a solitary into cultivating a selfish rather than generous heart."

"I'm afraid, Padre, that it's less my heart than my body that yearns to be entertained—and not by any experience of God. So powerful is my lusting after sensual gratification that it surely is gravely sinful. I confess that I don't feel any such lusting for God or the holy things of the Church. Yet I continue to be magnetically drawn to . . . well . . . that mystery of God of which you spoke. Pray for me, Padre, for as you can see, I am a very confused young man."

"Giovanni the Beloved, all God has made is beautiful and good, including sensual—and even sexual—desires. All love is from God; so why should we separate physical intimacy from a deep experience of

God? Is not all desire for what is good a form of our desire for God? At its heart is not this yearning an expression of the incarnation?"

"The incarnation?"

"Excuse me; I've slipped into theological language. The term refers to the reality of 'the Word made flesh.' The entire mystery of what we celebrate each Christmas is the presence of God in our flesh as it was fully present in the flesh of Jesus of Nazareth. And how should we respond to the great gift of this mystery? Each must respond to this deep longing in the way that God has created him or her to respond."

"When I reflect on the voice of God that says, 'Follow me,' it feels like I need to leave the world of my life in Assisi behind. There are days, Padre, when I think the only answer is that I should join a monastery where my hunger for the holy would be nourished. Maybe I should become a monk at your Benedictine Abbey. What do you think?"

"The Church, my young seeker, has successfully divided the world into two worlds, one sacred and the other secular. Each world wars against the other with the sad result that, like Assisi and other nearby Italian cities, they seem constantly in conflict with each other and within themselves."

"War,—yes, you've given a name to the whirlpool of conflict within me."

"The Church and the secular world exist as isolated islands, yet ironically they need each other more than they are at odds. But because of that conflict, when you are outside sacred space, you feel at risk of losing your soul to the devil, whose kingdom is this world with all of its vain pomp and silken seductions."

"Oh, I know that feeling only too well, but. . . ."

"Both the Church and the world claim to be the 'real world,' and so when you are deeply immersed in either one of them, the other seems unreal. Ah, yes, Giovanni, I can easily understand your desire to come and live within the secure confines of a sacred space like the monastery of Mount Subiaso."

"Isn't that the reason why you chose to be a monk?"

"I am monk by accident as well as by choice. My parents were poor and had several children for whom they felt responsible. When I was very young, they took me to the monastery and left me there as a child oblate who would later become a monk. They did so believing that I'd at least have three good meals a day and a safe, secure way of life. Even as a small child the monks recognized my intellectual gifts and guided

me along the path of becoming a monk, and then a priest, in the monastery. Since I came to the monastery as a small child, I knew no other kind of life than the world of the abbey. I was very innocent and naive about the ways of the larger world. As a young man, however, I freely chose to become a monk, and it was a good choice. It gave me a good education and a way of life that I've never regretted. Then, after many long years of service in the monastery, one day the abbot graciously agreed to my request to live out the rest of my days outside the monastery's sacred enclosures. . . ." Spreading his arms outward toward the forest around his cave, he continued, "And this, my one-man monastery hermitage here in creation, has taught me many important lessons. One of them is that I live in sacred space."

"Sacred? I see nothing that looks holy."

"Be healed," Antonio said softly, reaching over and touching Francesco's eyes.

Though he felt nothing unusual or saw no differently than before, Francesco stood up and looked out over the forest, with its stately green oaks and tall poplars, the birds fluttering among their branches. Then he lowered his gaze to the bottom of the tree trunks and the carpet of grass and wildflowers. "It's lovely," he thought, "but I see nothing sacred."

"Giovanni Francesco, take off your shoes!" the old man said, aware that Francesco had seen nothing unusual, "for the very ground upon which you stand is holy land."

"I don't know why, but if you'd like me to. . . ." He knelt down and removed his expensively crafted shoes. "Now what?" Standing up barefoot, he looked around, only to find that he was all alone. The old hermit had simply vanished. Scratching his head in bewilderment at Antonio's disappearance as well as the instruction to remove his shoes, Francesco looked down at the ground. "All I see is grass with patches of plain, old Umbrian soil, hardly the sacred soil of the Holy Land."

Once again wearing his shoes as he returned down the path to Assisi, Francesco's mind labored to unravel the snags in Antonio's words. He blinked his eyes once, twice, and a third time, yet he saw only groves of pine and poplar trees, fields of waving yellow sunflowers and rolling green hillsides with rows of grapevines. "Antonio called what I'm seeing 'sacred space,' like the inside of a church. And he spoke of his black, green-eyed cat Brother Nicoletto as a son of God. How does he do it? What's the secret to raising the veil of the ordinary—if,

indeed, such a veil does exist—so as to see the sacred beneath it? Perhaps if I rub my eyes, it will help the healing take effect." When he opened his eyes, he saw no differently. In a field beside the road was a gray donkey chewing grass. Shaking his head, Francesco moaned, "I must be blind, for I feel no brotherhood with that ass."

Before the towers of Assisi came into view, Francesco heard the pealing of the church bells signaling the prayer hour of vespers and the end of another workday. He was now joined by groups of field laborers with their hoes and rakes on their shoulders walking home along the road that wound its way upwards to Assisi. He paused and gazed up at the city perched on the spur ridge of beautiful Mount Subasio. Then he looked around at the waving sea of golden sunflowers, the verdant slopes with their clouds of silver-leafed olive trees and lush green grapevines. He noticed the three donkeys nibbling grass. Again touching his eyes in the way the holy Antonio had done with his blessing, he wondered if perhaps the healing takes time, which challenged his belief that miracles occur like a flash of lightning.

 **hapter 4**

ON THIS NIGHT, THOUSANDS OF GLISTENING STARS HAD
taken their assigned seats in the ebony amphitheater over Assisi
for the concert that was about to begin. On the stage below, Francesco,
carrying his lute, and his friend Emiliano were on their way to the
home of Angela Fibonacci. The Fibonacci residence, like those of most
of Assisi's wealthy merchants, was less a house than a fortress, with its
high stone walls and tall, shuttered windows high above street level.
The two friends stood in the narrow shaft of yellow light that escaped
from the partially open shutters of a second story window of what
Emiliano knew to be Angela's room. In the surrounding darkness,
Emiliano lit his small lantern, and Francesco began softly singing as he
strummed his lute:

O Angela, angel of Paradise,

fairest rose in your father's garden,

exotically scented enchanter of souls,

open your heart and your lovely ear

to this poor nightingale's song

that proclaims the passionate ardor

of your ever beloved Emiliano.

Open wide your heart, O Angela,

fairest rose in your father's garden,

to this poor nightingale's song.

He began strumming louder, and his voice grew in volume as well
as passion:

Ever eager Emiliano aches
to be near you, lovely Angela,
for you lovingly climb
like an encircling rose vine
up the ivory tower of his soul.
Ardent-hearted Emiliano yearns
for the blessed moment to arrive.
O come quickly, wedding night,
night of bliss, night of love,
when you will encircle his tower,
as the two of you lay as one
under a shimmering canopy
of a hundred thousand stars
on a love bed of silken bliss. . . .

The shutters opened, and Angela leaned out of her opened window and peered down into the darkness where the lantern's flickering light illuminated the smiling upturned face of her handsome betrothed. She knew that the hidden singer playing the lute in the darkness was Assisi's most gifted troubadour and her beloved's closest friend. Angela blew Emiliano a kiss, beaming with delight at this romantic treat.

O Angela, rare and fairest flower,
know how handsome, young Emiliano,
Assisi's own Bacchus of love's wine,
aches, O fairest of Fibonacci flowers,
to flood your fresh spring cup to the full
from the overflowing sweet juices
of his hanging clusters of grapes.
O Angela, most fair spring blossom,
who thirsts for such a love-rich nectar,
know that, like the radiant sun,
he yearns to rise and descend,
again and again with great delight
into your dark, hidden wine cellar,

so that you and he may become
drunk in a wild, lifelong abandon
on the finest Giacosa love wine,
intoxicated in delicious madness.
O Angela, the fairest Fibonacci,
how he yearns, like the sun, to. . . .

Abruptly, Francesco's song died a sudden death, slain by the crashing of shutters violently thrown open at the window directly above Angela's. In the center of a broad band of light that flowed from the window was the silhouette of a large man leaning out, shaking both his fists. The angry Signore Fibonacci cried out, "In the name of all the saints, who's making all that damn racket down there?" Instantly, Emiliano snuffed out his lantern and dashed back into the darkness beside Francesco as Angela's father continued, "The pox on you ruffians, noisy riffraff! Why are you awakening decent citizens at this late hour of the night? Whoever you are down there, stop! Respectable people are all inside their homes; only thieves and prostitutes are prowling about at this time of night. Away with you at once before I sound the alarm for the night guards!"

After Signore Fibonacci loudly slammed his shutters shut, Angela leaned over her window sill and threw down a red carnation tied with two long red silk ribbons before quickly closing her wooden shutters.

"Good catch, Emiliano. That flower speaks a thousand words, *caro mio*. Best that you and I be on our way, lest old master Fibonacci sets his dogs on us!"

"Alas, my heart is anchored here on the pavement below Angela's window, yet my feet are eager to save my skin. As discretion is the better part of passion, I agree that we should get away from here fast."

"If he had heard the words of your song," Emiliano panted as they hurried down the narrow street, "my future father-in-law would be after you and me with his club as well as his dogs! I'm glad it was dark enough so that Angela couldn't see me blush at the suggestive lyrics."

"You're right, my friend, I got a little carried away. But let's slow down; no need to run anymore—we're far enough away from the Fibonacci volcano. Still, I'm glad my words made you blush, because that means they touched a hidden place in your soul, even if we've been taught to be ashamed of our bodily desires. When I was at the

Chambery Fair in France, I learned how powerful poetic words can be. The way troubadours sang taught me how to express exotic sensuality with clever words that have double meanings. In fact, as your blushing suggests, masking passion with poetry makes it even more sensual. And I thank you, Emiliano, for the privilege of being your instrument of love and deep affection. It was fun composing that love song just for you, *caro mio*, and a delight to give it expression. But, the cost of all that singing is that it's made me very thirsty!"

"Well, Francesco, you've certainly earned a trip to Giacosa's wine cellar, and I'm glad you enjoyed composing that song. It seemed that without my speaking of them, you knew my most erotic and deepest desires. We share so many things, my friend, it's no wonder everyone says that we must be twins. It's not just that we dress alike or use the same expressions or. . . ."

"In France they say that true friends and lovers desire to imitate one another. The greater the love, the greater the desire to become like the other. I wonder if that's why the saints. . . ."

"O brother ruffian, in all of Assisi you are unique!" Emiliano said as he wrapped a powerful arm around Francesco's shoulder. "One minute you're singing sinfully lusty songs, the next you're talking about the saints. Now, as for thirst, mine at least matches yours. So, my comrade canary of the lusty lyrics, let us proceed to the finest wine cellar in all of Assisi."

"Emiliano, how lucky we are to have a hideout like your father's cherished wine cellar," Francesco said as they walked down the long rows of wine barrels and racks of bottles. When they came to the far end of the cellar, they sat on the stools at the old table. Emiliano opened a bottle of Rufino Chianti and began generously filling their cups.

"Down here," Emiliano said, "no one can hear our conversations. It's like a mountain cave den for two young wolves like us."

"To your happy marriage, Emiliano!" Francesco declared as he raised his cup. "May the juicy wine of your love never turn to vinegar."

"Friend, I know this is going to sound silly," Emiliano said hesitantly, "but . . . I have a proposal. It's not an easy one to put into words."

"Go ahead, as long as you're not proposing that we have a double wedding. I'm not. . . ."

"No, it's not that. It has to with what you said earlier about the French saying how lovers and good friends imitate one another." His chest swelled as he filled his lungs, as if trying to gather the strength to speak his proposal aloud. "The truth is, I don't want to get married!" After he got this revelation out, he tilted his head back and emptied his cup.

"Not get married? What's wrong, Emiliano? I don't understand—you love her, don't you?"

"What I want to propose, Francesco, well . . . er . . . is that . . . you and I become monks together!"

"Monks! Emiliano you can't be drunk yet—we only just started drinking! That's crazy—have you caught old Strapazzate's sickness? Tell me, Emiliano, why don't you want to marry your beautiful Angela?"

"So I can save my soul!" he blurted out and then buried his head in his hands. "I'm so confused, Francesco, I don't know what to do. I truly love Angela, and I'm eighteen, almost nineteen; it's time to settle down and begin a family. One by one, all of our companions are getting married—there are only a few of us single ones left."

"You're right about that. There are only a few big fish like you and me left to be caught. But, Emiliano, haven't you already swallowed that sharp hook?"

"The devil fishes with *that* hook and its long fat worm! Don't laugh at me, Francesco, I'm deadly serious. I want to save my soul. Why else would anyone enter a monastery or become a priest? But think about it, my friend, if you and I became monks together in the same abbey, we could live side by side as friends for the rest of our lives."

"It would be more accurate to say that we'd be *buried alive* side by side in some dreary old monastery!"

"But don't you remember what the priests taught us at San Giorgio's? That sex before marriage is a sin—and even sex between a husband and wife is sinful, only not as serious. We had to memorize St. Augustine's words about a woman being the gateway to hell. That means even my beloved Angela would take me to hell. Isn't that what the Church teaches?"

"I guess it does, and I've struggled with that a lot myself. Yet the apostle Peter became a saint, and he was married—don't the Gospels speak about his mother-in-law? If he's one of the greatest saints, isn't it possible to be married without having to worry about saving your soul?"

"Don't forget, Francesco, that Simon Peter 'left everything' and followed Jesus. Isn't leaving his wife and family precisely how he became a saint? Name for me one saint of the Church who was a married family man. Go ahead; I dare you to come up with just one!"

"Well, let's see. . . . I can't think of one right now, but that doesn't mean there aren't any. I'm not a scholar of saints. How about the saints in the Old Testament, like Abraham, Jacob, and Joseph?"

"They're not saints—they're Jews. Anyway, they don't count or else we'd have names like theirs. Do you know any Christians baptized with names like Abraham or Isaac?"

"All right, but didn't Jesus go to the wedding feast of Cana? Wouldn't his presence have made marriage holy? And if making love is the gateway to hell, he surely wouldn't be at the threshold of hell working miracles, would he? As the son of a wine merchant, you surely remember that miracle!"

"I do, and it says to me that if you're married it takes a miracle to save your soul! It has to be miraculous. After all, if sex in marriage isn't evil, how do you explain those harsh conditions that follow Extreme Unction? After being anointed by a priest, if the sacrament works and you recover your health, the Church requires that you must remain celibate for the rest of your life!"

"I know that," he laughed. "Why else would people call it the Last Rites? You'd only want to be anointed if you knew for sure you were crossing over death's doorstep."

"It's not funny, Francesco. This is serious business. It's about hell or heaven. If marriage is as holy and good as you are saying, then explain to me why it isn't one of the sacraments of the Church?"

"I don't know why. I'm no theologian, but I've heard them say that some day the Church may make marriage a sacrament. And even if it isn't a sacrament, Emiliano, God is love, and so surely God blesses every union of two persons in love with each other. For me, love itself is a sacrament!"

"You're too romantic. Love leads to sex, and so your argument leaks like an old wine skin. Marriage is still only a concession to lust for those who are too weak to embrace celibacy. And it has little to do with love! It's just a business arrangement between the two families. You and I both know about those sad marriages where the couples don't love one another. I've given this a lot of thought, Francesco, and it seems that

saving your soul is almost impossible if you're married. So, I say that you and I should become monks and live a holy life!"

"You are crazy, Emiliano! You're as insane as that old Scrambled Eggs hunchback to keep proposing that idea. Like you, I don't want to go to hell, but I know in my bones that God isn't calling me to join some monastery or to become a priest.

"At the same time, Emiliano, I can feel, down to my bones, the tension you feel about your life choices. There are more than a few moments when I think I'm as crazy as old Strappazate. What did the ancients say? 'Friends are two persons with one soul.' You and I must share the same soul since we're both so confused about what we should do in life. Part of me wants to march off to war to fight for glory and fame in the new conflict that's brewing with neighboring Perugia. Then there's another part of me that longs to be a troubadour, to play my lute and sing romantic ballads from a lover's heart. And, like you, my friend, part of me wants to live a life that quenches my thirst for holiness. Perhaps I can combine them. After all, St. Martin was a soldier who became a saint; maybe there was also a troubadour who became a saint." After taking a long draft from his wine cup, he added, "Ah . . . right now I can't think of one, but there surely must be one."

"I admire your desire to be a warrior knight—I don't think I have enough courage to be one. The thought of going off to fight in some war and. . . ."

"Emiliano, it requires greater courage to be married than to be a knight! I'll go off to fight in the war with Perugia, and then in a few weeks or months I'll be back home again. War is a game played by nobles and gentlemen where the days of peace far outnumber those of fighting. Let's see," he paused and began counting off on his fingers, "no fighting at night, since the Church's *Pax Dei* forbids fighting between vespers in the early evening until after the next day's morning prayer and Mass. Then there's no fighting during the forty days of Lent; no warring on Sundays or the Holy Days—and we know that they're a lot of them! Then, if you include the Twelve Days of Christmas and the fifty days of the Easter season, what do you have left? But the struggle of marriage takes place all 365 days and nights of the year! A toast to you, my brave friend, who is about to enter the lifelong battlefield of marriage!"

After they both emptied their cups and refilled them, Francesco continued, "Emiliano, it'll take more than a warrior's courage to face

the warfare of marriage. Your wife will move into your home with you, your parents, and the rest of your family. Ah, then the slings and arrows will begin to fly between mother-in-law and daughter-in-law, and between siblings and in-laws. Finally onto the field of nuptial combat will come all the crying children. Oh, no, *caro mio*, it is I who admire *your* courage, for I lack the heroism for such a prolonged, sustained conflict. You, not I, are truly a brave man.

"And I know, Emiliano, that you love Angela. I think all this talk about monasteries is just a diversion from what you know to be your real destiny."

"I fear you're right, my friend, but I still can't see how my soul can be saved if I marry. But enough talk about me! I'm eager to hear about your plans after the war with Perugia when you will make your triumphant return like some conquering Caesar. Then what do you want to be?"

"I want to be . . . a saint!" Francesco gasped at the word that had just emerged from his mouth. Like a wild bird escaping from a cage, it had sprung off his lips and flown about the wine cellar with a screeching, "*saint, saint, saint!*" It echoed over and over across the long, arched ceiling of the dark wine cellar as the two friends sat staring in astonishment at one another.

"*P*adre, where did that word come from?" he pleaded with Antonio as the two sat together at the entrance to his cave. "I couldn't believe my ears last night. I was astonished when I heard myself say out loud that I wanted to be a saint! While it only startled poor Emiliano, it frightened me! As soon as I could, I ran all the way up here to see you, the word still burning like a red-hot coal on my tongue."

"Giovanni, could it have been an answer to your prayer?"

"Impossible! It's never been among the life choices I've entertained, for what sane man would ever desire to be a saint?"

"I agree—no sane man would. But, Giovanni, you must fast from using the word 'impossible.' It limits you, and, more importantly, it ties God's hands. And as for who would want to be a saint, don't you think everyone should? Isn't becoming a saint the primal vocation of every child of God? Whatever work or profession one pursues in life is only the workshop for the labor of becoming holy."

"But, Padre, wouldn't becoming a saint mean that I'd have to deny myself—isn't that what Jesus required of his disciples? And doesn't such denial require becoming a *nothing*? For as long as I can remember I've wanted to become *something*. I've longed to be a heroic knight; for my father to be proud of me; to be a real man, the kind he could love."

"Indeed, the Master did say that we must deny our very selves, take up our crosses and follow him—that such denial is the way to holiness. But before you can deny your self, Giovanni Francesco, it is absolutely necessary to have a self to renounce! To give a gift, one must first possess it. So, what self do you have to give away?"

Francesco dropped his head at this question, too embarrassed to respond. "Don't be ashamed, my young friend. You're no different from many in my abbey. I've known many monks who were mired down in their spiritual growth, stalled on the way to holiness because they had skipped over an important stage in life. They had entered the monastery as mere children or young men, before they had developed real personalities. They were lacking in any real status or rank, or any real self that they could deny. They erroneously thought that by entering the abbey and taking their vows they were denying their selves. Truly denying your 'very' self, as Jesus asked of his disciples, doesn't mean abstaining from food, drink, or even sex. It requires the supreme surrender of your very person: disinheriting yourself of name, family, fame, success, accomplishments, nationality, and even your religious identity. Believe me, I know that such surrender doesn't come easily and doesn't come prematurely. It was not until very late in my life that I myself was able to take the absolutely critical step of denial that paradoxically leads to the fullness of life and the discovery of your real self. Indeed, sainthood requires denial of self, but it also requires having a self to deny."

"But isn't wanting to make something out of yourself, wanting to be someone famous, the sin of pride? Isn't the desire to stand above others, to accomplish something great, to be unique among others a grave sin—and the very opposite of what sainthood means? Aren't saints humble, and doesn't humility require becoming the lowest, taking the last place?"

"Humility means being unpretentious, but it also means truthfulness. It means being authentically who you truly are. Look over there at my garden; see that plot of flowers next to the vegetables? I love to grow flowers, for beauty is as essential for life as food. Is it a sin when

each flower blooms as beautifully as it can? Each of my flowers is stunningly beautiful—not so it can outshine the other flowers, but simply to bloom with the beauty she was given by her Creator. Take those delicate and enchanting purple irises over there. They don't care a speck if anyone sees them; they are glorious, even if God is the only one who ever appreciates them. My flowers do not strain to make themselves beautiful. They simply allow themselves to unfold as God created them, as they absorb the warm Umbrian sun and the cool kiss of the moon, as they drink in the sweet rain and soak up the earth's juices. Giovanni, learn a lesson of holiness from the flowers in how they take in the world around them. You and I are like those purple irises; we must soak up the richness of the world, rejecting none of God's gifts, being nourished by everything around us."

"But isn't the world evil, the domain of the Devil? How can. . . ."

"Giovanni, those irises are saints because they do the will of God just by being flowers, by living out the possibility God placed in their seeds. As for the world being the domain of the Devil, didn't Jesus say the kingdom of God had arrived here on earth? Didn't Christ's love transform a world gone awry? So, like these flowers planted in God's soil, grow into sainthood, drinking in all the world around you, gulping it down, and then transforming it through love."

"But isn't sainthood and holiness reserved for priests and monks?"

"Giovanni, that answer sounds like a diversion from owning your destiny. The greatest vocation in life isn't priesthood; it's humanhood. Unlike the flowers, you and I can resist being saints. We have a choice, just as I believe Jesus of Nazareth had a choice either to unfold the awesome presence of God in his flesh or leave it unborn. If he didn't have that freedom, then he was never truly human. He was awesomely beautiful because he chose to be the fullness of who he was."

"My head is spinning, Padre, with this talk about sainthood. First you told me I lack a self to deny so that I can become fully alive, and now you say I'm some unique creation of God. If all that's true, then what's my problem?"

"Giovanni, you haven't bloomed yet! Go home—go home and bloom."

"*F*ifty, plus twenty, plus. . . ." Pietro Bernadone was hunched over a table in the rear of the cloth shop, whispering to himself as he scribbled with his quill feather pen, adding up the day's sales.

"Father, excuse me. I hate bothering you while you're balancing the day's profits, but could you and I talk about something rather important?"

"Francesco, is it really that important," a frowning Pietro looked up, "that we must talk about it at this very moment? I must complete. . . ."

"Father, I want to go to war!" he blurted out, nervously twisting and straightening a piece of fine Flemish wool. "I want to go off and fight in the war that's just been proclaimed by Assisi against Perugia. I'm almost twenty years old now. It's-time-I-do-something-mean. . . ." Catching himself, he forced himself to speak more slowly, "Father, it's time in my life for me to do something meaningful." Under his breath he said to himself, "for me to bloom."

"My son," Pietro replied, staring up at his son who now was a man, "yes, we do have time to talk." Pushing aside his accounting scrolls, he said, "Go and bring that bottle of wine from the back shelf and two cups. Then we'll sit down, and your father will share with you some good wine and some good wisdom, both of which require years to mature." When Francesco returned, Pietro generously filled both cups. In obvious delight at being able to play the role of the wise father, he raised his cup and said, "Son, 'to life,' as our Jewish friends say." After they drank from their cups, Pietro added, "Speaking of the Jews, always remember that war is never good for business! That is, unless you're a merchant selling swords and armor, or you're shrewd enough to be a merchant who sells money. We merchants could learn a lot from those clever Jew moneylenders who make a fortune loaning out their money—naturally at very high interest rates. And financing wars can be very profitable. Otherwise, son, peace is always good business. Another toast: Here's to *pax* and profit!"

After sipping his wine, Francesco lowered his head and gazed into his cup as if studying the small pool of red wine, hoping to see swirling around in the blood of the grape the words he wanted to speak.

"My son," Pietro said, reaching over and placing his hand on his son's shoulder. "If you truly desire to go off to war against Perugia, and this is not just some passing fancy, well, then you have my blessing. I'm very proud of you."

His head shot upward, "Oh, Father, thank you for your blessing. I couldn't leave without it."

"More than my blessing," he said, standing up as tall and distinguished as any bishop. "Tomorrow, I, Pietro de Bernadone, will

buy for you the finest war steed and the finest armor in all of Umbria. My son must be the best attired of all the knights of Assisi, which is only befitting for the son of the noble house of Bernadone." Francesco's heart throbbed. It felt as if it filled his entire chest as his father placed both of his large hands on Francesco's shoulders. "But as you well know, I am a businessman. We didn't grow rich through stupid fiscal management. I must always balance my costs with my profits, for am I not a shrewd merchant? So, my Son, I require of you a solemn promise."

"Anything, Father! Ask anything of me that you wish, and I will promise."

"Excellent, as I expected from an obedient son. Promise me that . . ." squeezing Francesco's shoulders even tighter and looking him directly in the eyes, he continued, "Promise me that you will not get killed!" Then, to Francesco's great surprise, his father, with some embarrassment, awkwardly embraced him.

*T*he marriage of Emiliano and Angela was fashionably new— which was appropriate, since they both belonged to the emerging new class of wealthy merchants. After the usual ceremony at the bride's home, in which the fathers exchanged signed wedding contracts and the young couple pronounced their vows, Emiliano and Angela wanted to go to church. They wished to have a priest pronounce a blessing and sprinkle them with holy water as husband and wife. As the best man, Francesco stood next to Emiliano at the entrance of the Cathedral of San Rufino. The cathedral piazza was filled with a festive crowd of family members, friends, members of the merchants' guilds, neighbors, and the curious who had gathered to witness this new ritual following the traditional marriage ceremony. The crowd roared its approval when the bride and groom kissed each other publicly for the first time, the official sign of sealing the marriage.

Then, everyone departed from the piazza for the real wedding celebration: the lavish banquet and dancing in the inner courtyard of the Fibonacci home that had been festooned with long, draping garlands of flowers. The festivities lasted all that day and well into the evening. Emiliano's father served the finest vintages from his wine cellar, and the long banquet tables seemed to groan under the weight of all the food heaped upon them. A quartet of string minstrels played joyously as colorfully attired young people danced in the center of the

courtyard. Around its edges elderly women dressed in traditional black sat visiting while little children exuberantly ran about playing.

"No fear of this being another wedding of Cana," boasted Signore Giacosa. "At this wedding feast the bride and groom need not fear running out of good wine!"

"You are a most generous father of the groom," Signore Fibonacci said lifting up his wine goblet. "Blessings on our two children."

"Blessings in abundance, good fortune, healthy children, and a long life to the couple," added the fat, black-cassocked parish priest.

As Francesco joined the group, Giacosa inquired, "Tell us, Francesco, when will we be invited to your wedding? Since you and my son have always been like twins, yours can't be far away, eh?"

After the laughter, the fat parish priest said, "Ah, the rumors I've heard around the piazza aren't about a wedding. They're saying that soon you'll be going off to fight in our war with Perugia. So, gentlemen, I propose another toast." Raising his goblet, the cleric said, "To Francesco and the glorious honor of Assisi, and to all her brave young knights!"

"May all our young men," added Signore Fibonacci, "and especially you, young knight Bernadone, bring glory upon yourself and our noble city of Assisi. By not allowing Perugia to bully us because we are smaller than she, you are defending our honor. We'll show those Perugians they can't push us around."

"And let us pray," added the rotund parish priest, switching his goblet to his left hand so he could hastily trace a sign of the cross over Francesco. "May God protect you, and all of Assisi's warriors, and bring you all home safe in body and in soul."

"Indeed, gentlemen, he *will* bring glory to Assisi," Pietro Bernadone declared, stepping forward and placing his arm around his son's shoulders, "and great fame and honor to the house of Bernadone." All the men loudly agreed and raised their goblets again to Francesco. Though he was blushing, as a parched desert soaks up a spring rain he gladly drank up the praise of these significant men of Assisi, especially his father. His heart was as happy as any bridegroom's, for his childhood dream of knighthood was about to be realized. While his dear friend Emiliano would be enjoying his honeymoon, Francesco would depart in three days on his own honeymoon of sorts, gloriously marching off to war with Perugia.

The string quartet had ceased playing and had joined those who had been dancing at the banquet tables. Emiliano called out over the noise of the table conversations, "Sir Knight Francesco, if you would pay us the honor of music, my dear friend. Please, treat my wife and me and our wedding guests to some of your magical music."

Pietro beamed proudly as Francesco walked to the center of the courtyard with the lute and bow that he had purchased for him. Dressed in his favorite tight scarlet and blue hose and tunic, with a long pheasant feather stuck jauntily in his scarlet cap, Francesco acknowledged the crowd of wedding guests. He began by gracefully bowing toward each of the groups of guests around the courtyard, and then bowing deeply from his waist toward the bridal couple. Raising his bow in a sweeping gesture to touch the center of his forehead, he then swept it dramatically out toward the groom and bride seated at the far end of the courtyard. As the crowd applauded politely, he placed the lute under his chin and slowly lowered his bow onto its strings. The music that flowed from his lute was so hauntingly beautiful that the little children stopped their noisy playing and joined in the solemn hush that descended upon the wedding celebration. It was as reverent as the silence at any Mass. The swallows and larks that had been fluttering and chirping about the courtyard quickly landed on the red tile roofs to perch in rapt attention along with the once-cooing pigeons. Even Signore Fibonacci's hounds, which had been romping around, now sat erect with their heads slightly tilted in a listening pose. It almost seemed that the gentle breeze had ceased softly rustling through the hanging garlands of flowers. The only movement was Francesco's body swaying rhythmically with the melody, as his bow, which was guided more by his heart than his hand, skimmed across the lute strings. The sound that emerged possessed an angelic voice filled with the awesome beauty of another world. Tears overflowed Angela's eyes as his lilting music saturated with great love opened her heart to all the wonder that was to follow on this her wedding night. "Even heaven does not have music like this," thought Emiliano as he kept his eyes focused on the ground, attempting to hide the tears rolling down his cheeks.

*E*ar-shattering was the raucous, hellish music at the Devil's wedding uniting the armies of Perugia and Assisi in bloodshed. The music of this nuptial of the damned was crammed with the dissident, deafening clashing of sword against sword and the hammering of clubs

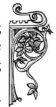

and lances upon body armor. No one was dancing to the rolling cadence of the drums of war on the battlefield of Collestrada outside Perugia, and the pounding only partially covered the agonizing screams of the mutilated and dying.

The newly arrived nineteen-year-old Francesco was in the rear guard of Assisi's army, a hodgepodge of noble and gentleman knights mixed together with hired mercenaries, all joined in battle with their Perugian enemies at the Ponte San Giovanni. Even from where he waited to enter the fray, he could hear the screams of "Holy Mother of God, someone help me, please," and "I'm dying—for God's sake, get me a priest." Mixed with these clear cries of agony was the less distinct cacophony of dying screams from men and horses. Several yards ahead he could see a foot soldier whose stomach was ripped open, intestines coiling out of him in a pool of bright red blood. There was another man whose head had been sliced off, blood spurting from his neck. As men-at-arms marched before him in billowing clouds of gray dust, he sat clad in the finest armor upon a magnificent horse. That afternoon as the two armies charged one another at the bridge of San Giovanni, Francesco learned that war is a nightmarish trip to the lowest levels of hell. Appropriately, it would be here at Ponte San Giovanni, at a bridge that bore his name, that his romantic images of knighthood were beheaded and died in writhing agony. His previous poetic images of the breezes flapping noble pennants to the heart-stirring music of trumpets and drums had never included the gory details of death displayed before him at this moment. Those dreams of graceful pageantry never included the butcher-shop panorama of the bloodied heads and hands, or the arms and legs being ripped from their bodies. Never had he seen human bodies cleaved open with guts spilling out into mud turned crimson by rivers of blood. He sat in his saddle, stunned by the horrific sight. He was paralyzed by the piercing screams of the wounded crying out for help, as well as the empty, open-mouthed silence of the broken bodies that had been hacked to death in this unfolding apocalyptic drama of hell now released to rampage over the soil of Umbria.

At that moment came the command he had so longed to hear— "Forward"—ordering him and those beside him into the battle. A traumatized Francesco sat statue-like in his saddle, frozen with fear, his sword still unsheathed, his untested lance hanging limp at his side and the proud pennant of Assisi now crumpled in the dirt.

 Blinded by the swirling clouds of dust from the newly engaged battle before him, he felt the earth beneath his horse begin trembling as it does at the first shocks of an earthquake. He realized with panic, however, that this was no earthquake when he heard the thunderous sound of a warhorse's hammering hoofs. Straining to see through the blinding clouds of pale dust now eerily illuminated by the sun, suddenly it seemed like that large shimmering pinwheel of the sun had created a gaping hole in the clouds. Then, to his petrifying horror, out of the blazing heart of the furnace of the sun rode a large, heavily armored knight whose tunic bore the symbol of Perugia, the black griffin, a lion with the wings and claws of an eagle. The mounted warrior was wildly charging at him swinging a spike-headed iron mace. The fierce knight was upon him in an instant. His heavy mace came hurling down with deadly impact into his target's chest armor, causing the magnificently clad human statue riding on Francesco's horse to come crashing to the earth in a deafening explosion of clanking armor and the screeching of shattered pride. Then everything went deadly silent and dark for the Knight Bernadone, as that once-sunny day became a starless, moon-naked, ebony midnight.

"Family name?" snarled the clerk without looking up as he sat arched over a small wooden table, his quill pen in hand ready to transcribe on his parchment page. Francesco realized he was in a small, dark room deep in the damp bowels of the great fortress castle of Perugia. An oil lamp on the table sputtered as it gave off a flickering golden glow that tried to enhance the skinny shaft of yellow sunlight attempting to squeeze through the narrow slits of a barred window. However, these two faint sources of light did little to illumine the darkness of the small room. Facing the clerk and flanked by two large soldiers, Francesco sensed the presence of a fifth person somewhere behind him in the dark shadows.

"I demand," Francesco began, struggling to sound self-assured and bold, even though his hands were tired behind his back, "to know what you've done with my horse and armor!"

"They are no longer yours!" replied the clerk, his eyes still on the parchment, "They and all the rest of your possessions now belong to the Lord of Perugia. Moreover, the prisoner is advised never again to dare to demand anything! Now, once again, state your family name."

"I am Giovanni Francesco, son of Pietro di Bernadone of Assisi."

"You mean the greedy cloth merchant whose shop is near the main piazza of Assisi?" spoke a velvety voice from behind him. "The same Pietro Bernadone who pretends that he's some kind of nobleman?"

"My father," Francesco answered, straightening his shoulders and standing as tall as possible, "is the head of the largest guild in Assisi, and he is the greatest cloth merchant of Umbria. He is also. . . ."

"Also, I believe," returned the cultured and crafty voice, "very fond of his son." As Francesco attempted to turn his head to see who was speaking, the voice continued, "Do not turn around! Guards, insure that the prisoner only faces forward, and if he even attempts to turn around again. . . ." Francesco immediately obeyed as he felt a large muscular hand seizing his throat.

"I'm sure that Pietro, the Great Bernadone," the silky voice continued, "will gladly pay a nobleman's, if not a king's, ransom for his darling son and princely heir. Now, Prince Bernadone, you are invited to become a houseguest of his Eminence, the Lord of Perugia. Guards, escort this prisoner to the dungeon where he can join the other prisoners from Assisi."

With the crashing echo of the massive iron door slamming shut behind him ringing ominously in Francesco's ears, he stood squinting, attempting to survey his new home. There was only a feeble, pale light filtering down through two small iron-grated openings near the ceiling of the dungeon—making it difficult for him to orient himself. One thing in the environment was immediately clear, however: the sickening wave of stench from the unwashed, sweaty bodies and the accumulation of human urine and excrement. It was far more horrible than the breeze coming off Assisi's new dung and garbage dump. Slowly, as his eyes adjusted to the semidarkness, he began to perceive the crowded space in which he was to be imprisoned with a multitude of men. He began recognizing among those imprisoned some of his companions at arms, those with whom he had proudly marched off to war against Perugia.

"Angelo, Antonio, Benvenuto—good friends! I'm so glad you're alive and safe," he cried embracing them, rejoicing that they were still alive, even if bruised and bloodied from battle.

"Soon, Francesco, you'll see," Angelo said, "our families will ransom us out of this hell. You especially, since your father is a rich

merchant. He'll never allow his son to be locked away in this stinking prison."

"So, Gentlemen," Francesco said, bowing deeply before them with a wide sweep of his hand, "while we await our liberation, let us entertain ourselves with a bit of mirth and song. Since singing holds magical power to vanquish this appalling stench of Perugia, let us sing. As a warrior, alas, I left home without my lute. But fear not, for even if the Perugians have stolen my horse and armor, they're unable to steal my voice. So, friends, let me begin by using the oldest instrument in all the world."

Just as he previously performed for his friends gathered around the bubbling fountain in the Piazza del Commune, now he delighted his companion inmates with song and story. He was able to remain as free inside prison as he had been outside by entertaining his fellow prisoners in a variety of roles: as a humorous joker, a spellbinding storyteller, and a minstrel of comical and naughty songs. He was also a magician, who by his creativity made the white rose of hope bloom out of nowhere. His powers of enchantment were able to muffle the dungeon's stench and lessen the pain and soreness of the warriors' battle wounds.

What they first thought would be only a few days of imprisonment, soon grew into weeks, and then multiplied into months. One by one the prisoners' families began ransoming them, but as the months aged into seasons, Francesco remained a hostage in Perugia. At night, laying on his vermin-infested straw bed, he would hear the echo of the words spoken from behind him on the day he arrived at the fortress: "Pietro, the Great Bernadone, will gladly pay a nobleman's—no a king's—ransom for his darling prince heir." He knew his father loved him greatly and that his mother would be pleading with his father to pay the ransom so he could return home. So, he asked himself, "Why this long delay in my release? Is the price of my ransom so great that it truly is a king's ransom?"

"Signore Bernadone, what news of Francesco?" inquired Emiliano, who entered the Bernadone cloth shop all bundled up in a heavy cloak because of the bitter cold of winter. "He has been away so long a time."

"No news, Emiliano. No doubt the poor lad's suffering in this harsh winter, too. I don't remember one like it."

"Angelo, who went to war with him and was also captured, told me after he returned that Francesco was keeping everyone's spirits high with his singing. He is so good at. . . ."

"Yes, he's good at singing, but one can't make a living and provide for a family by singing! Even the birds must labor to gather their food."

"They say, Signore, the Perugians have set a great ransom for his release."

"God help us, Emiliano, you've heard correctly. For months, as you know, they wouldn't even negotiate with me, and now they want a king's ransom! My son isn't Richard the Lion-Hearted, yet the ransom they demand from me is worthy of a monarch. Ten years ago when Richard was returning from the Third Crusade and was captured in Germany, King Henry VI set his ransom at 100,000 pounds! To raise that ransom the English had to collect taxes from all their merchants and even the common people! Emiliano, who can I tax?"

"I have a little money, and I could take a collection from among his. . . ."

"No, Emiliano, that wouldn't even put a dent in the ransom. Besides, it is my responsibility, and I can only hope that those damn greedy Perugians will lower the ransom. But enough sad news. Tell me how things are with you and your new wife."

"Wonderful, Signore Bernadone! She is beyond my dreams. Thank you for asking. But now I must ask your pardon, Signore. I've enjoyed visiting with you, but I really must return to the shop. My father will be wondering what has happened to me. I pray that somehow the Perugians will lower Francesco's ransom. Until we meet again."

*F*rancesco's heart felt as if it were an empty wine bottle now that his friends had departed, leaving him companionless. He was the only remaining hostage from Assisi; all the others had been ransomed by their families or by death. That winter, more than the bitter cold filled the fortress dungeon, as new prisoners were daily added to the dungeon. These were not members of the nobility or gentlemen knights, but were the poor and uneducated, petty thieves, swindlers, the insane and accused heretics awaiting trial. The most recent to be imprisoned were four brutal highway robbers. They were former mercenary soldiers who had fallen on bad times—that is, times of peace! Their fighting in small local city wars had given them an appetite for violence and brutality, so now in the absence of war they turned to robbery and plunder. Besides

 the fact that they enjoyed being sadistic, their new profession was far easier than having to do hard labor. Unfortunately for them, and for Francesco, they were careless during a recent robbery and were caught by the Perugian guards.

Francesco continued by his joyful singing and storytelling to lift the sadness of most of his fellow prisoners. These uneducated peasants—often day laborers in the mines and fields—understood neither French nor Latin, and so he reinvented himself as a troubadour. As an educated son of a wealthy merchant, he had previously not had any direct social contact with the *minores,* the lesser or little ones, of society. Yet his strong desire to reach their hearts enabled him to simplify his style and language quickly. As he did, he discovered to his delight that his native Italian was as poetically beautiful as French, and certainly freer and more sensual than Latin. Still, he often found it difficult to entertain his new friends because his voice was frequently drowned out by the loud, obscene remarks of the highwaymen. They took diabolic pleasure in being offensive, even in inflicting pain, especially when others appeared to be enjoying themselves, and particularly when Francesco was telling a story or singing. Daily the highwaymen humiliated the weaker prisoners, brutalized them, or even stole their meager rations of food. With each passing day the dungeon of Perugia grew more and more like the lowest pits of hell.

This subterranean section of the castle had not always been a dungeon. Originally it was used as an underground storage area. Extending down a corridor along the east side of the dungeon were a series of three-walled enclosures that had previously been separate storage spaces. After his Assisi friends had left, Francesco began using one of these small walled enclosures as his place to sleep, and then also as a place to pray. Loneliness as well as having endless time with nothing to do weighed heavily on him, and to lift the burden he began praying. It didn't come easily, not like learning to play the lute or composing romantic songs. Need, being the mother of prayer, he began praying prayers of petition, daily begging Christ, the Blessed Mother, and especially St. Leonard, the patron of prisoners, for his release from prison.

"Saint Leonard, holy patron of prisoners of war, petition our blessed Lord to soften my captors' hearts so they will allow me to go home. Ask God to send an angel to guard me from the evil that is lurking about in this terrible place, a menacing evil that daily grows

more ominous. Oh, how I wish that I had one of my father's holy relics of yours to protect me.

O my Lord and Savior, bless and keep my mother, Pica, and my dear father, Pietro, well and safe. Watch over my beloved friend Emiliano and his wife, Angela.

Holy Mary, Mother of God, pray for us poor banished children of Eve who are suffering in this vale of tears. Pray for us sinners."

Loud shouting by two prisoners who were arguing and swearing profanities at each other interrupted his prayer. The words "and at the hour of our death" lingered like the scent of incense in his mind. As if they were hands lifting him up out of the dungeon, those final prayer words carried him over the red tile roofs of Assisi toward the cave hermitage of Padre Antonio. Vividly he recalled his last visit to the monk's hermitage just before departing to fight in the war with Perugia. He had gone to visit the old hermit to ask his blessing. His cheeks spread in a broad smile as he recalled that visit.

Arriving at Antonio's cave, all he saw was Nicoletto curled up at the entrance sleeping. "Where is Antonio," he wondered. "I've only a few hours before I must depart for Perugia. Perhaps he's gone to visit his monastery, or maybe. . . ."

"Giovanni Francesco, why are you so anxious?"

The voice came from above. Startled, he looked up through the openings of the tree branches, but saw only a few puffy white clouds drifting across a sapphire-blue Umbrian sky. "The *voices*," he thought with foreboding.

"Giovanni, up here!" Francesco joyously recognized the voice. "Up here, to your right."

"Padre, why are you sitting way up there in that tall pine?"

"You might say I'm getting a bird's-eye view of my hermitage—and of life," he giggled. "I'm piously practicing being otherworldly."

"You could also break your bones if you fell from such a height, especially at your age."

"Giovanni, you sound just like Father Prior, who always likes to say, 'Act your age, act you age.'"

"But, Padre, it's dangerous being up there, you could get killed. . . ."

He had never seen an adult sitting up in a tree. The fact that the adult was a priest made it especially strange. He could almost hear his father saying, "Men do not play around at climbing trees."

"Our Holy Father Benedict in his Holy Rule says, '*Memento mori*—Remember that you die!' So if I'm tempting death, I can also be obediently remembering."

"I'm sure that Saint Benedict never intended that his monks risk their lives doing foolish things like. . . ."

"Like going off to war, like being a knight about to engage in fierce and bloody hand-to-hand combat, eh, Giovanni? Remember, the Lord says that those who live by the sword die by the sword."

Feeling like a mouse trapped in the paws of Nicoletto, Francesco dropped his head to his chest. "Antonio is right," he pondered, "and I could die in this war. But if I die defending the honor of Assisi—now that would be a glorious death and not one as foolishly childlike as falling from a tree."

"Padre, I've come to ask for your blessing. This very day I am to depart as a gentleman knight with the army of Assisi to do battle against Perugia."

"Yes, I know. I've heard."

"Will you give me your blessing? While I'm proud to be man enough to go to battle to defend the honor of Assisi, I know it could be dangerous, that I could even be wounded. . . ."

"'Could?' My dear Giovanni, I assure you that you *will* be wounded—no one goes to war without being wounded!"

Fright flared up within Francesco, surprising him. He thought he had securely bolted that door in his mind behind which slept the snarling, horrible fears of what might happen to him in war. Antonio's words had now set them clawing and scratching to get out. Death for him wasn't an issue, for it was too remote—only old people die. The source of the clawing within him was the fear of being wounded—defaced with ugly hideous scars, crippled by losing an arm or leg. He shuddered at the thought that Padre Antonio had prophesied he would be wounded.

"Padre, you're a priest; tell me, is killing in war a sin? Some say that Jesus forbids fighting and war, yet the Church has blessed war against the infidels and allowed knights to do honorable battle with one another. Is it permissible for a Christian for a good reason to become a warrior and go off to war?"

"That's not a question I can answer. Both the question and answer belong only to you. To find the answer, follow your conscience, for God has placed its guiding voice in each of us. As for your other

request—yes, I will give you my blessing, for you are truly in need of God's benediction."

Francesco knelt, and from the priest's perch high overhead the blessing of God descended like gentle rain, more from Antonio's heart than from his lips.

Bidding Antonio farewell, Francesco had hurriedly retraced his steps back home for the grand departure of Assisi's small army to Perugia. The wind rustling through the leaves on swaying branches seemed to be chanting, "*Memento mori, memento mori, memento, memento*—Remember, you may die." In all his excitement of going off to war as a knight, he had never given a thought to the fact that he might actually die in battle. Antonio's words from the Rule whirled around him like an icy winter wind, freezing him stone still on the path at the thought of his death. Then, the fear of actually dying conjured up images of his ultimate fate in the scorching, agonizing fires of hell because of his sins, especially his never-confessed mortal sin of Chambery.

He turned around at once, his feet almost flying back up the path toward the hermit's cave. Surprisingly, he found Antonio seated outside the cave entrance waiting for him.

"Padre, I can't-go-off-to-war-I . . . have-to-must . . . confess. . . ."

"Catch your breath, Giovanni. Come over here; sit beside me."

Instead, he knelt, instantly emptying his heart: "I confess to you, Padre, that I have missed Mass; I've doubted the teachings of the Church; I've made fun of the priests; I've been jealous; and I've failed to say my prayers." Antonio tenderly placed his hand on Francesco's shoulder as he nodded his head and waited patiently. The old confessor knew the power of shame, which always reserved for last the worst of faults. "I had thoughts of lust; I've sung songs whose words may have caused others to sin in thought, using words so sensual that by my singing them I myself was aroused, enjoying sexual pleasure; and. . . ." He stumbled, feeling the red-hot poker stirring the fires of shame in his heart. "When I was in France, I slept with a . . . er . . . I had sex, made love, five years ago, twice, bless me, Padre, for I have sinned."

"A woman or a man?"

"A woman! But I was. . . ." Then he poured out the entire story as sweat dripped off his forehead.

"Yes, anything else burdening your heart?"

He was silent, the red-hot poker again jabbing inside him, "Once, my friends were going down to a brothel at Spello. They kept egging me to come along . . . I was ashamed not . . . I sinned."

"I see. Anything else burdening your heart?"

"I've sinned alone, with myself . . . many times. That's all."

He slumped to the ground, heaving a great sigh of relief as if he had given birth to a giant boulder. It was strange: He felt so ashamed, yet so free! "Regardless of how severe my penance will be," he thought, "even if Antonio refuses to ever see me again, I'm free of that burden." Antonio only nodded his head in understanding as he wiped the sweat off Francesco's brow with the sleeve of his tunic.

"Go in peace, Giovanni. Your sins are forgiven. God forgave you that very night at Chambery and each of the other times, but you hadn't forgiven yourself."

"But I never confessed them to a priest!"

"Giovanni, right now, how are you feeling?"

"Wonderful, I feel so cleansed, so free."

"Remember that feeling. From now on you must become an instrument by which others can feel just as you do now."

"I'm afraid to ask, but for such horrible sins, what is my penance?"

"'Horrible?' Do not play God, my young friend, by judging the degree of sinfulness in your deeds. I know that priests judge the worst of all sins to be those of the flesh, but I seriously question if God does. Remember when I told you that the greatest of all sins is not to become the person that God created you to be? When you return from Perugia, if you wish, we can talk more about what happened at Chambery and at any of those other times, but for now, Giovanni Francesco, you must be on your way or else you will be left behind and miss your opportunity to prove your manhood!"

"Yes, Padre Antonio, you're right. So, quickly, then, whatever it is, please give me my penance and then absolve me."

"You've already done your penance, Giovanni. Guilt itself is more painful than any hair shirt I might give you, for guilt is a private torture chamber more painful than any public penance. Five years of carrying your guilt is quite enough penance. Now, go in peace." And he made the sign of the cross on Francesco's forehead as he pronounced the Latin words of absolution. Embracing the old hermit with enormous affection as they parted, Francesco ran free like a child down the path

as old Antonio called out after him, "Pax, Giovanni. Go in peace—and return in peace."

Seated in the dirty straw of his prison enclosure, Francesco touched his forehead as if to revive the old hermit's blessing. *Memento mori*, he silently echoed to himself, feeling as if he had been buried alive in the rotting stench of this tomb of a prison. Death was now real for him, after the bloody carnage of the battlefield of Collestrada and after having held in his arms his fellow prisoners in their last gasping moments of life. He recalled those who had died separated from their family and without the comfort of the Last Rites of the Church, and that caused him to begin praying: "Eternal rest grant unto them, O Lord. Forgive their sins and shorten their time in purgatory. Comfort their families, and may their souls and the souls of all the departed rest in peace." Then, remembering his own dire circumstance, bits and pieces of the psalms he had memorized in school now began cascading from his lips: "The angel of Lord encamps around those who fear him. . . . They gather together, they lie in wait. . . . Behold, this poor man cried, and the Lord heard, and helped him out of all his troubles."

As he prayed petitions for himself and others, his imagination drew a picture of himself as a beggar outside God's heavenly door, imploring for the needs of his fellow prisoners, for the sick, lonely, and mentally deranged. While he found pleasure in praying for others, he had not lost his revulsion at being so filthy. He loathed the dungeon's stench, despised being pressed closely in on all sides by the sweaty, stinking bodies of other prisoners. Having always prided himself on being immaculately groomed and dressed, now he had to endure not being able to bathe his grubby and lice-infested body. The once elegantly tailored tunic he had worn beneath his knight's armor was now reduced to dirty, sweaty tatters after being worn day and night for over a year. He looked at his grime-encrusted hands and black fingernails and thought that with his dirty, scraggly beard and long, tangled hair he surely must look like old Strapazzate.

One day in early spring—it must have been spring, since it was no longer freezing cold—a dark-skinned young man with a gold earring in one ear appeared at the opening of Francesco's enclosure. "Singer of songs, I am a fellow musician."

"You're new here in the guest house of the duke of Perugia. What's your name?"

"Actually, I'm a guest of Holy Mother Church. The bishop of Perugia dumped me here last night on charges of being a sorcerer, and I'm awaiting trial by a Church court. As for my name, ah . . . I have many names, but you can call me Jacopone, formerly of Naples, once of Orvieto, and now of Perugia."

"You move around a lot."

"My people belong nowhere—and everywhere they happen to be. I now happen to be here, but not for long. However, for the moment you may call me Jacopone of Perugia."

"I am Francesco di Bernadone of Assisi. You say you're charged with sorcery?"

"Along with being a swindler, pickpocket, horse thief, disciple of the Devil, worker of magic. . . ."

"Enough crimes for one man. You don't look all that sinister, even if you have been thrown in here by the Church. Nor do you look Italian."

"I'm Romany, or, you might say, a gypsy. We've given ourselves the name gypsy because it means 'from Egypt.'" Waving his hand in circles in the air, he added, "Ah, the exotic motherland of the occult, the magical and mysterious. People are always starving for something occult and magical."

Francesco nodded his head, remembering well the consequences of his own hunger for the magical at the Chambery Fair. "Well, you are the first gypsy I've ever met."

"We're new to Italy, only passing through on our way to new lands and new opportunities. The Romany have no native land; we're people of whatever land we are passing through, devout members of whatever religion belongs to that place. Our elders tell us we originally came from Northern India and Tajik, but who knows. Old folks love making legends. Since we're a people of the road, forever on the move, in the summer we live in tents along the roadside, and in the harshness of winter we find whatever shelter we can. We enjoy the beauty and hospitality of nature."

"That sounds like a wonderful life. I'd love living as you do, Jacopone. I've dreamed of being a wandering minstrel."

"There's a difference, Francesco. Your French and Italian minstrels belong to some city or country, even if they go roaming about. We gypsies do not belong, and for that reason we are suspected, feared, and even hated. Decent, hardworking people do not take kindly to

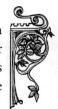

homeless wanderers. Unless you want trouble, like the kind you're in now, my young Italian friend, don't become a wanderer. In our migration northward through Italy, the Church and local governments have made our lives difficult. They judge all wanderers to be dangerous."

Jacopone reached over and fingered the tattered remnants of Francesco's once beautiful tunic. "Once upon a time this was very expensive material. Only nobles or rich merchants can afford such fine clothing. Since your family obviously has wealth, why are you here in prison? And from the sad state of your clothing, it appears you've been here a very long time. I don't understand."

"I fear I have a great ransom on my head, perhaps more than my father can afford. I wonder how much longer I'm going to be in this stinking prison!"

"Ah, perhaps I can be of help with your wondering, even if fortune-telling is the reason I'm here with you in prison." Reaching inside his tunic, he removed a packet of cards, saying, "I hid these from the guards who threw me in here. With these, my young Italian minstrel, I can tell the future, and your fortune—naturally, for a slight fee."

Francesco hesitated, remembering the priests warning about it being sinful to engage in the black art of fortune-telling. "If you want to know your future, you'd better say so, for unlike you, Francesco, by tomorrow I'll be long gone from here."

"I thought you told me you had to stand trial before a Church court for sorcery. How can you be free by tomorrow?"

"We gypsies have thicker blood than you Italians. Unlike you, my family will insure my release. And how will they do that, you ask? I suspect that at this very moment they're bribing a couple of prison guards. Tomorrow as they escort me through the crowded marketplace on the way to the bishop's court, a great fracas will break out in the merchants' stalls. I can see it: a grand rampage of fleeing, screaming women, vegetable carts being overturned, men shoved to the ground, a frenzy of barking dogs—all created by my brother gypsies so that the guards can claim they were overpowered. And I, your humble servant Jacopone, will escape in the chaos. Now, *do you* or do you *not* wish to know what fortune the cards hold for you—yes or no?"

"But isn't the knowledge of the future known only to God—and the Devil? Fortune-telling is forbidden by both the Bible and the Church."

"Ah, it is, it is, and that's why those damn priests had me thrown into this stinking hole charged with being a sorcerer. But the charges are unimportant. I could just as easily have been accused of poisoning the holy water font, or causing mold to form on the host, for we gypsies are the target for all the fears and hates of the people. Now, for a small fee, I will unveil for you your future."

"I have no money and nothing of any value. But I could give you my ration of food this evening. Would that pay for my fortune?"

"Alas, have I fallen upon such hard times that I must stoop to such indignities as sharing my mystical wisdom for a bowl of Perugian sludge? All right, it's a deal. I'll eat double the slop of the day, and you'll go hungry, but I wonder which one of us has the better deal!"

Sitting crossed-legged before Francesco, with great flare, Jacopone began to lay cards facedown one after another, saying something in a strange language about each of the twenty-one cards. Finally, he placed the twenty-second and last card on top of the others. Then he picked them up and shuffled them all together again. Raising the pack of cards to his forehead, he prayed again in that strange language and then spread them out one-by-one facedown in a semicircle in front of Francesco.

"So, tell me, what is my fortune?"

"Patience is required," Jacopone replied, "and silence." He slowly moved his right hand over the top of the twenty-two cards until he stopped and touched one of them. "And . . . your fortune is . . . ," he intoned in a deeply solemn voice as he turned over the card in such a way that it faced Francesco . . . "to be the Fool!" Staring straight at Francesco was the Fool card, the twenty-second card of the gypsy deck, the only one devoid of numerical value, having just the image of the Fool on it.

"The Fool! What kind of fortune is that?"

"The cards do not lie! As for its meaning—who knows? You could become like us, an entertainer moving from place to place, an itinerant jongleur, a clown. Here in Italy in the *commedia dell'arte*, the street theater, you have your minstrels and clowns traveling in small troupes performing from town to town. But, alas, all fortunes are not good. It could portend a dark destiny of you becoming a grand fool, the butt of every joke."

"But surely there must be something more to my future—like, when do I get out of here? What else do the cards say?"

"You want more wisdom for only a bowl of slop? And speaking of what's fit only for pigs, even now I hear the guards opening the iron door to bring the evening banquet to dump in our troughs."

The only supper Francesco had that night was nibbling at his bizarre fortune revealed by the gypsy. On one hand, it seemed to be the fulfillment of his dream to be a jongleur and minstrel. Yet on the other, the thought of being the foolish butt of every joke was something too horrible to stomach.

The next morning when the accused gypsy was taken out of the dungeon, Francesco wondered if his prediction about being rescued by his gypsy clan might be coming true.

*A*s Francesco's imprisonment continued, he spent as much time as possible in his small enclosure. While it was cramped and one side opened to the large room, it provided a shred of privacy and relief from the constant, deafening racket of the other prisoners. Among them was one who was insane, a middle-aged man from Perugia who claimed to hear mystical voices. Another prisoner had told Francesco about his history. He once had a very promising future. The son of a wealthy merchant in Perugia, in his late teens he began suffering violent seizures. These attacks would throw him to the ground, where he would lay unconscious for some time. It was at these times that he began hearing voices. The physicians bled him and tried all their cures, but without success. Equally ineffective were the efforts of the priests to exorcise him. He refused to wear any clothes—in obedience, he said, to his voices—and began walking the streets stark naked. This so scandalized the citizens of Perugia that his poor father was forced to imprison him.

Here in the dungeon the insane man continued to go about naked, and his voices also kept speaking to him. Now they were telling him that he was the rightful Pope and that the other one in Rome was only a pretender to the papal throne. So the prisoners had named him Pope Adam II. Added to the usual raucous racket in the dungeon, the naked pope of Perugia wandered about shouting oaths of excommunication at some prisoners, while giving his papal blessing to others. At any moment he might abruptly cease bestowing a pious blessing and begin ranting about the approaching apocalyptic end of the world. The four highwaymen took a perverse pleasure in inflicting physical cruelty on him. If Francesco happened to be nearby, he would attempt to protect

the deranged man. However, that would only make him the target of the robbers' blows and kicks.

"O Holy Knight of Assisi," the madman shouted one day frantically running into Francesco's enclosure. "The Archangel Michael has just told me to come to you. Michael, the greatest of all of heaven's angelic warriors, told me, 'Your Holiness, go with great haste to the Holy Knight of Assisi who has been kind to you, and tell him he is in immanent danger. Danger, yes, danger. . . .'" Reaching down, he picked up a piece of dirty straw from the pile on which Francesco slept and solemnly presented it to him. "Here, my son, take this most holy relic from the crib of Bethlehem, a piece of sacred straw from the manger of the Divine Infant. Keep it close to you at all times, all times, for this holy relic will protect you from the great evil that is. . . ." Stopping, he closed his eyes and tilted his head as if listening to something. "Yes, I understand." Then, turning back to Francesco, he said, "They say, child of God, that you must flee at once to Egypt where you will be safe until, the . . . er . . . until . . . whatever-his-name is dead. My son, I will give you the papal blessing: May the blessing of Almighty God, in the name of the Father, and of the . . . the . . . er . . . well . . . whoever." In the middle of tracing an extravagant sign of the cross, he paused with his right hand midair, and again turned his ear up. "Yes, Lord God. What is it? Of course, I am your obedient papal servant, your vicar here on earth." After listening in silence for a moment, he returned to Francesco and said, "O, noble knight, please excuse me. It is expedient that I depart at once. The Lord God has commanded me to go forth to lead the next crusade to rescue the Holy Land."

As the poor man ran away, Francesco placed the dirty piece of straw behind his right ear and said to himself, "I don't need a papal prophecy to be told that this stinking annex of hell is dangerous. Fighting among the prisoners is a daily event, as they squabble over food, sleeping places, or some imagined slight. Then there are those truly dangerous highway bandits, especially their leader, that hulk of a man with a missing ear—the one they call Citriolo, the cucumber. Of the four, he most delights in tormenting the weaker prisoners, especially the poor, naked insane man." His anxiety, however, was now heightened by the babbling warning of Pope Adam II of Perugia, because he remembered an Assisi folk saying: God speaks through the simpleminded, the children of providence.

The Perugians may have imprisoned Francesco's body, but his creativity remained as free and vital as ever—evidenced by his decision one day several months earlier to baptize his prison enclosure. Realizing that both dungeons and caves are underground places—the only difference being that you freely enter one and that you're thrown into the other—he decided to convert his dungeon into a hermitage cave. Pouring some of the filthy water from his wooden drinking cup into his hand, he said, "I baptize you, my prison enclosure, and dub you as my hermitage cave." Then, with priestly pomp, he began sprinkling the water in the three directions of his enclosure, saying, "In the name of the Father, and of the Son, and of the Holy Spirit." It surprised him how such a simple ritual seemed to alter the ugly reality of his imprisonment. Since that time he had truly experienced his three-sided cell as a hermit's cave.

He smiled to himself at the thought of a cave hideaway, since previously he would have shunned being alone. Now here in prison he had come to enjoy it. "A hermit's cave," he pondered, "what did Padre Antonio say when I asked him why he was perched up in that tree? That's right, he said, 'It gives me a bird's-eye view of my life.' This dungeon retreat has already given me a new way to look on my former life. Things I once thought essential—beautiful clothing, fine food and wine, my glorious lute—all these mean little now compared to being free." As the fighting and brutality increased among the prisoners, he began to think of himself as the hermit in hell.

Very late one night when the rest of the prisoners were asleep, Francesco was awakened by a warm surge of breath next to his face. A voice reeking of decaying teeth hissed in Francesco's ear, "You enjoy being our little minstrel of song, dance, and riddle, don't you, Francesco of Assisi? Well, master of riddles, I've a little riddle for you to solve." By the light of the pale moon descending from the small window near the top of the dungeon wall he was able to faintly discern the face of Citriolo, the husky highwayman, who was crouched like some great animal over him.

"Yes, pretty boy," snarled a second bandit, whose body straddled his feet, "Here's our little riddle for you to solve: What isn't there any of here in this prison?"

"Wine?" Francesco managed to gasp. ". . . or maybe good pasta or cheese? Or perhaps flowers?"

Chapter 5

"GOOD DAY, SIGNORE BERNADONE." EMILIANO EXTENDED his greeting as the two met on the street leading into the San Rufino cathedral piazza. "What good fortune to meet you as I'm delivering an order of wine to a customer. Any news of Francesco?"

"The news from Perugia is not good," Pietro said sadly, shaking his head. "I have just received a letter that Francesco is seriously ill."

"Oh, no! Not the plague, I pray."

"No, not the plague, but whatever it is, he's very sick. I was informed by the duke of Perugia's chancellor that my son has been seriously sick for about eight weeks. I've sent a messenger bearing a return letter asking that doctors be engaged to attend to Francesco. I included a large sum of money requesting specifically that they hire the famous Jewish physician, Abraham of Perugia. I've not as yet told his mother anything about this. She worries too much already, and until I make arrangements. . . . But, Emiliano, tell me: How are things with you and your wife?"

"This news about my dear friend Francesco deeply troubles me, Signore. I pray he will be well and will return home soon. As to your question about me and my wife, the news is good, very good! From all the signs, it seems that Angela may be with child. It's still early, but all the women in the house believe it to be true. So, we're all very excited."

"Congratulations, Emiliano! Now you're really a man! When Francesco gets back from Perugia, if only he would get married too. He needs a family to make him responsible. May God bless you, Emiliano, with a son, a strong healthy boy just like his father."

"Thank you, Signore Bernadone, I hope your prayer is answered, for it is mine also. If I'm lucky enough to be given a son, I shall name him Francesco. Now, if you will excuse me, Signore, I must deliver this wine. Until we meet again."

"*Pietro*, you can't do that! It's against the laws of Holy Mother Church!" a horrified Pica wailed when Pietro informed her he had retained the services of a renowned Jewish physician to tend to their son's sickness. "The Church forbids Christians to seek the medical services of Jewish physicians."

"Woman, shut up with that silly church talk! I'm the head of this house and family, so mind your business and stay in the kitchen. God, how I wish the Church would mind its own business of tending to souls and stay out of science, medicine, and the marketplace!"

Meanwhile, in Perugia, the warden of the dungeon, aware of the precarious ransom value of his one remaining hostage from Assisi, had him moved to a small cell adjoining the dungeon. He provided water and soap along with the services of a barber to see if these might improve the lad's health. They did not. He also allowed the physicians hired by Francesco's father to visit and treat his special prisoner. Following their extended examinations and treatments, Abraham of Perugia, the foremost physician of Northern Italy, and his two assistants reported to the warden that they were mystified by the unusual affliction plaguing this young prisoner.

"This disease is something we have never encountered before," Abraham of Perugia said. "First of all, the young man suffers from cycles of high fevers alternating with chills, followed by sweating, dizziness, and severe fatigue—all these may be symptoms of a disease known as *mal'aria*, 'malicious air,' the foul air that creates marsh fever. If the lad is to recover from it, we recommend a good diet, proper care, and much rest. However, if that diagnosis is correct, it will likely return again and again later in his life."

"You're suggesting, then, that he be released and returned home?"

"To cure his *mal'aria*, yes." Then, raising his upturned hands in the air, he added, "However, that isn't his only sickness. It seems he is suffering from something even more severe and even more mysterious. Whatever it is baffles the three of us. This strange malady leaves him alive, yet he is as lifeless as a corpse. He clenches his teeth and clings to a single dirty strand of straw, refusing to let anyone remove it from his tightly clenched fingers. He cannot or, perhaps more correctly, *will not*

speak and refuses all but token amounts of food or drink. Yet he constantly requests buckets of water."

"Buckets of water, Signore Abraham?"

"Ah, a most abnormal compulsion. He orders it several times a day, and since the jailer is under your orders to provide whatever he needs. . . ."

"Does he drink the water?"

"No, sir, he bathes in it, again and again, using a sponge. Yet he isn't dirty. Attempting to cure his strange malady, we've tried bleeding the patient, but soon stopped that procedure, for it only weakened his condition. As physicians we are accustomed to seeing the most recent diseases and plagues from the Orient, like leprosy, which the returning crusaders brought home with them. However, the strange plague afflicting your prisoner—in our combined opinion—deals more with the soul than the body." The other two physicians nodded solemnly in agreement with this last diagnosis. "Perhaps," he continued, "the source could be evil spirits, some unusual form of diabolic possession, or even *malocchio*, the evil eye—if you believe in such superstitions, warden. These sicknesses of the soul, however, can bring about the patient's death just as easily as any disease of the body. Some learned colleagues in our profession at the University of Paris believe they are the original source of all bodily afflictions. Be that as it may, your prisoner's malady is deadly serious. So, after much discussion among us, it is our considered opinion that you send for a priest to perform an exorcism on him!"

When the duke was given the report of the eminent Jewish physician and his colleagues, he grew fearful that his lone Assisi hostage would die before he could reap any financial benefit. He instructed his chancellor to negotiate a lower ransom payment as quickly as possible, low enough to be profitably rid of him while he was still alive.

*P*ietro was horrified—biting his lip to control his anguish—when he saw his son carried in by the litter bearers he had hired to bring Francesco home from Perugia. His heart ached at how gaunt his son looked as they gently helped him off the litter. The change of clothing Pietro had sent for him hung limply on the skeleton frame of his body. He was as pale as snow, and while he tried to smile, his once-magnetic eyes were as lifeless as two brown stones. Pica wailed at the

sight of him, screaming as she flung herself back against the wall, fiercely pounding her head with her fists.

Yet what two exorcisms had failed to do, his liberation from the dungeon of Perugia and return home to Assisi was now beginning to achieve. His mother slowly nursed him back to health with her medicine of loving attention—as well as rich, tasty pasta, hot herb soups, and his other favorite dishes. In those first days after his return, Francesco appeared to be suffering from enormous fatigue and slept both day and night. Pica took up her vigil at his bedside and attempted to comfort him when in his nightmares he was again kidnapped and imprisoned back in Perugia. He talked in his sleep, whimpering like a child or even screaming aloud, "Rats, those filthy rats are crawling all over me . . . get them off!" Or, loud enough to awaken himself, he would shout, "Get your hands off of me . . . stop, stop. . . !" As the long days of his recovery slowly dragged by, Pica was able to see the beginning of the healing affects of the ancient medicine of good food and rest; Francesco was gradually growing physically stronger as he gained back some weight.

Soon he was healthy enough to venture outside their home. Assisted by a cane, he began walking about Assisi to regain his strength. Whenever asked about his imprisonment, whether by old friends whom he encountered on his walks or at home by his father, he would speak only in general, abstract terms. One day, weary from walking, he sat down to rest outside the church of St. Giorgio, choosing a place on the low stone wall that offered a broad view of the valley below. As he gazed over the silver tops of the olive trees, he began weeping. "I am an orphan, an orphan. I don't belong anywhere or to anyone, not even to myself. Who am I? What is happening to me?" Wave after wave of tears expressed better than any words his deep melancholy, the lonely isolation of being a foreigner in his native Assisi, a stranger even to himself.

"As I blindly grope my way out of the sour valley of emptiness, failure, and disappointment, I feel as if I'm aimlessly wandering in my own limbo, a lonely dweller in the Valley of Tears. How I wish I were strong enough to go and visit Padre Antonio, but I can't make that long climb up to his hermitage. Will I ever be my old self again?"

*S*pring of that year in Assisi witnessed not only the rebirth of creation and the blooming of flowers but also the rebirth of

Francesco Bernardino's delight in life. It felt, he told Emiliano, like Easter—as if a giant stone had been rolled away from the tomb of his depression and sickness, allowing his former flamboyant personality to rise up anew. He returned to his former life as the town's troubadour, playing his lute and making nightly rounds to rowdy parties and taverns. His friends were happy to have their jubilant King of Feasts back. Emiliano, however, discerned in him what the others failed to see, a strange shadow that partially eclipsed the once radiant sun of his friend's former enthusiastic vitality. He also sensed that a different person was slowly emerging from his former self. This new Francesco he saw now sought the company of Assisi's poor, her beggars, day laborers, and dung collectors. And just as surprisingly, these outcasts sought out his company.

"I'm worried," Emiliano told Angela one night. "In some ways Francesco is the same man I knew before he went to Perugia, yet somehow he is becoming a different person. I can't explain it, but I feel it. He's recovered from his sickness and is once again the center of the party life of the unmarried young men of Assisi, and he easily makes new friends, yet. . . ."

"Yet?" she asked after a long silence.

"Among those new friends are the poorest of our poor. He can sit for hours visiting with peasants and even the dung collectors. Then yesterday, I happened to come upon him as he was upbraiding some peddler who had been beating his donkey with a stick. Francesco chased the peddler down on the street, grabbed the man's stick, broke it in two over his knee, and threw the pieces at the peddler. As he did, he cursed the man in words I can't repeat to you."

"I've always thought of Francesco as a gentle person."

"Yes, so have I. But there is more than just that change in disposition. Pietro told me he is worried about Francesco's melancholy moods. When he sends him to deliver an order of cloth, Francesco often doesn't return for hours, sometimes not till sunset. When his father questions him, all he does is shrug his shoulders.

Feeling guilty for his son's long imprisonment in Perugia, Pietro tightly reined in his urge to reprimand Francesco for his failure to attend properly to his work. He had warded off his temptation to apologize to Francesco for the long delay in paying his ransom and to

tell him how much he personally had agonized over Francesco's imprisonment. Pietro Bernadone couldn't do that because he had his own creed, and the main dogma was: Apologizing is a sign of weakness; men do not apologize or make excuses. However, his reluctance to criticize his son was pushed to the limits one day by an incident that happened in front of their shop. Francesco was seated at the entrance playing his lute to the delight of a couple of customers when a peddler of songbirds passed by their shop. Across his shoulders was a sturdy pole from which hung cages made out of small tree branches. Inside the cages were small songbirds. The birds were chipping away as the peddler chanted his singsong sales pitch about his feathered wares. Francesco leaped up and ran to the peddler. Pulling a handful of coins from the purse hanging from his belt, to the shock of the peddler, Francesco handed him the money, purchasing every one of his songbirds. Attracted by this unusual sale that was in progress, a small group of people gathered around Francesco as one by one he opened the cages and released the songbirds, shouting loudly, "Be free, brothers and sisters, go home to the treetops." Then, he wildly began stomping on the cages, smashing them into pieces while shouting at the top of his voice, "No, no, no! Never should any child of God be caged." Pietro rushed out and made flimsy excuses to those gathered outside his shop. While embarrassed, he was more frightened by his son's bizarre behavior.

$\mathcal{N}$ow strong enough to visit Padre Antonio, Francesco climbed up to the monk's mountain hermitage where the old monk enthusiastically greeted him. "Giovanni, Giovanni Francesco, how wonderful finally to see you again after these many months. I've prayed for you daily since I learned from passing hunters that you had been taken prisoner in Perugia."

Francesco overflowed like a rain barrel in a downpour, emptying his heart about his time in prison and even more about his inner state since returning home. He described his agonizing feelings at being an alien in his own land, his depression about not being what he had once been, and yet not being someone new. Expressing his relief at no longer being imprisoned in Perugia, he talked about his increasing fear at being in the dungeon of some loveless arranged marriage, as well as his suffocating panic at spending the rest of his life jailed as a merchant.

"Giovanni, it pains me to see how great is your suffering, and I sense that you're only beginning to uncover the layers of your pain. It's as if some unspoken darkness still imprisons you."

Francesco said nothing, but only nodded in silence, for the door to the part of his mind that needed to express itself was bolted not only with shame but also with intense anger. Understanding Francesco's reluctance to go deeper into that darkness on his own, Antonio continued, "Yet suffering, while difficult to endure, also has a hidden gift. It's like having labor pains, you might say, so that something new can be birthed. For that new self to emerge, however, something old must die, and that's always so painful. You have a destiny that's pregnant within you, Giovanni. Indeed, each of us has a purpose in this life; no one lacks some significant work to accomplish in God's great divine design. If your destiny is not to be stillborn or, worse yet, aborted—which sadly happens to so many—you must let the Spirit of God be the attending physician at your birthing. Let the Spirit of Consecration change what is presently so painful inside you into a grace—the graced gift that lifts the veil covering your life destiny. God passionately yearns to work good out of evil, even out of your suffering, but that transformation must always be accomplished with your help. No miracles are going to fall from the heavens without your help."

Again, Francesco only nodded in agreement. For some time the two men sat in silence under the thatched porch roof at the entrance to the hermit's cave. While Francesco sat silently, his heart wordlessly screamed, "Nothing good can ever come from such despicable evil."

Finally, Padre Antonio spoke up, "God longs to speak to us, if only we can be quiet long enough to hear. Perhaps, Giovanni, what you are looking for you are seeking in the wrong places. Find a quite place where you can make love to silence. I assure you, she is a beloved who will reveal what you are seeking."

*A*nother drab day in jail, Francesco thought as he sat in the family cloth shop. Just at that moment he heard a shout from the front door: "Francesco, I have wonderful news!" Emiliano leaped into the shop. "Just this morning Angela had a baby boy!"

"I'm so happy for you, Emiliano! I hope and pray both mother and the baby are all right."

"Yes, they are, thank God and St. Margaret. My mother tied a relic of St. Margaret to Angela's birthing bed, since from ancient times St. Margaret has been the patron saint of childbirth, and we all prayed. . . ."

"A boy! Congratulations, Emiliano! Now you are truly a man," Pietro joined the conversation. "I overheard your news, and I am so glad for Angela's safe delivery. Ah, Francesco, you also should be a father and know the joy of having a son of your own. Your mother and I would be overjoyed to have a grandson—perhaps one who would look like his grandfather, eh? Emiliano, encourage your closest friend here to get married; explain to him all the joys of being a husband and father."

"Your father's right, Francesco, marriage is truly wonderful. But I doubt you could be as lucky as I to have found such a wonderful, loving wife."

"I'm so happy for you, my dear Emiliano. You're twice blessed to have such a good, loving wife and now a son!"

"Thank you. But I've come to your shop not only to tell the good news, but to also ask a great favor of you: Will you be my son's godfather?"

"Oh yes, *Padre* Emiliano!" Francesco exclaimed, embracing him. "I'd be greatly honored to be his godfather. What name have you chosen for his baptism?"

"Angela and I have agreed to name him Francesco Emiliano Giacosa—naturally!"

"I am doubly honored, *caro mio.*"

"His baptism is to be the day after tomorrow—we want it as soon as possible so he can be cleansed quickly of original sin. I'd never want to risk my son dying in such a condition."

The large Giacosa and Fibonacci clans, along with numerous friends, crowded around the baptistery of the Cathedral of San Rufino as Emiliano presented his infant son for baptism. Since he was being baptized so soon after his birth, Angela was still resting at home. After the priest had performed the various anointings and the numerous exorcisms removing the evil spirits from the infant, the godparents held the baby Giacosa over the marble font.

"With what name is this child to be baptized?" asked the priest as he held a silver seashell filled with baptismal water over the infant.

"Francesco," Emiliano beamed proudly.

"That's not a saint's name!" snapped the frowning priest. "You must choose another name, a saint's name!"

With a sigh soaked in sadness, Emiliano answered, "Then my son shall be baptized with the name Giovanni Emiliano Giacosa."

Francesco smiled, for he also had been baptized Giovanni, and his chest swelled in joyful pride that he was the godfather of his dear friend's son. He thought to himself, "My godson is being baptized in the same baptismal font in which I myself was baptized more than twenty years ago." While the priest continued praying the Latin prayers of the ritual, Francesco's mind was elsewhere. He had noticed that recently this kind of distraction was becoming more frequent; some simple, innocent encounter could plunge him into deep thought. As he held his godson, little Giovanni Giacosa, he thought, "What if someone would actually live out his or her baptism—not just becoming a member of the Church, but living as a person full of the Holy Spirit, like our Lord Jesus did after his baptism?"

"Doest thou believe in the Holy Ghost?" the priest's question directed at him and the godmother flung him back into the present moment. "We do believe!" they both answered. As he gazed down at the child in his arms, he pondered, "Do I, Francesco, really, truly believe in the Holy Ghost? Do I believe I was baptized into the very same Spirit as was my Lord, given the same Spirit that then led him into the desert? My God," he shuddered, "think of what would happen to someone for whom that was true!" These strange ponderings were suddenly aborted as the priest loudly pronounced the Latin blessing concluding the baptismal ritual.

eavy were the financial losses suffered by Pietro Bernadone in paying his son's ransom, but of a greater concern to him was his son's perpetual restlessness. "I'm a practical man," he told his wife, "and I live in a world of action rather than thought. So it's time I began seriously planning the arrangement of a good marriage for Francesco. A good marriage will force him to settle down and begin to take life seriously. He's twenty-one years old, far too old to remain single."

"If he's not eager to be married," Pica replied, "perhaps, Pietro, he may still become a priest or. . . ."

"Nonsense, woman, I can't think of anything worse than for him to become a priest! Now let's be serious. I'm sure that I can find some nobleman who is badly in debt and who has a decent unmarried

 daughter. Such an arrangement would provide our son with a wife who has noble blood and even a title. She could produce a son who would have a noble name, a name of great honor. Ah, that would be worth more than gold and. . . ."

With a loud crash, the door to their sitting room slammed open against the wall as Francesco rushed into the room with the force of a violent windstorm.

"Father, Mother, I am joining Walter de Brienne, commander of the papal armies of Innocent III."

His parents sat stunned at his announcement. "The armies of the Pope?" gasped his mother.

"I volunteered to go and fight against the German Emperor, Otto of Brunswick, who has seized Apulia, intent upon capturing the papal territories in the center of our country."

"I heard in the piazza," Pietro said, "about that devil Otto tricking the Pope, and instead of coming here to defend the papacy, as he had promised, he's laying his greedy hands on the surrounding papal territory. Those damn ravenous Germans swarmed over the Alps like a plague of locusts, trying to grab up our Italian lands, claiming that we're part of their Holy Roman Empire. For once I support the Pope. He should drive those damn Goths into the sea and be rid of them."

"This afternoon in the piazza," Francesco said, "when I heard a messenger from Rome calling for recruits, I volunteered to go as a squire. If I prove to be brave in battle, they've promised I'll be made a knight. And I promise you, Father, that this time I'll not disgrace you. I shall return home in triumphant glory. Father, please, give me your permission."

"Francesco, I wish I were younger so I could fight Otto myself. But as for you going off to war again, I also wish I were a king! Then I could afford such a son as you. This is so dangerous and so expensive: You must give me time to think. Now, you and your mother must leave me alone so I may consider your request."

Pica and Francesco withdrew as Pietro sat rubbing his chin, pondering. He felt a stab of guilt for failing to pay his son's ransom more quickly, followed by a sting of shame and responsibility for the tribulations Francesco had endured in prison. "He has never blamed me, true," he thought, "yet I still feel guilty for how long a time he was forced to remain in prison. Perhaps by now agreeing to this his newest desire, plus all the money needed to pay for it, I can finally resolve my

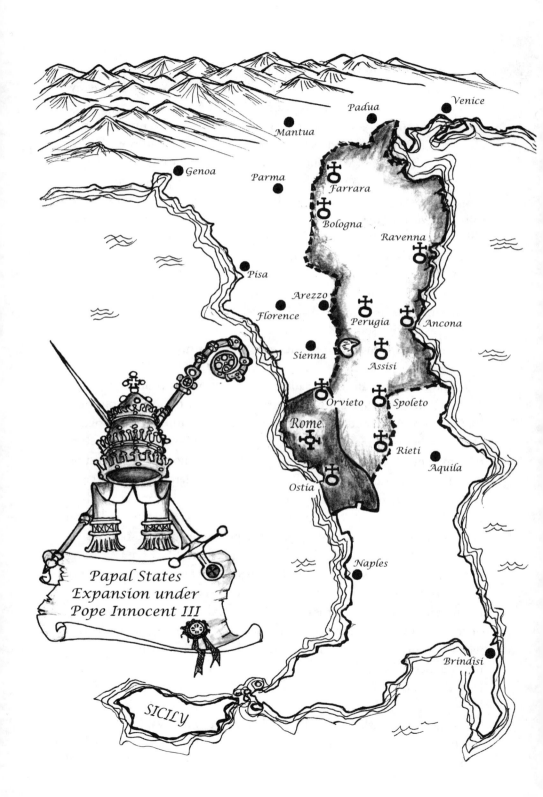

Mantua

Padua

Venice

Genoa

Parma

Farrara

Bologna

Ravenna

Pisa

Arezzo

Florence

Perugia

Ancona

Sienna

Assisi

Orvieto

Spoleto

Rome

Rieti

Aquila

Ostia

*Papal States
Expansion under
Pope Innocent III*

Naples

Brindisi

SICILY

guilt by making him happy. And perhaps this time the experience of going off to war will truly mature him as a man."

Pietro called the two back into the room, saying, "Yes, you have my permission, and my blessing, my son. I love you very much, and may this consent to this your newest wish be a sign to you of my affection. However, my blessing and permission come with a condition: When you return home after winning your knighthood fighting for the Pope, it is my desire, and your mother's as well, that you get married, settle down, and seriously embrace your life as a merchant. Now, my son, off to battle with Walter de Brienne and his papal troops, but do not get killed." Dramatically patting the large purse that hung down from his belt, Pietro concluded, "And this time, my son, don't get captured either!"

"Francesco," his mother added, wiping her eyes, "may good Saint Rufino, the patron saint of Assisi, as well as the Holy Mother of God guard you in your service to the Pope. My son, I will obtain a holy relic for you to take with you to insure your safe return."

rancesco sat tall in the saddle, mounted on his proud war horse and attired in his shiny new armor. He and the other volunteer soldiers from Assisi and the surrounding area had gathered in the piazza of the Cathedral of Saint Rufino to be blessed by Bishop Guido before they marched south to fight on behalf of Pope Innocent III. Standing in front of the cathedral doors, flanked by all the clergy from Assisi and the neighboring towns, Bishop Guido prayed a solemn prayer for their victory in the cause of the Pope and for the soldiers' safe return. As the bishop prayed, Francesco slipped his hand under his chest armor to touch the silver case containing a bone relic of Saint George that hung on a silver chain fastened around his neck. His mother had specially obtained this relic of the patron saint of knights and warriors who was the favorite saint of the crusaders. "I wonder," he thought, smiling as he touched the relic, "if Bishop Guido's father was 'riding Saint George' when Guido was conceived!" He was tickled by this term referring to the practice of sexual intercourse when the woman is on top, which legend humorously promised was the infallible way of begetting a bishop.

When the bishop concluded his prayer, he walked past the mounted knights and squires and their men-at-arms, sprinkling each of them, as well as their weapons and horses, with holy water. Then, as all

the bells in the cathedral tower began jubilantly peeling, the entire company of mounted knights and squires slowly departed in procession from the piazza. As they rode down the narrow, twisting streets of Assisi toward the main gate, citizens leaned out of windows waving and cheering over the triumphal marshal music of drums and trumpets. Francesco felt convinced that this time he would return home as a hero, for was not Francesco di Bernadone now a soldier in the service of His Holiness Pope Innocence III? Would not God bless such a holy mission as this?

As Assisi's detachment of warriors began their journey southward toward Spoleto, where they would join up with the army of Walter de Brienne, the omens were not good. They had barely passed the city gate when a black magpie flew overhead squawking down at them.

"Evil omen!" shouted a young squire shaking his fist at the black bird. "'Tis a bad sign to see a magpie as you're setting off on a journey. It's a sure sign someone will die soon."

"I don't need any magpie to know that," snarled Signore Lorenzo della Casa, the knight for whom Francesco was squire. "I thought we were departing to go to war. War means killing, and it especially means certain death for the dim-witted ones who recklessly place themselves in the path of danger."

"I rubbed the hunchback of old Strapazzate," replied another squire, "as I passed him on my way to the bishop's blessing at the cathedral. Everyone knows that brings good luck, since touching a deformity—which is evil by nature—brings you the secret power to ward off those unseen dark forces of nature."

"I did that too," replied another squire. "His hunchback holds more luck than a bishop's blessing."

"God help us," declared Signore della Casa. "Am I going off to war with a bunch of superstitious old women? Stop all this childish babbling about good and bad luck. It's only a weak attempt to mask your fear. And if you're afraid to die, why did you agree to go off to fight in a war? I assure you, if you believe that touching something evil brings you good luck, well, lads, you're in for a flood of good luck, for you'll shortly have no shortage of evil to touch! Soon you'll meet face-to-face with the most hideous evils of killing and senseless, bloody butchery. And, lads, if there's any good fortune to be found in that, it's only to be found in escaping from it alive, with all one's limbs intact."

At a crossroads between the cities of Spello and Foligno the troops were forced to pause briefly to wait for a large flock of sheep crossing the road in front of them. Francesco cried out, "Look, comrades, a flock of sheep, how fortunate! It's an omen of good luck on a journey when you come upon a flock of sheep in your path."

"He's right," shouted another man. "Sheep are good luck. Shepherds say that on Christmas morning their sheep bow three times to the east. A shepherd friend of mine told me it's the gospel truth; that he personally had seen it happen more than once."

"Before I left home, my father gave me this," said another youth, holding up a small bone. "It's not the relic of a saint—it's a sheep bone! Shepherds always carry one of these to bring them good fortune. My mother says it's because our Blessed Lord was called the Lamb of God."

"What the hell!" groaned another knight. "May the saints protect us, for we *are* doomed if we've set off for battle with a flock of whimpering sheep instead of a troop of real fighting men. Would you men—or should I say *boys*—stop bleating like sheep about your superstitious omens and portents! For it is Fate and God that will determine our fortunes. Sober up and attend to yourselves, lads, or go back home!"

As the company of warriors and their attendants from Assisi traveled southward, Francesco was absorbed in wondering if he could actually kill another man or if he would be too sheep-like. "I hope I can do it," he thought. "I so want to be a brave knight, to prove to my father my manhood when faced with great danger. I cannot—I *must* not—be a coward." These thoughts awakened the memory of his visit with Padre Antonio before he departed on this expedition. He had gone for the hermit's blessing and to confess again so that he might receive Holy Communion. Like almost everyone else in the pews, he never received Holy Communion at Mass, for who of us can be worthy enough to take the Body of Christ on our lips? Those on their deathbeds—after their full confession—did receive Holy Communion, as did many departing for battle. However, his mother had pleaded with him to attend Mass and go to Communion before he left for war, and so he had come to visit his friend and confessor, Padre Antonio. After his first experience of war in the horrible battle of Perugia, he was anxious and fearful about going off into battle again, even if he was fighting as a soldier of the Pope. He recalled the look of surprise on

Antonio's face when he asked him about the morality of being a soldier and drifted off into the memory of their conversation.

"*F*ew people even ask such a question, Giovanni, in these times when the popes mount huge armies to go off to war against the Saracens. The popes have promised that all warriors who die fighting in the Crusades will be forgiven all their sins and will go straight to heaven. So, especially coming from a young man who dreams of being a knight and a champion, yours is a most unusual question."

"Well, until now, Padre, I've never even thought about the morality of war or the crusades. Wars and fighting have always existed. While I've chosen to go to war again, where perhaps I'll have to kill others—even if it is in service of the Pope—I'm beginning to wonder if I'll be able to do that. Over the past few months I've had an increasing desire to imitate Jesus, but didn't he say we were never to return injury for injury and that we are to love our enemies? Doesn't that mean not going to war against them? How can I faithfully follow Jesus and yet kill or maim those who will be my enemies in war? And what if I should die with another man's blood on my hands?"

"A desire to imitate Jesus, Giovanni? How closely do you want to do that? Do you also want to get yourself crucified?"

"No, of course not! What I mean is: How am I to live out his words about nonviolence? How can I follow him and at the same time be a soldier in the papal army? That's a contradiction I've just begun to wrestle with."

"Ah, Francesco, you're not alone! Christianity has struggled with that for ages! Forgive an old teacher if I wander down history lane, but there is an ancient teaching from the early Church that said if Christians were forced into the military service they could not wear a sword. Then in the fourth and fifth century, the canon of Hippolytus declared that a Christian could not voluntarily enter the army. However, if the state compelled a man to join and he was issued a sword, he was forbidden to use it to shed blood. Other theologians at this time began talking about what they called a 'just war,' suggesting that killing is justified if you are defending your home or family. But even in those days the purpose of war was peace. Nevertheless, in time, as with many other teachings of our Lord, the Church continued watering down his words until it became not only permissible but

honorable for Christians to become soldiers, as long as they practiced moderation and piety."

"Moderation, you mean in killing?"

"It does sound strange, doesn't it, Giovanni? As everyone knows, it's a great example of impractical theology. How is moderation possible when you're fighting in the fierce heat of hand-to-hand combat? So, while Christians could become soldiers, around the end of the fourth century the great theologian St. Basil taught that if a warrior killed someone in battle, then his hands became unclean, since another man's blood was on them. These soldiers had to abstain from Holy Communion for at least three years."

"Three years!"

"Yes, while that would hardly be a harsh penance today, in those days faith was still vibrant and people received Holy Communion at every Mass. Sadly, most of us today feel too unworthy to receive it. As a result, that restriction is no longer an effective punishment for drawing another's blood."

"If I carry a sword and shed another's blood, will I still be forbidden Holy Communion for three years, even if I'm on my deathbed?"

"No, that regulation is no longer observed, but I personally think its implications still apply to us, even if today's popes speak of the Holy Crusades as being just wars. St. Augustine taught that 'One does not pursue peace in order to wage war; he wages war to achieve peace.' He went on to say that if you wage war you should do so in a 'peaceful disposition,' so that by defeating your enemies you can bring to them the benefits of peace.'"

"Was Saint Augustine saying we should be instruments of war so we can sow peace? That doesn't make sense."

"Ah, indeed, Giovanni, in our complex and violent modern world it would seem better not to strive too faithfully to imitate our Blessed Savior in never being violent in word or deed. Among Christians, only monks and clergy are bound by Christ's teachings about violence, and in many cases the clergy completely ignore it. Being a faithful son of the Church today seems to translate into using your sword in war to slaughter others. It's not the only aspect of being a Christian that we've watered down into weak wine. . . ."

*F*rancesco was brought back to the present moment when his military column halted to make camp near Foligno on the old

Roman Via Flaminia. It had been a long day in the saddle. Following their evening meal, several of his comrades came and encouraged him to join them on their trip to the city to "visit the ladies of Foligno." Though Francesco knew two of the soldiers, he declined. He had no desire to go down that road again. While it began with exotic fascination, it ended in frustration. Besides, with immanent death a real possibility, he wasn't about to tumble back into sin.

After suffering the embarrassment of their crude, taunting responses to his refusal, he went and joined his mentor knight, Signore Lorenzo della Casa, who was sitting alone at one of the campfires.

"Signore, may I join you?"

"If you wish, Francesco."

"With your permission, I would like to ask you a question: When you go off to war, as we are now, are you afraid?"

"Do I look like a fool? Of course I'm afraid. I fear not returning to my wife, my family, and my home. I fear for my soul. I fear being dismembered. I fear dying in excruciating pain. Son, only idiots claim they do not fear the slashing sword—and especially their own death. But brave men conquer their fears before they set out to conquer their enemies. As for those who profess heroism and valor in facing the enemy, they are only fools eager to live short lives!"

"How about the omens, Signore, at the beginning of our journey; they were not good. I fear. . . ."

"Omens are omens. They are only signs. And signs can be read however one wishes. Is it not silly to say that it's good luck to see seven magpies at the same time but bad luck to see one magpie? What nonsense! You could just as easily say that seeing seven magpies means seven times bad luck. For many, especially the simpleminded, superstitions are beliefs more powerful than any Church dogma. They are much more a sign of fear than of insight. If our superstitious young companions are so vexed about dying, let them run home to their mommies. War is a terrible, dreadful reality not to be trifled with."

"Signore, if war is as fearful and evil as you suggest, is it perhaps then contrary to the will of our Blessed Savior?"

"As regards the wishes of my Savior, is not Holy Mother Church the aqueduct of them? And so when it comes to war, she says the water is pure!" Then, laughing, he added, "For those who drink it. If you ask why I go off to war, it is because I fear boredom more than I do death." He laughed again before continuing, "Yes, being a warrior is dangerous,

but if you're cautious, watch your back, and are vigilant not to play the hero, ah, then war can also be a grand adventure. War keeps both man and sword from getting rusty, which can happen so easily when you're a householder in some quiet village. As for what our Savior taught about violence, well, that is meant more for nuns and priests than for us lay folk, eh?"

"Signore, you speak of conquering the fear of death? How do you do that?"

"Ah, lad, some die too young, and, sadly, most die too old. Blessed are those who die at the right time, and so are able to die victorious after having lived a full life." Slowly shaking his head, he added, "Sadly, in times of war many a beautiful soul is blown off the tree before it's ripe."

"Blown off the tree?"

"All of us are but fruit hanging on a great Tree of Life. Some fruit is ripe, some still green, some worm-eaten, while the toothless ones among us have already begun to rot. When the wind of God shakes the Tree of Life, the stems of some of the fruit snap and they fall, while the rest of us hold on for dear life. Sickness, disease, and old age are like a gentle breeze; they bring death in a natural course, when it is time for us to let go. But with war, death comes like a fierce, powerful storm, quaking the tree, causing many to fall to their death before their due season, some still green and tender."

"Signore, unlike some of the squires, I've already been to war and have seen the evil of which you speak. Yet I so long for fame and honor. I want to be like you and become a knight by my valor and bravery."

"Francesco, do not let your desire for glory blind you to the grim reality of war. Remember that War is one of the four horsemen of the Apocalypse. Alongside his brother, Old Death, the bony rider on the pale green horse, they charge into every battle and gobble up both the brave and the cowardly. Ah, but the worst and saddest of all deaths come to those who have never lived. And that's why these squires—like many of their friends back home—are afraid to die: because they've never lived! If you strive to live in such a way that when you die your spirit will glow like a dazzling sunset, then you will be a true champion. That word 'champion' comes from *campus,* for 'field,' and, indeed, champions are the last ones to leave the field of battle. The greatest among them leave as victors whose deaths are sunsets so glorious that the light of their lives spans centuries."

"I would love to die as such a champion. Thank you, Signore della Casa. What you say reminds me of what my confessor, Padre Antonio, told me before I left on this campaign. He said that war tends to grow on a man like a habit. What in the beginning one finds detestable, by repetition, begins to be pleasurable. Eventually, it can be done without guilt."

"Indeed, lad. But let us not over-philosophize about war! I promise you that when you come face-to-face with a man lusting to kill you, you'll do what is natural, regardless of whether it is moral or immoral, holy or hellish. Francesco, you have more questions than there are stars in the sky. Enough of them for now, please. It's time we both slept before the sun rises upon us. Good night."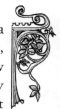

All the next day the company of knights and squires rode southward before camping that evening outside of Spoleto. Francesco tossed and turned throughout that night in a fitful sleep. He dreamt vividly of the dying heretic maid of Montelimar he had seen on his way home from the Chambery Fair. In his dream he saw the flames instantly igniting her hair into hundreds of twisting flames. As she was being engulfed in a tower of crackling fire, a voice in his dream cried out, "This maid is a champion. See, she renounces not her beliefs, even before the fury of hell." He awoke with a start, aware that, indeed, the flaming sunset of her dying had followed him all the way to Italy and perhaps would stay with him his entire life. When he finally fell back asleep, he was plunged into a nightmare of reliving the battle of Collestrada outside Perugia. He was walking across the battlefield littered with wounded bodies and men dying in pools of their own blood. Then, in horror, he was dragged down even deeper into the pit of his terrible dungeon nightmare. He dreamed he was fighting in a great battle, standing waist deep in a river of blood, bravely slashing his sword to the right and the left, hacking off men's heads, arms and legs, while overhead in the clouds sat Jesus weeping. He could hear the voices, *his voices*, speaking in a jumble of Latin, French, and Italian, so that their words were scrambled into nonsense. Then a giant black magpie flew down and perched on his head before beginning to pick ferociously at his scalp. Finally, just before dawn all these night fantasies blended together, transforming themselves into a giant black snake that coiled around and around his body, choking all the breath from his lungs.

At sunset two days later, as the bells of the Cathedral of San Rufino were peeling out the call to vespers, with his head slumped down on to his chest armor, the solitary figure of Francesco Bernadone rode dejectedly down the cobblestone streets of Assisi. Unlike the triumphant departure for Spoleto in which jubilant cheers were showered down from the balconies and open windows, now the acid rain of taunting laughter, jeers, and loud whistles of derision came pouring down upon him.

"Francesco di Bernadone, the Prince of Cowards!"

"Look—a little man wearing a big man's suit!"

"No, he's not a little man! He's a little woman in man's clothing!"

Underneath his armor Francesco was wearing the prickly hair shirt of shame as his horse clopped down Assisi's narrow, twisting streets. Heading home through the drenching cloudburst of ridicule, he moaned inwardly, "I am the Fool. The gypsy Jacopone told my fortune accurately when he showed me the Fool card in the dungeon of Perugia. He was right: I am the Great Fool of Assisi. Forget about being an entertaining minstrel clown; my fate is to be the butt of the jokes of all Assisi." When his horse finally stopped at his front door, Pietro stood like a giant pillar filling the doorway, silent as stone, his face throbbing red with shame and anger. He extended his arms toward Francesco with the palms of his hands open and uplifted as if they were waiting to be filled with some explanation.

"On the old Roman road just outside Spoleto," Francesco mumbled, head down, unable to look up at his father, "I heard voices . . . they said. . . . I'm so sorry, Father, I. . . ." Unable to explain, he leaped off his horse and fled into the gathering darkness of night. Outside the city walls, as he ran down toward the olive groves, his ears pounded with the echoes of the Spoleto voices:

"Love your enemies. Never return injury for injury."

"You really want to go to war again? Remember Perugia."

"Francesco, whom do you serve by killing—man or God?"

"Who is your true Liege: the Lord Christ or the Pope in Rome?"

"Come, follow me. Those who live by the sword die by the sword."

Then to these voices was added an echo of Signore della Casa's powerful voice, "Attend to yourself, or go back home." He ran faster, attempting to outdistance the voices. Then he heard a voice that didn't just speak, it yelled at him. It was the same voice that had sliced deeply through his heart that night at Spoleto. "Your destiny lies not in fighting a battle for the Pope; it is hidden back in Assisi. To find it, you must return to Assisi where God will shake you so violently that you will come tumbling down off the Great Tree. You are to die, but not in battle. Go home, Francesco, and die!" Stumbling down the hill as he dodged the low-hanging branches of the olive trees, he clamped his hands over his ears and shrieked, "I'm going mad, mad, mad!"

*G*ossip in Assisi, like gossip anywhere, must be new to be interesting. Soon the chattering in the piazzas about Francesco's desertion and shameful disgrace was replaced by fresh scandals. As crowds from the surrounding villages and townsfolk filled the main piazza at the weekly Saturday market, the gossip around the merchant stalls was about new disgraces. The crowds exchanged stories of recent rushed marriages to cover up pregnancies, news of the death of this or that well-known person, rumors of supposed adultery, and stories of the sexual affairs of this or that priest. Even Francesco outwardly appeared to have forgotten his shameful retreat from Spoleto before even a single battle was fought. He faithfully resumed working with his father in their cloth shop, and he returned to his former life as the King of Feasts. He never told a person about the voices he heard at Spoleto, not even Emiliano. It had become clear to him that hearing voices when no one was present—as did old Strapazzate—was a sign of madness or diabolic possession.

Although Assisi's citizens soon forgot his disgrace, Francesco did not. Beneath his brilliantly colored clothing he now secretly carried three ugly wounds that had stigmatized in his soul: Chambery, Perugia, and Spoleto. As when a clay jug dropped from a rooftop is shattered beyond repair, so now was his youthful idealistic dream of becoming a champion knight. Feeling the knobby scabs of three painful secret wounds, he began spending more and more time roaming in the dense forests of Mount Subasio. One day, instead of climbing up into the forests, he chose to walk down into the olive groves and fields just below the walls of Assisi. He loved to walk through the brilliant yellow sea of waving sunflowers and was headed in that direction as he descended along the old footpath leading from the city walls. As he approached the dilapidated little chapel of San Damiano, he was startled by a loud, shrieking voice:

The Lord of Hosts said unto me, "Haggai, say to him,

'You have drunk your wine, but have gotten no joy.

You have clothed yourself, but have not been warmed.

You have accumulated silver, but your bag is filled with holes. . . .'"

Looking up in the direction of the voice, he saw Strapazzate standing at the top of the chapel's half broken-down stone wall. Dressed in his usual filthy rags that made him look as if he nightly slept inside some sooty chimney, the old beggar began wildly waving his arms and shouting again:

"Haggai," the Lord of Hosts says, "Speak for me:

'Who is left among you that has seen my house

in its former glory? And how do you see it now?

Does it not seem like a pile of ruins to your eyes?'

Tell them. No, you must tell *him*, Haggai . . .

'Go up into the hill country; bring timber

and rebuild my house . . . rebuild my house. . . .

The seed has not sprouted, the olive tree has not borne. . . .

So I have chosen you, says the Lord of Hosts . . .

You, I have chosen, you, I have chosen, you . . . you.'"

As Strapazzate's last words faded away, he began wildly whirling around and around. Then, to Francesco's surprise, he jumped off the high wall down into the chapel. Fearing that by this fall he had broken some bones, Francesco rushed into the stony skeleton of the old chapel. As he stood in the center of the dusty golden sunlight pouring in through the broken-open roof, the only person he could see in the chapel was hanging on a large Byzantine cross—the crucified Christ. Quickly he traced upon himself the sign of the cross, whispering, "O Lord, bless poor crazy Strapazzate."

Francesco repeated the old hunchback's vivid, bizarre words, "Haggai . . . rebuild my house . . . clothes that do not warm . . . wine that doesn't bring joy . . . who is left that has seen my house in its former glory? I have chosen you, chosen you . . . you. . . ." As these words etched themselves into his memory, he wondered who this Haggai was. He'd never heard of him before. The words sounded like

Scripture, but since Strapazzate had spoken them, who knew where
they came from? And was the old crazy man talking to him?

He decided to go and visit Antonio. As he climbed into the dense
forest toward the old monk's hermitage, the words, "The seed has not
sprouted; the olive tree has not borne," were buzzing like flies around
his mind. What seed? What olive tree?

"*G*iovanni, Haggai, indeed, was one of the Hebrew prophets, a
lesser known prophet whose writings fill only a few pages in the
Bible. From my former days of teaching Scripture to the young monks,
I vaguely recall in the writings of Haggai verses like the ones you just
spoke. But I should really correct myself—I didn't teach Scripture; I
simply attempted to present it to those young monks. For those youths,
Haggai, like the other prophets, was dusty and dull with old age. Like
all young men, they tended to judge what is old as stale and boring.
Now, if they had been allowed to read King Solomon's exotic Song of
Songs, ah, then those lads might have lit up brighter than candles.
Unfortunately, the Lord Abbot doesn't permit his young monks to have
access to *that* book of the Bible, and many older monks fear reading it
lest they be tempted to sin."

"Padre, back to old Strapazzate at San Damiano—he jabbered on
about some house God was telling Haggai to rebuild. What house?"

"He was referring to the temple in Jerusalem, and he was calling
the Jews to rebuild it after their exile in Babylon. That would have been
five hundred and some years before the birth of our Savior."

"So his prophecy was fulfilled, since the temple was around in
Jesus' time."

"Even though spoken long ago, God's word remains a sharp two-
edged sword that slices and slashes across every age. That sword never
dulls—for did not Haggai's words, 'The seed has not sprouted,' slash
open in you a questioning wound?

"Well, I do feel like a dead seed or a barren olive tree. I'm so
depressed by this barren emptiness that I feel."

"Be grateful to old Strapazzate, for he may have given you a great
gift with his crazy ranting from the book of Haggai. Are you not,
Giovanni, a passionate seed aching to sprout? Before you break forth
into bloom, you first must endure the darkness of being buried in the
earth. You must allow yourself to know the emptiness before you can
be full and fruitful." Standing up, he went inside his hermitage cave

and returned with an empty wooden bowl, placing it gently in Francesco's hands. "A small gift to heal you."

"You only have a couple of bowls. I can't take. . . ."

"I have two other bowls, one for myself and one for you whenever you and I share a simple meal. Please, take this one." He held the old hermit's bowl with a combination of reverence and confusion, wondering what he was supposed to do with it.

"A riddle, Giovanni: Does the emptiness of your bowl cause it to be sad or feel depressed? Rather, is not its emptiness an essential aspect of what it is? Is not, therefore, its emptiness a kind of fullness—containing a richness of endless exciting possibilities of what can fill it? It can become full of wine, soup, stew, or any of a hundred things. You, Giovanni, are an empty bowl filled with the possibilities of all your dreams—being a glorious champion, a wandering troubadour, a minstrel of love ballads, as well so many other things you can't even begin to imagine. And I've got a surprise for you: Your seed is sprouting! I'm convinced that Assisi's own Haggai, old crazy Strapazzate, knowingly or not, has spoken the truth when he said that God has chosen you."

Something inside Francesco was released with Antonio's words. Clutching his simple wooden bowl with great joy, he almost danced all the way home to Assisi, improvising songs to give voice to his newfound happiness:

> A noble knight surely I'll not be,
>
> but a joyful wandering minstrel,
>
> singing of love's great mysteries
>
> in faraway lands and o'er the sea.

Once again Assisi's own troubadour began enthusiastically entertaining his friends and everyone else who gathered in the piazza to hear his passionate songs. For him, any excuse, however feeble, was sufficient cause to absent himself from his work in the family cloth shop, a fact that greatly disturbed his father.

"Son, I've found the ideal wife for you!" Pietro announced one day as Francesco returned to work several hours late. "She will bring good connections of great value to our family and our business. The time has come, and a good wife will help to anchor you where you belong." At these words his fist came down with a thud on a large pile of woolen

cloth. Then, raising his hand and sweeping it in a wide circle around the shop, "Someday soon, my son, all this will be yours. You must become a responsible merchant and start to invest yourself in this enterprise, or else you will die in abysmal poverty—and not only you! Your mother and I aren't young anymore, and unless you begin to apply yourself at once and become responsible. . . ." Francesco was standing next to a bundle of cloth and setting his lute upon it, he listened attentively, silently nodding his head in agreement—either in agreement or simply acknowledging and pondering his father's anxieties. The two men looked intently into each other's eyes.

"Take your good friend, Emiliano. Isn't he happily married and proud to have a young son? He's becoming a respectable merchant, learning as he daily labors beside his hard-working father. Why can't you be like him?"

After anxiously pausing for a moment, the Bernadone patriarch exclaimed, "Francesco, stop playing with that old wooden bowl and answer me!" Unconsciously, Francesco was rolling around in his hands Antonio's wooden bowl, which he had taken off a nearby shelf.

"Where did that old bowl come from? It looks like the bowl that old crazy Strapazzate uses to beg for food door-to-door."

"It was a gift . . . a friend . . . gave. . . . Excuse me, Father, I fear my old Perugia marsh fever is flaring up. I can't breathe—I must have some air, or. . . ." He quickly ran out of the shop clutching the empty wooden bowl. With tears streaming down his cheeks, he ran up the narrow, twisting cobblestone streets that led toward the north gate. "It's not the marsh fever," he mumbled. "I was suffocating back in the shop from a fear of being trapped there, trapped in a marriage with someone I don't. . . ." He came to a sudden stop, as directly in front of him was one of the garbage-dung carts parked sideways across the narrow street, blocking his path. The dung picker was stooped over, sweeping up a pile of horse droppings. Francesco vaulted over him, holding his breath against the stench, and hit the street again running toward the city gate.

He came to another sudden stop after passing under the archway of the opened gate—it was so abrupt that he almost lost his balance. For there, standing in the dark shadows of the wall, close enough to touch, was a leper! Francesco almost vomited from being so close to the hideous leper. He had always found them to be intolerably disgusting, with their horrible, disfigured faces and their nauseating bodies covered with oozing wounds. All his friends knew that he had been known to

go a mile out of his way to avoid passing close to a leper. Whenever he happened upon one, even at a distance, he would rush home to bathe, trying to wash off any possible contagion.

"Bread!" begged the disfigured leper. "Bread, for Christ's sake."

"How dare you come here so close to the city!" Francesco demanded, holding his cloak over his face to ward off any possible infection. "You know well that the law forbids lepers to venture this close to any city."

"I know, young signore, but starvation makes a man do crazy things. Please, some food, for Christ's sake."

"Do I look like a baker? I don't have any bread! Now, go away. . . ."

"I'm starving, Signore. Please, I beg you."

"Here, then," he said, reaching into the purse hanging on his belt, "take these coins and get out of my sight." Francesco hurled his handful of silver coins as far as possible up the road that led up into forests of Mount Subasio. As the coins came splattering down in a shower of silver rain onto the dusty roadway, the leper awkwardly and painfully hobbled off on his one good leg, eager to gather them up. Whirling in the opposite direction, tightly holding his nose with the fingers of one hand and his wooden bowl in the other, Francesco began running down the path that led to the olive groves on the southeastern slopes below Assisi.

Upon reaching the tumbled-down chapel of San Damiano, he paused, panting, to rest outside the old abandoned shrine. The deserted chapel, he thought, looked like a busted stone barrel with its broken walls and half shell of a roof exposing the inside to rain and sun. He carefully peered inside, half-expecting to see crazy, old Strapazzate lurking somewhere inside. Then, as if some strange hand pushed him from behind, he entered the rundown chapel. Walking toward the altar, he frightened a flock of birds, which with much flapping of wings flew up and out through the open roof. He felt a need to kneel before the dust-covered, abandoned altar, which was splattered with white bird droppings. As he did so, he placed his wooden bowl on the floor beside him. For a long time he knelt silently, staring up at the ancient crucifix that hung above the unused altar.

"My Liege Lord, I feel just like this old church of yours," he prayed, raising his arms toward the large patches of blue sky visible through the broken-down roof. "I too feel broken down, empty, and abandoned.

The joy of my usually happy spirit has flown out through the holes in my soul. Everyone wants me to become something that I don't want to be, and worst of all, Lord, I don't even know what I want to be!" As often happened, his prayer spontaneously formed itself into a mosaic of remembered bits and pieces of psalms:

> O Lord, hear my prayer, listen to my plea . . .

> My spirit faints within me, my heart grows numb . . .

> Hide not your face from me . . . come and show me . . .

His prayer words were now tethered by heavy sobs: "Show me the way I should walk, for to thee I lift up my spirit. . . . O God, come quickly to my assistance. Show me the work I am to do."

Like a spring rain shower, his sobbing slowly ceased, leaving behind only a predawn-like stillness as he peered intently at the serene figure whose arms were extended on the cross. Gazing at the face of the crucified Christ, he felt a peacefulness that calmed his heart. He was struck by how the almost naked body hanging in agony seemed to exude an overwhelming serenity that was now seeping into Francesco's skin. As this sense of tranquility filled him, he closed his eyes and settled into a deep silence.

His body told him he had been absorbed in that silent state for a long time when he felt the need to shift from kneeling to being seated. With his legs crossed in front of him he sat on the stone floor, caught like a fly in the silken spider web of the stillness of San Damiano. While this blessed stillness was a new experience for him, it lasted a long time—though he didn't know how long, because it possessed a timeless quality. He did know, however, that he didn't want it to end, especially this great bliss that he now felt staring at the crucifix.

What he found most unusual was that while he was so absorbed in this peaceful rest, his senses were simultaneously as keenly sharp as a razor. To him the gray aged stones in the wall behind the hanging cross now appeared to glisten with the sweat of the bulging strength of wrestlers in a tournament. His flesh tingled as he felt the silky texture of his blue and yellow tunic in a way he never had before. While engrossed in the stillness, he could hear the afternoon songs of birds outside the chapel; their voices resonating as crisp and clear as if they were singing their early morning greeting to the rising sun. His nostrils

drank in the potent basil-scented breeze surging into the abandoned chapel from the meadows surrounding San Damiano.

"Rebuild my house," he heard a voice that seemed to be coming from the figure on the crucifix. "Can't you see that it's falling down?" The voice so startled him that he couldn't distinguish whether he had heard it with his ears or his heart. He quickly turned around to see if perhaps old Strapazzate was lurking in the shadows. He saw no one. Terrified, he turned back toward the crucifix.

"Rebuild my church . . ." the voice again declared as clearly and distinctly as any human voice.

"Rebuild?" he asked, looking down at the two pale, soft hands of the son of a rich merchant. Even if the voice had been a command he must obey, he questioned what he knew about working with stone or wood, or, for that matter, about any kind of physical work. He looked up again at the figure of Christ on the cross and opened his arms in an expression of hopelessness. He cried out, "Indeed, Lord, I prayed for you to 'show me the way I should walk,' but I'm confused—was that voice really yours? More than confused, I fear I'm becoming like naked Pope Adam of Perugia or pitiable old Strapazzate. Painted images of Christ on wooden crosses do not speak—that's a plain and simple fact for those who are sane." It occurred to him that perhaps it wasn't a voice, but only the rustling of the breeze or the lingering echo of the insane ramblings of Strapazzate. Other than the singing of birds outside, everything remained as still as the serene face silently looking down on him from the cross.

"Yet even if I'm not going mad and it was your voice, how could I ever accomplish what you ask? How could I ever be capable of rebuilding this tumbled-down chapel? Now, if you had asked me for songs and stories, ah, perhaps I could shape and build them rather well. But as for wood and stones. . . ." He sat in the inner tension of that silence and carefully studied the figure on the cross whose large, sad eyes seemed voicelessly to echo, "Rebuild my house!" Then he gasped in terror, for the facial features of the crucified Jesus began to rearrange themselves before his eyes. The flesh of the face on the cross gradually twisted and reshaped itself into Francesco's own face! Spellbound, he continued watching as the previously static, painted body on the cross began writhing in spasms, as if attempting to escape from the nails that fastened it tightly to the cross. Then, just as suddenly as all this had begun, the image on the cross once again became the static and serene

figure of Christ. Jumping to his feet and grabbing his wooden bowl, Francesco cried aloud, "God, help me, for I am losing my mind!" He felt he had to go at once to see Antonio. His entire body was twitching in dread as he quickly traced upon himself the sign of the cross, turned around and began running out of the haunted chapel.

When he got outside, he stopped in his tracks, amazed. When he had entered the chapel, the noontime sun was almost directly overhead; now it was more than halfway across the western sky. Soon this day would be over, and so he began sprinting toward Antonio's hermitage on Mount Subasio. As he ran, he prayed he would not encounter the hideous leper he had met on the way to San Damiano. While the wooden bowl in his hand was empty, his mind was filled with a whirlpool of baffling thoughts and terrifying fears. At the drowning center of this violent vortex was the haunting image of the crucified figure on San Damiano's cross. He again saw the face of the crucifix becoming his own.

*A*s he gasped for air, panting heavily, his heart pounding, it felt good to be seated outside Antonio's hermitage, to have his mentor's arm around his shoulders and to hear his reassuring voice. "Very unusual, yes, Giovanni Francesco, most unusual, but don't say anything more. First you must catch your breath—and your soul."

Some moments later, after Brother Nicoletto had climbed up into Francesco's lap and looked up at him almost knowingly with his large green eyes, Antonio continued, "Now, let us go back to the beginning, and this time, relax, take your time, and speak slowly. You say that while visiting that little abandoned chapel, you heard a voice that seemed to be speaking to you, but there was no one else present?"

"Yes, Padre, the voice was as clear as yours is now, and it distinctly said, 'Rebuild my church.'"

"When you first began pouring out this story to me, I thought you said you heard the voice saying, 'Rebuild my *house.*'"

"I think the voice said 'house' one time and 'church' another time. It repeated the phrase several times, and I was frightened and somewhat disoriented. This will sound crazy, but I actually attempted to persuade the voice that I couldn't rebuild the chapel because I know nothing of carpentry or stone masonry. I belong to the guild of cloth merchants, not the guilds of masons or stonecutters. I could have gone on to say that the work of the guilds is strictly limited, so that even if I knew how

to rebuild the church, it would be illegal for me to work as a mason or carpenter."

"Giovanni, I understand the restrictions of the guilds, but let's return to the voice. Are you sure old Strapazzate wasn't hiding somewhere nearby, playing tricks on you? Wasn't it there at that chapel that he proclaimed to you the words of the prophet Haggai, 'Rebuild my house'?"

"At first I thought it was him too. I looked all around but saw no one. And I'm sure that I was alone in the chapel. Yet I fear I'm as crazy as the old hunchback. Sane people do not hear voices speaking out of thin air. Recently I've becoming suspicious that I'm not normal; there must be something wrong with me up here," he said, tapping his head.

"Normal, you're certainly not! But you're not crazy either. In your haste to make sense out of what happened at San Damiano do not rush to the wrong conclusions. Once again, Giovanni, start at the beginning, and do not leave out a single detail."

Step by step, Francesco retold his story, beginning with his unpleasant discussion with his father about marriage and being a merchant, which led to his physical sense of being suffocated. He described his difficult meeting with the leper and his hurried flight from Assisi in an attempt to find a quiet place to think. He told Antonio about his long time spent in silence and prayer and how in the midst of his profound rest he experienced his senses being heightened to an extraordinary degree. As he finished his story, he asked Antonio, "Was that a supernatural experience, and, if so, what did it mean?"

"Personally, I prefer to call it *supersensual*. Saying *supernatural* can give a distorted idea of how we experience God—it's kind of angel talk. As to the meaning of your experience, I'd be a poor confessor and guide if I told you what I think it means. The meaning as well as the message was intended for you.

"I see disappointment in your eyes, Giovanni, but it is you who must prayerfully unravel its significance for you. Perhaps I can help, however, by offering a context for your consideration: For those with practical minds, like your good father, hearing voices out of thin air is not real. Reality, for such persons, is touchable, rational, and logical. However, there's another reality that is intangible but equally real, and it can be experienced right alongside our commonsense world of logic and natural law."

Francesco was nodding, trying to consume what Antonio was saying as the old hermit went on, "It's true that the mind plays tricks, and so the voice could have been no more than the herb-scented breeze you mentioned. At the same time, we can hear in many ways—not only with our ears but also with our heart. When our thoughts become so empowered by our emotions, they actually seem to speak aloud to us. Then, there's another much less common possibility to consider. . . ."

After a long silence, Francesco asked, "And the other possibility?"

"*Unio mystica!*"

Chapter 6

FRANCESCO'S EYES BULGED LARGE WITH A BEWILDERMENT that shriveled up his tongue.

Antonio saw the young man's face contorted in confusion, and so he softly repeated the term "*mystica*," almost singing it. Then he began gently to translate and explain. "*Unio mystica* means 'mystical union,' but don't let that name frighten you. It simply refers to the saints' experience of their mysterious union with God. I can see you're ready to object that you're no saint, but allow me to continue. Some of these experiences happened to ordinary people, the milder forms are frequently felt by those who become so completely absorbed in the ritual of the Mass or in their prayer as to experience a deep sense of serenity, peacefulness, and unity with God. And contemplatives who engage in long hours of focused prayer, following many days of fasting and privation, can experience a profound *unio mystica*. It can sometimes include seeing visions or hearing voices, as a number of saints have reported."

"Saints! Antonio, you said it again. I'm not among their number. I'm a sinner."

"Didn't you tell your dear friend Emiliano that you wanted to be a saint?"

"True, but that word just sort of sprang to my lips. I love things like beautiful clothes, music and dancing, fine wine and good food far too much ever to be a saint. I lack a hunger for the great penance required—it would too difficult to be a saint."

"Difficult to be a saint? Not at all, Giovanni! All you have to do is hate—hate your flesh, its passionate impulses, the enjoyment of festive meals and delicious wines. Add to that a hating of laughter, song, and

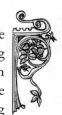

being joyful. Refuse to smile and always wear a pious face, while punishing yourself with long months of strict fasting and inflicting harsh punishments on your body. The monastery was full of such saintly pretenders, which is the reason I enjoy living out here in the woods as a hermit. Appearing to be a saint isn't hard work; becoming your true self—that's what's difficult. Authentic saints, Giovanni, are natural, while sanctimonious saints are artificial."

Seeing that Francesco was edging forward on his tree stump, Antonio said, "Hold the idea that's eager to leap off your tongue for just a moment, Giovanni. As I said before, each of us has been designed to be a saint from before birth. That image of sainthood is imprinted on our souls like a pattern for creating a fine garment. We're all supposed to become saints, whether or not we see visions. Your experience of seeing the face of Christ turning into your face may suggest a pattern for beginning the work of becoming identified with your Savior by living as he did. Such an identification is indeed possible and requires no special training, no miracle or grand divine invitation setting you apart. It only requires love, because lovers seek to be one with their beloved!"

Francesco no longer felt a need to say anything. Sitting there speechless, he felt his body still trembling slightly from his bizarre experience in the old chapel. And now the words of Antonio were sweeping him away, as if he was tumbling end-over-end like a log in a flooded river.

"Giovanni, are you not being drawn to be intimately identified with the Suffering One on the cross—as well as with those suffering ones who share his body? The great mystery of the Body of Christ is that the suffering beggar at the crossroad is one with the suffering beggar on the cross."

"Christ was no beggar! Our Lord died heroically, begging for nothing as he hung nailed to the cross dying for our sins!"

"No, my youthful friend, you're wrong. While his death certainly was heroic, Jesus died begging for our love. He died begging you, Giovanni, and each of us to love him as he has so passionately loved us. And when it comes to love, are we all not beggars? Some hold out their hearts like empty cups, begging for them to be filled with another's lifelong commitment of fidelity. Others beg for their cups to be filled with power and authority, which they mistakenly think will make them

lovable. Others beg for sexual pleasures, or to be accepted, or to be needed, yet in the end we're all begging for the same thing—love."

"I'd forgotten, Padre," Francesco said eagerly, "that Jesus *was* a beggar on his cross when he petitioned God: 'Father, forgive them, for they know not what they are doing.' He was begging God to give the gift of pardon to those who had caused him such great pain and shame."

As Antonio quietly nodded his head in agreement, Francesco's second wound, his imprisonment in Perugia, began to ache. Ashamed of those awakened memories, he buried his face in his hands, mumbling, "Forgive them, Father, for they did not know what they were doing."

"Giovanni, are you simply quoting Scripture, or are you praying that God forgive someone who has caused you crucifying pain?"

Though he didn't answer out loud, the two men sat in silent communion as the purple twilight shadows softly descended, indicating the end of the day. Finally, Francesco ended the silence. "Thank you, Padre, for your patience. I believe I'm beginning to understand what I must do. It seems the crucified beggar of God is now begging me to restore his little neglected chapel of San Damiano. Perhaps I'm supposed to raise the money needed to pay the masons to do the work. I'm not sure, but I do feel strongly that this task is what God desires me to do."

"Spirit-messages are never simple, Giovanni. They require serious reflection to untangle their true meaning. However, I affirm your taking upon yourself this work of charity in rebuilding San Damiano chapel. It sounds like a good beginning point in your new life quest. The ancients believed it is often better to work our way into new ways of thinking than to think our selves into new ways of living. To put it more simply: First, use your hands, then your mind will follow. So, I would encourage you, despite the laws of the guilds, to consider beginning the work yourself without hiring workers. Work is good for the soul. As our holy father Saint Benedict taught, '*Ora et labora,*' Prayer and work. When these two are married, they create a healthy, balanced life. One without the other can easily lead us astray. Labor implies getting our hands dirty, which returns us to our primal vocation of being laborers in Eden's garden."

As Francesco looked down at his clean fingernails and soft, white hands, he painfully recalled how filthy they had been in the dungeon

of Perugia, and he wondered if he could actually embrace the tasks of a common laborer. Notwithstanding Antonio's advice, he was inclined to raise the needed money to hire guild workers to do the labor. "I'm not sure, Padre, which will be more difficult for me, the *labora* or the *ora*, since I am unskilled in both. I tried praying when I was in prison, but. . . ."

"Try again; you're still in prison."

"How am I still imprisoned?"

"Just as you were locked away in Perugia, so each of us often imprisons a part of ourselves. In a dungeon deep within us we confine our unpleasant memories and those dark, unmentionable urges we've judged unfit or too dangerous to see the light of day. Deep prayer is like a sacred staircase that leads down to a radical honesty about our whole selves. But do not fear, Giovanni, for as our Lord told us, 'The truth will set you free'—and I might add to his holy words that the truth will heal you."

"Does the healing of truth bring serenity?"

"Serenity is the outward peacefulness of the holy ones that results from their liberation. You will gain serenity when you are released from all the labor of having to constantly guard what's held prisoner in your inner dungeons. Self-acceptance, even in your darkest areas, allows you to relax, to be free of perpetually having to defend your propped-up public image. When you stop wearing a mask, you're able to let go and just be yourself, and that freedom is what many call serenity."

"I long for that kind of peacefulness, but I'm afraid to descend into my dungeon and accept what's chained up down there."

"Let go of your fear, Giovanni. The descent is gradual; the veil hiding what you fear inside you will be raised when you're able to face whatever is there. Moreover, instead of trying to be courageous, simply dedicate yourself to prayer.

"But look, my young friend, this day is almost over—enough talking."

"Yes, I must start for home. I've been gone far too long."

"Before you depart, I want to give you a blessing." Reaching over, Antonio touched both of Francesco's eyes and said, "Be healed!" As they stood up, Antonio added, "Now, let me accompany you part of the way."

As the two walked silently along the path that led to Assisi, Francesco wondered about the healing blessing. "That's the second

time Padre Antonio has blessed my eyes. I guess I still can't see whatever it is I'm supposed to see."

When they reached a junction in the road, Antonio said, "Giovanni, soon Sister Night will be wrapping us in her ebony cloak. It is time I headed back to my hermitage."

"And I must quicken my pace to arrive at Assisi before they shut the city gates and I find myself locked outside." The embrace of the two friends was long and full of affection. As Francesco departed for home, he felt renewed and grounded by the old hermit's love. In the east a crescent pale-blue moon was rising majestically in the rose and turquoise twilight sky as he leisurely walked down the path, reflecting on the extraordinary events of that day. He refused to force himself to hurry in order to reach the city before the closing of the gates. He knew that, if necessary, he could find another way into the city, and it was too important for him to absorb the grace of the moment. His thoughts were centered on a new hunger, to hear more about *Unio mystica*. Then his thoughts and imagination skipped to the Christ figure on the cross telling him to rebuild the old, ruined chapel and all the problems that request raised for him. He wondered how he was he going to accomplish the task. He felt personally unfit to do it. And how would he raise the needed money?

As he walked, an uninvited guest appeared and distracted him from his thoughts about repairing the chapel—a painful flashback of his imprisonment in Perugia. He tried to shake the memory from his mind, but it stubbornly refused to leave. Then he recalled Padre Antonio once telling him that a good way to handle distractions in prayer is to entertain them. Quoting the Rule of Benedict that all guests are to be received as Christ, he had encouraged Francesco to entertain distractions like guests, since they often come bearing gifts. Although Francesco didn't think he was praying at the moment, he thought his memories of Perugia were certainly distractions. So he decided to entertain them as he would any guests—by singing:

> Welcome, my uninvited guests from hell,
>
> raggedly clothed, unwashed and unwanted.
>
> Black are your fingernails and hands with grit;
>
> your unwashed body stinks worse than garbage.
>
> Welcome, my uninvited guests from hell.

Let me entertain you on my invisible lute.

Enjoy this melody I'm pretending to pluck

as my fingers nimbly play upon thin air,

while my voice sings of shame and hate. . . .

His imaginary lute suddenly disappeared, and his minstrel melody halted mid-song, as he sang the word "hate." He was surprised that such a malice-laden word had sprung from his lips. It seemed to have arisen from the dungeon deep inside his heart. Disturbed by its appearance, he acknowledged that he still felt intense hatred toward those bandits for what they had done to him. He hated himself for having allowed them to overpower him, even though they were so much larger and stronger than he. He felt a piercing shame and guilt— shouldn't he have tried harder to fight them off, even if it might have meant his death? Did his lack of such resistance make him guilty of serious sin? He felt an impulse to confess to Padre Antonio and tell him all that had happened in the dungeon of Perugia.

As Francesco looked up, there looming before him was the dark silhouette of Assisi's city walls and towers. He had been so absorbed in thought that he didn't realize how far he had walked. "The city gates will be closed by now," he thought. "I'm sure, though, that I can enter through the western gate near the prisoner's cemetery, the gate used by the garbage-dung collectors. At this time of night they will just be completing their work." That gate was indeed open when he got there, and he sneaked into the city unnoticed.

He awoke the next day feeling fresh—and also as if he were on fire. He felt a burning need to share with someone his haunting fear that he was going mad, an urgent need to speak with someone besides Padre Antonio about his strange experience at San Damiano. Later in the day he found an excuse to absent himself from the shop, and he hurried over to the Giacosa wine shop to talk with his friend Emiliano.

"You'll find him down in our wine cellar," said Signore Giacosa. "Thank God our family business is expanding so much that we have to enlarge our wine cellar," he added, folding his hands as if in prayer. "Ah, God is good!"

 In the wine cellar he found Emiliano moving large, heavy wine barrels, his sweat-soaked tunic clinging to his body, revealing his muscular chest and arms. "Francesco, *caro mio*, what a wonderful surprise!" he exclaimed, wiping his forehead with his tunic sleeve. "If you've come to help, you had better go home and change your clothes first," he laughed, gripping Francesco by his shoulders with both of his hands. "I'd give you an embrace if I wasn't all sweaty."

"*Caro mio*, I've come because I urgently need to talk with you. I must tell you about the strange things that have happened to me." As they stood in the wine cellar, Francesco uncorked his heart and poured out the entire story of his experiences at the little chapel of San Damiano. He spoke about the voice he had heard and how the face of the Savior had changed into his own face. He shared his fears that he might be going mad but said that, regardless, he would attempt to do what the voice had asked of him. Then he collapsed to sit on a wine barrel.

"So you're going to rebuild that old church, Francesco? That will mean new timbers and slate for the roof, as well as new stones for the walls, since many of the original ones have been carted off to build or repair houses here in Assisi. You'll also have to hire stonemasons and carpenters, and they'll be expensive. They won't be interested in your job because they're already employed full-time repairing the eastern city walls and constructing that new house on the Via San Gregorio. And the money—will it come as a charitable work from the cloth merchants' guild?"

"You're a very practical and astute man, Emiliano, and as you describe it I feel overwhelmed by the task. But as for the stonemasons, I feel that the voice was speaking directly to me, and it implied that somehow the repair work was to be my personal project. I'm caught between feeling that it's my personal responsibility and wondering how could I ever rebuild that chapel. I'm excited and confused; as soon as I awakened this morning I knew I had to come and speak with you. Yet, despite my confusion and my sense of inadequacy—and this may sound pious—I truly feel that if Christ really spoke to me, then God will provide a way for me to do it. Just what that way will be, however, I have no idea."

"Can I help you, my friend? Is there anything I can do?"

"Indeed, Emiliano, for a short time you could loan me your body in exchange for mine! When I've finished rebuilding the chapel, I will gladly return it to you with interest!" They both laughed, and Emiliano gave him a large, sweaty hug.

As they walked toward the stairs leading up from the wine cellar, Francesco turned toward Emiliano and earnestly added, "There is something I would ask of you, Emiliano. Please don't begin to think that I'm becoming another Strapazzate, and please don't stop being my friend."

"Never. Don't ever be afraid of that," he responded as he escorted Francesco outside.

When they bid each other farewell, Francesco left behind a worried friend. Emiliano stood deep in thought, wondering if his friend's old Perugian sickness was beginning to affect his mind. He had remained silent about his belief that sane people do not hear voices speaking to them from crucifixes. Yet so deep was his love for Francesco that he could suspend the judgment that his friend was losing his mind. He hoped that maybe in a mixture of stress and a momentary return of his Perugian fever, he had only imagined the whole thing. "Indeed," he thought, "Francesco has the most vivid imagination of any man I've ever known, and perhaps. . . ." He slowly traced the sign of the cross upon himself, whispering, "Lord, please help my dear friend, and help me to continue to love him—even if he does go mad."

As Francesco was walking back to the family cloth shop, he was so lost in prayer and thought that he saw or heard nothing along the way. He was discouraged at what he considered his complete lack of the personal physical skills and strength needed to rebuild that chapel. As he walked, he prayed for some divine insight or intervention that might enable him to execute what he was being asked to do. In the midst of that prayer, he reflected on his last conversation with Antonio. He dryly smiled to himself as he thought, "I believe I'm beginning to know what it was like for Jesus to beg his Father prayerfully on the cross. All I can do is beg God for assistance in rebuilding San Damiano." Then, suddenly, he had an idea. "I could use that old bowl Antonio gave me to collect the money to pay for the needed labor and materials." He broke into a run, racing to get the bowl and his lute. Hurrying back to the Piazza del Commune, he sat on the stone lip of the fountain with his empty wooden bowl beside him. Accompanying himself on his lute, he began to sing his plea:

Oh please, kind sir, silver for your Savior,

most noble sir, grant to your Lord a loan,

a handful of coins that tinkle and shine,

to hire stonemasons and purchase new stone

to repair our beloved old Damiano shrine.

Kind sir, gentle lady, and you young lad,

please, you astute merchant with extra coins,

God's house is roofless, broken and sad.

Please give a gift to rebuild San Damiano.

As the afternoon leaned toward evening, his wooden bowl remained empty. The merchants and citizens of Assisi had thrown not a single coin into it. They only shook their heads, smiling in disbelief at the sight of Francesco begging. In place of coins, they tossed comments at him. One merchant said, "What will that Bernadone lad think of next?" And the merchant's son added, "This has to be one of his new jokes." A well-to-do matron asked, "Truly, I ask you, whoever saw a beggar dressed like a prince?" And another merchant remarked, "I call it madness. Why in heaven's name should I donate even the smallest coin to rebuild that old abandoned chapel that no one ever uses?"

Laying down his lute, Francesco continued his begging song, but now he moved about, holding out his empty bowl to those strolling across the piazza. Near day's end, he spied ragged old Strapazzate entering the piazza from the far side carrying his begging bowl. As Strapazzate approached the bubbling fountain, Francesco could see that his bowl was filled with hunks of bread and food that housewives had given him. The young minstrel's poetic begging song evaporated on his lips as the foul-smelling old beggar stopped directly in front of him, stared right into his eyes and then peered down into his empty bowl. "Ah, Tommaso of Spello," Francesco asked, "do you have any messages from God or any words of wisdom from the saints for me today?" The old hunchback swayed back and forth for a few moments, and then grinning a toothless smile, he began singing,

Oh, please kind sir, some silver for your Savior,

please, young sir, give an ear to your Savior;

it's time to change the way your life is driven,

for heaven's Holy Lender once cleverly said,

"To everyone who has, more will be given,

and they will grow rich and be well fed.

But, alas, the one without, what little he has

will be taken from him, leaving not a shred."

The Lord comes, but you have nothing to yield.

He'll say to you: "Lazy servant, full of fear,

Fool, you've buried your talents in a field."

Dig up the field, go find the treasure dear.

If not, tremble at the Holy Lender's wrath,

For he will say, "Now, lazy lout, lose even the. . . ."

Strapazzate continued wordlessly humming his little tune as he took up Francesco's wooden bowl and began running his finger around and around the rim. Then, raising it high above his head, he repeated the words of Jesus, "'Even the little he has will be taken away from him!' Yes, poof, gone, defunct! So, farewell, until we meet again, Signore Beggar Bernadone."

Francesco easily recognized the parable of Jesus that Tommaso of Spello had woven into his song, for it was his father's favorite parable. Pietro always claimed it gave the Holy Savior's stamp of approval to those merchants who cleverly used their money to make more money. He especially enjoyed repeating the part about the servant who had wisely invested his money to double his silver talents and was rewarded by being welcomed to share in his master's joy. Pietro interpreted it as an infallible sign that shrewd merchants such as himself would have high places in heaven.

After his unproductive day of begging for money to repair the chapel, Francesco rejoiced to see his friend Emiliano, who was entering the piazza leading one of the Giacosa mules to which had been strapped a large wine barrel. "Emiliano, my dear friend, could you spare a few coins for your poor beggar friend's worthy cause?"

Amused at the sight of his wealthy friend with a beggar's bowl, Emiliano replied, "I'd hate to see a good friend go home empty-handed, so I will gladly contribute, but on one condition—agreed?"

"How can I refuse?"

"Good, here are some coins for your fund, but you must promise to come and have dinner with my wife and me." Before waiting for a response, he dropped several silver coins into the empty bowl. "Other than church on Sunday, we've hardly seen you since you returned from Spoleto. Please come, and bring your lute to sing for us."

"Of course, Emiliano, I would love to come to dinner at your home. And thank you for your contribution—the first.

"Also, Emiliano, you are right; it's been far too long since we've spent some real time together. My mother tells me that since your beautiful Angela gave birth she has grown even more lovely. And, of course, I'm eager to see little Giovanni. Is he growing up to look like his father?"

"You mean little Francesco? That's what we call him, and, yes, he grows bigger every day. He's such a delight to us. Please come soon to visit our home."

"I promise, and now you must be about your work and I about mine—begging." As Emiliano departed to deliver the barrel of wine, Francesco looked down at the few silver coins in the bottom of his bowl, and his heart echoed Strapazzate's words, ". . . but the one who has not, what little he has will be taken from him!"

The next day Francesco chuckled with delight at the amusing contradiction of being a beggar attired in clothing as fine as any nobleman's. As the son of one of the city's most influential merchants, those he approached for money could not dismiss him as easily as they would a poor, dirty beggar hobbling on crutches. While some found his role change from Assisi's King of the Feasts to its Prince of Paupers amusing, his father did not.

"Francesco, while we are not nobles," Pietro moaned in near exasperation, "we are one of the most respected families in all of Assisi. Am I not the head of the Guild of Merchants? Now, however, I've become the butt of Assisi's jokes. You shame me, my son, by begging for money from my friends and fellow merchants. Tongues in Assisi are wagging at your impossible story about that crucifix talking to you! Francesco, are you going mad? Are you now the son of Strapazzate? Don't you care that you've disgraced your real father?"

"But, Father, I'm begging for God!" Francesco surprised himself with the conviction with which he spoke. "I'm only collecting funds to

rebuild the fallen-down little chapel of San Damiano. Is that not a noble, even a holy, cause?"

"Begging for money to rebuild churches," Pietro shouted, slamming his fist down on the table with a loud crash, "is the work of priests and monks. You say that God told you to rebuild it, but why would God ask that? We already have too many churches, and those we have aren't even filled on Sundays and Feast Days! If the bishop allowed that old chapel to fall into disrepair, then it's his responsibility, not yours! Son, your responsibility is here," he proclaimed, stomping his foot, "here, here, right here in this shop! Your work isn't rebuilding dilapidated churches, it's selling cloth and learning how to run our family business." As Pietro paused to catch his breath, Francesco waited patiently, for he knew that his father's sermon wasn't over yet. While he knew what was coming next, today his father seemed to have run out of patience and was more vehement and unwavering that Francesco marry and become responsible.

"No, indeed, Francesco, restoring old San Damiano is not your business! What really needs rebuilding is your life, and, my son, it badly needs restoring! I propose that what God was really saying to you was, 'Francesco, repair the house of your life. Become sensible and practical.' So, if you must beg, Francesco Bernadone, I say good, but go begging for a good wife! In fact, I intend to begin. . . ."

The tolling of the death bell of the Church of Santa Maria called the two Bernadones to an instant truce. They both knew that Death was a frequent visitor in Assisi, where, as in any city or village, so many mothers died in childbirth and so many children died at an early age. But this grim tolling bell cast a particularly ominous foreboding over both of them. Their premonition was soon confirmed when Albertino Compagni ran panting into their shop.

"Poor Filippo Villani has died," he said quickly, tracing the sign of the cross upon himself. "As we all know, he has been sick. But today he grew much worse, and his wife called for the priest. He was given the Last Rites and died peacefully shortly afterwards. Eternal rest grant unto him, O Lord. . . ."

"And may his soul," father and son joined in, "and the souls of all the faithful departed rest in peace."

Even before they could conclude with an "amen," the ever-practical Pietro said, "I must attend to the details of his funeral at once. I will go to each of our guild members to begin making arrangements. It is our

responsibility to pay him the proper honor that is due to a longtime member of our distinguished cloth guild. Francesco, take over the shop. And you, Albertino, come with me as we apply ourselves to one of the most important duties of our guild, the funeral and burial of one of our members.

*E*veryone remarked at how impressive was the funeral of Filippo Villani. People spoke of how stately was the ritual of his coffin being borne into church on the shoulders of his brothers of the Merchant Guild, all of whom were attired in their finest clothing and their magnificent black-hooded cloaks. They placed his coffin reverently on a raised platform in the center of the church. Clerics came forward with large, ornate silver candleholders bearing orange funeral candles as tall as a man, placing three on each side of the coffin. The tall candles looked like luminous honor guards standing at fixed attention. The Cloth Guild had arranged for a Solemn High Mass to be sung by three vested priests and for Assisi's finest choir to chant his funeral music. Like the strains of angels, the choir's beautiful, ethereal voices lifted up the ageless Latin chants that were filled with grave and somber foreboding:

> Have mercy on me, O God,
>
> according to your great mercy.
>
> In your great clemency blot out my iniquity;
>
> wash me completely from my guilt,
>
> and cleanse me, O God, from my sin.
>
> Against thee only have I sinned;
>
> I have done what is evil in thy sight.

From his student days at San Giorgio's, Francesco knew those Latin words of Psalm 51 by heart. He wordlessly joined in singing them with the choir:

> Behold, I was born in guilt,
>
> and my mother conceived me in sin.
>
> Turn your face from my sins,
>
> and blot out all my guilt . . .
>
> blot out all my guilt. . . .

"Blot out all my guilt." The anguish of that entreaty echoed across the church and found a home in the family, friends, guild members, and even the curious who were gathered, for each of them had been schooled to accept the unhappy reality of death as going into the grave heavily guilt-laden. Francesco's heart went out to old Filippo, who was naked in his coffin except for his burial shroud. "Naked we come into this world," Francesco reflected, "and naked we depart from it, for only bishops are fortunate enough to be buried fully clothed in their episcopal robes. We come into the world with nothing, and we leave it empty-handed, except for priests who are buried with their chalices."

"Good Filippo," Francesco leaned over and whispered to Dino Compagni, "doesn't leave this world naked or empty-handed. He is robed more magnificently than any bishop, attired in his countless good works, his great charity, and his generosity to the Church."

"Yes," Dino snickered. "Instead, it's the family of Filippo Villani that's left empty-handed—so much poorer now that he's dead. Did you hear that in his will Filippo gave enough silver to the Church to pay for twenty-five years of Masses to be said for his soul. Twenty-five years—imagine what that costs! It'll put a hole as big as a city gate in their family purse. It's a wonder his sons aren't singing a dirge for themselves instead of for him."

"He was a pious man and feared greatly for the salvation of his immortal soul," Francesco answered, partially shielding his mouth with his hand.

"Why, for God's sake?" Dino replied not very softly. "I'll bet he never committed any sin greater than failing to say his night prayers." Then, jabbing his elbow into Francesco's side, he added, "Not like you and me, eh, Bernadone?"

"Shush," Francesco replied, embarrassed because people were turning around and frowning at them for talking during a Mass for the Dead. As his attention returned to the Mass, Francesco's conscience elbowed him, "What about your soul? How many years of Masses will it require to blot out your guilt and enable you someday to escape purgatory—or, if you're not careful, risk ending up irrevocably in hell?"

The three priests at the altar were wearing the traditional heavy black vestments. On the broad stiff back of the main celebrant's chasuble, embroidered in silver thread on black velvet, was a large white skeleton holding a great curved sickle. That symbol of death was the focal point for all eyes. At the skeleton's feet were crisscrossed clusters

of white bones, and above its skull was a circle of thorns bearing the initials IHS, from the Latin for Christ our Savior. The ancient funeral Mass of the Dead was a heavily solemn ritual, waterlogged with sorrow, while gloom and doom were interwoven like shadowy threads through the repetitive prayers pleading for divine mercy toward the dead sinner. Grim and mournful as graveyards were the melodies of the hymns and chants, each of them amplifying the dark travesty of death being the final punishment for Adam's sin. In his sermon the priest mirrored the ghostly image on the back of his chasuble, speaking only of God's wrath, urging prayers for the soul of deceased, who was now consigned to carry into his grave the heavy burden of debt for his sins. He ended his very long sermon by shaking his bony finger at the large crowd of mourners, saying, "Awake from your sleep! Death comes like a thief in the night to steal your life. Repent today, do penance while you still have time left. Who among you will be next to find Death at your door?"

*T*he smell of incense from the funeral seemed to cling to Francesco's clothing as he stood again with his father in the shop. Attending Mass always put his father in a foul mood, even though he only did so for funerals and a few great feasts. Pietro was mumbling to himself as he rearranged the piles of cloth, complaining about how "those damn priests never weary of trying to frighten people with their venomous, guilt-inducing talk about the fiery punishments of hell. Why don't they ever speak of heaven? Isn't it as real as hell?" Pietro wasn't shy about his beliefs, and his son knew them well. He believed in God and in justice—after all, was he not a merchant, one who knows that commerce could not exist without justice? He did not believe in the Church—he had told his son numerous times that the Church is only for those men who don't know what to do with that gift hanging down between their legs, or for women and children who are easily deceived and frightened by priests.

So Francesco was surprised when he said, "Son, I hope you heard what that priest said this morning about the time being short and the need to wake up. That's exactly what I was saying to you right here in our shop before we learned about poor Filippo, God be good to his soul. Just as we heard the news, I was telling you about the time for your marriage being long overdue. You are almost twenty-four years old, and. . . ."

"Yes, Father, after I repair old San Damiano, I will. . . ."

"The repair of that church is none of your business. Here, this cloth shop is your business! Someday, like old Filippo, I shall die, and then who will run this shop? And if I should die before your mother, what would become of her? Do you want your poor mother to become a beggar—not one asking for money to rebuild some crumbling shrine, but needing to buy bread for her very survival?" Silently father and son stared at one another. While his father had won this contest by his stinging guilt-producing arguments about his mother's welfare, Francesco wasn't willing to concede final defeat. His father's lower lip curled up, clamping his mouth shut, as he ferociously wrestled within himself over the various possible solutions to the exasperating dilemma of the immature son who stood before him.

"I shall leave tomorrow morning," he announced pontifically, the wrestling match over, "and personally go down to Spoleto to deliver an important order of cloth. Upon my return I shall immediately begin making the arrangements for your marriage! I estimate that my trip to and from Spoleto, including the time there, will require three to four days. While I'm away, you shall be in complete charge of our shop! Furthermore, you will be here working the entire day, except for the siesta times—no walks in the woods outside the city and, especially, no nonsense of begging in the piazza. Is that clearly understood?" Pietro whirled around, not waiting for an answer, and stomped to the back of the shop.

Francesco stood helpless as he pondered the sentence just delivered by his father that had now transformed the cloth shop into a dark, gated anteroom of a prison. His ears vibrated with the crashing echo of the large iron prison door of Perugia being slammed shut behind him. Then the *voices* spoke again, only this time it was some ominous unseen magistrate solemnly intoning, "Giovanni Francesco di Bernadone, you shall be imprisoned here in this small cloth shop for the rest of your natural life as a merchant, with no hope of any pardon or release by a ransom—no matter how great it might be. May God have mercy on your soul."

His right hand instinctively sprang up to his throat in an attempt to ward off being suffocated. He frantically ran outside, gasping for breath. Then he began madly fleeing down the narrow street as if chased by the devil. He stopped briefly, leaning against a wall to fill his lungs, before again running down the twisting cobblestone street and

out the main gate. Turning right, he almost tumbled down the hillside because he was running so fast as he headed toward the olive groves and the ruins of San Damiano. As he entered the little chapel, he paused and looked up through the gaping roof that opened to the sky and felt a wave of peace wash over him. Still panting, he dropped to his knees, where he prayed for an hour or more.

"No voices spoke," he thought as he stood up, "but I now feel strong enough to return to my work at the shop." Then he said aloud to the crucifix, "Yes, I will prove to my father that I can be responsible, and by doing so I will make him proud of me." Tracing the sign of the cross on himself, he added, "I will even return to Assisi with a sense of playfulness and delight and will do my work with joy." Climbing the hill toward the gate, he began singing aloud a favorite cheerful French song and continued singing all the way to the city.

Halfway down the street to the cloth shop he could see that a small group had gathered and were intently watching something. Curious, he stopped and looked over the shoulders of those in the back rows. The onlookers had surrounded a peddler sitting at a temporary makeshift stall with a couple of dozen caged larks. Francesco watched as the traveling peddler was heating a long steel needle over a small fire burning in an iron pan. Then, as his young assistant held one lark securely in both hands, the bird peddler began directing the now red-hot needle toward the eyes of the bird.

"What in God's holy name," Francesco cried out, "are you doing?"

"Signore," the peddler said, looking up as he held the glowing needle, "naturally with this red-hot needle I am about to blind this lark. It is common knowledge, as you know, that a blinded lark sings infinitely more beautifully and divinely, and so. . . ."

"Like hell you are!" Francesco yelled, pushing his way past the surprised spectators and springing toward the peddler. With a swift and well-directed kick at the peddler's small stool, he sent the man tumbling to the pavement and the needle into the air. Then Francesco shoved the stunned young assistant into the wall, releasing the lark in the process. As the dumbfounded peddler struggled to his knees, Francesco was ripping open the birdcage doors and shooing the larks out of their cages, crying, "Fly away, my sister and brother larks!" As they quickly soared up into the sky, he called out, "Fly away to freedom, for only freedom, and not being blinded, makes your song divinely beautiful." He began jumping up and down on the wooden

birdcages, causing the onlookers to draw back in fright. Then he straddled the terrified and bewildered bird peddler, scowling and shaking his fist at him and saying, "How brutally sinful to mutilate helpless larks, making them prisoners of blindness for the rest of their lives. Even if those birds would escape from their cages, without sight they couldn't live in nature." Raising both his arms high in the air as if ready to bring them down on the peddler in a rain of violence, he screamed, "Heaven cries out for your punishment for such a vile, depraved sin! Even to think of thrusting a red-hot needle in their eyes is diabolically sinful!"

By this time the crowd of spectators had swollen twofold with the addition of those drawn to all the commotion in the usually peaceful town of Assisi. One man shouted, "Watch out, everyone! He must be possessed, the way he's smashing those cages." Another added, "That's Francesco, son of Pietro Bernadone, who people say is going mad."

"I am mad!" Francesco shouted at them, "not insane, but terribly angry! What has made me so furious is this traveling peddler's viciously sinful butchery toward these innocent birds."

"No, Signore, it is you who have sinned!" answered the peddler now standing and brushing himself off, while his young assistant still crouched down against the wall. "By stealing from me my rightful day's earnings and destroying my property, it is you who have sinned. It is you who are guilty. Doesn't the new Commune of Assisi have laws protecting her merchants, even those who are visiting your city?"

"Yes, yes," a bystander shouted in reply. "The bird peddler is right! You have broken the law by setting his birds loose and are at fault for his loss of property. Those birds belonged to him and were not yours to do with as you please! Just because you're the uppity son of that rich Pietro di Bernadone, you think you can prance about Assisi doing whatever you please and whenever. . . ."

"Here," snarled Francesco, throwing a handful of coins at the peddler's feet. Almost physically shaking with rage, he exclaimed, "There's more money there than you could ever have gotten from selling your flock of blinded larks." As the peddler knelt and quickly began picking up the coins on the pavement, Francesco added, "And furthermore, you are forewarned: I am a member of the Guild of Cloth Merchants, and I will demand that the Commune of Assisi banish from our streets such cruel monsters as the likes of you. Now get out of here." Then, turning away, he stomped off toward the cloth shop,

muttering aloud, "Sinful, mortally sinful, to mutilate a child of God by purposely blinding it." As he was vigorously striding up the street, he could hear comments from the group of spectators behind him.

"Did he call those larks children of God?"

"Yes, and he also called them sisters and brothers."

"If he's not already mad, he'll soon be! Mind my words."

"Poor Pita, how she must suffer. Ever since young Bernadone returned from the war in Perugia he's been acting very strange—and even more so since his return from Spoleto."

"I'd say it was more than strange. His behavior is like one possessed by the devil! Did you see how violently angry he became, stomping on those cages? And that furious look on his face as he threatened the poor peddler—it looked so diabolic!"

"Once he was such a nice young man, so friendly, always singing and so happy. Now he's attacking poor peddlers and ranting about birds being his sisters."

"Wait and see, I predict he'll soon be hearing voices, just like poor old Strapazzate."

Francesco was frightened. He had even shocked himself by the passionate intensity of his anger toward the bird peddler. He had never been so angry before, never so filled with rage as when he was stomping on those cages. As he turned the street corner, he stopped to quiet the hammering of his heart. He now felt terror at the ferocious beast he had somehow released from within him. He breathed deeply, trying to quiet the inner rage awakened back there when he was actually on the verge of physically attacking that peddler. Perhaps those people back in the crowd were right; perhaps he was becoming crazy.

After his father departed for Spoleto, Francesco displayed real talent as a merchant. He was cheerful and pleasant to the customers who stopped to examine the fine cloth and soft wools in the Bernadone shop. He naturally possessed all the talents needed to be a successful merchant: personality, perceptiveness, charm, and humor. One person departing from the shop remarked, "That young Bernadone could sell holy water in hell." Whether or not the customers purchased any cloth, before they left the shop he would always smile warmly, hold out his wooden bowl, and say, "Please, some silver, a few

Cortona

Gubbio

Perugia

Assisi

Lake
Trasimeno

River

Tiber

Spello

Main Road to Rome

Foligno

Orvieto

Spoleto

Terni

ORA LABORA
ET

Rieti

Assisi and
the Cities of Umbria

to Rome

Aquila

coins to help purchase stones to rebuild the broken-down chapel of San Damiano."

While some grudgingly dropped a few coins into his bowl, resenting being trapped by this charming, smiling merchant beggar, others only laughed, patting him on the back, thinking it was some kind of joke.

The appearance of Emiliano entering his shop on the third day after his father's departure sent Francesco's spirits soaring. "*Caro mio*, how marvelous to see you again. Take a look at your friend—behold the respectable merchant my father's always yearned for. He'd be proud, eh?"

"I can see, my friend—and I can hear. The gossip is that you are, indeed, a shrewd merchant, but also still a beggar—even if a respectable one rather than the usual dirty, raggedly clad kind." Francesco beamed a large smile and graciously bowed. "They also say that you gave the *malocchio*—the evil eye—to some people in the crowd when you . . . er . . . became rather upset, shall we say, about that bird peddler."

"You're kind to say 'upset.' I don't know what dark passion came over me to become so angry."

"You're a passionate man, my friend. But, tell me, how large is your charity fund to rebuild San Damiano?"

"About the size of little Francesco, I fear. Since I had raised such a small amount, the other day I decided to go and visit the workers from the stonemason guild who are repairing the eastern wall of the city to ask if they would volunteer their labor. They only laughed and shouted down from their scaffolding, asking me if I would in turn volunteer to clothe their children and put food on their tables. Then their guild master came down off the scaffold carrying his mortar board, walked over to me, and asked me to hold out my hands, saying he was going to give me a gift for the chapel. When I eagerly did so, he dumped into my hands all the wet mortar off his board! Then he placed his large sweaty hands on my shoulder and solemnly proclaimed, "I, Giraldi Pulci of Assisi, master of the Stonemason Guild, do this day officially install you, Francesco Bernadone, as a brother-member in our Stonemason Guild. Thou art hereby granted all the rights and privileges of our guild, to labor from dawn to dusk—in dust, I might add—upon any forsaken, collapsed old shrine, rundown outhouse, or cow shed that thou shalt come upon." Then all his brother masons up on the scaffolds cried out 'Amen' and began clapping loudly, hooting and whistling at me. Emiliano, I was so embarrassed."

After Emiliano left, Francesco returned to his double mission of being a good cloth merchant and a good beggar to pay the stonemasons to repair San Damiano.

"No," one customer snapped angrily, "I will not donate to your foolish fund. Why should I part with my hard-earned money! The only ones who use that chapel are the birds! Why in God's name should we. . . ."

"Friend, you yourself have said why we should do this—'in God's name,' that's why!" he responded with an enchanting smile. "So in God's holy name, please, sir, can you donate a few coins?"

As fire leaps across a thatched roof so did the news that the Bernadone cloth shop was now under new management, and people began flocking there. Most of these, however, were not customers eager to buy cloth or to donate to San Damiano. They were Assisi's very poor, the blind, crippled, and street beggars. Previously, they had been fearful for their lives even to approach the Bernadone shop lest they be beaten away with a broom or club by an angry Pietro, accompanied by his famous acid shower of curses. Now they came hopeful of help. And they left not disappointed, for Francesco gave away money, food, and even some of his own clothing that was almost new yet no longer in style.

A neighboring cloth merchant, standing at the door of the Bernadone shop, shook his finger at Francesco, saying, "The presence of those dirty, vermin-covered poor here in your shop, Francesco, is not good for business! What decent man will come to buy goods from you if he must stand next to the pests of society? No one who is sane wants such flea-infested scum rubbing against him. Didn't your father ever tell you that the first dogma of cloth merchants is, 'Fleas and moths love cloth—thou shall not let them eat up your profits'?" Francesco nodded in agreement and was about to speak when the merchant continued, "Also, young Bernadone, don't mix religion with business. Didn't your father ever teach you that? If your father were here, he'd not tolerate what is going on in his shop!"

It occurred to Francesco that the dogma the merchant quoted about fleas and moths was more sacred to the cloth merchants than the dogma of the Holy Trinity—and far easier to understand. The warning

 of the visiting merchant, however, didn't hinder his generosity to any of the poor who came to the shop, and none ever left empty-handed. He found twin joy in being responsible for the work his father had entrusted to him, while at the same time being responsible for the work of begging and caring for the poor that his Lord and Savior had entrusted to him.

Gossip has wings. As swiftly as pigeons flying cross the piazza, accounts flew across Assisi concerning the Bernadone marriage between selling cloth and begging for money. One such hearsay pigeon fluttered down and landed on the balcony of the second-story dining room of the bishop's house next to Santa Maria Maggiore Church. The floor-to-ceiling wooden shutters were opened wide to welcome in the cool air as the bishop and three of his priests sat eating their evening meal.

His Excellency Bishop Guido, a stately man in his late fifties, bald except for a few clumps of white hair that floated like small puffs of clouds over each ear, was seated at the head of the table. His face was striking, but his eyes were perpetually empty of expression. Such inscrutable countenances were as common among the high prelates of the Church as they are among the diplomats of princes and kings. These men had throughout their lives carefully crafted such impenetrably silent faces, which seemed as indispensable to their professions as swords to knights. Their expression must never give a clue to what they were actually thinking, and since the eyes are the portals of the soul, they must especially remain mute as to the hidden thoughts and emotions transpiring within.

"Monsignor Carafa, a busy day?" Bishop Guido asked the chancellor of his diocese, who was seated at the opposite end of the long table.

"Yes, Bishop, it was," replied Monsignor Paulo Carafa, dabbing his thick lips with his white linen napkin. "I was occupied most of the day with checking the accounts of the rent collections on the local olive groves and vineyards owned by the diocese. Then I had to attend to the necessary dispensation papers from Rome so that Duke Eugenio can marry his second cousin. The day's most unpleasant task," he said as he again briefly dabbed his lips with his napkin, "was having to resolve that sticky problem"—he once again paused briefly, this time for effect—"connected with the death of the parish priest at San Pietro."

Monsignor Carafa was the epitome of the clerical official. His aristocratic face was crowned by neatly trimmed black hair, and

although he was only in his early forties he was already quite portly. Carafa was characteristic of ambitious clerics who eagerly strove to climb higher up the episcopal ladder by ardently cultivating relationships with the wealthy and those in high places who might advance their career fortunes. To the bishop's right was seated Padre Giuseppe, whose countenance was as pale as their white tablecloth and as delicate as the fine plates from which they ate. Seated directly across from Giuseppe on the bishop's left was the young, newly ordained Padre Tomas, who was the bishop's secretary. Still boyishly slim, his face was like a cream-colored page of new parchment as yet unsigned by age and experience. Padre Tomas was youthfully eager to please his superiors.

"You refer, Monsignor," Padre Tomas said to Carafa, continuing their conversation, "to that conflict with the dead priest's wife, who, I hear, now refuses to move out of the parish house at San Pietro?"

"Padre Tomas, please, it was not his wife!" Bishop Guido said with an upraised right hand. "Canon Law requires all priests to be celibate, so it is impossible for a priest to have a wife. As you well know, for more than two hundred years, since good Pope Benedict VIII, the law of celibacy has been a requirement for all ordained subdeacons, deacons and priests."

"Excuse me, your Excellency, I'm sorry for my unfortunate choice of words. She was . . . rather . . . what the people call his 'hearth mate.'" The white pigeon perching on the balcony cooed.

"Whatever name you give her," Monsignor Carafa dryly replied, "we all know that the law of celibacy is not observed, if by it you mean complete abstinence from sex! Since the Second Lateran Council in 1139 issued the first binding laws against clerical marriage, Pope after Pope has unsuccessfully tried to enforce the clerical promise of celibacy that includes complete abstinence from all sexual relations." Spreading his arms with upraised hands, he added, "Ah, but nature is nature. I agree with the statement made some years ago by our own Italian Bishop Rathurio that if the Church was to excommunicate all unchaste priests, all she would have left to administer the sacraments would be altar boys!"

Padre Giuseppe giggled and quickly covered his mouth with his napkin, shooting a hasty glance at the bishop, whose attention was focused on breaking a piece of bread. "We who are seated at this table," Carafa continued, "know well—as did the dead *padre* of San Pietro—

that almost all those peasant priests have a woman to share in the hard work of farming their small plots of land . . . ," adding with a broad smile, ". . . and to share their beds."

"However," Padre Tomas spoke up, "even if priests are not sexually celibate, they cannot legally be married. And so when they die, the property of the Church doesn't go to their. . . ."

"Tomas," Monsignor Carafa smirked as he interrupted him, "I'm delighted to see that you were awake during your studies! You are correct: Even if clerical celibacy isn't observed fully, it does accomplish its original purpose of protecting the lands and property of the Church from being inherited by the 'wives' of priests or their children. They can preach all they like about the spiritual implications of celibacy, quoting old St. Jerome's flawed theology about Adam's original state of virginity being all men's natural state. Or they can refer to his bit of pious history that marriage only appeared in Eden after Adam and Eve's fall, making it part of the bitter fruit of Original Sin." Carafa swung his gaze between Tomas to Giuseppe, viewing them as eager students at the table of a brilliant professor. Relishing his role as the knowledgeable teacher, he continued without pausing, "Jerome, as we know, also taught that virginity is the highest state possible in this life and is, therefore, closer to God. But doesn't that theology make you wonder how on earth old Jerome thought humanity would ever continue if everyone sought to be closer to God? However—and correct me, Bishop, if I am in error—this elevated state of spiritual perfection was never the original or primary intention of the Church's celibacy legislation, which is perfectly clear: Bastards can't inherit!" Padre Giuseppe's eyebrows shot up into his hairline as he covered his mouth with his hand at Carafa's use of the word "bastard" at the bishop's table.

All the while, Bishop Guido continued slowly chewing on a large piece of bread to avoid being involved in the discussion. As usual, his face and eyes revealed nothing, though he groaned inwardly, thinking that once again his dinner had been taken hostage by these tiresome priestly discussions about celibacy. He lamented so often having to endure priests hashing over this same old subject. He wondered what had happened to stimulating discussions about philosophy, theology, and spirituality. Then his eyes came to rest on the large platter of fruit and cheese in the center of the table. As he eyed a round, plump melon on the platter, it reminded him of the breasts of Monsignor Carafa's mistress. "I'm not blind," he thought. "I'm aware of their clandestine

relationship, even if most are not. Actually, I find Carafa's woman to be most distasteful. It's shocking the way she dresses at Mass—or, rather, *fails* to dress! She loves wearing those stylishly low-cut gowns that expose her large, melon-like breasts to any man with a hungry eye! Shameful! Ah yes, my dear Carafa, it is not only simple peasant parish priests—those unlearned in theology and Latin—but also clever canon lawyers and even cardinals that have their women . . . or boys."

"Your Excellency chews his food very slowly," Padre Tomas ineptly attempted to add to the table discussion. "My mother always taught me to eat slowly, saying that it's good for one's health." Bishop Guido nodded to him with a smile as he continued slowly and silently chewing. Fearing that his remark had sounded inane, Tomas felt impelled to redeem himself by saying something of significance. As he quickly rummaged for some fitting item of conversation, the white pigeon perched on the balcony railing again cooed loudly. "Have you heard," he said, beaming a wide smile of relief, "the stories about the most recent antics of Giovanni di Francesco, the son of the cloth merchant Pietro Bernadone?"

"For God's sake, what has that reckless, idly rich youth done now?" asked Monsignor Carafa heaving a dramatic sigh. "It is beyond me why Signore Bernadone tolerates his son's refusal to grow up! The sons of the other merchants of Assisi are all taking *their places* in society." Carafa's emphasis on "their places" clearly revealed his strong belief in the validity of ancient feudal class divisions. At the bottom of that societal structure were ignorant peasants and common laborers. Next came craftsmen, artists, and merchants, and at the top of the pyramid were knights, nobility, and educated churchmen like him. "Peasants, knights, and Church," he thought, recalling an old saying, "The world is divided into the sheep, the watchdogs, and the shepherds."

Giuseppe saddled onto Tomas's comment about Francesco Bernadone, adding, "Some time ago young Francesco came to see me on a matter of conscience but not of confession. He told me he had been hearing mystical voices and came seeking my wisdom as to their meaning. Well, naturally, I told him that God was calling him to be a priest and. . . ."

"A priest! For heaven's sake, Giuseppe," Carafa snapped, pointing his spoon like a lethal weapon toward the now-startled priest. "Whatever were you thinking? That lad lacks the intelligence, and,

even more, he is devoid of the basic common sense needed to become a priest."

Struggling to regain some credibility, Giuseppe launched into another subject: "Your Excellency, I want you to know that I've begun employing the new custom at Mass that is now so popular in Venice—elevating the host and then the chalice after the words of consecration instead of at the end of the canon prayer. This so helps the faith of the common people in seeing the living miracle taking place through our hands, but which is hidden from them because our backs are to them. I think we also should begin to adapt the other Venetian practice of ringing small bells at the consecration so that those who are elsewhere in the church will be alerted to the very moment the miracle is occurring. I heard the other day that in Spello as a very holy monk was saying Mass the host actually bled! And at Mass in Foligno, they say that during the elevation someone saw a small babe with a halo in the host. Isn't that wondrous? This new century will surely bring us many new kinds of devotions that will inspire the people, don't you think?"

The bishop merely smiled and nodded at him. Inwardly, he thought, "What kind of strange theology of the Eucharist has given birth to these pious personal devotions of the priests that only serve to elevate their status in the eyes of simple people?"

"Padre Giuseppe, if you please," snapped Carafa. "Before your interruption we were not discussing pious devotions at Mass but the case of Giovanni Francesco Bernadone. I tell you that there's more to this case than meets the eye. In these troubling new times we must all be vigilant and discerning about those who hear voices."

"Today, crossing the piazza," said Tomas, eager to share something with his superiors that they did not know, "Bernadone's friend Angelo, who was one of his companions at the battle of Perugia, told me that Francesco is begging for money to rebuild that broken-down old chapel at San Damiano. For a couple of days now his father Pietro has been away on business in Spoleto and has left his son responsible for their cloth shop. But people are saying that rather than selling his father's cloth, he's more engrossed in collecting alms to repair San Damiano."

"Will someone enlighten me," replied Monsignor Paulo, raising his wine cup to his lips. "Why would our little village entertainer and local prodigal son want to repair that useless old chapel?"

"Angelo told me, in confidence you understand," Tomas said, his face beaming with delight as he prepared to tell his choicest piece of

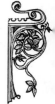

gossip, "that Francesco had privately told him . . ." he paused momentarily to insure that he had their complete attention ". . . that one day he had stopped to make a visit at San Damiano and that the crucifix that hangs above the altar in the chapel . . . well . . . it spoke to him!"

"Spoke to him!" Carafa almost gagged on his wine.

"Yes, he told Angelo that the figure on the crucifix said to him something like, 'Rebuild my church.'" Tomas dramatically leaned back into his chair and turned toward Bishop Guido with the eager eyes of a hunting dog holding a duck in its mouth looking up at its master. Bishop Guido said nothing but was only looking calmly down the table at Monsignor Carafa.

"A talking crucifix?" Carafa blurted out in a voice rife with sarcasm. "O my God, what next? May the saints protect us from those who hear personal messages from God! Ever since Christ ascended into heaven, God has spoken only to Holy Mother Church, and then the Church informs her faithful children what is, or is not, the will of the Almighty. Let us pray that this tale of Angelo is either groundless gossip or one of his pranks, for which he is notorious. For if what he reports is true, then our own Francesco Bernadone is not only immature and naive, he is also very dangerous!"

"I find him so joyful and creative," replied Tomas. "He's so enthusiastic about everything he does!"

"Heretics are enthusiastic!" said Carafa, pointing his table knife at Tomas. "God's faithful have no need of enthusiasm or creativity. They only need to say their prayers and be obediently submissive to the Church. Tomas, my young friend, as a priest you've much to learn. And as a beginning, I urge you to beware of those who are all fired up with enthusiasm and zeal."

"Yes, Monsignor, I suppose you're correct," Bishop Guido interjected, surprising his table companions by breaking his long fast of speaking. "But after all these centuries of obedient submission, doesn't the Church seem so . . . ah, how shall I say it . . . so lifeless? If only our faithful and our priests had a greater love of God and more zeal for prayer and good works. And as for young Bernadone being enthusiastic, do we not on the Feast of Pentecost pray that the Holy Spirit will come down upon us—and I suppose that means all the Church—and fill our hearts with fiery zeal?"

"Of course, Your Excellency, I agree with all you say," replied Carafa like a clever chess player cautiously calculating his next move. "Yes, indeed, the zeal of the Holy Spirit is essential for the Church to inspire bishops like yourself and our Holy Father the Pope. What I was referring to is the misguided enthusiasm of ignorant laypeople for miracles and for . . . ," shooting a glance at Giuseppe before he continued, ". . . hosts that bleed. And especially to be watched is the dangerously zealous preaching of demonically inspired heretics, whose words are flaming torches of error thrown into the hay-filled barn of the Church. Those so-called 'reformers' go about causing great chaos among the people, encouraging them to abandon God's ordained order within society, proclaiming that anyone, even common laypeople, can interpret for themselves the meaning of Scripture. Like the pox, the French and German diseases of heresy are being spread right here in Italy, even in Assisi. We all must be attentive, watchful for the first signs of such danger to our faith."

The bishop slowly cut off a piece of cheese and began chewing it, while Tomas sat red-faced, embarrassed by the chancellor rebuking his immaturity and lack of knowledge. Across from him, Giuseppe was squirming, attempting to remove Carafa's stiletto remark about bleeding hosts.

"Voices from God, " Carafa continued, "are heard by agents of the devil whose long, ass-like diabolic ears are easily tickled by grievous error. Didn't that French heretic merchant Peter Waldo of Lyons claim that God had spoken to him, calling him to reform the Church, to go about poor and barefoot proclaiming the Gospel to common people? May the Holy Mother of God protect us from any such merchants," he pronounced, slowly scanning the faces of the others at the table, "or *sons* of merchants who claim that God is speaking to them. At first such voices may appear innocent or even pious, with messages like, 'Repair my little chapel.' But, mark my words, tomorrow God will be telling him. . . ." He left his sentence unfinished as he dramatically traced the sign of the cross upon himself.

The pigeon perched on the balcony suddenly fluttered up and flew away. Shortly thereafter, the clerics' evening meal ended, and the four retired to their rooms.

Chapter 7

"O HOLY SAVIOR," GUIDO PRAYED WITH HIS HEAD BURIED in his hands as he knelt on a wooden kneeler before a large crucifix hanging on the wall:

Hear this prayer of your unworthy servant Guido, for how urgently your Church does, indeed, need to be rebuilt—to be rebuilt by being reformed. Perhaps, O Lord, you are speaking to us through this young Francesco Bernadone. For, sadly, so many of the clergy are scrawny of soul, satisfied in striving to live no higher than their married parishioners. They're poorly educated in theology and scripture, and are impotent to stir up any love for you. As a result of their low level of religion, instead of loving you, the common people fear you! On the other hand, those priests who are educated only seem ambitious for power, itching for high positions, lording it over the very people they're supposed to be serving. Pardon my judging them, but they seem far more interested in accumulating wealth, in wearing rich clothing, and enjoying good food and fine wines than they are in personal prayer and devotion.

Then, sighing deeply, he again raised his head to look directly at the crucified figure hanging on the cross. After some moments of silent gazing, he continued his spoken prayer:

O Christ, help this old poor soul, your weary son Guido. I dare not ask for something as miraculous as you, my Lord, speaking directly to me—as it seems you did to our Francesco Bernadone—but I long that you would make known your

holy will for me. You've made me the shepherd of your people of Assisi so I might lead them along the right way. I know all too well that heresy is a sin that leads the innocent astray, but isn't apathy a greater sin, Lord? Didn't you say that you vomited the lukewarm out of your mouth, and are not too many of us lukewarm in our love for you?

He let out another great sigh and shifted his weight from one knee to the other before returning his gaze to the crucified one.

Not only is poor little San Damiano tumbled down in disrepair, so is your larger Church, your Body, your Bride, for whom you shed your blood, O Lord. It has fallen into disrepair by centuries of concessions. Her once holy seamless robe is stitched together by compromises and is filled with the moth-eaten holes of hypocrisy and duplicity. Her theologians are able to rationalize away the challenges of the Gospel, watering down your fiery words into harmless gray ashes to justify their living lavishly like noble princes instead of humbly in the pattern of your simple poverty.

Lord, look with pity on us poor sinners, for we all share in the sins of the Church—each of us. Send us reformers like Giovanni the Baptist and prophets of reformation like Isaiah and Jeremiah. Pour forth your Holy Spirit once more upon your Church so as to renew it again and again—to reform each and every one of us sinners.

He paused, again looking at the figure hanging on the cross, this time expectantly, but he still heard no voice speaking to him. He opened his hands, his fingers upraised toward the crucifix, aching that they be filled with an answer to his plea for a reformer. He then prayed his traditional evening litany of petitions for the people of his diocese, those sick, suffering and dying, the poor and, finally, his clergy. He ended this litany by remembering the priests of his own cathedral household:

Keep young Tomas innocent and unsophisticated as long as possible, for he holds much promise so long as he remains free of cynicism. Temper Paulo's obsession with legalism and free him from being such a rigorist when it comes to the failings of others while so easily excusing away his own faults.

And as for pious Giuseppe, be with him, Lord, for he means well but is so absorbed in that pious new rite of elevating the host and chalice after the words of institution at Mass, and with the ringing of those bells so the people can see the 'living miracle' of the Eucharist. Would that the ringing of bells called the people to come forward to receive Holy Communion—and to live out the Eucharist in their daily lives—instead of only piously watching what is taking place at the altar. What I fear, my Lord, is that if this kind of devotional sentiment spreads, it won't be long before they'll be displaying the host containing your Bread of Life for the faithful to adore, like it was some kind of trophy.

Forgive me, Lord, for my judgments, but it so saddens me to see your Church slipping further and further away from the apostolic tradition, and from its core truth. I'm distressed as well by the theologians who have begun to distort the *mystery* of your body and blood by forcing it into their over-intellectualized, nonunderstandable language. I'm saddened to learn that in some universities they're now talking about the various necessary conditions for validity, about what constitutes essential elements for the Eucharist, and even the precise words that must be used along with the proper intention of the priest. Are these theologians forgetting that when the early Church Fathers spoke of the Eucharist, they were referring to everything from the offering of wine and bread through the words of consecration to the actual act of receiving Holy Communion—that all of it is the Eucharist? How can they reduce that infinite reality into their tiny and exact intellectual boxes?

Wearily he sank his head down to his chest and was lost in a great silence, aware only of his deep breathing. Then, a smile slowly spread across his face as if he had indeed heard a voice speaking to him some wonderful good news. "Yes," he said aloud, "you've sent us someone who will be a living Eucharist, whose entire life will be a Eucharist of your love and joy. Of course, how stupid of me! We don't need some radical reformer. We need a *transformer*, someone who radiates your joy, for the greatest transforming power in the world is your joy!"

 Having completed his night prayers, with attentive devotion Bishop Guido slowly traced upon himself the sign of the cross. Then, heaving a large sigh, he stood up and walked over to his bed, aware that he was feeling many years older than his actual age. He carefully removed his fine woolen bishop's cassock and placed it on a hanger. However, he did not remove what he secretly wore underneath it—his penitential hair shirt. As he laid his head back on the pillow, he whispered the ancient prayer:

> Save us, O Lord, while we are awake
>
> and guard us as we sleep
>
> that we may watch with Christ
>
> and rest in peace.

Daily life in Assisi was rather dull. It was no surprise, then, that the news "Padre Matteo is coming to Assisi!" streaked like lightening across the city. Padre Matteo Parini of Perugia, the famous and fiery preacher whose mere appearance drew huge crowds, was coming to speak at San Giorgio's that very Sunday afternoon. Francesco had agreed to accompany his mother Pica, who was excited at the prospect of hearing this most renowned preacher in all of Umbria. Because Padre Matteo would be speaking in Italian and not in Latin, which was always used when giving a sermon at Mass, this was being called an "instruction." That distinction, however, only increased the interest among the common folk.

In a way San Giorgio's was the wrong choice; the church was far too small for the large crowd that attempted to jam inside. Yet the site chosen wasn't an accident, for Padre Matteo himself had selected it. Being shrewd in psychology, he knew how crowded spaces help create a mob mentality. Being Sunday afternoon, most husbands accompanied their wives because the talk held more promise than staying home and watching their fingernails grow. At the appointed hour Padre Matteo appeared wearing a long black cape. Its high collar framed his lean, angular face and accented his long, hawk-like nose, which protruded down from bushy dark eyebrows. He was tall and thin, with an ashen ascetic-appearing complexion and pale blue eyes, which to those in the front rows at San Giorgio's looked like frozen icy ponds.

So many were jammed inside the church that those who didn't arrive early were forced to stand outside the doors. While most of these were prepared to strain to hear his words, there would be no need to cock their ears, for he began to bellow so loudly that he was audible even to the aged deaf.

"Evil, my beloved citizens of Assisi," he proclaimed, "diabolic evil creeps up to the gates of your once-innocent city even on this very Sunday. It slithers among you, poisoning your hearts and stealing your souls. When God looks down upon Assisi, he weeps bitterly that you have allowed the Christ killers—the Jews—to be tolerated in your midst. Jews, Jews, Jews! You all know very well how their homes and businesses are here among you. Beware, you parents! Guard your children, for right here in nearby Spello, only last April, during their Passover, the atrocious Jews of that city tortured and slaughtered an innocent little boy, making him the spotless lamb of their Seder meal—and then they ate his flesh!"

A loud gasp rose up and then a groan fell upon the crowd. They had heard rumors of such things, but here was a priest of God, who wouldn't tell a lie, speaking to them of an actual event that had taken place in nearby Spello. Fearfully, the mothers clutched their children even more closely.

"On my way here to speak to you, I stopped to pray at a church in the small village of San Paulo. The priest himself told me that his devoutly pious villagers had recently captured a Jew who had stolen his church's sacred chalice, which had a consecrated host in it!" Another loud gasp escaped from the crowd, and Padre Matteo continued with even greater intensity, "Blessedly, the villagers who caught that Jew promptly hung him from a tree before he and his fiendish Jewish friends were able to use the chalice and the sacred host in their devil worship. You priests who are present here today, guard well the sacred vessels of your churches lest the Jews of Assisi plunder them for their sacrilegious and diabolic rituals!

"Blind Jews, who refuse to see the truth! Christ killers, who have deliberately rejected our Lord's message of salvation! These greedy, profit-sucking Jews sinfully loan out money to merchants at exorbitant interest, violating God's laws and Holy Mother Church's prohibition of usury!" Pausing for effect, Padre Matteo made a wide sweep of his hand

across the church and then dramatically pointed toward the ceiling, exclaiming, "Doesn't heaven cry out for their punishment? Why, good Christians of Assisi, why do you allow them to live among you? Become instruments of God's wrath so that they will feel the consequences of their own bloodthirsty lust to have our beloved Lord crucified. Recall the Gospel story of Christ's passion that you hear every Good Friday, how the good Roman governor Pilate, after finding Jesus innocent, washed his hands of our Lord's blood. Yet the crowd of Jews cried out, 'Let his blood be upon us and upon our children!' It's in the Gospels, how the Jews cursed themselves and all their descendents down through the ages with the blood of Christ. So why do you allow them to live in comfort and peace among you? Why?"

Many in the crowded church shot glances at each other, for the priest was correct. They did know the homes of Jews living in Assisi; some even knew them as neighbors. Although their number was small, they were easily recognized by their strange customs. While forbidden to own land, to belong to any guilds, or engage in many crafts, the Church and the commune did tolerate their presence in the city. Francesco, however, was concerned, for though he was aware that Jews had ordered the death of his Lord, he knew that the Jews with whom he did business were not evil, murderous people. As a youth, he and the other boys had engaged in the traditional Good Friday fun of throwing rocks at the doors of the Jews who lived in Assisi, but it had always made him uncomfortable. And while he had previously heard some of these same rumors about the terrible crimes of Jews, the ones he personally knew were friendly and productive citizens of the city, people whom his father often praised for their shrewd business skills.

"Moreover, wickedness and evil immorality breeds like the plague among you. Why do you allow it? You fine citizens of Assisi are not an ignorant people. You know very well that among you are those who practice the devil's arts—I speak now of witches! The good priests of San Giorgio church have told me about one you all know—the sorceress Gaspara Frezzi, who lives at the foot of the hill upon which this very church rests, in a hut down in the olive groves. Does she not call herself a healer? And do not many of you go to her for cures? If she cures you by her mixture of herbs and little packets of magical ingredients, does that not prove she is a witch? Only God truly heals! Only the holy oils of the Church heal, not the herbs and magical medicines of witches who are in league with the devil. This Gaspara is

one of those crazy, possessed women who have traded in their souls to Satan for the secret knowledge of herbs and healing, conjuring oils. There are persons among you here in this church," and he pointed three or four times out into crowd, "who have reported to the priests that you have seen her on a moonlit night hovering midair over the cross atop this very church! Beware you good fathers, for your young daughters are in grave danger! These witches will sell love-spells to the sinful, lusting men of Assisi; they, in turn, will be able to cast a spell over your virgin daughters, inducing them into the sin of adultery!"

The fathers present in the church—a rare occurrence, indeed, because it wasn't Easter or Christmas—began casting fearful glances at their daughters, anxious about the violation of their virginity before a proper marriage. The young unmarried women, for their part, wondered if such love-spells might make them begin to ache so madly for love that they would throw prudence out the window.

"Furthermore, you must be on guard, citizens of Assisi, for among you are those, who, in league with Satan, would cast the worst kind of spell over you—the spell of heresy! From France and Germany these vipers of Satan are descending into Italy, worming their way into Florence, Perugia, and even here into Assisi. These ravenous wolves dressed in lamb's clothing style themselves as 'reformers' of Holy Mother Church. They promote poverty as a virtue and castigate our beloved, faithful bishops and priests, even the Holy Father in Rome, the Vicar of Christ. They spread the hell-seeds of heresy by saying that ordinary laymen and laywomen—yes, women—can preach the Gospel, forgive sins, and even make the Body of Christ present in bread and wine. As they spread all these lies and evil doctrines, they claim they are only following in the footsteps of our beloved savior, Jesus Christ. O decent and faith-filled citizens of Assisi, keep your ears open and alert for such heresy and report it at once to the authorities.

"Faithful children of the Church," he raged rabidly, mustering all his oratory skills, "I would fail in my sacred duty as a priest if I ended this admonition to you without addressing the hideous evils of adultery, fornication, and masturbation! Yes, those whose hands are guilty of these sins cast themselves headlong into the scorching fires of hell that are more intense than any volcano's burning lava. And there are even among you those who are guilty of . . ." pausing, he began sweeping his arm like a hay-sickle over the heads in the crowd and then

solemnly traced upon himself the sign of the cross as he continued, "the unnatural, beastly sin of sodomy."

The crowd was now being fed with the food they secretly had hoped would be on the menu of the famous preacher. They cared little about heretics or even witches, but what fascinated them were the unmentionable sins of the flesh. The mere naming of these conjured up vivid images that brought them excitement, a strange pleasure even as they were being condemned as sins. "You parents out there, beware of allowing your young sons to go off as pages and squires on the crusades, for they will. . . ." His powerful voice faded into silence as he sunk his head into his hands, moaning deeply as if in pain. "The deepest and most painful rings of hell are reserved for those who are physically attracted to those of their own sex. Those who perform unnatural acts with persons of their own sex are sentenced to the lowest pits of hell. Since the days of Sodom and Gomorra, when the Almighty rained down his vengeance in scorching brimstone and searing fire upon such sinners, God has continued to curse them to a fiery destruction."

Padre Matteo now held captive the crowded congregation inside San Giorgio's by preaching about those things too shameful even to speak about to another soul. Matteo knew the ancient law: The more despicable and unspeakable the evil, the more intense its fascination.

His instruction had lasted over two hours, and whenever he sensed that his audience was losing interest, he would cleverly insert some hair-raising horror like a story of sodomy among crusader knights or a Jew asking to buy a consecrated host from a depraved priest. Toward the end of his long diatribe, sensing that the crowd was wearying, he inserted, "As we all know, our young Italian men are attracted to women with blond hair—which, of course, is not natural for us Italians. The prostitutes of Venice, aware of this enticement, cleverly lure their prey by bleaching their hair blond." He paused for a moment before adding, ". . . by using a secret solution made of human urine!"

Padre Matteo ended his instruction by dramatically leaving the pulpit and going directly to the altar where he knelt and prayed in a loud voice that God would guard Assisi from the snares of the devil, from heretics, witches, prostitutes, and sodomites. Then he stood, turned, bestowed his priestly blessing upon the assembly, and quickly departed behind the altar into the sacristy.

As the crowds departed, excitingly discussing his presentation, Francesco asked, "Well, Mother, what did you think of the famous Padre Matteo Parini?"

"I shuddered, Son, at some of those horrible stories he told us. But he is a powerful preacher to whom God has given great gifts for moving the hearts and souls of others."

"Yes," thought Francesco, "but move them in which direction— toward or away from God? From the very beginning of his sermon I could sense something darkly dangerous about him, even if he is a priest. While it was impossible for him to look directly at each person in such a crowded church, I had the intense feeling that he was staring directly at me. And try as I might, I couldn't shake off a growing sense of an ominous darkness slowly spreading through the church. Like that engulfing black clerical cloak he was wearing, I felt an almost tangible evil surrounding him. It frightened me; it felt as if he had come to Assisi seeking me out, intending to destroy me." As Francesco tried to reassure himself, telling himself that his imagination was simply becoming too active, his mother tugged at his arm that was intertwined with hers.

"Francesco, after his sermon did you see those men who went up and surrounded him? Do you think they were wanting him to hear their confessions?"

"I saw them, Mother. I'd wager they were approaching him to become his disciples, asking if they could join his secret fraternity, which I understand is known as 'the Watchmen of Orthodoxy.' More often, they're called Parinians, after his last name, Parini. The actual membership of their fraternity is known only to their grand master Padre Matteo and to other Parinians. They pledge themselves to purity and prayer, and to guard the Church against heresy, witchcraft, and immorality. People say there are small secret groups of them in most of the cities surrounding Perugia and elsewhere in Italy. After today's sermon, I expect there will soon be one of his fraternities here in Assisi."

"Well, Son, even if Padre Matteo is a priest, I don't believe that poor old Gaspara is a witch! When you returned from Perugia so terribly sick, I went to her without telling your father. She gave me some healing herbs that I know helped nurse you back to health. After Padre Matteo's sermon today, I prayed for her—especially that some

men, fired up by his talk, wouldn't go down to that poor old widow's hut in the olive groves and harm her."

"Mother, I'm sure God heard your prayers—and that he always does. Please don't stop praying for me as well, that I find the path God wants me to follow." This was no idle pious petition, for he was keenly aware that tomorrow, or the day after, his father was due home from Spoleto.

"Giovanni, I haven't told you this before, but I believe it's possible that you really did hear our Savior speaking to you about repairing San Damiano. But never tell your father I told you that. You and I both must do whatever your father says, for he is the head of our family, and. . . ."

"Jews, Jews, get the damn Jews!" When Francesco and his mother heard these shouts coming from behind them, they turned and saw a band of men running from Piazza San Giorgio. "Drive the Christ killers out of Assisi," they were angrily yelling as they ran past.

"Poor Jacob and Rachel and their children," whispered Pica. "They're Jews, but they are so kind and considerate, and they're such good customers of our shop. I hope and pray," she said as she made the sign of the cross, "those men are not going to attack their home."

"Francesco, pray to Saint Bibiana," a smiling Angelo said at the entrance to the Bernadone cloth shop. "It looks like you've got the biggest hangover in Umbria, and only the patron saint of hangovers can help you now!"

Raising his bloodshot eyes up to heaven, Francesco dutifully prayed, "O Saint Bibiana, come quickly and heal me of my morning-after ravages." Turning to his friend, he said, "Angelo, I could hardly get out of bed to come to work this morning; my head was splitting after last night's wild party at the tavern. I drank so much wine that my temples are still pounding like a bunch of credit collectors at the door."

"Last night, you were finally the old Francesco again!" Angelo beamed. "How wonderful it was to see you so joyful again, so full of jokes and laughter—and that wild dance you did on the table top with. . . ."

"No, Angelo, I was only full of wine. You said I was dancing on top of a table? I don't remember that part of the evening. And with whom was I dancing? No, on second thought, don't tell me who it was or what I did afterwards," he added quickly, recalling the sermon of Padre

Matteo about the future that awaits those who commit fornication. "If I don't know, then I can honestly deny it ever happened."

"Well, good luck with your hangover, Francesco. Personally, I've never had much success praying to Saint Bibiana. I've always preferred the confirmed cure for morning-after hangovers—another bottle!" Laughing, Angelo waved good-bye, saying, "Let's get together again tonight at the tavern."

Francesco only nodded and waved as his friend left the shop. Alone with his thoughts, he hoped his head and stomach would soon recover, for it was possible that his father, who had been away for four days now, might be coming home today. As he refolded some cloth, he reflected, "I got really drunk last night—on purpose. I kept on drinking in a futile attempt to drown my unhappiness and forget what was awaiting me when my father gets home." Looking around the shop, he thought, "I've been responsible. I've worked faithfully here each day in the shop making money for us." He removed a small box from under the table, and as he had done numerous times in the past days, he counted the money he had collected to repair San Damiano.

"Is this the shop of the famous Pietro Bernadone?" asked a stranger in the doorway. "And are you his son, whom I am told by the merchants of this city, is a shrewd businessman."

"I am Francesco Bernadone. What may I do for you?"

"I'm passing through your most beautiful city, and I'm wondering if you might have any good bargains for a poor traveling cloth merchant such as myself."

"*A* good and prosperous day to you, Signores Compagni and d'Ascoli," Pietro joyfully greeted his fellow merchants as he descended the narrow street into Piazza Rufino. "Gentlemen, how fortuitous to encounter such good friends as you upon my return. Come and join me over a cup of good wine to celebrate the handsome profit I made from the sale of my cloth in Spoleto. Moreover, my friends, I return with a further promising profit for the future, for I have begun negotiations toward a good marriage contract for my son!"

"I regret turning your wine of joy into sour vinegar," said Guittone, "but while you've been away, Pietro, that son of yours has been begging alms with one hand while selling your cloth with the other! After someone has donated to his cause, he promises God's blessings; and the

 larger the donation, the most expressive he is about the size of the blessing!"

"Pietro, the next thing we know," laughed Albertino, "besides your shop having the finest cloth in Umbria, you'll also be selling indulgences and relics of the saints—perhaps the relics of the True Cross!"

"Also," Guittone said, patting the purse hanging from his belt, "we've heard rumors that the Bernadones are selling their finest cloth at the lowest prices in all of Umbria! What ever happened to our guild rules about not underselling our brothers?"

"I know nothing, nothing, about these things, but, alas, you've confirmed my fears. I beg your pardon, gentlemen. I must return at once to my shop to find out what has been happening in my absence. Please excuse my haste." Shamefaced, Pietro bowed to them as he stormed off toward his shop. As he quickly exited the piazza, he could feel the sting of their laughter, as well as the ridicule of unseen others stabbing him repeatedly in the back. Only moments ago, his tongue had tasted the good news of his Spoleto trip. Now, however, as he hurried down the twisting cobblestone street to his cloth shop, his mouth felt filled with vomit.

When he arrived, he found Francesco seated outside the cloth shop encircled by children. He had his lute under his chin playing it like a fiddle with a bow as the clapping children merrily danced to his happy music.

"Francesco, stop this nonsense at once!" Pietro shouted so angrily that the children took flight like a flock of frightened pigeons. "Come inside this moment—I demand an explanation!"

"We didn't have any customers right now, so I. . . ."

"No! I'm not talking about those silly children. On my way here as I passed through the piazza, I was shamed to my soul by my brother merchants, who told me you had turned our shop into a beggar's booth. And they said something about selling our wool at the lowest prices in Assisi. You know the rules of our guild!"

"But, Father, what else was I to do?" he said, forgetting his hangover. "I had to beg. How else am I to collect the necessary funds to rebuild the chapel? And since I've collected so little, I decided to sell our Flemish wool to a traveling merchant at one-quarter of our normal price."

"What?" A stunned Pietro collapsed into his chair as Francesco recounted his story of the visit by the merchant who had been passing through Assisi and his idea of obtaining the money needed to buy building stones by selling their fine wool to him. He explained to his father how it was kind of a loan, and how he would repay it with interest after the chapel had been rebuilt.

"Come with me," Pietro exclaimed, leaping out of his chair and grabbing Francesco by his wrist. He dragged him to the storage room at the rear of the shop and roughly pushed him inside the small, dark windowless room. Slamming the door and bolting it, he snapped shut the sturdy lock. "I do not know what else to do with you," Pietro said, panting as he leaned against the locked door. "You're lazy—you sneak away from your work to spend entire days roaming in the woods. Now you've given away our finest and most expensive wool for almost nothing! And you haven't stopped there! Beyond my financial loss, you've robbed me of my reputation, making me—your father, Pietro Bernadone, the leader among all the merchants in Assisi—the butt of the biggest joke in the city! I know they're all laughing at me, even if they do it behind my back."

"But, Father," he called out from behind the locked door, "I was only. . . ."

"Silence! I don't want to hear any more of your excuses—or any more of your madness! You've looted what does not belong to you for your own purposes. That's robbery, and I demand justice. You'll repay all the money you've stolen from me while I was away in Spoleto, and you'll make full restitution for all the money I've squandered on your dreams of knighthood, including that enormous ransom I had to pay to Perugia. Only by such public actions will I ever be able to regain my honor. To insure that I get justice, I will request a meeting of the Assisi commune as soon as possible. I will ask them to sit in judgment over your crime. I am taking you to court—for I will have justice! Sadly, I now realize that as your father I have failed you, Giovanni, by loving you too much! Yes, I have failed to discipline you severely enough to help you grow up to be a real man, a man who is responsible and honest."

In the pitch darkness of this new prison, what pained Francesco most was that his father had addressed him using his baptismal name, Giovanni, instead of Francesco. He had never before called him Giovanni, and that name, which was taken from the beloved disciple,

now paradoxically pierced Francesco's heart with its implied razor-sharp rejection of him as his father's beloved. "Giovanni, Giovanni, Giovanni, Giovanni," his father's voice sounded in his mind as mournfully as the tolling of Santa Maria's death bell now reverberated off the unseen walls of the darkened storeroom. Tears began streaming down his cheeks as he regretted he had ever begun begging alms for San Damiano. His heart felt swollen in shame at being so stupid as to sell their finest wool so cheaply, causing his father, whom he admired and loved so much, to reject him so completely.

A small bit of light and sound entered the storage room from the narrow crack under the door. He was able to guess the time of day by the muffled voices and sounds he could hear from out in the cloth shop and by the tolling of the church bells. Unlike Perugia, this new prison was comfortable and clean, and he could sleep on bundles of soft cloth instead of filthy, flea-invested straw. Toward the end of his first day he heard the voices of his father and mother arguing.

"Pietro, please let him out of that storeroom," his mother pleaded. "Why are you keeping him prisoner in his own home? The poor boy must be hungry by now. Can't I bring him a little bread, cheese, and wine?"

"No!" Pietro snapped back at her with absolute authority. "He is a thief, and thieves deserve to be imprisoned! Woman, don't you know the boy gave away my finest Flemish wool for pennies, cloth for which I had paid dearly? That son of yours is a thief! Not only has he stolen my wool, he has robbed me of my honor. And any man without honor in his own city is, indeed, bankrupt! Once a man's pride and dignity have been stolen, he becomes a pauper. My mind is firmly set. I'm going to arrange for the court of our Assisi Commune to hear my case against your son."

"Oh, Pietro, don't do. . . ."

"If I don't, Pica, then my word is weaker than water, and I'll look twice as foolish as I do now. Perhaps, God willing, after being locked up in there for a couple of days, he may come to his senses. I don't want to take him to court and publicly punish him, but besides my pride I have also become bankrupt of patience."

"Pietro, I beg of you, please give him a little time to ponder his errors before you go to the commune. He's a good boy; I know he'll repent. Please, can't I bring him at least a little bread and wine? And

perhaps also his beloved lute? When he plays it, he seems to be able to think more clearly. It may help him come to his senses."

"I'll think about it. But for now, Wife, this discussion is ended! I want to hear nothing more about it from you. Return upstairs to our living quarters, while I attend to some important work here in the shop. And, woman, stop that crying. Perhaps tomorrow; we'll see."

*O*n the second day, Francesco's silence was broken by the snapping open of the lock. As the door creaked open, a broad slice of daylight flooded into the darkness of his storeroom prison. As his eyes attempted to adjust, he was able to discern his father's hand in the beam of light at the doorway placing a loaf of bread, a hunk of cheese, a small jug of wine and his beloved lute on the floor of the room. Then, without a word, the door was quickly closed and the lock snapped shut.

Even more than the bread, Francesco was delighted to have his musical instrument. Like a blind man he sat in the darkness strumming his beloved lute. Before long, however, he stopped, for even his music wasn't making him feel any better. Needing to sort out what was happening, he laid aside his lute. "Perhaps I should do what my father wants," he thought, "and become a respectable merchant, and even get married. I should forget about repairing old San Damiano, especially since I'm the only one who seems to care if it is rebuilt. Maybe I should forget about following my inner call and the voice I heard from the cross, forget about my dreams of being a troubadour, and live a normal life." He sat for a long time in the darkness that seemed to mirror the absence of light within his heart. He was even beginning to doubt that he actually had heard anything in that chapel.

As when he was imprisoned in the darkness in Perugia, he began to pray. Once again lyrics of old ballads remembered, as well as poems, words of Jesus, and short selections of scripture became the pantry for his prayers. Out of that storehouse there now arose an ancient hymn sung on the feast of Pentecost, to which his own words were intertwined. As he took his lute in hand, in the darkness his fingers found the right strings as he began singing:

Come, Holy Spirit, Creator blest,

and in our hearts take up thy rest.

Come, Holy Spirit, and set me free

from this great plight that now confronts me.

Which of my fathers shall I obey?

The father I have loved from my birth,

or the Father of my Lord on the cross?

As a son of both, whom do I obey?

The one who asks me to build

my life as a respectable merchant,

or the one who asks me to rebuild his church?

Come, Holy Spirit, inflame my soul for both,

to give due respect to my earthly father

and to love my unseen Father

as did my Lord Jesus—unto death.

Guide me to love both of my fathers

and honor them as you commanded.

Come, Spirit of God, as you did long ago,

spiraling down into that upper room

where our Lord's fearful disciples

were hiding behind locked doors.

Come, now, O Spirit of Courage,

to your poor, fearful son of Assisi

held captive behind this locked door.

Set my heart ablaze, ignite my tongue,

engulfing it in flames like Peter's and John's.

As the fingers of his left hand danced across the strings, his right hand was strumming the melody faster and faster, bringing the notes of the old familiar melody of Pentecost into harmony with the strains of his soul. The fast-paced, ever-quickening rhythm of music caused his thoughts to form themselves into pictures. He saw the Spirit's licking tongues of flames raining through the roof of the locked room and down upon the fearful Apostles. Then this fiery Pentecostal fresco began reshaping itself into the image of the hungry flames consuming the youthful body of the heretical maid of Montelimar. At this mental picture, his fingers froze on the strings. He felt a resurgence of admiration for that girl whose convictions were so strong that she was

able to endure such a terrible, agonizing, fiery death rather than deny her beliefs. And he heard a voice within saying, "Francesco Giovanni Bernadone, do you have the same courage of your convictions?"

The muffled sound of the evening church bells announced to Francesco that another day had slowly passed in his prison storage room. As time passed, his conviction grew that the Spirit of God was beginning to answer his prayer. As slowly as the pale blue and amber light creeps over the morning horizon, so gradually did the answer dawn within him as to which of his two fathers he must obey. Any previous doubts had now vanished, and he knew with absolute certainty that he must obey the voice of Christ on the cross, even at the expense of alienating his father Pietro. However, instead of bringing him a sense of peace, the answer to his prayer now soaked him in dread, and so he began to pray passionately:

My Liege Lord, I am your humble vassal.

To you, my Liege, I pledge my complete loyalty.

I heartily promise never to depart from you;

come searing fire or the sword, I'll not flee.

Now on bended knee, I beg for a weapon.

Grant to me, my noble Liege and Savior,

the Spirit's sword of courage, with which

you armed your timid, cowardly disciples,

and also the brave maid of Montelimar.

Francesco straightened his back, feeling great pride in the realization that in this darkness he had mysteriously been raised to the noble rank of a knight of Christ. He traced upon himself the sign of the cross, as if he were being invested with an invisible red crusader's cross. More than on his chest, that sign was imprinted upon his entire body and soul. "Yes," he thought, "my dream of being a champion has come true, even if it's in a new way that I don't yet completely understand."

Then, as quickly as this stunning insight had come, it was gone. It was now replaced by the frightening specter of his impending trial. He visualized himself standing before the rich merchants who comprised the commune of Assisi. He was naked of charm, disarmed of power, stripped of status.

The commune court reserved the right to deal with all crimes against business and violations against personal property—and was doing so in a new way. The ageless way had been the Church's method of judging guilt or innocence by seeking some sign from heaven. It might be by a duel, where God would decide the winner, or an ordeal of fire, in which divine justice would allow the innocent to escape unharmed. These new practical-minded businessmen found that method of judgment to be stupid. In their commune court, innocence or guilt was based upon the testimony of witnesses, not hearsay or supposed supernatural acts of God. These citizen courts handed out especially harsh punishments to those who stole property. Francesco was also aware that some judges found perverse pleasure in turning up new and creative punishments. He remembered one time in particular when a judge decreed that a thief's ear should be nailed to a cartwheel and then ordered the wheel to be sent rolling down a hill. He shuddered as he recalled how his father had derided the humiliated and severely punished thief.

His image of that courtroom filled with richly dressed merchants reminded him of what he could not see—his own stunning clothing. In the darkness of this storage room he could only touch the costly fabric of his gorgeously tailored tunic and experience upon his body the feel of his luxurious leg hose. He dearly loved wearing the richly colored, handsome clothing his father had given him. "Even before Spoleto," he thought to himself, "I was aware that I wore my fine clothing to cover my shame. My dashing way of dressing covered my physical deficiencies. It was more than just being stylish; it gave me a sense of importance and even grandeur. My clothing has been covering up my sense of inadequacy, my inner vulnerability and nakedness. It's sad that I've only been able to see this now in the darkness of my homemade prison."

The darkness opened his eyes to even more truth that humbled him: how the girl in the moonlit paradise of Chambery, as well as Emiliano and many others had called him "passionate." "Yes, I'm passionate," he announced to himself, "passionately selfish and passionately proud. I've greatly enjoyed being the King of the Feasts, as my companions call me. I've taken hidden delight in being the center of attention and being a leader. Yes, I'm passionate and also *stubborn*. Whatever happened in our wild stunts and celebrations had to be *my* way, what *I* wanted. It was a case of 'do it my way or leave.'" He buried his head in his hands and moaned, "And it's my stubbornness that has  gotten me into this situation."

It was three days into his imprisonment when he heard the key turning in the lock. As the door opened, a wave of blinding light came rushing in upon him. "Can I come out now?" Francesco asked, shielding his eyes.

"Yes, if. . . ." Pietro snorted, fully blocking the doorway, ". . . if you have finally come to your senses!"

"I understand. Yes, Father, I do believe that I have come to my senses."

"Before you take one step out of that storeroom, know that your fate depends upon the answers you shall give to these three questions. First, have you abandoned completely all this nonsense about repairing that old church? Second, will you promise to work faithfully, day after day, here in our shop until you've made full restitution for the wool that you practically gave away—that you stole from me? And third, will you agree to marry the woman that I have selected as your wife?"

"Ah, Father, you present a trinity of questions, and just as there are three persons in one God, I have one answer for all three queries: No!"

"With your own mouth you have condemned yourself, Francesco! You are a thief, and I will have my justice in the courtroom of the commune of Assisi!"

"If I am a thief, then God shares in my guilt, which makes my crime one that can only be tried in a Church court. The money I got from the wool was not for me personally—it was to go to the Church, for the repair of San Damiano chapel! Therefore, if you insist that I be judged, I demand my rights to be judged by Holy Mother Church in the court of our Lord Bishop of Assisi."

Gasping in disbelief, Pietro slammed the door shut and bolted it. More shocked than surprised, he sat down on a stool to sort out his thoughts. While greatly distressed at his son's answer, his practical business mind speedily began to grasp the potential profit in Francesco's demand to be tried by a Church court. "Yes," he thought, "that way I'll be spared the embarrassment of having to drag him in front of my fellow merchants of the Commune court. Bishop Guido is a reasonable, practical man who can be counted on to act justly. And when it comes to the sin of stealing, does not the Church teach that a thief must make full restitution? Moreover, even if I don't regularly attend Mass, am I not a most generous benefactor to the Church? Yes,

yes, my son's idea of a Church court may, indeed, turn out to be the best resolution. I have nothing to lose, for I shall appear there as the injured parent. And I will regain my reputation in Assisi when Bishop Guido judges, as would any good confessor, in my favor, requiring that Francesco make full restitution to me."

Speaking through the locked door, Pietro said, "As you wish, then, Francesco. I shall make that concession and allow Bishop Guido to judge your case of robbery. I'll go at once to the cathedral and make the necessary arrangements for your trial. And I shall have justice!"

In the darkness, Francesco exhaled deeply. Then he took his lute into his hands and began singing a prayer:

Thank you, my Liege Lord,

for your assistance. But I pray

that you stay ever skin-close to me,

for this is only one small victory.

Yes, the contest has only begun,

and I must still stand before the bishop.

Come quickly, O Spirit Lawyer,

and help me prepare my case.

The odds are stacked against me,

or else my father would not have agreed.

The judgments of Church and State

both lean toward my father's way.

Only heaven's court will rule for me,

but, alas, I can't wait till Judgment Day.

Come, O Lord, get me off the hook.

Provide me with some wise defense

not found in any holy or legal book.

It must be something so dramatic and bold,

so clear that the bishop will have no choice.

Gently laying aside his lute, he said, "Ah, my beloved Lady Lute, whose soul is so beautiful, what would I ever do without your inspiration?" Then, lying back next to the lute, he allowed his mind to

wander wherever it wished. As sleep crept up on him, he mused, "It's strange, but resting here in this darkness, I feel like an infant inside some great womb, waiting for my time to come forth." Moments later, his thoughts vanished as sleep embraced him with her soft nothingness.

*M*onsignor Carafa sprang like a cat at the opportunity to arrange for the Bernadone trial. When Pietro had come to him requesting a day in court, he smiled to himself as he thought, "This is a God-sent opportunity to make an unmistakable statement to the populace about the authority of the Church." He immediately stated to Pietro that it would be necessary for the case to be conducted publicly in front of the old Cathedral of Santa Maria Maggiore rather than in the privacy of the bishop's house. Pietro eagerly agreed, for the more public the trial, the greater would be his vindication. Carafa ordered the construction of a special wooden platform upon which the bishop would preside over the trial surrounded by the clergy of the various churches of Assisi. Carafa took an almost sensual delight in preparing this trial. He wanted it to provide an elaborate display of the ancient authority of the Church as the ultimate influence in society.

"In these turbulent times," he told Padre Giuseppe, "when the merchants of cities are assuming so much control over civil affairs, it is essential that they and all the citizens be reminded that the Church holds final authority over their lives."

"You're so right, Monsignor," said Giuseppe. "I've even heard reports that some of these new merchant-controlled city-states have actually challenged the legitimate authority of the Lord Bishop! In one case those arrogant merchants even defied the Pope, boldly asserting that God was the only one they needed to obey."

"It is our sacred duty," Carafa declared, "to insure that such a disastrous state of affairs will never happen here in Assisi. Indeed, this trial of the thieving prodigal son of Pietro Bernadone gives us the perfect opportunity to display Holy Mother Church to these peasants in all her splendor and supremacy."

*T*he warm afternoon sun flooded Piazza Santa Maria as its old tower bells chimed out the hour. As the echo of last bell was fading away across the piazza, Monsignor Carafa led a solemn procession of robed priests out of the cathedral to the platform erected in the piazza. His Excellency Bishop Guido, escorted by Padre Tomas,

solemnly processed through the main front doors wearing his tall miter and gold ceremonial cope and carrying his gold, bejeweled bishop's croizer staff in his hand. After they had ascended the three steps to the top of the platform, Bishop Guido was seated on his faldstood, the backless folding chair used for officiating at solemn liturgical occasions. Padre Tomas sat on his left and Monsignor Carafa on his right, with the rest of the priests behind them. At the bottom of the three steps facing the clergy stood Pietro di Bernadone alongside his son Francesco. Behind them in a close grand semicircle stood the almost jubilant crowd that filled the piazza. The great crowd, which numbered into the hundreds, was largely the work of Carafa. His agents had spread gossip about the nature, time, and place of the trial everywhere in Assisi and throughout the surrounding area. The balconies and windows of homes that ringed the piazza were also crowded with aristocrats and the wealthy seeking some novel and distracting entertainment. They had purchased permission to view the proceedings of this intriguing trial from the homeowners' balconies. The crowd in the piazza below was comprised of average merchants, commoners, and the poor, all of whom were in a feast-day, carnival mood, hoping that this extraordinary public trial would provide some entertainment in their drab daily lives. While the women gossiped, their husbands were placing wagers on the verdict in this unique trial between God and justice.

As master of ceremonies, Monsignor Carafa called loudly for silence, and when the noisy crowd grew quiet, he opened the trial by piously reciting a prayer to the Holy Spirit for guidance. Following his prayer, he read a lengthy legal declaration outlining the canonical authority of the Church over all matters, both spiritual and temporal. Paradoxically, the boring legalistic drone of his proclamation was drowned out by the mere silent presence of Bishop Guido. He sat calmly with an almost regal composure—his gold-trimmed white miter, along with his heavy, ornate golden cope and tall bishop's croizer loudly and powerfully proclaiming the authority of the Church in Assisi. As Carafa droned on, Bishop Guido was wearing an invisible smile behind his inscrutable face, for he was well aware that symbols are far more powerful than words.

As the trial proper began, it was Pietro Bernadone's turn at oratory. With great passion he presented his case against his son, claiming that

Francesco had stolen what was Pietro's rightful property by selling his most costly wool at a ridiculously low price. He demanded full restitution, quoting the seventh commandment about stealing and piously adding a reference to the fourth commandment about children being bound to honor and obey their fathers. As he enthusiastically unfolded his case, Pietro unconsciously began to ascend the steps of the platform until he was standing just one step below the top level, on which the bishop and clergy sat.

Bishop Guido glanced to his right and took unexpressed delight at the shock on the face of his chancellor, who interpreted Pietro's action as an audacious display of presumption. For Carafa, it reflected the escalating sense of equality the merchant class presumed to have with the clergy. Bishop Guido, on the other hand, felt compassion for poor Pietro. "What was stolen from him," Guido thought, "wasn't his fine wool or even his money—it was his pride. Ah, yes, among us Italians, a man's honor is his greatest fortune. Money can always be returned, but what can restore a man's honor once it has been lost?" As he looked down at the two men in front of him, he saw a potential vendetta germinating in the womb of this conflict between father and son. "Sadly, we Italians are also famous for our vendettas." He straightened his back as if to shift the weight of the wisdom he felt that he must exercise, for in his hands had been placed the fate of a family. How he responded could well tip the scales in starting or preventing a private little war that might rage on for generations to come.

When Pietro had finished presenting the details of his case, Monsignor Carafa nodded to Francesco, indicating that it was now his turn to address the court. He spoke in a loud clear voice so that all could hear, retelling the strange story of how the crucifix at San Damiano had spoken to him. This public confession of what previously had only been a rumor caused a flutter of murmuring to ripple across the crowd. Francesco continued, pouring out his confusion about how he should obey the command of Christ to repair the tumble-down chapel, as well as the story of his futile efforts at begging alms to buy materials and pay workers. As he was speaking, to everyone's surprise, Bishop Guido stood up from his faldstool and handed his golden crozier to Padre Tomas. Then the bishop slowly descended the platform steps until he reached street level, where he stood face-to-face with Francesco.

"Son, please tell me," the bishop asked as the sunlight glistened off his gold-trimmed miter, "how did you know that this voice you heard was our Blessed Lord's?"

"Because, my Lord Bishop," Francesco said with dancing eyes, "the voice was filled with love and longing. And who else but God would want to rebuild an unused, broken-down chapel? Certainly not the devil, would he?" At this remark, spurts of laughter erupted in the crowd, and faces began smiling. Excitement grew, for now this trial was beginning to provide what they had come for—entertainment.

"Reasonable response, Giovanni Francesco," Bishop Guido nodded in agreement. "But do you not also believe that the Lord God spoke to us through Moses when he commanded that we honor and obey our parents? It is one of the greatest and most beautiful commandments of God, and your father is right in demanding that, as long as you live under his roof, you must honor and obey him. You are not married and have no family or home of your own; so you're still under his authority. And more importantly than honoring your father, you are to love him, for he is the source of your life, your very existence."

The crowd leaned forward, intent upon Francesco's answer to these wise words. Pietro was smiling broadly at the bishop's statement as he descended to street level and stood now beside his son and the bishop. Along with Pietro, the rest of the parents in the crowd were pleased, and several were nodding their heads in agreement.

"Your Grace," replied Francesco, "I do honor my father Pietro and love him very much. Yet is not God also my Father? Am I not bound to give greater obedience to God than to any other authority, even my earthly father?"

Monsignor Carafa grew anxious and began fiddling with his cassock buttons. Francesco's words about giving ultimate authority to God were precariously close to the erroneous doctrine those new heretics were proclaiming. Did his words, "any other authority" also include the authority of canon law and of the Church? Carafa could feel sweat beads forming on his forehead—and not from the heat of the sun. "What dangerously wild utterance," he thought, "would this irresponsible youth speak next in the hearing of all these people? Perhaps I was mistaken to stage a public trial. It might have been better in a secluded room in the chancery where outsiders couldn't hear such dangerous statements." Although he was sitting motionless, it felt to him like an earthquake: The ground was less sure beneath him as

circumstances seemed to be slipping out of his control. A sickening feeling of terror gripped him, for he saw it as essential to have a firm grasp over every situation. In fact, he had elevated control into his cardinal virtue. And at this moment, Carafa's carefully planned career and his dream of advancing to the office of bishop, if not beyond, felt threatened.

The spontaneity of the scene that was unfolding, which was so disturbing to Carafa, was delighting Bishop Guido. It was a refreshing change from the repetitive sameness of liturgical rituals and his predictable episcopal duties. The warm, still afternoon was unexpectedly visited by a fresh breeze blowing gently across the piazza, and as the bishop inhaled it deeply he wondered, "Has Monsignor Paulo's opening prayer inviting the Holy Spirit been answered?" He looked at the young man who stood before him. The dancing sunlight was causing the golden threads in Francesco's flaming scarlet tunic to shimmer and sparkle. As usual, the merchant's son was resplendent in the finest clothes, even though they were a bit wrinkled because he had been locked up for days in the storage room.

"Bishop, I have prayed," Francesco continued, "asking God what I should do. And I feel my prayers have been answered. I am confident that I've been called to love and serve my heavenly Father more than my earthly father." Then, turning to Pietro, he said softly, "Dearest Father, know how deeply I love you, and how I've longed for—ached for—your approval and blessing. Yet I must be faithful to the answer God gave me in my prayer. I am firmly convinced that, even though the way is not entirely clear, somehow I must obey the voice of our Lord speaking to me from the cross."

At these words, Monsignor Carafa turned around, rolling his eyes upwards in mock shock toward the priests seated behind him on the platform. The bishop pondered the scene that had unfolded. This enthusiastic young man who stood before him had just spoken with confidence about God answering his prayers. "Is it possible," Bishop Guido thought, "that he could be God's answer to my prayers?" He was greatly disturbed over the escalating abuses in the Church, and, along with a small group of his brother bishops, he had decided to petition Pope Innocent III to call another ecumenical council. The Church was burdened with so many problems: the clergy's disregard of their promises of celibacy, the lack of authentic devotion, the absence of zeal, the shameful selling of indulgences and the abusive trafficking in relics.

These bishops felt that only a general council of the entire Church could address these abuses, yet now he wondered, "What if an ecumenical reform council isn't the answer? What if our real need is for a reforming ecumenical saint?" *Ecumenical*—that old Greek word spun around and around in his mind. "What a strange title for a saint," he thought, "*worldwide?*" As these thoughts swirled around in his mind, his hidden penitential hair shirt began itching, and he wondered if it might be a sign from God.

Like a swimmer rising quickly to the surface from the bottom of a deep pool, Bishop Guido returned his attention fully to Francesco, who was now removing a small leather bag from inside his tunic. Handing it to Bishop Guido, he said, "Your Excellency, here is all the money— though it isn't much—that I've collected in alms to rebuild San Damiano." Then turning to his father, he embraced him and kissed him on both cheeks. Reaching inside his scarlet tunic, he removed another small leather pouch and said, "Here, Father, is the money from the sale of your fine Flemish wool, which I intended to use to rebuild the old chapel. It is far, far short of the full value of your fine wool. So, to repay the amount that I owe you, and to reimburse you for all my other debts, I now wish to hand over to you, in full, my family inheritance." Pietro frowned, nodding silently as he took the bag of money, quite certain that his son wasn't finished yet. The crowd was hushed, leaning forward, also sensing that something significant was about to happen.

"Father, I love you so, more than you can ever know," Francesco said, placing one hand on Pietro's shoulder. "And I wish it were possible to repay you for all your gifts: a good home, my schooling, my beautiful lute, my expensive ransom from Perugia—and, most of all, your great affection for me symbolized by these beautiful clothes that I wear." Then, placing his other hand on Pietro's shoulder and looking into his eyes, he added, "Now, Father, as a symbol of my inheritance I give all of them back to you!" To the shock of everyone, he quickly stripped himself naked of all the clothing he was wearing and dropped them at his father's feet. His father's jaw dropped, and he stood opened-mouthed, awestruck. Bishop Guido's eyebrows shot halfway up his forehead, and the crowd gasped loudly at the sight of Francesco standing there stark naked and smiling as innocently as Adam before the Fall. Quickly, the women and girls in the crowd covered their faces

with their hands, though more than a few peeked through their fingers. From the windows and balconies of the surrounding homes, the wealthy women turned away giggling. Among this group was twelve-year-old Clare, the daughter of Lord Scifi. Unlike the others, she did not turn her eyes away, as she was fascinated by her first sight of a naked man. However, her mother Lady Scifi quickly seized her arm and pulled her away from the window.

Down below in the piazza, standing in the first row of the crowd directly behind Pietro was Francesco's mother Pica. With her head buried in her hands, she was sobbing uncontrollably in great agony. Many in the crowd later remarked that she looked just like the holy icon image of the Sorrowful Mother of God wailing at the foot of the cross. Bishop Guido instantly stepped forward and wrapped the naked body of Francesco inside his large, golden cope. It was a gesture that spoke either of modesty or affirmation. As Francesco stood wrapped inside the ceremonial cope, the saintly bishop smiled, aware that this seemingly bizarre incident was not a spontaneous act but was, rather, high drama. To him, the fact that Francesco so swiftly stripped off his clothing meant that he had surely practiced it before. Such a radical and premeditated act of renunciation also confirmed the bishop's belief that symbols speak louder than words and that Francesco's stripping off of his clothes was a profoundly spiritual gesture.

To Bishop Guido's—and everyone's—surprise, the naked twenty-four-year-old Francesco suddenly broke free from the bishop's cope, turned, knelt on one knee and kissed the bishop's ring. Then, jumping to his feet, he turned and ran through the stunned crowd, which parted before him like waves before the oncoming prow of a ship. Reaching the end of the piazza, he disappeared like a darting young deer down a twisting narrow street toward one of Assisi's gates.

Chapter 8

YOUNG FRANCESCO WAS DELIRIOUSLY INTOXICATED AS HE
ran through the pine forests, drunk on freedom and surprisingly
unashamed of his nakedness. "See, my brother pine trees and sister
wildflowers," he joyfully sang out, "I'm just like you. Look at me: I'm
wearing only what God gave me at my birth." Taking deep breaths, he
filled his lungs with the liberation-soaked air that swept across his
unclothed body. More than just freed from the restraints of clothing,
he felt emancipated from the expectations of his father and of the
others in Assisi.

"Assisi," he thought, halting on the path, hit hard by a sudden
realization. Whirling around, he looked back at his beloved hometown:
Its red-tile roofed homes and churches looked as if they had grown out
of the rocky slopes of Mount Subasio. "What have I done?" he asked as
he began sobbing. "How can I ever return to my beloved Assisi and see
my father and my mother?" Behind his tear-filled eyes appeared the
image of Pica in the piazza at Santa Maria Maggiore as she swooned to
the pavement, shrieking in shame after he had stripped himself naked.
Then, he was struck by another painful awareness. "And you, my
beloved Emiliano, now we shall forever be parted. Oh, how I shall miss
you! I've also orphaned you, my precious lute, you whom I cherished
more than one of my limbs. By returning to my father all he had given
me, I've lost you, the tongue of my heart."

As he realized the extent of the consequences of his renunciation,
he was gripped by an overwhelming sense of homesickness. That pain
was about to propel him back to Assisi to repent of his radical action,
to beg forgiveness of his father and mother and promise to do anything
to return to their graces. Then, suddenly, he heard a lark singing. Her

voice was sweeter than any songbird's he could ever remember hearing. Her joyful song worked the miracle of reawakening his joy in being free. He let out a heavy sigh and turned his back on the distant view of Assisi, resuming his climb up into the forest. With each step he took, the balance scales began tipping away from extreme sorrow and regret back toward intoxicating joy. "At last I'm free," he thought, "able to become myself instead of having to be what others want me to be." His jubilation, however, did a sudden somersault as he said, "But now that I'm free to be whoever I wish, who or what do I wish to be?"

Within moments that old companion question was joined by two new ones: Where am I going? and Where will I live? Before he could answer, he came upon an oval shaped pool of water, probably eight feet wide, surrounded by dense leafy undergrowth with patches of small blue flowers scattered around its edges. From higher up on the mountain a small stream was slowly trickling over moss-covered rocks into the pool. Francesco noticed a couple of earth-worn paths in the grass, perhaps made by deer, fox, and other animals that came to the pool to drink. Gazing down into the clear water, he was amazed to see a naked young man looking back at him. Guided by some inner urge, he slowly began descending into the pool, allowing its cool waters to swirl around his body and sensually caress his skin with its wet fingers. When he was waist deep in the pool, the waters reminded him of the scene when he was acting the godfather of Emiliano's infant son and the priest asked, "Do you wish to be baptized?"

"I do," he shouted to the surrounding trees. Then he repeated the words used by the baptizing priest, "Receive the sign of the cross upon your forehead and upon your heart." As he signed himself on his forehead and chest, he thought, "Just like the crusaders, I now wear a cross upon my chest." As the water level reached his shoulder tops and neared his chin, he continued, "Do you believe in Jesus Christ, his only Son, our Lord, who suffered, died and was buried?" He responded to his own question, "*Credo, credo,* I believe." Then the waters swirled over his head.

As he rose out of the pool, rivulets of water cascaded off his head and down his face. In the process, his eyes felt strangely cleansed. The forest now appeared to him as freshly new as the Garden of Eden. As the water trickled off his naked body, he was revisited by his old question of who he should be. Glancing down at himself, he laughed, "I feel like Adam. Perhaps I could be a new Adam—whatever that

means!" The sound of a snapping twig caused his question to hang suspended in midair. It was followed by the cracking of another twig being stepped on. As the sounds became louder, it was clear that whatever was approaching the pool wasn't a field mouse or rabbit.

"A bear!" The thought that it might be a bear or perhaps a wild boar alarmed him. He knew that there were many of both living in these wooded areas of Umbria. "No," he thought again, "it's more likely a wolf." He recalled stories of them plaguing the neighboring city of Gubbio. At that moment he saw a pair of fierce green eyes at the entrance of a path to the pool. Cautiously a large gray wolf began stepping forward, never taking its eyes off of Francesco's until it reached the opposite edge of the pool.

"Peace," Francesco said, his heart wildly pounding in fear as he held out his open hand toward the wolf. The eyes of the wolf slowly descended from the young man's face down his dripping wet body toward his feet. Then the wolf raised its head and spread its cheeks as if in a smile and vanished into the thick, green undergrowth.

"Giovanni, Giovanni," sang a grinning Padre Antonio, who was leaning on his hoe as Francesco came running up toward his small hermitage vegetable garden. "Giovanni Francesco—or better Giovanni Adam Bernadone—what happened to you? Have the bandits robbed you not only of your purse but also of your clothing?"

With the zest of a bubbling fountain, Francesco poured out his entire story of selling his father's fine wool, his imprisonment and the time of prayer-reflection in the storage room, the trial in the bishop's court, and finally his declaration of freedom in the act of returning his clothes to his father.

"Well, well, Giovanni, that's a remarkable story! But we must find you something more than a fig leaf to wear." Laying aside his hoe, Antonio went into his hermitage cave and returned holding an aged gray tunic made of rough cloth. "Here's my old spare garment. Father Benedict's holy rule says that a monk shall have two tunics, but by giving this one to you I'll be observing a higher rule, that of our Lord. When Jesus sent his disciples out to preach the Gospel, he ordered them to 'take nothing for the journey, no food, no money, not even a second tunic.' So, by your accepting this tunic, we'll snare two birds at once: Your nakedness will be covered, and I'll better live out one of our Lord's commands."

"But, Padre, I can't. What will you wear when you want to wash or repair the one you're wearing?"

"I wear what you're wearing right now. Now put on this tunic, not simply for modesty sake, but because clothing symbolically signals one's identity."

"Thank you, Padre," Francesco said, slipping the old gray tunic over his head. "It feels good, even if it's not as kind to my skin as my previous clothes or as refreshing as the breezes of creation when I was naked."

"Not a bad fit, Giovanni. It speaks boldly of what I sense you are becoming. When you were the son of a wealthy merchant, you dressed as one of the *majores*, the great ones. Now you're attired in the garment of the *minores*, the little ones, the poor and the peasants. This gray tunic is also the garment of hermits."

With his head cocked to one side, Antonio stood back admiring Francesco attired in the threadbare gray tunic. "In our society clothes do more than cover our nakedness. They instantly communicate our social status: The noble knight wears his armor, the priest his black cassock, the monk his religious habit, the physician his purple robe, and the prostitute her red dress. You can recognize a reformed heretic by the double cross on his cloak and the Jew by a yellow circle or the Star of David on his. A leper wears a black tunic, or perhaps a gray one like the one you're wearing, as well as a scarlet hat."

"You don't have a red hat to accent my outfit, do you, Padre Antonio? For I'm sure that I've become something of leper to my family—and to most of my friends."

"Giovanni, your jest contains more truth than you may realize. Those afflicted with leprosy experience their flesh slowly being eaten away by that horrible disease until there's nothing left. Be forewarned: At the end of this new path you're undertaking, you'll find you have nothing left of who you once were."

"But what path am I taking? And what did you mean earlier when you said that you sensed this hermit's tunic is a sign of what I'm becoming?"

"Ah, Giovanni, when you told me your story about stripping yourself naked of everything you possess, did you not say the idea for that bold gesture came as an answer to your prayers? Was it not, then, God who called you to choose the wishes of your heavenly Father instead of your father Pietro?"

"I guess so, but. . . ?"

"To renounce all your possessions, to leave all things, including your father and mother, is the first requirement of discipleship, even if you didn't consciously choose to become a disciple of our Lord."

"I only wanted to repair old San Damiano and to be. . . ."

"I know you had your own reasons for renouncing your possessions. God, however, is eager to lead us to our destiny and cleverly inspires us to take actions that have profound consequences beyond our comprehension in leading us on the divine path. Giovanni Francesco, you've taken the first steps on that path, and as a result I believe you will need to find the solitude and prayer life that belongs to a hermit. Those inner resources will help you both to see and embrace the consequences of your actions and to remain faithful to the path you're to follow.

"Giovanni, you are usually the one who asks all the questions, but now I have one. You are abounding in such joyful excitement over your newfound freedom, but don't you also feel some sadness and heartrending loss? For nothing in this life is free—especially freedom!"

"Yes, Padre, you are most insightful. As you surmised, part of me is grieving with great sadness, but is refusing to acknowledge the grief. I have no regrets about giving away my clothing and my comfortable life, but, oh, I shall miss my friends, especially my dearest friend, Emiliano. . . ."

"And? Surely your freedom cost you more than your clothing, lifestyle, and friends."

"Yes, already I'm missing my father, even if he and I couldn't agree on many things, and, of course, my mother, whom I've caused such pain and grief. Also, I feel loss in never again being able to return home to Assisi."

"And?"

"My lute, my beloved lute, how I shall miss her music and all the hours of enjoyment she gave me."

"Indeed, to leave all things for the sake of the kingdom of God is not easy. It's no wonder so few have the courage actually to do so. Such a complete surrender of everything requires either great madness . . ." opening wide his hands, he added, "or an enormous love of God."

"I wish it were for the love of God, but I'm afraid my only reason was to be free. To be honest, I doubt if I even love God. What I do

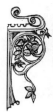

know without any doubt is that I'm terrified of God's wrath for my sins. . . ."

"To fear God is wise, for God is an unquenchable fire, and those who come too close are consumed by that fire. Giovanni, I can see the fright in your eyes, but you have no need to be afraid. The only thing that is incinerated in that fire is the dross of who you are—just the trash."

Antonio chuckled with glee, but Francesco gulped, for he was afraid that he was all trash, and after the fire what would be left? "The love of God often begins with fear," Antonio continued, "but when one has outgrown that childhood fear of a parental punishment, love can replace it. Love must always replace the fear of hell as the guiding rule of one's actions. But for that to happen it isn't patience that is needed, it's *passion*, great passion."

"I don't lack great passion. My problem, I fear, is that I have too much passion—like that time a few weeks ago when I became so violently angry that I flew into a rage. It seems that since my imprisonment in Perugia whenever I see someone abusing birds or beasts I become so enraged that I fear I'm possessed!"

"That's it, Giovanni Francesco—possessed! You've just identified how to free yourself from fear. Indeed, fear is a dark power that can take possession of us. But, paradoxically, being possessed is the surest way to escape the prison of fear.

"Fear, my young friend, is the most ancient—the great mother—of all evils. Our primal fear gives birth to all our other fears: our fears of death and of what it means to love; our fears that God will destroy us or demand too much of us. And especially because you're an Italian, you know well the fear we men have of being vulnerable, of close intimacy, of appearing weak if we cry. The ageless search for aphrodisiacs is an expression of our masculine fear of being sexually impotent. The child of that fear prevents us men from being spontaneous and playful, from allowing the eternal child within us to come out and play. As a result, we men fear women."

"Fear women? Why would we be afraid of women?"

"Because, Giovanni, women remind us of the feminine that slumbers ever so deeply inside each of us men. Sadly, we're taught to deny that God has placed within each man the ability to be motherly and compassionate. We fear that other side, that which is gentle, tender, and intuitive."

Overwhelmed by how he was possessed by his own fears, Francesco sat silently for a moment. Then he asked, "What did you mean when you said that being possessed is the surest way to escape the prison of fear?"

"To live in the glorious freedom of the children of God, we must allow ourselves to be possessed by God. You are passionately loved by God in a way no human lover could ever possibly love you, and returning that love does not involve prattling on in your prayers with words of sweet affection! Those who talk much of their love for God, easily deceive themselves. Remember, it is God who loves us so much more than we could ever love, who romances us, gently luring us ever deeper and deeper into being possessed! And such divine possession simply requires letting go!"

"But, Padre, let go into possession? I've always been taught that possession is an evil state. Are we not to fear being possessed—like witches and the insane that roam about foaming at the mouth? Why does the Church have exorcisms to cure the possessed?"

"Indeed, Giovanni, there are many poor souls who are imprisoned or possessed by any number of evils, and, often, those who are truly possessed by God are thought to be just as threatening as the mad and those who are considered demon possessed. Fortunately, the Church hasn't created rites of exorcism to cure those possessed by God!" Then, clapping his hands, he said, "Ah, Giovanni, enough of all this serious talk for now. Let us share some soup and bread, and a small cup of wine. I'm not sure about you, but I'm hungry."

As they ate their simple meal, Francesco shared with the old hermit the story of his unusual experience at the pool in the forest.

"I do not recall that particular pool, Giovanni, but there are several up here in these mountains. But yours is a most interesting and significant experience. And I find it fitting that you called yourself a new Adam."

"I was struck by how you called me Giovanni Adam when I arrived at your hermitage this afternoon. Did you say that because I was naked?"

"And missing your fig leaf!" Antonio laughed. "That was the obvious reason, but as we've reflected on your experience today, I think there are two other reasons. The first has to do with what happened to you at that pool. Was it not a baptism?"

"But I've already been baptized as a child when. . . ."

"Ah, yes, Giovanni, but just as it can take a lifetime to live into one's baptismal name, I often wonder how many times in our lives we need to experience baptism before we can release the full implications of our first baptism. You were not just baptized into the Church as a Christian. You were also plunged into the Spirit and fully into creation, and your baptismal experience in the forest highlighted these two aspects of baptism that speak of a new creation. So you truly did rise out of that pool as a type of the new Adam. The ancients called water the *'prima material,'* the primal substance from which all of creation emerged. It was not by accident that those words of your godson's baptism came back to you. I believe they were given to you so you could fulfill your rebirth as a new man. Some kind of new beginning was essential to complete your death in the Piazza Santa Maria before all of Assisi. You died more than symbolically, and you had to experience a real rebirth."

"That's a lot to reflect on, Padre. I shall ponder it more later. And your second reason for calling me Adam?"

"There's an old legend that at the birth of the Christ Child in Bethlehem an earth-shaking scream was heard across Italy and Greece, which then echoed through the entire earth. That cry was heard most clearly by those who till the land or herd flocks of sheep, and by all those who love creation: 'The great god Pan is dead!'

"Earlier today, Giovanni, around the time you plunged into that pool, something most unusual happened as I was praying in my cave. It began as if some great force was sweeping through the forest. As the roar grew louder, the great oaks began quivering violently, and the ground began buckling as if in an earthquake. Frightened, I peered out of my cave and saw large flocks of larks spiraling across the sky, and the sun—yes, the sun—began whirling like it was dancing. Then, all at once, everything became as deadly still as a graveyard. Not a leaf on the vegetables and flowers in my garden or on the trees moved. All was hushed; all creation seemed to be holding its breath, listening in expectation. I began to venture out of my cave, when out of that awesome stillness came a ferocious wind that began bending the oak trees toward the ground and blowing before it blinding clouds of gray dust, dead brown leaves, small twigs and branches. And then. . . ."

Awestruck, Francesco asked, ". . . And then?"

"Out of that ear-shattering, roaring wind came a voice that I would swear said, 'A new Pan is born!'"

"Are you implying that somehow I'm the rebirth of that lusty half-man, half-goat pagan god of nature?"

"Yes and no, my young friend. If by pagan you mean some diabolic or false god, the answer is no. Do you think, Giovanni, that in the perhaps hundreds of centuries before the coming of Christ, God was absent on our earth? Much of the ancients' experience of the sacred—which Christians today call 'pagan'—I like to consider not so much as diabolic or evil but as incomplete, since the fullness of God was wholly revealed only in the body—the flesh and blood—of our Lord.

"I know that much of this is a challenge to what you've been taught, and I'm not asking you to accept it, just to think about it. Christianity needs a new passionate Pan who can help us see forest and field as sacred, a new Adam who can open our eyes to the holiness of our bodies and all that God has created. And perhaps, in the divine scheme, you are God's chosen one to end that ancient earthen divorce. Your baptism was into Christ, whose cross was signed upon your forehead and upon your heart. The reason the legend says that Pan died at the birth of Christ was not that Pan was an evil that needed to be *replaced* but that at the birth of Christ the earth had now been *fully* blessed. At his passion and death on the cross and his resurrection, the earth would be *redeemed*. Because the imprint of Christ is upon you, perhaps within your heart the lustiness of Pan can be transformed into a pure passion for life, especially the life in forest and glen, flora and fauna. And perhaps through that transformation in you, the whole Christian world can fully embrace all of God's creation."

Francesco sat in silence, a bit overwhelmed at all that Padre Antonio had just suggested. They had talked well into the evening, and the sun was beginning to set. Antonio looked over at Francesco and said, "Alas, Giovanni, this old man is growing sleepy, and after all that has happened to you this day you must be also. Since you're now homeless, I invite you to be my guest and spend the night here at my hermitage. However, I'm afraid I've only one sleeping pallet. . . ."

"Padre, thank you for your invitation; indeed, for once in my life I am a homeless vagabond. Don't worry about a pallet; I'll sleep out here under your thatched porch. Good night, and again thank you for all your insights and wisdom."

*T*he next morning as the two men broke the fast of the night with a simple meal, Francesco asked, "Can we return to our

conversation from last night when you said you thought God may have chosen me to be a new kind of Pan?"

"Of course, Giovanni. Perhaps it may help to look at some of the history of how Christianity became divorced from God's creation, even though Christ came to redeem it. Indeed, it is unfortunate that Christianity is a town religion, a domicile dweller, and so is uncomfortable when it is outside in creation. The conversion to Christianity originally began in cities and came only slowly to the countryside. The peasants who labored in the fields or tended their flocks were the last to be converted to the faith and to surrender their worship of the old nature gods and goddesses. That explains the origin of the word 'pagan,' which in Latin literally means 'country-dweller.' Only God knows why the Church was so fearful of the power of those old gods of rivers, fields, trees, and animals, but it was. The Church's first crusade involved brutally crushing those old nature gods and goddesses, wiping them off the face of the earth instead of baptizing their primal wisdom. As a result, the good news of Christ became divorced from the earth and the seasons and all creatures. Sad, so sad. The psalms of David overflow with rich images from creation, but the Mass and the prayers of the Church are almost completely devoid of references to or images from nature."

"Padre, I thought rebuilding old San Damiano was a difficult task. How will I ever be able to remarry Christianity with creation?"

Padre Antonio shrugged his shoulders as he stroked his gray beard. "I don't know, Giovanni. But whatever God wishes you to do, God will show you the way."

Francesco returned to talking about his previous day's experience in the pool. He told Antonio how in tracing the sign of the cross upon his body he felt like he had become a crusader, a cross-marked warrior. In response, Antonio explained how the Church had adopted from the Roman Army both the word *sacrament* and the ritual of marking the baptized person with the sign of the cross. He told him how a new Roman legionnaire made a *sacramentum,* an oath or pledge, upon entering military service. By this oath he dedicated his life to the emperor or his commanding general. Often, following this oath of allegiance, the soldier was branded with the insignia of the general he had pledged to serve.

"So that invisible cross you traced on your forehead and body was the insignia of your Liege Lord," Antonio said, "that must now become a visible identification with your crucified Lord."

Francesco wondered what Antonio meant about the cross needing to become a visible identification. It was a frightening thought, and perhaps it was the reason why at that very moment he remembered the wolf he had encountered at the pool. He told Antonio how a large gray wolf had approached the pool from the other side and had carefully looked him over from head to foot as he stood dripping wet, and then how it seemed the wolf had smiled at him.

"I'm not surprised," old Antonio said as he smiled and nodded. "For it is said that animals can almost instantly know whether or not they are secure, and even more surprisingly they can sense holiness in a man or woman."

"But I don't possess holiness," Francesco answered quickly, "nor do I even pursue it."

"No, my dear Giovanni, but holiness is pursuing you! And not only holiness but also great suffering married to great joy, as well as peace wedded with agonizing conflict. Allow me to answer your question before you ask it; they're all pursuing you, even the frightening aspects, suffering and conflict, because they're the real teachers of greatness."

"But I was terrified by that wolf! He could easily have killed me."

"I'd wager that at first he was as afraid of you as you were of him. I would guess that wolf had never seen a naked man before. But as you extended to him your blessing of peace, a grace flowed out of you that caused the wolf to sense you meant him no harm. Who knows, you may have made yourself a new friend."

"The wolf?"

"A few years back," Antonio answered, "there was a group of Irish monks who stayed overnight at our abbey on their pilgrimage way to Rome. They told some of us stories of how St. Patrick had preached to the wolves. That led others to share tales of saints like St. Theodore of Sykeon, a little-known saint of the seventh century, who counted wolves and even bears among his friends. That was followed by stories about St. Anthony, the famous Egyptian desert hermit, who said that when he traveled, wild animals frequently would give him directions, and wolves came to his cave to share his bread."

"Well, Padre, I know of one hungry wolf cub from Assisi that has come to your cave!"

After both of them had laughed, Antonio continued, "Blessed St. Ambrose compared us humans to wild animals whom our Lord has tamed through the power of the Holy Spirit." Then, pointing a long

finger at his own chest, he added, "And here is one old wild beast that the Spirit has tamed." He laughed so loudly that it startled Nicoletto, who jumped out of his curled napping position at Antonio's feet and ran over to Francesco. When Francesco reached down to stroke Nicoletto, however, the frightened cat backed away.

"Did you see that, Giovanni? Creatures like Brother Nicoletto, or even that wolf you encountered, can be great spiritual teachers, for they force us to restrain our immediate inclinations and thus ultimately help us control our selfish desires. You had a desire to stroke Nicoletto, but at that moment he was too shaken to want any affection, and so he backed away. Brother Nicoletto is one of my mentors, and among the greatest lessons he's taught me is always to place the needs of others before my own. To learn his needs I watch carefully and observe how his body speaks to me: whether he's frightened or tired or hungry. When he's hungry for affection, for example, he announces his trust that I am not a threat by rolling over on his back and exposing himself without fear that he might be injured. Moreover, Giovanni Francesco, being attentive to the bodily messages of animals can help us do the same with people! We should approach others with great reverence, holding back tightly on the reins of our own needs and carefully listening to the sign language of others' eyes and bodies."

"Thank you, Padre, and you too, Brother Nicoletto. I hope that, like you, I may learn the lessons offered me by those I encounter, be they priest or wolf, monk or ass, peddler or peasant, friend or enemy. With God's grace I shall try to listen with my ears and my eyes."

They visited for several more hours, and while Francesco knew it was time for him to leave, he didn't know where he should go. He couldn't return to Assisi, and he couldn't stay with Antonio, since that would violate his old friend's solitude. Then he felt a nibbling in his heart and knew it was a revisiting of his mice-size doubts about his radical life decision.

"Padre, tell me," he asked, "did I do the right thing yesterday in the piazza at San Rufino by stripping myself of my possessions? I would feel better if I had your blessing on my new life as a hermit or whatever it is I'm supposed to be. Would you please bless me?"

"No, I will not, my young friend!" Antonio replied, carefully observing Francesco for the jarring effect of his words. "I'm afraid that by blessing your radical decision I would betray your newfound freedom and only enslave you again. It would set me up as a symbolic

father whose approval and blessing you so dearly crave!" Antonio's refusal caused the small mice in Francesco's heart to become as hungry as bears. They began eating large holes, making him feel deeply hurt, confused and sad.

"Giovanni Francesco, you have an enormous need for your father's affirmation. Perhaps Jesus faced a similar dilemma in his decision to live the new life God had called him to embrace. He may also have deeply longed for Joseph, Mary, and his aunts and uncles to bless him. But it seems he was denied that consolation, for in the Gospels his own family and neighbors thought he was crazy or possessed. Yet his ultimate blessing and affirmation did not come from a human source; rather, at his baptism he heard a divine voice that confirmed him. You would be wise to seek the same source of blessing, for unless you are affirmed at the core, you will never be free enough to do anything truly creative and new—and you'll never be free enough to fulfill God's destiny for you."

"I think I understand, and I'll try . . . but I still have my doubts."

"Lean over here," Antonio said to him. "I want to whisper a secret in your ear before you leave." When he had leaned close, the old hermit whispered ever so softly, "So did Jesus!"

Antonio stood at the entrance of his hermitage, watching his young friend depart. As the figure wearing his shabby gray tunic was slowly encompassed by the forest, Antonio thought, "He's so youthfully innocent and trusting." The old hermit recalled an event back when he was the infirmarian at the abbey. He had the privilege of being able to care for his confessor and mentor Padre Guittone as the old monk was dying. Guittone was renowned in the abbey for his holiness, and during these final days he and his spiritual companion, now nurse, discussed what they saw as the miserable condition of the Church. In their conversations Padre Guittone frequently returned to the same questions: Was a reformation even possible? And if so, who could accomplish it? Moments before he died, Guittone suddenly smiled peacefully and, taking Antonio's hand, said, '*Parvulus eos ducebit, Parvulus eos ducebit.*' Until this very morning, Antonio had thought that in those confused dying moments old Guittone had only been rambling, quoting a shred of Scripture. Now, however, he realized it had been a profound prophetic insight. After making the sign of the cross in a blessing over the disappearing Francesco, Antonio said aloud, "*Parvulus eos ducebit!*"

"Clap-clap, clap-clap." From up ahead on the road Francesco could faintly hear that most dreaded sound on earth—and it was growing louder. He had traveled no more than a couple of miles from Antonio's hermitage when he saw a man approaching who was dressed in a gray tunic wearing a scarlet hat. As the man drew closer, he began loudly shouting, "Unclean, unclean" over the "clap-clap, clap-clap" of his wooden clapper. At the same time, he struggled to hobble over to the far side of the road. Though Francesco attempted to keep as far away as possible, he couldn't resist looking at him. The leper's face, which he attempted to hide by covering it with his disfigured, diseased hand that was missing a couple of fingers, was a grotesquely half-human, twisted mass of bloody, oozing wounds. Francesco was now in the full bloom of handsome youth and had always placed great importance upon the beauty of the human body, especially the face. He felt his stomach violently begin to churn at the sight of this hideously disfigured man attempting to pass him invisibly on the opposite side of the road.

Instinctively Francesco's feet reacted by quickening their pace so he could swiftly escape from the repulsive leper. Only moments later, however, with an iron act of will, he forced himself to come to a dead stop on the road and turn around to look back at the leper, who now was standing in the middle of the road watching him. "Coward," he thought, as he felt the pain of his old Spoleto scab. "You've so eagerly embraced becoming one of the *minores*, the lowly ones, and now you're running away from this poor leper, who is the lowest of the lowly ones. You coward! You'll never become a champion by retreating from what you fear." Shame dug her spurs firmly into him, and he quickly began running toward the leper. The man became terrified at this seemingly bizarre behavior and began shaking his wooden clapper loudly and shouting, "Stay away! Stay away from me! Unclean, unclean!"

When Francesco reached the leper, he threw his arms around him and then, to his own surprise, as well as the leper's, kissed him on the lips. Francesco was stunned, for that kiss tasted as sensually sweet as the time years ago when he had kissed his beloved Emiliano at the doorway of the wine cellar. As his mind scrambled in an effort to comprehend such a mystery, the leper also reeled back, aghast in shock and horror at being kissed by this stranger. He whirled around to run away, but Francesco grabbed him by his one good arm.

"Brother, wait, don't run away. I'm Francesco of Assisi. Please, tell me your name."

"I am Benvenuto, the leper," he mumbled, raising his hand in an attempt to cover his disfigured face. "Are you some kind of madman? Why in God's name did you touch me—and kiss me? Are you blind and deaf? Can't you see I'm a leper?"

"I am your brother," answered Francesco, who found himself inspired to ask, "Perhaps you and I could travel together. Where are you bound?"

"Go away! I'm not your brother, and you don't want to go where I'm bound, for I am going to the tombs of Gubbio to join the living dead."

"I've never been to Gubbio. But I have heard of the retreat home for lepers nearby. It's as good a destination as any, for I'm not going anywhere. So, Brother Benvenuto, may I travel there with you?"

"That confirms it! You are mad, for only a man who has lost his wits would walk alongside a despised leper, an exile shunned by his own family and all the rest of human society."

"Aha, your own words have confirmed it! We are brothers! You see, I too am an exile shunned by my family and society. If I attempted to return to my home of Assisi, I'd be ostracized like any madman. So let's be on our way to Gubbio."

"I understand nothing of what you say, but I'll not object to your accompanying me, for even traveling with a crazy man is better than doing so alone—that is, as long as you're not dangerous. Whoever you are, I've kept the law and you've been forewarned, so I'm not responsible for the consequences."

Benvenuto's last words, "for the consequences," lingered in Francesco's ears, buzzing like angry honeybees. As the two men walked toward Gubbio, Benvenuto revealed the hidden world of lepers to Francesco. He told him of the shaming pain of being an outcast, of their being excluded from normal activities, like washing in a stream or drinking from a spring and even from entering a church—even though some cathedrals had peepholes cut in their walls to allow lepers to observe Mass. He went on to say that lepers were forbidden from entering any mill or tavern or coming close to any gathering of people. If they wanted to buy something, they were outlawed from touching the food or object they desired and could only stand at a great distance and point to the article. Merchants who sold them anything were forbidden to directly handle any coins without first purifying them in  a searing fire. When traveling, any time they would encounter someone upon the road, as Benvenuto had done with Francesco, they were required to announce their diseased condition by sounding a wooden clapper and calling out loudly that they were unclean. At all times they had to wear an identifying tunic and a scarlet hat so that even the deaf would know they were the abominable, untouchable ones.

"Benvenuto, I always introduce myself as Francesco from Assisi, yet you mentioned no city or village. Why?"

"I have none, for I'm dead. When you met me back there on the road, I was coming from my village church where I was given the Office of the Seclusion of the Leper. I had heard Mass while kneeling under the black pall used at funerals to cover the coffin of a corpse. The priest prayed for my soul and then threw a shovel of dirt onto the funeral pall as he prayed, 'Be thou dead to the world, but alive again unto God.' So, Francesco, you're walking with a corpse on his way to be buried with the other living dead of Gubbio."

Benvenuto's words about death ushered both men into silence. "Maybe," thought Francesco, "*I* should find some priest and ask to be given the Office of Seclusion. I know that if I walked down the streets of my city, I would be shunned as if I was a leper. So, Francesco of Assisi is now also among the living dead." Then, as his thoughts returned to his unexpected kissing of Benvenuto, he gently licked his upper lip with his tongue as one does after eating something sweet. Other than that one time with Emiliano, he had never before kissed another man on the lips. Why had he done it? Had old Antonio's emphasis on the presence of Christ in all creation and especially in the poor, inspired him to kiss the lips of Benvenuto's hideous face? His face held no likeness to any picture of Christ he had ever seen, yet that kiss was as sweet as his recollection of his *caro mio*. Could it be that in his spontaneous act of faith his true *Caro mio*, his beloved Christ, had kissed him?

Benvenuto hobbled along, wrestling with his own sack of thoughts: "What kind of strange man is this I'm traveling with? Why did he come close to me? Why did he touch me—and even kiss me? Clearly, the man is mad, so I must be on my guard as he walks side by side with me. But how could he not be concerned that by being so close he will not become infected with my disease? And how can he call me brother?"

So these two outcasts, one by nature, the other by the grace of God, continued together on their journey from the forests of Mount Subasio eastward toward Gubbio.

*f*rancesco remained in Gubbio for some time helping care for the sick and dying lepers. He washed and bandaged their open sores and fed those who no longer had hands. Daily he worked alongside a few brave monks and priests, whose deep compassion and even greater courage inspired them to care of the needs of those diseased outcasts who were shunned by the rest of society. And when the time came, he volunteered to become the bedside servant of the dying Benvenuto. After they had met on the road, they became dear friends, and Francesco considered it a privilege to care for him as he approached death.

During his new friend's last days, Francesco began feel a desire to return home to Assisi, and after the death of Benvenuto he departed from Gubbio. As he traveled, he realized that returning to Assisi would be impossible and instead chose to explore the forested ridges of Mount Subasio in the hope of finding his own hermitage site. About three miles away from Assisi in the dense forest he found a small cave suitable for his needs. Once he cleaned out the scattered bones left by some wild animal, he swept the cave clean and converted it into his very own hermitage. Then, in imitation of Padre Antonio, he gathered some tree branches and constructed a porch and a thatched roofed over his cave's entrance.

"Not too bad," he said, admiring his work, "for a man who doesn't know how to use his hands." That bit of self-praise, however, only reminded him of his failure to fulfill the command of the Christ to restore the old chapel at San Damiano. As those who live alone are prone to do, he began softly talking to himself. "But how can you even begin, Francesco? You have no money—can you build something out of nothing?" At a casual glance he saw around him all the building materials needed to repair the old chapel, but how would he be able to haul those large rocks protruding out of the mountain across the three miles to San Damiano? He recalled stories his mother had told him about saintly hermits who when they fasted were visited by angels. He decided to undertake a strict fast with the hope that God might send him an angel messenger to tell him how to accomplish this impossible task. As a hermit, his diet was already leaner than Lent, composed only

of roots, berries, wild herbs and a little bread he had earned working alongside peasant field workers. Now, desiring to be gifted by God with an answer to his prayer, he decided to begin a strict three-day fast, during which he would be completely alone in silence praying in his dark cave.

At the end of the first day he was gifted, but not with an answer to his prayer. He was blessed with a sense of freedom, for he now felt not the slightest desire for his former life of riches, luxurious clothing, and fine foods and wines. However, while his former life was now empty of meaning, he had not yet discovered a new life, other than being a hermit. The absence of food and activity, along with the prolonged solitude, caused old, forgotten memories to resurface. On the second day he recalled the times when Antonio had touched his eyes, saying, "Be healed," though he still hadn't noticed any change in his vision. The gift of this second day was a keen hunger, not for food, but to see whatever Antonio had hoped he would see. The third day was spent waiting and fasting; while nothing significant happened, Francesco did have a sense of quiet calm. At sunrise on the fourth day, however, after completing his fast, he came out of his small dark cave feeling like a newborn child emerging from a dark womb.

"I see nothing," he exclaimed in great joy. "I see nothing!" Whirling around and around with his outspread arms waving free, he sang out, "As I look at creation, I see no-thing! I no longer see things, only living beings. The fiery face of a living sun; the tall, aged oak brimming with life; pine and cypress trees and wild grasses swaying with life; small yellow and blue mountain flowers as animated as little children; and even these centuries-old gray rocks—they are not things; they're alive! It feels as if they are looking at me just as I am beholding them. They're not only alive; they seem to be shimmering with an awesome vitality!" Lowering his voice to a mere whisper, he said, "I have the sense that God is looking at me through each one of these members of creation." Then he fell to his knees in awe and adoration. As this profoundly moving experience gradually faded, he was left speechlessly stunned in wonder.

"*P*adre, Padre, I can see!" Francesco shouted as he came leaping with joy to Antonio's hermitage. The old hermit only smiled as Francesco joyfully poured out his story, first about his three days of fasting, solitude, and prayer, after which he had been graced with his

 brief but stunning gift of sight. Then, he told him about his meeting with Benvenuto and his time in Gubbio helping to care for the lepers, followed by his return to the forest on Mount Subasio to find his own cave hermitage. He concluded by expressing his anxiety about whether his awesome experience of new vision was only a trick of his vivid imagination.

"Welcome, Giovanni. That was quite a wonderful mouthful of occurrences! I didn't even have a chance to tell you how good it is to see you again after all this time. Congratulations, by the way, on your new beard. Besides making you look more like a hermit, your dark beard and black hair perfectly frame that charming face of yours.

"Now, as far as questioning your senses, my young friend, that is normal whenever something unusual—or, shall I say, otherworldly—happens to us."

"But it feels, Padre, almost like I'm betraying my beautiful experience by doubting it."

"Doubting isn't bad, for faith and doubt are twin companions of the soul that escort us through life. In fact, doubt can serve her twin sister. In the dialogue between the two, faith is clarified and finds a deeper ground of truth. You had an awakening—if fleeting—vision that all of creation is composed not of inanimate objects but of living beings. If your 'vivid imagination' makes you doubt that your experience was real and true, maybe it will help to see your new sight as a gift of God through your daimon."

"A gift from some demon?" Francesco asked fearfully.

"No and yes," replied Antonio, "I didn't say *demon*; I said *daimon*. A daimon is a divine spirit, once also called a genius. Unfortunately, in Latin it is also translated as an evil spirit, but in the original Greek, daimon meant a personal divine power.

"Before you think that this old hermit is merely talking through his hood, I should inform you that years ago in the monastery I taught a class in Roman Mythology to the novice monks. I'd tell them how, like the Greeks, our Roman ancestors, who long ago lived in Assisi and worshipped at the temple of Minerva that still stands in the main piazza, believed in daimons or geniuses."

"The temple with those beautiful Corinthian columns that's now used as a prison?"

"The same; it's over twelve hundred years old but, unlike me, is rather well preserved for its age."

Antonio proceeded to relate to Francesco how long ago the Romans believed that at each boy's birth he was given his unique Genius and each girl her Juno. He said that these divine spirits were given at birth to inspire and guide a person from the cradle to the grave, something like guardian angels. Then he told Francesco that he believed God had blessed him with a wonderfully creative genius, a divine spirit who was guiding him, and he advised him of the importance of listening to it.

When Francesco raised the question of how he would know if he was doing the will of God, Padre Antonio pointed out that term had been used by the Church to justify the horrible slaughter of war she had renamed the *crusades*. "People have used 'the will of God' to explain away every kind of terrible occurrence, from devastating crop failures to being born into lifelong slavery as a lowly serf or as a woman—and even the death of a child at birth, blindness, stomach pains, and plagues." He ended his litany of tragedies by declaring that it was nonsense to accept all these horrors as being God's holy will for us.

As he finished, Francesco wondered—not for the first time—if perhaps Antonio had lived alone too many years as a hermit and this may have been the cause of his outlandish, if not heretical, ideas. "Be that as it may," he thought to himself, "it is clear that Padre Antonio is a holy man, who is close to God, and that is why I have chosen him as my spiritual guide and confessor."

Having concluded his inner dialogue, Francesco said, "All right, but if blindness and terrible plagues are not the will of God, then what is?"

"As I understand the Gospels, the will of God is the *work* of God. We know we are doing the will of God when, like Jesus, we go about doing the work God has given us. I pray the Lord's Prayer this way: 'Thy kingdom come, thy *work* be done on earth as it is in heaven.' If you want to see God's will, Giovanni, look at the work you've done—and will do."

"My work? The only work I've done since leaving Assisi is helping care for some lepers at Gubbio. I've prayed and fasted, if you can call that work, but when it comes to my prayer, I'm as much a failure as I am at repairing old San Damiano."

"Never be the judge of your own prayer! Only God is fit for that work. When it comes to prayer, the only essential question is desire: Do you desire to pray? Do you desire to love God? Do you long to be as

intimately united as possible with your Lord? If you have that kind of desire, then you're praying. As my old confessor and spiritual mentor, Padre Guittone, was fond of saying, 'It is immensely better to desire God with great love than to be able to spout poetic prayers in praise of God or to experience flights of mystical bliss.' He would often. . . ."

"Your spiritual mentor?" Francesco asked with surprise.

"Of course, Giovanni! Do you think that fruit drops fully ripe off the tree? Naturally I had a spiritual director. Without a soul friend to whom one can open one's heart without shame, someone wise in the spiritual life, how can one fulfill one's destiny? And everyone's ultimate destiny is to become Godlike, to become a saint. Blest are those who have a friendship with a holy man or woman. I was especially blest to have Padre Guittone, a very holy monk, as mine."

"I feel equally blest," said Francesco, "having you as mine. But please continue with what you were saying about prayer when I interrupted you."

"Often what one judges as good prayer," Antonio continued, "is only that which makes one feel good. But, alas, such pious religious feelings soon evaporate. So, do not fret if you feel your prayer life is a wretched failure, for as long as you pray with great desire, your prayer is judged by heaven as great. Indeed, you cannot fail when you pray as does a little child. In fact, I feel in my old bones, Giovanni, that your future work will someday take the form of being a joyful messenger of the Gospel—and that you will do it as a child!"

"A child? Padre, I have struggled ever since my youth to grow up and become a man, as my father kept demanding that I do. Now *you* want me to grow down and become a child?"

"*Parvulus eos ducebit,*" Antonio said smiling.

"I would guess, my young friend, from your nonverbal response of tugging at the strands of your beard that your limited Latin leaves you confused. *Parvulus eos ducebit* translated means, 'A small child shall lead them.' It's from Isaiah's prophecy about a child of God—a new divine Pan, if you will—who would unite all creatures in Eden harmony. The Old Testament prophet gave us the beautiful image of the wolf playing with the lamb, and the lion and the calf browsing together in peace. Many years ago when I was the abbey infirmarian, I held in my arms a dying holy monk who prophesied using those same words, giving me hope that our decadent, lukewarm Christianity could be reformed."

"*Parvulus eos ducebit,*" Francesco repeated, "A small child shall lead them—not a pope or. . . ."

"Yes, a child, and you, Giovanni Francesco, are as childlike a person as I've ever known—in your innocence, your freedom to dance, burst into song, or laugh without sophistication. It's different from being childish, for you're a mature man with a child's heart. And with that quality you'll lead people to the realm of peaceful harmony Isaiah spoke about, where ancient enemies will live without conflict. More than a nature-loving, goat-hoofed Pan, you'll be a barefoot prophet to lead the Church to the magnificent discovery that it is indeed possible to live the Gospel. This and so much more I see pregnant within you, ready to be birthed. And I have no doubt that God's hand is upon you."

"Oh, Padre, with all my heart I wish I could feel that hand of God on me. Our Lord Jesus knew he had his Father's blessing, for a voice from the clouds told him, 'You are my beloved son, and upon you my favor rests.'" Then raising his arms up to the sky, Francesco said, "But the clouds do not speak to me!"

"But didn't Christ speak to you from the cross in the chapel of San Damiano?"

His head spinning from all his mentor had said about him, Francesco thanked Antonio for his affirmation and set off to return to his cave hermitage. Along the way, he pondered the things they had discussed. Perhaps it was Antonio's comment about him being like a child and how easily he could break into song that inspired him to begin humming as he walked. Yet before long, that humming awakened his sorrow at no longer having his beloved lute. Seeing a couple of old branches on the path, he leaned over, picked them up and broke off their side limbs. He raised one of the branches up to his chin, and using the other as a bow he pretended he was playing his beloved lute as he sang:

> My soul magnifies my Lord,
>
> for he has filled me with riches,
>
> with good things in abundance.
>
> My spirit rejoices in God my Savior,
>
> who has gifted me with a genius spirit,
>
> my own daimon to enthuse and inspire me.
>
> My soul rejoices in you, my God,

for you have unmagnified me:

You've shrunken me smaller than small.

So my heart and my soul sing joyfully

that I'm the least of the lowly,

who has become dear to your heart.

His song lifted his heart; so he continued playing on his imaginary lute and composing as spontaneously as a little child:

My soul rejoices in the Lord.

I'm not crazy or possessed.

I'm your troubadour of joy.

I'm your troubadour of joy.

He stopped singing only to watch the great orange orb of the setting sun, which was now hovering over the rim of the mountains and enveloped in clouds of incense-like gray-blue mist rising above the olive groves and vineyards of the Umbrian valleys. He was so absorbed in the stunning beauty of that scene that he was caught off guard by an unexpected visitor, old Claude, the lute maker from the Chambery Fair. He saw Claude as vividly as if he were actually standing in front of him. The old lute maker was smiling as mischievously as when he had shown Francesco that unique antique lute that lacked any strings. He had told him that such an instrument produced the most awe-inspiring sounds but was intended only for a great master. As Francesco looked at the two sticks in his hands, he understood what old Claude had meant when he said that to create truly inspiring music the musician must *become* the instrument. Then the ghostlike image of Claude vanished, leaving Francesco marveling at the magnificent instrument that had replaced his beloved lute. That awareness caused him to break into song again.

Francesco, you're to be a living instrument,

upon which joy and love may play their rich melodies.

To become God's instrument of the divine songs

of hope and peace, pardon and consolation.

You must always keep yourself attuned to the Spirit.

In the silence that followed his song he recalled how Claude of Chambery's original lute had been made from the enchanted wood of a lightning-struck tree whose soul had been scorched by heaven's fire. "The soul of this your humble instrument of Assisi," Francesco said wordlessly to God, "was also scorched by heaven's fire. On that day in the chapel of San Damiano your Spirit's lightning bolt struck me, and I burst into flames. There are times when I can actually feel on my heart those scorching burns of your fiery skybolt. May those searing scars never heal, O Lord, so that this lowly instrument of yours will always be inspired by the fiery passion of your spirit and the joyous music of your love."

FRANCESCO HAD BEEN BACK AT HIS CAVE FOR ONLY
A short time when he was shaken by the sound of a voice.
At first it called out faintly, and then louder and louder: "Francesco,
Francesco . . . Francesco of Assisi." Fearfully he traced the sign of the
cross upon himself and waited. After a short while, he heard the voice
again, only now much closer.

"Yes, what do you want?" Francesco called out as he stood at the
entrance of his cave.

"I've come to confess," shouted a man who began to emerge out of
the dense foliage and underbrush. To Francesco's great delight he
recognized the man as Emiliano. "I confess that I'm a heretic, and worst
of all," Emiliano said, drawing closer, "I don't want you to convert me
from my sinful ways!"

"Emiliano, *caro mio*, how marvelous to see you after all this time! I
don't know how I didn't recognize your voice."

"Come, long-lost bearded one, give your friend an embrace,"
replied Emiliano.

After a long and fervent embrace, Emiliano explained that he was
on a trip to Perugia to purchase wine and had detoured from the main
road to climb the mountain searching for Francesco. "Hunters," he
said, "reported having seen you at a distance and said that you were
living somewhere up here like a bear in a cave."

"Emiliano, oh, how I've missed you, ever since. . . ."

". . . You stripped yourself naked in the piazza that day, Francesco?
I was so shocked and confused by that. I was surprised and also hurt,
for I didn't. . . ."

"Emiliano, I wanted to come and tell you of my plans, but I couldn't. My father had me locked up as a prisoner in my own house."

"Your stripping yourself naked in front of everyone was so insane, and after your other strange behaviors it only confirmed my worst. . . ."

"Suspicions? That I'd lost my mind? No, I wasn't crazy, even though that fear has also haunted me. I'm sorry, my friend, but I still have no reasonable explanation for my actions. All I know is that it was the only way."

"That night after you ran out of the city," Emiliano lamented, "I was crying like a baby, convinced I had lost you for life. It was Angela who suggested to me that what you did may have been a kind of suicide, only one in which you were much more alive after you committed the act than before. When I saw you run naked out of Assisi, it was as if someone had cut off one of my arms. Yet through my tears I began to see that Angela was right, that now you were free to be whoever you had to be. So, *caro mio*, I had to come up here in the forest to see if I could get back my lost limb."

As the two embraced a second time, Francesco wept with joy. "My arms and yours can never be severed, Emiliano. You and I are united in a love that even death cannot divide."

Then, Emiliano eagerly fed Francesco's hunger for recent news from Assisi. He told him about his own family—that he now had a baby daughter named Victoria and how Francesco's godson had grown. As he shared other items of gossip, he carefully avoided talking about how Francesco's radical actions on that fateful day in the piazza had deeply affected both of his parents. Aware of Emiliano's discretion, Francesco did not question him about Pietro and Pica but instead focused on rejoicing over the news of Emiliano's baby daughter. When he did speak about his family, he told Emiliano how he had been too ashamed to return to Assisi to visit him for fear he would embarrass him by how he looked. He joked that his neighbors would have thought old Strapazzate had come begging at their door.

"Now," he asked Emiliano, "what was all that nonsense when you came walking up to my cave about you being a heretic?"

"Ah, yes. While my Angela remains as lovely as ever and the family wine business is flourishing, all is not perfect, for I fear I am a heretic!"

"You too? Then you and I truly are brothers, for I think that I've become one too. Tell me, *caro mio*, which of the teachings of Holy Mother Church do you now no longer believe?"

"I do not believe," stammered Emiliano, "I *cannot* believe any longer that enjoying sex with one's wife is a sin! There, I've said it out loud. So, you see, I am a heretic, for we both know how the Church teaches that sex is sinful, even in marriage—and especially if you take pleasure in it! Rather than sinning, when Angela and I make love, I feel like I'm in heaven or receiving Holy Communion! Oh, Francesco, this will sound like a damnable heresy, but it feels to me that there are three of us in bed: Angela, me, and God! Yet I'm still distressed by my guilt. There are nights when we make love that I lie there awake after she's fallen asleep wondering if perhaps I've been possessed by the devil. Dear friend, I could never have told this to any priest—he would have condemned me to hell."

"That's impossible, Emiliano! Once you're in heaven you can't be sent to hell, and you just told me you're in heaven right there in your bed in Assisi!"

"But the Church says. . . ."

"Emiliano, do you remember that conversation you and I had in your father's wine cellar before you were married when you wanted both of us to join a monastery, because sex was so sinful?" Laughing so vigorously that his whole body shook, he embraced Emiliano and then slapped him on the back, saying, "And now you're a believer! You're a true believer in the good news—and fortunate are you to have Angela as your angel of revelation—the good news that Christ has made all of life holy, including sex!"

Buoyed by his friend's wise words, Emiliano returned the affirmation. He spoke of his joy at being with Francesco again and how he was so inspired by Francesco's living in such poverty, expressing his desire to share in such a holy life. Francesco responded by saying that Emiliano's life as a married man was just as holy as his and that even as laymen they were both called to holiness. Even if one friend lived in a cave and the other lived as a family man, they both bore the penance of the cross, that marriage, as much as solitude, was a crucifixion. Emiliano had to agree that daily he was called to crucify his selfishness by placing the needs of Angela, little Francesco, and now Victoria before his own. Francesco smiled and suggested that Emiliano's penance was richer than that of hermits or ascetics because he couldn't take any pride in his renunciation of self, as it was part of the very fabric of married life.

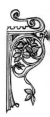

"Francesco, as beautifully as you speak about marriage," Emiliano said, "one would think *you* had a wife and family. You're certainly right about the cross of marriage, for I often find it painful not to demand that things be done my way. My father is always complaining that I give in too much to Angela's wishes and reminds me I should be the lord and master of my own house. He likes to repeat that for us Italians, the greatest of all fools—the butt of all jokes—is a henpecked husband. But, I'm not henpecked! Angela and I are doing our best to share in the work of rearing our children in the same way that we share our bed—in love."

"I'm proud of you, my friend," beamed Francesco. "Each of us, I believe, must embrace the cross of Christ in the way that enables it to enter our daily life—whether married or single, alone or in a family. Like you, I strive to live out the Gospels as best I can. Some time ago I heard Mass at Saint Mary of the Angels, and the priest preached on Saint Matthew's Gospel where Jesus called his disciples to go forth with nothing but the clothing on their backs—to practice complete poverty and to rely on nothing but the loving providence of God. Hearing that Gospel had a profound affect on me. I felt as if our Lord was speaking directly to me, calling me to live such a life of poverty. And now I'm really attempting to do that."

"Looking around this cave," Emiliano replied, surprised, "it looks to me like you've gotten off to a pretty good start! If this stark, Spartan living isn't poverty, what is? After what you did in Piazza Santa Maria Maggiore, other than that old, tattered tunic you're wearing, what do you own?"

"On that day I was really only seeking freedom from my father and his expectations of me, but now I feel a growing need to be naked of everything, a need to dedicate myself to live in the simplicity of poverty. But my path is different from yours, Emiliano. Together let us continue striving with all our hearts to live out the Gospels—me here in this cave and you as a merchant, father, husband, and lover."

"I will, I promise," Emiliano pledged. "But now, *caro mio*, I must be back on my way to Perugia. Thank you for again filling my heart with your fire." As they embraced in farewell, Francesco kissed him on the cheek, saying, "I love you, my friend."

Francesco accompanied Emiliano down to the road that led to Perugia. It was a symbolic walk, for the two friends had taken very different paths in life, yet they remained true friends. This meeting and

now parting in the forest of Mount Subasio was a watershed moment marking the point at which their youthful friendship became infallible, having withstood the test.

Seated at the head of the family table, Signore Fovorino Scifi observed Lady Ortholona Scifi as she corrected her daughter, "Agnes, dear, use only three fingers, not all of them—or use your spoon. Remember that you are a member of the aristocracy, and practice what you've been taught. Only common people use all their fingers to put food in their mouths."

"Agnes, maybe Father will buy you a fork," her older brother Roberto said, winking at her, "as well as one for each of the rest of us! Then we can dine as elegantly as Fiorenzo, son of Signore Pietro Baglioni of Perugia, with whom we stayed as guests during the civil unrest here in Assisi."

"Fiorenzo is not a man, not a real man," his father replied as he used three fingers in gracefully lifting a piece of meat onto his plate. "The way he used that effeminate fork of his, Fiorenzo Baglioni is more a dainty than a dandy. Imagine, actually eating with a little farmer's pitchfork—and a silver one at that! If wealthy ladies wish to flaunt their wealth by their silly use of forks, then let them do so. I only hope that my daughters will not fall victim to such foolishness. And as for you, my son, the use of forks is not manly!"

"Father, I was only jesting," replied Roberto, the eldest son, "simply jesting. I find a spoon and knife more than sufficient to help me eat."

"Indeed, Roberto," replied Signore Scifi. "Our holy priests even tell us that the use of forks offends our Blessed Lord, that they are sinful signs of excessive refinement. And these," he added as he held up his three fingers, "as the priests say, were given to us by Almighty God as being worthy to touch God's bounty."

The scene of this conversation was one of the most elegant dinning rooms in all of Assisi. As the Scifi family gathered for their midday dinner, pigeons cooed on the balcony ledge of their dinning room, whose double doors were opened wide to the warmth of the sunny piazza below. They dined on paparadelle, ribbons of meat-seasoned noodles with Parmesan cheese, which today was spiced by the extra seasoning of the latest gossip. At this noon meal the special garnish was provided by recent reports of the demented son of Assisi's leading wool merchant, Pietro Bernadone. Fourteen-year-old Clare Scifi, who daily was growing more beautiful, was more interested in the stories of the eccentric hermit than in her plate of paparadelle, even though at twenty-six Francesco was almost twice her age.

"They say he goes about barefoot along the countryside roads singing songs of God's love," said Roberto. "Can you imagine— barefoot! I mean with all the stinking horse and mule crap on the roads?"

"Signorino Roberto!" his mother Ortholona exclaimed in exasperation. "Have your tutors not given you and your brothers a fine education in Latin and the classics? You'll kindly use more appropriate language in the presence of your mother and sisters," she added, gracefully sweeping her hand in their direction. "Your sister is a Signorina, a noble lady, as are her younger sisters—they are not peasant barmaids! So please use more suitable expressions."

"Of course, Signora." Roberto said, bowing to her. "I apologize to you and to my sisters. I was only attempting to say that this crazy cloth merchant's son, who once had his head in the clouds, acting like some sort of troubadour-poet, now has his feet firmly on the earth—or rather in the muck. Surely he is mad; why else would he have actually gone to live with the lepers at Gubbio?

"Our mad Francesco," continued Roberto, "as I said, is now tromping about barefoot in the donkey-filth of the roads, talking to the peasants about God. Is all this not correct, Signore Scifi?" he asked, formally questioning his father, who was seated at the end of the table.

The noble patriarch of the Scifi house, Signore Fovorino Scifi, sat regally enthroned in a tall, ornately carved chair at the head of the family table. His finely tailored clothing enhanced his tall, slim figure and highlighted his aristocratic face, which resembled the classic form depicted on busts of Caesar.

"Roberto, it is not his feet that concern me!" Signore Scifi said placing his knife on his plate. "It's rather what he does with his mouth! Trouble is brewing here in Assisi if the reports about what he is saying are true. Our ancient social order is never endangered when people go to Mass and listen to the priest quote in Latin Saint Paul's words about 'the glorious freedom of the children of God.' However, when a barefoot vagabond dressed as one of the *minores*, the lowest of the classes, goes about in local village squares and along the highways talking to the peasants about that glorious freedom of the children of God—and does so in Italian . . ." he said, pausing briefly to scan the faces of the members of his family seated around the table, "then, there is serious cause for grave concern."

"But, Father," asked Clare innocently, "what harm can come from Francesco quoting the words of Jesus or his apostles from the Bible?"

"My beloved Signorina Clare," her father said with a smile that revealed his enormous affection for his beautiful young daughter, "nothing, of course, my dear, as long as those who hear such words spoken in the village squares pay no more attention to them than when they are spoken in church. But, my precious, the *minores*, the peasants, are many, and we, the *majores*, the nobility and the wealthy, are so few. Since the most ancient times, each class has known its proper place decreed to them at birth by our all-wise and blessed Lord. However, if the *minores* are encouraged to seek some new, glorious freedom, which implies living in a state other than the one they are presently in, well. . . ." Hunching his shoulders, he left his sentence unfinished as he raised his hands into the air in a gesture of complete helplessness.

"Clare," said Vita, her older brother in his late teens, "we live in troubling new times when the merchants are elbowing their way upward into our station in life. With their ever-increasing wealth they see themselves as *majores*. As for Francesco, it is beyond my comprehension why a son of a wealthy merchant, who could live in a better house than many nobles and enjoy good food and fine wine, would actually choose—freely choose, mind you—to become a poverty-infested peasant! He has to be insane!"

"Besides, Clare," his brother Roberto interrupted him, "surely you've noticed how at Mass these wealthy merchants' sons come dressed in more expensive clothing than even Vita or I. And that Pietro Bernadone took diabolic delight in dressing up his son in the richest

and most expensive of clothing tailored in the highest fashion, as if to shame. . . ."

"As I was saying before Roberto interrupted me," Vita broke in, "he must be mad, for he goes around with two old sticks pretending like a child that he's playing a lute. And the children, I hear, join around him in circles, dancing and singing as they would with any crazy man. Now, Robert, I've finished. If you want to say more, you can. . . ."

"Silence!" Signora Scifi said, tapping her knife on the edge of her plate, "I remind you that we are at table, and the two of you should treat each other with respect, in a manner befitting this fine meal."

"Father," Clare asked innocently, smiling at her father, fully aware she was his favorite, "are not the words of Holy Scripture always befitting to any meal or any situation? So with all deference and respect to you, Mother, may I ask why the glorious freedom of God would be such a terrible thing for the *minores*? Why can't they be free to do whatever they please? Also, if merchants are clever enough to use their God-given gifts to make money, why shouldn't they be able to live better lives? And, dear Father, I ask that you please be patient with me, but I have one more question. These new ways of which you spoke, why are they so dangerous?"

"My dearest Clare," Signore Scifi responded, "your father is no theologian who understands the complex implications of God's holy will and those words about the freedom of God's children. Perhaps someday we shall invite Monsignor Carafa or our good Bishop Guido to dine with us, and he can explain to you the passage from St. Paul and how it relates to our social order and to other religious issues. Scripture, my dear, was written a very long time ago, and maybe back in ancient days those words had an entirely different meaning. But I confess that your father doesn't know the answers. I do know, however—for I am a good Christian and a realistic man—that no one, not even the Lord Pope Innocent is free. We *majores* also have our restrictions; we are not free to do whatever we please. We have our feudal obligation to watch over the *minores*, a solemn duty to protect our servants and workers in our fields and vineyards from harm so that they can work and live in peace. Everyone . . ." he said, spreading his arms wide, "everyone, my dear, is bound to live out the obligations of their station in life. No one is free!" As he took a sip of his wine, her three brothers solemnly shook their heads in agreement. "Take the case of marriage, for example," he

continued after wiping his lips with his napkin. "Just imagine, Clare, the chaos in our world if young people like yourself and your sisters were able freely to choose who they would or would not marry?"

Clare did not reply but only glanced at her two younger sisters as she thought, "Why would it be so terrible if I had the freedom to choose whom I should love and marry?" Sensing the growing tension at the dinner table, Signora Scifi, with her usually graceful charm, introduced another subject that she felt was more suitable for the end of their meal as the servants entered the room to remove the dishes and bring in their dessert.

As those at table engaged in the after-dinner conversation, Clare withdrew deeply into her thoughts about Francesco. She remembered an evening when she was perhaps ten years old when he was playing his lute for a group of friends in Cathedral San Rufino Piazza. As she listened to him from behind closed shutters in her second-story room just above the piazza, a whole new world opened up for her. Peeking through the slats of her shutters, she could almost feel his magical powers that had attracted the group of young men of Assisi that had clustered around him. She loved it when Francesco sang romantic ballads in French—and especially when he daringly serenaded in Italian—for his voice was so pure and beautiful. Unlike other musicians of the day, his music blended the most recent styles with the old plainsong chant of church music to create a new, sweet harmony. To Clare, he was more gifted than any French troubadour she'd had ever heard. Her only regret had been that she couldn't be down in the piazza near him and instead had to listen from behind the closed shutters of her room.

Being at table, she suppressed her desire to smile as she recalled that warm afternoon when she and her mother had been guests at a friend's house that overlooked Santa Maria Maggiore Piazza. The events of that day were imbedded in every colorful detail in her memory as Francesco's proud father had marched him out to stand trial before the Lord Bishop Guido. Even now she could feel the shock that swept the crowd when he suddenly stripped off his clothing and stood naked before all of Assisi. Never before in her life had she seen a naked man. While it had taken place over two years ago, the vivid image of his beautiful naked body had not diminished in the least. She again saw him standing with his arms outstretched as if on a cross. Now that was glorious freedom! She cherished her memory of him being so free, so liberated, as he ran naked across the piazza through the crowd. Unlike the other women and girls who quickly turned their faces away, she had watched him until her mother dragged her away from the window. How wondrous it would be, she thought, if someday she could be as free as Francesco was on that afternoon.

As Clare began her dessert, she chewed more on her fate than the fruit and cheese she was eating. Being an unmarried daughter, she was imprisoned in her own home, protected by her brothers and the servants. "I'm not protected," she thought. "It's more like I'm guarded under lock and key, as if I were a common prisoner." She dreaded the approaching day when her parents would select the man she was to marry. Even more, she abhorred that fateful marriage day when her husband would become her new master, lord, and jailer. "Oh, yes," she thought, "I'll live in great luxury, wear expensive, beautiful clothing, and even become a mother, while married to some silly, effeminate, fork-using man like Fiorenzo Baglioni or to someone who is very rich and powerful, but. . . ."

"His poor father, Pietro . . . ," her father's powerful voice swept away her thoughts like a large broom, ". . . my heart goes out to him. A couple of days ago I visited the Bernadone shop to purchase some new cloth to be used by my tailor. I was shocked to see how he's aged. He looks ten years older. Alas, disgrace ages a man."

"And his poor mother, Pica," added Signora Scifi. "She now spends most of her time at church weeping. This terrible scandal has aged her as well; she's becoming as stooped over as an old widow."

Slowly moving his long, pointed index finger from one of his children to the next, Signore Scifi said, "My sons and daughters, never ever be the cause of such appalling shame for your dear mother as Francesco Bernadone has been to his poor parents." As inconspicuously as possible, Clare raised her right hand to her throat, as she was feeling suffocated by the frightening reality that she might well be a prisoner for the rest of her life.

*I*n the year of our Lord 1208, twenty-six-year-old Francesco sat outside his hermitage on a warm spring day watching two small birds busily building their nest. As they flew back and forth, carrying small twigs, he suddenly exclaimed with the glee of inspiration, "Thank you, Lord! You've answered my prayer! I don't need to collect alms to

repair your old, ruined chapel. Like these little birds I can go around Assisi picking up whatever is needed to rebuild your holy nest at San Damiano. You've showed me through these birds that I can do the work myself. And I won't even be violating any guild laws, for wasn't I made a member of Assisi's Guild of Stone Masons?"

Then, the two small birds presented him with a second gift: Watching how lovingly they labored together awakened his slumbering romantic idealism. "A knight," he thought, "dedicates his service to a noble Liege Lady, and troubadours likewise dedicate their songs and poetry to noble ladies. So, to what noble woman shall I pledge my service and dedicate myself?' That question sat in a corner of his mind waiting for an answer as he continued to watch the two birds lovingly build their home out of the poorest materials of old twigs and dry grasses. Then, leaping to his feet, he sang out, "I know, I shall pledge my love and service to my Liege Lady, Holy Poverty!" After a brief graceful dance, he dropped to one knee and raised his eyes toward the heavens, saying, "O God, my most holy Father, I humbly request permission to court your most beautiful and beloved daughter, Poverty, with whom I am madly in love. I aspire to serve her faithfully and honor her as my Liege Lady. I shall be her gallant knight defender and most humble servant."

Intoxicated with joy, he began wildly dancing, not with his feet, but with ideas. He took the hand of one idea and whirled it around before changing partners and dancing with another. He continued deftly changing partners in a fascinating dance of the impossible and unfeasible that somehow transformed into the possible and promising. However, his thought-dancing abruptly came to a stop as he wondered, "How can I truly court my Liege Lady Poverty unless I can give her a token of my love? Being the Noble Lady of Emptiness, she only loves poor gifts—and how can I become even poorer than I am now? What can I give to her as my love gift?"

His mind feverishly rummaged through the storage loft of his mind. "What do I still possess that I can give to woo my Lady?" A moment later his dark eyes glistened like polished ebony. "I still possess something of which I am most proud: my name Francesco Giovanni di Bernadone. That's something of great value! Yes, I shall give my name to my Liege Lady Poverty! I shall become just like Tommaso of Spello, who was known only as crazy Strapazzate the Beggar. Without a name of my own, perhaps they will call me Francesco the Beggar."

After doing some deeper rummaging through his soul's storehouse, he softly added, "I've a second gift to give, a far more costly one: my self-pride. It has prevented me from daring to venture back inside the gates of my beloved Assisi since that day I ran away naked through her gates. My pride has made me afraid of the shame of what people, especially my friends, would say, how they might call me Mad Francesco, the new Strapazzate of Assisi."

Then, drawing himself up to his full height, he slowly traced the sign of the cross upon himself and declared, "My Liege Lady Poverty, my beloved, I present to you these two gifts: my splendid, respected, and distinguished name, along with my self-important pride. Naked of both these ego garments and wearing only this old gray tunic and my desire to follow Christ, I shall depart from this hermitage and return to the streets of Assisi. God has opened my eyes to rebuild San Damiano in the way that birds build their nests, and so I shall gather up or beg for whatever building materials and stones I need. By becoming a beggar, one who is the most despicable of men, I, your humble servant, shall become more dear to you, my Liege Lady."

The old, dilapidated cart Francesco dragged behind him the very next day through the inclining, narrow, twisting streets of Assisi was dung-splattered and stank like an outhouse. With this discarded dung-collectors' cart he gathered up stray stones along with those he begged from laborers and householders and carried them down to San Damiano. He soon became a familiar figure wandering Assisi's streets and was quickly renamed Francesco the Beggar. He became a source of ridicule as he sang his beggar's song:

Stones for the Lord, large or small,

any unused, old leftover stones.

God will richly bless your gracious help

in rebuilding old San Damiano's nest.

Old timber beams or scraps of wood—

God will bless you for such helping gifts

as will the holy healer, San Damiano.

Each night before the closing of the city gates, Francesco would drag his stone-loaded dung cart down the hill to the old chapel where

he now slept and kept a prayer vigil. When he had gathered enough materials, he began what he called his sweat prayers, as he labored to restore the tumbled-down walls of the chapel. In the midst of his work, he recalled Padre Antonio talking about St. Benedict's motto, *ora et labora*, prayer and work. His new *labora* became his *ora*, and it was a most rewarding prayer, for as his hands grew more callused he could slowly see the results of his labor prayer. He was amused that his skill as a builder seemed to develop in proportion to the size of his calluses, and his only regret was that he wasn't able to lift the larger stones by himself.

While many in Assisi considered the barefoot man in the tattered gray peasant's tunic to be mad or possessed, as bees are drawn to flowers, many openhearted people were attracted to him. In time, volunteers came to help him, some simply in order to share in the joyous company, while others worked as an act of 'stone remorse,' a self-imposed penance for some past hidden sin. Piazza gossip in Assisi said that stone remorse explained why Bernardo of the wealthy di Quintavalle family had given away all his property to the poor and had joined Francesco to live in poverty in a thatched hut next to San Damiano. Tongues wagged and tasted the deliciously sweet honey of speculating about what weighty immoral sins might propel a wealthy young man to embrace such a drastic penance as barefoot poverty.

One summer afternoon as Francesco and Bernardo were dripping wet with sweat from their labor of lifting heavy stones, three men approached San Damiano. They stood at some distance from the chapel and began throwing stones at Francesco and Bernardo, shouting, "Sodomites, God has cursed you to the lowest levels of hell. Why are you polluting this holy chapel with your unnatural sins?"

"Peace, brothers," Francesco said with an upraised hand. "Why are you falsely accusing us of such shameful acts, and defaming our good work here?"

"We are not falsely accusing you," the tallest of the three shouted. "You're sodomites, two evil men living together in sin!"

"Good brothers," Francesco replied, "Brother Bernardo and I are no different from the monks of St. Benedict in the nearby monastery on Mount Subasio who pray and work alongside one another."

"Heretic! Liar!" one of them shouted. "Those monks have taken the holy vows of celibacy. Have you?"

"Who are you," asked Bernardo, "and why have you come here to defame us, when the work we're doing is for the glory of God?"

"You mean for the shame of God!" another shouted. "Unlike you, we are part of a holy cause. We are proud to be disciples of Padre Matteo Parini of Perugia, the defender of the papacy and the true faith. You, however, are agents of the devil. Know that we're collecting reports on you, how you go barefoot about the countryside, like those French heretics, preaching to the people about God. You are thieves, for you are mere laymen; you're stealing the duty that rightfully belongs only to priests. We've heard reports about how you've denounced priests and bishops for failing to live the Gospels faithfully, and even condemned the Pope for. . . ."

"We've never condemned anyone for how they follow the way of Christ," Francesco replied, "for our Lord said, 'Do not judge and you will not be judged.'"

"We're on our way to Perugia to report all these things about you sodomites to Padre Parini—yes, we're proud to be members of his holy fraternity. Unlike you, we're zealous to serve the Pope, to be watchmen of Christian morals and vigilant observers of the diabolic deeds of Jews and heretics."

After several failed attempts to reason with the three Parinians, Francesco turned his back on them, saying to Bernardo, "Evil has come to visit San Damiano, so let us beware but have nothing to do with these men. Arguing with such as these only feeds their hate and reinforces their beliefs—and arguing is not the way of peace. Brother, we are men of peace; so let us forget they are even here and return in silence to our work." Francesco turned and blessed the three Parinians, making the sign of the cross over them. Finding their taunts and accusations not acknowledged, the three men soon grew tired and departed.

As they disappeared into the olive groves, Francesco whispered a prayer, "Help me, Lord, for I didn't feel like blessing them; instead, I felt like heaping fire and brimstone on them. But you've said we're to bless our enemies, not fry them, and so with your boundless love, Lord, please supply whatever good may have been lacking in my blessing." As he helped Bernardo lift a heavy stone into place on the wall, he pondered, "There was a tangible presence of evil I could feel surrounding those men, and I pray it doesn't linger here. O Lord,

protect us from the venomous presence of such evil, for I fear it will surely visit again."

To the delight of both Francesco and Bernardo, they were soon joined by a third companion, a man named Giovanni. He was unlike them in that he was the uneducated son of nearby peasant farmer and from birth had been familiar with poverty. Giovanni was physically strong from having labored all his life and so was a great assistance in their construction work. Francesco found in Giovanni both a companion and a teacher, since the young farmer's son had a childlike simplicity and a natural humility. Daily Francesco was inspired to imitate him.

The novel activities happening at San Damiano, and the fact that the three men were living in adjacent huts, continued to stimulate gossip in Assisi, where each day was not only the same as yesterday, but an encore of yesteryear, if not "yestercentury." Soon the curious as well as the pious of Assisi and the surrounding towns came to see what was happening down at the old chapel. This age of transition was producing statues of the Mother of God that were said to weep, along with images of the holy saints whose eyes were purported to move. Such spiritual expressions attracted the piously hungry who were seeking some tangible affirmation of God's presence in the midst of their bleak and often suffering-filled lives. And San Damiano was no ordinary chapel, for not every church had a talking crucifix! Soon various reports of miracles and wondrous supernatural happenings at the old chapel spread across the countryside, fascinating those prisoners of the humdrum.

"Friends," Francesco announced to his two companions one day, "the reconstruction of San Damiano is completed! It has been a wonderful work, and I thank you for your help. Indeed, we have been graced by God's presence. Now that I've fulfilled my duty to the Lord Jesus, I think it's time for us to move on—and my hands are itching to. . . ."

"Mine as well," added Bernardo, "and I know just the place where we can heal that itch. Located a few miles down the valley is the little chapel of San Pietro della Sina. The local peasants call it 'Sagging San Pietro' since it is so in need of being restored to its original beauty and life."

While it was not exactly what Francesco had in mind, he joyfully agreed. So the three companions moved away from San Damiano to

San Pietro where they began rebuilding that small broken-down shrine. While there, sadly, a fourth joined their tiny community, Brother Death, who came to take away their new friend and companion, Giovanni. While the young farmer's son was strong of body, he became unexpectedly sick and died just two days later. His death was deeply painful for Francesco, for he loved this gentle companion, who in his uncomplicated, natural simplicity was such an inspiration. Brother Giovanni never had to struggle with spiritual disciplines to be humble and simple; he was already as naturally simple as any small child. Accompanied by many tears, Giovanni was buried next to the little chapel of San Pietro where they were now working.

Months later, just as they were finishing their repair of the San Pietro chapel, an invitation came from the Benedictine monks of the nearby abbey of Subasio to restore their small chapel dedicated to Mary of the Angels. To Francesco and Bernardo it seemed like a gift from God because at both San Damiano and San Pietro they had to deal with many visitors, which did not allow them the solitude they sought as hermits. So the first thing they did at this new site in the deep woods down below Assisi was to build two simple hermitages out of tree branches and grasses.

Saint Mary of the Angels, the chapel of Our Lady, was in great disrepair. Called the Portiuncula, "the little portion," it was an ancient chapel venerated because of apparitions of angels that had been reported there. Francesco was delighted that the chapel was dedicated to Mary the Mother of God, and the legend that angels had visited it only added to the mysterious beauty of this little chapel.

One day, in the midst of their work, a young man from Assisi named Pietro Catanii visited Francesco and Bernardo. He was a student at the university, and while at home during a break from his studies he had heard the stories about Francesco and Bernardo and their life of poverty. Upon meeting them and seeing their life and work at Portiuncula, he was instantly drawn to join them in their lifestyle of simplicity and prayer. Francesco warmly welcomed Pietro as their newest companion, which Bernardo found most curious, as Francesco was notorious in his distaste for books and higher education. While he never spoke openly of it, he believed that priests' higher education only allowed them to rationalize away the commands of the Gospel. However, Francesco, the eternal juggler of contrasts, considered the book-educated, intelligent, and logically minded Pietro a healthy and

charming compliment to his own spontaneous personality. Not long thereafter, the three companions were joined by a fourth, a young man named Giles. Like Giovanni had been, Giles was the son of a poor farming family and no stranger to poverty.

These early, unstructured days during which these four men lived, prayed, and worked together at Portiuncula were as enjoyable as a honeymoon. The order of the day perfectly fit Francesco's desire to live in the immediate moment, with each day holding a different mixture of time for physical work and time alone in prayer and solitude. And the day always ended with a warmly shared evening meal. It wasn't long before other men were attracted to Portiuncula and came asking to join them. They were drawn by the enchanting presence of Francesco, the simple and joy-filled community, and the opportunity to live a simple and free life. With the arrival of Leone, Rufino, Masseo, and Filippo, the companions now numbered eight.

"Our small group is beginning to grow," Bernardo observed one night as they sat together visiting after their evening meal.

"Yes, and it's a great joy for me," said Francesco, "to again share in the company of good friends."

Bernardo thought to himself, "My friend, Assisi's juggler of personal paradoxes, is a complex man. He balances being an introvert who enjoys and needs his times in solitude with the extrovert part of himself, the entertainer who thrives on the companionship of others."

"It's also a sign," Leone responded to Francesco's comment.

"A sign of what?" asked Rufino.

"That God's blessing," Leone replied, "is upon our little group, for the numbers of our brothers grow without Francesco recruiting new followers."

"Not followers, Brother Leone!" Francesco interjected quickly. "I never want followers or disciples—only friends and companions."

"Our small group does appear to be blessed by God," replied Pietro, "and since God acts with a purpose, should we not determine what work God has given us? And should we not consider forming a new monastic order?"

"I agree with Pietro," added Leone, "and I think our group should have a name."

"Why must we have a name?" answered Francesco, jumping quickly into the conversation like a fish leaping out of the water to catch a fly. "Why can't we just go on being what we are now? I speak

only for myself, but I'm simply trying to live the Gospel as I feel our Lord Jesus called his disciples to live it—without compromises and without fanfare! I do know that the Lord called me to repair his fallen-down chapel of San Damiano and to embrace the same poverty as his first disciples. So I've pledged to live without any possessions as a servant knight of my beloved Liege Lady Poverty." Then after falling silent as he looked from face to face, he added, "But, my friends, God said nothing to me about our little group, which has seemed to spring up on its own."

"I want to share this life you've been called to, Francesco," said Pietro. "Your joyful poverty and dependence upon the daily providence of God has transformed my life into a grand adventure."

Others in the group immediately echoed Catanii's desire to join Francesco in his life of poverty. He thanked them for their affirmation, saying that their companionship was a blessing and had confirmed for him that he wasn't mad. He was vehement, however, that they should not imitate him but Christ. He said that God was using him as bait, and encouraged them to swallow the entire hook rather than nibbling around the edges. Some of the brothers understood his talk of worms and hooks, but others didn't, and soon the discussion returned to how they should organize their life and their life's work.

"Brothers," Francesco said, "for me, living simply includes having a poverty of rules! Indeed, I believe God desires that we do more than repair old broken-down chapels, and I do feel that we are called to go forth preaching the Gospel." Recalling Padre Antonio's prophetic words, "*Parvulus eos ducebit,*" he added, "And we should preach it like little children using simple, sincere words."

"Like children?" asked a stunned Leone. "Who listens to children unless they are crying? Shouldn't we ask God to give us the great eloquence of famous preachers like St. Bernard, who stirred thousands to join the Crusades?"

"Rather, Leone," said Francesco, "let us strive to speak not just to ears, or even to heads, but to hearts. Let us pray for the gift of having tongues like birds so we can announce the glad tidings with the joyfulness of our sister larks—and, like them, never ask a penny for singing the praises of our Lord."

The discussion around the fire became like a soup pot, with each of the brothers adding his own ideas about what work he thought God wanted them to do. Francesco was amazed at how differently they all

saw the purpose of their tiny band. Yet he hid his astonishment, realizing how his dream of an unstructured life had created the openness for them to insert their own dreams into his dream. Then, an image of their little group being a boat without a rudder filled him with panic: He realized that the brother with the strongest oar could take their boat wherever he wanted it to go.

"As to the proposal that we become a new monastic order," he said with the authority of a helmsman, "I firmly believe that is not the course we should take! We are not monks or clerics; we're laymen—as were the first disciples of our Lord! And if our little band must have a name, I propose the Fraternity of Minores or the Brotherhood of the Little Ones. Just as beggars and prostitutes have their guilds, perhaps we could create our own and become the Assisi Guild of Holy Vagabonds of God."

"Vagabonds!" said Rufino. "They're nothing more than beggars. Are we to obtain our daily bread by begging?"

"Remember, Rufino," Francesco returned, "Jesus never told his disciples to beg for their daily bread—he said to pray for it. Like the *minores*, I believe we should survive by the sweat of our brows, laboring alongside the peasants in the fields to earn our food. We should never live on handouts and certainly should never accept anything from the poor, who have so little for themselves."

"But Francesco, didn't you yourself beg?" asked Rufino. "I heard that you once went about Assisi begging for stones."

"Rufino, man does not live on stones alone," Francesco said with a smile. "Those stones I begged were for rebuilding poor old San Damiano. While I never refused bread if someone voluntary offered some to me, I have never begged anything for myself. At the same time, being a beggar can teach many lessons. I learned how to be empty of myself; because I found it so humiliating to beg, it allowed more room in me for God. Begging also brings us into a holy communion with the unfortunate ones who have no choice but to beg: lepers, the lame, the blind, and the insane, all of whom are unable to work.

"So, my friends, with regard to Rufino's question, I don't believe we should beg for our livelihood; yet I firmly believe there will be many occasions for us to shrink our selves smaller in the eyes of others so as to make more room in us for our beloved Lord. Yet other than begging as part of the process of spiritual conversion, I propose that those who

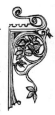

belong to Assisi's Guild of Holy Vagabonds should labor with their hands to obtain their food."

"But, Francesco," asked Masseo, "will we have our own rules and rituals, like the guilds, or should we take the vows of obedience, chastity, and poverty embraced by monks?" His question about taking religious vows sparked a lively exchange among the eight men about the value of vows, ending in a consensus that vows surely would be necessary.

"My friends," Francesco said, again grabbing the helm of their little boat, "your desire to take up the three religious vows is understandable. Since the days of St. Benedict that has been the spiritual path taken by those seeking holiness—but it's not mine! Brothers," he continued as he stood up and began pacing around the fire, "for me vows would be too confining, just as being seated limits one's movement. Understand that I am speaking only for myself, for Francesco, and not for any of you. And, indeed, for centuries many monks have become great saints by means of their vows. In fact, I personally know a living saint-monk who has embraced poverty, chastity, and obedience—my confessor, Padre Antonio. So if any one of you my brothers wishes to take those vows, you are free to join a monastery. I would hate to lose even one of you, but each man must follow the voice he hears—and you would have my blessing."

Several faces in the circle were now wearing expressions of sadness and loss. As Francesco surveyed the scene, his tone softened, and so did the others' facial expressions. "And yet, my brothers, perhaps we could find three . . . uh . . . promises, to guide us. Let's see, for myself, the first would have to be liberty. Yes, that would be a good pledge, for we must always be free to follow the Holy Wind, just as Jesus and his first disciples did. We can practice liberty by traveling without possessions or provisions for tomorrow so as to live in the glorious freedom of the children of God. Indeed, we'd be free as the wind, which our Lord said, 'blows whenever and wherever it wishes.' This liberty includes being free of all possessions, for, truly, we do not possess property—it possesses us!"

Giles was smiling like a little child. While he didn't understand much of what Francesco was saying, he was entertained by his flamboyant way of saying it as he strolled around the circle tugging at his beard.

"Equality!" exclaimed Francesco, his imagination flaring with a new idea that caused his hand to leave his beard and spring into the air. "That should be our second pledge! We can promise to live the same equality that marks our circle tonight—where no brother sits higher than another, whether we are as learned as Brother Pietro or as unlettered as Brother Giles. Among us there will be no Father Abbot or ruling prior who would be a master over the others. For did not our Blessed Lord call his friends to be humble servants to one another?"

Some of the brothers inwardly questioned how a group could ever exist without someone in command. Yet not one of them uttered an objection to Francesco's novel idea. They knew that, once inspired, the flow of this bubbling, creative fountain was not about to be plugged by any logical objection.

Francesco stopped his pacing and stood with his head titled back, thinking. Suddenly, he beamed with delight as he proceeded to announce their third oath: fraternity. He began almost dancing around the fire, and his voice took on a lyrical quality as he spoke with great enthusiasm about their third pledge. He went on about how they would love one another with the greatest affection, with more love than that which binds blood brothers. Flinging his arms out wide, he began whirling around as he talked about living as brothers to all men and women, children and to all of God's family. Their pledge of fraternity would call them to show great respect, and even reverence, to one another. This respect, he said, also would extend to bishops, priests, and monks—which surprised some in the group, who didn't find the clergy worthy of respect because of their lax morality—as well as to peasants, beggars, lepers, prostitutes, and Jews.

Bernardo swallowed hard as he thought, "Jews! And prostitutes? That will call down upon us a plague of Parinians eager to denounce us for being immoral heretics." Many of the other brothers had a similar difficulty accepting the idea of showing loving respect to the "Christ killers."

"In holy fraternity," Francesco continued, "we would behave like brothers to the entire family of God, treating with loving respect all our brothers and sisters: foxes and wolves, fishes and birds, pine trees and sunflowers." Then, throwing his head back as he gazed upward into the night sky, he continued his litany, ". . . and living in harmony with Sister Moon and her big brood of sparkling stars and with Brother Sun,

who has gone to sleep on the other side of the mountain." Dropping his arms to his sides, he poured out a loud stream of laughter, saturating the night with his great joy.

The brothers looked up at the stars, whose position in the night sky confirmed what their bodies were already telling them: that it was time to go to bed. As Francesco fell silent, one by one they edged away from the last glowing embers of the fire and went off to their individual huts. Brother Giles fell asleep amidst a cloud of confusion, for he hadn't understood much of what his good friend Francesco had said—or, for that matter, all the others' talk about monastic orders and vows. As he fell asleep, there was one thing about which he was not confused, and that was his great love for Francesco. He knew that he would follow him anywhere, yes, even to the gates of hell.

Pietro found falling sleep difficult because he had been mightily inflamed by Francesco's vision. Yet, by what strange logic, he wondered, would he be able to give the same measure of reverence to inanimate things like trees and stars as he held toward human brotherhood? He had never heard of any philosopher of ancient Greece or Rome who had proposed anything like it. Then he realized that Francesco was no philosopher but a poet! "If everything he was saying to us tonight was only poetry, then what harm is there in it?" Still, he tossed and turned as if a large rock shared his bed with him, for he couldn't reconcile the pledge of fraternity if it required them to show "loving respect" to Jews. "How can I honor those greedy, scheming Christ killers? That wasn't poetry! But perhaps Francesco was only carried away by his enthusiasm. Yet, as for the permission he extended for us to leave, how could I ever leave him? The man is inspired! That's the only reason I didn't return to the university but chose to became his companion. So with or without vows, with or without a name for our little group, I want to stay by his side as long as I live."

Pietro was not the only brother who did not sleep alone that night. Others tossed and turned with troubling questions.

Unseen by the others, Francesco continued walking past his hermitage and slipped away into the darkness of the night-cloaked forest. After the evening's discussion, he felt a particular longing for the solitude and peacefulness of the forest, to rest in its bands of pale-white moonlight that interlaced the blue-black shadows of the tall pines. The dark and light stripes of the forest reminded him

of the famous Cathedral of Orvieto, whose walls had alternating striped bands of white and dark marble. He felt the urge to genuflect, as if he were entering a church more beautiful than any cathedral. Coming upon a gnarled rock protruding from the earth, he knelt, placed his elbows on the rock and began to pray:

My Liege Lord, I need to go to confession.

Bless me, Father, for I have sinned this night.

I have caused great confusion in my brothers,

calling them, I fear, to a life that is beyond them.

I felt possessed—like the words were not mine.

Those strange ideas were flowing through me

as water goes down a ditch and out a pipe.

From where, O God, did those words spring?

What was the hidden source of those notions

that were dramatically new even to me?

Someone, something, took hold of me—

as one takes up a lute—and played on me

the song of those three radically new pledges.

Without thought did those wild new words

spring off my tongue like fiery sparks.

I was possessed—but by whom or what?

Was it your Holy Spirit or an evil spirit

who had me say that we must respect Jews—

stubborn unbelieving Jews, your enemies—

the Jews who crucified you on your cross?

O Lord, please forgive my seeming sin of treason.

For, like Judas, I feel guilty of betraying you

by asking the brothers to vow to love even Jews,

your enemies who shamed and crucified you.

O Lord, come to my assistance, I humbly pray:

Quickly resolve my disturbing doubts and tell me

from what source these disturbing ideas came.

He cocked his head to listen for a heavenly response but heard only the soft voices of the wind gently moving through the tall pines. He stood up and traced upon himself the sign of the cross. As he began walking deeper into the forest, his mood shifted. "How free—how gloriously free, I feel," he said aloud, "in this my Umbrian forest cathedral. Alas, it is more beautiful than the great churches of Orvieto, Florence, or even Rome. This timbered cathedral has pine pillars more graceful and elegant than any marble Grecian or Roman columns. Brother Trees, I feel your throbbing hearts stretching out limb and bark to touch the starry heavens." Then he knelt and kissed the earth, saying, "And sacred to my feet are you, my Sisters Grass and Moss, for you are the emerald marble floors of this divine cathedral."

Still kneeling, he raised up to his full stature, looking left and right. "If all the creatures I see are my living brothers and sisters, holy children of God, then the Church . . ." he paused, swallowing deeply, before repeating, "then the Church must be more than buildings! It must be greater than all her members and must also be. . . ." Jumping to his feet, he began running as one pursued by demons, terrified by some invisible evil he felt lurking in the dark shadows. As he ran through the striped bands of darkness and light, it felt as if something sinister in the darkness was reaching out, attempting to grab a hold of him. Sobbing so that his entire body shook, he began screaming, "Pagan! Everything I've been saying and praying is pagan, pagan, pagan!" Upon reaching the circle of huts, he hurried inside his hermitage. Panting, he now felt without a doubt that he must be possessed by a devil, for it seemed that all he had prayed and thought was pantheistic. Francesco did not sleep that night, but spent the remaining hours until dawn staring up at the hut's dark ceiling, longing for God to speak to him. Yet he heard no voice.

The Brothers *Minores*, or as Francesco enjoyed calling them, "the Brothers of No-Importance," or "the Insignificant Sons of God," had now grown by four, raising their number to twelve. They traveled as a troop, going about the countryside around Assisi preaching to any who would listen to them about God's great love. Sometimes Francesco would sing a song he had composed or tell stories from the Bible, enlivening them with his own colorful enhancements, or he might quote some of the sayings of Jesus. Whatever he said was spoken with great enthusiasm, and even greater joy, and after the band of twelve departed from a village, the people would comment on how the joyful spirit of the brothers would linger with them for days like an echo. No

priest or monk had ever spoken to the people about God with such joy. It was, indeed, a blessed relief from their usual sermon-diet about a wrathful God who sent crippling illness or blindness as punishment for sins, a diet that consisted of frightening tales about the tortures of hell, which was the inescapable fate of sinners. The villagers and field peasants would discuss for days the puzzle the brothers unintentionally left behind: How were these men able to be so joyous and filled with merriment when they lived in a poverty even greater than the pitiable lives of those to whom they preached?

All across Umbria stories leaped from village to village about the joyful poor man Francesco and his small band of barefoot brothers. Yet not everyone rejoiced. At the secret gatherings of the Fraternity of the Disciples of Padre Matteo Parini, the barefoot heretics of Assisi became the main subject of discussion. The Parinians began spreading dire warnings among the people about the evil of Francesco's heresies, and they shared lurid tales of the reported immoralities that pervaded the small group. In defaming Francesco, they found many allies among the village parish priests, who were envious of his popularity with their parishioners. They complained to their bishops about him preaching, a privilege that belonged only to them by right of their ordination, and they demanded that he be silenced. The local clergy joined with the Parinians in using every opportunity to frighten the people with exaggerated tales that compared Assisi's barefoot preaching layman to the condemned and damned heretic Peter Waldo of Lyon.

 hapter 10

NORTH OF THE HOLY CITY, THE AFTERNOON SKY WAS blooming with a summer storm, Rome was very warm and deadly still. White-capped grayish-black clouds tumbled atop one another, forming giant billowing florets of dark thunderheads. Cardinal Lorenzo Montino was standing at a floor-to-ceiling open window watching the magnificent display of the massive storm clouds when his secretary entered the room to announce the arrival of a visitor. Montino thanked him and returned to his desk. Even seated, Montino was an impressive figure. Tall of stature, bearing the classically handsome face of his noble Roman family, he had about him a quiet elegance and sense of authority. His dark eyes glistened with the sparkle of a keen intelligence, even if he found asking questions easier than engaging in discussions with people. He sat with his elbows on the desktop and his hands folded together in a pyramid shape that met in front of his chin, ready to receive his visitor.

"Your Eminence, Monsignor Cappellari," his secretary said as he ushered in a purple-robed cleric from the Roman curia—the court of the Pope.

"It seems, Your Eminence," Cappellari began the visit, "that Rome is about to be visited by a storm."

Cardinal Montino nodded graciously as he gazed over the top of the fleshy pyramid of his hands and said, "Yes, Monsignor, it does indeed. Just as Rome has been visited by them before, and surely will be again."

"Your Eminence," the purple-cassocked official of the Vatican responded with a wave of his hand toward the opened window, "I was

referring to that thunderstorm coming from the north. It holds the promise of much needed rain and cooler weather."

"Naturally, Monsignor Cappellari," Cardinal Montino responded with a faint smile. "To what other storm might I have been referring?"

"Perhaps the one that's presently brewing north of Rome up in the hills of Umbria," answered the curia secretary as he untied the red tape that secured a brown file. Removing several pages of parchment, he added, "Your Eminence, I trust, has read the copy of this report on Assisi sent to you from the Holy Office, and so are familiar with the charges. Naturally, Cardinal Uzielli of the Holy Office is gravely concerned about its contents and feels it is expedient that we act on this distressing situation as soon as possible."

Seated behind his large desk in a tall-backed, ornately carved chair, Cardinal Montino allowed his face slowly to form the thinnest line of a smile, whose life span was but a few seconds, as he asked, "Soon?"

"Yes, His Eminence Cardinal Uzielli emphasized the word *soon*."

"Monsignor, I was unaware that Rome ever responded quickly to anything. This being the Eternal City, we have, how shall I say it, an eternity in which to act."

The purple-robed bureaucrat adjusted his body ever so slightly in the chair, but other than that he gave no indication of any distress he might have felt at the pinprick of anger caused by this clerical game of cat and mouse. He placed the parchment pages of the report back inside his folder, for years of training in "the Roman way" had taught him the diplomacy of avoiding direct confrontation. His calm reaction said to Montino that he was prepared for the cardinal's response. He raised his hand, waving it in the air, as if directing a choir, as he said, "How true, how truly spoken, Your Eminence. That may indeed be the case with this Umbrian issue; however, I have come primarily on another errand. My superior, His Eminence Cardinal Pietro Uzielli, has requested that I extend to you an invitation to be his dinner guest tomorrow evening at his palace. I am to inform you that the cardinal has also invited his, and your, mutual friend, the learned prelate, Cardinal Ugolino di Segni."

Cardinal Montino responded with his classic thin smile as he stood up to signal that the visit had ended. "Monsignor Cappellari, please be so gracious as to express my gratitude to His Eminence for his most cordial invitation. Cardinal Uzielli is famed throughout the Holy City for his excellent wine cellar, his ever-inventive chef, and the beautiful

fountains that grace the gardens of his estate. Tell His Grace that I shall be honored to accept his invitation to attend the meeting . . . uh, excuse me . . . his dinner."

*T*he dinner gathering hosted by Cardinal Pietro Uzielli was typically superb, with a wide variety of rich foods and exceptional wines all presented with impeccable service. Seated at the head of the table, Cardinal Uzielli was not a physically imposing man, his body being of medium height and weight. What set him apart from others was how in his fifty-some years he had cultivated the face of a stern, uncompromising judge. His sharp, fox-like eyes seemed to look at you as if through the narrow visor of a warrior knight's helmet.

After his servants had cleared away the dinner dishes and the three cardinals were alone in the massive dinning room, Uzielli said, "You both have received a copy of a report sent to the Holy Office by a certain Monsignor Paulo Carafa, chancellor of the Umbrian diocese of Assisi." Lorenzo and Ugolino nodded their heads in acknowledgment as he continued, "This Monsignor Carafa shows great promise, and his detailed report sent to our office is most professional and comprehensive. Holy Mother Church is most blessed and fortunate to have such informants . . . er . . . dedicated servants as Carafa, as well as the pious fraternities of Padre Matteo Parini. They are steadfastly loyal to His Holiness Pope Innocent III in their vigilant ardor to expose heretics and all who threaten the stability of our Church and society in these troubling new times."

Cardinal Ugolino di Segni, who was seated to the left of Uzielli, was a nephew of Pope Innocent III, and as a cardinal prince of the Church had a potentially promising career ahead of him. He was portly of body from birth, with a round, pleasing face accented by a high forehead edged with receding black hair. While he was a nephew of the Pope, his elevation to the cardinalate was based on more than just his family connections, for he had a clever and keen intelligence as well as a natural, almost maternal kindness. As he sipped his wine, he pondered Uzielli's statement that these were troubling times. In response, he thought to himself, "My dear Pietro, troubling is hardly the word I would use to describe these times. Indeed, in the first years of this new century the Church is faced with enormous problems. Muslims still control the Holy City of Jerusalem and Islamic influences are quickly spreading northward from Spain into France and all of

Europe. Arabic numbers are even replacing the ancient Roman numerals because they are more efficient in business transactions. The Fourth Crusade was an utter debacle: Upon capturing Orthodox Christian Constantinople, the crusaders torched and destroyed it in a bloodbath of carnage and looting too horrible even to imagine."

"Whenever we present reports to him, as both of you are aware," Cardinal Uzielli continued, "His Holiness prefers that we include our personal recommendations. Pope Innocent is a most capable pontiff, yet, naturally, it is impossible for him to be fully informed on every subject and situation in the Church." For emphasis, Uzielli raised his hands, palms upward, in the classic Italian gesture of impossibility. "Since as prefect of the Holy Office I will be the one to present this difficult Assisi situation to His Holiness, I thought that perhaps you two could offer some recommendations. How are we to deal with the budding problem of this heretical prophet from Assisi named Giovanni di Francesco Bernadone."

"Prophet?" replied Montino, raising his eyebrows. "As I read that chancellor's report, I don't recall anything about prophesying. Perhaps I missed something?"

"Cardinal Montino," Uzielli replied in a voice edged with annoyance, "I was not referring to the kind of prophet who predicts the end of the world or the second coming but to the far more dangerous Old Testament kind of prophet! Monsignor Carafa gives us graphic details about the radical brand of poverty practiced by this man and his small band of disciples. While they have never taken the monastic vow of poverty, they've given away everything they own and voluntarily live in the direst of poverty. They've even gone so far to go about barefoot!"

"I did read that, Cardinal Uzielli," replied Montino with his famous thin smile, "but, pray tell, what is so dangerously prophetic about someone actually living out the words of Jesus spoken in the Gospels?"

"You know as well as I," snapped Uzielli, "that without having to preach a single word of condemnation, his living out of such radical poverty is shouting out a prophetic accusation against Holy Mother Church!" Extending his hands toward both his guests, he said, "Isn't he condemning each one of us—all the cardinals and bishops who fail to live in poverty while he goes about barefoot eating the daily diet of peasants? This time, I fear we're dealing with the cleverest of heretics, for although he's shrewdly instructed his disciples never to condemn any cleric, priest, or bishop, he challenges everything we stand for. By his living out of a total poverty and identifying himself with the *minores*—the rabble—he throws down a Gospel gauntlet at the feet of the Church."

"Gospel gauntlet?" asked Ugolino.

"My friends, please forgive me," Uzielli said as he rang a small silver bell. "Before I respond to your question, Cardinal di Segni, a thousand pardons for my negligence as your host. My mind was caught like a rabbit in the snare of this nasty problem of heresy in Assisi, and I apologize to you that I've forgotten. . . ." His voice trailed off as he rang the silver bell a second time.

As the sound of the bell's tinkling faded, a door silently opened, and a strikingly handsome young attendant entered the dining room. The servant's bronze face was crowned by shiny black ringlets of hair, and he was dressed in the fashionably tight clothing style of the day that defined the contours of his broad chest and muscular body. The colors of his leg stockings and his tunic were the royal purple and gold of the House of Uzielli, and the combination of hues enhanced his sparkling eyes.

"Your Eminence rang?" he said with a deep bow.

Without looking at him, Uzielli made a wide sweep with his left hand, indicating their empty wine glasses and said, "Sebastiano, go to the wine cellar and bring up a bottle of our aged Verdicchio dei Castelli di Jesu Montepulciano."

The servant bowed deeply. "At once, Your Eminence," he replied, withdrawing gracefully backwards out of the dining room.

"Where were we—ah, yes," said Uzielli. "Don't you see, Ugolino? The vast multitudes of the people are poorer than dirt, and their entire lives are spent in dismal poverty, misery, and great unhappiness. Yet is this not the will of God for them? By hard labor and the devout practice of their faith, however, they can find acceptance of their station in this life and rest in the next life. Now, into this divinely decreed order, into this world where, by original sin, man has been exiled to live in this valley of tears, suffering, and misery—painfully laboring to scratch a living out of the earth—comes this Francesco of Assisi. No ordinary preacher, he's barefoot, dressed in rags, and living in a poverty that is more profound than that of the poorest of peasants, and yet he is joyously happy—as happy as if he owned all the gold in the world!"

"Perhaps he's just empty-headed and simpleminded," replied Ugolino, gazing down into his empty wine glass. "Don't such people always seem to be happy? Yet I fail to see, Uzielli, how this Francesco of Assisi has thrown down this—what did you call it—*Gospel gauntlet*?"

"The gauntlet that he hurls in the face of the Church, dear Ugolino, is the beatitudes! 'Blessed are the poor, for they shall inherit the earth,' and the word *blessed* means to be *happy*! If the word of God is infallible, then the poor of the earth are fortunate, are blessed with happiness! If that is true, then why aren't all the monks and nuns who have taken the holy vow of poverty as deliriously joyous as he is? If being poor means being blessed by God, then why aren't the three of us and, indeed, the entire Church poor?"

"Good question," Montino thought to himself as he looked at the cardinal's lavish silver tableware, at the delicate, expensive wine glasses, the white linen tablecloth, and all the other luxuries of his extravagantly elegant dining room.

"Don't I recall, Pietro," said Ugolino, "that somewhere in the chancellor of Assisi's report it said this Francesco Bernadone admonished his small band of followers to show great respect to all priests and bishops, regardless of the morality of their personal lives? It said that he encourages the people to show the same respect. So it doesn't seem he's trying to turn the people against the Church."

Uzielli looked stoically at Ugolino, his eyes narrowing into slits, inwardly wincing at the awareness that his well-laid plans for this evening were being upset. It was becoming clear that these two cardinals were not going to be easily convinced to support his recommendation that the Pope order this Francesco of Assisi to Rome to stand trial for heresy. Like a sly fox he quickly maneuvered. "Recall that only thirty years ago," he said as he launched an attack from a more strategic and defensible position, "another merchant, Peter Waldo of Lyons, also claimed that God spoke to him. Like this merchant's son from Assisi, he too was a barefoot preacher who went about calling the ordinary people to live out the Gospels. He encouraged them to embrace the same poverty our Lord's first disciples practiced as they shared all their possessions in common. Because he was not a priest, he was forbidden to preach by the Third Lateran Council of 1179, but he and his followers ignored Rome and continued their so-called mission of preaching. Finally, he had to be excommunicated by the Council of Verona in 1184, but by that time it was too late to stop the spread of

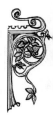

the disease of his heresy well beyond the borders of France!" A gentle rap at the door halted the cardinal's history lecture, and he answered, "Come."

His servant Sebastiano entered, carrying a silver tray that held a bottle of wine with dust still on it, indicating its age, as well as a bottle opener and three fine Venetian wine glasses. He placed a clean glass at each of the cardinals' places, and after gracefully uncorking the bottle he poured a small amount of wine into Uzielli's goblet and stepped back. As their host presiding over the elegant court ritual that would assure his guests the wine they were about to drink was not poisoned, Uzielli sniffed the aroma of the wine and then drank the small amount in his glass. "Ah, fit for the lips of the Pope!" he exclaimed, smiling, and then flipping his left hand toward the empty glasses of his guests. With courtly bearing Sebastiano gracefully moved from one to the other, filling each of the three crystal goblets with the pale white wine. Then, placing the opened bottle close to Uzielli, he bowed deeply and withdrew from the room, silently closing the door behind him.

"As I was saying," said Uzielli, eagerly resuming his history lesson now that they were alone again, "by the time the Church finally excommunicated Waldo it was too late. His French heresy-plague was already infecting Bohemia, Poland, and even Italy. If only Rome had not moved sluggishly with feet of lead!" Uzielli paused and lifted his wine glass, announcing, "A toast to our good Pope Innocent III: *Ad multos annos*, many long years and good health to him!"

After the three drank the customary toast to the Pope, before Uzielli could begin again, Ugolino took up the story. "Yes, as we know, his heresy spread from Lyons to the south of France, where it fused with the ancient third century heresy of the Manicheans. I find it amazing how heresies seem to possess the power of reincarnation. They can be snuffed out by the Church but reappear again centuries later, often blending with new ideas. Such, indeed, was the case with the ideas of Peter Waldo. These new French heretics denounced the Church, her sacraments, and the priesthood, and they resurrected the old Manichean teachings that the flesh and matter are sinful. They condemned the eating of flesh meat and the drinking of wine, besides declaring that all sexual desires, and even marriage, are from the devil. They now call themselves Albigensians or Cathars, the Pure Ones."

"And we are aware that on this past January 12," added Montino, "on the feast of Epiphany, the papal legate Pierre de Castelnau, whom Innocent III had sent to resolve the conflict, was. . . ."

"Murdered!" Uzielli forcefully interrupted, again seizing the subject like it was the tail of a serpent that he enjoyed swinging back and forth in front of his colleagues. "How despicably unthinkable to murder the Pope's legate! It is tantamount to an attempt upon the very life of the pontiff! This traitorous act was led by Count Raymond and those villainous French nobles who are secretly members of the heretical sect. The Pope had mounted a new crusade to cauterize the wound that daily poisons most of southern France with the pus and rot of the devil. My brother cardinals, if only Rome had acted to eliminate Peter Waldo the very moment that the Vatican smelled the stench of his heretical disease, then we would not be dealing with this devilish band of Albigensians today. That is why, Cardinal Montino, regardless of your personal feelings about this dangerous situation in Assisi, it is absolutely imperative that we act at once to silence . . ." pausing for brief moment, he let out a deep sigh before concluding his verdict, "to silence once and for all this dangerous Francesco Bernadone, our barefoot Italian Umbrian version of Peter Waldo."

Ugolino stood up with his glass of fine wine and walked across the room to look out through the window-doors that opened to the vista of the cardinal's carefully manicured green gardens. Bordered by rows of tall, slender pine trees, his elegantly groomed garden had geometrically patterned walkways of blond gravel that framed emerald-green grass islands containing arrangements of flowering fruit trees, trimmed shrubs, and marble fountains. He continued looking out into the twilight-tinged gardens as he addressed the other two men, "Yes, we must do something. The question is: How do we know the most prudent course? Pietro, may I ask: In your report from Assisi what did the bishop of that city say. . . ah . . . what is his name?" He paused in a moment of forgetfulness, tilting his head back as if the bishop's name would roll down onto his tongue from some remote corner of his mind.

"Guido," supplied Uzielli.

"Ah, yes, Bishop Guido," Ugolino said as he turned around and walked back to the table, "a saintly bishop, at least so I'm told." Then smiling as he seated himself again, he continued, "Rare today in the Church, and refreshing. Now, in order that we might present a truly prudent suggestion to the Pope—along with what the chancellor

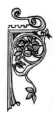

said—it would be helpful to know the thoughts of Bishop Guido on this barefoot preacher in his diocese."

"I agree, Ugolino," Montino quickly added. "As the bishop of that city, his opinions are most significant. I'm curious, Pietro: What kind of report did Bishop Guido send on this Francesco of Assisi?"

Uzielli leaned back in his chair, sipping his wine. "The bishop has not, as yet, sent us a report. I understand that he is elderly, and so. . . . I have not yet requested a report from the bishop because Monsignor Carafa's report was technically just in the form of a warning. However, his was not the only admonition. The Holy Office has also received numerous complaints from Padre Matteo Parini and the members of his various fraternities in Umbria. Now. . . ."

"Your Eminence," Montino interrupted him, wearing his famous thin line of a smile, "surely we're not rushing out to gather faggots to build a fire to burn this Francesco as a heretic based only on the accusations of a minor official from a small diocese in Umbria? And as for those dispatches from the Wolf of Perugia. . . ."

"Wolf? Are you referring to the pious Padre Matteo Parini with such a disparaging term?" asked a stunned Uzielli.

"I'm referring to that ravaging, sadistic black wolf," he flung his response back at Uzielli with surprising emotion. "And I'd think Rome should be more worried about his heresy. . . ." Then, as quickly as one blows out a candle, Montino resumed his usual serene composure. "I feel confident that my esteemed colleague Cardinal Ugolino di Segni will agree with me that our next step is to send an inquisitor to Assisi who can gather information first from the lord bishop of Assisi and then from the abbot of the nearby Benedictine abbey, from other clergy, as well as from the people."

Laying aside his napkin, Ugolino stood up from his chair and said, "I affirm your wise suggestion, Cardinal Montino. It would be prudent for us to know the thoughts of Bishop Guido concerning these accusations before initiating any charges of suspected heresy. Thank you, Cardinal Uzielli, for your marvelous dinner and your zealous concern for Holy Mother Church. In these, as you said, 'troubling times,' we cannot be too vigilant. I regret that the hour is growing very late, and Montino and I must be on our way home. As we all know, the streets of the Rome are most dangerous late at night."

Uzielli retired to his bedchamber in a foul mood. While he removed his fine scarlet robes, he found it impossible to take off the pricking under-tunic of defeat in which he felt he had been invested by his two brother cardinals. As a powerful, high-ranking prelate of the Vatican, it was a most unusual experience for him. More painful than any hair shirt was not having his every wish and desire instantly obeyed. "Damn them for their clever maneuvering," he thought as he rested his head on the silk pillows. "With all their talk of prudence, they are delaying, if not jeopardizing, my carefully constructed case of heresy." Uzielli's irritation over this Assisi case was connected to something far more important than the simple heresy trial of some barefoot nobody. For by means of this case he was hoping to maneuver himself into the role of Champion of the Orthodoxy, one who would be eminently well suited for the highest office in the Church, the papacy. "In the end, however, I will win," he mused. "Then the Pope will acknowledge my vigilance in protecting the purity of God's Holy Church, and that in turn will elevate my stature among the other cardinals."

Unseen by Uzielli at that moment, a hairline crack silently began to appear in the velvet-brocaded fabric wall-covering beside the cardinal's great ornate bed. The crack slowly grew larger until, with only the slightest creaking sound, a tall section of wall swung open revealing a hidden passageway.

"Ah, Sebastiano," Uzielli said softly in a voice sweet as honey.

*A*ntonio could not make out the identity of the dark silhouetted figure standing at the entrance of his cave, and so he asked, "Who's there?"

"Padre, it's Francesco. I'm not disturbing you at prayer, am I?"

"No, Giovanni Francesco, please come in, come in. It will be easier for you to come to me than for me to come to you," he chuckled. "It seems, my friend, that my sinful past is catching up with me. Forgive me for not recognizing you, but the light was behind you and my eyesight is fading rapidly. It seems to grow worse daily. But, now, tell me, what brings you to visit this old hermit?"

"I'm badly in need of some of your wise counsel," he said, sitting beside the straw pallet of his old friend.

"Wise counsel? Giovanni, if wisdom comes with age, it does so at a cost," he said, holding up a gnarled hand. "If I have any wisdom, I'm paying for it with the curse of the crippling of my hands and the

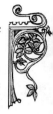

stiffening of my knee joints. Now, please give me your arm and help me walk outside to sit in the fresh air."

After they were seated outside under his porch arbor of branches, Francesco wept as he poured out his grief at the recent death of his mother. His friend Emiliano had come to Portiuncula to tell him that, stricken with the pestilence, she had died within hours and was quickly buried. "How I wish, Padre, that I could have seen her before she died so I could have attempted to explain my act of renunciation."

"It's hard not knowing if she ever approved or even understood," Antonio reflected back to him. "Being aware of a mother's loving acceptance, regardless of what we may have done, is a great blessing. It's not a gift we easily receive, even when we leave all things to follow Christ. Once again, Giovanni, God seems to be asking even greater poverty from you."

Francesco agreed and sat silently for a moment. Then he related how Emiliano told him that his father had been so shamed before all Assisi on that day when Francesco stripped himself naked that he had his only son declared insane and banished him from his family as if he was a leper, one of the living dead. Then when Francesco returned to Assisi as a grubby beggar dragging an old dung cart collecting stones, people said Pietro was shamed to his very bones. He publicly announced that his son had died and would take his customers outside the shop and point to a pile of stones, telling them it marked the grave of Giovanni Francesco.

"A grave?" asked Antonio.

"Yes," Francesco answered, "Emiliano told me that our neighbors saw my father take my beloved lute outside the shop and stomp it into pieces. Then they watched him dig up some cobblestones, throw the shattered pieces of my lute into a shallow hole and then pile stones on top of the site. As stories of my begging for stones from his merchant friends grew, so, it seems, did his shame—and it consumed him like leprosy. He even spoke of leaving Assisi and moving to Rome or Naples where no one would know that he was the father of Mad Francesco of Assisi. But Emiliano said that my father simply socially moved away from others, going deeper inside himself until he became a living ghost of the once proud, robust Pietro Bernadone."

Francesco's last words were swept away in a great flood of tears, as he began crying uncontrollably. Antonio neither did nor said anything in response, understanding that Francesco's great sorrow could cleanse

his guilt for bringing such pain and shame into the lives of his parents, whom he so loved. As Francesco sobbed, holding his head in his hands, Antonio reflected on the enormous price this young man was paying to live out his conviction that God had called him to holiness. "Francesco's price has been all the higher," he thought, "because it is a sanctity no sane person could embrace—one might call it a sacred insanity. To follow Christ by giving away his prized clothing, his expensive lute, and his heritage of wealth has been insignificant compared to the final surrender of his most precious gift: the love of those he had loved and who once had loved him. Besides bearing the colossal cost of living out his convictions, he is now overwhelmed by the staggering price paid by his parents, particularly the loss of their honor—which is so important to us Italians—as well as their reputation and status in their community, and even their very will to live! What person of sane mind—if he or she knew the entire cost—would desire to be so possessed by God?"

"Emiliano had even more bad news," Francesco finally said, wiping his face with the sleeve of his tunic. "He told me about the growing frenzy in Assisi around the devil and the persecution of those thought to be possessed. He related the story of how the old healer Gaspara Frezzi had been burned alive as a witch. One night while she was sleeping in her little hut down below Assisi in the olive groves, someone came and boarded up the windows and doors and then set the hut ablaze. The next morning a field worker found the smoking ashes. From a branch on a nearby scorched olive tree there hung a board on which one word was painted: Sorcerer. People believe that members of the Fraternity of the Parinians are responsible, but because they're so powerful no one is willing to accuse or condemn them. I wept when Emiliano told me about it—what a terrible way to die. She wasn't a witch or someone possessed by Satan, but just a harmless—and even a generous and helpful—old woman."

"Oh, I'm so sorry, Giovanni," Antonio said. "I know the news of your poor father's pain must wound you deeply. And what a hideous tragedy is the death of that poor old woman who was an innocent victim of the diabolic evil of which men are capable."

"I don't understand how those followers of Matteo Parini can be so hateful, especially when they claim to be defenders of the faith of Christ."

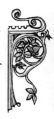

"Alas, Giovanni, evil is often the handmaiden of religion, especially when religion makes her members constantly aware of their sinfulness and perpetual unworthiness rather than the mercy of God. Instead of preaching love, she uses evil to frighten the multitude into complying with the commandments and following her creeds and dogmas. The result is usually a rigid legalism and a fixation on evil."

"That, Padre Antonio, is what I saw the Sunday Padre Matteo first came to Assisi and I accompanied my mother to hear him preach. It seemed to me that he was filled with the venom of a deadly viper. Forgive me, God, for I know it is wrong to judge him like that!"

"Our Blessed Lord encountered just such evil in the Pharisees and religious leaders of his day," Antonio replied. "He reserved a similar term for those hypocrites who cleverly appeared to be concerned about holy things as you used to describe Matteo Parini and his followers. He called them 'a den of vipers.'"

"Just as those religious leaders were determined to put Christ to death, Padre Antonio, it seems that Matteo's followers are obsessed with destroying me."

"I'm afraid it has ever been so, Giovanni. Since the beginning of time when Light appeared on earth, the Darkness has detested it and sought to destroy it—as when the serpent of Eden twisted innocence into a lie. But good and evil are not just mortal enemies in an eternal war; they are next-of-kin, like Cain and Abel. Mysteriously joined to each other, they exist within each of us! If we deny our own inner darkness, we become like serpents and strike out at others—especially those who are innocent. Like the Pharisees and the Parinians, we send out our own secret wickedness and the venomous desires of our hidden darkness. We all know the mild form of this denial expressed in the old adage that goes, 'Tis easier to weed your neighbor's garden than your own.' When it gets more serious, however, the results—as in the case of poor Gaspara—are often deadly."

"Padre, I don't want to deny the darkness within me. I want to see 'the plank in my own eye,' as my Lord and Master said. In fact, as you were talking, I felt a need to dedicate myself to bringing Christ's light into any situation where I find darkness."

"Ah, my young friend, that is true innocence. Your baptism in the forest, which sealed you as a child of God, allowed you to say that. But, indeed, you need to keep renewing your first baptism, for just as it was

in Eden, all goodness and innocence can be twisted and perverted into evil.

"Giovanni, you might think of good as being a ladder in which the farthest rungs extend into the light, with the darkest evil at the other end, and each rung progressively darker as it moves away from the light. For example, each of the seven deadly sins begins as something good and natural. Lust begins as passionate love, but when drained dry of true caring for the other it becomes the evil of exploitation. Gluttony begins as our God-given delight in eating, but by greed for pleasure it grows out of control and becomes distorted into sin."

"I can see, too, how enterprises that start out good can turn sour."

"Indeed," Antonio responded. "The Crusades are a good example. They began with the noble cause of insuring that Christian pilgrims could safely visit the holy sites in Jerusalem—as had been possible under the previous Muslim rulers. But eventually the Crusades became hideously evil wars bent on massacring Muslims and driving them out of the Holy Land. With my own eyes I saw the holy cross of the crusaders distorted by the vices of Christian warriors until the ends of the crossbar were twisted upward like horns and the pole of the cross became like Satan's staff."

"Padre, you never mentioned that you had gone off on the Crusades. How was it possible for a monk?"

"It's not something that's easy for me to speak about. It was hardly edifying to watch our Christian soldiers murder, rape, and plunder as savagely as any infidel. But as for how I got there, it was fifteen or so years ago, in the early 1190s, when I heard the Pope calling for priest chaplains to minister to the crusaders. Being an idealist, I asked Father Abbot if I could leave the abbey to become a priest chaplain, and he gave me permission to be away from the monastery temporarily."

"How wonderful to administer the sacraments to. . . ."

"Ah, that's what I thought! But I'm afraid that when the crusaders left home, along with their wives they also left behind their spiritual needs. My crusader years were largely a school where I learned that a diabolically cold-blooded beast secretly lurks deep within even the most civilized and noble of men. There were a number of knights who were as idealistic as I was at the start of the venture, but most of their innocence was washed away in the bloodbaths in the Holy Land. By the end, the only time most of the crusaders wanted a priest was if they were dying."

"I've always dreamed of visiting the Holy Land and especially Mount Calvary, where our Lord was crucified.

"Although the Third Crusade was a disaster, Giovanni, and the crusaders failed to recapture Jerusalem, their failure didn't prevent me from visiting the site of Christ's crucifixion." Antonio's gnarled hand slowly traced upon himself the sign of the cross as he painfully continued, "O Merciful God, rob me of my hideous memories from Calvary. More than just seeing the hallowed hill upon which our Savior died, I actually saw him being crucified again and again. I witnessed countless horrors of Calvary in the slaughter of innocent women and children and in the torched ruins of shops and homes that been looted and burned by our so-called Christian knights. To my everlasting shame," he went on, beginning to wave his gnarled hand back and forth as if attempting to wipe away his memories, "I was forced to stand at the foot of a thousand crosses and witness the savagery of Christ's crucifixion."

"I've heard terrible stories about the Crusades before, Padre," Francesco said, "but the brutality was always condoned because our enemies were infidel Muslims, who were said to be more brutal and savage than one could imagine."

"Indeed, Giovanni, there was savagery on both sides, and, to be sure, the Muslims live in a very different world than Christians and practice a very different religion—they were very real enemies. But Christ told us to love, not to butcher, our enemies. As hard as that is to do, living out the Gospels always bears fruit, sometimes in God's wondrous, surprising, upside-down ways. In my case, if I had not gone to the Holy Land, and if I had not had an open heart toward the enemy, I would never have met the Sufis, a group of Islamic mystics and holy men. They dressed like the poor in garments of rough brown cloth, and they would spin themselves into ecstasy, dancing wildly round and round until they would whirl themselves into an alignment with God, whom they call Allah. They translated for me some of their poetry and prayers, which were full of a wonderfully intense vitality and passionate love for God."

"A scary thought just occurred to me, Padre Antonio. I have a sense that God may be asking me to love the Parinians so that I might find some sort of blessing like you found with the Sufis."

"Ah, my friend, now we're getting close to the heart of the matter. Do you remember how repulsed you were by lepers, and then how

revolutionary it was when you embraced Benvenuto? Do you think you can embrace evil in the same way you pressed leprosy to your bosom?"

"I'm not sure, Padre. I don't know if the Parinians would even let me embrace them."

"I'm afraid you're right, Giovanni. You're not likely to find your blessing in the form of a warm response from the Parinians. It's much more likely to be an inner blessing. Think of how you have been blessed by living out Jesus' first beatitude: 'Blessed are the poor, for theirs is the kingdom.' It seems that now you are being asked to find happiness in the last beatitude: 'Blessed are you when they persecute you and utter every kind of slander against you because of me. Rejoice and be glad.'"

"I've been able to meet Lady Poverty with joy, but how do I respond to persecution with rejoicing?"

"With much of what you're already doing, Giovanni, especially being childlike in your faith. But also, be prepared! Remember how Jesus told his disciples to be innocent as doves but also as shrewd as serpents. The more you become the light, the more the darkness will attempt to crush you, to snuff you out like a candlewick. So be prepared for evil to come Portiuncula. Saint Mary of the Angels, renowned for its angelic visits, will soon very likely be visited by demons."

Francesco shuddered, wondering what demons would visit him and his brothers. Recalling his recent problems with the structure of his small band, he said, "My first response, Padre, is that I should end the brotherhood and run away from this gathering evil!"

"Running away," Antonio replied firmly, "will only allow the evil to devour you—it would not only satiate the Parinians, it would even please some of my own brother monks who believe you're tinkering with the devil! Not long ago I spent some time back at my abbey of San Benedetto when Father Abbot sent two monks to bring me back to the monastery to be examined by our brother infirmarian because he was concerned about my health. Under obedience, I had to go, if only to ensure the abbot that I was still in good enough health to continue living alone as a hermit. Anyway, I spent three days at my monastery and. . ." he paused to chuckle, ". . . I heard all sorts of outlandish tales about you and your wandering band."

"What kind of tales?"

"Well, some monks told me how you were going about the countryside condemning the great wealth of the monasteries like ours,

telling the people that St. Benedict would turn over in his grave if he could see the riches of his monks today. They said you had compared the corruption of the papal court to a stinking sewer and that the Holy City should be renamed Sodom City. You were also reported to have had a private vision of heaven ceaselessly weeping day and night over the scandalous sexual immorality of our priests."

"I never said any of those. . . ."

"I know that, but I have more to tickle your ears. What really upset some of our monk priests was how you and your companions were preaching the Gospel even though you are not ordained and that you were doing it outside of church at crossroads and in village squares. They called you our Italian Peter of Waldo and predicted that your zeal for heretical doctrine and dissent would soon surpass the apostasy of that famous heretic of Lyons. Saliva practically dripping from their lips, they gleefully repeated rumors that Pope Innocent III was going to call you to Rome to stand trial for heresy."

Francesco sat saddened and shocked, but before he could open his mouth to protest, Antonio continued his story, "And some even found your joyfulness to be sinful!"

"My joyfulness sinful?"

"I'm afraid so, Giovanni. Certain monks have accused you of inciting people to sin by laughing, saying that you've encouraged your companions to spread mirth and joy wherever they go. Some have quoted you as saying, 'Lord, make me a happy instrument of your joy, so that where there is sadness I can spread laughter and merriment'!"

"But, Antonio, why do those monks believe merriment and laughter are sinful?"

"Unfortunately, it comes from a narrow understanding of the Holy Rule. In it St. Benedict has a chapter on silence where he says, 'As for coarse jokes or frivolous talk or making people laugh, these we condemn to be forever barred in all places, and for such conversation we do not allow a disciple to open his mouth.' Some of the monks judge all laughter as sinfully vain and foolish, pointing to Benedict's saying that one of the signs of humility is 'if a man is not ready and quick to laugh, for it is written in Scripture that the fool lifts up his voice in laughter.'"

"But doesn't St. Paul command us to rejoice always? Don't the monks. . . ."

"Ah, my joyful Giovanni, there's more. St. Benedict goes on to describe the last stage of humility: 'A monk, when he speaks, does so gently and without laughing.'"

"Without laughing? You mean the final state of holiness is to be joyless?"

"Benedict concludes by saying that wherever a humble monk is in the garden, in the fields working, in prayer or on the road, he keeps his 'head always bent, eyes fixed on the ground, reckoning all the time how guilty he is of sin. . . .' So now perhaps you can understand why many of my brother monks are shocked when they hear reports of you dancing or playfully pretending that two old sticks are your fiddle and bow as you sing joyful songs of your own creation that cause little children and peasants to laugh. Their monastic training has formed them to judge you as a vain show-off and a witless fool, and I don't mean the entertaining minstrel kind. For these monks, salvation, prayer, praise of God and all of life are deadly serious issues. But I beg you, Giovanni Francesco, not to be harsh in evaluating my brothers. They are gnarled old trees who, when they were tender young saplings were shaped by their spiritual teachers into the people they are today."

"I fear I wouldn't last very long in the monastery," Francesco said. "I enjoy laughing too much."

"Well, why do you think," Antonio said with a chuckle, "I left the abbey to live out here as a hermit? Holy Benedict designed his monastic system to be a school of the Lord's service, and when one lives it correctly it teaches unique and invaluable lessons in how to live virtuously, like the arts of compassion and prayer, and the necessity of placing others' needs before one's own. Just as with the Crusades and other things that begin with good intentions, in time that monastic formation of learning how to be a saint can easily be distorted, abused or even deforming. Still, never forget all the good that monasticism has done, and all the saints and holy men it has—and is—producing. "

"Padre, as a son of St. Benedict, you're a living example of that for me."

"Ah, Giovanni, I confess I'm not a very humble son of Holy Father Benedict. For there are days when I'm overcome with laughter at my clownish clumsiness in attempting to be holy, and I find myself giggling aloud about my stupidity."

"Thank you, Padre. As usual, you've informed and encouraged me. While not knowing what St. Benedict said about laughter, as a child I

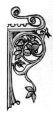

too was taught that laughter is wrong. But like other things I've been taught I shouldn't do, I did it anyway. When I was in school, the priests at San Giorgio disciplined us with rods whenever they caught us having fun. I remember how one cranky old priest named Padre Federico, whom we called Padre Raisin Face, would constantly harangue us. 'Stop this frivolity!' he liked to say. 'Our Lord and Savior Jesus Christ never laughed. Nowhere in the holy Gospels does it say that he even smiled—so wipe those silly grins off your faces. Be sober, dwell only upon your sins, and you'll find nothing to laugh about!' How sad when people feel that the good news of our Savior must be lived as sad news of sin and damnation, making religion so somber as to be joyless."

"I agree," Antonio said, "and the blame hardly belongs to Saint Benedict alone. The seemingly boundless joy that you embody contradicts the teaching of most of the great spiritual masters. Their message is: Saints do not dance! Saints do not laugh! Saints are humble; they never sing or entertain people or draw attention to themselves. Saints pray with tears and weeping, not with gladness and. . . ."

"I'm glad I don't seek to be a saint!"

"Sometimes, my young friend, I think that's the best way to become one. You would be wise to beware of the maggot of saintliness that insidiously worms its way into the hearts of pious people. As you daily have to pick lice off your body, so every day in your prayers search for the maggot of false piety that burrows into the soft fruit of your soul to feed on any goodness it finds. Whenever you find this nasty vermin present in your good deeds, do not hesitate to purge it with the most painful of acids. But you must remain vigilant, for while you may be purged of it for a short time, that mystic maggot invariably returns."

"What is that purging acid of which you spoke? I fear, Padre, that I'm in need of some of it."

"Ah, again, Giovanni, it's the purging acid of inner poverty and innocence. Paradoxically, in that acid is present the mystery of good that comes out of evil. It involves the painful recollection of our sins, our stupid mistakes, the times when we did what seemed right and good at the moment but later we realized we were being deceived by our own lust, pride, greed, or anger. This acid of a childlike spirit frees us to laugh at ourselves and at life. It allows us to know joy even when we're old and ailing—and even when we're persecuted."

"A little while ago," said Francesco, "you mentioned you had heard a rumor at the abbey that the Pope was going to call me to Rome to

stand trial for heresy. Well, Padre, I'm afraid that is no rumor! When Emiliano visited me, he told me that there was also trouble brewing for me in Assisi. Along with the slanderous stories the witch-hunting Parinians are spreading about me, he said that now a priest inquisitor from the Holy Office in Rome has come to Assisi to investigate me and my little band of brothers. Emiliano said the inquisitor had already questioned Lord Bishop Guido and now was inquiring about me from the priests, merchants, and aristocratic families of Assisi. He had even come to Emiliano's family wine shop asking him all kinds of questions about me because people had reported that we were once the closest of friends."

"Ha, I'm not surprised at the special attention you're receiving, Giovanni Francesco," Antonio laughed. "You're becoming famous—or, rather, infamous!"

Their conversation was interrupted by someone down below in the forest loudly calling out Francesco's name. The shouts continued and were soon joined by a more distant voice crying out, "Father Francesco. Father Francesco."

"Someone is looking for you, Giovanni," Antonio said, "and urgently."

"That first voice sounds like Brother Bernardo," replied Francesco, "and the other. . . ."

"Francesco, where are you? Francesco, where are you?" The first voice was coming closer.

"I'm up here at Padre Antonio's hermitage," Francesco shouted back, concerned about why his brothers were so anxious to find him. In a matter of moments Bernardo appeared out of the forest running up toward Antonio's hermitage.

"I thought you might have come here," Bernardo said, panting heavily. "I've never been up here before, but I thought. . . ."

"Bernardo, this is Padre Antonio, my confessor and guide," Francesco said. "And, Padre, I want you to meet my dear friend and brother, Bernardo, who was the first of my comrades."

Once again, shouts rose out of the dense forest: "Father Francesco, Father Francesco."

"That's Brother Giles," said Bernardo. "He and I came up here to find you." Cupping his hands around his mouth, he called out, "Brother Giles, I found him! I found him! Go home, Brother Giles, and we'll join you back at Portiuncula." Then, turning back to

Francesco, he said, "You must come quickly, for we have great trouble back at Portiuncula."

*W*hen Francesco arrived at Portiuncula, he was warmly greeted by his brothers. But the warmth of his welcome was rapidly chilled by the disturbing problem that Bernardo had briefly told him about as they hurried down the mountain. Masseo and Pietro were standing guard, armed respectively with a shovel and hoe, defending the front door of the chapel of Saint Mary of the Angels.

"He's inside, Father Francesco," said Masseo, raising his shovel. "What are we to do?"

"Brothers, first, please take that shovel and hoe back to our garden. As our Lord's disciples and men of peace, weapons—even improvised ones—have no place here."

"But those men chased him here with clubs and swords," Masseo said. "Didn't we have a duty to protect him?"

"You have done what is right, Brother Masseo—as have all of you—in attempting to protect the innocent. But now we need to do more than what is right; we must do what is better. We must do what God desires."

The brothers proceeded to tell Francesco the whole story of how they had been doing some planting in their small vegetable garden when old Strapazzate came running out of the trees screaming that he wanted to be given sanctuary. Safely reaching the chapel, he turned in the doorway to face the group of armed men who had been chasing him and shouted, "God's house . . . sanctuary . . . sanctuary . . . God's house! You can't touch me here." Then Brother Masseo, who had been using a shovel, along with Pietro, still carrying his hoe, ran to the chapel door and stood between Strapazzate and the five angry men. Pietro announced to them the rules of the Right of Sanctuary, which forbade them from entering the chapel and harming the old beggar. After he demanded to know why they were chasing Strapazzate, the men, who were Parinians, answered that they were going to take him to Perugia where he would stand trial for diabolic possession. By that time the rest of the brothers had joined Masseo and Pietro to form a human barrier in front of the chapel. Frustrated and angry, the Parinians departed, saying they would soon return with reinforcements to seize this man who had sold his soul to the devil and was possessed by Satan. The brothers concluded their story by saying that this had

 happened several hours ago and that surely the Parinians would be returning at any moment.

"I will go into the chapel," announced Francesco, "and speak to Tommaso. Bernardo, please come with me. Meanwhile, the rest of you brothers, please return to your work in the garden."

As Francesco and Bernardo stepped into the small dark barrel-vaulted chapel with its faded frescos, a frightened Strapazzate asked, "Is that you, Holy Prince of Beggars?"

"Yes, Tommaso of Spello," Francesco replied. "I am pleased that you found a safe place here in the lap of our Lady of the Angels. Now, tell Brother Bernardo and me what happened."

"Friendly Francesco, God's beggar with holy lice," Strapazzate said, falling to his knees directly in front of Francesco, "I go to pray at martyr's shrine of holy Gaspara's ashes in Assisi's Garden of Gethsemane down below San Damiano's chapel—you know the spot, eh? Then, they come—to gloat there. Evil men, men with wicked hearts, the wicked ones of Parini. They see me kneeling at Gaspara's Calvary. I can see . . . see. . . ." Then he sank his head down to the chapel floor.

"See what, Tommaso? What did you see?" asked Bernardo.

"I see their hearts—bad, oh, very bad. Hate me," Strapazzate answered. "I start to run . . . they block my path back to Assisi . . . I think of the good man Francesco of San Damiano—run to his house here with Holy Mary of the Angels."

"That was wise of you, my old friend," Francesco answered, lifting Strapazzate to his feet. "Here in this house of God you will have sanctuary, and my brothers and I will. . . ."

"Father Francesco, come quickly. They've returned!" Brother Giles shouted from outside the chapel. "Come quickly; tell us what we should do."

Assuring Strapazzate of his safety, Francesco and Bernardo stepped out of the chapel and stood with their backs against the closed door. There, facing them, was a band of perhaps twenty-five or thirty armed men. One of the Parinians shouted that they had returned to seize Strapazzate and take him to Perugia to stand trial for witchcraft and diabolic possession. Their leader was a large man attired completely in black from head to foot with a black hawk's feather in his cap. He proudly identified himself as Girolamo de Verrocchio, the grand guardian of the Fraternity of Matteo Parini. Then he produced a

document from Padre Matteo bearing the seal of the Bishop of Perugia ordering the apprehension of the demon-possessed Strapazzate of Assisi. Francesco boldly stood his ground, declaring that since Saint Mary of the Angels was within the Diocese of Bishop Guido of Assisi, only he and not the Bishop of Perugia could sanction such an arrest in violation of the ancient law of sanctuary. Confident that Bishop Guido would never give his permission, Francesco told the Parinians to go to Assisi and return with a proper document from Bishop Guido if they wanted to seize Tommaso.

In response, the Parinians withdrew a short distance and held a council, while the ten brothers drew closer to Francesco and Bernardo.

Following their brief conference, Girolamo de Verrocchio stalked forward until he stood nose to nose with Francesco. "The *Right of Sanctuary*," he snarled, his right hand gripping the handle of his sword, "granting refuge inside a consecrated place for those fleeing persecution, is merely a pious custom. You may assert that it is a law of the Church, but does the Church grant sanctuary to the devil? Does the Church allow demons to pollute sacred places? No! And neither will we agree to sanctuary for this henchman of the devil. So, step aside, beggar, or we'll take you and the rest of your rabble along with us to Perugia to stand trial for heresy." He paused and sneered wickedly as he saw the fright written plainly on some of the brothers' faces.

"Peace, my brother," Francesco responded quietly. "I beg you to. . . ." But before he could get another word out, Girolamo raised his black-gloved hand and signaled. At once the mob of armed men rushed forward, roughly shoving Francesco away from the chapel door.

"Sacrilege, sacrilege," the brothers shouted as the Parinians stormed into the chapel, violating the sacred space by carrying not only their weapons but also their intent on doing harm. In only moments, they came outside dragging the helpless Strapazzate, who was screaming, "Sacrilege, sacri-ledge, oh, sacke-vege. Child of Providence, do not harm. Not I—you are the henchmen of the devil—you Parini pests. Count the cost . . . for God has counted one-by-one my every hair. No sparrow falls from Mother Mary's lap without heaven. . . ."

"Your own babbling mouth," snarled Girolamo, "condemns you as guilty of being possessed by Satan himself and, thereby, filled with the very wickedness of hell. So what need is there for any trial?"

"I agree with Your Lordship," Strapazzate announced boldly, suddenly and surprisingly now beginning to speak free of his usual

jumbled language, "for your own mouth has declared me to be a fit candidate to become a disciple of Matteo Parini. I thank you for counting me worthy to be received as the newest member of the vile fraternity of loyal Parinians."

"Contemptible ass! Despicable slanderer," screamed Girolamo. "Why should we bother to take him back to Perugia for trial? Let's hang him right here from the nearest tree."

"You can't! God wills it not!" Strapazzate answered, bowing his head down and stretching out his neck. "Before you dragged me from the House of Holy Mother Mary of the Angels, she told me that it is God's will, to be done here on earth as in heaven; that I must die like the Apostle Paul. So here is my neck: Behead me!"

"Only nobles may be beheaded or die by the sword," someone in the mob shouted. "You're not worthy to perish so painlessly. *Minores*, commoners like you, die like dogs by being hanged."

Two of the brothers had slipped back and returned with the shovel and hoe. They now stepped forward in a brave but foolhardy attempt to save Strapazzate, but Francesco held up his hand, stopping them. Falling to his knees, he said, "Brothers, we must not resist evil with evil. Christ has forbidden us to return violence for violence. Come, all of you, join me. Let us kneel down and pray that poor Strapazzate be spared."

So the brothers knelt and began loudly storming heaven with their prayers. Over their voices, old Strapazzate could be heard screaming, "Please, Holy Francesco, save me! Do not let them hang me. In God's name, please do not let them hang me!" But on this day heaven, it seemed, wasn't listening to their prayers or to the pleas of poor Tommaso of Spello. The mob of Parinians dragged Strapazzate over to a large tree not far from the Chapel of Saint Mary of the Angels, and throwing a rope over a strong branch, they hanged him. As Francesco prayed, he looked out over the heads of the jubilant mob to see the old hunchback beggar of Assisi twisting slowly and lifelessly from the noose at the end of the rope. As he beheld that grisly sight, he recalled Padre Antonio's words that the day was coming when demons and not just angels would visit Saint Mary's at Portiuncula. That day had come all too soon.

*T*he brothers reverently washed the dead body of Strapazzate, clothed it in one of their tunics and buried him beside the Chapel

of St. Mary of the Angels. For his grave Brother Giles made a crude wooden cross and carved *Tommaso of Spello* on it. Francesco spent the rest of that day with the brothers as they tried to comfort one another after the shock and horror of the hanging.

The next day he returned to Padre Antonio's hermitage, where he wept unashamed as he poured out the ghastly story of Strapazzate's lynching. He spoke of his agony at being powerless to say or do anything that would stop the Parinians from hanging poor Tommaso. He anguished over the seeming impotence of their prayers, and he asked why even God seemed powerless to prevent the horrible death of an innocent man. When he had finished his story, Antonio proposed that they simply sit in silence, allowing their unutterable prayers to usher them into the healing presence of God.

After a very long time Antonio spoke. "Giovanni, what you did was right," he said, sensing that this was the question burning in Francesco's heart. "By seemingly doing nothing, you were doing what God wanted. Your only other choice was to use force to rescue him, and even if by some miracle you had overcome that mob, one evil is never defeated by another evil. If we are to be God's instruments of peace, then we must be careful not to get in God's way—and that is never easy for us to do. We're all too eager to see immediate success from our deeds, and to quench our thirst for a quick victory by using whatever means are available. 'To be a good instrument of God, don't get in the way'—that was the difficult lesson I was taught by my confessor Padre Guittone. 'Be patient,' he'd say to me, 'for God's justice always comes, but it comes in God's time.' It is not difficult to pray to be an instrument of peace. What is difficult is refusing to exchange being an instrument of peace for being an instrument of expediency, especially in order to prevent some violence or injustice that's taking place directly in front of you. Being peaceful at a distance—ah, that's easy. What is difficult is remaining peaceful right in the midst of conflict."

"I learned something of that lesson personally yesterday. Wanting to protect Tommaso of Spello painfully tested my desire to be a peacemaker. This is the third beatitude we've talked about in the last two days, and it may be as challenging for me as trying to rejoice in the midst of being persecuted. It feels like a noose is being tightened around my neck, just as it was around Tommaso's. It feels like the mob is after me too. And I'm concerned about the inquisitor from the Holy

Office. I wonder if I should I go to Rome to speak directly with the Pope."

"As you consider your course of action regarding the Vatican inquisitor, I should briefly finish telling you the gossip about you that is going around the cloister walkway."

Padre Antonio told him the stories circulating through the abbey about Francesco offering Holy Mass for his brothers and forgiving their sins—as well as those of the peasants and villagers who asked him to hear their confessions. Francesco responded that he knew that priests were ordained to say Holy Mass, but admitted that he had led the brothers in remembering our Lord's Last Supper. He told Antonio that in doing so he felt he was only being faithful to the Lord's instruction to "do this in memory of me," and he didn't see that being any different from Christ's other admonitions, like the one that says, "Sell your possessions and give the money away to the poor." He said that whenever one of his brothers or some peasant approached him wanting to confess to him, all he had done was listen with compassion and then repeat to them the words of Christ, "Go in peace, your sins are forgiven." Since on Easter night Christ had given his disciples the power to forgive sins, Francesco believed that as one of his disciples it had also been given to him.

"I can't argue with your reasoning," Antonio said, "because it's supported by hundreds of years of theology and tradition. Distinguished theologians like Thierry of Chartres proposed much the same thought. And the great St. Bernard of the last century said, 'There is no necessary connection between consecration and sacramental ordination.' Even today at the beginning of the thirteenth century, when it comes to the consecration of the Eucharist or absolution of sins, there remain many places where no absolute distinction is made between laity and ritually ordained. Indeed, the Instructions for Holy Communion for the Eleventh Century, which I might add have never been overruled by the Church, even used feminine pronouns!

"So, Francesco, as the leader of a spiritual community, you're like abbots and abbesses who are confessors to their own monks and nuns. One abbess, Hildegard of Bingen, a famous mystic and preacher, who before she died thirty some years ago in 1179 made a preaching pilgrimage to admonish lax priests, was said to be the celebrant of the Holy Mass for her nuns. Yes, scholarly theologians and liturgists have taught that when the words of consecration are spoken over bread and

wine, these earthly elements are transformed into the Body and Blood
Christ, regardless of whether the speaker is ordained or a lay man or
woman.

"At the same time, Francesco, while you have tradition and
sacramental theology behind you, that doesn't mean you won't be
condemned for what you are doing. For, indeed, the times are
changing. Rome, the monks say, will soon clearly define who can, and
cannot, be ministers of the Mass and confession."

"Thank you, Padre," said Francesco. "I appreciate your words of
warning as well as affirmation. I didn't know all that theology or history
of the sacraments. I only was doing what in my heart I felt God was
asking of me.

"But tell me, Padre, what else are they saying about me at the
abbey?"

"The other gossip, Giovanni, was about all the legends that are
springing up across Umbria: how you've tamed wolves and mad dogs
with only a smile and how flocks of larks sing along with you whenever
you sing—and even a few miracles of healing cripples."

"That kind of talk is really amusing," Francesco said with a smile.
"No, Padre, I'm afraid I'm just a sinful man who can't work miracles or
tame wild beasts."

"I'm glad to hear you say that. Indeed, not to forget your mistakes
and sins is the best cure for the mystic maggot we talked about, the one
that gnaws at holy people, feeding on the fruitfulness of their lives. And
it seems, my young friend, that your life work is becoming very fruitful.
The monastery was humming with rumors that at least a hundred men
have left their wives and families and have given away their money to
the poor to become your followers. Tell me, Giovanni Francesco, how
many followers do you actually have?"

"Twelve. There are only twelve of us, like the apostles, and we all
count the Lord Jesus as our teacher and master."

"Twelve is indeed a mystical number. But I'm curious, my once-
upon-a-time hermit and lover of solitude, how many more followers
can you fit into your little boat before it begins to sink?"

"You know, I don't plan ahead," he lamented, resting his forehead
in his left hand. "I only live in the moment. I try to greet each new day
without marking out a course, welcoming it as something new and
exciting. I've pre-planned none of this—not even having a single
companion, let alone a community of them. It all just happened! There

are times when I've wanted to run away, to go somewhere far away and just begin again, alone. That need to escape feels especially strong now that Rome has sent an inquisitor to collect evidence that I'm some kind of heretic—and all these terrible false stories you've just told me. . . ."

"Yes, I can understand how painful all this must be for you, Giovanni—the scrutiny from Rome as well as your discomfort at having to manage a community. It's one thing to attract those who wish to come and share your life, and something far different to lead them as wisely as a Saint Benedict. He possessed the twin gifts of being a holy man, whose deep solitary prayer drew others to join him, and at the same time being a competent administrator and leader. His Holy Rule is proof of those twin gifts. Yet few are those who posses both.

"Now, Giovanni, as to you wondering whether you should go to Rome to seek the Pope's approval, as Padre Guittone used to say to me, 'Never let your opponent choose the place and time to confront you. Rather, meet him when you are prepared and have the high ground.'"

"So, Padre, you think that before I'm ordered to Rome I should go there and tell the Pope about the crucifix at San Damiano and ask for his blessing?"

"It would be wise to meet the Pope before you are called to Rome. But as far as seeking his blessing, Giovanni, son of Pietro Bernadone, whose blessing are you seeking? In desiring *Il Papa's* blessing, you've moved up that youthful need of yours many notches higher, seeking the affirmation of the ultimate earthly father, yet isn't it the very same need for paternal approval? How can you be the joyous troubadour of the glorious freedom of the children of God if you're always imprisoned by your need for the approval of your natural father, a father confessor, a father abbot or even the holy father in Rome?"

Chapter 11

THE RED-TILE ROOFTOPS OF ASSISI SEEMED TO BE STAINED a vibrant blood-red by the setting sun as Bishop Guido sat looking out his window. "Pope Innocent III," he thought, "is perhaps the greatest man of this century. He's more than the Bishop of Rome; he's also a prince more powerful and politically shrewder than the vast majority of kings. As the Vicar of Christ—the new title he has begun to use in his papal position—he does not hesitate to use his power and influence to force emperors and kings to their knees, employing the spiritually and politically potent trump card of excommunication."

His thought formed into words as he said aloud, "Was it by a cast of the divine dice or the spin of the goddess Fortuna's wheel that the powerful and great Innocent III and lowly Francesco Bernadone should find themselves together on the stage of life at this critical time? Ah, when God throws dice, they are usually loaded!" Standing up, he turned from the window and walked toward the doorway, praying, "O God, whose wisdom appears as folly to us poor mortals, it seems you've pushed your servant Guido, the sinner Shepherd of Assisi, out upon that same life stage, giving me the role of a bit player in your great drama. O God, come to my assistance as I now go down to my cathedral to meet Assisi's now infamous son, whom I believe may be your chosen one for this age."

Francesco secretly came to the Cathedral of San Rufino as soon as possible after Padre Tomas, the bishop's young secretary, had visited Portiuncula. Tomas had come wearing a hooded cloak and, without identifying himself, had asked to speak to Francesco privately. The two walked a short distance from the cluster of huts before Tomas disclosed his identity to Francesco.

"My Lord Bishop Guido," Tomas said, "has enjoined me to come and speak with you secretly, as he was most anxious not to put anything in writing. He asked me to relay to you this message: You are to come at once to meet with him, for the situation has taken on the greatest urgency. As far as possible, you are to come to Assisi without being recognized."

"I will do as he wishes. Where and when am I to meet with him?"

"Go to the baptismal font in the rear corner of the cathedral, and he will meet you there right after vespers this afternoon. Bishop Guido also instructed me to tell you that you are not to speak with anyone of this meeting, not even your companions, for the matter is gravely dangerous."

"I will do as my Lord Bishop wishes. Thank you, Padre Tomas, for coming as his messenger."

"I am honored that my Bishop entrusted me with this mission and especially pleased that it has provided me an opportunity to meet you. I've heard many wonderful things about you and how you are making religion come alive for our people. Perhaps I could return some time when we can visit longer?"

"I'd enjoy that," Francesco said. After bidding Padre Tomas farewell, he returned to the community cluster of hermitage huts. Finding Brother Leone, he asked him to explain to the brothers that he felt the need to be absent from their evening meal to walk alone in the woods. Remarking that the evening might be cool, he put on a large cloak with a hood.

The feeble pale light of that dying day softly filtered down through the high windows of the old, gray-stone cathedral. At that sunset hour the worn pavement stones of the floor were streaked with long purple shadows cast by the wooden scaffolding that had been erected to paint a series of new frescoes on the upper walls of the cathedral. Francesco stood hidden in the dark shadows of the deserted cathedral as he was approached by a figure wearing a gray pilgrim's cloak with a large hood pulled down to hide his face.

"*Pax*, peace, my son," the bishop greeted him. "Thank you for coming to see me on such short notice." Then in hurried, hushed tones he continued, "Francesco Giovanni, this is the first I've seen you since that day five years ago when you renounced your wealth, but I have often thought of you and have heard many stories about you. The followers of Padre Matteo Parini have come to me on several occasions

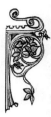

with outlandish stories about you, wanting me to condemn you and your ideas. I have steadfastly ignored them because it is my belief that you've been sent to us from God. The exact mission God desires of you I am not sure, but I have regularly prayed for you and your safety."

As Francesco bowed his head, acknowledging his gratitude for the bishop's support, he thought, "You're not alone in your uncertainty about my mission, Bishop. I'm just as unsure as to what I'm supposed to do."

"Francesco, I've asked you to come here so I can warn you," the bishop continued, "because there are those in the highest positions at the Vatican who are eager to arrest you and all those associated with you."

"Arrest me?"

"Yes, on the charge of h-h-heresy!" His voice trembled as he said the word. The bishop confirmed what Francesco had heard about a Roman priest inquisitor and two secretaries from the Holy Office coming to Assisi to collect oath-bound statements concerning Francesco from the clergy and people. Some of his priests, the bishop sadly confided, who were eager to advance themselves in the eyes of Rome, were reporting to the inquisitor gossip about him as if it was fact.

"My Lord Bishop," Francesco whispered, "you are a holy man who is wise in the ways of Rome and the Church. Tell me what you think I should do."

After anxiously glancing over his shoulder, the bishop said, "Giovanni Francesco, I feel that God's hand is upon you, and I believe you are being led by the Holy Spirit. When I consider the mission you were given by our crucified Lord in the little chapel of San Damiano to 'repair my church,' my heart longs for it to be expanded to rebuilding the entire Church of Christ."

Francesco nodded silently at the bishop's words, but inwardly he was overwhelmed by the magnitude of such a task and apprehensive about the implications of being led by the Holy Spirit. He was also frightened of the dire consequences of being found guilty of heresy.

"As to my advice about this heresy investigation," continued Bishop Guido, "aware of the seriousness of such an inquiry by the Holy Office, I've been praying about how I might best be of assistance to you. After all, Francesco, you are one of the flock for whom I bear responsibility before God. The answer that constantly surfaces in my prayer is that you should go at once to Rome, not waiting to be taken there in chains. Go as quickly as you can, even tomorrow if that is

 possible. And when you get to Rome, you must demand to speak directly to the Pope himself, not to anyone else, not even to one of the cardinals. You must speak only to the great Innocent III. He is a man of vision who is deeply concerned about stopping the sinful trafficking in relics and desirous of correcting the shameful abuses of his priests. Did you know that the Pope calls the bad priests 'dogs'? I am convinced that it is God's design, and no accident of fate, that you and Pope Innocent are linked together at this moment in history. But again, I repeat, you must refuse under any circumstances to tell your story to a lower official in the Vatican and are to speak directly to the Pope."

"My Lord Bishop, thank you for your advice, but I am only a simple layman—and a barefoot one who looks like a common beggar. How will I ever be able to speak directly to the Holy Father? Surely the Successor of Peter does not grant audiences to beggars?"

"You must have faith and trust, Francesco. God works the impossible, and as unlikely as it may seem, if you have faith, God will make it happen! One more thing: Innocent was educated as a lawyer, and so is well organized in both his politics and his prayer. He is an excellent Pope partly because he excels in the details of administration. For this reason, I'm quite certain he will ask you for the rule of your new community. Every religious order has its rules of life since they're necessary to insure proper order and stability in their communities. So you must be prepared to present to him in writing the charter of regulations that govern you and your little band of brothers."

"My Lord Bishop," Francesco replied, smiling, "our only rule is following the rule of the Gospel given us by our Lord Christ: 'Sell what you have and give it to the poor. Never return injury for injury. Bless your. . . .'"

Placing his hand on Francesco's shoulder, the bishop said tenderly, "Yes, I know, Francesco, and that is most beautiful. But I can assure you that His Holiness—and others who are powerful in the Vatican—will. . . ." The bishop stopped as a door slammed somewhere up near the altar, and the sound echoed down the long, dark canyon of the cathedral. "That may have just been the wind, but we can't take a chance. You must go at once, for you and I must not be seen talking to one another." As Francesco knelt before him, the bishop blessed him, tracing the sign of the cross over him. "Now quickly, Francesco of God, go in peace." Francesco took the bishop's hand and kissed his episcopal

ring with more affection than he would have shown a holy relic and then, shadow-like, slipped out the door.

Bishop Guido remained standing in the dark shadows of the painter's scaffolding, waiting to see if anyone would appear. "Quite likely," he thought, "it was only the sexton closing up the sacristy for the evening." As he waited, he looked across the nave at the old frescoes painted many years ago on the opposite wall of the cathedral. His eyes slowly traveled along the scenes, from the betrayal and arrest of Jesus in the garden of Gethsemane to his trial before Pilate and finally his death on the cross. As bishop, he had now commissioned an artist from Florence to paint frescos on the wall directly above him. These new frescos would depict other events leading up to the passion and death of Jesus. Walking from the shadows out into the center of the long empty canyon of the cathedral, he turned and smiled with satisfaction at the first almost-finished fresco. "Bishops," he thought, "have the opportunity to create great treasures that will inspire faith today and for generations to come." His hope was that his commissioning of these new frescos as well as his encouragement of the youthful Francesco would be such a gift to the Church, now and for future generations. In the evening twilight he gazed up at the new scene of Jesus cleansing of the Temple. He wondered if the young man with whom he had just talked would make that fresco prophetic.

*I*n the year of our Lord 1210 Francesco and his small band of eleven companions began traveling on foot from Assisi to Rome. They had departed very early on the day after his meeting with Bishop Guido. Soon they joined the crowds at Orvieto on the main highway to the Eternal City of Rome. This main road to the most important city in all of Christendom was crowded and colorful; there were chanting pilgrims carrying banners of their village patron saint, Irish monks and prisoners in chains on their pilgrimages of penance, along with German and French merchants on foot and horseback, their mules piled high with their goods. They shared the road as well with serfs freed of bond, monks and nuns on errands to Rome for their communities, and ragged, dirty beggars. It seemed that Francesco and his small band belonged to this latter group rather than the clerical gentry on horseback. These were the richly attired lord abbots and princely bishops accompanied by their household guards and traveling courts of servants and clerics. It is said that all roads lead to Rome, and it is also

true that all kinds of peoples traveled them: unemployed soldiers, tinkers, papal postmen and knights on their way to the Holy Land, giant wagons groaning under the weight of marble being transported to some great Roman church that was under construction, outcasts and outlaws, colorfully clad minstrels, medical quacks with their miracle cures for everything from baldness to bad teeth, along with market-bound cattle and sheep.

Francesco appeared to be deaf to the bedlam of singing pilgrims, bleating sheep and the shouts and curses of wagon drivers. He was absorbed in composing a rule of life for his small band of brothers. The minstrel in him began composing a song, using the various instructions Jesus had given his disciples as if they were notes in his ballad of the Rule of the Little Brothers.

At noon, the band of brothers paused alongside the road to rest and share some bread, and Francesco used the time to dictate his rule to Pietro Catanii. Before they had departed from Portiuncula, Francesco told him to bring along his pen, ink and parchment because the bishop had told him that he must submit a written rule to the Pope. "Pietro, please read the rule back to us," he said after finishing his dictation, "and tell me what you think of it." Addressing the rest of the group, he added, "And, brothers, I also want your opinions."

Clearing his throat, Pietro began:

> The Rule of the Little Brothers of Assisi is the Gospel Rule of our Lord Jesus. Those who join the Little Brothers shall sell all they own, give their money to the poor and then live in poverty. The brothers shall joyfully proclaim the Good News barefoot, without sandals, carrying no money, and having no clothing other than one tunic.

> The Little Brothers shall offer no resistance when attacked, will never return evil for evil or insult for insult. They will love their enemies, bless their persecutors, and never judge others or speak evil of anyone. They shall pray without ceasing, giving thanks always and for everything. Their suffering they will keep hidden so as to be merry and rejoice always.

> The Little Brothers shall never worry or be anxious about tomorrow's needs. They shall be like the birds of the air and the lilies of the field, dependent only upon God's holy and

loving providence for their needs. Ever watchful for the kingdom of God, they shall repent and do penance so as to enter into the kingdom. The Little Brothers shall love one another, will love all they meet as brothers and will be the servants of others. They will love God with all their heart, soul, mind, and body, and they shall believe in the Good News by living it daily without compromise.

Pietro looked up from the parchment, smiling, and the other brothers looked at one another as if asking with their raised eyebrows, "Is that all?" A few of them were familiar with the detailed Rule of St. Benedict, which covered every aspect of daily life, but this rule of Francesco's was more a song than a set of rules.

"Francesco, you asked me what I think?" Pietro asked. "Well, I think it's a rather nice synopsis of the Gospels," he said, laughing lightly.

"What's a synopsis?" asked Giles.

"Our friend Pietro is having a little fun with me," Francesco replied. "What he means is that our rule is a brief summary of the Holy Gospels. As a farmer's son, you could understand synopsis as being like a pile of good grain that's left at harvesttime after you've separated the chaff and stems from the wheat by shaking it through a thresher's winnowing basket."

Giles understood perfectly the word Pietro had used after Francesco's analogy. Yet he innocently asked, "But is that bad or good? I hope that means it's good, since we've come all this way to get the Holy Father's blessing. Besides," he said, grinning broadly enough to show his many absent teeth, "by going to Rome we can gain one of those large indulgences that will take away all our years in purgatory!"

"Let us not disappoint our brother Giles," Francesco said, "by sitting the whole day along the roadside and so delay him from gaining one of those great Roman indulgences. It's time we returned on our journey. But as we walk, let us continue our conversation, for I want to hear your opinions of our new rule."

"I think," Leone said, beginning the discussion as they again joined the throng on the crowded highway, "that we should add to that rule the three vows of chastity, poverty, and obedience. The members of the other religious orders like those of St. Benedict and St. Augustine take those holy vows."

"Leone, dear friend," Francesco replied, "haven't we already spoken numerous times about those vows? Doesn't the Gospel contain all that is necessary for salvation and for holiness? If Jesus had felt explicitly taking those three vows to be essential, would he not have had his disciples do so? Why is a vow of chastity necessary for unmarried men such as us, since God requires that we live chastely? Wouldn't our taking a vow of chastity be like wearing a hat on top of a hat?"

Giles giggled, but Leone didn't smile, for he had no response to Francesco's questions. The brothers walked in silence until Leone spoke again, "Somewhere in our rule, shouldn't we include a statement about our habits, about their identifying design and color? You can instantly recognize and distinguish a Benedictine from an Augustinian monk by. . . ."

Francesco shuddered inwardly, for the closer they came to Rome the more he felt his once glorious freedom eroding away. "Habits, Brother Leone," he said, "are the religious clothing of clerics and nuns. We are laymen. Jesus never told his disciples to dress the same as each other, but only to love one another! If we must have a habit, let it be a habit of loving one another and all people, for then even if we are naked everyone will recognize us as the Little Brothers of Assisi."

Giles giggled again at the image of the twelve of them going about naked preaching the Gospel.

"Leone, my friend," Francesco said, "I don't mean to make light of your concerns, but I just don't understand why we need habits more distinctive than what we're wearing right now. Look around us at the poor traveling on this road; do not the tattered tunics we wear identify us with the children of God, the *minores*, the poorest of the poor?" He stopped and stood on one foot as he held the other up in the air, adding, "Look at our feet. Don't they speak loudly of who we are? Even the poorest of peasants on this road are wearing sandals. So let our bare, dirty feet—along with our great love and abounding joy—announce our identity to one and all."

*T*heir last day on the road to Rome was drawing to a close as a weary sun, exhausted from its day-long travel across the sky, was slumping behind the mountains to rest. Off in the distance the brothers could see the Eternal City of Rome as they left the highway to make camp for the night. As exhausted as the sun after another long day of walking, they sat around a fire. As they ate their skinny meal, they again returned to discussing their rule. Francesco remained firm in

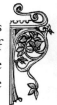

his insistence that they live their life of absolute poverty not as monks but as a brotherhood of laymen. In the midst of their discussion one of the brothers asked if Francesco's pledge of equality didn't mean that the group as a whole had the right to decide what should, or shouldn't, be in their common rule.

"Brothers," said Bernardo, who had once known the soft feel of the finest cloth and fur-trimmed winter wool upon his skin, "I respect Francesco's desire for equality among us so that each man's opinion is as valuable as the other's. However, I propose that we agree to allow him alone to compose the rule that he wishes to present for the Pope's approval. None of us would be sitting here tonight around this fire outside the gates of Rome if he had not inspired us by his life of great joy and if we did not share the conviction that the Spirit of God was leading him. Am I not right?" The brothers all nodded silently. "If we did not think that Francesco was inspired by God, why would we have left all things to join him? While many people have thought that he is mad or possessed, we have seen the finger of God upon his life. So, dear comrades, let us all now trust in his prayer-inspired vision for our way of life."

The brothers' response was silence—not the silence of a begrudging acceptance but of agreement with the truth of Bernardo's assessment of the basis for their common life. As they settled in to sleep for the night, Francesco was grateful for what his loyal friend Bernardo had said, yet his gratitude was moth-eaten. He remained conflicted, on the one hand, by his commitment to a simple rule reflective of the Gospels, and, on the other hand, by his feeling that his singlemindedness was a violation of the principle of equality he wanted the brothers to share. He was totally convinced that God had called him to lead a radical Gospel life without compromise, and the beautiful words of Brother Bernardo had given him the confidence to be the sole author of their rule. Yet his sleep that night was fitful, as he was caught in the tension between equality in the group and charismatic leadership. And he wrestled with a recurring fear: Was the radical life of poverty that God had called him to embrace not something that others could reasonably live out? And if that haunting fear was true, would he not then drown in a sea of his brothers' compromises?

The next morning, upon entering Rome, Francesco and the little band of ragged, barefoot brothers invisibly walked directly to the magnificent piazza of the Pope's Lateran Palace. They were

overshadowed by great pomp of the richly attired lord abbots and bishops, who were accompanied by their elaborate entourages of soldiers, servants and clerics, some of whom had shared with them the highway down to Rome. The papal troops at the entrance gates to the courtyard of the Lateran Palace stood at attention and saluted with their lances as these elaborately attired clerical dignitaries passed through the gates.

When the officer attired in the plume-adorned helmet and highly polished armor saw Francesco and the brothers, he snapped, "Beggars, be off with you. If it's handouts you want, go around to the kitchen entrance at the rear of the palace."

"Sir," replied Francesco, "we have come all the way from Assisi to speak with the Holy Father."

"Lice-infested beggars! I said, be off to the rear entrance!" the officer shouted, raising his arm toward Francesco in a mock attack. "Or else!"

So Francesco and the eleven left the front gates and walked around to the rear of the palace.

"No, you do not understand," Francesco said to the servant at the papal kitchen door. "We are not hungry for bread. Allow me to introduce myself. I am Francesco Bernadone, and these are my brothers. We've come all the way to Rome from Assisi to speak to our Holy Father, Pope Innocent III. Would you kindly inform the Holy Father that we wish to speak to him?"

"Naturally, my Lord," replied the apron-attired servant at the kitchen door. Bowing deeply, he added, "How fortunate that you've come to the right entrance, for, indeed, His Holiness is here."

"Wonderful," replied Francesco. "God is good."

"But, alas, my lord, I must sadly inform you that His Holiness is presently occupied with the noon meal. He is attending a big pot of boiling noodles to ensure they are *al dente*. If the Vicar of Christ wasn't so busy with this matter of grave importance, I'm sure he would grant you an immediate audience. Since that's not possible, may I instead offer you some bread?"

Francesco, whose stomach, like those of his companions, was empty, swallowed his pride. "Thank you, you are most kind. We are grateful to be blessed by the generosity of the Lord Pope and by you one of his most gracious servants. May God reward you for your generous compassion and kindness toward the poor and hungry."

The next day they returned to the rear kitchen door of the papal palace, and again the day after that, petitioning to speak directly to the Pope. Each time, all they received was bread. After the third day's disappointment his disheartened companions were ready to return to Assisi, convinced they were never going to be able to speak to the Pope.

"Did not our Lord say to pray with faith?" Francesco asked the brothers as they sat eating their bread outside the kitchen. "He said to 'ask and you shall receive . . . knock and it shall be answered.' Brothers, we must have faith not only great enough to move mountains, but even great enough to move the Pope's servants so they will petition him to speak to us. Let us continue knocking."

"Mountains would be easier to move," Bernardo said, placing his arm around Francesco's shoulders. "But let us keep knocking on the Pope's door, even though I'd wager that God will more quickly answer those who knock on his heavenly door."

*S*eated on the papal throne was a tall, dignified man whose very presence commanded respect. His dark, intent eyes gave the impression they could effortlessly pry into a man's heart, stripping him naked of pretense. His eyes perfectly fit his face of noble refinement, a face as autocratic as any of Rome's once powerful Caesars. Yet it wasn't as perfectly balanced as the countenances of the idealized Greek and Roman statues. On the right side of his face, his cheek lines dropped noticeably lower than on the left. The right side reflected the sternness of an autocratic ruler, while his left side seemed more rounded, as if a smile was about to appear and express his gentle spirit. Pope Innocent was fully aware of his unique face, as well as the reason for its distinctiveness. While he was the most powerful man in all of Christendom, if not the world, and although he looked upon himself as "the judge of all men who can be judged by none," there was within him another, very different person. His face reflected the secret of his two diverse personalities, even though everyone in the papal court—everyone except the astute Cardinal Lorenzo Montino—seemed unaware of the second personality.

Outside the papal throne room, on the other side of the doors at the far end of the hall, was a domed, marble-walled antechamber. There, on wooden benches lining the walls, sat the cardinals' private secretaries and personal valets who served as their trusted couriers. The antechamber also was crowded with bishops and their secretaries, noble

princes, and dignitaries awaiting their audiences with the Pope. This procedure of having to wait in the high-ceilinged, ornate antechamber worked the old Roman magic of enhancing the already awesome authority of the Pope.

"Your Holiness," said a cardinal stepping forward to the throne with a petition, "your papal legate whom you sent along on the Fourth Crusade has asked your permission to dispense knights from fulfilling the personal vows they swore to recapture Jerusalem. His report states that only the more devout knights are requesting your dispensation, since the others have already departed, grabbing as much booty as possible."

"Granted," the Pope sadly replied with a sigh. "This entire Crusade has been a disaster. Those greedy, plundering Venetians manipulated the expedition by sacking their rival city of Zara in Dalmatia. God grant us absolution for the rape of the cities of Zara and Constantinople. Your Eminence, send to our legate the necessary documents of permission and our blessing bearing our seal."

"Your Holiness, regarding requests for your permission," Cardinal Uzielli said, stepping forward, "I have serious concerns about a request from an Italian bishop for the celebration of the Mass for the feast of, . . ." pausing, he scanned the document in his hand, ". . . that pious French devotional called 'the Immaculate Conception of Mary.' My concern is with the orthodoxy of this novel devotion that has now spread here to Italy from France." Uzielli was robed from head to toe in brilliant scarlet, including his broad-rimmed hat, which at the moment was hanging down his back from an elaborate gold and green twisted silk cord. He was the only cardinal present who was dressed in this manner, and all the other cardinals thought he made a striking impression dressed entirely in that shade of red. More than a few of them desired to be likewise attired.

"As your Holiness is aware," Cardinal Uzielli continued, "since this feast is based on the concept of Mary the Mother of God being completely free of any taint of original sin from the very moment of her conception, that it is . . . well . . . most controversial."

"Yes, of course," the Pope responded, being a scholar himself. "We are aware that the great theologian Saint Bernard of Clairvaux, even though he had a great personal devotion to the Mother of God, was opposed to such a doctrine." Then, looking over Uzielli's head to where the other cardinals were seated, the Pope said, "Cardinal Montino, please approach us, for you are known as a spiritual theologian learned in such matters, and are in a position to offer us some wise counsel on this question."

"Your Holiness," said Montino, rising after kissing the Pope's ring, "I wish that I were, indeed, learned in such matters of the spirit." Standing alongside Uzielli, he could almost tangibly feel the resentment flowing from his scarlet-robed brother cardinal, whom he knew desired no assistance, since he had already prepared a solution to this question of orthodoxy. "However, Your Holiness, as to the question of this Marian devotion raised by my distinguished brother cardinal, my personal theology is the same as that of St. Bernard and many other theologians. I agree that this rising Marian devotion detracts from the redemption of our Lord Jesus Christ. Original sin is a human condition. If we endorse a feast that declares that Mary, even though she was the mother of our Lord, was completely free of original sin from the moment of conception, are we not then implying she was not really human? And if Mary was not essentially human, was she then divine?"

"Naturally that would be heresy!" Uzielli replied instantly, eager not to be eclipsed by Montino. "Although lacking the endorsement of Rome, this pious feast of the Conception of Our Lady has been celebrated for the past hundred years in various English and French monasteries. Yet even pious feasts can be extremely dangerous because. . . ."

"*Lex orandi, lex credendi,*" Montino said, completing Uzielli's sentence as he graciously bowed to him. "What we pray is what we believe."

"Precisely," Uzielli replied. "As my distinguished colleague in the College of Cardinals has just stated, that has been and is the long-standing norm of Holy Mother Church. Yet this feast of Mary being immaculately conceived lacks the important required criterion that the custom in question must be contained in the apostolic tradition. The Holy Office is required to keep an ever-diligent and watchful eye on new devotions and carefully attend to the precise wording of the prayers and devotions of the Church. For these reasons, I urge that Rome take immediate action, and. . . ."

"And your opinion, Cardinal Montino?" asked the Pope.

"Your Holiness, do nothing! Do not take on this thorny issue yourself. Rather, present this doctrine of Mary being free from original sin to our theologians and scholars at the great University of Paris, renowned for her philosophy and theology. Also, present it for

examination to the scholars at the great University of Bologna, your own alma mater, and allow them to debate the implications of how this devotion might greatly diminish the redemptive incarnation of our Lord Jesus Christ and usher in the rebirth of the pagan Mother Goddess."

"I beg to disagree," said a frustrated Uzielli. "If we give this matter over to the scholars, with their endless theological hairsplitting distinctions, it might take centuries to reach a decision. Would it not be more expedient if Rome acted at once to forbid this unorthodox Marian devotion?"

"Your Holiness," Montino said, "if you suppress this emerging, popular feast, it will be regarded as an imperial papal act, but if you allow the learned doctors of theology to explore it thoroughly, it will be seen as a pastoral decision. I am personally against elevating the Mother of Christ to a sinless status because the devotions and piety of the common people soon would raise her up to a status above even that of her son. Then again," he continued after a brief pause, "theology is a living organism, and, who knows, perhaps what today appears as unorthodox may in centuries become orthodox. Personally, I believe that our Lord was most explicit that our prayers reach the Father through him—and through him alone. The common people, who are untrained in the finer distinctions of theology, may begin to bypass Christ in asking Mary to intercede for them. And I am concerned, as I said, that in this expanding devotion to Mary as the sinless Mother of God, the ancient pagan Mother Goddess cult is being resurrected. But, as for the present celebrations of this Immaculate Conception feast, I would say it is quite harmless if observed in a few remote monasteries. Monks tend toward such devotions to the Mother of God perhaps because they are celibate men living closely together and separated from women. . . ."

"Cardinal Uzielli," the Pope interrupted him, "it is our wish that you reply to any further requests regarding this novel devotion by saying that other than in those monasteries presently observing it, the Holy See counsels that our bishops prudently refrain from introducing it. Now the day is quickly passing; what is the next item?"

"Your Holiness," Uzielli replied, "the Holy Office is gravely concerned about the spread of certain errors attributed to Joachim of Fiore, who, as you may recall, died only two years ago in 1208. While he was purported to be a pious man renowned for his . . . visions . . .

sadly, such mystics who report hearing voices or seeing visions are too often blinded to the orthodox truths of the faith of Holy Mother Church. It now seems that Joachim's ghost is afoot among his followers, known as the Florentines, who are continuing to teach his erroneous doctrines on the Trinity."

Pope Innocent nodded his head in agreement as he listened, aware, at the same time, of how his scarlet watchdog of orthodoxy appeared to be taking mouthwatering delight in his work of rooting out heretical errors. The case of the Italian Cistercian Joachim of Fiore reminded the Pope of that mystic's prediction that the year 1260 would usher in the Age of the Holy Spirit. Joachim prophesied that this would be an age of great religious revival and reform. "Fifty years from now is too long," the Pope pondered. "We could use such a Pentecostal reform right now instead of having to wait half a century."

"And, your Holiness," Uzielli continued, "the Holy Office continues to receive complaints from the bishops of France and even from some here in Italy about simple laymen and laywomen—saying Mass and forgiving sins. While these persons are usually pious leaders of religious groups, and while there is an ancient tradition that permits such a practice, we feel that it is a dangerous situation. We strongly believe it requires the Church immediately and precisely to define that only ordained male celibate clerics are. . . ."

"Thank you, Cardinal Uzielli," the Pope again interrupted him. "As usual, you keep us well informed on the most recent serious problems to which we must attend. We are grateful for your guiding wisdom and loyal defense of the Church in these most difficult times that overflow with bad tidings—and for your most prompt attention to every problem that visits the Eternal City." Uzielli smiled with delight as he slowly and reverentially backed away from the papal throne.

"I have more favorable news for Your Holiness," said Cardinal Montino, who had remained standing at the papal throne. "You spoke of your pleasure at the speed of my brother cardinal's attention to problems. In that vein, I am pleased to report the good news that your recent document to King John of England was delivered by a papal courier to Canterbury in only twenty days, and that includes your messenger's crossing of the English Channel!"

"Ah, Cardinal Montino, that is very good news indeed," the Pope beamed. "We're only ten years into this new century, and already it shows signs of becoming an age of rapid communication. We must

adapt ourselves to the swiftness of this new time in which not only documents and strategic information, but even the news of daily events can travel so rapidly across Christendom."

Cardinal Montino smiled to himself, encouraged by the Pope's delight in new things. He continued by reporting on the amazing progress of the construction of Paris' new Cathedral of Notre Dame. The Pope listened eagerly to Montino's report because as a student at the University of Paris he had personally visited the construction site of the cathedral, which had been begun three years after his birth. Montino read to the Pope a report from the bishop of Paris, who said that if work on that great cathedral continued at the same rapid pace he expected it to be finished in only forty years. He also reported that the Cathedral of Chartres, the first to use the innovative flying buttresses that enabled the church's walls to rise to unbelievable heights, was due to be completed in only ten years, in 1220. As he spoke of these new cathedrals, Montino used the increasingly popular word "Gothic," which formerly had the derogatory connotation of "barbaric," to describe this new form of architecture that was now so popular beyond the Alps—and so different from the classic Italian style of churches.

While Montino spoke of cathedrals, the Pope's thoughts lingered on the news that his bull of interdiction had already arrived at Canterbury. "King John's arrogant rejection of my papal nominee for the bishopric of Canterbury has forced me to place the entire country under an interdict that will prevent any of his subjects from receiving the sacraments. And I can be assured that his subjects, being faithful sons of the Church and fearful for their immortal souls, will refuse to obey any order of their king until he bends to Rome. That," the stern autocratic side of the Pope thought with delight, "will force King John into submission. . . ."

"Your signature is required, Your Holiness," a member of the papal court requested as he stepped forward with a handful of documents, "on this decree, and on this annulment, and also here on this appointment of a new bishop." As the Pope signed the documents presented to him, he continued thinking about England and the mild contempt in which he held this island country, as it was only recently civilized. "Where," he thought, "would those barbarians—who once painted their faces blue—be if Rome had not conquered and civilized them? Now, all these centuries later, Rome, under my pontificate, will once again bring the English to their knees." Various cardinals approaching his throne with their ecclesiastical business interrupted these thoughts about England.

Chapter 12

WHILE THE POPE CONDUCTED DAILY VATICAN BUSINESS, across the papal throne room, Cardinal Montino pretended to scratch his head so he could privately speak to Cardinal Ugolino from behind his raised silk sleeve. "My 'ears and eyes' in the Pope's kitchen have informed me that Cardinal Uzielli's so-called heretical barefoot preacher, Francesco of Assisi, is here."

"Here in Rome?" Although Cardinal Ugolino's face was expressionless, his whispered voice wasn't. "Where?"

Montino held a handkerchief to his mouth and coughed lightly to cover his response. "Even now, Francesco and his small band of followers are at the back door entrance to the kitchen of this Lateran Palace!"

"Do you think," Ugolino replied quickly, "that I should send my trusted secretary to bring him inside?"

"No need. I've already anticipated your desire, my old friend. I've instructed my secretary to usher them with all secrecy to the small chapel right down the hall from the antechamber. I propose that I stay here to keep an eye on that crafty fox Uzielli while you go to the chapel. Question this Francesco and see what it is that we are actually dealing with. I trust your intuition, Ugolino."

"Ah, my dear Lorenzo, you are always a step ahead of me," Ugolino whispered with the thinnest of smiles. After a brief pause, he rose and departed from the throne room, unnoticed by the cardinals busily clustered around the papal throne.

About an hour later, Montino observed the private secretary of Cardinal Uzielli hurrying into the throne room and whispering something into Uzielli's ear. Whatever he said brought a perplexing

 look to the cardinal's face. Montino suppressed a smile as the tall, ornately carved doors of the antechamber opened to Cardinal Ugolino, who proceeded with brisk decorum directly to the papal throne. He waited patiently while some nobleman completed his papal audience and received the Pope's blessing.

"Your Holiness," Cardinal Ugolino said quickly, before the papal chamberlain could announce the next dignitary, "please pardon the rudeness of this interruption. I know you have a crowded agenda of audiences today, but the urgency of the Holy Spirit prompts me to. . . ."

"Ah, my good Cardinal Ugolino," smiled the Pope, "rarely are our days interrupted by an issue carrying the immediacy of the Spirit! You have captivated us with your Pentecostal preface; please enlighten us."

Bowing slightly, Ugolino continued, "Your Holiness, we're all aware of your zealous wish to reform Christ's Church, your desire for a spiritual revival."

The Pope nodded in agreement as he thought, "Indeed, I am, Ugolino, and I've begun making plans for a new ecumenical council to deal with that reform." The serious tribulations of the Church quickly paraded before him: widespread abuses in the practice of celibacy, the need for a better-educated clergy, the need for canonical distinctions to define proper ministers of the Eucharist and Confession, the laxity of the people toward the sacraments, and the necessity to address certain questionable doctrinal and theological thought advanced by the likes of that mystic Joachim of Fiore. He had already drafted a proposal that would require all the faithful, under the pain of mortal sin, to confess and to receive Holy Communion at least once a year. Inwardly he groaned, fearing that even if he called general councils of all the bishops of Christendom from now until all the cows came home, any new regulations they might decree would be like old women—toothless! He knew from experience that such new Church laws did not make Holy Mother Church pregnant with new life but only with hoards of canon lawyers and scribbling clerics. All the while, nothing would change in the spiritual life of the Church.

"We are aware of your pastoral concern. . . ." The Pope became conscious that he was hearing the faint voice of Ugolino as if it were coming from another world, and so he turned the focus of his attention away from his thoughts and back to the cardinal standing in front of him. He considered Ugolino to be a good man, a prelate of integrity, one whom he could trust and whom he knew possessed a personal dedication to him. ". . . as well as your keen interest in new inventions and ideas. One example being your wish for replacing the old Roman numerals with their new Arabic counterparts, particularly because of their innovative use of the number zero. . . ."

"Like bread being buttered," the Pope thought, "these cardinals feel they must prepare me for what they are going to present." The Pope calmly interjected, "To the point, my good Cardinal Ugolino, to the point."

"Yes, of course, Your Holiness. I feel impelled to take the most unusual step of presenting to you what may be a gift of the Holy Spirit and an answer to our prayers. That gift comes in the form of Francesco Bernadone, a young man of Umbria from the city of Assisi. He comes to Your Holiness with the blessing of his pastoral shepherd, Bishop Guido of Assisi. After visiting with him briefly myself, it seems clear to me that he also comes with the blessing of God."

Eagerly leaning forward in his throne chair, obviously intrigued, Pope Innocent said, "We would, indeed, like to meet any man who comes to us so blessed." Cardinal Ugolino bowed, and as he crossed the throne room toward the doors, the antechamber buzzed with the animated and even excited whispering of the assembled cardinals. Cardinal Uzielli wasn't excited, he was furious, for his secretary had just informed him who it was that Ugolino was about to present to the Pope. Beneath his mask of unconcerned calm he was outraged at being foiled again, but the only indication of his anger was in his lap. There, hidden by his scarlet silk cassock, his hands were clenched into tight fists as scarlet-red as his cardinal's robes.

The first to gasp in disbelief were the purple-robed papal courtiers who opened the large doors of the antechamber to Cardinal Ugolino as he escorted what appeared to be a shabby beggar in an old gray tunic into the papal audience hall. Accompanying them in an incongruous procession were eleven other ragged, barefoot beggars. An audible murmuring-wave of shocked disbelief spread from the doors over assembled cardinals and clerics all the way up to the papal throne—with three exceptions. Cardinals Montino and Ugolino were smiling, as was Pope Innocent III. The moment the Pope saw the young man in the tattered gray tunic, he felt an inexplicable surge of excitement race up his spine, causing a smile to appear on his face, which he quickly hid by his raising his right index finger to his lips.

 As Francesco and his brothers knelt in awed respect, Cardinal Ugolino formally presented them to Pope Innocent. Then in simple and somewhat faulty Latin, Francesco told the Pope the story of the message he had heard from the crucifix about restoring old San Damiano. He spoke passionately of his conviction that God had called him, and now his little band, to live the same kind of life to which Jesus had called his first disciples. As Francesco spoke with great enthusiasm about their rule of life, the Pope moved his index finger from his lip upward to his right nostril, at the same time bringing his thumb to his left nostril in a gesture that suggested he was pondering deeply. Then he squeezed his fingers together, discretely closing the papal nostrils. The Pope thought about Ugolino saying that this Francesco was a gift from heaven, yet to him the aroma of this divine gift was more reminiscent of the papal stables. Around the crowded, windowless room full of cardinals and dignitaries, a sea of silk handkerchiefs began to appear everywhere.

"Holy Father," Francesco said as he handed the Pope the parchment on which Brother Pietro had written their rule, "my brothers and I humbly ask that Your Holiness bless and approve our rule of life, which we believe God is calling us to live out."

As the Pope lowered his thumb and finger from his nose, he smelled something more than unwashed bodies in dirty beggar's robes and feet that reeked of a mixture of animal dung and the muck of the road. Innocent III was not the most powerful man in all of Christendom by accident; he had a sixth sense by which he could sniff out what was in the hearts of other men. He possessed the ability to detect the hidden stench of deceit or trickery, but in this poor man kneeling before him the only inner scent he identified was sanctity.

Pope Innocent questioned Francesco about his Rule of the Little Brothers, suggesting that it seemed vague, that it was rather brief and lacking in precise details. It was obvious that he was not prepared to be surprised by the young beggar's response. Unlike the cardinals and bishops with whom the Pope daily dealt, Francesco immediately countered the Pope's objections by asking him if he also thought Jesus had been vague and too brief in the Gospel rules for his disciples. To all the cardinals' amazement, the Pope and Francesco engaged in a stimulating exchange in which they respectfully disagreed over his rule of life, until the Pope held up his hand indicating that their discussion had ended.

"Your Eminences," Pope Innocent III asked, addressing the collection of cardinals, "you are my wise counselors. What are your opinions on the novel and simple rule this man from Assisi has proposed in living out the Gospel of our Lord without compromise? Should we grant him our papal approval?" The Pope's keen eyes scanned their faces, waiting for one of them to respond. Like small children, the assembled cardinals were eagerly ready to play that favorite game of the Roman papal court, "Guess What the Pope Is Thinking." Whenever the Pope asked their opinion, the game's winner would be the first cardinal to think of the correct decision, which, of course, was the same one that the Pope had already reached. The sport of this game was especially appreciated by the brilliant pontiff presently seated on the throne of Peter, for he knew precisely what should or should not be done, and so had little need of their counsel.

"Ah, a Gordian knot indeed!" said Cardinal Uzielli, the master of diplomacy and court intrigue, sweeping forward in a rustle of silken robes as he approached the papal throne. "Your Holiness is faced with a most difficult problem. Unlike Alexander the Great, who, as legend says, cut that famed knot in two, I fear that you will not reach a resolution to this question from Assisi with a single, bold, decisive stroke. The moment this son of the Church presented his rule of life for your approval, I prayed to the Holy Spirit to guide you in this potentially complex issue. I feel confident in speaking for each of my brother cardinals when I say that we all are praying that you be granted the wisdom to make the right decision, Your Holiness." He bowed gracefully to the Pope and then continued, "As Your Holiness knows only too well, these are the most difficult, troubling, and confusing of times, when it seems that heavenly voices are being heard by everyone. A mere forty years ago the apostolic Church had to judge the validity of the so-called 'Pious Men of France!'" Uzielli turned briefly and smiled at Francesco and his companions, who were kneeling before the Pope. "These pious men—and women—whom the French bishops reported were running around naked in the woods, living in leafy huts, claimed they were embracing the beatific poverty of the Gospels! Beatific! They disregarded and denounced the Holy Sacraments, the Priesthood, and the Church's hallowed state of Matrimony, and they ended by rejecting the authority of their bishops and even of the Vicar of Christ! History has proven how radical religious movements that diverge from the conventional customs and traditions of the Church

carry the seeds of potential heretical dissent. Please note that I do not wish to pass judgment, and point only to the possibility of heresy. So, Your Holiness, my brothers of the College of Cardinals petition that the Holy Spirit inspire you to discern the will of God wisely and rightly in the case of this barefoot young man."

"Uzielli, you clever old fox," thought the Pope, "you Roman rascal. You've cleverly presented to the cardinals your negative response to my question by comparing this Francesco of Assisi to the heretical Peter Waldo and his poor men of Lyons without even mentioning him by name. With your sly comments about the pious men of France, you've tilted those fence-setting cardinals over to your side, and you've piously disguised that maneuver as a prayerful concern for my discernment of the will of God." Glancing slowly around the room, Pope Innocent asked, "And the rest of you, my cardinals, what is your opinion about granting our approval to this new community of extreme poverty? How shall we decide this question which your distinguished colleague, Cardinal Uzielli, described as a Gordian knot?"

"Your Holiness," Cardinal Montino said as he approached the papal throne, "With your permission, and Cardinal Uzielli's, I would like to speak for myself. While indeed troubling, these new times are also fresh and invigorating times. The Church must adapt to new times—as you yourself have said, today's rapid communications require that the Church adapt to new ways of thinking." Turning to face the assembled cardinals, he continued, "And, my brothers, as the leaders of the Church we should not fear what is new, for did not our Blessed Lord say, 'Behold, I make all things new'?" Again facing the Pope, he said, "Perhaps this young man from Assisi and his companions who kneel here before you may be part of a newness of the Holy Spirit. Perhaps he is part of the answer to our prayers for the rebirth of a love for God that slumbers today because of clerical abuse, sin, and apathy. Your Holiness, you've asked for our opinions, and I humbly suggest that in our anxiety or haste for some quick resolution we use no Alexandrian sword. I respectfully propose that you temporarily delay your final decision until—with the support of my and my brother cardinals' prayers—you have had sufficient time to ponder prayerfully the fate of this new spiritual community that has been presented to us this day by Francesco of Assisi."

"I agree," Cardinal Ugolino replied quickly as he stepped forward, "with that wise proposal of Cardinal Montino. My humble suggestion,

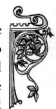

Holy Father, is that you invite Francesco and his brothers to return here tomorrow or the day after for your decision." Then, turning to Francesco, he said, "If the Holy Father agrees with this proposal, I shall make arrangements for you to be guests at a nearby Benedictine monastery until he shall call you back. There you will be properly fed and have a decent place to sleep."

"We do, indeed, approve of the wise proposal you and Cardinal Montino have brought forth," the Pope replied. Then, looking kindly down at the small group of poor men in ragged tunics kneeling before him, he said, "Francesco, lest your petition become lost in the Vatican's notoriously sluggish offices renowned for misplacing requests for centuries, it is our wish that all of you return tomorrow. At that time we will you give you our decision." Raising his right hand, he concluded by saying, "Now, go in peace with our blessing, Francesco Bernadone and the Brothers of Assisi," tracing over them the sign of the cross.

Montino and Ugolino, along with Francesco and his brothers, bowed to the Pope. As they were departing the papal throne room, Cardinal Ugolino said softly, "When you return tomorrow, Francesco, you may come to the front gates of the papal palace. I assure you that this time you and your brothers will be received there with honor and respect."

*U*nlike their previous nights in Rome, the eleven Little Brothers of Assisi slept on good beds after enjoying an excellent monastic meal. Francesco, however, spent the entire night in a prayer vigil in the abbey chapel, fervently begging God to inspire the Holy Father to grant his blessing and approve their way of life. Meanwhile, on the other side of Rome, Cardinals Montino and Ugolino dined together as they discussed the amazing events of that day and the possible resolutions and implications of the Pope's decision on Francesco's request.

"If the Pope agrees to grant his approval," Ugolino said, "he will surely have to make some compromises to placate the powerful force of cardinals allied with Uzielli. We can only hope and pray for the sake of the Church that the Pope decides in favor of Francesco, and then that our young friend from Assisi will be willing to accept Innocent's conditions for his approval."

"I agree with your assessment of the political situation," Montino replied. "Even now, Uzielli is surely gathering a camp of his supporters

from among the most influential cardinals, whom the Pope can't ignore, but. . . ." Montino sat with his eyes closed in silence, slowly nodding his head.

"But what?" asked Ugolino, feeling anxious because of his friend's unfinished sentence.

"To me," Montino replied, "Francesco did not appear to be the kind of man who makes compromises—with himself, with the Gospels, and even, I fear, with the Pope. Though I greatly admire that quality in him, I don't know if he is willing to modify his Gospel vision."

"Oh, Montino, I hope you're wrong about that, but I sensed the same thing. Francesco's dream seems to mirror that of Peter of Waldo, and, sadly, because Peter refused to compromise with Rome he sealed his fate—and doomed his dream. May Francesco of Umbria not follow Waldo's path of rebelliousness. When I met with him ever so briefly today before presenting him to the Pope, I had the profound sense that I was in the presence of a. . . ."

". . . Saint?" asked Montino. "Yes, that was my impression too, Ugolino, even though I didn't speak with him privately as you did. Just being in his presence, I sensed his holiness and was attracted by his unique simplicity. I was in awe of how innocently and honestly he disagreed with the Holy Father. And, Ugolino, more than admiration, I felt shamed by him!

"Shamed? How, Lorenzo?"

"Saints shame us! Their purpose isn't so much to edify us as to shame us, even if the truly holy ones never desire to embarrass anyone by the intensity of their love. So, yes, I was shamed by his passionate zeal and his uncompromising commitment to the work he feels God is calling him to undertake. But his most outstanding and challenging quality is his enthusiastic and deep love of God. Ugolino, I don't have that kind of enthusiasm, love, or trust in God's providential care. Perhaps it's my age or the harvest of all my accumulated years of countless little concessions. Yet I know that age isn't an excuse: I was a compromiser even when I was his age. I knew when it was prudent, for my own interests, to remain silent—or, even worse, to agree with those in positions of authority when they were compromising the truth. How refreshing it was today when Francesco didn't play our little Roman game of "Guess What the Pope Is Thinking" by trying to conjure up the correct answer to match the decision already made by the Pope. No,

he honestly told Innocent what he thought and was bold enough to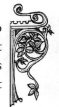
undiplomatically disagree with the Pope over his rule of life. I find it
delightfully paradoxical that he so beautifully embodies our pontiff's
name. Yet at the same time that such childlike innocence shames me, it
also inspires and challenges me."

"Lorenzo, I agree with what you say about Francesco, but don't be
so stern on yourself. You've done so much good by your career in the
Church. You've used your influence and position to. . . ."

"Ah, Ugolino, my dear friend, you echo the famous absolution that
each of us saint-failures grants to ourselves for being only lukewarm
lovers of God. Then, into our soft, comfortable, compromised lives
comes a Francesco of Assisi, and we abruptly find ourselves confronted
with the reality of being lackluster lovers."

"You said he inspired you," Ugolino replied. "I was inspired as well.
Perhaps the Church can be too if . . . if only he escapes from the
clutches of Uzielli."

"And Mad Matteo of Perugia . . ." added Montino.

"Padre Matteo Parini," Ugolino replied with animation. "I've
wanted for some time to ask you what you meant at our dinner with
Uzielli about Parini being the 'Wolf of Perugia'—and that he, not
Francesco, was guilty of heresy."

"Ah, the suave Lorenzo," Montino began, "the clever, diplomatic
Montino, slipped! It was a rare incidence, for I always carefully guard
the door to the cellar where my private, unspoken opinions and
judgments are hidden. But that manipulating, opinionated Uzielli
brings out the worst in me. As to why I called Matteo the Wolf of
Perugia, it is because our Lord warned his disciples about the vicious
wolves who would come among them, and he wasn't speaking of the
four-legged variety. Matteo and his rabid pack of wolf-cub disciples are
ravishing the easily swayed sheep among the faithful by preying on
their fears, prejudices, feelings of guilt and self-hate. My imagination
shudders to picture the scope of the diabolic evil that could engulf the
Church if Matteo and his hate-filled vigilante disciples were given a
license to 'reform' the Church by searching out her heretics. These self-
appointed champions of orthodoxy and so-called reformers are all cut
from the same cloth. They see grave evil in the sins of the flesh, in
sexual acts, but never in the immoral and unjust acts committed by the
powerful and rich upon the poor, in their exploitation of the peasants.
The Church has seen the likes of them before and, sadly, will have to

suffer them again in every age. But I ask you, Ugolino, how might evil more effectively infiltrate the kingdom of God to spread its wickedness than by wearing the gleaming white vestments of an anointed acolyte of God?"

The two men sat for some time in silence. Ugolino was surprised, even slightly stunned, by the intensity of feelings expressed by his usually serene and peaceful friend.

"That's a very perceptive insight," Ugolino finally said, "and I'm afraid you are all too accurate. I was intrigued as well by your comments about Matteo being a heretic. How did you mean that?"

"We profess in our faith that God is love and also that God is almighty. Scripture tells us that divine goodness fills creation, yet according to the doctrine preached by Matteo Parini the world is crammed with diabolic evil. The conclusion of his preaching is not that God is ever present, but, rather, that it's the devil who is everywhere, and who is as powerful, if not more powerful, than God. In short, the Parini heresy is that the evil itself has become God! The theology of his heresy is a vicious circle: What is pleasurable is sinful, and since pleasure is impossible to avoid, one is always in a state of sin. It says that since human nature is sin-tainted and since what is natural cannot be avoided, people are naturally drawn to evil and must be resigned to their fate of living in sin."

"But, Lorenzo, didn't the sin of Adam and Eve give the devil free rein to roam the world doing evil, leading people into temptation?"

"Yes," answered Montino, "evil is present in the world. But what about the grace God has poured into the world, especially through the person of Christ and Christ's Church? Those like Matteo who ignore the power of God's grace, who vehemently preach against the horrible sins committed by others and call down the vindictive wrath of God upon them, *become* hate-filled! They project what they hate in themselves upon others because they find those inclinations that secretly lurk within them to be so despicable and intolerable."

"And along comes Francesco of Assisi. . . ."

"Yes, the complete opposite of Matteo! Francesco is filled with a joy and love you can sense simply by being in his presence. His simple rule reflects the love and gentleness that he himself radiates. I know the Pope also felt Francesco's uncomplicated holiness. I could see it in the pontiff's mysterious doubled-sided face.

"But, enough for now, Ugolino. The hour is late, and it is time for me to leave. Thank you for your excellent dinner and gracious hospitality, which provided the two of us an opportunity to reflect on this most historic day."

On the other side of the Holy City, Cardinal Uzielli was conducting a secret conclave of a very select group of cardinals. Those cardinals whose loyalty he could count on were gathered at his palace for dinner in order to conspire about how they might sway the Pope not to confer his approval on this budding young heretic and his unwashed, stinking friends. Uzielli told his brother cardinals that this Francesco from Assisi, who claimed to hear God speaking to him, was but the first symptom in Italy of the dreaded disease of Peter Waldo's heresy that had already ravaged France. He waxed eloquently to them about that Gothic plague of so-called reformation that was brewing north of the Alps and now was beginning sweep down upon the Italian Church—and threatening to infect the whole Church. He described in lurid detail how Francesco had demonstrated his complete poverty by brazenly stripping himself stark naked before the bishop, clergy, and entire populace of Assisi—including women and innocent children. He concluded by quoting with relish from the secret reports of Padre Matteo and his Parinians, which stated that the barefoot heretics of Assisi showed every indication of being a greater threat to the Church than the Waldensians had ever been. The time, he said, to chop off the head of the serpent was now—right now, before it grew as large as Italy itself.

That same night, across the Tiber River in the Lateran Palace, Innocent III had retired after completing his night prayers in chapel. His sleep, however, was troubled, as he was assaulted by strange dreams that awakened him several times. After one dream, unable to return to sleep, he arose and walked to the open windows of his room. He stood looking out upon the sleeping city of Rome and reflected, "I usually find that major decisions come easily for me. Without a second thought, I am able to excommunicate a rebellious king, decide to convene an ecumenical council or even make my nephew a cardinal. Why then do I find it so difficult to make a decision about this simple barefoot preacher from Assisi?"

He began recalling pieces of his disturbing dreams. In one, he had been praying in his chapel before his crucifix when the Christ figure on the cross slowly changed into the barefoot preacher Francesco. The crucified figure in an old gray tunic was speaking to him, but for some unexplainable reason he was deaf and couldn't understand anything being said. Then Francesco freed himself from the nails and jumped off the cross, but as his feet hit the floor he turned back into Christ, who came and stood at the foot of the Pope's bed. "O Innocent, my vicar on earth," Christ said, holding out his pierced hands, "are the poor sheep of my flock now so lost that you must make a law binding them under the threat of mortal sin to come and feed on my body at least once a year? O Innocent, my lost starving sheep are also your sheep. Good Innocent, my shepherd, how could they have wandered so far away from me?"

Then Innocent recalled his last dream, which had so rudely awakened him. In that dream the Pope found himself wandering alone in a dense forest somewhere in France when out of nowhere a naked Francesco of Assisi came running through the trees. Then from all directions countless other naked men and women quickly crowded around him and began dancing together. Innocent had awakened from the dream, his entire body shaking in fright, when he recognized that one of the dancing naked men was he himself! Wearily shaking his head, the Pope turned away from the window and returned to his bed. As he pulled the covers over his chin, he wondered about the meaning of his bizarre dreams. Only slowly did he fall asleep again, anxious that he might have more of these dreams.

The day following his first audience with the Pope, Francesco knelt to kiss the ring of Cardinal Ugolino after the cardinal had escorted Francesco and his brothers from the papal throne room into the antechamber. Ugolino smiled as he gave his blessing to the small group of twelve that knelt encircling him. Then he lifted Francesco to his feet and invited the others to stand as well. Placing a bag of coins into Francesco's hand for food on their way home, he wished them a safe journey to Assisi and returned to the papal throne room.

Francesco's friends encircled him, each of them talking to him at the same time. Unbeknownst to them, the strange little group of barefoot street beggars became the center of attention of that crowded papal antechamber. The richly dressed bishops, noble princes and their

entourages awaiting audiences with the Pope stared in speechless disbelief at the group of beggars. From the benches along the walls lined with the cardinals' private secretaries and valets, a loud buzzing of gossip arose as if from a row of beehives. The bishops' and dignitaries' disbelief turned to shock when the leader of this band of beggars leaped into the air and shouted with joy. As his brothers formed a wide circle around him, he began flipping into the air, turning somersaults as skillfully as an expert tumbler. In the midst of one leap he cried out, "The Pope gave us his blessing! The Holy Father approved of us! *Deo Gratias!*"

"*Deo Gratias!* Thanks be to God!" his companions began chanting in a joyful chorus as Francesco danced as spontaneously as a carefree child. His companions began clapping in rhythm as he whirled around in ecstatic joy before leaping upward, turning a cartwheel into a handstand and springing back onto his feet.

"This ragged buffoon," said one of the cardinals' purple-robed secretaries in a loud, snobbish voice, "thinks he is in a public market. How shameful! You would think that this crude, farm-bred beggar and his unwashed, barefoot companions would show more respect to the house of His Holiness Pope Innocent III!" His comments were affirmed by several of the bishops and princes who stood nearby.

Stopping with one foot dangling in midair, Francesco turned and gracefully bowed to the man, saying, "No disrespect intended, Very Reverend Monsignor, either to His Holiness or to any one of you. Forgive my uncontrollable joy that is too great to be contained, for I've been so favored by our blessed Holy Father, Innocent III. Whenever the Holy Spirit seizes me, alas, I become unaware of where and even who I am." Then he knelt on both knees, bowing toward the cleric as he said, "Please pardon my rude behavior. I apologize to each one of you for any disrespect shown to the Holy Father. Holy bishops and priests, I ask that you pray for me, for I am a sinner and, alas, it seems, a dancing sinner." The assembled high dignitaries simply stared in silence as he jumped to his feet, bowed to them from his waist and, with a wave of his hand, cried out, "Come, Little Brothers of Assisi, let us depart and dance our way home!"

As the twelve poor men joyfully left the ornate papal antechamber, the room did not just buzz, it veritably rumbled like a young volcano being birthed, as the clerics and dignitaries present began talking at the same time about what had just happened in front of them. However,

one person in that room sat in silence, trying to absorb what he had just witnessed. He was confused, since for no explainable reason he felt as if he had fallen in love—and with, of all persons, that dancing, barefoot man in the gray tunic. The young man was also bewildered because as a house servant to one of the princes of the papal court his daily world was marked by Byzantine-like deviousness and intrigue. To survive in such a scheming world required that his every action and word be carefully preplanned. Never before in his life had he seen anyone so spontaneous and free, and he wondered if this quality of naturalness and freedom was what had enchanted him. He smiled, revealing his beautiful white teeth as he reflected, "For me to be attracted to someone as dirt poor and raggedly dressed as that man is ridiculous!" Such were the thoughts of Sebastiano, Cardinal Uzielli's valet.

A lumbering, heavy wagon being drawn by a team of mules and escorted by mounted papal soldiers and several cassocked clerics was directly in front of the band of Little Brothers, who were homeward bound on the chaotically crowded highway out of Rome. Through the clouds of gray dust being raised by the wagon and its mounted escort, the brothers could see a large bronze casket in the center of the wagon. It was secured by heavy ropes, and its lid was marked with a wax seal bearing the papal coat of arms. That official seal along with the papal troops and clerical escorts testified that the casket contained the relic of an entire body of a saint martyred long ago. It was likely on its way to be placed beneath an altar of some new cathedral under construction in Germany.

"Brothers," Leone said, waving his hand back and forth in front of his face in an attempt to brush away the dust clouds coming from the rumbling relic wagon, "God is surely with us, for His Holiness Pope Innocent blessed our little community and gave us his approval."

As the others chattered in gleeful agreement, Pietro said, "Yes, Leone, but not in writing. The Pope only blessed our work, which isn't the same as granting an official document of papal approval and sanction."

"Who needs anything in writing?" asked Giles, who couldn't read. "A man's word is his word; isn't that right?"

Pietro put his arm around Giles, saying, "Yes and no, my brother. Without an official document bearing the Pope's signature and seal—like that relic up ahead of us—what proof do we have of what he said

or didn't say? But we do have witnesses, and very important ones, of his blessing on us. So, brothers, please forgive me and do not let your logical-minded brother dampen your joy by raining legalism down on it. We got what we came to Rome for: We received the Pope's blessing, and Brother Giles got his indulgence for visiting the tombs of the holy apostles Santi Pietro and Paulo!"

"Heaven, here I come," shouted Giles with childlike glee.

While all the brothers continued in a jubilant spirit, Francesco was no longer buoyant. He felt sick to his stomach, and if his soul could have vomited it would have done so right there on the road. After his initial burst of great joy, he now groaned inwardly as reality settled in. The cause of his agony was on the top of his head. He reached up and touched the spot that expressed the great cost he had paid for the Pope's approval and blessing. That morning when they returned to the Lateran Palace the Pope told him that he would approve and bless their community only if he and his brothers were tonsured as clerics of the Church! Tonsured—that stipulation sliced like a sharp stiletto through Francesco's heart, slaying his great dream of a lay spiritual community. "How foolish of me," he thought, "to have forgotten my father's adage, 'Nothing in life is free!'" He could still feel the prickling pain of his agonizing memory of kneeling in front of the Pope, who was waiting for his answer as a host of voices within were screaming for him not to compromise his beloved dream of following Jesus just as his first disciples had—as a layman. As those inner voices shouted for him to refuse to abandon his vision, he could feel himself surrounded by an oozing, sinister darkness bent on destroying him. At the same time, streaking toward him out of that darkness he felt streams of luminous grace. One of these streams seemed to flow from the man seated on the chair of Peter.

Francesco recalled how at that moment the sands in the elaborate golden hourglass on a stand next to the papal throne seemed clogged at its narrow neck, making time appear to be standing still. He had spent a nightlong vigil prostrate on the pavement floor of the chapel intensely praying for the grace to accept whatever would be the will of God. Now on his knees in front of Pope Innocent, he wondered: Was it the will of God that he be tonsured as a cleric? Was it God's will that along with everything else he had renounced he must now also forsake his cherished dream of a small band of poor laymen preaching the Gospel? On the other hand, he wondered if refusing to compromise was what

God really desired of him. Meanwhile, he felt again the impact of the intensely powerful eyes of the impatient Pope that were wordlessly demanding his answer.

"Your Holiness, I plead with you not to insist that we be tonsured," Francesco begged with his arms outstretched toward the Pope. "Please, oh, please, Holy Father, allow us to remain simply laymen like our Lord's first disciples, like Santi Pietro and Paulo and the others."

The Pope shook his head in a silent no. On his one condition he would not be swayed. And so, desperate for the Pope's approval, Francesco did what he had done so many times before for his own father, Pietro Bernadone.

"Holy Father, I submit to your wishes," Francesco answered sadly in an act of blind faith that felt like he was leaping off a high cliff. "I accept your will that I and my brothers be tonsured."

Then in the presence of Pope Innocent III and all the cardinals, a bishop used silver scissors to clip away hair, leaving a small circle on the crown of each of the brothers' heads. Using a razor, the bishop removed the remaining stubble, creating a small, round bald dome. Now they were no longer laymen. By the ritual of tonsure they were now clerics of the Church, just as were monks, priests, and students studying to be ordained. He closed his eyes because they still stung from the sight of the piles of their hair scattered on the floor at the papal throne.

The sounds of loud shouting and noisy commotion abruptly ended his recollection of the tonsure ceremony, and he opened his eyes to see what was happening. On top of the relic wagon directly in front of them an apparently fanatical or crazy man was hugging the large bronze casket containing the saintly relic. He must have seen that the wagon was carrying a large relic of a saint, for he had climbed up on it and now was wailing, "Grant me a miracle, O holy saint! Please, grant me a miracle!" Then he began lavishing kisses on the ornate bronze casket, saying, "O Saint whoever you are, heal me. Cure my illness."

The priests escorting the relic were shouting for him to get away from the relic casket as two sturdy soldiers of the papal guard jumped off their horses onto the wagon. They began wrestling with the demented man, who was clinging tightly to the ropes that secured the casket to the wagon. The wagon driver halted his mules, stalling the relic wagon in the middle of the road. The roadblock was completed by the large crowd of travelers who quickly gathered around the wagon, adding their voices to the tumult and enjoying this unexpected island

of excitement in an otherwise dull day of travel. The soldiers finally violently yanked the half-crazed man off the ropes, and after giving him several hard slaps to the head, they tossed him off the wagon into the roadside ditch. At that, the wagon driver cracked his whip and shouted at his mules, causing the heavy wagon to lurch forward. The crowd dispersed, and the roadway returned to its normal chaotic movement.

"Francesco, did you see what happened to that man?" Leone said. His shock turning into glee, he added, "Those soldiers couldn't do that to us—we're clerics now! It would have been a mortal sin for them to strike us as they did that madman. Aren't we lucky that the Pope insisted on tonsuring us? We can travel free of fear from such attacks."

"That's true," answered Francesco. Indeed they were protected from any bodily abuse. They were likewise immune from being hauled before civil courts, since as clerics they could only be tried by Church courts. Yet Francesco mused on how Christ didn't have any clerical immunity from being slapped, scourged, abused, or spat upon by Roman soldiers on Good Friday. And the *minores*, the vast majority of the population, did not have protection from the physical abuse of their landowners and stewards. So why should he and the brothers be sheltered from physical mistreatment?

As his brothers chatted with one another, Francesco returned to thinking about the distressful effects of the tonsure ceremony. "I wonder if the requirement to be tonsured was Pope Innocent's idea, or had it originated elsewhere in the twisted maze of the Vatican? From the first moment I encountered Cardinal Uzielli during my meeting with the Pope, I sensed his intense dislike for me. It seemed he held a real disdain for lay people in general. Cardinal Ugolino warned me that Uzielli possessed the will and the power to manipulate various elements within the papal court. Yes, it's likely that Uzielli was my enemy in the papal court—I could sense his desire to destroy my dream, and perhaps even me." Francesco wrestled with that realization for a time and then said softly to himself, "If he is my enemy, then, as Christ commands, I must love him and pray for him. So, God of all graces, I ask you to bless Cardinal Uzielli with good things and your richest blessings."

Having finished that brief prayer, one he would repeat frequently in years to come, he returned to thoughts about being tonsured. "The Holy Father told us that we had to be tonsured to protect us from physical harm because we could so easily be mistaken for common street beggars. But I suspect the real reason was that the Pope had been

forced by Uzielli's forces in the curia to make a compromise arrangement. But why would they have demanded tonsure? Was it so that the brothers' and my activities would be under the Church's thumb? Or was Uzielli hoping that like Peter Waldo I would also refuse to compromise and then the Holy Office could prosecute us as renegades of the Church?"

*A*s they traveled, Bernardo and Francesco were walking together behind the others. Bernardo leaned over to Francesco, who was still silently absorbed, and quietly asked, "Francesco, you're deeply disappointed about us being tonsured as clerics, aren't you?"

"Thank you dear friend for asking," he softly replied so the others would not hear. "You know me well, and how much I treasured my vision. Sadly my dream of a community of dedicated laymen is now as dead as the body of that martyred saint up ahead in the bronze casket! At first I was intoxicated with joy that the Holy Father had affirmed us and our work, but after leaving Rome I've become more depressed with each step I've taken. I feel I've somehow betrayed God, for in my bones I've always felt that the vision I had was God's dream. Oh, dear friend Bernardo, pray that I've done the will of God by consenting for us to be tonsured."

The two continued walking together in somber silence for some distance. Then, suddenly, Francesco's face was illuminated like the dawn. He broke out in the cheerful smile of an optimist upon whom the sun never sets for long. "But, Bernardo, being tonsured doesn't prevent us from being prayerful poor men who go about doing good work. I was just thinking that our brotherhood needs a simple motto like the Benedictine monks' '*Ora et labora*, Prayer and work.' In the Acts of the Apostles, Peter, the first Pope, said that Jesus of Nazareth 'went about doing good.' As I reflected, that short phrase made a deep impression on me. Those words are so simple and yet also so profound: 'He went about doing good.' In a flash of insight, it occurred to me that I could compress them into '*Pax et bonum*, Peace and good,' as a possible motto or slogan for our band of Little Brothers. So, Bernardo, what do you think?"

"I like it! Our purpose, as you've often said, is to imitate our Lord as closely as possible. And those words, 'Be peaceful and do good,' not only sum up his life but also perfectly define our course in life."

"Oh, Bernardo, I hope the rest of brothers feel as you do. I love the vision of us going about spreading peace and doing good everywhere. How wonderful our lives would be!"

"It is exciting, Francesco!" Bernardo smiled as he thought to himself, "That's my beloved and creative friend—always the tumbler minstrel acrobat. Even when he's been tripped and has fallen, he is always able to bounce back up and land on his feet, laughing. I myself was devastated by having to be tonsured—if I had wanted to be a cleric I would have entered some monastery. Alas, as much as I was shaken by the Pope's demand, Francesco's wound went much deeper. Yet in the midst of a sea of sadness over the death of his dream, he's found a source of great joy. In the process he's sowed the seeds of joy in the sad soil of my heart. When I was locked in the darkness of doubt about our fate, he lit the lamp of hope-filled faith about our future. It's no wonder I chose to follow him."

Chapter 13

THE TWELVE BROTHERS LEFT THE ROAD TO SPOLETO AND
entered a small village to rest and purchase bread and wine
with some of the money given them by Cardinal Ugolino. After they
finished their simple meal, Francesco stood up to address the small
crowd of townsfolk lingering around the fountain in the village square.
He began by telling them to rejoice because the kingdom of God had
arrived—and had come even to their village. Calling them to do
penance and believe in the Good News, he spoke fervently about the
love of God. He talked about how the divine love had become flesh in
our Lord Jesus Christ and in each one of them as well, and how it was
wondrously present even in all creation and all creatures. These
uneducated villagers listened with a rapt attention, mesmerized by his
lyrical voice, which was filled with intoxicating life and conviction. His
words flowed together as if in a song, sometimes spontaneously
forming into rhymes and always filled with images as vivid as a
masterful fresco. This barefoot beggar in the old gray tunic enchanted
the crowd with his unpretentious yet charismatic charm. He was like a
human sponge that had absorbed into the flesh of his body the words
and very person of Christ and now was effortlessly squeezing that grace
out as liquid music for these peoples' souls. Never before had any priest
in the pulpit spoken to them about the love of God with such
immediacy and genuine passion.

As they left the village to resume their journey to Assisi on the
congested highway, Rufino said, "Francesco, those people were
spellbound at your words. Since we're also to preach the Gospel, would
you teach us how to preach as you did back there in that village?" In
unison, several other brothers echoed that request, "Yes, teach us all
your secret."

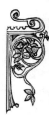

"It's no secret," Francesco answered with a smile, "but I might offer a few little suggestions. First, desire with all your heart to fill your every word with the fire of God's Spirit. Then, on top of those zestful, fiery words add generous amounts of the honey of joy, because the message God wants us to preach is good news! That requires, my brothers, that our words be as pleasant and gloriously sunny as the tidings of great joy the angels proclaimed at Bethlehem. Finally, incorporate into your message the seductive charm of a troubadour enchanting his lady love."

"Why," Francesco added, "don't you preach to us as we're walking, Rufino."

"The kingdom of God is among us," Rufino began. "Do penance and believe in the good news, or else you'll go to hell. . . ."

"No, no, my dear friend," Francesco interrupted him. "Where is the love or joy in those words? Alas, it seems the Pope tonsured your tongue as well as your head, for you're speaking just like a priest!" At that, all the brothers laughed.

"Please, Francesco, let me try," said Brother Silvestro. Filling his lungs deeply, he began to shout aloud, "The kingdom of God has come, brothers and sisters, so do penance and believe in the glad tidings that God loves you. . . ." Other travelers on the road immediately began gawking at them, as if wondering, "Who are these beggars yelling about God?"

"Silvestro, Silvestro, my brother," Francesco interrupted him with his hands covering his ears, "lovers do not shout at one another! Nor are we deaf! Brothers, let's get off this crowded road and go over to that field where the harvesters have just finished working. I'll show you a practical lesson I learned about preaching." When they were all seated together along the edge of the field, he said, "Now, Silvestro, do you see the flock of birds feeding out there on the wheat grain the harvesters left behind in the stubble? Preach to them!"

"To the birds?" he asked in astonishment.

"Yes, our Lord told his disciples, 'Go into the whole world and proclaim the Gospel to every creature.' Indeed, Silvestro, 'every creature' means more than men and women. It includes fish, frogs, dogs, and even birds. So now, Silvestro, try proclaiming the good news of God to our brother and sister birds."

Silvestro again inhaled deeply and began in his booming voice, "Brother and sister birds, the kingdom of. . . ." With much loud

squawking and flapping of wings, the flocks of birds swiftly rose from the stumble field and flew away.

"You see, Silvestro, you've frightened those little birds," Francesco said. "That's the practical lesson I spoke about. When we preach, we're not announcing a war or shouting a fire alarm, even if that's how many priests preach. We are to be God's enchanters. We are to make the Gospel as temptingly delicious as the finest meal, as seductive as any sins of the flesh. Please sit down, Brother Silvestro, and allow me to tell all of you a story.

"When I was living as a hermit back in the early days before you joined me, I tried preaching to the birds. You've no doubt heard about that, but I confess it didn't happen the way it's being broadcast around the countryside. I was attempting to follow our Lord's command to preach to all creatures and decided to begin with birds. Don't feel bad, Silvestro, for my experience was just like yours—they all flew away with my first words. When I told my monk-hermit friend and confessor about my failure, he surprised me with a story about a Muslim holy man named Najmuddin Kubra. I should tell you that while at the Crusades my confessor Padre Antonio met some Muslim holy men named Sufis, the Islamic brotherhood that practices mystical prayer. These holy men told Padre Antonio about Najmuddin, who died about sixty years before I was born. He was a man of deep prayer, and one of the great Sufi teachers. He was also famous for taming a ferocious wild dog, and he preached their holy book, the Qur'an, to the birds of the air."

"An infidel holy man? That's a contradiction in terms!" exclaimed Masseo.

"Brothers, do not be shocked. My spiritual teacher, Padre Antonio, who taught Scripture in the abbey and is a learned man, helped me overcome my prejudice toward the infidels. He quoted St. Peter, who said that 'God shows no partiality! Rather, in every nation, whoever fears God and acts uprightly is acceptable to him.' So if God doesn't show partiality, I've tried to practice impartiality myself, and I now believe that saints can be found as well among those who are not Christians."

They all sat silently as they attempted to swallow this novel teaching. Then the birds that had been startled away returned and again began feeding in the wheat stubble field.

"So, I thought," Francesco continued, "if that holy Muslim preached to the birds, I would try to do so myself. I began by

attempting to preach to the larks in the forest of Mount Subasio. I spoke in Italian with a bird accent—softly, gently and so sweetly as not to frighten them. In time they actually appeared to be listening. So, from the birds I learned how to speak of the love of God in a way that not only larks but even the most timid among people would not be frightened away and would be able to listen. Therefore, whenever you preach, speak to the people as if they were a flock of pigeons."

"Let me try," said Pietro standing up. "Dearest friends, rejoice! I bring you tidings of great joy, for the kingdom of God is at hand. Repent and believe." Along with Francesco he glanced out at the field, and to his amazement and delight not a single bird had flown away.

"Good, Pietro, good. Now . . ." he smiled and stood up, adding, "try to speak your words as if they were music. Look upon yourself as a musical instrument, a lute whose strings are being stirred by the bow of the Holy Spirit as it slides seductively across them." Then he began beckoning with his outstretched hands as if gracefully luring some invisible woman toward himself. "As that happens, you are seducing the hearts of your listeners into the very arms of God."

"Beloved children of God, repent, for the kingdom has come," Pietro began. "With the greatest tenderness and affectionate love, our God has invited you to come and build your nests in his holy heart."

"Excellent, Pietro! That's the way we should lure people to God." Then he pointed toward the road and said, "Look, brothers, the road is beckoning us to return to it and to our journey home. It's time we were on our way."

The twelve newly tonsured clerics reentered the road as a tiny gray stream flowing into a cultural river inundated with every kind of humanity, as well as horses, cattle, and sheep. Each brother in their little band was preoccupied with his personal thoughts. Some, like Leone, rejoiced inwardly that they were now tonsured clerics. Others were saddened that they now wore a religious haircut. Still others were continuing to chew on the tough piece of possibility that there might actually be saints among the accursed infidels.

Approaching them in the road's southward flow was a mounted company of the Knights of St. John of Jerusalem on their way to Rome. They were dignified knights who had vowed obedience only to the Pope and were responsible for policing the pilgrim routes and operating hostels for pilgrims. Shortly after they had ridden past the brothers, a strange group of half-naked men began pouring out onto the main

highway from a side road. They were chanting flagellants, stripped to their waist, flinging whips back and forth as they lashed their own bodies and those directly in front of them. As these blood-splattered men trudged past the small band of Little Brothers, they were mournfully singing "*Kyrie eleison*, Lord have mercy on us." Many of the travelers on the road, including a few of the brothers, regarded these penitents, with their bleeding, self-inflicted wounds, as living saints. Such pilgrimages of public penance, in which men, and even women, would scourge themselves bloody for their sins and the sins of others, had recently become a common sight in towns and on the highways.

"I noticed, Pietro," Francesco said after the weeping flagellants had passed by, "that in your preaching back there, when you quoted our Lord, you used the word 'repent' instead of 'do penance.' I've never heard that before; may I ask why you changed it?"

"When I was at the university, one of my teachers, who was learned in Greek, taught us that 'repent' is the correct translation of the original word used by our Lord. A learned scholar, he explained to us the difference between doing penance, like the flagellants we just saw, and repenting. He encouraged us to go to the library and study the manuscripts of such theologians as Hugh of St. Victor and. . . ."

"Books!" Francesco lamented with a loud sigh heavy with disdain as he placed his arm around Pietro's shoulder. "I fear that book learning only confuses us. I'm grateful that books are so scarce—for they can only be created by being handwritten, copied by scribes one letter at a time. But God is good, for those bound manuscripts are so expensive that our little band of brothers would never be able to own even one of them. While monasteries have their scriptoriums and universities their libraries, I ask you, Pietro, do any of those books make the monks or scholars any holier?"

"Francesco, I know how you dislike books and feel they're harmful to the spiritual life, but the library at the university had marvelous works by great mystical scholars as well as books of science and alchemy. Christian monks in Spain are translating into Latin the Arabic translations of Greek scholars like Aristotle and Plato, along with the works of medicine and astronomy that have been lost to the West for centuries."

"Let them be lost! Who is the lesser for not having such knowledge clutter up his or her mind? I do not need to read or study Aristotle or Plato to know that we are all sinners who must do penance today for

our sins, like those flagellants, so as not to suffer for them in the next life. And, Pietro, whether we call it repenting or doing penance, is there really any difference in what we must do for our souls to grow closer to God?"

Pietro turned and glanced back toward the procession of flagellants, whose plaintive chanting was now barely audible as they were engulfed by the multitudes thronging on the road. Turning back to Francesco, he said, "Those men that passed us are certainly doing penance, and quite likely among them are believers of the new pious teaching that such self-inflicted pain replaces any need for confession—and is even equal to receiving Holy Communion. Sadly, for many of those penitents such self-inflicted punishment of their flesh, such bloody repentance, is becoming a religion of its own. As to your question about how repentance is different from this kind of penance, I would suggest, dear friend, that repenting means doing what you and I and our brothers have done. It means changing one's life not only by turning away from sin but also by returning to God and the ways of God."

Francesco listened thoughtfully to Pietro since he loved him very much. However, it was as easy for Pietro to read Francesco's face as it was to read a manuscript. He knew that his friend practiced many painful personal penances. Like the flagellants, it was by inflicting pain on his flesh through fasting, sleeping on the hard frosty earth, rolling naked in the snow in the bitter freezing cold or other acts of self-denial that Francesco did battle with evil spirits and the urges of his flesh. "He may strongly disapprove of books," Pietro thought, "but ironically he himself is a book! He's an open book that's easily read by the learned or the completely unlettered!"

"I'm not as educated as you, Pietro. I'm only a stubborn donkey who has to be driven up the rocky road to heaven, and nothing makes this old ass hurry along like the sharp sting of the whip!"

Pietro thought, "I love the man—perhaps because he's such a skillful juggler of paradoxes who somehow can keep the most extreme contrasts in balance. In the morning he's dancing in joyful abandonment like a fun-loving minstrel in the antechamber of the Pope and by the afternoon of the same day he's admiring those blood-splattered flagellants."

As Francesco and his companions walked northward past the massive, towering fortress of Spoleto, he could feel the pain of an old

wound. The very sight of Spoleto rubbed against the crusty scab of the painful memory of his desertion from the papal army bound for Apulia, a memory that reminded him of the death of his dream to be a knight. It was here that his voices had told him not to seek glory in war but to go home. That Spoleto wound now oozed with the acid-like memories of his disgraceful return to Assisi where he was ridiculed as a deserter, a coward and a failure. In Rome, kneeling before the Pope, he had listened for his voices to tell him what to do, but they did not speak. It occurred to Francesco that failures, especially the embarrassing public ones, are able to inflict deep invisible wounds that never completely heal. He wondered if some of those so wounded are forced to carry their stigma of shame to their graves.

Unconsciously, he raised his hand and touched his tonsure; his finger slowly tracing its way around the circle of shaved bare skin on the top of his head was like feeling another failure. He again wondered if his consenting to become a cleric was another mistake, another Spoleto failure, another death of a dream. Being a cleric now made him part of the hierarchical Church. He was more intimately linked to Holy Mother Church, whom he loved even if some of her clergy and hierarchy caused her to be bloated fat by their sumptuous life and covered her with the ugly sores of immoral corruption. He couldn't help loving her, for she was the Bride of Christ, even if he thought she was a whore. "O Lord, forgive me for that judgment of her and seal my lips that I may never ever speak that thought aloud. But she is a whore who has gone to bed with conniving, corrupt princes, with cruel, ruthless emperors and depraved, decadent clerics. Yet, down through the centuries she has carried in her silken prostitute's purse the Holy Sacraments and the Gospels of your Son Jesus Christ. And if, O God, because of her sinfulness you had wiped her off the face of the earth— as you did with wicked Sodom and Gomorra—how would I have ever known the joyful message of my Savior? Your Son did not condemn the whores of his day but, rather, shared their company at meals. So if I am to follow him, then I shall not judge the Whore of Rome and shall humbly share her company as a cleric."

Upon their return to Portiuncula, the Little Brothers of Assisi needed no papal document of Rome's approval, for the peasants gave them all the approval they needed. To the *minores*, that small shaved circle on top of their heads spoke louder than any piece of

parchment from the Church. Monsignor Carafa, however, knew the difference between a blessing and formal recognition, and he continued gathering evidence about what he saw as a dangerous, if not heretical, movement. Even if Francesco had the bishop's ear, Carafa had the ear of the great and powerful Cardinal Uzielli. While the chancellor stood at his office window looking out over Piazza Santa Maria, his mind's eye was looking inward. On his desk behind him was a sealed packet just delivered by a courier of His Eminence Cardinal Uzielli containing instructions for him from the Holy Office. He was advised to continue carefully documenting all the activities of this band of tonsured laymen. "An interesting choice of terms," Carafa thought, "'tonsured laymen,' yet the Cardinal is correct in that they are only ignorant laymen with no intention of entering any religious order and certainly no capacity to engage in the studies necessary for ordination to the priesthood." Yes, with the blessing of Rome, Carafa would be most vigilant in documenting all the words and deeds of this budding heretical movement—for the good of Holy Mother Church as well as the benefit of his personal future."

*S*eated at her dressing table, Clare Scifi needed no mirror to know she was a beautiful young woman. Nor did she have a need to add artificial hair to her own natural hair, as did the women of high fashion, or to wear those stylish new dresses that heightened a woman's figure by pressing up her breasts. While her clothes accentuated her natural beauty, she would have been just as beautiful if she was dressed in rags—and even more so if she were naked, which was how she secretly dreamed of being. She turned around as her younger sister, Agnes, entered her room.

"I have two choices," Clare said to her. "Like you, I can consent to Father's will and be wed in an arranged marriage with someone I do not love and, most likely, won't even know. Once married, my behavior will be according to the code that has been anciently carved in stone."

Agnes giggled and began repeating in a singsong voice the memorized code for a proper woman.

> The proper wife shall walk bearing her head straight and tall
>
> but with her eyes lowered, looking to the ground
>
> four rods ahead of her.
>
> She shall not turn her gaze from left to right

or glance from place to place.

She shall not laugh in public so as to appear to be silly,

and she also shall not look at or speak to any man

she encounters on the street or in church.

And she shall eat her food using only three fingers.

As her sister recited those verses, Clare mockingly paraded across the room, mirroring the walk and bodily behavior required by the wifely code. When Agnes got to the part that said, "And legally she is a minor, in the custody of her husband, who is permitted—nay, encouraged—to beat her frequently for her own good," both girls giggled and then began chanting together,

Beat me more, my love, for my own good, beat me.

Hit me with your fist and kick me with your foot.

More, more, my love, for it will do me much good.

Then Clare threw herself on her bed, sighing, "No, Agnes, it's not funny! We both know many women who are married to hell. For most women marriage is a prison in which they are jailed in their own homes, powerless except for the small authority they exercise over their servants and children—and that awesome authority of selecting the menu for family meals." She stood up from her bed, her voice boiling over like a pot of water on the stovetop, "Agnes, why shouldn't we be as free as men to come and go as we please? Free to do whatever we wish, to marry whomever we wish." Stamping her foot, she said, "If only I had been born a man!"

"God's will," Agnes said with a shrug of her shoulders, which only caused Clare to stomp her foot even more loudly.

"It's God's will I was born a woman. I accept that. But the way in which I am forced to live as a woman is not—NOT—Agnes, God's will! It's only the will of men!"

"The Church teaches that it is in the Bible, so . . ." her sister replied, "it must be God's will."

"The Church," thought Clare, as she walked over to the window. "That's the second of my two choices, the only other one open to women." She could join the convent, as had her aunt, and become a cloistered Benedictine nun. "Ha," she laughed, "if I did that, my father would be furious, for the enhancement of the family fortune requires that I enter into a financially profitable marriage arrangement." Indeed, if she absolutely insisted on joining the convent, her father and mother, as devout people, would be helpless to prevent her. The convent! The very thought of it filled her with a bitter taste as she slowly began running her fingers through her beautiful long dark hair.

*A*ntonio's hermitage looked abandoned. The small vegetable garden was untended and weedy, the thatched porch roof needed repair and his black cat Nicoletto was nowhere to be seen. Francesco stood peering into the darkness of the cave. "Padre Antonio," he called out. "Are you at home?"

"Is that my Giovanni?" came a quiet voice from out of the darkness of the cave hermitage. "Come inside, Giovanni. How wonderful it is for this old man to have a visit from such a famous person as yourself."

"Padre, you're teasing me," Francesco said fondly as he entered his old friend's darkened hermitage.

"Giovanni Francesco, welcome! As you can see, I'm fasting from lighting my lamp this month—and, alas, I'm also abstaining from rising to embrace an old and dear friend."

"I'm sorry to hear that, Padre. Your joint afflictions have grown worse?" Francesco asked as he sat on the ground next to Antonio's mat.

"Yes, they have, and you're also looking at a true hermit now. My beloved Nicoletto has gone to God, as I shall soon. I wept as I buried him out there in my flower garden and found a stone to mark his grave. He and I shared so much, and now I grieve the loss of his companionship. But daily I thank God for the gift of the many years we shared together. Not only has my Nicoletto left me, my eyes are also leaving. By the day, it seems, my sight grows dimmer. In here I know where everything is and can easily make my way around by feeling, but I so miss tending my little garden. However, I'm not complaining, for God has so graciously gifted me with a good life. And even now in the growing darkness I'm experiencing a greater closeness to God—and a wealth of time with which I can reflect on God and my life."

"Padre, you're a ceaseless teacher to me. You're able to find something to be grateful for even in the death of your beloved Nicoletto and the diminishment of your bodily powers."

"Francesco Giovanni, if I was truly wise, I wouldn't be wasting what little time I've left in life dwelling on my past adventures in the Holy Land and Spain. I would use it all to ponder my sins and to pray.

"But enough talking about me. Now, my young friend, tell me about yourself. Every week a monk from my abbey visits to keep a check on me, and so I've heard rumors about you and the Pope! Yet when it comes to stories about you, what is fable and what is truth is difficult to discern," he said with a chuckle. "So, from your own lips, is the gossip true that you, Giovanni of Assisi, personally spoke with the great Innocent III?"

"No fable, but a miracle, Padre, that I, a nobody, was able to speak personally to the Holy Father—and, even more, that he blessed and gave approval to our band of Little Brothers."

"Alas, Rome, the Mother of Indulgences," Antonio hummed and then added, "does not indulge in giving away things for free! I'm sure that your papal blessing cost you something." Then he reached over and touched the top of Francesco's head. "Ah, just as I feared. For her favors and dispensations the Vatican usually requires money. You're lucky, Giovanni Francesco, that all they required of you was a little hair!" As Antonio laughed loudly, Francesco was glad the light inside the hermitage was so dim, for his blushing felt all too palpable.

"Do not be ashamed, my dear friend," Antonio said, touching Francesco's cheek tenderly. "Rome isn't ready yet for zealous, holy laymen—and even far less prepared for fervent, holy laywomen. Pope Innocent is a shrewd and realistic man, but he is also a man of vision; otherwise he would never have given his blessing to you and your little community. I'm an old monk, and from my years of observing the serpentine entangled politics in the monastery, I can assure you that hidden behind the scenes in Rome there were powerful forces at work both for and against you."

"I did, indeed, feel some of them, Padre, especially the powerful dark forces. And I've been praying for the people behind those forces. Our Lord told us to love our enemies, and I believe that's necessary even if they are among the highest ranking prelates of the Church."

"Good! I'm pleased to see that you've not been spoiled by Rome. Your conniving opponents in the Vatican need your prayers. By scheming against you and your dream, they're obstructing a work of the Holy Spirit, and that, Giovanni, has the most serious spiritual consequences. You presented the Pope with a predicament in which he had to gamble that you were not some budding heretic, as I suspect you were portrayed by a number of his powerful cardinal advisors. If you are a gift from God and the sunrise-hope for new life in the Church—

as he and a few cardinals surely believed—he had to find a way to placate your enemies inside the curia." Then Antonio reached out to grasp his wooden cup and took a sip from it. "Every society needs to protect its stability and traditions while it slowly adjusts to change. The Church is the bedrock of tradition and so naturally fears change and creativity, yet she cannot prevent the coming of change and so is rigorous in assuring that creative newness is never given free reign."

"But is not God as ever-creative as the seasons that change, one after another?'

"True. God is always freshly creative. However, change for us humans is difficult, and the Church wisely knows how change can bring hardships to many and ignite destructive social conflict. So she attempts to control change by discouraging or restraining the rise of creative individuals like you! Her survival style tends to emphasize regulation and conformity, and that is what she did in requiring your new community to become part of the time-honored clerical state. Alas, Giovanni Francesco, if only Holy Mother Church could trust that her faithful—even in the earthquake-turmoil of great change—can learn to adjust and grow with change. If only she could be free of her great fear of new, creative expressions of the tried and tested, and allow herself to be guided by the dynamic, ever-fresh, creative Spirit of God."

Francesco pondered the wisdom of Antonio's words about change and the Church. As he did, a previous remark Antonio had made earlier in the conversation jumped into his mind. "Padre, a few minutes ago, didn't you mention something about your adventures in Spain? Did you travel to Spain as well as to the Holy Land? As a monk how was that possible? How were you able to do such expansive, adventuresome things in an institution so committed to stability and tradition?"

"Giovanni, you can string questions together like sausages—so many, so quickly. First, God has gifted me with a wonderful, full life and the courage to create my own history instead of being a helpless victim of fate. To answer your last questions briefly, I simply asked for permission to leave my monastery to go to Spain! Before being a chaplain on the Crusades, while I was the abbey guestmaster, I met a Spanish nobleman from Cordoba who was on a personal pilgrimage to Rome. During his stay at our abbey, he and I visited about his country. He told me about the wondrous libraries in Spain that contained Latin translations of works by Muslim scholars on philosophy, astronomy, mathematics, and medicine that far exceeded any existing in

Christendom. Of course, I had a special interest in the medical texts because just before I was guestmaster I was the infirmarian of the monastery."

"Padre, I've always marveled at how many different jobs you held at the abbey. It doesn't sound very efficient to be constantly reassigning monks to different duties!"

"Monks are rotated from position to position partly so that they won't become attached to anything, even their work. In my case, however, I found that the variety kept me fresh and creative and also expanded my knowledge. As infirmarian, I acquired some learning in the healing arts and knew that the abbey would benefit from the medical literature that existed in Spain. So I proposed to Father Abbot Placid that he send me to Spain to acquire whatever I could of this new medical knowledge, especially since the brother infirmarian at the time was a very timid monk who didn't want to go outside the abbey. Father Abbot was years ahead of his time, much like Pope Innocent, and he did not hesitate to approve my proposal."

Antonio paused and inhaled deeply, saying, "Even to this day I can smell the scent of the orange trees of Spain—may I go to my grave with their aroma in my nostrils. But I must return to my tale: My mission to Spain was beneficial for our monastic library and our infirmary, but it was even more fruitful for my spiritual life. In Spain I discovered Muslims, Jews, and Christians all living peacefully side-by-side, even if the nonbelievers were somewhat restricted by the Church. The freedom of this social intermingling allowed them to enrich each other with gifts of science, art, architecture, and even spirituality, and in this cultural exchange the Christians gained far more from the Muslims than they gave. While in Spain I was blessed to meet members of Islam's mystical order of the Sufis—you might recall my speaking about meeting them in the Holy Land. You would find them fascinating, Giovanni Francesco, for they are devout laymen dedicated to deep prayer and to living in the original spirit of their scriptures, the Qur'an."

"I do remember you speaking about them, Padre, particularly about one of their spiritual masters who used to preach to the birds."

"My troubadour friend," he said placing his arm around Francesco's shoulder, "your heart would melt like fat in a frying pan if you could hear their gorgeous prayer poetry that sings of their love for God, whom they call Allah. And because they write in their native tongue instead of Latin, their love lyrics are even more passionate and

sensual. It's no wonder that their poetry has greatly influenced the love ballads of our Italian and French troubadours."

Like a bright spark struck from a block of flint, Francesco felt in his heart the passionate heat of a kindling desire to go to Spain. He wondered if God was speaking to him in this newest desire.

"Padre, I could listen to you talk for hours about Spain. Once again you've inspired me, and I only hope I haven't tired you out with all my questions. I have more, but I'll save them for the next time I come to drink at the well of your wisdom. Now, I must return to Portiuncula and my brothers."

"Thank you, Giovanni Francesco, but it is I who am grateful for your visit. It's has been a feast for me, and I appreciate your coming all the way up here to visit this old man. Even though I fear this old "well" is running dry, it delights me to see you and your bucket at my door. And please pray for me and for forgetfulness."

"Forgetfulness?"

"Yes, my friend, since your prayers are powerful, pray that my Father Abbot will be kept so busy with matters of grave importance in the abbey that he'll forget about his old hermit monk. I dread that day when he'll send two stout brothers to escort me back to the abbey—for my own good. So please pray, and return soon."

*O*n the Fourth Sunday in Lent a large crowd was gathered in the Cathedral Piazza of San Rufino, for word that Francesco Bernadone was going to preach after vespers that Sunday had quickly leapfrogged across Assisi. The crowd in the piazza that day was composed of citizens, merchants, and an interesting mix of the curious and spiritually hungry. The windows of the homes bordering the cathedral piazza were overflowing with the wealthy and the aristocrats eager to hear this unusual son of Assisi, who recently had so impressed the Pope in Rome. If the Great Innocent III had given him an audience, why shouldn't they? Since his return, the city had buzzed with the hearsay that the numbers of the Little Brothers of Assisi had more than doubled and were now close to fifty, a sign of God's blessing as well as the Pope's.

Standing alone in front of the cathedral doors, Francesco faced out toward the large crowd. Unseen by him and the throng in the piazza, seated well back from the open balcony doors of a friend's second-story home that faced into the piazza, was a secret guest, Bishop Guido, who

was as much a praying presence as a witness. Francesco's heart throbbed, as he was apprehensive of speaking before such a large crowd composed of his fellow citizens, associates, and old friends. He saw Emiliano and his wife standing midway back in the crowd, and he waved and smiled at them. He was also able to recognize his father's old friends and fellow merchants, Albertino Compagni and Guittone d'Acsoli, who now looked much older and grayer. As he scanned across that great mass of people, he looked for one particular face, hoping against hope that he'd see his father.

He took a deep breath soaked with prayer, asking God to inspire him, and then he began preaching. Almost instantly his mounting anxiety was transformed into dynamic energy as he spoke to the people about the love of God. Right from the start his words were aflame with passion as he spoke about the great commandment to love God with all one's heart, soul, and body, and to love one's neighbor as oneself. He compared God's intense love for each one of us to those fiercely hot forest fires not uncommon in Umbria that could roar up mountainsides making pine trees explode into living torches. While preachers had expounded upon that same commandment for more than a thousand years, on this late afternoon in Assisi Francesco's words were as dynamically compelling as the day when Jesus first spoke them. As orange tongues of a forest fire leap across dry forest timber, so the hearts of his listeners were set ablaze with a freshly invigorated awareness that all the many laws of God and the Church were fulfilled by Christ's one law of love.

"Yet love cannot be a commandment!" he declared boldly. "For what foolish lover would ever make a law ordering his beloved to love him? That would be madness! Love can never be compelled, nor can one barter for love as if it were a bolt of cloth or a cow. So, neighbors, as God's beloved who are called to live in the glorious freedom of the children of God, we must ask if God blesses our marriage arrangements. Does God bless any barren union of a man and woman who do not love each other yet are vowed to remain faithful in their marriage union until death?"

Many in the crowd began frowning, and even Francesco was shocked at the words that had suddenly sprung to his tongue. Whenever he preached, he would never prepare what he would say beforehand, for had the Lord Jesus not told his disciples that the Spirit would inspire their speech? His words confirmed the secret belief of

many women in the crowd that God would not bless unhappy, parentally arranged marriages that imprisoned them for life with a man who didn't love them and who was often physically abusive. Many of the men present also shared a distaste for this age-old custom of arranged marriages. Those who could afford to do so would often allay the bitter reality of such marriages by having a mistress or two. The poor, on the other hand, would have their occasional affairs with village whores and peasant maids. Yet, whether rich or poor, by their sins of adultery they all felt they had one foot in hell. By contrast, wives had no such outlet for love and sex. If they were discovered in any infidelity, according to the ancient Italian code of honor, their family's reputation required satisfaction in the form of their death!

"Love is no cruel hunter who entraps another," Francesco continued. "Love never rapes or forces itself upon another who does not desire it. God is our prime example of how we are to love one another." Here his words of passion and compassion became lyrical: "God stands beneath each of our windows like a youthful troubadour singing of his enormous love for us. He says:

My dearest beloved, love me as I love you,

for all the fires of hell are only glowing embers

compared to the roaring furnace of my sacred heart.

I long that your heart might mirror mine,

so that you would passionately love me

with the wild abandonment of a young lover.

Love me in each and every one of your loves,

for in loving each other you love me

in that glorious freedom of the children of God."

As Francesco spoke, his hands became words themselves. His whole message—voice, body, and soul—bewitchingly drew the hearts of his listeners to the Sacred Heart. He seduced them into his song of love that now was overflowing from his heart like a rushing mountain stream after the spring rains. Even those who disagreed with him about the ancient custom of arranged marriages were swept up in his song. Then, without warning or the usual preacher's pious conclusion, he was finished. While the crowd was recovering from his sudden ending, he

turned and entered the cathedral, followed by his brothers. It was now the late-afternoon, and as the sun was casting elongated shadows upon the cathedral façade, the people in the crowd began draining out of the piazza for their homes. The wealthy who had listened to Francesco from the open windows of their balconies returned to their businesses or departed for their evening meal—except for one young woman, Clare Scifi. She delayed joining her family for supper and stood at the open window looking down on the almost-deserted piazza. Tears, not of sadness but of great joy, were trickling down her cheeks, for on that afternoon she felt as if she had been wooed by God, courted by God's Spirit of Love.

As she turned away from the window, wiping the tears from her cheeks, she saw her life in a radically new way. Only that morning, she thought, her home had felt like a jail that mirrored the lifelong domestic prison of her potential marriage. This afternoon, however, Francesco, the barefoot troubadour of God, had magically cast a spell on her. She had been freed in the act of falling in love. This caused her to see her bedchamber, and the entire Scifi palacia, as a beautiful waiting room foyer to God's bridal chamber. Clare felt her body throbbing with a new sense of emancipation as she lingered in the echo of Francesco's words about "loving in the glorious freedom of the children of God."

Meanwhile, inside the slowly darkening cathedral, Francesco knelt in prayer as his brothers formed a protective ring around him, shielding him from those eager to tug at his sleeve, begging for his prayers or some cure for their troubles. His companions knew from experience how exhausted he would be after the soaring heights of his preaching, having filled all his words with a totality of his heart, body, and soul. As he knelt praying, his weary body slumped back onto his heels and his head drooped to his chest, causing the brothers to tighten their circle of sanctuary.

"Francesco Bernadone," said a man speaking over the top of the heads of the brothers. Deaf to their objections, he continued, "I was deeply moved by your beautiful words about the love of God. . . ." As Brother Leone took the man's arm and began escorting him away, the man added, "Please, may I speak with you? I need to ask you a question."

"Thank you, sir, for your kind words," Francesco said as he stood up and moved outside the circle of his brothers. As he approached the

man, who was accompanied by Leone on one side and a young lad on the other, he said, "But, stranger, I prefer that both of us thank the Holy Spirit, who spoke through me. I detect by your speech that you're not a citizen of Assisi, and your uniquely festive and colorful attire confirms that."

Looking down at his tunic, which was splattered with a lavish variety of brilliant colors, as also were his face and hands, the man replied, "Thank you for speaking with me. Allow me to introduce myself: I am Jacobi of Florence, and I'm the painter who has been commissioned to create the frescoes up there on the wall of this cathedral. And this lad is my apprentice, who is learning the secrets of the craft." The lad nodded and smiled, using his hands to imitate the stirring of paints.

"Well, Jacobi of Florence," Francesco replied as he gazed up at two large, newly completed frescoes high up on the cathedral wall, "I'm no expert at art, but I think you're an excellent painter. What a wondrous gift you've been given by God. I wish I could paint as beautifully as you do."

"A redundant wish, Francesco," Jacobi said with a bow, "since you're already a gifted painter! I speak from a place of understanding, for this afternoon I left my work up there on the scaffold to hear you speak and. . . ."

"You were working on Sunday?" asked Brother Leone. "The Creator rested on the seventh day and commanded us likewise to rest from our labors on Sunday!"

"Some may call what I was doing work. But before you make up your mind, let me ask you a question: Does God cease his work of creating on Sundays? If so, then who works so creatively on the seventh day making the flowers to bloom with beauty and the wheat to grow so that we may have bread to eat on every other day of the week? Like God, I don't consider creatively engaging my craft to be working on the Lord's Day. After the Holy Masses were finished today, since the cathedral was empty until vespers, my apprentice and I returned to painting the frescos. Moreover, the Lord Bishop is most eager that these frescos be completed. . . . Anyway, Francesco, I called you an artist because this afternoon I didn't hear a single word you said—rather, I saw your words!"

"Jacobi," Brother Giles asked, "how are you able to see words, which are invisible as the wind?"

"Any other day, brother, I would have agreed with you that words are invisible. However, today as Francesco spoke I saw pictures as vividly as if they had been painted by the finest of artists."

"Jacobi of Florence," Giles replied, "poor Giles of Assisi is confused by your words, for my eyes don't see what yours do. I only saw my dearest friend Francesco in front of the cathedral speaking to the people about God."

"Do not be concerned, Brother Giles," smiled Jacobi. "I was only using a figure of speech. Your friend Francesco is a great artist who uses words instead of brushes to paint. He dips his tongue into the paint pot of his heart to create indelibly beautiful images."

Turning to Francesco, he continued, "I watched you artistically mixing your palette, Francesco, sometimes using the soft, gentle colors of spring and adding to them the scarlet red flames of the setting sun on an autumn day. You paint words as passionate as the summer's warmth and as peaceful as a winter's snow. Your fiery words," he said as he patted his heart with his paint-splattered hand, "have inspired in me a burning desire to paint as vividly as you speak. And that brings me to my question, Francesco: What must I do to paint as you speak?"

"Perhaps, brother Jacobi," Francesco said, "you have answered your own question: A great artist paints by dipping his brushes into the paint pot of his heart. While I am not an artist, after looking at your two completed frescos, I might make a humble suggestion. I would surmise that you paint in the style taught to you when you were an apprentice like this young lad. If you wish to paint with even greater vitality, then you must move beyond what you were taught, even beyond what people expect—otherwise, you'll remain a prisoner of what is." As he looked up, he added, "These images you've painted are stunning in their beauty; they say more than most preachers could say in a lifetime, but. . . ."

"Yes, go ahead, but what?" asked Jacobi.

"I wonder how the figures in your painting could somehow move and appear more alive. I am a musician and not an artist, but I think music holds a clue. Musical notes in themselves do not move the soul; it's the movement of the notes, the rhythm of the music, that creates the kind of living melody that speaks to both ears and soul. So, Jacobi, in answer to your question, just as songs without rhythm would be flat and lifeless, I would suggest that before you paint you move into a place of prayer and of music so that your painting may flow with melodic

rhythm. Paint as does the Holy Creator, in whose living frescos of creation we see people, trees and animals alive, swirling with energy, pulsating with life." Francesco began shaking his hands as if he was suffering from the tremors as he said, "Life, Jacobi! Creation throbs with life, with living energy. Ah, if you could paint like that, then your frescoes would truly be enchanting.

"But, alas, my friend from Florence, it is growing late, and my brothers and I must be on our way home to Portiuncula."

As Francesco and the brothers departed, Jacobi stood at the base of his scaffolding looking up at his completed frescoes. He thought, "Francesco is right; in creation everything does throb with life, and I would love to infuse my frescos with a sense of rhythm and movement. To achieve that effect, however, I would need to paint images in a third dimension to give them a sense of depth. Perspective—to see as the eyes see—is what they need to elevate them from being flat and lifeless. But, alas, the ancient code of the Artist Guild permits only two-dimensional images. My Guild would excommunicate me for so radically violating. . . ." Suddenly remembering his young apprentice, he said, "Come, lad, it's time for supper. I'm sure you're hungry."

*O*utside the cathedral and across the piazza, Bishop Guido had slowly gotten out of the chair in which he sat listening to Francesco preach. As he did, his body reminded him of his age, but his heart felt like the *Song of Songs'* young lover, who comes to his beloved leaping like a stag over the hills. As he departed, Bishop Guido expressed his gratitude to his host for providing him with a place that allowed him to listen to Francesco unseen by the crowd. As he descended the stairs to the piazza, his heart was filled with gratitude that his love of God had been renewed by what he had heard that afternoon. He was pleased as he stepped into the piazza to see that it was deserted; his identity would also be adequately hidden by the dark purple shadows of twilight. As he walked home, he pondered, "If only my peoples' hearts were as moved this afternoon as was mine!" Then, inspired, he announced aloud to the deserted street, "I shall invite Francesco to preach in my cathedral at Mass this coming Palm Sunday. While, technically, he can't preach at Mass because he's not a priest or a deacon, am I not the bishop?"

Bishop Guido smiled as he thought, "Ah, Monsignor Carafa, the Guardian of Orthodoxy, will strongly disapprove of that. He'll quote

canon law to me, saying that Francesco can speak to the people on street corners and in the piazzas but that as a layman, even a tonsured one, he is forbidden to preach at Mass. Of course, he will add that violation to the little report he is compiling for the Vatican. Tonight at supper I will announce to Paulo that I am planning—no, that I have decided—to grant a dispensation to Francesco to preach at Mass this Palm Sunday. Then I can be assured as Holy Week begins that at least in my cathedral the cross of Christ will be preached with great love and fire."

Chapter 14

THE LITTLE BROTHERS HAD BECOME BIG! LIKE thunderhead clouds quickly billowing on a hot July afternoon, so had the band of the Little Brothers now swollen to more than a hundred members. Francesco had begun sending the brothers off in pairs to preach the Gospel in nearby villages and cities, like Cortona and Spoleto. When the remaining brothers at Portiuncula gathered for their meals, they sat in small groups, according to Francesco's desire, so they could be more like brothers in a family.

"Brother Francesco," Bernardo asked as a group of ten brothers sat in a circle ready to eat their noon meal, "will you pray our meal blessing?" At the mention of a meal blessing, the brothers seated in the circle reverently bowed their heads as Francesco began:

O Bread of this meal, bless our hearts with the glowing warmth of Brother Sun, who ripened you as wheat into the fullness of life.

Bless us with the liberty of the wind that swayed your stems,

heavy with grain, rippling them like golden waves in a yellow sea.

Bless us with vitality, O meek vegetables from our garden,

fat with earth's humbleness that breast-fed you into nourishing life.

May we who feed upon your flesh and drink your rich life-giving juices become living food to nurture others' souls and spirits.

 By now, not a single head in the circle of brothers was still bowed, since Francesco's blessing had caused all of them to spring upward in astonishment. He, however, continued praying with closed eyes, unaware of their reaction:

Finally, O Beloved Creator of all things good and delicious,

make us drunk on heaven's noble wine of gratitude and joy

as we eat these gifts of holy food before us, always mindful

that we are to be gifts of your bread of life to one another.

We pray in the name of the Father, and of the Son

and of the Holy Spirit. Amen.

"Brother Francesco," asked Brother Leone, looking at the vegetables in his bowl as if they were poisoned, "how can you ask that our bread and vegetables bless us? If we are to eat this food without harm to our souls, shouldn't we keep our focus on asking God to bless it in order to release it from the clutches of the devil?"

"I agree with Brother Leone," said Elias, who had just recently joined the Little Brothers. Raising his finger to push a strand of hair behind his ear, he added, "Father Francesco, while poetically colorful, your meal prayer was rather unconventional."

"It's *Brother* Francesco," he replied. "Please, Brother Elias, do not call me 'Father.' I am your brother in Christ." Then Francesco tore off a piece of the bread and, holding it solemnly in his hand, bowed with reverence toward it as if he were about to receive the holy host of communion.

A frown creased Elias's forehead as he observed Francesco's silent gesture of reverencing common bread as if it was somehow holy. Brother Elias was in his late thirties, lean of stature, and of medium height. His most striking feature was his quick, darting eyes, which suggested his sharp, ever-calculating mind. While typically Italian, his facial features were uncommonly rigid and unexpressive. Elias seldom smiled; he was a serious, practical man whose personal life and daily communal tasks at Portiuncula revealed his love for organizing things. His fondness for orderliness, which bordered on fixation, was unconsciously expressed in his quirk of rearranging strands of hair over his ear.

"*Brother* Francesco, then," Elias replied in a condescending tone, "please illuminate us. Be a lamp to shine some light upon our ignorance regarding this mystery of how common food can bless us."

"Brothers, by our prayers of blessing we do not make creation holy. It has been holy from the very beginning when God pronounced all created things to be *good*, which is the same as holy. And any taint of sin upon creation that resulted from Adam's fall from grace was washed away by the holy blood of our Savior."

"I'm no theologian," replied Elias, "but does the Church not teach that all creation and all the world were cursed by the sin of Adam and Eve? We no longer live in paradise—this is Umbria, not Eden! Heaven's dispenser of graces, Holy Mother Church, by her numerous blessings of secular things, ransoms them from Satan's possession. By our prayerful blessings of material things, by sprinkling them with holy water and making the sign of the cross over them, we call down the blessing of God upon them, even if our blessings can never come close to those of priests or have the sanctifying effect of saints' relics. Sinners that we are, by these daily blessings we share in the ransoming of this fallen world from evil spirits."

The other brothers sat listening in silence as they ate, since never before had they seen any brother openly challenging Francesco as Elias was now. Though Elias had only been in the brotherhood for a short time, that didn't prevent him from asserting his strong personal opinion on almost every issue in the community. His boldness in expressing himself and his air of certainty had attracted a group of the newer members like bees drawn to a scented flower. They admired his ironclad convictions, which fed their need for an authoritarian leader. Bernardo and Pietro, the first two followers of Francesco had rather easily adapted to the diversity of personalities Francesco had unconditionally welcomed into their brotherhood, but they found Elias to be as irritating as a hangnail. Yet despite their dislike, and even distrust, of Elias, in the spirit of Francesco's desire that all the brothers would live in mutual love and respect, they struggled to love him. Pietro, however, was convinced that when Elias had joined the Little Brothers he came with some very definite ideas about what its shape and direction should be. He was troubled by a haunting premonition that Brother Elias would someday indeed shape the brotherhood according to his preordained vision.

"Brothers," Francesco said as he stood up, "I too am no theologian but only an instrument in the hands of God, one who allows the bow of the Spirit to play whatever song it wishes upon the strings of my heart." Then, chuckling, he pretended to hold a lute up to his chin, and drawing an unseen bow across the lute's invisible strings, he began to sing:

O God, you created our earth

not as an object to judge or condemn,

but as a great bowl into which you might pour

all the great love of your holy heart and soul.

Oceans, mountains, and rolling fields,

grape vines, olive trees, and apple trees,

birds, fish, wolves, and sheep,

and, finally, man and woman

are, simply and wonderfully, vessels

that you have filled full of your life.

You, our Father, became our Brother

to share our pains and sufferings,

to enjoy human play and pleasures,

as you enfleshed your great love for us

in our Brother, Jesus Christ.

O Lord, bless our eyes and hearts

to see your face in all of creation,

to see every aspect of our life

as cross-consecrated, twice sacred.

Thus blessed, let us genuflect in humble awe

before the sacred hidden in the simple.

Pietro tapped his ear with his finger, for he could have sworn that in the slight breeze stirring the leaves of the nearby trees he had heard a chorus of the thinnest voices singing *Amen*. "Ah, what tricks," he thought, "the wind plays upon us as it gently sways the trees."

Tucking a strand of hair behind his ear, Elias turned and walked away without saying a word—and was quickly followed by two of the

brothers hurrying to catch up to him. Francesco watched them depart engaged in deep conversation. He thought to himself, "Brother Elias, I don't blame you for being confused by my prayer and my ideas. Even my beloved old friend Leone, who has been with me for so long, is still easily shocked—and I don't blame him either. Not long ago I too was blind to the Divine Mystery present in creation and common earthen things. I never would have judged a tree to be a tabernacle holding the presence of God. But I've changed and can . . . no," he corrected himself, ". . . this new awareness is not anything of my own making! Rather, I've been gifted with a second-sight by which I can sense. . . ." His spinning thoughts abruptly ceased, and he smiled as he realized, "Ah, it is you, my beloved Padre Antonio, whom I should acknowledge, for your healing of my eyes has at long last occurred! This recognition prompted him to say a brief prayer of gratitude for the wise guidance of his old friend and mentor, who had blessed and inspired him and had patiently allowed his spiritual insights to unfold in God's own time. To that prayer he added another, asking God to gift his brothers with the same healing of their eyes.

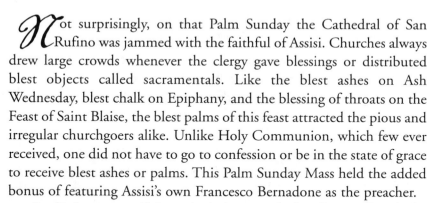

*N*ot surprisingly, on that Palm Sunday the Cathedral of San Rufino was jammed with the faithful of Assisi. Churches always drew large crowds whenever the clergy gave blessings or distributed blest objects called sacramentals. Like the blest ashes on Ash Wednesday, blest chalk on Epiphany, and the blessing of throats on the Feast of Saint Blaise, the blest palms of this feast attracted the pious and irregular churchgoers alike. Unlike Holy Communion, which few ever received, one did not have to go to confession or be in the state of grace to receive blest ashes or palms. This Palm Sunday Mass held the added bonus of featuring Assisi's own Francesco Bernadone as the preacher.

So the long nave of the cathedral was packed wall-to-wall with the faithful. They stood holding palm branches that had been blessed at the beginning of the Mass by Bishop Guido. The clergy and local nobility seated around the altar in the elevated sanctuary at the far end of the nave joined the faithful in standing as the deacon of the Mass began reading the long Palm Sunday Gospel of the Passion of Christ. Since it was in Latin, the reading was incomprehensible to the people, and so they used the extended time to ponder the magical and miraculous powers of the palm branches they were holding. Of all the sacramentals of the Church, they were considered the most potent. Folk belief held

that wherever they were placed, be it over a doorway or behind a cross, they possessed the power to banish evil spirits, turn away destructive lightning and even deflect the curse of the evil eye cast by an angry neighbor.

As the deacon completed the long Passion Gospel, the crowded cathedral began to hum in anticipation as the people watched the Master of Ceremonies, Monsignor Carafa, place a tall, white miter on Bishop Guido's head after he sat down in his high-backed episcopal throne. Then, wearing his tattered gray tunic, a barefoot Francesco Bernadone stepped out from behind a large pillar. He walked to the middle of the elevated marble sanctuary platform and bowed reverently to the high altar; then, turning, he bowed to the Lord Bishop. A hush as solemn as a funeral pall fell over the crowd.

To the surprise of the clergy and everyone else, Francesco remained standing in the middle of the sanctuary instead of ascending the ornately carved marble pulpit. "My Lord Bishop Guido, Right Reverend Monsignors, Reverend Fathers, and noble Lords and Ladies," he said in a strong, clear voice, as he graciously bowed to each in turn, according to the Roman tradition of acknowledging the presence of dignitaries. Then turning to face the vast field of faces packed in the cathedral's long nave, he said, "My brothers and sisters," bowing to them with the same reverence he had shown the clergy and nobility. A slight but audible murmur arose from the crowd, for never had they seen any preacher bow with such deference to the common people before beginning to speak. Some women also smiled at one another at Francesco's break from custom, since the faithful always were addressed by preachers simply as *Brothers* or *Sons* of God.

"Today, here in our Cathedral," Francesco said as he stepped closer to the people, "the Lord Jesus rides into our very midst as he passes through Assisi on his way up to Jerusalem to die. And as he does, he longingly calls out to each one of us, 'Come, my beloved one, accompany me as I go up to the Hill of Calvary, and so show that your love for me is stronger than death.' This Holy Week, let us not abandon him by simply being consumed in our mundane cares and usual affairs. Know that the days of this holiest of weeks are laden with gifts, for God has turned upside down heaven's great hourglass, reversing the flow of time some twelve hundred years, bringing us right into the heart of our Lord's life! Let us not miss this opportunity to accompany Christ as he

carries his cross to his death, to be buried with him so we can share abundantly in his Easter joy."

As Francesco was preaching, Bishop Guido glanced up at the new fresco of Jesus' Entrance into Jerusalem. On this Palm Sunday it seemed the peasant Jesus of Galilee in that fresco had come alive, had leaped off his painted donkey and jumped down into the sanctuary where he now stood in the person of Francesco. With his arms outstretched as if on a cross, Francesco pleaded with the multitude in that green sea of palm branches, "'Come, follow me,' calls out our Blessed Lord today. So, my fellow citizens of Assisi, let us do so, and go up to Jerusalem and die out of love for him."

Clare Scifi's heart was exploding in joyful love as she listened to Francesco speaking with such profound simplicity and great passion. She was so moved by his words and presence that at that very moment she would eagerly have mounted the cross to be next to her beloved Lord. As she tightly clutched her blest palm branch to her breast, her eyes fixed solely on Francesco, she sighed faintly. Her father, Fovorino, heard her sigh and turned to look at her where she was standing next to her brothers in the row behind him. Then he discreetly elbowed Signora Scifi, and using his blest palm branch as a pointer, he directed his wife's gaze over his shoulder to their youthful daughter's face, now luminously translucent with the unmistakable glow that is created only by being in love. His daughter's gleaming face greatly distressed Signore Scifi; it felt to him like a destructive plague of swarming locusts devouring a field of golden grain. For Signore Fovorino, that endangered harvest field had a vested interest well beyond his daughter's personal fulfillment. It involved his long, delicate negotiations for his daughter's marriage contract that would greatly enhance the Scifi family fortunes. Signora Scifi also readily perceived the telltale signs of love luminously written across her daughter's glowing face. She was likewise distressed, since she correctly surmised that the source of that glow was the poor, barefoot preacher Francesco.

"To each of us," Francesco continued, his voice quivering with emotion, "our Lord Jesus pleadingly calls out, 'Come, my beloved, and follow me. Share not only in my hosanna triumph but in the agony of my cross.' Yes, today, Christ challenges us not simply to wear his cross like the crusaders' symbol on their banners and tunics, but to bear it in our very flesh." Then, extending his arms wide and his palms outward toward the vast congregation, he slowly turned from his left to his right

as he said, "Besides carrying his cross, are there any here among us willing to have their hands and feet pierced as did our beloved Savior?"

Much more than the words he spoke, this barefoot man in the shabby tunic had a radiant presence about him that embodied what he preached. Not all his listeners, however, were fascinated and enchanted by his passionate message. Monsignor Carafa thought to himself, "This man is possessed! Satan himself has sucked his tongue! Only demonic possession can explain his uncanny ability to seduce the hearts and minds of the people. Its written all over their faces, especially the young men and women: They are bewitched, diabolically enthralled. This heretic beggar entrances even the bishop."

"Jesus the Divine Lover calls to each of us," Francesco continued as he himself was being swept up in the exchange of excitement between himself and the crowd. "'Come to my nuptial bed of the cross and join me in being transfigured into the passionate glory of God.'" At the very moment he spoke those words, Clare Scifi was suddenly gripped by the realization that her fate had been sealed for life. She would follow this man whom she loved and become his first woman disciple! She embraced that decision as wholeheartedly as if it had been a Church dogma, and the only questions that remained were when and how. Clare knew her lightning-quick choice wasn't rational. Yet when is love logical? Besides, she bore no blame for her choice; that guilt belonged to the Great Fisherman who had baited the hook with a lure too tantalizing not to swallow.

Clare's entire body shuddered; her spine tingled at the thrill of Christ personally calling her to his nuptial bed of the cross. As quickly as a lady's fan is folded, twelve hundred years were creased together, and she found herself transported back in time to a road leading up to the Holy City. She experienced herself surrounded by a large cheering, palm-waving crowd as Jesus, dressed in a gray peasant tunic, rode by on a small, docile donkey. That Palm Sunday in the year 1212, as her ears reverberated with the roar of Jerusalem's loud shouts of "Hosanna! Blessed is he who comes in the name of the Lord!" eighteen-year-old Clare was suddenly seized by the Holy Spirit. In the midst of Francesco's sermon, to the horror of her parents and family and the shock of those around her, Clare shouted out loudly, "Hosanna! Blessed is he who comes in the name of Lord! Hosanna! Hosanna! Blessed is the chosen one who comes in the name of the Lord!"

Francesco stopped preaching; his mouth hung open speechless at this unexpected outburst that came out of the crowd, which was now itself stunned into silence. A moment later, from the back of the cathedral, a voice cried out, "Hosanna! Blessed is he who comes in the name of the Lord!" Then, from about halfway down the nave came the same shout. It was almost immediately echoed by other voices, until the entire crowd began chanting over and over, "Hosanna! Blessed is he who comes in the name of Lord!" In his great haste to halt this spontaneous expression of enthusiasm, Monsignor Carafa tipped his chair over backwards as he jumped to his feet. Appalled at this interruption that threatened to kidnap the ancient order and decorum of the Roman Liturgy, he rushed to the bishop's throne as if the cathedral had caught on fire and shouted over the din of the crowd, "Bishop Guido, begin the Creed! For God's sake, Bishop, begin the Creed."

As the escalating, enthusiastic chanting of Hosanna swelled up like thunder, Bishop Guido, the good shepherd of Assisi, wisely realized that his beloved faithful were not yet ready for a real-live Pentecost. So he stood up and solemnly intoned, *"Credo in Unum Deum,"* and to his and his chancellor's relief, the choir immediately began singing the creed of the Mass. Because of generations of habit, the entire congregation joined in. Francesco was also relieved, after being shocked by the effect his preaching had had on the crowd, and he quickly disappeared, retreating from the sanctuary. One voice among the hundreds was not singing the ageless Creed: Clare was softly repeating, "Hosanna! Blessed is he who comes in the name of the Lord! Blessed is he whom I shall follow—in the name of Lord."

Bishop Guido had recognized the voice that first shouted "Hosanna." He was a frequent dinner guest of the Scifi family, and a year or so ago Clare had asked him to become her confessor. Standing at the altar with his hands folded as he waited patiently for the choir to finish the long Offertory hymn, he reflected on his personal involvement with both Clare and Francesco. In his visits with her as her spiritual guide, she had described her anguish over the prospect of her father arranging a marriage for her. She had also spoken of her desire for a deeper spiritual life and even her attraction to Francesco and his band of brothers.

The usually prayerful Bishop Guido found it unusually difficult on that Palm Sunday to remain focused on the text and ritual of the Mass,

for his mind was being constantly visited by thoughts of Clare and Francesco. During the extended and elaborate singing of the Sanctus hymn before the Canon, he recalled the scene that morning when Signore Scifi invited him to Palm Sunday dinner with his family. "After dinner," he mused, "Clare and I, as is our custom, can visit in private. Then, if what I feel has happened to her this morning is indeed true, I must at once get word to Francesco. . . ." A cough, followed by a soft thumping sound, interrupted the bishop's planning. Those sounds sprung him back into the present moment, where his Master of Ceremonies, Monsignor Carafa, was tapping his finger on the opening page of the large missal, signaling him that it was time to begin the Canon prayer.

*T*hat Palm Sunday night, after the sun had slipped behind Mount Subasio, the twilight western sky was spectacularly stained purple and orange, and an almost-full moon of the spring equinox was rising in the east across the valley. Hidden by the twilight's purple shadows, Clare Scifi let herself out of her home through the short door known as the Death Door. Only a few feet high, these doors, found in most houses of the day, were used only to carry out the dead. Clare smiled, realizing how tonight that exit seemed appropriately named for her. While as dead as any corpse to her former life, she was abounding in youthful enthusiasm and eager to be born into a new life.

Leaving her home behind as the growing darkness blanketed the narrow, twisting cobblestone streets, she ran toward the Garbage Gate, which was always the last gate in Assisi to close. She wasn't frightened by the darkness, for her heart was so full of joy to be on her way to Portiuncula that it had no room for fear. That afternoon Bishop Guido had assured her that he would send word to Francesco so he would be prepared to receive her. The chilly fingers of the April wind whipped back Clare's long cloak, rippling the dress she was wearing beneath it. With a dramatic flare worthy of Francesco, she had chosen to wear her favorite white dress, feeling that she was like a bride going to meet her divine beloved Lord at Portiuncula. As she approached the Garbage Gate, now silhouetted against the twilight sky, she reflected on her conversation with Bishop Guido after dinner. When she told him how that morning at Mass she had decided to become a follower of Francesco, he affirmed her decision, telling her he was convinced that God was calling her to live a uniquely holy way of life. He said that he and Francesco had already discussed the possibility of women joining his movement and that he thought Francesco was now ready for this next leap of faith. Aware of her father's absolute inflexibility regarding her impending marriage arrangement, he also told her he felt in his bones that she must act at once, even that very night, or else he feared the door of opportunity would be forever barred and bolted. Clare needed no excuse to hurry to join Francesco and told the bishop she would indeed escape that night. Upon reaching the Garbage Gate, she was relieved not only to find it still open but also to find waiting in the shadows two of the Little Brothers whom Francesco had sent to escort her safely to Portiuncula.

*B*reathless in anticipation, Clare stood in the darkness outside the chapel as one of her escorts opened the door to Saint Mary of the Angels. Clare silently gasped with delight as the chapel door slowly swung open, revealing what was for her a vision of heaven descended to earth: the old stone, barrel-vaulted chapel with its faded frescos aglow in the yellow light of her bridal party. Francesco had selected his eleven original followers to be present for this historic moment. They were standing like the wise virgins in Jesus' wedding parable, holding clay oil lamps whose dancing flames filled the small chapel with warm amber light. Clare slowly walked inside, followed by her two escort-brothers, who closed the door behind them. Francesco smiled broadly as he came forward and assisted her in removing her dark, hooded cloak. Then he stepped back as she adjusted her now-revealed veil. All in white, she was so stunningly beautiful with the lamplight shimmering off her dress that it seemed to Francesco their little chapel had again been blessed with an angelic visitation. The awe of the brothers at her remarkable beauty was quickly replaced by their jubilant cheers of welcome. Then Brother Giles stepped forward and presented Clare a bouquet of white spring blossoms he had handpicked. Leaning

forward, she kissed him on the cheek, so flustering Giles in a mixture of joy and embarrassment that he spilled some of the oil from his lamp. As Francesco turned and walked to the altar, Brother Bernardo extended his arm and escorted Clare to the front of the chapel as the other brothers followed.

Francesco began by leading them in the Lord's Prayer, after which he spoke briefly on how he felt it was God's will that Clare was being drawn to share in their lives of total poverty and preaching the Gospel. He said that this night was Clare's marriage feast, when she would be wedded to her Liege Lord Jesus Christ and also become a bridesmaid of Lady Poverty. He spoke of his belief that God's will in heaven was being done this night, that this was a baptismal feast of the birth of his dream of a sisterhood of women to share the brother's vision of joyful poverty. Then he invited all of them to kneel and pray silently that the unquenchable fires of the Holy Spirit's love would descend on Clare as she became the first Little Sister of Assisi.

Francesco stood up and faced Clare as she knelt on the cold pavement stones. Then he asked her if she was freely choosing to renounce all wealth and power and to embrace the life of a Little Sister of Assisi. In a clear voice she announced that with the help of God such was her desire. In the glistening yellow glow of the burning oil lamps and the lighted candles on the altar, Francesco gracefully removed her white veil and handed it to Bernardo. Pietro then took a pair of shears from the altar and handed them to Francesco, who looked at Clare with questioning eyes. After she nodded her consent, he solemnly began clipping off her beautiful long hair, which fell soundlessly to her feet like clumps of brown clouds. When he was finished with the shears, he invited Clare to her feet. Even with her closely cropped hair, she was as radiantly beautiful as ever in her long white dress. Francesco then nodded to the other eleven brothers, and along with Francesco they all turned to face the chapel walls with their backs to Clare. She proceeded to remove and fold her long white dress and to place it and her shoes on the altar to the left of a gray tunic and coarse rope. As she stood naked, with her arms outstretched in the form of a cross, she recalled the day seven years ago when Francesco had stood in the piazza just as naked as she was now—only on that day hundreds of pairs of gawking eyes were staring at him. She felt fortunate in her complete renunciation of her family and its wealth that the only eyes beholding her nakedness were the flaking, faded eyes of the Mother of God and

the angels and saints in the fresco behind the altar. She paused and looked down at her youthful, unblemished body with great joy, for she had long dreamt of being just as she was at that moment. Then, with a curious, almost sensual pleasure, she solemnly slipped on the long gray tunic that was identical to those worn by the brothers.

"We praise you, O Christ," Clare jubilantly declared, signaling that she had completed her change of clothing, "who by your holy cross has redeemed the world." Francesco turned around and smiled; then he placed a light gray shawl as a veil over her head as Brothers Bernardo and Pietro ritually tied the coarse rope around her waist. One by one, the brothers followed Francesco and welcomed Clare with a kiss of peace. Her heart throbbed with the joy of a runner victoriously crossing the finish line, for now her dream had come true: She had become the first woman member of Francesco's newly created Second Order. Francesco was also elated, for his dream of a parallel community of poor women had now begun to bloom. He was confident that other young women would soon be joining Clare.

That night, however, his joy was tempered by the likelihood that once they learned about Clare, some of his newer members would disapprove, especially Brother Elias. Yet had not Saint Benedict's own sister, Saint Scholastica, begun a community of women religious as a twin to her brother's order for men? And did not the Gospels speak of how women accompanied Jesus and his apostles as they went about preaching?

His thoughts were interrupted by the rhythmic sound of snapping fingers and feet tapping the pavement stones—an activity begun by Brother Giles, whose peasant background said that such a glorious occasion demanded a folk dance. Whenever the common folk wanted to express their joy at a good harvest or a friend's wedding, they did so by dancing, for the poetry of the body could say what tongues couldn't. The rural people believed that these communal dances had the magical power to create what their bodily steps and movements imitated: fertility for the bridal couple and fruitfulness for the grains sown in the earth. As Giles introduced one of those ageless folk dances performed at weddings and at spring planting seasons, the vivacious leaping *galliard,* the brothers responded instinctively to his rhythmic beat by reaching out and taking the hand of the brother on either side. While Francesco and the ring of dancing men circled Clare, the barefoot Bride of Christ spontaneously began moving her feet and clapping her hands

to the melodic beat. She beamed with joy as she thought, "This is, indeed, my wedding night—and the spring planting festival when the seed of Francesco's dream has been sown in my soul. May it bring forth a great harvest of holy laywomen dedicated to Christ."

Then, Brother Giles broke free of the circle of hands and spiraled into the center of the ring. Taking Clare's hand, he danced her into the ring of brothers as Francesco spontaneously began leading them in singing an Alleluia chant in anticipation of Easter Sunday, just six days hence. When they were all exhausted from dancing and rejoicing, they bid one another good night as Francesco sent Clare with an escort of two brothers to her temporary residence at the Benedictine Monastery Convent of San Paolo, where her aunt, Sister Bono, was a nun. Francesco and Clare had agreed that she would remain with her aunt until the brothers had the opportunity to create proper quarters for her and any future women members at San Damiano. Francesco was confident in sending her off to the Benedictine Convent of San Paolo that Sister Bono would insure Clare's safety in case her father and brothers might attempt to remove her physically from the convent.

*T*wo weeks later in Rome the priest secretary of Cardinal Uzielli entered the cardinal's office and handed him a sealed packet. Upon recognizing the wax imprint seal, Uzielli dismissed his secretary from the room with a wave of his hand. Then, as if he were unwrapping a long-awaited gift, the cardinal broke open the packet's wax seal bearing the imprint of the coat of arms of the Diocese of Assisi. He smiled in anticipation as he unrolled the document and read:

> *Blessings and salutations to His Grace,*
>
> *Giovanni Cardinal Uzielli.*
>
> *Your Eminence,*
>
> *Your most obedient servant Paolo Carafa, as you requested, writes to report the recent activities of Francesco Bernadone of Assisi and those associated with him. His Order of the Little Brothers, as he now calls his movement, has recently grown to more than two hundred followers. Those seeking to be to be identified with Francesco are all attired in the same gray hermit robes girded at the waist with a common rope.*

This past Palm Sunday, contrary to the laws of Holy Mother Church, Francesco preached at Mass in Assisi's Cathedral of San Rufino, as Bishop Guido had given him a special dispensation to do so on that occasion. However, I fear this action will only set a precedent for these barefoot common preachers, who are unschooled in theology, Scripture, and moral law. They, like the followers of the French heretic Peter Waldo, claim the Spirit of God inspires them to preach to the people in the vulgar tongue.

Recently, while preaching outside in the cathedral piazza, Francesco cleverly caused confusion in the hearts of the simple people by telling them that the law of love supplanted both the commandments of God and the laws of the Church. Being tonsured, he gave them the impression that the Church was granting them license to engage in libertine sensual and sexual expressions.

I am fortunate to have reliable sources inside the Benedictine Convent of San Paolo near Bastia. They have reported to me that presently residing within that convent is one Clare Scifi, the teenage daughter of the wealthy Signore Fovorino Scifi of Assisi. She is barefoot and wears the same poor gray tunic as Francesco and boasts to the nuns that she is the newest member of his new Second Order of Poor Women. I assume that the Vatican never gave permission for the formation of such a band of women, or as chancellor I would have been informed. My sources in San Paolo reported that her father and his sons have unsuccessfully attempted to remove her from the convent. Signore Scifi is grievously distressed, since by running away from home to join Francesco, his daughter has ruined a most suitable marriage he had arranged with a widowed nobleman from Spoleto. My sources also report that Clare and Francesco have had several intimate meetings in the convent, and the scandal of this arrangement has now spread beyond the walls of San Paolo to the surrounding countryside. Speaking of her relationship with Francesco of Assisi, Clare has been heard to say—and I quote verbatim—"After God, he is the charioteer of my soul." This shocking statement, of course, carries the strong sexual implications that this alleged holy man is somehow whipping into a frenzy the wild horses of her lower nature.

It is also being reported in Assisi that a crew of his brothers is presently building living quarters at San Damiano for Clare and future women members.

Knowing of your Eminence's vigilance for the good of the Church, I hope this report will supply valuable information for your investigation of Francesco of Assisi. Be assured that I shall continue to inform you of all future developments in this burgeoning case of heresy and immorality that has such potential danger of scandal and grave harm to Holy Mother Church.

May our heavenly Lord bless Your Eminence with grace and peace in the name of our Savior and Lord, Jesus Christ.

Your obedient and humble servant,

Monsignor Paolo Carafa of Assisi

Sealed on April 8 in Eastertide,

in the Year of the Lord 1212,

at the Chancery of the Diocese of Assisi in Umbria

Uzielli dropped Paolo Carafa's letter on his desk, rubbing his hands together with the glee of a small child who has just been given a shiny new toy with which to play. "Ah ha," he laughed, "a woman—my little poor man now has himself a woman! To be victorious in his case of heresy and this threat to the Church, all I need do is to let nature, his lower nature, take its course." As Uzielli leaned back in his chair, his face bore the glorious glow of anticipated Roman triumph.

"Mother Abbess," Francesco said as he quickly stood up—as did Clare and Sister Bono—when the stately black-robed woman entered the small room where the three had been visiting. The abbess wore the black habit and veil of a Benedictine nun. Its distinctive starched white wimple and head covering tightly framed her aristocratic face. Her silver, jeweled pectoral cross, which hung from a silver chain around her neck, spoke of her authority and power, a primacy that equaled that of a lord abbot. Being the son of a cloth merchant, Francesco noticed that her nun's habit was made from an expensive quality of fine black wool.

"Please be seated," the abbess said, motioning with her hand toward their chairs. "I regret that I've been delayed in personally

welcoming you, Clare, but I have just returned after being away for two weeks in Perugia. I was visiting a most generous benefactor, who has given us several large olive groves and has kindly agreed to build a priory daughterhouse for our monastery." She continued as she fingered her silver cross, "Upon my return today, Sister Prioress informed me that our humble convent was hosting an illustrious guest and a renowned visitor. We welcome you Clare, lovely niece of our Sister Bono and daughter of the famed Signore Fovorino Scifi of Assisi." Then after a slight bow to Clare, she made a similar gesture toward Francesco as she said, "And we are honored that our humble monastery convent has the distinction to have as our guest the famous Father Francesco, founder of the Little Brothers of Assisi."

"Thank you, Mother Abbess," Francesco replied with a reverential bow, "but I am only Brother Francesco, and not a priest. I am, however, deeply in your debt and that of the other nuns of the Convent of San Paolo for the gracious hospitality you have extended to Sister Clare of my new order."

"I was aware," she said, "that . . . uh . . . Sister . . . Clare arrived here attired in the same clothing . . . I mean . . . habit . . . as you and your companions wear. So I understand, Brother, that you have begun some kind of a new religious order for women?"

"Yes, Reverend Mother," he replied quickly, "but until Sister Clare asked to join us, it was only a dream. Long have I desired for dedicated laywomen to join with us in our work of preaching the Gospel and. . . ."

"'Preaching,' Brother? Did I hear you correctly? Do you mean as in preaching the Gospel?"

"Yes, Mother Abbess. While that may sound unusual, it is my belief that since God gave the gift of speech to both men and women, women also should be able to proclaim the Gospel! Moreover, Mary Magdalene was the first evangelist of the good news; our blessed Risen Lord himself sent her to proclaim to his apostles the joyous news that he had risen from the grave." Unperturbed by the distressed look that raced across the fine features of Mother Abbess' face, Francesco excitedly rushed on, "Besides preaching, there are numerous ways to proclaim the Gospel, such as nursing the sick, visiting those in prison, feeding the hungry, and clothing the naked, since these and all acts of compassion loudly sing out the good news."

As Francesco spoke, Clare's eyes sparkled like precious gems reflecting the rays of the sun, and she pondered how wondrous it would

soon be to go about the countryside doing just those things. She could visualize her own small group of Little Sisters traveling the roads alongside Francesco's Little Brothers and sharing his message of glorious freedom.

"Mother Abbess," Francesco asked with longing eyes, "will you grant permission for Sister Clare to remain here until we are able to construct proper convent quarters for her and other women near the chapel at San Damiano?"

"I gladly grant permission," she replied, "for Sister Clare to remain as long as necessary within the walls of our humble monastery of San Paolo." As Francesco and Clare beamed, she continued, "However, I must say, Brother Francesco, that I understand little of what you've said about proclaiming the Gospel. Yet I've learned over the years that God's ways are not ours." Then, when her left hand rested lightly on her silver pectoral cross, she raised her right hand and traced the sign of the cross over them, saying, "May God bless both of you, and may the Holy Mother of God watch over your dreams. Now, I ask that you excuse me, for it is necessary that I attend to some pressing convent matters. God be with you."

As she departed, Francesco and Clare stood up, joyful and grateful at Mother Abbess' blessing and permission for Clare to dwell there as long as necessary. As the abbess walked down the long convent corridor, she wistfully whispered to herself, "Innocents, oh, may the Mother of God watch over you. You are such dreamers, such innocent young dreamers. Today, alas, it seems from the reports I heard in Perugia that all of Christendom has fallen in love with innocence."

Chapter 15

REGALLY ATTIRED IN HIS SCARLET SILK ROBE, UZIELLI
arose with a flourish after kissing the Pope's ring. "Your
Holiness, I regret to inform you of a most serious situation brewing
across the Alps to the north. Our agents in Germany report that a mere
boy, not yet twelve, named Nicholas, claims to have received a vision
from God calling him to launch a crusade of children!" He paused to
notice that this news had caused the Pope to raise his eyes upward as if
he was trying to see through his graying eyebrows. "Sadly," he
continued, "reports from France inform us that another lad, roughly
the same age, a shepherd boy named Stephen of Cloyes, claims he also
was told by Christ to lead a crusade of children to rescue the Holy Land
from the infidels. One group from Germany and another from France,
each composed of thousands of children, are now marching southward
toward the Mediterranean."

"Children!" exclaimed the Pope. "Insanity! The concept is beyond
belief. Are we convinced that these reports are accurate?"

"Yes, Holiness," continued Uzielli, "and the lads leading these
crusades say that the reason the previous four Crusades have been
failures is because of the grave sins of the adults involved in them. They
say that God will bless them, for children are innocent of sin."

"Not innocent—naïve!" exclaimed an exasperated Pope. "And even
if those mere children survived crossing of the Alps, how would they
ever be able to get to Jerusalem?"

"We've been informed," Uzielli continued, holding a scroll of
parchment in his hand, "that these boy leaders have been promised in
a vision that angels will guide them and that when the thousands of
small children arrive at the seaports of Genoa and Marseilles," he

paused, raising his eyes in a gesture of hopelessness, "they will not need to hire ships, for the Mediterranean will divide before them as the Red Sea once did for Moses."

"God have mercy on us!" the Pope moaned as he collapsed backwards into his throne and sunk his forehead into his left hand.

"That's not all, Your Holiness. Our agents report that this marching multitude of children is daily being joined by pious and ignorant parish priests along with peasants and vagabonds. The crusade of Nicholas may now number close to twenty thousand and that of Stephen is perhaps as high as thirty thousand. Both Germany and France are full of pious stories about the children being accompanied by flocks of songbirds and clouds of butterflies."

"Dispatch a papal legate at once. No, send two!" shouted Innocent as he sprang forward in his chair. "Send them northward with all speed, one to Germany and the other to France, where they are to inform these children and all those accompanying them that Pope Innocent III commands—the Vicar of Christ, in the Name of God, absolutely commands—they desist from this pious insanity. They are all to return home at once—and grow up!"

"Other disturbing news, Your Holiness. It concerns the barefoot reformer from Assisi named Francesco who two years ago knelt here asking you to bless and affirm his charismatic work of poverty and preaching. While his original group of twelve has now grown more than two hundred and. . . ."

"His little brotherhood has grown to more than two hundred members?"

"Yes, Your Holiness, and while two years ago when you wisely insisted that the first twelve be tonsured, unfortunately no provisions were made at that time regarding any men in the future who might choose to follow such an unseemly. . . . But as a result, the majority of his new followers are not tonsured. I have presumed to anticipate your response, Holy Father, and so have sent orders for the local bishop, Guido of Assisi, at once to tonsure all these and any future new followers."

"Yes, Cardinal Uzielli, you have wisely foreseen my wishes! You are, indeed, a most prudent and judicious son of the Church; you're my second right hand."

"Thank you, Your Holiness," Uzielli said, bowing graciously and turning slightly to allow his secretary to hand him another document.

"We have received only troubling news about this group in Assisi, and I regret to inform you that in his movement there are now *women* involved."

"Women, living with those men?"

"Not precisely, Your Holiness. However, since narrow is the line between closely associating with and commingling with, it is difficult to discern the actual truth. I've received this document from Monsignor Paolo Carafa, Chancellor of the Diocese of Assisi, informing the Holy Office that having women involved with his movement is causing scandal among the faithful of that area. His report states that there has been intimate dancing involving both sexes. He also writes that Francesco himself has become involved with a certain nobleman's daughter who ran away from her home to be with him." Uzielli dropped the letter to the floor and raised his hands palms up in a gesture of hopelessness.

"How sad, " the Pope replied, heaving a heavy sigh, "for we felt that he was to be a spark to enkindle a renewal of devotion and faith among us, the sign of reform so urgently needed in these troubling times. Cardinal Uzielli, as always I rely on your prudent advice, and since you have presented us with this unfortunate matter, you surely have some prudent counsel."

Uzielli bowed deeply at the Pope's words, partly to conceal the face of a smiling jackal.

*T*he sun had risen and set more than twenty times at San Paolo in the Umbriam Apennines Mountains when Francesco came to visit Clare.

"I'm sorry, Sister Clare, that the work of constructing your convent at San Damiano has been again delayed, but the brothers promise me that soon you will be able to move there. However, I have some good news, for Brother Pietro told me only yesterday that two women in Assisi stopped him on the street asking how they could join you and our new order of Little Sisters. Isn't that good news?"

"Truly it is. But please, Brother Francesco, tell the brothers to hurry, for I don't want to stay behind the walls of this convent any longer than absolutely necessary. I feel like a bird that has escaped from a golden cage only to be cooped up in a convent cage. I ran away from home to live in your joyous freedom and holy poverty, but these women here hardly live lives of poverty!"

"But, Sister Clare, they've taken vows of poverty. . . ."

"In name only, I'm afraid. Many of the nuns are the surplus unmarried daughters of nobles and wealthy merchants, and they continue to live as they did before entering the convent. They possess private property, wear jeweled rings and costly broaches, and have comfortable, finely appointed accommodations. After our prayer times, which are only pious, empty interludes in their day, they engage themselves only in fine needlework and embroidery—and in gossip about others in the community. Some nuns have pet lap dogs, and one nun even has a pet cat." Clare's voice became tinged with the typical medieval disgust for cats, believing them to be familiars of witches and, thus, diabolic pets. "A cat, can you imagine that in a convent? They even go on feast day excursions!"

"Feast day excursions?"

"They call them 'pilgrimages,'" replied Clare, "but that's only a pious excuse to leave the convent and go off traveling, accompanied by their servants, to far-distant shrines and holy places. And while coming and going, they visit exotic places and enjoy the sights of the world. Yet I don't condemn them, for many of them faced the unwelcome prospect of being married to a man they didn't love, being forced to bear batches of children, and like myself, ran off to the convent."

"Clare, you ran to God!" he replied instantly. "I've heard your words about wanting to love and serve our blessed Lord. And I've seen the devotion in your eyes and your face as well as in your life choices. By choosing to become a Little Sister, you were living out the words of Jesus to come and follow him by leaving father, mother, family, and all possessions behind."

"Francesco," Clare said, taking his hand as a large tear began to trickle down her cheek, "you make it all sound so holy and good! I have a confession to make, for here at San Paolo I have had the time and the courage to face the truth. I left everything not for God—but for you!" Seeing the surprise scrawled across Francesco's face, she hurried on, "I wanted to enjoy your glorious freedom to do whatever you wish and go wherever you want. Don't laugh, Francesco, but I saw myself also as a joyful troubadour, a woman troubadour! The reason I ran away from home was because I was enchanted by you and your dream. I'm sorry to disappoint you—and if you only knew how much I've wished that, like you, God had spoken directly to me from a crucifix."

"Clare," he said, softly placing his hand on her shoulder, "please don't cry—or question so harshly your vocation to be a bride of Christ. At the Last Supper our Lord didn't create the wondrous gift of his Holy Body and Blood out of thin air! He took ordinary bread and common table wine and filled them with himself. By doing so, he showed us the way God works in our world. In Jesus we see that the Spirit of God takes our most common human urges and the ordinary everyday things of life and transforms them into channels of God's grace. Oh, Clare, whatever your motives may have been, look upon them as being like common bread and wine and then let the Holy Spirit consecrate them—and in the process change you.

"Now, no more tears!" Francesco said, standing up. "Open yourself to being overshadowed by the Holy Spirit as was the Holy Virgin so you can become a simple handmaid of the Lord."

As Clare stood up, the two friends engaged in a warm and longer-than-usual embrace. As she felt her body firmly pressing against his, Clare experienced a transforming surge, as if somehow in that embrace an exchange of their souls had taken place. After Francesco departed, Clare pondered the passionate sensation in her breast of his unconquerable and resilient spirit, wondering if something lay ahead that would require that invincible spirit to grow in her.

*F*inally, the convent at San Damiano was completed, and as Clare moved in, two women from Assisi and another from Spello accompanied her. To her delight, within days her younger sister, Agnes, joined her in what the people of Assisi were now calling the Convent of the Poor Clares. She hated that name, preferring they be known as the Little Sisters of Assisi. Her friend Francesco was equally disturbed when the townspeople began referring to his brothers as Franciscans, and he didn't attempt to hide his anger.

Soon after Sister Clare had moved to San Damiano, Francesco groaned inwardly, his heart scourged at the news of the latest "poverty of spirit" being demanded of him. The news on everyone's lips in conversations at Portiuncula and the piazzas of Assisi was that Rome would not tolerate anything so radical as religious laywomen freely wandering about the countryside preaching or performing works of mercy. With the greatest haste the Vatican had dispatched an envoy to Assisi ordering Clare Scifi and any other women present or future living at San Damiano to be pontifically confined within a cloister.

Many people in Assisi loudly applauded Rome's decision, having judged as insane Francesco's idea of unmarried women roaming the countryside. Bishop Guido should have been the one officially to perform the solemn sealing and locking of these women inside the convent enclosure, but because of sickness he was confined to his bed. So, to his personal delight, Monsignor Paolo Carafa, acting with the authority of the Vatican and in the name of the bishop, had the honor of sealing shut the cloister enclosure. He pompously read the Latin papal document and translated it to the crowd of townsfolk that had gathered at San Damiano. It called down instant excommunication and the soul's damnation on anyone who dared violate the nuns' cloister. The only exceptions to entering the cloister were in rare emergencies, and then only with the written permission of the bishop. Having completed the ceremony, Carafa rolled up the scroll with a smirk as he thought, "Another stake in the heart of that heretic!" He had immediately read between the Latin sentences of the Vatican document and seen the hidden tactics of his patron Cardinal Uzielli. Now if Francesco and Clare wished to have their little clandestine visits, they would have to do so through a small, iron-grilled window set in a stone wall. Carafa smiled as he walked back up the hill toward Assisi and even chuckled as he thought, "Her silly dream of being a wandering companion of that heretic is now a stillbirth! With the continued help of God the growing heretical pregnancy of these poor men and women of Assisi will likewise soon be aborted."

That day, unseen by the crowd, Francesco stood among the olive trees, looking up at San Damiano as he wept. "My poor Clare," he moaned, "how appropriately have the people named you 'poor,' for after you've given everything else up, Rome has stolen your dream of living in the glorious freedom of the children of God. How long can you survive without suffocating, caged up in that grilled cloister? You're too young to be walled up, estranged from all normal human contacts, forever robbed of the joys of wandering among the sunflowers in the fields and tromping over the rolling roadways." Then, recalling his long imprisonment in the dungeon of Perugia, he cried aloud, "O dearest Clare, whose soul is linked to mine, if what has happened to you had been my fate, I would be clawing with my fingers, tunneling out of San Damiano. For if, like you, I were caged up as a bird, I would soon die. So, my dearest friend, know that I understand if you must abandon our fragile dream of the Little Sisters."

In the following weeks Francesco was so hedged in with tasks that he was unable to visit Clare at San Damiano. Every time he turned around, the brothers were hounding him with questions about how to find necessary materials for the construction of new huts or cloth for new habits. The chore of feeding and housing the ever expanding brotherhood created a myriad of problems that were added to his ongoing responsibility of interviewing each new applicant.

"Father Franthisco, can I join and be your friend?" asked a middle-aged man whose high brow accentuated his sunk-in eyes and large, blunt-ended nose. He spoke with a lisp through large protruding lips from which drips of white saliva drooled. "I lovthe God. God lovthes me. God lovthes you;" wildly throwing his arms outward, he added, "and lovthes everything, even little things."

"Your name, brother?" Francesco asked, smiling.

"Luigi, I'm Luigi of Foligno," he answered, showing his large, twisted buckteeth, "I made long walk here. I've other namthes villagers call me—not nicthe ones. I lovthe God, I lovthe hard work." He held out his large, callused hands to Francesco, saying, "I work hard, hard, very hard, if I become one of your brothers."

"Luigi, for the love of God will you leave your family and give away all your possessions to the poor?"

"Got none! No family," and patting his belt, he added, "no purse—see? So, Holy Franthisco, can I live with you?"

"Yes. Welcome, Brother Luigi, to the family of the Little Brothers. Now, go and speak to Brother Elias, who will give you one of our tunics and show you some work by which you can give glory to God." After Francesco embraced him, Brother Luigi joyously danced off, wobbling like a big, awkward duck.

"Next," said Francesco as he welcomed a young man in his mid-twenties. "Do you desire to love God with all your heart and soul and your neighbor as yourself?"

"Yes," replied the eager young candidate.

"Have you given away all your possessions to the poor, and are you now willing to live in holy poverty?" asked Francesco.

"Yes," answered the young peasant who clearly owned nothing.

"And my third and final question is, what is your name?"

"I was baptized Giovanni, and our farm was near Montefaico."

"Brother with the beautiful name of Giovanni, welcome to the Little Brothers of Assisi," beamed Francesco as he embraced the lad.

"Now, go to Brother Elias, who will give you one of our habits and assign you to one of the communities of our brothers."

A short distance away from the chapel, Pietro stood beside an oak tree observing his beloved Francesco. "For him it's all so simple," he thought, "no examination into their motives or former lives. Correctly answer two simple questions about loving God and renouncing any worldly goods, and you're an instant member. So easy, no year of novitiate, no Holy Rule to memorize and observe, no rules other than those of the Gospel. My dear friend Francesco hates rules as much as he hates having to resolve the tangled problems of organization. I believe he would rather suffer from the plague than have to endure the administrative details of operating Portiuncula. More than once he's told me, 'Truly, Pietro, what a gift God has given me in Brother Elias, who is so skillful in organizing things. I don't know what we would do without his gifts in attending to the smallest details. If it were not for his abilities, I would never have time to pray or be in solitude.'"

Pietro closed his eyes and pondered, "Among Francesco's many gifts, perhaps his most striking gift is his innocent belief in the goodness of every person. On the other hand, he can suffer from blindness to their dark sides—particularly with Brother Elias and a few of the others—and I fear that will someday cause him great pain. What first appears as a gift may turn out to be a curse for him and his dream. His childlike innocence—or perhaps it is his spiritual maturity—allows him to accept people just as they are at the moment, and so he doesn't question an applicant's past life or his reasons for wanting to be a Little Brother. Unfortunately, not all who are eager to join us have the highest spiritual motives. Vagabonds and even outlaws have discovered how easy it is to become instantly respectable simply by putting on our gray habit. In these matters Francesco is either naively unaware, or I suspect he chooses not to know about the activities of some of his followers. Former beggars find that once they're dressed in our gray tunics people don't curse them anymore when they come begging for food or money. And just as the nobility and wealthy merchants often donate large amounts of money so that priests will say endless Masses for their souls, so the poor folk rejoice at the chance to give away food or a few coins to our brethren, asking only that the brothers pray for them. By so doing, they hope to have the same chance of reaching heaven as the rich. . . ." His reflection was cut short by the voice of Brother Elias, who was loudly shouting as he came running up toward the chapel.

"Brother Francesco," Brother Elias angrily roared, "would you explain how you were able to accept into our order a stupid, clumsy clod like Luigi? How are we ever to gain respectability in the Church and the local community if we continue to accept such unsuitable members as him? Anyone can see he's not right! My God, Francesco, don't you ever. . . ."

"Calm down, Brother Elias, calm down." Francesco said, trying to reassure him, placing his hand on Elias's shoulder. "What do you mean that Brother Luigi isn't right? What's wrong? True, he's no scholar like Brother Pietro standing over there, but he loves God, and didn't our Lord say that the kingdom belongs to those who are like children?"

"He's deformed! He's misshapen in body and mind," Brother Elias snapped. "He's ugly and ignorant—and clearly came out of the womb that way. It's obvious that the people of his village got rid of him by sending him here to us at Portiuncula. He must be sent back to Foligno at once, this very day. It is totally beyond my comprehension how you could ever have accepted him into our order."

"I accepted you, didn't I, Brother Elias?"

Elias's eyes flared with intense anger, his face flushed scarlet red, and he whirled around and stomped away. As he did, Francesco turned and retreated inside the chapel of Our Lady of the Angels. Having witnessed the entire exchange, Pietro only sighed deeply, shaking his head as Francesco walked away.

About an hour later, Pietro entered the chapel and in the dim light could see Francesco lying prostrate on the pavement. Hearing the creaking of the door as it opened, Francesco raised himself up to a kneeling position and turned around.

"Ah, dear friend, Pietro," he said, using his sleeve to wipe his cheeks of tears. "What an ass the brothers have for their leader! Brother Elias is right—I do not use prudent judgment in so many things. Yet I honestly don't see any reason why poor Luigi couldn't find a home with us." Then Francesco sat back on his heels, shaking his head, as Pietro sat down beside him on the floor.

"Pietro, I'm not suited—nor will I ever be—for the task that God has placed upon my shoulders," Francesco moaned. "Asking me to order all the details of our daily life is like asking a donkey to sprout wings and fly. And, indeed, I may be as dumb as a donkey, but I don't understand either why Elias is so vehement about the brothers needing to be respectable in the eyes of the Church and society. Does anyone

show respect to the *minores?* Isn't that what our name Little Brothers implies—that we are insignificant, lowly-regarded *minores?*"

Pietro placed his arm around Francesco's shoulders, silently nodding his head as he allowed his old friend to unburden his heavy soul. Pietro understood something of Francesco's distress, for he was also homesick for their early days. Daily he was feeling more and more like an alien in the large brotherhood.

"Not that long ago, in this small chapel, Pietro," Francesco said, looking around, "we danced in such ecstatic joy as we celebrated Sister Clare joining us and the beginning of our Second Order of Poor Women. Today, my heart wants to wail a dirge for the dream that was entombed in San Damiano when our sisters were cloistered. If I were a priest, I'd also give Last Rites to our brotherhood, for I fear that my beloved dream for the brothers is dying as well."

The two friends stood up and walked toward the chapel door. They were surprised that before they could open it, the door swung open from the outside. There, in the bright sunlight, stood Emiliano Giacosa.

"*Caro mio!*" exclaimed Francesco, his sadness instantly transformed by the sight of his old and beloved friend. As they embraced, Francesco felt moisture on his cheeks; drawing back, he saw that Emiliano was crying. "Dearest friend, what's wrong?"

"My Angela and little Victoria are dying," wailed Emiliano. "They've been struck down by the pestilence. Oh, Francesco, I've come for help."

"Emiliano, I will do anything; but if they have the pestilence, what?"

"Come and hear Angela's confession! I went to our church without success, for the priests refuse to enter our home; they are fearful they will catch the pestilence that has come to Assisi. On our street alone, three have already died, and the commune wardens have painted large white crosses on the doors of their homes—warning all to stay away. Please, Francesco, come, for God's sake, even if the pestilence is deadly, and hear her confession."

"I'm not afraid of the pestilence, Emiliano—it's that I'm not a priest!"

"You are a man of God, and everyone says that God hears your prayers. I've heard that you've forgiven the sins of others. Now I ask you

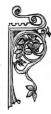

to come and grant absolution to my beloved Angela. Please, *caro mio,* we must go quickly!"

So Francesco and Emiliano ran back up the road to Assisi. As they wildly raced through the narrow, twisting streets, all who saw them coming with tear-streaked, anguished faces quickly cleared a path for them. Turning the corner onto the street of the Giacosa wine shop and home, Francesco saw that the shutters on the windows of all the houses were tightly shut and large, hideously ominous white crosses were splashed across the doors of three of the homes. Emiliano screamed, for there were two wardens with a bucket of white paint at his front door. Roughly pushing them aside, he and Francesco rushed upstairs to the bedroom, which was heavy with the stench of sickness and death. Angela's face was covered with beads of sweat and was as white as the sheets on the bed. The only sign of life was her large brown eyes, which briefly sparkled at the sight of Emiliano and Francesco. Emiliano then looked over to the small bed in the corner. Seeing a white cloth wrapped around the form of a small child, he wailed, "Our dear little Victoria, O God, no! We're too late—may God have mercy on her soul." Angela's large eyes filled with tears that trickled down to mingle with the drops of sweat on her cheeks as she softly moaned.

"Dearest Angela, my beloved," Emiliano said, leaning down close to her face, "Brother Francesco has come to hear your confession and grant you absolution. You are pure, my beloved, as sinless as the lilies of the field, but I know that you desire to confess. I'll step outside on the stairs until the two of you are finished." As she weakly nodded, he kissed her on the lips, then turned and nodded to Francesco, who stepped forward with tears streaming down his cheeks. He sat on the side of Angela's bed and cradled her in his arms, leaning his head down close to her mouth.

A short while later Francesco called Emiliano back into the bedroom. As he came in, he heaved a great sigh, for while Angela was smiling faintly it appeared to him that she looked much weaker. Sitting beside her on the bed, he leaned down, kissed her and said, "Our darling little Saint Victoria is with God in heaven, my dearest one, and praying that you will be spared. Please, Angela, don't die; little Francesco and I need you. Beloved Angela, you are my life." And he began kissing her again while Francesco stood next to him, weeping.

A thin smile briefly crossed Angela's face, and then her breathing stopped. Francesco leaned over, closed her eyelids and traced the sign

of the cross over her as his lips moved in a silent prayer. With a loud shriek, Emiliano threw himself onto the bed and embraced Angela tightly in his arms. Francesco left the room, closed the door, and sat outside sobbing at the top of the steps.

The very next day Angela and Victoria Giacosa were buried. Because of the great fear of the pestilence, only three attended their funeral: Emiliano, his twelve-year-old son, Giovanni Francesco, and Francesco. Since no priest would come, Francesco performed a burial, reflecting in his prayer on how Angela and Victoria were now among the Communion of Saints and how they shared in the resurrection of Christ. Even though Angela and Victoria had not been declared saints in the Church's eyes, Emiliano agreed fully with Francesco's prayer. As he was finishing the double burial service, Francesco recalled once hearing that the dead rest more quietly if you sing a song over their graves. So he sang two songs, one for little Victoria and one for Angela. As Francesco beautifully and spontaneously sang, composing the words and music as he went along, Emiliano remembered the night years ago, before he was married, when Francesco had sung outside Angela's window.

When the prayers and farewells to the beloved dead were finished, Emiliano invited Francesco to a funeral meal at the home of his father-in-law, Fibonacci. Francesco thanked him but declined, and after their poignant departure, walked slowly past many graves until he came to the grave for which he was looking—the one belonging to his mother Pica. He knelt and prayed for her soul and then stood and sang a song over her grave, wishing her rest and peace. In the last verse of his song he tenderly expressed his wish that his mother was now one with God and that she now understood—and even rejoiced in—her wayward son, Giovanni Francesco.

*S*everal weeks later, Emiliano came dragging his heavy cross of grief down to Portiuncula. After he and Francesco had walked a distance into the woods away from the small city of the brothers' huts, Emiliano asked, "*Caro mio*, you are close to God. So, tell me, why? Explain to me how I have sinned. How have I so grievously offended God to be punished like this? What evil could I be guilty of to have my great treasures taken away from me, my beloved Angela and my precious little Victoria?"

"God does not send plagues and pestilence as punishment for our sins," Francesco replied, "even if the priests call them the means of divine punishment. At least the God that I love does not inflict horrible sicknesses or other evils on us for our sins."

"Oh, Francesco, do you remember when I told you how much Angela and I enjoyed making love together? Do you think that's the sin which caused God to send the angel of death to our door? I should have listened to the Church and. . . ."

"No, don't think that way, my dear friend. While I may have once thought that, I have come to realize how false a notion it is."

"Then why?" asked Emiliano. "There are some in Assisi who say that the Jews have poisoned our wells. Still others say a troop of gypsies who recently camped outside the city left the pestilence behind, and still others say it is a curse of God because Assisi didn't send more men to fight in the Crusades."

"An emphatic *NO* to all of them, Emiliano! No such reasons explain the mystery of death and disease. If they were a chastisement from God, then I would be an atheist! I could no longer believe that Jesus was the son of that kind of cruel, vicious God, and I firmly *do* believe that he was God's son."

"But, Francesco, the Church teaches us. . . ."

"I'm sorry, Emiliano, I am no longer able to reconcile the God that some people in the Church preach about with the God that Jesus sang about and revealed in the living ballad of his merciful deeds and presence. For me, at least, the two are often at odds, and I've chosen to believe in the God of Jesus."

"But Angela and Victoria—why?"

"Why? Why does anything in creation die? Perhaps death is one of God's great secrets. I don't know, but somehow it must be a mysterious part of life."

As the two old friends walked and talked, Emiliano began to feel the first healing scab forming over the top of the gapping, bleeding wound of the deaths that had ripped him asunder. Francesco encouraged Emiliano to grieve and, at the same time, to dream about what he and his son, Giovanni Francesco, would now do with their lives. He even proposed that he should stay open to the possibility of remarrying. Emiliano shook his head, saying his heart had no room for dreams, for it was overflowing with tears, that it was impossible even to think of remarrying any time soon, if ever. Then Emiliano stopped

walking, took hold of Francesco by both shoulders, looked him in the eyes and told him that now that Angela was gone what he really dreamed of doing was coming to join him as a Little Brother! What he really desired to do was to sell his wine shop and give away all his possessions—but he knew that he couldn't. Living in total poverty wasn't possible for at least eight to ten years, when his son would have reached manhood and married. Tightly squeezing Francesco's shoulders, he pleaded with him, "Isn't there some way that, while caring for my son, I can become one of the Little Brothers?"

Besides being held by the strong grip of his dear friend Emiliano, Francesco also felt himself being seized by a more powerful force—the rebirth of a dream. As if his heart had been given wings to soar skyward, he had been visited by an inspiration to form a companion group of Little Brothers composed only of laymen like Emiliano. He was so excited and enthused by the gift of this new idea that he kissed Emiliano, who had been the vehicle of this inspiration. As impulsively as usual, without giving any thought to the details or implications involved, he eagerly poured out to Emiliano his germinating dream of a companion lay order that along with the orders of brothers and sisters would form the third side of a triangle, a trinity of orders. Emiliano was equally excited, immediately captivated by this prospect of somehow once again being closely involved with his friend, and he urged him to say more about it.

As he spoke to Emiliano, Francesco began composing offhand, starting to give shape to his original inspiration. "The members of the new Third Order of the Little Brothers of Assisi would be laymen, intimately united with the brothers and sisters in the first and second orders yet living in the world, continuing to practice their professions and trades. They would not be clerics, as the Church forced our band of brothers to become. And because of family obligations they would not pledge poverty, but only to live simply and be generous in sharing with the poor. They would preach by their example of living the Gospel in the midst of making a living, and prayer would be an essential part of their daily life." Francesco was so excited that he broke into dance and joyful song, for he saw this brotherhood as a resurrection of his original dream of a lay community. The two friends talked about this newest dream as they walked back to Portiuncula. On the way they made a critical decision together.

Upon arriving at Portiuncula, Francesco and Emiliano entered the Chapel of Saint Mary and the Angels and then barred the door. In a private ritual they knelt before the altar as Francesco prayed for the Holy Spirit to descend upon Emiliano and upon this his newest dream. Then Francesco took off his gray tunic and Emiliano his clothing. The two stood naked before God as Emiliano pledged to live in the spirit of poverty as a layman, a father, and a merchant, as one who was in the world but not of it. He pledged to follow a pattern of daily prayer, to pursue holiness, service, and the complete nonviolence that Jesus asked of his disciples. Then with his own gray tunic the naked Francesco solemnly invested his oldest and dearest friend into the brotherhood and addressed him for the first time as Brother Emiliano Giacosa. After the two had embraced and exchanged the Kiss of Peace, Emiliano accepted Francesco's invitation to become head of the Third Order with the title of Servant Brother Emiliano. Emiliano took off Francesco's gray tunic and returned it to him, and then dressed again in his own clothing. At the door of the chapel, before they parted, he also accepted the responsibility to create a simple prayer ceremony by which anyone who wished to join could be received into the Brotherhood of Penitence, which was the name they chose for the lay community.

That very afternoon Francesco hurried to the convent of San Damiano to tell Clare the news about Emiliano and the creation of the new lay community. Then they visited about Clare and daily life at San Damiano. Francesco rejoiced as she unfolded her story. He could see how God was working good out of Rome's requirement that she and her companions be cloistered, since they were now real hermits of prayer, just as Francesco had so longed to be. He was overjoyed that she and her companions were living out his original vision of a small group dedicated to poverty and prayer in a community of love and peace. Clare shared with him her fiercely adamant intention that she and her sisters continue to live a life of true poverty without any compromises, and in hidden ways to live lives according to the Gospels.

After departing from the convent to return home, he stopped and looked back at the cloistered walls of San Damiano, and for the second time that day his heart exploded in joy. Flowing over those stone walls and out into the valleys and fields of Umbria, the eyes of his heart could see a springtime wind of grace and prayer laden with the seeds of a vibrant freshness of new spiritual life. "For indeed," he said to himself with pride, "daily Sister Clare is busy creatively consecrating the constriction of being cloistered. Her loss of freedom is being transformed into true spiritual greatness."

pon reaching Portiuncula, he was surprised to find Count Orlando waiting to speak with him. The two men withdrew from the others and talked for some time in private. Then Francesco called together a group of the brothers and made an announcement, publicly expressing his gratitude to the count. The brothers received his announcement with amazement, but said nothing until they had escorted Count Orlando a short distance from their small city of huts at Portiuncula. Brothers Bernardo and Leone did not attempt to disguise their bewilderment at Francesco, who previously had been so vehement about their strict observance of poverty. For now he had just accepted from Count Orlando the gift of an entire mountain!

"A mountain!" exclaimed Bernardo, "you accepted the count's gift of a whole mountain?"

"My brothers," Francesco said with a smile, "as soon as I made my announcement, I could read your eyes as if they were small round pieces of parchment. I saw the shock and disbelief that Brother Bernardo has just expressed. But allow me to explain. I did not agree to receive Count Orlando's generous offer of beautiful Mount La Verna as a gift, but only to borrow it, to accept it temporarily on loan from him. When we are finished with La Verna, we'll give it back to the count or to his estate."

"On loan, or owned, with all respect, Brother Francesco," replied Bernardo, "to me they sound the same!" Then, raising his hands and waving them as if to ward off any explanation, he added, "And don't try to blind me with your famous brand of Bernadone logic. I have known you long enough to appreciate your endless juggling of contradictions—and also to trust that you are guided by the Holy Spirit. But to swallow a mountain—dear Francesco, that's the biggest test you've given me yet. Now tell us, what are we going to do with a mountain?"

"Thank you, Bernardo, for your expression of trust and love. I don't have to own a mountain to be rich; I'm already a very rich man to have such good and faithful friends as you to support me, regardless of how crazy and illogical my decisions appear to be. I'm not a man of logic or practicality, but of prayer and spontaneity. I couldn't resist

Count Orlando's offer because I've recently begun to hunger for the old days when I had hours and days of solitude. The opportunity to use La Verna as a hermitage was like a gift dropped from heaven. When I'm off on that mountain, I'll be out of reach from the endless needs of the brothers for me to make decisions, free from the demands of the ever-growing number of people wanting to talk to me. This old heart," he said, tapping his chest several times, "tells me that Mount La Verna will become very important to me and to all of us."

*F*rancesco did, indeed, retreat to the remote solitude of La Verna, but not for long. A refreshed and ebullient Francesco returned after two weeks of solitude and made an announcement that again tested the ability of Brother Bernardo and the other brothers to accept the radical contrasts in his personality.

"I am going to Spain!" Francesco announced as casually as if he had told the brothers he'd decided to go to nearby Perugia.

"Spain?" exclaimed a shocked Brother Leone.

"Spain?" Brother Elias echoed Leone in a tone of voice more filled with interest than surprise. "How long will you be gone?"

"Brother Francesco," said Pietro, "if you leave us to go to Spain, who will lead us while you're away? Spain is very far from here, and the journey is a dangerous one—you could encounter bandits, fierce wild animals, or even the deadly plague. Whatever will we do if you don't return?"

"Brothers," Bernardo snickered, "let us not think about ourselves, but about our brother Francesco's needs for prayerful solitude. He longs to dwell as a hermit and to find God in seclusion, so let us rejoice that on the highway to Spain he'll be gifted with unbounded opportunities and empty spaces for the peace and quiet he needs for his meditation."

"If the road to Spain," Brother Giles wondered aloud, scratching his head, "is like the one we took to Rome, I think that Father Francesco will have a really hard time finding a place of quiet solitude big enough to put down his toe."

"Beloved Giles," replied a grinning Francesco, "your brother Bernardo is only having a bit of fun with me; don't take him seriously. He's using humor to playfully point out the opposing forces that wage war inside this brother of yours who equally loves community, solitude, and the freedom of the open road."

The next day Francesco departed for Spain: barefoot, with no traveling bag, money, staff, or even one of the brothers as a companion. Before he left, to the great displeasure of Brothers Pietro and Bernardo, he appointed Brother Elias to make any decisions in his absence concerning practical matters at Portiuncula. And over Brother Pietro's own objections of being unqualified, he appointed Pietro to be responsible for the spiritual needs of the brothers. Then, gathering a special group of his brothers, he knelt and asked them to bless him. Tears ran down his face and those of his old friends as one by one they placed their hands on his head and called down God's blessing on him during his travels. When he stood up, he joked with them that he was only going to Spain, not to his death. None of them laughed, however, and Leone felt certain he would never again see his old beloved friend in this life. Then, blessing them and all the brothers dwelling at Portiuncula and those away preaching, Francesco simply turned and started on his way. The brothers marveled that he walked with the lively bounce of a man at least ten years younger than his thirty-one years.

After he had disappeared from view, his old friends began openly discussing the real reason why he was going to Spain, as Francesco had only given a variety of vague reasons. Brother Leone proposed that his actual intention was to go on a pilgrimage to the shrine of St. James at Santiago de Compostela in Spain, which, after Rome, was perhaps the holiest of all the shrines in Europe. Pietro expressed his feeling that Francesco needed a break from the frustration and exhaustion of dealing with all the details of the brotherhood that had now reached the size of a small army. Bernardo spoke last, suggesting that even Francesco himself didn't know exactly why he was going, but he thought that part of the reason was a need to escape to the freedom of the open road because he was being suffocated by the very success of the brotherhood. "Francesco," he told them, "is like a lark that hates being caged, even if he himself provided all the sticks to make his cage."

In Assisi wild rumors about Francesco's journey were as numerous as fleas. One of them said he had gone off to Spain to join the Crusades in the Holy Land, where he hoped to die as a martyr at the hands of the infidel Saracens. Another tale suggested that since he himself was so innocent he had gone off to the Children's Crusade, led by the two twelve-year old boys, that he was headed for Genoa and then to walk across the Mediterranean Sea to the Holy Land. There were also the

nasty rumors that Francesco's radical ideas were leading him not to Spain but to southern France where he would join the heretic Albigensians.

*L*ess than a month later, Francesco was part of the noisy throng on the same crowded road to Marseilles that long ago he had taken with his father on their way to the Great Fair at Chambery. He reflected, "Sixteen years ago I traveled this same road—only I was riding a beautiful horse and dressed as a merchant prince, the apple of my father's eye and the heir to his merchant's business and fortune. Now look at me—anyone would take me for a beggar! Then I was treated with respect, while today children have fun throwing stones at me, farmers' dogs bark and snap at my feet, and the wealthy merchants mounted on their steeds—and even their servants—look down on me with disdain." Coming to a turn in the road, there before him was the old wayside shrine of the three Magi. As sixteen years ago his father and their caravan had paused there to pray, so now Francesco knelt in prayer, gazing at the faded fresco of the three kings pointing to a great star. He prayed aloud, "Kingly Saints Melchior, Gaspar, and black-skinned Balthasar, bless my journey to Spain and bring me back home again to Assisi. O God, I give you thanks that, just as you did with the Magi, you've given me a star to lead me to Christ, except that mine appeared not in the eastern night sky but inside the walls of San Damiano. And, Heavenly Father, I've never been happier in my life that I now am following that star, even though it was so painful leaving those I love in Assisi."

As he stood up and rejoined the clamor and confusion of the crowd tramping along the highway, he reflected on how easily that crowd of strangers busy with their own affairs had provided the same privacy and solitude as his mountain hermitage—he was that hungry for solitude. Walking in the congested "hermitage," his thoughts returned to his most recent visit with Clare at San Damiano. Vividly before him was her tearful and confused face as he attempted to explain his burning desire to travel to Spain. He could sense her unspoken desire to escape San Damiano and enjoy the freedom of the open road with him; it felt like her fingers were clinging to his tunic. He was no more able to give her a logical reason for his burning desire than he was with his brothers. He could only speak of the fire that had been enkindled in his heart to visit Spain, yet Clare understood. "Trust the fire!" she said as she wiped tears from her eyes, "For God speaks to us in fire. My dearest friend, I

believe that with patience someday you will know why that fire has been set ablaze within you, for God rarely speaks complete messages to us. And I also believe—and don't laugh—that our Lord God enjoys playing the game of cutting up his messages to us into little pieces. Then he scrambles them all together in his hat and gives them to us one piece at time, not necessarily in any coherent order. The game requires that we try to guess the full message as quickly as possible by praying over the random pieces we've been given. As you do that, my beloved soul companion, trust the fire."

When he stood up to leave, Clare asked him for his blessing, and he agreed, upon the condition that she also bless him. As he now reflected on that final visit, Francesco kissed his fingertips and rejoiced that he could still feel the touch of her tender fingers. Because of the cloister's iron grill, the only way they could have physical contact when exchanging their blessings was by joining their fingers through the bars of the grill. As Clare's fingers touched his and she spoke her blessing, he experienced it flowing into his fingers as sweetly as honey and as gently as a calm breeze.

There was now no gentle breeze but a strong west wind blowing along the road to France. It was raising great brown clouds of blinding dust, all but hiding from view those tramping the path with him. Francesco pulled the hood of his tunic over his head as far down as possible to shield his eyes from the flying stinging bits of dust. His present blindness led him to recall his final visit to say good-bye to his old mentor, Padre Antonio, before departing from Assisi.

"Who's there," Antonio had called out from inside his hermitage.

"An old friend," Francesco answered.

"Giovanni de Francesco! How wonderful it is to these old ears to hear your voice," the old man answered, "Come in, come in, dear friend."

Even in the dim light, Francesco was shocked to see how infirm his old mentor and confessor appeared to be. He had aged significantly since their last visit. He saw that Antonio's eyes were coated in a bluish-white glaze and guessed that he was now almost completely blind. He could see that Antonio's hands were gnarled and crippled by his joint affliction.

"As you can see, Giovanni," the old hermit said with a broad smile, "I've been confronted with a new adventure. One would think a man my age had completed his accomplishments—ah, but God has sent me

off on a new search to find the Divine Mystery. In my earlier years I've found God in Scripture, in the mystery of the Eucharist, in my monastic companions, in my prayer and meditation, in my travels and encounters with those who were so different from me. And I've found God here in my hermitage, in the wonders of creation and then most wondrously in you, my beloved Giovanni Francesco. Now, when I'm ready to die and find some rest, there comes the greatest of all quests: to find God in my diminishing five senses—in my loss of hearing, my blindness, my painful, aching joints, and having my independence robbed by my lack of mobility. There—in a few rambling sentences you know everything new in my life. So now, tell me about yourself and your religious community." Then chuckling, he added, "Any new stunts of holy madness, my young heretic, to prompt more investigations from orthodox Holy Rome?"

"My newest madness is that I'm going to Spain!" Francesco had blurted it out without thinking of how that news might affect his dying friend.

"Spain! Ah, the land of mystery and holy wisdom. How wonderful!" Antonio's enthusiasm surprised Francesco. "Pardon an old man's pleasure," he continued, "since such occasions have been rare recently, but I'm so pleased that the seed of that madness planted in your heart right here in this very hermitage has now taken root and begun to sprout."

"Yes, Padre, you're the guilty one," Francesco said, "with those stories of your abbot sending you off to Spain. Your tales were not so much a seed as a spark that enkindled a burning desire within me. I've come to say good-bye and also to ask if, as a parting gift, you have any words of wisdom for me."

"My trip to Spain," he said, "or Hispania, as we monks referred to it with its old Roman name, deeply influenced my spirituality and my whole life, and I pray that your trip will do the same for you. As for wisdom," Antonio said, nodding his head in silence for some time, "I have two parting pilgrim gifts for you to tuck into your sleeve. First: Memorize—inscribe in your heart—the words the Holy Spirit placed on the Apostle Peter's lips in the Acts of the Apostles, 'I see that God shows no partiality. Rather, in every nation whoever is in awe of God and acts in an upright way is acceptable to God.'"

Francesco repeated those verses slowly and then said, "Padre, I've inscribed them on my heart and will keep the inscription fresh by

repetition, though I don't fully understand their significance. Yet I will keep them in focus, for you have been such a wise teacher, who has given me so many wonderful seeds of insight to nurture and change my. . . ."

"Giovanni, no, no! I have only been a channel of the Divine Mystery. If you've grown in the wisdom of God and now see differently than before, you must thank the Source, not the aqueduct. Now, allow me a little playfulness as I give you a departing riddle as your second gift: To come home from Spain as a rich man, you must go to Spain as a poor man."

Francesco laughed loudly. "Ah, Antonio the Jester, 'tis a riddle, indeed, for am I already a poor man! I shall depart for Hispania with only the tunic on my back, no traveler's bag, no food or money, no staff and no sandals. Is the answer to your riddle of becoming poor that I should go to Spain totally naked?"

"There are holy men in the world," Antonio replied, nodding, "whose poverty includes the renouncing of all clothing! They go about naked both day and night, even as they walk the roads! I know you've embraced Lady Poverty more radically than has any monk, yet I suspect that part of you remains as rich as any wealthy wool merchant's money chest."

"That's as much a riddle as the first one. I'm sorry, but I don't understand what you're trying to tell me."

"To begin with, my beloved Poor Man of Assisi, even if you go about barefoot and dress more poorly than any peasant, your poverty may be only skin deep. Your father gave you an education befitting a wealthy merchant. You've learned mathematics, history, and even Latin—not well, I agree, but you can read and speak it. You learned French and have a wealth of musical and poetic gifts—so you're hardly poor. But remember my pilgrim's riddle: To come home from Spain as a rich man, you must go to Spain as a poor man."

"I suspect," Francesco replied as he slowly struggled to digest this heavy farewell meal of insights, "you're hinting that I must embrace an even greater state of poverty."

"If you wish to be truly rich, you must be willing to give away even your greatest treasure," Antonio answered in a solemn tone as he reached over and—even though sightless—tapped directly on Francesco's heart. "Your beliefs!"

Chapter 16

THE HIGHWAY'S DEAFENING CLAMOR—THE SOUNDS OF sheep, horses and mules, of peddlers hawking their wares mixed with the angry shouts of cattle drivers and the songs of singing pilgrims—was not loud enough to drown out Antonio's last words to Francesco. Perhaps on that ancient Roman highway to France there were still ghosts of Roman legionnaires marching to Gaul, but Francesco had no doubt that he was accompanied by a ghost, the holy ghost of his old confessor Padre Antonio, who kept repeating to Francesco the suggestion that he might need to yield even his beliefs. Francesco the Pilgrim continued to wrestle with the meaning of those words of his old mentor. Did Antonio mean his cherished religious beliefs? More than ever, Francesco longed with great passion to embrace Lady Poverty, yet was it possible that the sacred teachings and dogmas of the Church were preventing him from being truly poor? And how was the renunciation of his remaining treasure, as Antonio had implied, necessary for him to be rich in wisdom? He groaned aloud as he thought, "If I give away my religious beliefs, what would I have left upon which to structure my way of life, my prayer, my understanding of life and the world, and even my hope of heaven?"

As he walked, it seemed appropriate that after leaving Assisi he had allowed the hair on the top of his head to grow in again, excusing himself by saying he lacked one of his brothers to shave his tonsure. Now, like the hairs atop his head, the doubts of his mind filled the sacred faith-space of his soul.

By late afternoon as the sun was quickly plummeting toward the western horizon, Francesco reached the village of Sainte Jean Le Pont, not far from Toulon on the road to Marseilles. As signs of sunset

 appeared, the crowded highway quickly began to empty out. Those with money retired to inns in the village, the traveling nobility and bishops to the homes of local nobles, and monks and priests to the nearest monastery or religious house. The vast majority of the travelers prepared to spend the night just off the highway as they gathered around their evening cooking fires. While Francesco could have asked to join any of these small groups of people camping along the road and would have received some food, he found himself attracted to a fire flickering some distance away from the road at the edge of a nearby wooded area. As he walked toward the fire around which several people were gathered, he recalled the words of Clare, "Trust the fire. God speaks to us in fire."

Trusting that the fire was a good sign, Francesco was unprepared for his hostile reception. "Be off with you, you dirty beggar!" shouted one of the men seated by the fire, a large, angular man wrapped in a great black cape. "There's no food here for the repulsive likes of you. Go eat with the beggars in the ditch, or with a swift kick I'll send you off to your heavenly reward—or off to hell, tattooed with welts from the largest stick I can find."

"Trust the fire, but it doesn't appear that God is speaking to me in this one," Francesco thought. Still, impelled by his sense of trust, he stepped closer and began to smell the supper cooking on the fire, which was surrounded by six rough-looking men.

"Brothers, the peace of God be with you," said Francesco.

"And, beggar, may the mischief of the devil be with you," roared a large man with a heavy black beard and long hair, "and the blessings of the evil eye be upon you." His companions around the fire all laughed as a tall, skinny man picked up a stone and, with perfect aim, threw it, striking Francesco on his left shoulder.

"Peace, my brothers. I come in peace," Francesco replied, rubbing his sore shoulder as he stood just outside the circle of the firelight.

"Do you think," asked a man with one good eye and an empty socket where the other should have been, "that like a lot of those pilgrims he's got a heavy purse hidden under that ratty robe he's wearing?"

"Good question, Bruno. Let's strip him of his robe and find out," laughed the tall, skinny man who had thrown the stone at him. "And if he doesn't, then we can send him off naked and sell his tunic."

"Your brain is as skinny as your body," joked a stocky, muscular man wearing a large-brimmed leather hat. "That ragged tunic he's wearing isn't worth the stealing. At least when last I was in the market lice weren't bringing a penny." Then, shaking his fist at Francesco, he said, "Go away, road scum, and take your filthy fleas with you, or. . . ."

"Not too quick, mate," snarled the fifth man who had the face of a weasel. "I say that before we send him off, we have a little bit of fun with him."

"Brothers, I come in peace. I was drawn by your fire," Francesco replied, eager to get away as quickly as possible, since he was beginning to feel the throbbing pain of his old Perugian wound. As he started to back away, he said, "You're right. I've made a mistake, and I should be on my way back to. . . ."

"No! Don't leave us just yet," said the sixth man in a commanding voice. As he stood up, the firelight revealed that he was as tall and muscular as Emiliano. Curving down the right side of his face from his eyebrow to his jaw was an ugly scar that disfigured what would have been a handsome face. "Friends of the devil," he said, "let us not be hasty. This stranger in the night may actually be a brother in our guild of mischief. While he may have been drawn here by our fire, perhaps it is the sweet aroma of felony that really attracted him. I sense in him a budding capacity for crime." Then, cocking his head to one side, he added, "But from the seedy looks of him, he's fallen on hard times, or . . ." he laughed before finishing his thought, "they've fallen on him. So, stranger, if you think you can be a companion in crime, come and sit with us, and we'll find out if you're deserving of some of our supper."

As Francesco stepped inside the circle of the firelight, he felt naked under the piercing gaze of the six men. While his legs wanted to run away, some inexplicable force kept him there, and, smiling, he sat down on a vacant log downwind on the smoky side of the fire.

"Stranger, tell us what trick or skill you can bring to our group," asked the small man with the weasel face. "Are you a highway robber, a common village thief, a purse snatcher, a peddler of fake relics, maybe a murderer for hire, or perhaps just a rapist for fun and pleasure?"

Before Francesco could answer, the skinny man spoke. "Now, as for me, I'm a skilled snatcher of purses, and a real master of the craft— especially at hangings and heretic burnings. Ah, them's the best times to snatch a purse, for a good hanging or witch burning arouses people even more than having sex. All hot and bothered, they forget about their purses dangling from their belts. But from the looks of you, I'd say you're no purse snatcher; your fingers are too short!"

"Look at him, the guy lacks the eyes of a wolf," added the one-eyed man, "so he can't be a hired assassin. From the looks of him, I'd bet tomorrow's take that he couldn't kill a bird."

"But, brothers, I am a thief," Francesco replied with a thin smile, "and I belong to an Italian brotherhood of thieves."

"Prove it! Show us what you've swiped today," the scar-faced man said in a voice of authority that made it clear to Francesco he was the leader of the band. "Then we'll know you're worthy to share supper with our brotherhood."

"Friend, today hasn't been as good as other days," Francesco said, pausing to look up at the night sky now beginning to fill with glistening stars, "but I hope by a couple of my deeds today I've been able to steal at least a piece of heaven."

The circle of heads to his left and right stared at him in disbelief, as if an invisible magician had played tricks on their ears. Then they glanced at each other to see if anyone understood what he had said. Before any of them could speak, Francesco jumped up and began singing a bawdy song from his younger days of drinking and wenching in Assisi. Without a break, he followed that song with a lewd song, before moving into a romantic ballad.

"Beautifully done," declared the scar-faced man, applauding when Francesco finally stopped. "It's been a long time since we've heard such beautiful singing around our campfire, and. . . ."

"Other than," interrupted the large, heavyset man with the black beard, "the jingle, jingle of stolen silver coins. Now that, lads, is music to these old ears."

"Shut up! And don't you ever interrupt *me* again when I'm speaking," shouted the scar-faced man. Turning back to Francesco, he

said in a normal voice, "Stranger, allow me to introduce myself. I am Jacques Coeur, the leader of this band of noble gentlemen of the road."

"And I am Francesco of Assisi," Francesco responded with a bow of deference to Jacques as if addressing a prince or a prelate, "at your service."

"He looks more to me like Francesco the Sissy," snickered the one-eyed man, initiating a roar of laughter among the others.

"Shut up, buffoons!" shouted Jacques. "You knaves of the devil and knights of burglary, pray tell, where are your courtly manners? My eye perceives in this beggar who has joined us tonight a most unusual man—a talented, if tattered, troubadour. So I, Jacques Coeur, judge him worthy to be our guest and companion at this evening meal. Give him a bowl of stew meat and bread we borrowed from that distracted roadside cook, for he's honestly earned it by his singing."

As a hungry Francesco devoured his stew and bread, the bandits, who ate even more ravenously than he, began telling wild tales of their exploits of stealing and wenching in taverns, interspersing the most vulgar sexual jokes. Then they began ridiculing the Pope and the Church and jesting about their lust to have sex with nuns. A silent Francesco found himself a prisoner of fear. He wrestled with his instinct for survival, which required that he remain silent, and his obligation to preach about Christ's purity of heart, nonviolence, and their need to repent and change their ways. As fear firmly held his tongue, he stared into the fire looking for an answer, reminded of Clare's words about God speaking in the fire. As the flames leaped and danced, causing scarlet sparks to spiral up like shooting stars into the night sky, Francesco was reminded of another campfire, the one on his last night at the Chambery Fair. His hidden Chambery wound began bleeding guilt, and he recalled the words of Jesus, "Let him who is without sin cast the first stone!" That night Francesco did not preach to the six about nonviolence or their need to repent their lives of stealing and dissipation but only spoke to himself, "Clare was right: God speaks in the fire."

"Noble Gentlemen of the Imperial Court of Satan," Jacques solemnly announced, "since tomorrow is hurrying toward us, let us likewise hurry to our beds." In the fading light of the dying fire, the men began rolling up in their blankets for the night, and as they did Jacques asked Francesco if the two of them might go for a brief walk together. As the two strolled away from the glowing orange embers of

the dying fire and out under the star-crowded sky, they started a conversation that lasted late into the night.

The next morning as the sun was just peeking over the horizon, Francesco prepared to join the other travelers now beginning to pour onto the highway. As he departed, he thanked the men: "May God bless you for your kindness and hospitality to this poor beggar." Holding up his right hand, he added a blessing: "And may Saint Dismas open your hearts." Then he turned and began walking across the field toward the highway.

"Ha, what a joke he was!" the weasel-faced man said as they watched Francesco walking away. "Trying to pass himself off on us as a brother thief! Imagine trying to fool the likes of us. He's no more a thief than I'm a. . . ."

"You're wrong! He's a master thief," replied Jacques as he watched Francesco join the other travelers on the highway. "In fact, brothers, I believe he's one of the cleverest thieves I've ever met."

The men silently began gathering up their gear, not daring to contradict their leader. Jacques Coeur stood silently following the slim figure in the gray tunic as he disappeared into the multitudes now clogging the highway.

"Ah, yes, he's a great thief," Jacques said to himself, "and I'm sure there are many who have and will have their hearts stolen by him. And how do I know? Because he has stolen mine!"

*I*t was not long before Francesco was passing through the French seaport of Marseilles. The entire city was alive with anticipation at the arrival of the Children's Crusade. In a few days more than thirty thousand children would march into the city from the north led by the shepherd boy Stephen. The normal population of Marseilles was already swollen by vast throngs from neighboring villages that had come to see a repeat of the miracle of Moses crossing the Red Sea. Everyone knew about God's promise to the lad Stephen that thousands of innocent children crusaders would walk dry-shod across the Mediterranean to the Holy Land. The town authorities and leading merchants were alarmed over how Marseilles could possibly feed and house so many thousands of hungry children, but they couldn't forbid them entrance to the city because the populace saw them as divinely sent. While Francesco was tempted to remain in Marseilles so he could witness the wondrous miracle of the parting of the sea, his heart

overruled that desire and compelled him to continue on his journey to Spain.

As he traveled the road from Marseilles to Montpellier, he was secretly pleased that his tonsure was almost fully hidden. While a tonsure would have given him added protection, he delighted once again in being one of the *minores*. Francesco's highway prayer was saying his Pater Nosters, using a common piece of cord in which he had tied one-hundred-fifty knots to keep count of his Our Fathers. For the peasants and common people, who couldn't read, these recitations of the prayer Jesus taught his disciples was a substitute for the one hundred and fifty psalms of the Divine Office that monks prayed daily. Francesco's custom was to pray three Pater cords each day, one set for his brothers back in Portiuncula, a second for Emiliano and the eternal rest of his wife and daughter, and a third set for Clare and her needs. While peasants and the poor used a knotted cord to count their prayers, the nobility used polished precious stones as counters on their cords. Lacking pockets in his tunic Francesco tucked his prayer cord into the rope-belt that girded his tunic, and at other times he had it tied around his waist underneath his tunic.

At almost every village where he stopped, the news was all about how Pope Innocent III had broken the stubborn King John of England by his threat of deposing him. French villagers enthusiastically spoke of how the Pope had offered the English crown to Philip Augustus of France. They were delighted that King John had been made impotent by the Pope's excommunication, which included all John's subjects. Now to save his throne he would have to come crawling on his knees to the great Pope Innocent.

After passing through Montpellier, Francesco used the coastal road that curved southwest toward Narbonne. Just northwest of that city was Toulouse and just beyond it was fortress city of Albi, which held a commanding position on the left bank of the Tarin River. Albi, a fief of the counts of Toulouse, was the hotbed of the Cathar religious movement, whose members were called Albigensians. Travelling in the midst of this region of heretics, Francesco daily shared the road with increasing numbers of mounted knights who had responded to the call by Pope Innocent III to mount a crusade not against infidels but against the French Christian heretics in southern France. Villagers along the way bragged to Francesco that this French Crusader army

now numbered more than two hundred thousand, the majority of whom were from northern France.

As the high stone walls of the ancient city of Narbonne came into view, Francesco rejoiced, for he was hungry and weary from walking. A village priest, whose Mass he had attended the previous day, told him that the people of Narbonne were known for their arrogance, proud that their city, originally called Narbo Martius, was the first Roman colony in Gaul a hundred years before the birth of Christ.

"Halt, you there in the gray tunic!" demanded the captain of a detachment of mounted knights guarding the main gate of the walled city of Narbonne. "State your name and business in this city."

"Peace be with you, noble knight. I am Francesco Bernadone of Assisi in Italy," he replied to the mounted, plume-helmeted officer attired in gleaming chest armor. "I come in the name of God seeking shelter for the night within your city walls before continuing my travels southward to Spain."

"And no doubt for food as well," replied the captain. "And unless you've a hidden bag of coins under that dirty, tattered tunic, how will you pay for food and shelter? If, indeed, you are a beggar, then turn around and go back to Montpellier or wherever it was you came from. Narbonne already has all the poor and beggars it needs without letting another one sneak into the city."

"You are correct, sir. While a beggar, I'm no ordinary one," answered Francesco. "I'm a beggar of our Lord God, whose beloved Son called us to preach the Gospel, to embrace holy poverty, and to lay down our weapons so we might live in peace."

"A preacher!" whistled one of the knights. "Yet he's not attired in the beautiful black and white habit of Dominic of Guzman's band of wandering preachers from neighboring Toulouse."

"Dominic?" asked Francesco. "I've not heard of him or his wandering preachers."

"They are God-fearing, learned, and devout men," answered the knight. "In the service of Holy Mother Church they've astutely attempted to reason with those damn Albigensians in order to peacefully bring them back to the true faith."

"For sure, he's not one of them," said another mounted knight. "Just look at him: barefoot and wearing that dirty, old tunic."

"France is nauseous unto death," snarled the captain of the guard, "with wandering beggar preachers like you! For all we know, you could

FRANCE

Albi

Toulouse

Montpellier

Rhone River

Arles

Marseilles

Toulon

St. Raphael

Mediterranean Sea

Narbonne

SPAIN

The French
Coastal Pilgrim's Road

be one of those damned Waldensian or Albigensian heretics that have been swarming like locusts over this part of France. We're told that in the southern region of Lanquedoc, from the lower Rhone River to the Pyrenees Mountains, more than a thousand towns and villages are now Albigensian. Our responsibility is to keep heretics, lepers, and beggars from entering Narbonne." Turning in his saddle toward the foot soldiers standing on either side of the large gateway, the captain said, "Take this beggar, or whatever he is, to the archbishop's palace to be questioned by Dom Pierre, the Cluny monk in charge of the *Inquisito,* the inquiry of the Holy Office."

*E*scorted on either side by a soldier, Francesco descended a flight of some twenty steps down into a long tunnel-like underground room illuminated by oil lamps and blazing pitch torches. At the far end was a long table at which sat three black-robed Benedictine monks. Francesco's two escorts remained at the bottom of the stairs as he walked forward. Approaching the table, he saw an inkpot, quill feather pen, and blank parchment pages in front of the monk on his left. The face of the monk seated in a tall-backed chair in the middle was as drab as a slab of pale cheese, while his eyes danced with the angry flames of a zealot. Francesco stood in silence in front of the three monks as their eyes scrutinized him from head to foot. During their prolonged silent inspection, which Francesco felt was intended to terrorize him, he prayerfully looked for help toward the crucifix mounted on the table before him.

"I am Dom Pierre, inquisitor of the Holy Office," the monk finally said, "And you are?"

After Francesco gave his name and place of birth, Dom Pierre began firing questions at him, one after another as quickly as a master archer. Francesco deftly attempted to dodge the more dangerous ones. "Do you believe in the miraculous powers of the relics of saints? Do you believe in the absolute spiritual and temporal authority of the Pope? Do you believe in all the Holy Sacraments of the Church, especially the Holy Priesthood?"

As Francesco confessed his belief in each of these, he noticed the monk scribe making notes on his answers. Dom Pierre continued, "Do you believe that the Pope has the power from God to grant indulgences from the treasury won by Christ on his cross, indulgences that *do* reduce the years of suffering in purgatory?" After a pause Dom Pierre

added, "And mindful that these two witnesses will verify your statement, tell me, Francesco of Assisi, what are your beliefs about sex?" He paused again as if he were rolling the word *sex* around on the tip of his tongue, savoring the very sound of it. Then he folded his hands in a prayerful position and looked at Francesco over the tops of fingertips as he waited for his response.

The monk scribe sat with his quill pen poised, ready to record his answer. For a fleeting moment, Francesco again saw the silent courageous Maid of Montelimar chained to the stake piled high with dry kindling wood as a black-robed monk—similar to Dom Pierre— offered her a last chance to recant her beliefs. He had frequently thought of her remarkable courage, wondering how he would respond if his deeply held beliefs were ever challenged. That time had come as he now found himself in front of a French court of the Inquisito similar to the one the maid must have faced.

"I believe that God created sexuality as good and beautiful, like all the rest of creation," Francesco answered after taking a deep breath filled with a prayer to the Holy Spirit for guidance, "but that Adam and Eve by their disobedience. . . ."

"Francesco of Assisi, are you married?" Dom Pierre interrupted him, pointing his finger at him. "Ah ha, your face spoke before your lips! Tell us why you are not married. Is it because you are one of those 'Pure Ones,' the damned heretics of Albi, who do not marry because they believe that marriage and *sex* are of the devil and so are always sinful?"

"Holy Mother Church blesses marriage," Francesco answered, "and so it can't be sinful, at least mortally. The reason I'm not married is because I have pledged to be the spouse of Lady Poverty, and I belong to a religious community called the Little Brothers of Assisi."

"Never heard of it! And are you making fun of us? How can one be the spouse of a virtue?"

"No, I wouldn't make fun of you. And our brotherhood was blessed by the Holy. . . ."

"Do you eat meat?" the prosecutor cut him off. "Meat, animal flesh, Francesco—like all real men, do you enjoy succulent roasted lamb and good beef?"

"I had some beef stew just yesterday," replied an increasingly anxious Francesco, for the people he had met on the road told him the

Albigensians believed that eating animal flesh is sinful. "I believe in the Church's teachings and am a faithful son of Holy Mother Church."

"I wonder if," said Dom Pierre, "you truly are, since you stand here before us barefoot and dressed in tattered clothing. Do you believe the possession of property is sinful? Or do you believe it is the will of Almighty God that all men, including the Church of Christ, can own and enjoy the possession of property?"

"I do not believe it is sinful to own property."

"Don't lie to me! What you really believe shouts at me, as you stand there penniless in dirty rags. You're aware that these heretics regard the possession of private property as sinful, aren't you? That makes them and their diabolic teachings a public crime to the social order as well as a heinous infection in the body of the Church. Tell me," he inquired, leaning forward over the table, "are you one of *them?*"

"No, I am not! God has declared all creation to be good and that would include personal property," Francesco replied, carefully choosing his words. "Yet some, for the welfare of their souls—like Benedictine monks—take the vow of poverty so that they might share and enjoy things in common. While not a monk, I try to live in the holy poverty that Jesus taught. . . ."

"We are not interested in your interpretation of Holy Scripture," Dom Pierre interrupted him. "The Bible isn't important! It is the dogmas, doctrines, and laws of the Church that, without any error, contain all of the eternal truth revealed in the Scriptures and the teachings of Jesus Christ. What does interest me is your beggar-like poverty. While you claim to be Italian, you speak French far too fluently—so perhaps you're really French and a secret follower of the heretic Peter Waldo of Lyons. To me, my barefoot stranger, you look just like one of those heretical Poor Men of Lyons who secretly go about preaching their false doctrine. I demand that you tell me: Are you one of *them?*"

"Dom Pierre, I swear I'm not a follower of Peter of Waldo. I speak French because I am the son of a merchant who married a French woman while trading at fairs in France. For business reasons he had me learn the French language. And now I'm only traveling through France as a holy pilgrim on my way to Spain."

"Spain!" snapped Dom Pierre. "Are you going there as a supporter of Pedro of Aragon, the Spanish hero of Navas de Tolosa?"

"I'm sorry, but I know nothing of him," Francesco responded as he again glanced with an unspoken prayer at the face of the agonizing Christ on the crucifix.

"Pedro gloriously defeated the infidel Mohammed III, the Amir, winning a great victory for the Holy Faith at that battle of Tolosa. Now, however, he has become the Judas of Aragon, since even at this moment he is marching north to assist his kinsman, the Duke of Toulouse. That viper of Satan has allowed the heretics to flourish in his domain and along with others of the nobility is a secret member of that immoral sect of Albigensians. That Spanish Judas Pedro is marching north to fight against Simon de Montfort, the commander of the Crusade and the glory of France's knighthood, who is now approaching Albi and Toulouse to chop off the head of that great serpent coiling itself around all of southern France. Our Holy Father, being a man of peace, has only resorted to war when all his peaceful efforts to bring back his lost French sheep failed, the final straw being when they murdered the Pope's legate."

"I confess, Dom Pierre, that I know nothing about these political affairs of kings and dukes and their wars. I pray you judge me innocent of anything to do with heresy and allow me to continue on my way."

"You may leave, Francesco," he replied, "but you are either with us or you are against us. For we are the Chosen of God, and we are engaged in a great apocalyptic battle between good and evil, between God and the devil, a war in which no one—*no one*—can be neutral. For now, you may go."

With an enormous sigh, Francesco bowed deeply to Dom Pierre and to the other two monks, turned, and walked toward the door. As he began climbing the steps, the inquisitor sprang his trap.

"Francesco, you *are* Italian, am I not correct?"

"Yes, I am Italian as I have said, from the city of Assisi," Francesco responded as he turned to face the three monks.

"Then surely you are familiar with the Italian Evil Cat game, are you not?" asked Dom Pierre from across the long room. "Help my memory: How is that game played?"

"A man is stripped bare to the waist," Francesco replied haltingly, "and enters a cage with a common cat where he attempts, with only his bare teeth, to kill the cat. His hands are tied behind him, since he's forbidden to use his hands or feet."

"Ah, I am sure that the crowds must greatly enjoy such sport," replied the inquisitor watching Francesco with the eyes of a hawk. "How wonderfully thrilling it must be, and so dangerous, for a man could easily lose his eyes or become disfigured by the claws of a frenzied cat. And I can imagine the number of coins wagered on such a game and the great fun when the man finally chews the cat to death. Tell me, Francesco of Assisi, did you enjoy watching the Evil Cat Game?"

"I . . . err. . . ."

"Careful, our Italian visitor, how you answer that question," the monk cautioned as he stood up, "for those vile, damned Albigensian heretics not only teach that eating animal flesh is sinful but that so is any harm done to dumb animals. They treat cats and animals with the same kindness they show to their friends and neighbors." Then, waving his hand back and forth in the air, he said, "No need to answer my question! You have already done so! Even from here I can read in your eyes that you indeed share their heretical beliefs." Before Francesco could open his mouth to speak, Dom Pierre shouted, "Guards, take the prisoner, who is now charged with suspicion of heresy, to the dungeon, where he will be held for observation and further questioning."

"And my name is Jean Baptiste de Lorris," replied a fellow prisoner after Francesco had introduced himself. "Welcome to Ecclesiastical Prison of Narbonne. You are, I assume, a guest of Rome's Inquisito, as are the rest of us being detained down here."

"I'm no heretic, sometimes a doubter of the faith perhaps, but. . . ."

"Careful, my Italian friend," he replied. "If I were you, I wouldn't speak aloud that you doubt anything the Church teaches—and I certainly wouldn't openly criticize or make fun of her. I'm a poet whose only crime was to write one humorous, double-meaning poem about social problems, fake relics, and pious superstitions that only mildly questioned some of the positions of the Church, and I've been locked up down here for three years."

"Three years!" Francesco gasped, feeling his throat constricting as if he were being strangled.

"Better than being burned at the stake or perpetual imprisonment, eh?" replied Jean Baptiste with a wave of his hand. "Pope Innocent III has declared heresy to be an act of high treason against God. That verdict makes it equal to treason against the king and so is punishable

by death. But I'm still alive, and there's still hope. So far I've only confessed to being a poet, and so I hope someday to see the sun again."

"But why are you being held so long without any judgment being pronounced?"

"Spiritual intimidation, holy terrorism! My indefinite imprisonment is a tool of the Roman Holy Office to terrorize other poets and writers into avoiding even disguised allusions about the evils in the Church or the social order. I contemplated confessing, but I refuse to stoop to denouncing my brother writers and poets as heretics, which is the easiest way to freedom. Yet since I'm not an obstinate heretic and am only being held under suspicion, someday, if I'm lucky, I may be released with only a penance of public scourging, long fasting, and prayers. Or I may have to make a penitential pilgrimage to Rome. That's if I am lucky. But part of their intimidation is keeping us unsure of how severe the final verdict may be. So this Frenchman is taking the safer course and just waiting it out with the hope that they'll release me. Francesco, the Church is clever in how she strikes terror in the hearts of her sheep to keep them from straying. And for those who have drifted, she employs a holy war of extermination to frighten the other lost souls back into the fold.'"

"I believe that Jesus forbade war, even holy wars, as well as the use of all weapons, whether physical or emotional," Francesco said. "Our Lord said, 'Never return violence for. . . .'"

"Be careful of speaking about what you believe or don't believe, my barefoot Italian friend, for down here even the walls have ears! I caution you not to quote Jesus when you're questioned next. For those monk inquisitors the Bible is a two-edged sword: They use it to slash and hack any way they wish. When I was sentenced to stay down here for 'further questioning,' that monk inquisitor twisted Jesus' parable about the servant who buried his talent instead of investing it, saying I had failed to properly employ my talents as a poet to praise God and his Church. Then he quoted the master in the parable, saying to me, 'You useless fool,' and he told his guards, 'Throw him into the outer darkness, where there will be weeping and gnashing of teeth.' In my case, it was the inner darkness of this stinking dungeon, where, I can assure you, there *is* weeping and gnashing of teeth."

As Jean Baptiste and Francesco huddled secretly in a far corner of the dungeon to discuss Dom Pierre's grilling of Francesco, it became apparent that the poet was an educated man and also versed in

 Scripture. They whispered their wonderings about how the Church could denounce the heretics of Albi for their teaching on marriage, since the Church herself taught that sex, even in marriage, was at least a venial sin. Also inconsistent was condemning the heretics for considering private property to be sinful—Dom Pierre claimed that it was a crime against the social order. Yet wasn't the Church's elevation of the monastic vow of poverty as a superior way of life committing a similar crime against the social order? When Francesco raised the issue of the heresy of Albigensians not eating animal flesh, Jean Baptiste only smiled, saying, "I guess the heretics read the Bible!" Then he loosely quoted from the Book of Genesis: God told Adam and Eve that they were to eat every seed-bearing plant and fruit from the trees, but that the flesh of animals wasn't included in Eden's diet. The two men laughed, joking about how what was diabolical heresy for one Christian might be divinely inspired orthodoxy for another.

Then Jean Baptiste made a most thought-provoking statement: "We're told how dark, dangerous, sinful, spiritually vile, and even grossly immoral are the teachings of the Albigensians. Why, then, are they embraced by learned men, members of the nobility, and the common folk in a hundred villages and towns in southern France?" Francesco did not have an answer.

In the course of his internment, there was more than just the gnashing of teeth. Francesco often heard the screams of prisoners being tortured in the dungeon while they awaited further questioning. He followed the advice of Jean Baptiste and suppressed his growing questions and doubts about the Church—and now even about God. For perhaps the first time he was disturbed by the contradiction between the God of love that he believed in and the kind of God imaged as the master in the parable, who would throw into the outer darkness of weeping and gnashing of teeth a man whose only apparent crime was burying his meager talents.

After three days and nights in the dungeon of Narbonne, with fear and trembling Francesco answered the call to appear before Dom Pierre. To his great relief he was told he had been judged to be more a misguided fool than a heretic. While the court had never heard anything about his religious community of the Little Brothers, which he claimed had been blessed by the Pope, they had not found him adamantly clinging to any heresy. However, to insure that he remain

steadfast in the True Faith, and for the good of his soul, they sentenced him to a penance of six hundred Lord's Prayers a day for six months and to fast for forty days. Dom Pierre's final words were a stern warning never again to return to Narbonne. He reminded Francesco that only the Apostolic Church of Jesus Christ possessed the truth and that the teachings of all heretical sects and other religions were only demonic lies. Finally, he sternly admonished Francesco not to engage in discussions with—or even come into contact with—the Jews and Moslems of Spain, since they were the depraved enemies of the True Faith.

Leaving Narbonne, Francesco rejoiced like a lark released from a cage as he continued his southward journey toward Spain. When he reached Perpiganam, the road began leaning to the southwest as it ascended the foothills of the Pyrenees Mountains. As he stopped to rest at villages along the way, he heard horror tales of the unspeakable cruelties inflicted by both sides in the crusades raging around Toulouse and Albi. The French crusaders fought with savage gusto in weeding out heresy. Defending their lives and religious beliefs, the Albigensians, in turn, exercised deplorable brutality. He heard grisly stories of how knights looted the property of those even suspected of heresy. He himself had seen several instances of such looting along the road between Montpellier and Narbonne. A few miles from Narbonne he also overheard a band of French knights bragging about killing heretics. They joked about how lucky they were to go on a crusade without having to leave France. They were able to claim the same rich indulgences from the Pope and promises of plunder as they would in the hot, fly-infested Holy Land facing the fierce Muslim armies.

Francesco purposely chose to walk apart from others and easily enclosed himself inside the silence he called his highway hermitage. In that solitude he wrestled with God over his doubts. "O God, would you explain to me," he spoke softly, as if to the dust of the road at his feet, "how a Christian warrior wearing the cross of Christ on his tunic can slaughter another Christian or steal his property and not consider it sinful because his victim is a suspected heretic?" God didn't answer.

"Please explain to me, God," he continued, "how your Church can torture those suspected of heresy. Day and night in Narbonne I heard the screams of prisoners being tortured by those who claim to be your servants. My fellow prisoners told me the monks of the Inquisito justified their torture by quoting your Son's parable about the

unmerciful steward who had his large debt pardoned by his master but then in turn refused to forgive a lesser debt of a fellow servant. The master in the parable, whom the priests say represents you, handed over his evil steward to the torturers until he should pay his debt in full. Tell me, are you a God who tortures people, or are you a God of compassion?" Again, God did not answer his question.

"I also confess to you, my Lord God, that I do not agree with your Church's way of dealing with heretics. Her justification is borrowed from the practice in medicine of cauterizing a diseased limb with red-hot irons to heal the patient, and when the patient doesn't respond to this treatment then the limb is amputated from the body. By so doing, isn't the Church waging war against its own body rather than healing it? And isn't this acting contrary to what your Word Made Flesh said when he told us to bless and love our enemies? If the Church judges heretics as her—and your—enemies, then should she really wage holy wars against them? And even more puzzling are her war martyrs: How can the Church grant a full indulgence that frees her crusader knights from purgatory if they die while killing others? Lord God, you know better than I that I am a man of contradictions, but even I cannot reconcile the glaring contradictions between how Jesus says we are to act and the actions of your Church." God did not answer any of Francesco's questions, and like nasty fleas they continued to nibble at and torment him until the sights and activities along the road distracted him.

He crossed over the mountain passes into Spain and followed the highway southward toward Barcelona, glad to be past the conflicts of southern France and also eager to discover whatever treasures Spain might have to offer him. He felt his spirit flourishing as he breathed the freedom of being on the road again and of experiencing the unique Spanish culture, an exotic blend of Jewish, Moorish, and Christian influences. His enjoyment increased when he reached Malgrat de Mar, where the road wound its way along the seacoast. The cries of sea birds and the expansive vistas of the waves crashing against the rock cliffs seemed to cleanse his mind of the doubts that were challenging his faith. Crossing the fertile plain that lay between two rivers, Francesco approached the walled fortress city of Barcelona, which was perched on a gentle slope facing the Mediterranean and backed by a great amphitheater of bluish gray mountains.

Significantly, he entered Barcelona through the stone archway of the main city gate on Wednesday of Holy Week, the eve of Tenebrae, the three night services at end of Holy Week. At these services the psalms of sorrow and the lamentations of Jeremiah were chanted, concluding with all the church candles being snuffed out. Francesco was deeply moved by this Tenebrae's mournful chanting, which anticipated the crucifixion of Good Friday. He was especially taken when the silence that shrouded the darkness in the cathedral was shattered by the loud noise of the monks slamming their choir books and stamping their feet, gestures intended to imitate the convulsions that beset all of nature at the moment of Christ's death on the cross.

Appropriately, the sky was overcast with gloomy low gray clouds on that Good Friday as Francesco stood in the enormous crowd packed shoulder to shoulder in Plaza de Antonio Maura for Barcelona's Good Friday Passion Procession. Even as it approached from a distance, the sound of the funeral dirge, with its countless muffled drums and the crackling of a chorus of wooden clappers, was soul-stirring. The somber mood was reinforced by the striking absence of the usual clanging of the cathedral tower bells, which had been tongueless since Holy Thursday and would not be rung again until Easter Sunday. The procession entered the plaza like an immense purple and black serpent, on whose back stood swaying, towering sacred figures. Hundreds of purple-robed penitents masked in tall, pointed hoods bore on their shoulders platforms draped with black cloth and topped with brightly painted wooden statues. Perhaps twenty feet tall, these included saints like Spain's famous *Santiago*, St. James, whose very name was the rallying cry of Spanish soldiers, and St. Mary Magdalene standing atop the seven withering crimson dragon-like demons from which Christ had freed her. There was the good thief St. Dismas being carried heavenward by an angel from his cross, and a host of other saints. Next to last in the procession came a large purple-robed image of the thorn-crowned Sorrowful Mother of God with dozens of swords sticking out of her breast. The final figure was an even larger image of the thorn-crowned person of Christ, whose body was covered with red streamlets of blood as he shouldered a gigantic cross. Behind the statues came a long double line of chanting hooded monks carrying tall, dull-yellow funeral candles, followed by the black-robed clergy, with the archdeacon holding aloft a relic case bearing the nail that had pieced the right hand of Jesus. Finally, escorted by members of the nobility

and the knights of Catalonia and Aragon, their brilliant robes covered with black capes, came the Archbishop of Barcelona carrying a gold- and jewel-enshrined relic of the True Cross. At the sight of the relic passing by, the crowd traced the sign of the cross upon themselves. The sight also quickened an eager longing in the people's hearts, for the high point of Good Friday occurred at the end of the Mass when they were able to kiss this most sacred of all relics, a splinter of the True Cross. As a lover of theater Francesco was swept away by the flamboyantly colorful pageantry and passionate piety of Spanish Catholicity, and he felt it evaporating all his previous annoyance with the Church. Fittingly, he found himself being physically swept away by the surging multitude as they carried him forward toward the great cathedral at the end of the plaza. When the surging tide of eager worshippers that carried Francesco reached the threshold of the cathedral doors, they came to an abrupt stop, for the massive crowd already jammed inside blocked all forward progress. Francesco was squeezed between those already packed within and the crowd behind, which continued pushing and shoving to get inside for what the people called the Good Friday Mass. While the Good Friday service included the Passion reading in Latin, its highlight was the adoration of the cross. After several forceful but futile attempts by the crowd outside in the plaza to break through the logjam at the doorway, the shoving and pushing finally ceased.

"I've felt like this a lot recently," Francesco thought. "Not completely inside or outside the Church, suspended between powerful forces greater than myself. "Did my blessed Lord Jesus," he wondered, "on his Good Friday long ago, feel as do I now: caught between belonging inside the Temple and being forced outside of it—and also stuck somewhere between heaven and earth?" Stymied on the threshold, Francesco was deeply disappointed, for he had so longed to kiss the relic of the True Cross on which his beloved Savior had died for him. He felt thwarted and heartbroken that he was unable to go inside for the adoration of the cross. In his mind Easter Sunday was dwarfed by Good Friday's reality of Christ's crucifixion and death, which was the nourishing fountain of his spirituality and his personal devotion. Being trapped under the high stone arches of the great cathedral doors, he could hear nothing of the ancient Good Friday ritual going on inside, yet he tried to pray. His prayers were pierced by a keen sense of loneliness at being separated from his brothers in Assisi. He used the

pain of his isolation as an opportunity for communion with his beloved Lord, who had been deserted to suffer his passion and death on the cross alone.

Finally, the dam broke as the crowd inside the cathedral began shoving its way out at the end of the Good Friday Mass. The Plaza de Antonio Maura was soon transformed into an enormous sieve as in somber silence the vast crowds began flowing out in all directions. They departed as mournfully as from a beloved's funeral and made their way home to their Black Fast evening meal of bread and water. As a stick is swiftly carried along on a fast-moving stream, so Francesco was swept out of the plaza and down the Via Layetana, where it was all that he could do to keep from stumbling or being swept down some narrow, twisting side street. Unlike the previous mixture of women and men—without being aware of how the tide had shifted—he now found himself part of an angry mob of men, some of whom were armed with clubs.

The silence of Good Friday around him was shattered by loud shouts: "To the ghetto! To the Jewish ghetto! Get the Christ killers." Some of the mob began pulling cobblestones up out of the street and the shouting on all sides swelled into a roar of angry fury. "This way to the Jewish ghetto. Kill the Christ killers! Death to those dirty, scheming Jews." Francesco was terrified. It seemed incongruous and diabolical to be so suddenly kidnapped out of the solemn, prayerful silence of Good Friday and made a prisoner of this moving hell of hate, this mob thirsty for blood and violence.

In this regard, Spain was no different from Italy. Francesco had long known of this ugly Good Friday tradition, when the authorities turned a blind eye to the violence of mobs against Jews. The sport of Good Friday was to stone Jewish homes and shops as well as any Jews found out on the streets. And, of course, it was easy to recognize Jews, for by law they had to wear a yellow patch or the Star of David on their cloaks—and in some places even a horned cap of the devil. Had not Francesco himself, as a youth, engaged in the mischief of throwing stones at the homes of Jews in Assisi? Yet the gray-robed beggar now being swept along in the raging torrent of hate toward Barcelona's Jewish ghetto was not the same man as he was those many years ago.

"Look, there's one!" screamed a man near Francesco as he pointed down an alleyway leading off the narrow street. Francesco saw that he was pointing at an old man with a long white beard, whose cloak bore a yellow Star of David. The man stood with his back against the brick wall that sealed the end of the alley, with no way to escape. Shouting, "Stone that damn Christ killer," like a pack of barking dogs who had trapped their prey, the mob shoved its way down the alleyway toward the terrified old man, carrying Francesco with them.

The cornered, white-bearded Jew crossed his arms over his face and cried out, "Please don't! For the love of God, please. . . ."

"Filthy pig of a Jew! You've got Christ's blood all over you. You deserve to die for killing Jesus," screamed one of the men as he began beating the Jew over the head with his club. The others joined in by pounding him with the cobblestones they had gripped in their hands.

"Stop! In the name of our Blessed Savior, stop!" shouted Francesco as he flung himself bodily in front of the old man to shield him from their abuse. "Christ forbids us to. . . ."

"Another Jew! Only this beggar Jew forgot to wear his yellow star!" the man with the club yelled out, his club temporarily suspended in the air. "And this bastard Jew even dares to use the holy name of Christ in vain." Then he started raining down blows on Francesco's head and shoulders, and the others added their cobblestones. As the angry insults and the blows of the club and stones repeatedly fell on Francesco, he did not raise his arms to shield himself but rather used them and his whole body to protect the old Jew. Soon, it seemed to Francesco that it started raining blood, and the old brick alley begin to swirl around and around as the cobblestone earth at his feet and the gray sky overhead began tumbling end over end. Sucked into a tortuously painful vortex of blurred images, he was finally swallowed up in his own personal Tenebrae of black-shrouded silence.

"SHALOM!" FRANCESCO FAINTLY HEARD A VOICE AS HE struggled to reach through the fog of his unconsciousness. As his vision cleared, he realized he was lying in a bed; standing over him was a well-dressed young man about his age holding a jar in his hand. Francesco's body ached all over, especially his head and shoulders. "You've suffered many injuries to your head and body," the man said, "but the physician who just attended to you assures us that you will heal without any permanent damages."

"Who are you?" Francesco asked, trying to focus his eyes and his mind. "Where am I, and how did I get here?"

"My name is David Jacob of Barcelona, and our family owes you a great debt of gratitude for coming to the rescue of my father Samuel. It is now Friday afternoon, several hours after your attack, and you are in the Jewish ghetto of Barcelona as a guest in the Jacob home."

As Francesco slowly raised his head from the pillow and looked around at the room, David continued telling the story as he applied ointment from the jar onto the wound on Francesco's forehead: "When you collapsed from the mob's beating, you fell on top of my father, who had also fallen to the ground. Father pretended he was unconscious, and after the attackers gave both of you a few kicks, they departed, having exhausted their hate. As soon as they were gone, Father ran and got help to have you carried here to our house and have your wounds treated." As David began wrapping a long white bandage around Francesco's head, he went on, "Your tunic was ripped and bloody and is now being washed and mended. When we bathed the blood off your body, we could not help but notice that you are not Jewish."

"You're right, I am not Jewish," Francesco responded, "but today I am ashamed to be Christian. How is your father?"

"He received a bad blow to his head and has some bruises and cuts, but he fared far better than you since you shielded him from most of the mob's abuse. It's amazing to us that, being Christian, you should have risked your life to save a Jew. We are grateful for your heroism. Now, drink some of this wine. It is laced with healing herbs and it will kill some of your pain."

"Thank you," Francesco replied, drinking from the cup. "You are most kind to a complete stranger—and a Christian one at that." Then, after he had emptied the cup, he lay back on the pillow and closed his eyes. As the drugged wine began erasing his pain, he slowly sank into sleep.

"*D*o you feel like joining us for dinner? You must be hungry." The woman's voice awakened Francesco. "It is now sunset, and the family would like to welcome you to our dinner table." Opening his eyes, Francesco saw a beautiful, young, dark-haired woman holding some clothing in her arms. She explained to him that his tunic was still drying and that she had brought some of her brother David's clothes for him to wear to dinner. As she departed, she smiled and said that when he was dressed he could join them in the dining room at the end of the hallway.

Still very stiff from his beating, Francesco slowly got out of bed and began to dress. With each movement his entire body reminded him of his beating. When he had finished dressing, he slowly made his way down the hall toward the voices. Entering the room, he beheld a marvelous table covered with a white linen tablecloth and laden with many dishes of food. In the middle was a large platter of roasted lamb with a silver candlestick on either side, the candles still unlit.

"Come, Francesco, and meet the man whose life you saved today," David said, pointing toward the head of the table, "Samuel Jacob, my father." At the head of the table was the same white-bearded man Francesco had attempted to protect in the alley. His white beard and thick head of white hair framed a vigorous face, upon which age had written lines that spoke of strength and wisdom. Even with the narrow white bandage that circled his forehead, to Francesco he looked as majestic and dignified as images he had seen of the patriarch Abraham.

"*Shalom,* my savior, welcome!" Samuel said with a broad smile that caused his white eyebrows to dance upward toward his bandage. "My son David tells me your name is Francesco Bernadone and that you're from a city in Italy known as Assisi." Gesturing toward the empty chair on his right, he added, "Come up here, my son, and stand next to me for the Sabbath blessing. As you can see from all the wonderful dishes of food and the roasted lamb, this is no ordinary Friday night Sabbath dinner. Tonight is the eve of the Passover Sabbath. We celebrated Passover just two nights ago as the first full moon of spring blessed Barcelona. So this is, indeed, a most holy Sabbath meal."

Aching from his injuries, Francesco slowly walked to the end of the table and stood behind his chair next to Samuel. "I know you must be in great pain," Samuel said, "since your wounds were much worse than mine. I do not know words to express my gratitude to you for risking your life for me, a complete stranger. We are all honored to have you as our guest at this Sabbath meal." Francesco acknowledged Samuel's gratitude, but he groaned inwardly as he looked at the feast spread out on the table. "What pains me more than my bruises and wounds," he thought, "is that this is, indeed, no ordinary Friday night. It's Good Friday! On this night the meal for us followers of Christ is only dark bread and water after a long day without any food or drink."

"Samuel, I am honored by your hospitality and kindness," Francesco said, "but, you see, this is Good Friday, and. . . ."

"Ha, Francesco!" Samuel chuckled, his eyes flashing playfully. "How should I forget," he said, lightly tapping the white bandage around his head, "This reminds me that today is Good Friday!"

As the two discussed the meaning of this holy Friday, the rest of the family stood at their chairs, waiting for the meal to begin. Francesco told Samuel how for him to eat on this fast day, especially the meat of a lamb, would be a serious, even mortal, sin.

"Yes, yea, I see your moral problem," Samuel answered, nodding his head. "Yet how strange must our two religions appear to the one God whom we both adore. For one of us it is a day to feast, for the other it is a day to fast! I understand your dinner dilemma, for if I were to be a guest at your Easter Sunday table and you served me ham, how could I eat it without sin? Yet, as your guest, how could I, without transgression, refuse what you offered me? Food, wonderful food—that which brings us together, alas, also separates us. But, as you see, Francesco, my family is waiting for the meal to begin; so let us visit

after the Sabbath blessings and the meal has begun. Then I want you
to explain to me how your religion considers eating meat on this Good
Friday a mortal sin, and yet how on this same day your priests can
condone and even encourage your people to act brutally—and perhaps
mortally—in stoning innocent Jews like myself. Is that not mortally
sinful?"

Francesco stood silently looking down at his plate, knowing that he
would be unable to answer Samuel's question, for it was an
unanswerable question that was also raging inside his heart.

"Today, Francesco, you risked your own life to protect me, so I am
in your eternal debt. In our seeking to repay you, you must forgive us
poor Jews," he said, motioning with his hand down the festive table.
"We show our love and gratitude to people by feeding them. Our
gratitude becomes the delicious bread, rich wine, and succulent lamb
of the meal. I long for you, Francesco, to feast on my gratitude that is
enfleshed in that lamb and bread. You would make this old Jew very
happy if you could eat something, even if only a bite or two, since
words are too weak to carry the heavy load of my gratitude. But, my
Italian savior," he said, placing his arm around Francesco's shoulders
and looking at him with tenderness, "know that I'll understand if you
choose not to eat any of our food, for we children of Abraham, like
you, follow our conscience regardless of the cost."

After Samuel's wife had prayed the ageless ritual blessing and lighted
the Sabbath candles, Samuel intoned the blessings over the cup of wine
and the large loaf of braided Shabbat bread. Samuel's family sang the
sacred Hebrew songs welcoming the Sabbath as the Bride of God, as a
guest to their table. Seated on Samuel's right, Francesco was the first to
be given the Sabbath wine cup, and as he drank from it he was not
prepared for the profound sense of the sacred that accompanied the act.
After being passed from person to person, the Sabbath ritual cup finally
returned to Samuel, and Francesco was deeply impressed as he watched
old Samuel drink solemnly from the Sabbath goblet with a reverence
greater than he had seen in many a priest drinking from the sacred
chalice at Mass. After the ritual toast, as the plates of heaping food were
being passing around the table, the joyful, festive spirit of the dinner was
shattered by the clatter of a shower of stones crashing against the
shuttered windows of the dining room.

"Francesco, we are told," said David, "that in their Good Friday sermons your priests encourage your people to throw stones and even to set fire to our homes and shops. And, indeed, on this Friday of the full moon of spring, which you call holy, is when anti-Jewish attacks are always the most severe. I've attempted to convince my Father, the other Jewish merchants in our ghetto, and the elders of the synagogues that we Jews of Barcelona should follow the example of the Jewish community of Bezier. Each year they take up a large collection of money from all the Jews and present it to the city leaders in order to buy protection during Holy Week. The authorities then must either bribe their priests or strictly police the streets, for no abuse or harm comes to the Jews of Bezier. But why must we citizens of Barcelona have to bribe. . . ."

"I wish I had an answer to your question, David. I'm ashamed of how Christians treat your people on Good Friday—or on any day. I believe such acts of hate are contrary to the will of God, for our Lord Jesus absolutely forbade all acts of violence and even angry words." Then, as he saw he was about to be passed the platter of roasted lamb, Francesco realized he had to make a decision. The sick and wounded were excused from the Black Fast—and he qualified for that dispensation—but abstaining from meat on Friday was a primary prohibition of the Church. So as he was handed the platter of lamb, he prayed to the Holy Spirit to inspire him to do the right thing, to do what God wished. He was escorted by his conscience across the toll bridge between a law of the Church and the law of Love. He paid a double toll: the cost of giving up the reward of the warm feeling that comes from being a faithful, law-abiding Christian and the Church's assurance that by abstaining from the meal he was acting in a morally right way and so deserved heaven.

"I'm honored, Samuel," he said with a nod to his host as he paid the double toll and ran across the bridge of his conscience by lifting a large piece of lamb onto his plate, "as a guest at your table to be offered this gift of your love and gratitude." Samuel smiled and nodded back to Francesco.

Inwardly Samuel was amazed as he thought, "This man is truly unique: Twice in the same day he has acted heroically." As the elegant and delicious dinner continued, Francesco ate one appetizing dish after another as he thought, "Did not my Lord and Savior Jesus freely partake in the food and drink of just such a Seder feast as Samuel has prepared tonight? And, surely, doesn't the glorious freedom of the children of God include the freedom of conscience?" Yet lingering at the recesses of his mind was a fear that later he'd be haunted by his deeply entrenched belief that eating meat on Friday, especially Good Friday, was a grave mortal sin that could doom him to hell.

Francesco's fear did not materialize that night, and he slept well, not only because of the full, delicious meal he had eaten but also because Samuel had instructed David to give him a night cup of herb-laced wine. Midmorning of the following day, still a bit stiff from his beatings and now wearing his freshly laundered and mended gray tunic, Francesco sat in Samuel's study. Although a fresh bandage was wrapped around Francesco's head, Samuel no longer wore his, and Francesco could see the newly formed scab on the old man's forehead along with several black-and-blue bruises. In the course of their conversation Francesco asked the profession of his host and was told that he was a banker. It became clear to Francesco that he was a leading member of Barcelona's group of wealthy Jewish merchants who, like his own father, Pietro, exercised great power in the city. Samuel explained to Francesco that he had risked being out on the streets on Good Friday because he was visiting an old and dear friend who was dying. His intention had been to be safely back home before the cathedral services ended, but he had misjudged the time, and in trying to escape from the crowds coming down the street he had mistakenly run down a dead-end alley.

"You were a true hero," Samuel said. "You came to my rescue and saved my life, but I've been wondering what motivated you. You are a most remarkable man, and while I know many tolerant Christians in Barcelona, you are the most unusual Christian I have ever met!" Glancing down at Francesco's bare feet, he said, "At first I thought that perhaps you had lost your sandals in the brawl, but David tells me you declined the gift of sandals he offered you, saying that you always go barefoot. He also noticed that you had no purse of money. And when he offered you a large purse of money in gratitude for saving my life, you refused to accept it, even though you did so in a most gracious way. So while you appear on the surface to be only a penniless, shoeless beggar, I perceive something . . . mystical . . . in you—that you are a man of deep prayer."

"I do love to pray, Samuel, and I have to say from watching you at the Sabbath blessings that you are a man of profound prayer."

"Ah, I wish your impression was correct, Francesco. At least let us say that I love praying more than I value money, even the excitement of making money by banking! Does that surprise you? While I told you I was a banker, I should have said I'm a former banker, for not long ago I handed over my banking business to my son David. Now I am able to spend many hours a day in prayer and study of the Torah. Today is our Sabbath, when we Jews would usually attend the synagogue, but we have prudently suspended our services on this Saturday after Good Friday out of fear of attacks by the Christians. So we pray and study the Torah in our homes. After Easter Sunday when it's again safe to walk the streets, I will daily join the few other elders who gather in our synagogue to pray and study together the Scriptures and the teachings of our scholars. Among my favorite texts, one that I've committed to memory, is by our own Spanish rabbi Solomon Ibv-Garibrol, now dead for almost two hundred years." Closing his eyes, Samuel prayed:

O Holy One, we know you exist,

but the hearing of the ear cannot reach you,

nor the vision of the eyes.

You existed before time began and continue to exist

without a place in which to abide.

Your secret is hidden and who shall attain it?

So deep, so deep, who can discover it?

Thou art God, all things are your servants and

worshippers. . . .

Samuel paused and looked deeply into Francesco's eyes, saying, "'All things,' the great Solomon of Spain said, 'are God's servants, even the birds and beasts—all things, from the smallest pebble to the tallest mountain, from a single drop of water to great oceans.' When I meditate on that truth and as I handle the things of creation, I am in awe at how a flower or pebble is a worshipper of God just as I am. But allow me to continue his prayer:

Your servants are those who walk clear-eyed

on the straight path, turning neither to the right nor the left,

till they come to the court of the king's palace.

Thou art, indeed, the All Holy One,

who upholds your unity among all creatures.

"Those are beautiful words, are they not, Francesco? 'Your unity,' embraces every creature." Then Samuel paused, as if his mind was watching all of earth's creatures parade past him. "Ah, such a mystery that they are united in the same Mystery, although each has a different name. I try to walk clear-eyed, as wise Solomon said, wherever I go, so that I can see the All Holy One within each person and each creature I encounter. Remaining clear-eyed requires great effort, especially when you're looking at those who hate you or are eager to physically harm you. It requires seeing through layers of hate and greed—to seeing beyond the vision of the eyes. . . ."

"You mean like trying to see God in those hate-filled men who attacked you yesterday?"

"Yes! And you, Francesco, must also have seen them in this way, for while you've not spoken about such clear-eyed seeing, I haven't sensed any anger in you toward those men who beat you unconscious."

"I've tried to forgive the attackers and have asked God to bless them, for my Lord, Jesus Christ, expects me to do that as one of his disciples. Yet, while I've prayed for them, I still find it difficult to understand the reason for such vicious hate that seemed to possess them."

"Ah, I'm afraid the answer is found in the ugly, twisted-limb family tree of violence," replied Samuel. "Ignorance is the mother of fear, and she, in turn, gives birth to anger. Anger's son is violence, and his monstrously deformed son is war. Sadly, the tree of ignorance is fertilized by our religions when they apply the manure of hellish lies and half-truths. All religions like to claim that their God makes laws forbidding their members to have any social contact with those of other religions. They make it a sin to share worship with those who believe differently, claiming that their religion, being God's favorite, is superior to every other one. They prohibit 'us' from being neighbors with 'them,' a mentality that accounts for why we Jews are forced to live separately in our ghettos. And why is that so? Because if we were

neighbors, we might discover we are very much alike, and we might begin to like one another—or even, God forbid, love each other."

"Yes, we're usually taught that we are to love our neighbor," Francesco said, "as long as our neighbor is one of 'us.'"

"Both you and I are bound by God's law to love our neighbor, but you're correct that being a 'neighbor' is commonly interpreted as being of the same clan, family, or religion. Jewish merchants and bankers often exploit Christians and Moors while being compassionate to their fellow Jews. And, speaking of loving, you know well what would befall you, Francesco, if you happened to fall in love with my beautiful daughter Rebecca. Some seventy-odd years ago the Council of Auvergne decreed: 'If anyone'—meaning any Christian—'joins himself to the Jewish wickedness in conjugal partnership . . . a Christian woman with a Jew or a Jewish woman with a Christian . . . they shall forthwith be separated from the communion of the Church.' We Jews are no better, for we treat just as badly any of us who might marry a Christian. Here in Spain where Jews and Christians live together somewhat in harmony, it sometimes happens that two young people of different religions fall in love, but, oh, the terrible tragedy that follows!"

"Yes, Samuel, I'm aware of that prohibition, and also as a youth I frequently heard the words of the great theologian St. John Chrysostom quoted, 'The synagogue is a bordello . . . a hiding place for unclean beasts.' I grew up thinking that Jews were the lowest of all beasts, inferior to cattle and wild beasts since you were 'unclean.'"

"We're hearing rumors, Francesco, that here in Spain they're going to clean us up with a good bath! The Church, we've heard, is about to propose decrees that Jews in Spain must be forcibly baptized. As a friend of mine says, that means choosing the water or the sword. And, of course, all of this is very much connected to our discussion on violence. It is just another expression of the horrible beating we experienced yesterday. Indeed, that sadistic violence was born in the beginning of time when Cain killed his brother Abel. Ever since then each act of brutality, murder, or war has simply been another form of brother killing brother."

"Yes," Francesco said, "I've never thought of war and violence in those terms, but it's true, isn't it? You're a wise man, Samuel, and I'm glad we met—even though on my way to Spain I was warned by a monk in Narbonne not to have any contact with Jews or Moslems, that they are vile enemies of the Church. . . ."

"I'm glad you didn't heed that warning, Francesco, for I believe we come closest to experiencing the All Holy One in the kind of profound and human life experiences we've shared—in partaking a meal together as we did last night and in searching for the meaning of life as we are doing now. Seated next to you last night as you heroically went beyond the laws of your religion to eat of my gratitude, I truly experienced the presence of God in your act of unselfish love toward me."

"And, Samuel, I likewise felt God's presence as I witnessed you drinking from the Sabbath cup."

"Amazing, isn't it, Francesco, how our deepest human experiences become the Holy of Holies of the Temple wherein God dwells? Not a sanctuary of stone but human moments of simple joy and great ecstasy or even times of great pain and agonizing loss, when for a brief instant we experience. . . ."

"Samuel!" gasped Francesco, "What you just said about encountering God in great suffering reminded me of something I had forgotten. Yesterday afternoon when those men were beating me, just before I lost conciseness, at that moment when I couldn't endure any more pain, there was a . . . flash!" As Francesco lowered his head into his hands and his fingers felt his bandage, Samuel sat silently waiting for him to continue. Slowly raising his head, Francesco finally spoke, "Oh, Samuel, I saw God—no, for a flickering moment I felt absorbed, as if I were immersed by or in the Divine Reality—and then everything went black."

"Francesco, I believe you did see God—with the eyes of your soul. As holy Solomon Ibn-Garibrol said, God cannot be seen with human eyes. When the soul is enlightened, sight, sound, touch, smell, even knowing are instantly condensed together into a direct, if fleeting, experience of God. No one has ever seen life—what we see is the invisible Mystery active in living creatures. The same is true with seeing God. God is life, so when we meet life in its absolute fullness—ah, the presence! Rather than looking in temples and tabernacles, I believe it's best to search for the All Holy One in the most profoundly real of human situations: the agony of giving birth, the ecstatic sexual union of lovers, the delicious sharing of meals, at our sharpest peaks of pain. Yes, I believe God became present to you in that critical instant when you were most human, when your fragile mortality hung by the thinnest of threads. I am also convinced that you experienced the

Divine Presence because at that precise moment you were ready to give the supreme gift of your life for another son of God!"

The two sat silently a long time as if allowing warm yellow waves of the spring morning sun to flow through the open window into the study. In that shared silence Francesco pondered, "Ever since the crucifix at San Damiano spoke to me, I've so longed to have another such experience. Yet one wasn't to be mine—until yesterday. It was unlike the first encounter, which happened in a church and in intense prayer. This one was vicious and even diabolic. Yet it was just as powerful and intense a spiritual experience. In fact, it was more awesome because my encounter at San Damiano was with my Liege Lord Christ, and yesterday it was with an indefinable and inexpressible God."

Finally, Francesco spoke out loud, "I would like to return to our discussion about prayer. I sense you are a man of exceptionally deep prayer, which makes me aware of how shallow is mine. I long to discover how to pray with great intensity."

"I believe, my friend," Samuel answered slowly, "that longing itself is the secret. The longing of the soul is the great power that creates all truly good prayer—at least that is what our holy rabbis teach. Longing for ultimate unity with the All Holy One is the inner fire that fuses together soul and body, mind and heart. In order to pray as deeply as *you* wish to pray, the rabbis teach that it is necessary to enter into each single word of your prayer. They would counsel you to view your prayers as little boats that carry you to the Divine One, and then to invest your prayer as fully as you can with love and devotion—with a passionate fire. When your prayer boat is crammed with such ardor to the point of sinking, then if you pray even a single word of that prayer, it will send you straight across the ocean of space and time into the very heart of God!"

Francesco shivered as an almost ecstatic chill raced up his spine. Listening to Samuel speak about being so totally absorbed—body, mind, and soul—in praying, it was apparent to Francesco that his Jewish host indeed strove to live in such a way, completely investing himself in his prayers.

"The soul," Samuel continued, "ascends to God on a prayer with two wings, both of which are needed to raise one up to the All Holy One. The right wing is the passionate love of God, and the left wing is holy fear, awe, and adoration of the Unspeakable One."

"Yes, yes, I agree!" Francesco added eagerly.

"Along with that," said Samuel, "let me share another secret. It involves becoming 'clear-eyed,' as Solomon Ibn-Garbirol said, so as to be able to see the *Shekhinah,* for, ah, then. . . ."

"*Shekhinah?*" asked Francesco.

"The *Shekhinah* is the glory of God, the glorious presence of the Blessed Holy One that resides in all of creation. She is truly glorious— and I say 'she' because the ancient ones perceived the Cloud of Glory enclosing the All Holy One to be feminine. To perceive her shimmering glory you have to open your eyes to every event, every person, and every moment of life with a longing to be filled with her. My dear Francesco, the *Shekhinah* is wondrous indeed!"

After they had talked several hours, Samuel proposed that they rest before the evening meal, and so Francesco returned to his room. As he lay on his bed looking up at the ceiling, he smiled in deep gratitude for the two men who had helped to remove the scales from his eyes, Padre Antonio of Mount Subasio and Samuel Jacob of Barcelona. Pondering on the great wisdom of Samuel and the kindness of his family, Francesco recalled the words of Jesus, "By their fruits you shall know them. Good trees bear good fruit, not thorns and thistles." The word "thorn" reminded him of Dom Pierre, and he smiled wryly as he reflected on the monk's statement that only the Church possessed the truth and that he should not speak to any Spanish Jews and Moslems because their beliefs were only lies!

*T*he next day was Easter Sunday, and Francesco was grateful as he prepared to leave Samuel's house that that while his forehead was still black-and-blue, the wound had formed a large scab and a bandage was no longer necessary. He had also regained his strength, even if his shoulders were still black-and-blue from the bruises he suffered in his beating. The spring morning's crisp air was filled with the jubilant peeling of the many church bells of Barcelona announcing that it was Easter Sunday. With that joyful ringing in the background, Francesco thanked Samuel and his family for their most generous care and hospitality. As the family gathered at their front door to say farewell, Francesco raised his hands toward them and asked God's richest blessings upon Samuel and his family. Then Samuel asked Francesco if, since he had refused any monetary reward, he would at least allow his host to bless him as the patriarch Jacob had blessed his sons. Francesco nodded

 humbly and knelt at the threshold as the white-haired Jew, like one of the patriarchs of old, closed his eyes and prayed silently. Then, imposing his hands on Francesco's head, he pronounced the blessing of Jacob:

> May the God of your Father, help you,
>
> the God Almighty, bless you
>
> with the blessings of the heavens above,
>
> the blessings of the abyss below,
>
> the blessings of breasts and womb,
>
> the blessings of fresh grain and blossoms,
>
> the blessings of the everlasting mountains.
>
> And may the delights of the eternal hills
>
> always rest upon your head and brow.

Everyone in the family answered "Amen." When Francesco stood up, his cheeks wet with tears, he and Samuel held each other in an ardent embrace. As he walked down the street, he turned around several times to wave to Samuel and his family, who continued to see him off from their door.

Exiting through the large stone gate of the Jewish ghetto, Francesco found the streets filled with festively dressed people on the way to or from Mass. Many were joyfully exchanging with one another the Easter greeting, "Christ is risen. Alleluia!" As he stood in the gateway deciding which way he should go, a fat, richly dressed man, apparently a merchant, and his wife walked past him. The merchant paused and said to him, "Bad choice, beggar! You must be a stranger in this city to try to go begging *there*—that's the Jewish ghetto! Those damn stingy Jews wouldn't give you the time of day, let alone any alms. Here, my good man," the merchant said as he held out one small coin to Francesco. "Since it's Easter, I'll break my rule." Francesco smiled, shaking his head as he declined the gift, and turned and walked down the street.

Being Easter Sunday, Francesco felt that he really should go to Mass. Yet as he explored that feeling, he was surprised to discover that what he felt was more an obligation than a real desire. Walking toward the cathedral, in his mind he went from door to door using the question-mark shaped key "Why." Finally it opened the right door: "I feel the same way about going to Mass as I would if I'd been invited to eat a meal after having just completed a large feast-day dinner. But

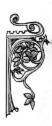

why?" Then the scene of Good Friday night at the Jacob family table appeared vividly to him. He reflected on how much he had enjoyed the ageless ritual Sabbath feast and the delicious roast lamb, as well as his loving communion with Samuel and his family and the long Holy Saturday conversation about prayer and the *Shekhinah* of God. "I've already been to Easter Mass!" Francesco exclaimed aloud just as he was arriving at the entrance to the Plaza de Antonio Maura. "And it was a real feast of resurrection for both body and spirit," he said as he turned away from the plaza and began walking toward Barcelona's southern gate. At that moment, the quiet morning erupted with the jubilantly clanging bells of Barcelona's cathedral, announcing the Easter High Mass. Francesco smiled broadly and shouted out, "Christ *is* risen, Alleluia!"

*L*eaving Barcelona, he continued traveling southward along the coastal road leading to Valencia. As he walked, he took delight in the colorful throng of travelers moving along it in both directions. Unlike the roadways of Italy and France, this Spanish coastal road included wealthy Muslim merchants, easily identified by their turbans and multicolored brocaded cloaks. It was filled as well with Spanish merchants, both Christians and Jews, mounted knights with long yellow and red streamers flowing from their lances, rainbow-colored traveling minstrels with tiny jingling bells on their caps, dark-skinned beggars, black-robed Benedictine monks and clergy, and with pilgrims and travelers of all sorts. Francesco found the moving multitude as colorful and diverse as the crowds at the Chambery Fair.

Spotting a large cluster of yellow daylilies blooming alongside the road, Francesco walked over to admire them. "Sister Lilies, how beautifully are you attired, radiant with the *Shekhinah* glory of God. Your splendor reminds me of how my beloved Lord Jesus Christ said that even I—poor, barefoot Francesco of Assisi—am robed more beautifully than are you, my sisters!" Looking down at his worn gray tunic, he grinned and said, "Sister Lilies, I fear I need to be more clear-eyed, for even though it is freshly laundered, all I see is a drab, patched donkey-gray tunic." Then, laughing out loud, he blew a kiss to the lilies and continued on his way to Valencia. As he walked, he began reflecting on Jesus' words about not being anxious over what to wear but to live in the rich poverty of the providence of God. "It's paradoxical," he said to himself, "how at this moment I'm so much

richer yet so much poorer than I ever was in Assisi. By following Padre Antonio's encouragement to empty my heart of my belief that Christianity exclusively holds the treasury of truth—as well as divesting myself of my childhood prejudice against Jews—I've been greatly enriched spiritually. Samuel of Barcelona confirmed my belief that God is present in all of creation, and I'm so much richer because of his wisdom about prayer and religious prejudice." He paused to thank God for his mentor Padre Antonio's parting gift of St. Peter's words, "For, indeed, God shows no partiality; rather, in every nation, whoever fears God and acts uprightly is acceptable to God."

"Yet, while richer in so many ways, I also feel poorer because of the absence of my brothers and all those I love in Assisi. Here in Spain at the westernmost edge of the world, I especially miss my beloved companions Bernardo, Pietro, Leone, and the ever-delightful Giles. More than ever before, I also miss *caro mio*, Emiliano, and I wonder if any other men have joined him in our Third Order of the Brotherhood of Penitence. I wonder, too, how Clare is surviving cloistered life at San Damiano." As he drank in the intoxicatingly beautiful panorama of Spain's coastal lands, he knew how much she would have enjoyed walking this road beside him. "Ah, *cara mia*, Clare!" His reflection halted suddenly as he realized he had never before addressed Clare as *cara mia*, "my beloved"! It had been no slip of the tongue, for Clare had truly become most dear to him. "How rich I am," he thought, "to have the love of Emiliano and my brothers as well as the love of this beautiful woman." His joy was doubled because he knew that love was mutual. It seemed odd that he literally had to come to the ends of the earth to become aware of that love. This newly discovered treasure found a voice as he burst into song:

> My soul magnifies the Lord.
>
> My spirit rejoices in God my Beloved,
>
> who has gifted me with poverty's great riches—
>
> which stripped me of all possessions,
>
> yet gave me all creation as my rich heritage.
>
> Great is my *Shekhinah* Spirit Guide,
>
> who in the mystery of the divine plan

has led me to the edge of the world,

where maps end and the abyss begins,

to find the fortune of an even deeper poverty,

not of gold, silver, riches, or belongings,

but in the very absence of those I love.

At the bottom of my pit of poverty

hangs a golden bell whose rope

is tugged at by those in far-off Assisi,

awakening my too complacent heart

to discover God's loveliest treasure

hidden cleverly in the hearts of all those I love.

My soul magnifies the *Shekhinah* of my Lord,

whose poverty made me so wondrously wealthy.

"O thank you, my Lord Enrico," said Brother Elias, "and may God richly bless you for your most generous gift that will allow us to continue to build proper living quarters for the brothers. Lord Enrico, you're an answer to our prayers. And I know if Father Francesco were here to receive this gift, he would call down a shower of heaven's choice blessings upon you and your family."

The nobleman smiled, graciously bowing, "Ah, my good Brother Elias, it is my pleasure and honor to be of some small service to the noble work that our Blessed Lord has given to the Franciscans of Assisi. My gift of money is only this servant of God's small way to share in your many good works."

"I can assure you, my Lord, that Almighty God will bless you abundantly for your generous gift," replied Elias, "just as we continue to be blessed with an endless stream of men eager to join us."

"Upon his return," answered the prince, "Father Francesco will be surprised and greatly pleased to see not only how his new order has grown in members but to witness all these beautiful new buildings. Now, my good Brother Elias, I must be on my way. I regret that I am unable to share the approaching hour of prayer with the brothers." As Elias returned from escorting Prince Enrico down to the roadway, he

found his way blocked by Brother Leone, who was standing in the middle of the path with his mouth open, about to speak.

"Brother Leone," Elias said as he brushed past him, "I don't have time now to discuss your ongoing objections with my projects. Not today, perhaps tomorrow, or some other day. I'm sorry, but. . . ."

"You're sorry!" Leone replied, trailing closely behind the retreating Elias. "I'd bet Father Francesco would be more than sorry. He'd be very angry—even if he wouldn't show it! He would not approve of all these new stone buildings or how you've changed our meals. And he would most certainly disapprove of how you're assigning some of brothers to study from books instead of working with their hands. You know how Francesco feels about books!"

"Please, Brother Leone, my hands are too full trying to tend to the needs of this day to talk with you now. Portiuncula can't run by itself, and I believe that I was the one whom Father Francesco placed in charge before he left. Now, I'm already late for a meeting with our architect," he said roughly brushing past Leone to enter a partially completed residence being constructed by some of the brothers.

At the same time, a short distance from Portiuncula in the convent of San Damiano, Sister Clare was meeting with her small community to discuss how they should deal with the new women asking to join their convent of Little Sisters. Seated around the table with Clare were her own blood sister Agnes and the four other members: Sisters Pacifica, Benvenuta, Cecilia, and Philippa.

"Sisters, we must be careful," Clare said, "not to grow too large too fast, lest we be robbed of our precious possessions of poverty and prayer."

"Sister Clare," asked Cecilia, "who would steal them from us?"

"Sister Cecilia, they would not literally be stolen," answered Clare, "but they would be lost in making compromises required to pay for the clothing, feeding, and housing of our members—as I understand is happening over at Portiuncula while Father Francesco is away. It is also very likely that some new members would easily become weary of our simplicity of life, viewing it as too harsh. Then, slowly, one step at a time, our communal life would take on greater ease and comfort."

"I'm having enough problems with Rome," she thought to herself, "without the added pressure from within our convent to make our life more comfortable. I'm convinced the Church is set on changing us

because the Pope and his cardinals believe that our radical poverty is too harsh for women, whom they perceive as the weaker sex. Pope Innocent sends me a continuous stream of messages demanding I write a more lenient rule for our order. So far I've delayed him, but how long can I do that? Oh, how I wish Francesco was home again, for I so need his wise advice."

"Sisters," Clare continued, "if we are to follow authentically in the footsteps of Christ, we must remain just as faithful and dedicated to our times of prayer as we are to our times of caring for the poor and sick who come to our convent door. Let us be wise virgins and not be blinded by our good works, tempted to expand the time we spend doing good deeds by shortening the hours of our prayer. Both prayer and good works are absolutely essential if we are to live a holy life. Only a strong personal and communal prayer life will protect our ears and hearts from giving in to the voices of our families and all those eager for us to adopt increasingly secure and comfortable lifestyles. While cloistered and thus forbidden to go out freely among the people, we can joyfully—and more loudly—preach the love of God by our hidden prayers and poverty."

The five sisters nodded in agreement. However, Sister Benvenuta privately questioned how they could be joyful when they had to eat every day like it was Lent and wear habits made of such coarse cloth. She could understand that following the crucified Christ meant having to suffer, but she failed to find any joy in their harsh penances.

"Now, let us decide," said Clare, "how we shall respond to that nobleman who left such a generous gift on our doorstep yesterday while we were in prayer. Also, we need to divide up the various work duties of our convent and determine who will share in the responsibility to care for the needy."

"Sister Clare, why are you asking us to make those decisions?" asked Pacifica. "In the Benedictine convent Mother Abbess makes all the decisions."

"Because Sister Pacifica," Clare smiled, "I am not a mother abbess, and we're not Benedictine nuns! We are the Little Sisters of San Damiano, and as such we are like blood sisters in a family. Brother Francesco told his brothers that no one should be a master lording it over the others, for Christ told his disciples to be servants to one another. The same is true for us women disciples here at San

Damiano—no one here will be a superior to the others. Now, let us together decide how we will properly arrange the work and prayer of our lives."

It required time to reach a consensus as the sisters haltingly reached an agreement not to accept the generous gift intended for their convent and carefully decided how to divide their household duties equally. For Agnes and Philippa this new equality was intoxicating, while the other three thought it took too much time and effort. At the end Sister Benvenuta spoke her mind, saying that it made more sense for Sister Clare just to tell them what to do, since married women and even Benedictine nuns simply did what they were told. After this long and difficult meeting, Clare went to the chapel to pray. As she knelt down, she felt compressed under her concerns that half of her little family found her ideas about communal living difficult. She shuddered at the thought that what was happening to the Little Brothers might also happen to her community.

"Gracious Christ, my Liege Lord, " she prayed, her eyes focused on the same painted crucifix that had spoken to her beloved friend Francesco, "this handmaiden of Lady Poverty pleads with you for help. Show me how I can be obedient to the wishes of the Pope without being disobedient to you and the Gospels. My beloved crucified Savior, I know in my heart that you have invited me into the same total poverty you called Francesco to embrace. Tell me how I can be obedient to the Church and remain faithful to you. I've surrendered my freedom by being cloistered; so please tell me how I can prevent them from taking away my holy poverty as well. O Lord, speak to my confused heart."

The famous talking crucifix of San Damiano looked down on her with sealed lips. After a long, painful silence, Clare continued, "My Liege Lord, I've heard stories of holy women in France who belong to new religious groups that freely live in the stark poverty of the Gospels they believe God is calling them to embrace. Yet, to do that they were forced to abandon Holy Mother Church. Surely, you will show to me another way. With the sisters here in. . . ." From the back of the little chapel came a soft cough, alerting Clare that her attention was required. So she abruptly ended her prayers with the sign of the cross and turned to face the chapel door, where her sister was standing.

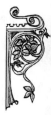

"Clare," Agnes said, "excuse me for interrupting your prayers, but Emiliano Giacosa, the wine merchant from Assisi, is at our door asking to speak to you. He said that he is a good friend of Francesco and. . . ."

"Thank you, Agnes," Clare said standing up. "Please tell him I will visit with him in the grill room." Turning again toward the crucified figure on the cross, she nodded her good-bye. Then she went to the small room with the iron-grated window that opened out to the visitor's room.

While Clare and Emiliano had never met each other before, their mutual love for Francesco enabled them to become instant friends. They both relished the opportunity to speak openly of their affection for him. Then they expressed their mutual concern about where he was now and their worries about his safety. After they prayed for his quick return, Emiliano stated the purpose of his visit: He asked Clare if she could help him form a lay Sisterhood of Penitence as a companion to the lay brotherhood that Francesco had created. Emiliano eagerly spoke about the scores of men who had almost immediately approached him asking to become lay members of the brotherhood—and how the numbers of those inspired by the joyful spirit of Francesco had grown into the hundreds. He laughed as he said that it seemed his days were now split between selling wine and interviewing new members. He went on to say that numerous women inspired by Clare and her small band of women at San Damiano had also begun coming to him asking about a sisterhood for laywomen.

"This is an answer to a prayer," thought Clare, thrilled at the idea of being able to stretch beyond the walls of her cloistered enclosure to help lead women to live holy lives in the spirit of Francesco. In her enthusiasm she reached out with both hands and gripped the iron bars of the cloister grill-window that separated her from Emiliano. She told him that she would most happily do anything that was needed to begin the sisterhood and begged him to tell her all about his Brotherhood of Penitence. He explained how the lay members promised to shun personal luxuries and vain dress and pledged themselves to live in the spirit of poverty, generously sharing their goods with the poor and needy. They were also dedicated to pray daily in communion with those of the other two orders; yet, inspired by Francesco's free style, they did not follow any set form of daily prayer. Emiliano's face beamed like a sunrise as he suggested that Francesco would be proud his Third

 Order was becoming just as controversial as his first two orders. Since it included men from all levels of society, some churchmen and nobility who were still clinging to the old feudal system had openly denounced the brotherhood as socially destructive. Its members came from all levels of society—merchants, servants, craftsmen, nobility, and peasants—and yet all pledged to treat each other as equals. Their most radical pledge was not to carry weapons or engage in any fighting.

Clare didn't need to be told why that was revolutionary, for men rarely traveled without weapons because of family vendettas that had lingered for generations or the perpetual feuding between cities like Assisi and Perugia, or the constant threat of highway robbers. Only clerics and nuns had been expected to live out the radical demands of Jesus in the Gospels. As the laymen of the brotherhood embraced these Gospel values, they encountered opposition for entirely different reasons than Francesco did in his early days. Certain local nobles and city authorities had come to Emiliano's wine shop to express their outrage that the lay members of the brotherhood had refused to bear arms if Assisi went to war. These officials informed Emiliano that his pious guild, brotherhood, or whatever it was, had been judged to be dangerously subversive and that they should expect public abuse and the probability that they would have to pay special taxes.

As Emiliano spoke of the Third Order's spiritual rebellion, his face glowed like the sun, and Clare's countenance beamed like the luminous full moon as she listened. She could see how their pledge not to bear arms or break the peace might have a significant impact on the continuous Italian intercity squabbles that inevitably turned into wars. She hopefully envisioned how it might end the senseless crusades as well as undermine the ageless tradition of Italian vendettas.

Conscious of the need to observe the rules of the convent, Clare informed Emiliano that they had used up the allotted time for their visit. Emiliano promised to return soon, and as he parted, his large hands gripped the iron grill bars, affectionately touching Clare's slender fingers still clinging to the grillwork.

Chapter 18

AS FRANCESCO WAS PASSING THROUGH CASTELLO DE LA Pana on his journey south from Barcelona, he paused to listen to a group of Catalonian minstrels. He was magnetically drawn by their unique, fiery music. When they told him that it was a blend of Spanish and Arabic melodies, whose lyrics were strongly influenced by Hebrew poetry, he sighed, wondering why religions couldn't do what these Spanish troubadours had done with their music. He continued following the coastal road—or, rather, was led along it as a donkey is led by a rope. Ever since his Barcelona experience, he felt he was being almost physically guided—as if while he was asleep one night someone had tied around his waist an invisible rope that was pulling him ever southward. As he approached Valencia on the banks of the Turia River, he had the feeling he was entering the Garden of Eden, for surrounding the city was a vast fertile plain with groves of orange, lemon, and mulberry trees. Here, for the first time he tasted the succulent delights of citrus fruit. The child in him also delighted in how these fruit trees looked laden with little orange and yellow suns. He marveled at the long, narrow ditches that the Moors had created to carry water to the orchards and how silkworms had been introduced and cultivated to provide a profitable silk trade. Francesco learned that the Moors were the Spanish descendents of the North African Berber and Arab Muslims who had invaded Spain in 711. They established a distinctive Spanish-Arabic civilization that had deeply influenced Spanish architecture, art, and agriculture for five hundred years.

Colorful Valencia fit his childhood image of an oriental city, with its many white Moorish-style homes, domes, and picturesque towers. While passing through the city, he met a man who eagerly told him

stories of the legendary El Cid, who, some two hundred years ago as a knight in the service of the king of Castile, had defeated the Moors at Valencia. As the man proudly spoke of this great Spanish hero, in his heart Francesco momentarily felt a faint breeze of his youthful dream of knighthood. When that wisp of a breeze quickly vanished, he knew it was time for him to depart from Valencia, for he felt the invisible rope around his waist tugging him forward. He left Valencia knowing that he had moved beyond his youthful dream of being a heroic champion. Now he was pursuing something new, the dream of becoming a great lover of God. In some mysterious way the treasure of wisdom or understanding, or whatever it was he was now seeking, was essential to his larger dream. As he walked in solitude, he was glad he didn't have to explain his quest to anyone, for one reason, because all it amounted to was a direction—south! Secondly, any reasonable person would think him a madman if he said he had an unseen rope tied around him like a halter that was leading him to the destination where the treasure was buried. While it hardly seemed logical, Francesco had no doubt that the hand of God was at the other end of his lead rope. His only concern was that he would be clear-eyed enough to recognize the buried treasure when he stumbled upon it. In the midst of the many doubts he had experienced on his journey, he still felt confident he would return to Assisi a richer man than the one who left. His trust was based on the fact that he had already uncovered the first part of the cache of riches in the most unexpected of places; it had been buried in Barcelona's Jewish ghetto in the person of a wise and holy man named Samuel. Although he had failed to find any more of the wealth he was seeking in all the many dusty miles he had walked since then, his journey was, nonetheless, filled with promise.

The southern road following the seacoast now leaned eastward as the land jutted out into the sea, forming a broad peninsula. When the coast-hugging road reached its easternmost point, he paused and looked out across the vast expanse of water toward Assisi. His heart quivered with a longing for home and for those he loved. While his travels in France and Spain had been filled with adventure, he greatly missed his brothers and even the landscape of Umbria. Then he turned his back on the sea and followed the road as it curved back to the southwest on its winding way past orchards of oranges, olives, and date palms. He soon entered the seaport city of Alicante and climbed the

low hills filled with white flat-roofed houses that formed a crescent around the city's large harbor. As he gazed into its deep blue bay, he hoped that perhaps he had reached his final destination. His invisible rope had other plans, however, and continued pulling him through the city and out onto a road that wandered away from the seacoast and inward toward Murcia, into the mountains of southern Spain.

Approaching Murcia, he sensed that he wasn't far away from the southernmost tip of Spain. His intuition was confirmed when he was told the distance was about the same as he had walked between Castello de la Plana and Murcia. Since his final destination was unknown, he now wondered if he was being pulled to the end of Spain where he could easily sail across the narrow strip of sea to Morocco. Was the treasure he was seeking buried in the Islamic world, in the deserts of North Africa? Then, as he stepped through the arched stone gate of Murcia, he stumbled, gasping for air. It felt like all his breath had been squeezed out of his chest. He slumped down beside the gateway, panting, as an astonishing sensation washed over him. The invisible rope that been leading him ever southward had disappeared. He inhaled deeply again and stood up, feeling like an untethered donkey that had been set free to roam the countryside.

While this powerful experience at the city gate strongly suggested that Murcia was his destination, he questioned if it had only been a passing physical affliction or simply an indication that he was weary of wandering and just wanted to return home. "No," he thought, "this is where I was led—but why, I'm not sure."

Murcia lay in a low, fertile plane surrounded by a range of purplish-blue mountains. It was called the Garden of Murcia, and its lushness resembled the lands around Valencia. There were also orchards of orange and lemon trees here watered by the Moorish system of irrigation. He found the local wine a bit rough to his taste, but that was compensated for by the fact that the local honey was far more delicious than any in Umbria. He also quickly recognized the excellent quality of the Spanish wool, linen, silk, and cotton in the local marketplace. What thrilled him more than anything else, however, was the people of Murcia. Like Catalonian music, they were a harmonious blend of Christians, Moslems, and Jews living together in seeming peace and good will. Yet while the sights, sounds, and experiences of this new world were all wonderful, they were not what he had walked all this way to discover. He thought, "What I seek here is hidden. If I am to

find it, I must be patient and prepared to spend some time in this place."

Having decided to remain in Murcia until he discovered the treasure he sought, he determined to earn his own bread by being a day laborer in the orange orchards. The orchard managers came each morning at sunrise to the plaza and hired the poor who came there hoping to be hired for the day. Throwing in his lot with those local *minores*, Francesco enjoyed his physical labor as well as simply being in one place after his months of walking the roads. His daily work provided him with food for body and soul as he wedded his hand labor with his heart labor of constant prayer. At the end of each day, a weary Francesco would join his fellow day laborers in the cool breezes of the plaza of Murcia as they ate the evening meal they purchased with their meager pay.

A week or so after arriving in Murcia, Francesco sat alone after a day's work, resting with his back against the plaza wall, with half a loaf of bread, a hunk of yellow cheese, and a wooden cup of Spanish red wine. At the sight of the evening star in the eastern sky, he sighed and said to himself, "Ah, the Vesper Star." Its radiant presence drew him into quiet prayer. He prayed silently his own adaptation of the Canticle of Mary, proclaiming how his soul magnified the Lord and his spirit rejoiced in God, his most generous Savior. He was interrupted halfway through his canticle by the Muslim call to prayer: "*Allah akbar!* I bear witness that there is no god but God, and Muhammad is his prophet." Since coming to Spain, he had grown accustomed to these loud calls to prayer broadcast five times a day from the mosque towers. At each of these invocations all Muslims would kneel and prostrate themselves toward Mecca in prayer. He found this Islamic duty an excellent reminder for him to pray and wished Christians had similar short prayer times during the day. "Perhaps," he thought, "upon my return to Italy, my brothers and I might begin such a practice. We might pray the Canticle of Mary at the sunset ringing of the church bells. . . ."

These thoughts came to a halt as his attention was directed across the plaza, where a group of seven or eight men, having finished their prayers, were returning to their activities. One of them, an attractive young man wearing a white turban and a coarse, brown, patched cloak remained where he had been praying and now was staring at Francesco. After a few moments he walked across the plaza to the place where Francesco was eating his meal on the stone pavement. The man

appeared to be in his mid-twenties, perhaps six or seven years younger than Francesco. He had nut-brown skin, full, rounded lips and thick, black, arched eyebrows that almost joined one another at the bridge of his nose, intensifying the impact of his luminously piercing brown eyes. His pitch-black mustache and beard sharply contrasted his white turban and accentuated his triangular face.

"I have a shovel and pick," the turbaned stranger said, more with his piercing eyes than with his lips. "You might find them useful in uncovering that secret treasure you're seeking, brother!" Francesco sat open-mouthed, stunned by this Muslim's insightful offer. "I addressed you as brother," he continued, "because when I saw you from across the plaza in your tattered gray tunic, you looked like a brother *qalandar*. I've come over to meet you in order to feed my curiosity, since gray isn't the color of our brotherhood and also because you do not wear any head covering. So to satisfy my curiosity, please answer my question: Who is the great one, Jesus of Nazareth or the Prophet Muhammad?"

"Neither," Francesco replied. "Only God is great!"

"Ah, I was not wrong! You are a brother, even if you're not a true believer."

"Now, it is I who am curious," said Francesco. "Do you possess some kind of occult knowledge? How did you know I was seeking a treasure? Please, sit and join me, and tell me something about yourself. I am Francesco of Assisi, of the order of the Little Brothers of Assisi."

"Thank you. My name is Ali Hasan, and I am a *qalandar* and brother of the Sufi order," he said, seating himself next to Francesco on the pavement. "The little brothers of where?"

"Assisi in Italy; we are an order of brothers pledged to follow Jesus without compromise in his call to poverty, peace, and preaching the Gospel. My mentor back in Italy, Padre Antonio, who has visited Spain, told me about the Sufis, but he didn't mention anything about *qalandar* Sufis."

"*Qalandar* is simply an Eastern name for holy beggars," he said as he laughed and playfully threw his head back. "We're wandering Sufis, who, like you and your brothers, practice poverty. We're also known for our whirling dances, by which we seek to be united in ecstasy with Allah, and so we are sometimes called whirling dervishes. As to your question about why I offered you a pick and shovel, your eyes betrayed your secret. Eyes, Francesco, speak louder than lips, and your eyes told me that you're seeking a hidden treasure." Then, leaning in very close

to Francesco's face, he said, "And I can read your eyes because I'm seeking the same hidden treasure. In Islam we believe the reason that God created the earth, seas, stars, planets, sun, and the moon was because he wanted to be found! Allah the Playful," he sang out, waving his arm to encircle the plaza and all that lay beyond it, "delights in being childlike and loves engaging in a great game of hide and seek! So, my new beggar friend, if I may call you that, do you want to join me and play games with God?"

"Yes, Ali, I would take great delight in joining your play with God. But first, please tell me more about your order of Sufis; why you wear brown cloaks and. . . ."

"Once upon a time," Ali Hasan said, fastening his deep brown eyes on Francesco, "there lived a great prince named Ibrahim ibn Adham. One day he was riding his steed when he heard a voice say to him, 'It is not for this that I created you; it was not this that you were commanded to do.' Three times he heard those words spoken to him before he came upon a common shepherd. Dismounting from his fine Arabian steed, he asked the poor man if he would exchange clothing. So the shepherd gave the prince his rough woolen garment, and he gave the man his fine clothing, horse, and all the gold in his purse. Then Ibrahim proceeded to walk on foot to Mecca. Thus is the holy legend of how we Sufis began and why we wear this rough brown wool clothing belonging to the poorest of the poor.

"We Sufis seek a rich poverty. Instead of desiring treasures of the purse, we lust after those of the heart, especially the riches of a mystical experience of Allah!" Running his tongue across his upper lip, he grinned at Francesco and said, "We also treasure chance encounters—such as ours—for by means of such meetings we're given a taste of the Beloved One. Above all, we value intimate unity with our Beloved and spiritual growth more than we value religious rituals and ceremonies. We're not conventional Muslims, for we seek the Spirit not the letter of the Prophet's teachings. His call to holiness is too often compressed into rigid laws over which religious lawyers spend hours and even days splitting hairs concerning some minor detail in the Qur'an."

"The Qur'an" asked Francesco.

"The scriptures of Islam. The Qur'an contains the words of life that Allah revealed with all the freshness of an oasis pool to the Prophet Muhammad. Regrettably, with time our Muslim scholars, influenced by Greek logic and philosophy, began framing their teaching of the

Qur'an in these terms. We Sufis, however, are not interested in philosophical ideas but endeavor to live in the original spirit of the Qur'an, which breathes with the fiercely independent wind of the desert where Islam was born. We sons of Allah live outside the arid rigidity of Islamic law, which only continues to grow more imposing and complex with the birth of each new religious lawyer."

"Ali, you must be my twin!" Francesco replied, his heart throbbing with excitement. "I feel exactly as do you and your Sufi brothers, for Christian theologians and priests have similarly compromised Jesus' teachings in the Gospel."

"*Injil* is our name for the Gospel teachings of the prophet Jesus, through which Allah the Merciful revealed his message of love and peace directly to his son, the prophet Jesus. Of him the Qur'an says, 'Allah bids you rejoice in a word from him. His name is the Messiah, Jesus the son of Mary. He shall be noble in this world and in the next, and shall be favored by Allah.'"

"Ali, you amaze me. I didn't realize Muslims believed in Jesus! I was always told you were infidels."

"We do believe in Jesus, yet we believe Christians have departed from his original teachings. We reverence him as a great prophet and also as the Messiah, and like you we reverence Mary as his Virgin Mother. We especially honor Jesus' teachings on poverty and justice, for they complement what is taught in the Qur'an. We Sufis seek to live out authentically the requirements of justice found in the Qur'an, and by our poverty and presence we oppose the sinful ways the rich ruling classes oppress the poor and weak."

"Ali, my friend and brother," Francesco said wrapping his right arm around Ali's shoulder and hugging him, "What a treasure I've found here in Spain! You and I are sons of the One God, and are true brothers, even if you're a disciple of the Prophet Muhammad and I a follower of Jesus Christ. But, forgive me. I've been so engrossed in our conversation that I've forgotten my duty of hospitality and have failed to offer you some of my bread and wine."

"Thank you, but I must tell you that we Sufis are notorious drunks, and when we're intoxicated we become wild men! So, bread yes, wine no—for we Muslims are forbidden to drink wine."

"I apologize, Ali. I didn't know that," Francesco said as he wondered how one could get drunk without drinking wine.

"Don't fret over such a small thing. While we Sufis are forbidden to drink, we strive to be perpetually drunk. So, after sharing some of your bread and cheese, what do you say the two of us get drunk—I mean really drunk?"

At this invitation, a ball of fire seemed to erupt at the base of Francesco's spine, shooting upward until it reached the top of his skull where it exploded outward in a shower of sparkling stars.

While Francesco usually slept under the stars or in some hayloft, this night would be different. Ali had practically demanded that he come to sleep at his place. As they left the plaza Ali explained how because he was a homeless wandering *qalandar* he had been given a free place of lodging by a pious Moorish merchant of Murcia. Recognizing Ali as a wandering holy man, the wealthy merchant had insisted that he stay in the empty little house of his former caretaker, saying that the Sufi's presence would bring blessings from Allah upon him and his family.

When they reached the wealthy Moor's home, it was dark. A silver crescent moon looked down on them as Ali led Francesco around the large main house and past the stables to the caretaker's small house. By the light of a clay bowl oil lamp that Ali lit upon entering, Francesco could see that the house was only a single room, as starkly bare as his hermitage at Portiuncula. It contained only a wooden bowl and drinking cup, a jug of water with a large washbowl and a towel, and a sleeping mat on the floor. Pointing to an old rusted shovel and pick leaning against the wall in the dark shadows, Ali said, "They were here when I arrived. Being a treasure hunter, I left them here as holy symbols. Because they are actual tools, they do not violate the passage of the Qur'an that forbids the display of images.

"Now, before we retire," Ali said, removing his brown cloak, "as a guest in my humble home, I ask that you be seated on the floor and allow me to perform a desert ritual of hospitality." As Francesco sat down, Ali poured water from the jug into the large bowl, knelt in front of him and began soothingly washing his feet, cleansing them of the grime of the streets and the dirt of the orchard. The unhurried, gentle washing of his feet and the coolness and freshness of the water was so sensually pleasurable that Francesco slowly reclined backwards until he was laying flat on the floor. His eyes closed as muscle by muscle his entire body began relaxing. After Ali had massaged his feet and dried them with the soft cotton towel, Francesco was so tranquil that he

wished this desert hospitality ritual would never end. Then, in an instant he became fully alert! His eyes popped wide open, and he quickly raised himself up on his elbows as Ali began affectionately kissing his feet.

"'How beautiful upon the mountains,'" Ali said, rising up to look at Francesco with those piercing brown eyes, "'are the feet of him who brings glad tidings, announcing peace, bearing good news.' Francesco, my brother, in these words the Prophet Isaiah has spoken of your beautiful but callused feet." Then his fingers soothingly kneaded Francesco's soles as he said, "When I first saw you tonight in the plaza I was struck by how, unlike everyone else, you wore no sandals! It occurred to me that while I go barefoot only in the mosque, you had either embraced a truly radical poverty or had come to see all the earth as holy land—or perhaps both! So, I had to meet this secret son of the Prophet." Then he leaned down and again began lavishly covering Francesco's feet with kisses, which caused Francesco to be apprehensive and embarrassed. A short while later he announced that it was time to retire and motioned toward the single sleeping mat.

Francesco objected, "Thank you for offering me your sleeping mat, but I'm used to sleeping on the floor. I'll just lay down here."

"No, come over here and sleep on the floor beside my mat, for those who sleep closely side by side exchange breath and soul!" Blowing out the oil lamp, he added, "So, my brother, as we sleep let us enter into a communion of souls."

*T*he next morning Francesco awoke feeling oddly drunk and yet very keen and clear, his heart pounding with excitement and feeling ten years younger. While the two had not touched a drop of wine, he was intoxicated with joy and the excitement of being enraptured by love. He did not return to work in the orange orchards that day or the days that followed. Instead, his time was absorbed with his new friend, Ali Hasan. Day and night they were inseparable. They were like arid deserts soaking up each other's spring rains of spiritual gifts. They spent entire days retreating in silence and endless hours sharing their spiritual dreams and insights in prayer, as well as exchanging stories of saints and spiritual masters of their two traditions.

"Francesco, from what you've told me of your community of Little Brothers," Ali said, "it reminds me of a Sufi order founded by Najmuddin Kubra the Greater, which he called the Greater Brothers.

He was a renowned Muslim spiritual master in the middle of the last century who tamed wild animals simply by his presence. Once when a vicious mad dog was about to attack him, he calmed the dog simply by looking upon it with love! Najmuddin also preached to the birds who, it is said, sat quietly listening to. . . ."

"Yes, I know, Ali. Padre Antonio told me about Najmuddin and his brotherhood. I wonder, Ali, how God can say the same thing to different people, people who are separated by vast distances and, even more amazingly, who belong to different religions. Samuel, the holy Jew of Barcelona, your holy Najmuddin, and now you, most of all you, my friend, echo the secret songs of my heart. Samuel of Barcelona believes Judaism is the true faith. I believe that Christianity is the only true faith and you believe. . . ."

"As a Sufi I believe the only true faith is Love!" Ali replied. "*Allah Akbar*—God is great! Being great love, and since love is lavish, the Holy One is excessively generous in sharing sacred secrets with all of his beloved, regardless of their belief, as long as they listen. Can truth be the possession of only one religion?"

"*Allah akbar!*" Francesco exclaimed with great delight.

"Allah *is* great! The answer to your question, Francesco, of how a spiritual gift that is revealed in one heart can be echoed in another heart far away is to be found in prayer. Words of prayer soaked in passionate love and faith spoken in Persia or Spain can reach all around the world and. . . ."

"Around the world, Ali? Don't you mean across the world?"

"Francesco, you speak as if the earth is flat!"

"What do you mean? Everyone knows the earth *is* flat. By coming here to Spain, I've come to the very edge of the earth. Not far beyond the coast of this country is an abyss. Nothing. . . ."

"Francesco, wait! While to common sense the world seems flat, when I was a student in Salamanca we studied Arabic translations of texts written fifteen centuries ago by Greek scholars who showed that the earth is round, a sphere." Seeing the total disbelief that filled Francesco's eyes, Ali continued, "Allow me to explain. My family lived in Granada, and my father, desiring that I follow in his profession and become a physician, sent me to study under the finest teachers in Spain at Salamanca. But I found geography and the philosophy of Aristotle far more interesting than medicine, and while a student at Salamanca I met a holy Sufi master. I was nineteen, and I fell in love—with Allah.

To the great disappointment of my family, I became the wandering *qalander* Sufi whom you see before you now. After that brief history, allow me to return to the shape of the earth. Our Muslim scholars translated the writings of the Greek astronomer Eratosthenes, who lived three hundred years before the birth of Jesus and nine hundred before the Prophet Muhammad. Eratosthenes lived in Alexandria, that famous Egyptian city of scholars, and there conducted experiments using the length of the shadow of the sun to prove the earth was not flat. At the same time he was able to measure the circumference of the earth. Geographers of his day employed his findings to construct globes showing how the earth appears . . . ," he said, motioning outward toward the sky, "from out there."

Francesco sat opened-mouth, dumbfounded, finding such an idea to be as incomprehensible as the doctrine of the Trinity. All that Ali was saying was contrary to logic, common sense, and his most basic beliefs and understandings. As he sat there, he recalled that Padre Antonio had told him about the need to be poor of his beliefs if he desired to return a wealthy man. Now he was being challenged to become the poorest of the poor, to embrace a poverty that seemed to deny common sense, the Church, and the Bible.

"Fifteen centuries ago," Ali continued, "that brilliant scientist Eratosthenes wrote that it was quite possible to reach India on the other side of the earth by sailing across what is called the Western Ocean from right here in Iberia. Another scholar of Alexandria named Strabo, who lived a hundred years after the Prophet Jesus, said the only reason explorers haven't sailed around the world is because of a lack of resolution or a fear that they would run out of provisions. So, Francesco, you have not come to the edge of the earth by coming to Spain, only to edge of the known world."

"That's impossible—and it's heresy!" exclaimed Francesco wide-eyed. "I recall vividly when I was a boy studying at San Giorgio's and our priest-teacher took our class up to the library of the Benedictine Abbey on Mount Subasio to see a map of the world. The monk scribes had laboriously hand-copied the famous *Orbis Terrarum,* the wheel map of Isidore of Seville. As we climbed up to the monastery the priest told us how scholars like the great St. Augustine and Venerable Bede had denounced the ridiculous pagan Greek idea that the earth was round as heretical since it was contrary to the Bible. He quoted St. Paul about the apostles' words going forth 'to the ends of the world,' saying

that a round earth couldn't have ends! He then quoted other passages from the Bible and sternly warned us that those who dared to believe in the ridiculous idea theologians called 'the abominable heresy of the roundness of the earth' could be burned at the stake as heretics. And even if the Bible didn't tell us the earth is flat, common sense would!"

"Francesco, common sense also says that creation is just creation, yet both of us see that it is invisibly filled with the Beloved—why else would we be treasure hunters? Moreover, while Allah is great, we humans are small. We think with little minds, and worse yet we love with little hearts."

"You're right, Ali," Francesco said. "More important than the shape of the earth is the shape and size of our hearts. Indeed, our hearts are too often much too small. I've heard that Spanish Catholic rulers, while they allow Moors to worship in their mosques, treat Muslims as an inferior class and force them to live in separate areas and pay special taxes."

"Little hearts are not limited to Christians!" replied Ali. "Whenever Muslims control a city or area here, they make Christians live in segregated areas. Where Muslims are rulers, they even control the appointment of your bishops, and any children born of mixed Christian and Muslim marriages must be Muslims. Furthermore, we Muslims are forbidden under the penalty of death to become Christians!"

"How God must weep at all the evil we do in his name," Francesco moaned, "launching crusades against one another, raping, murdering, burning people at the stake. If only others could experience the kind of love that you and I have found—the love that makes us one in a friendship. . . ."

"That kind of love, Francesco, grows larger hearts. It is only with large hearts that we have eyes to see what unites instead of what divides us one from another."

*A*nd so the days flowed quickly one into another as Ali and Francesco shared their hearts and souls. Ali introduced Francesco to a favorite Muslim hot drink called *qahwah* made from the bean of the kaffa plant they had discovered in Ethiopia. As he sipped the hot, stimulating beverage, he pondered on how his countrymen hated these people as infidels, yet how rich a culture they had. They had so much wisdom in spirituality, so much new knowledge of science and

medicine, so many creative ideas like irrigation, silk production, and this new hot kaffa drink to offer to Christendom. For Francesco, the scales didn't seem balanced. Though he felt Christ was the greatest of riches, Christendom seemed to have so little else to offer to Islam. He also sadly realized that when he returned home he would have to bury in his heart many of the riches he had discovered here in Spain, for his brothers in Assisi would think he had gone completely insane. They could no more accept the Islamic idea that the earth is round than they would appreciate his discoveries of prayer and holiness in the world of Jews and Moors. And he shuddered to think how the Church would respond to most of his treasures. He would prayerfully have to decide which of them to share and which to conceal in his heart when he reached home. The very thought of home made him suddenly yearn to be back in Assisi again. While all that was happening was so rich, freshly new and wondrous, he began aching for the old and familiar. Part of him hungered for home, and another part of him was equally thirsty to remain with Ali. Together they had explored so many frontiers in friendship, the love of God, and sacred wisdom.

Being a perpetual wanderer, Ali sensed his friend's urge to return home and surprised him by saying, "Francesco, before you go, let's have one more great adventure, one final joyous exploration, eh? Let's really get really drunk by visiting with an Islamic saint, a *sha'ir* named Rashid the Inspired, sometimes called Rashid the Mad. I heard that he lives in the coastal city of Cartagena, not far southeast from here. Who knows what treasures may be buried in Cartagena for both of us?"

"Ah, *caro mio*, brother Ali, you know how to set aflame my curiosity—as well as read my mind and heart. So, let us go to Cartagena and the sea. In Italy, you can't visit with a saint—they're all dead! But you Moors have both living and dead saints!"

The two holy traveling beggars made a strange pair on the dusty highway from Murcia to Cartagena, one dressed in brown and the other in gray, one turbaned and the other bareheaded and barefooted. As they walked, Ali told Francesco that he was not alone in being homesick, that he himself wanted to go home—only not to Granada. He felt the growing need to imitate Ibrahim ibn Adham, the prince who had renounced his wealth and had first worn the coarse brown cloak of the Sufis, and walk to Mecca! Then he told Francesco more about whom they were going to visit, explaining that a *sha'ir* was revered as a mad saint, a poet-seer who expressed himself often in

rhyme or parable-like verse and who was believed to possess supernatural power and knowledge. While such mad saints appeared to be half-witted, they were really soul-witted—soul-eyed. Their clairvoyance often stunned visitors, as they revealed information about private affairs that could not be known by any natural means.

"As you might guess," laughed Ali, "those who are fearful that their hidden secret affairs will be revealed choose to avoid such saintly madmen."

Upon hearing of this holy man's various powers, Francesco himself was having second thoughts about meeting him. He was about to say this to Ali when a band of Christian knights appeared on the road from Cartagena. As they approached, it was obvious from their suntanned faces, battered armor, and faded tunics that they were returning from the Crusades, having sailed from Egypt to the famous port of Cartagena. As they rode by, one of the knights hurled a curse at Ali, to which he replied with a blessing.

"You did just as Jesus taught us, returning a blessing for a curse," said Francesco.

"I know, and I was also imitating Allah the Compassionate, who never returns a curse to those who curse him or use his name in vain. In my blessing for that crusader, I prayed that his eyes be healed, for he suffers from the most ancient of eye diseases, the inability to see as does Allah, who looks upon both him and me as sons."

The exchange between Ali and the crusader turned the subject of their conversation to war, a reality in which both Christians and Muslims were fiercely engaged. Francesco believed that Jesus had forbidden all forms of violence, including war. He lamented that Christians had dispensed themselves from that inescapable prohibition by making Muslims the enemies of God. Ali told him how the Qur'an taught that war could only be waged to preserve religious values, avoid oppression, or protect the weak. The Prophet had explicitly forbidden attacking women and children, killing animals, or even destroying trees in war, and he said that as soon as an enemy sued for peace all hostilities must cease.

"Muslims," Ali said, "are no different from Christians or Jews. They just as easily act contrary to the teachings of the Prophet by claiming that killing the enemy is the will of Allah."

"*Deus Vult*—God wills it," said Francesco. "It is the same with us, for with that cry Pope Urban II launched bloody wars between our

brothers. Like Allah the Compassionate, the God whom Jesus taught about does not will war, with its senseless destruction and slaughter of the innocent. But why, Ali, do so many of our brothers fail to see that?"

"Their eyes are rigidly narrowed into pinholes, Francesco. There is an African saying, 'Never give a sword to a man who can't dance.' What great wisdom! Dancing requires that one be flexible, elastic enough to know when to separate oneself from the majority that claims some action is the will of God. Allah the Merciful can mold those who are supple of heart into the very shape of his own heart."

"Blessed are the flexible of heart," Francesco exclaimed, "for they shall be peacemakers. But why are so few elastic of heart?"

"Allah is compassionate, which means that his heart is supple and expandable enough to include all: the good and bad, sinners and saints. The majority of our brothers choose not to believe in such an inclusive God."

So the two friends talked of war and peace as they approached Cartagena, a city perched at the end of a very narrow isthmus of land joining it to the mainland, a location that provided natural protection with the sea on both sides and a lagoon on the west. Among the many ships at anchor in the port, Francesco saw several flying the white crusader pennant with its red cross, and for a brief moment he felt his old desire to go to the Holy Land. Upon entering the Muslim section of the city, Ali was directed to the house of the *sha'ir*, whom the local people called Rashid the Fool. At the end of a narrow twisting alley they came to a white house with a brightly painted blue door, which Ali explained was the color of paint used to ward off evil spirits. He knocked several times, but no one answered.

"Perhaps Sha'ir Rashid isn't home," said Francesco, secretly pleased that no one had responded to their knocking, for he wasn't sure after hearing of the clairvoyant powers of a *sha'ir* that he really wanted to meet Rashid the Fool.

"I am the Door! The Prophet Muhammad is the Door! Allah is the Door!" came a loud voice from directly behind them. Turning, they saw a white-bearded man in a large white turban behind them. He was dressed in a long, loose cloak, which once, it appeared, had been the simple brown garb worn by Sufis. Now, however, his cloak was so multicolored as to be dazzling to the eye, covered as it was with patches of every known color, many of which had been sewn on top of other patches. Around his neck he wore long strings of beads, and he was carrying a tall staff that had a number of long, narrow shreds of many-colored cloths attached to its top.

"*Salaam*, peace," Ali greeted him with a bow. "*Salaam* be with you, Rashid."

"*Salaam*," Francesco echoed, also bowing. As he did, he noticed that Rashid was wearing only one sandal.

"And *salaam* to both of you strangers, for there is more than enough peace to go around because Allah the Generous is not stingy." Pointing toward his door with his beribboned staff, Rashid said, "Come, enter my humble home, but leave your common sense at my doorstep, for you certainly won't need it inside." After being seated on small carpets facing Rashid, Ali explained who they were and why they had come to see him. Rashid replied with a smile that filled his entire face and caused his white beard to fan outward wildly. When Ali was finished, Rashid closed his eyes and began singing with great emotion:

> That day Love came.
>
> He set my heart aflame,
>
> And my heart exalted,
>
> Magnifying its sweet fare.
>
> The joy tree of my mirth
>
> Love uprooted that day.
>
> Yet sweet is his delight,
>
> Silver blossomed my desire.
>
> His face my heart beheld,
>
> My soul drowning in oceans
>
> Of sparkling jeweled stars
>
> Greater than the night sky.
>
> Heart afire with desire,
>
> Every single breath of my soul
>
> A glowing ember that flames,
>
> For my Lover of all loves.

"Such is the prayer of Attar Farid En Din," said Rashid, opening his eyes as he raised his hands in a gesture of bounty, "a Persian mystic alive even to this day, so I am told. I quoted the spirit if not the precise words of his prayer, and if I may. . . ."

"Please go on," urged Francesco, fascinated by Rashid.

"I will continue with a prayer by Dhu'l-Nun Al-Mirsi, a Sufi mystic who lived in the ninth century:

A fever burns my heart,

Ravages every body part,

Vanquishes my strength,

Smolders in my soul

Through day and night.

O favor me so I may live

Only for thee, my Beloved,

And make sweet with ease

The rigors of my poverty.

"Thank you, Rashid," Francesco said, "How wonderful are those mystic words of the poet. They beautifully express my desire never to lose the fever that smolders in my soul, so that in my poverty I may live only for my Beloved."

"Rashid, my companion Francesco knows that I am a curious Sufi," said Ali, "so I beg your indulgence as I ask the meaning of those many long strings of beads you wear around your neck."

"If you seek an indulgence," replied Rashid as he tapped Ali on his white turban with his staff, causing its long, colored ribbons to dangle in front of Ali's face like rainbow-colored rain, "beg one from the Pope in Rome, not from me." Then, as he chuckled, he said, "You ask the meaning of my beads, and I will answer your question with another question. Why do you carry a *Subha* of ninety-nine beads with a leader bead and a tassel?"

"As you know, Rashid, those beads represent the ninety-nine names of God that are mentioned in the Qur'an, while his hundredth name is unknown to us lowly mortals. I use my beads to pray, as Francesco here prays with his cord of one hundred and fifty knots."

"Admirable!" Rashid replied as he began fingering his strings of beads as if they were the strings of a lute, "But Allah has more than a

hundred names, so *Allah Akbar*, Allah is great and glorious and has more names than there are stars in the sky." Then he again began singing:

> Allah of ninety-nine-thousand-and-one names,
>
> Ah, Allah of endless names.
>
> Allah who is unnameable,
>
> And in whom all names are included.
>
> Ah, Allah, the great and ardent Lover,
>
> Aroused are you by any names
>
> Ad-libbed by adoring, tipsy lovers
>
> Intoxicatedly addicted to you.

"Those drunk on the wine of God's love," Francesco said, "are so witless as to pray without ceasing, for all their words are the names of God."

The two holy beggars asked questions of Rashid and listened as he sang, recited poetry, spoke in riddle and jest, and quoted various Sufi mystics. Lost in that sacred conversation, Francesco also lost all sense of time until Ali nodded to him, indicating it was time for them to depart. When they stood at the threshold and Rashid had taken both of Francesco's hands into his old, liver-spotted hands, he looked deeply into his eyes and said, "I go about with one foot bare and the other sandaled because I still find it difficult to stand always on holy ground. Yet in here," he said as he tapped his heart, "I know that it's all sacred, but I forget up here," he added as he tapped his head, "since evil and selfishness have contaminated so much of the land. Yet, you, my Sufi Christian, it seems, are able to sense you're on holy land everywhere! I perceive that for you every bush is gloriously aflame, dancing with the Presence. I admire you." Then, turning to Ali, he said, "Brother Sufi Ali, you and I would do well to imitate your unique friend and go barefooted, for is not all the earth sacred ground where we encounter the Sacred One? By going about barefoot, our brother Francesco is vulnerable to sharp stones and thorns, and also to people stepping on his feet—and heart. Yet one who goes about so vulnerable is surely awakened to the primal humility of creation, for none of our lowly brother and sister creatures wear shoes. Being humble and thus close to the earth makes one a true messenger of peace."

"A messenger of peace, Rashid?" Ali asked.

"Yes. Being fully conscious that you are always standing on holy land in the presence of God, you could never raise a sword to kill another person. Christians and Muslims who kill each other today in the Holy Land are blind," he said as he jerked his turban down over his eyes, "blind to the presence of the All Holy One. And their feet are as numb to the ground beneath their feet as are the feet of poor lepers. Popes, kings, and crusader armies are as obsessed with recapturing the Holy Land as our Sultans and their armies are with retaining possession of it." Then, leaning over to him, he softly said, "So must we be, Ali! We must be just as obsessed with reclaiming, retaining, and reverencing all the earth as Holy Land."

Ali again indicated to Francesco that it was time for them to leave, and when they reached the doorway he bowed and said, "Holy Rashid, before we depart, please give us your *baraka*." Turning to Francesco, he whispered that a *baraka* was a blessing given by Muslim prophets and holy persons. It was a special blessing or power that flowed directly from Allah through sacred objects or holy persons. It was also released by touching the *Ka'ba*, the black stone of Mecca, and by touching the tombs of saints and, thus, was the reason for the pilgrimages Muslims make to those places. As Ali and Francesco bowed deeply, the old man placed his hands on their heads. When Rashid blessed him, Francesco felt a surge of warmth enter his scalp as if the hot sun was beating down on his head. After they wished peace to the old man and had walked some distance from his door, Rashid called out to them to wait as he came hurrying down the street toward them.

"Francesco, my Christian Sufi," he said, placing both of his hands on Francesco's shoulders, "after blessing you back there, I felt a voice commanding me to prophesy." Looking directly into his eyes, Rashid solemnly said, "I say unto you, the day will come when thousands will come on pilgrimage to your tomb to be healed and to be gifted by your *baraka*." Then Rashid smiled, quickly turned around, and skipped back to his home.

*A*s they left the walls of Cartagena behind them, they walked in silence, and Francesco fearfully pondered the implications of the departing prophecy of the old *sha'ir*. Ali and he then spoke of how Rashid had inspired and challenged both of them to remain free of the greatest of all temptations, that of appearing normal, to resist the holy temptation to fit into an acceptable norm of holiness, even that of holy beggars. They both agreed that his bizarre dress and behavior wasn't that of an insane person but rather came from being somewhere beyond logic and reason. They recognized in Rashid a soul that was free, one who because of a constant attunement to the divine had been rescued from sleepwalking. And his "madness," in turn, helped keep him awake, ever aware of God in each moment of life. Ali told Francesco how he felt Rashid embodied the Prophet Muhammad's words, "One moment of conscious reflection is more valuable than seventy years of ritual prayer."

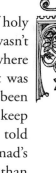

Then, as the end of the day approached, their discussion shifted to the subject to their friendship and the joy it had brought both of them. Never before had either of them found another soul so like their own, and when Francesco spoke of how he found Ali to be such a wondrous gift, Ali only replied, "*Allah akbar.*" As sunset approached, they walked a short distance off the dusty highway and into a grove of trees, where they found a grassy spot as a place to sleep. As the sun was setting, Ali prostrated himself facing southeast toward Mecca as he recited his ritual evening prayer, and Francesco joined him, prostrating himself upon the earth as he recited his favorite evening prayer, the Canticle of Mary. Standing up, he told Ali he had grown fond of that Islamic position of prayer; that he found it more powerful than kneeling because it allowed his entire body to pray in adoration and wonder.

"And surrender!" Ali added, "Prostrating oneself is the ancient eastern position of one who unconditionally surrenders to a conqueror, giving up with no reservations! The very word *Islam*," he told Francesco, "means surrender or allegiance to God, and a Muslim is simply the name of one who surrenders to God. Ah, Francesco, my Christian Sufi brother, supreme among all religions, regardless of which creed we espouse, is *Islam*, for living in unconditional surrender to Allah is the greatest of all of religions! Whether Jew, Christian, or Muslim, one must completely surrender to become one in heart, mind, and soul with the Beloved." Placing his hand over his heart, Francesco swore that he would not forget the great importance of surrendering, saying that for the rest of his life he would be a Christian-Muslim. In turn, Ali swore that from this night onward he would be a Muslim-Christian. Then, laughing at the seeming sheer madness of their oaths, the two friends embraced each other fondly as the first evening stars appeared in the turquoise sky.

As they lay side-by-side on the grass, the half moon pouring liquid silver down through the leaves, they spoke of the soon-approaching time when they would be separated, Francesco departing for Italy and Ali for Mecca. "That will be a painful day," said Francesco, "when we must say good-bye for the last time."

Ali replied, "Those who truly love one another never say good-bye for the last time!" As thousands of small stars spiraled overhead, dancing along their ageless night sky paths, the two friends fell asleep, utterly intoxicated on the strongest of soul wines.

The next morning when Francesco awoke, he was shocked to discover that he was alone. He quickly looked around the grove of trees, thinking Ali might have awakened early and gone off to pray. To his disappointment he could see no one else in the grove. Then, glancing down at the ground where they had slept, his heart stopped! There, neatly placed side-by-side, were Ali Hasan's sandals. Francesco felt his heart flattened as he realized his Sufi *caro mio* must have slipped away before dawn to save both of them from the usual parting promises and expressions that could never convey the depth of their great love for each other. As he stood holding Ali's sandals in his hands, he remembered Rashid's challenge to Ali to imitate Francesco, being vulnerable and humble by going barefoot.

"My beloved Ali," he said, kissing his friend's sandals, "you have left me forever to go wandering in the world as if inside one gigantic mosque, prostrating yourself to Allah in all places and before all you encounter. Wherever you are, dear one, on your way home to Mecca: May God bless you and protect you in the name of the Father, and of the Son and of the Holy Spirit." Finishing four signs of the cross, one in each of the four compass directions, he heaved an enormous groan, feeling his soul had been turned inside out. Then, facing the rising sun, he said aloud, "Now it is I who must be on my way home—to Assisi."

Returning to the highway, he began walking back toward Murcia. On the road he recalled what Ali had said about surrender being the cardinal virtue. So he surrendered to the poverty of being unable to say good-bye to his beloved friend and tried to find some good in being so sadly dispossessed. Walking through the streets of Murcia toward its northern gate, it felt to him that those beautiful, piercing brown eyes of his friend were lovingly fixed upon him. As he departed from this city where the two of them had first met and become soul mates, he was convinced that Ali was watching from some hidden place. When

he finally left through the city gates and began taking the road northward, he reflected, "Ali was right to leave without saying good-bye. While we hardly lack the words, it is impossible to say a final farewell to someone you love, for after being joined in true love you can never ever be separated from that person." A short distance beyond Murcia's gates, Francesco turned and shouted, *"Allah akbar!"* As he shouted it again and again, that Muslim cry of "God is great" contained all his wonderment and gratitude for the many rich spiritual treasures he had discovered with Ali, both there and in Cartagena. With tears streaming down his cheeks, he turned his back once and for all on Murcia as his broken heart took him by the hand and led him northward up the road to Valencia and beyond toward Barcelona and eventually to Assisi.

As he journeyed toward the city of Alicante, however, his heart sought healing by reliving his adventures with Ali. Perhaps it was the heat of the sun that caused him to remember a rainy day in Murcia when during a sudden downpour he had ducked under an overhanging roof to avoid getting wet. Still standing in the rain, Ali grabbed his arm and joyfully cried, "Come, Francesco the dim-witted, let's dance in the rain." Pulling him out into the heavy downpour, he added, "so we can be soaked with sky!" Like children hand in hand, the two of them began dancing round and round in circles in the cascading waterfall of rain. Finally, soaking wet, exhausted and unable to dance another step, they fell down laughing and rolling together in the mud. That memory released Francesco from any need to appear normal to his fellow travelers, and he raised his arms and began dancing. First slowly, then with increasing speed he danced freely, kicking up brown clouds of dust as, dervish-like, he whirled in the middle of the road. Fearful that this peaceful-looking beggar had gone mad or was possessed, his fellow travelers quickly moved away from him. Even after he had stopped dancing, they kept a safe distance from this strange man.

Then the wings of memory once again lifted his feet off the road to Alicante and carried him back to the time when he and Ali were traveling the road to Cartagena to visit Rashid. As they had crested a tall hill and, for the first time, saw before them the vast blue Mediterranean Sea, which extended all the way out to the horizon, Ali had grabbed Francesco's arm and said, "Francesco, look, isn't it magnificent? After we have visited the *sha'ir*, let's go down to the shore, not simply to walk in the foam-tossed waves as they come running into

 the beach. No, let's run out and dive into those crashing high waves and plunge down, down, down, all the way to the bottom of the sea to find the fabled Pearl of Great Price." Francesco told Ali that he didn't know how to swim and that if he dove in he would surely drown. And Ali replied, "Yes, of course! How else does one find the Pearl of Great Price?"

At this, a recollection of Jesus' words rushed into Francesco's soul: "He who tries to save his life will lose it, and he who loses his life for my sake will save it." He wondered if a greater treasure awaited him in Assisi, one that would require that he lose his life.

That night, preparing to go to sleep under the stars, he recalled those nights when he and Ali had slept beside one another, sharing, as Ali had said, "their breaths and their souls." That commingling of souls must have happened at a very deep level, he reflected, for even now when Ali was physically absent, his face, voice, and words were as vivid as when the two friends had been together. He knew their souls had been wedded to one another and wondered what the consequences of such an intimate communion might be.

Chapter 19

SILENTLY THE SEWING NEEDLE STITCHED TOGETHER A minor tear in the red silk cassock of Cardinal Uzielli. Canaletto sat in the good light near an open window to help him see more clearly as he deftly mended the cassock so that not a stitch would be visible. As the majordomo of the cardinal's house he frequently performed such intimate tasks for the cardinal. Canaletto himself was needlelike, in body and also in speech. He could be as sharply piercing as a needle in his sarcasm and criticism and so was feared by the servants under his authority. Slender and pale of complexion, he kept his black hair closely cropped in the Roman style of the Caesars and must have been quite handsome in his youth. Now in his late thirties, age had stolen his youthful attractiveness, leaving behind those telltale signs of middle age. As he sat sewing by the window, Canaletto was attired in his usual floor-length black tunic that accentuated the gold chain and medallion of the cardinal's coat of arms, which he wore as a sign of his authority. His skill with a needle was symbolic of his ability to weave together the various tasks of the cardinal's household, mending whatever might be amiss among the household servants and adroitly intertwining the fabric of events to benefit both his patron, the cardinal, and himself.

"Well, well, if it is not His Eminence's favorite valet," Canaletto said, looking up from his sewing as the door opened and Sebastiano entered the room. "Sebastiano, it should be you and not I repairing the cardinal's cassock. It's time you began to learn to do such delicate stitching."

"True, my dear Canaletto, but how could I match your art in hiding your mending so that a cassock appears to have never been torn? Indeed, and that's only one of the more obvious of your many talents that guarantee your position here as the master of the cardinal's entire household and confidential affairs. So, Signore Majordomo Canaletto," he said with a sweeping bow, "I salute you, your many artistic talents, and your lifelong position."

"Indeed you should, my young Sebastiano! And wipe off that grin! Have you forgotten that you yourself are one my works of art? You wouldn't be dressed in those expensive clothes like a prince and living a comfortable life in this fine house if it not for Canaletto!" Inserting the needle deeper, he added, "If it were not for me, you'd be living with your pigs, dirt poor and hungry in that insignificant village where I discovered you."

"I cannot argue with that," Sebastiano said, rolling his head back and forth as if to say, "So what does that mean today?"

"Like a master sculptor who is able to perceive the beautiful Greek god Adonis hidden in a crude block of marble, I saw great possibilities in you as an uncouth peasant teenage boy with dirt-encrusted fingernails. So I brought you to Rome, scraped and polished away all the dirt and grime, taught you how to speak and walk, how to carry yourself, how to gracefully wait on table, how to dress, and how to. . . ."

"Make love, right?" Canaletto did not reply or even look up as he continued to concentrate on his sewing. "And, my dear, clever Canaletto, I'm sure that after all your months of sculpting you were well rewarded for all your artistic labors when you presented, shall we say, your work of art to Uzielli. . . ."

"His Eminence! How dare you refer in such a familiar way to your lord and master! Watch your tongue—and your step—young man, or you may soon find yourself back herding pigs. Go look in the mirror, Sebastiano; you'll see that you're not growing any younger, and one of these days, sooner than you think, you will lose your. . . ."

"Place in bed? Canaletto, is that what happened to you? Only you cleverly greased the slide out of bed so that you would slide upwards instead of out the door, eh? As for looking in the mirror, I do that daily, and I assure you the cardinal will not soon desire to replace me. Now, while I have found this conversation to be interesting, I beg your leave, Signore Canaletto. It is time that I be 'about my father's business,' as

Uzielli's confidential messenger." Then, bowing deeply from the waist, he chanted, "So, Signore Majordomo, until we meet again."

Sebastiano had lied. He walked some distance down the first floor hallway from the room where Canaletto sat sewing and stopped at an open window, where he deeply inhaled several times. He needed that fresh air, for he'd felt as if he were being suffocated in that little room with Canaletto. He was distressed because he *had* looked in a mirror, and the mirror told him that, while in his early twenties, he was no longer a handsome, youthful boy. He had grown into a man. A handsome one, true, but a man and no longer a boy. Canaletto was too accurate, and Sebastiano was no fool. The mirror told him that his days in the house and bed of Uzielli were slipping away as quickly as the grains of sand in an hourglass. When would he be forced to imitate Canaletto's denial of aging by dying his hair? He had accidentally walked in on Canaletto one day as he was preparing the ageless remedy of Roman senators for hiding their graying hair, Pliny the Elder's recipe of boiling leeks and walnut shells. "Does growing old mean self-blinding?" he wondered. "Didn't Canaletto see that the dark color of his hair didn't match the age of his skin?"

He then continued walking down the hallway until he came to a window that looked directly out onto the fountains. There, he was again assailed by the dark specter of aging that would sooner or later bring his descent from his present privileged position. Because he had nowhere else to go if he was sent away from the cardinal's household, Sebastiano wondered where his descent would stop, how humbling his eventual situation might be. Sebastiano did not see the elaborately groomed gardens or their fountains, for he was looking inward, reflecting on his life. Uzielli was more than old enough to be his father, and while the cardinal had been generous and affectionate, he didn't love him. He was sure that Uzielli didn't love him, for Uzielli only loved Uzielli. Yet Sebastiano was as fond of him as if he had been his father, for his own father had died when he was a small child. The cardinal gave him money to use however he wished, as well as a comfortable life that allowed him to wear stylishly beautiful clothing, sleep on a soft bed, and eat good food. Yet what he truly needed and wanted was to love someone; he ached to be able to give away his heart in a truly passionate love.

 Watching the fountains' intricate dancing waters, he reflected on how clever Canaletto was, how he had elaborately schemed to attain and retain his position as the cardinal's majordomo. He could easily envision Canaletto traveling across the hill country around Rome searching in the small villages for his replacement. Then the fountains' dancing waters reminded him of a day some five or six years ago. He vividly recalled that morning when he was seated in the papal antechamber and witnessed that joyfully uninhibited man in the tattered gray tunic dancing so freely. As Sebastiano wondered what had happened to him, his attention fixed on one the gardeners, a young man about his age, digging around a shrub a few yards from the open window where he stood. His gardener's tunic clung to his sweat-soaked body, and as he raised his right hand to wipe away the sweat from his brow he turned toward the window and saw Sebastiano looking at him. He smiled slyly, and Sebastiano returned the smile with a nod, inwardly speaking a wordless greeting, "*Amoretto.*"

"Little love," Sebastiano thought as he walked away from the window, "is not what I desire. What I really lust for is a great love."

*I*n the cardinal's private study, a floor above the window where Sebastiano had been standing, Uzielli sat reading a coded letter that had just been delivered. Leaning back in his chair, he exclaimed, "Marvelous! King John of England has handed over his crown to the papacy and declared himself a vassal of the Pope. I must see that my English agents are rewarded for insuring that I receive this important news before the Pope." He continued to decode the secret message about how King John had also agreed to pay a tribute to the Holy See to the sum of one thousand marks annually. Placing the document on his desk, he pondered how long it would take a papal courier to reach Rome with this news! "I must move quickly," he said to himself, "to make the most of the news of this wonderful situation, bringing in my allies in the curia."

Standing up, he rang a small silver bell for a servant to attend him as he dressed for his special meeting with a select group of the cardinals. When his favorite valet Sebastiano failed to appear, he rang again, this time more loudly, as he thought, "Now, if I were Pope, I would. . . ." That thought was interrupted by the appearance of a servant other than Sebastiano, who began dressing him for his meeting. As Uzielli was being dressed, he reflected, "Pope Innocent will not live forever, and if

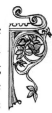

I am to succeed him I must zealously build strong alliances with the other the cardinals. I can guarantee their loyalty with generous gifts on the one hand and on the other by possessing potentially damaging secret information about their private lives. A potent combination!" he thought as a thin smile crossed his lips. "For some time—through his numerous informants in the households of my brother cardinals—my devoted aide Canaletto has been able to gather a store of secret personal information about various members of the College of Cardinals. This, plus the knowledge he has gleaned about what gifts they greatly value, will be most useful when the time comes, the time for the cardinals to elect the next Pope." Finally dressed in his favorite formal attire, he departed for the meeting of the cardinals whom Innocent III had commissioned to prepare the schema for his forthcoming Fourth Lateran Council.

"*A*n impossible task to complete in such a short a time!" moaned Cardinal Antonio Bellini, who sat with four other cardinals and their secretaries at a large table covered with documents in the Lateran Palace. "I wonder why the Pope is in such a hurry? He has given us only a little over a year to prepare all the position papers for this council he has decided to convene. The year 1215 will be upon us before we know it."

"And this will be no ordinary ecumenical council," replied Cardinal Montino. "It will be a great council, truly ecumenical—not only will all the bishops in the world attend, but priests and even laymen are to be invited. Indeed, Innocent has designed a council that will be refreshingly and delightfully catholic."

"My present count of the list of those invited numbers more than twelve hundred," moaned Bellini, "and the Pope keeps adding to it! The list includes the Patriarchs of Constantinople and Jerusalem, 71 archbishops, 412 bishops and 800 abbots, along with all religious superiors, various noble lords representing the crown heads of Europe, as well as a number of laymen chosen to attend." Heaving a great sigh as he wrung his hands, Bellini added, "How am I to provide suitable lodging and food in Rome for all these dignitaries, their secretaries, servants, and large entourages, not to mention attending to the seating and protocol at the council?"

"Do not worry, Cardinal Bellini," Cardinal Ugolino di Segni said. "You have a great task, but we shall all see that you do not bear that

heavy burden alone. Your concerns mirror the many issues the Church faces today. Those issues demand a general council of the whole Church, and that means a truly catholic response and not simply one from the bishops."

Smiling diplomatically, Cardinal Uzielli said, "His Holiness, guided by the Holy Spirit, is eager that this council should resolve the recent dangerous discussions about the Holy Eucharist. He wants the council to make a definitive definition about the Holy Eucharist, one that requires an oath of allegiance, under the pain of sin. As Your Eminences are aware, there are those today who speak in . . . how shall I say . . . in either mystical terms or in a too material sense of the True Presence of Christ in the Holy Eucharist. There are those northern barefoot heretics dressed in rags in Germany and France who are scattering upon the wind seeds of doubt about the Real Presence. They and their followers must be condemned by name."

"For centuries—perhaps until the last century," replied Montino, looking at Uzielli, "our Lord's words in the Gospel about the Eucharist, 'This is my body; take and eat. This is my blood; take and drink,' have been sufficient. Why do we now need to. . . ."

"Heresy, Lorenzo!" snickered Uzielli. "Surely you're aware that there are many who deny that the Eucharist is physically the Lord's body because it looks and tastes like bread. The wisdom of Aristotle has provided us with a new and proper explanation: transubstantiation."

"What will that Greek philosophical term," replied Montino, "possibly mean to the common people—and even to most of our simple parish priests?"

"Fear not, Lorenzo: We shall explain to them that it means the substance of the bread and wine is changed into the body and blood of Christ while the outward appearances of the bread and wine, their taste and feel, remain unchanged. If we make it a dogma, then regardless of how difficult it is to comprehend, they will not question it!"

"His Holiness also wants us to address the problem of the faithful not frequenting Confession and Communion," Cardinal Ugolino said in an effort to avert the rising conflict between Montino and Uzielli. "The Holy Father feels that we must make new laws requiring all the faithful to make an audible confession to a priest at least once a year and to. . . ."

"That's if they are in the state of mortal sin, correct?" asked Montino.

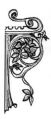

"Naturally," Uzielli replied with a smirk. "But, my holy Cardinal Montino, who can go longer than a year without committing a mortal sin?"

"In addition," continued Ugolino, "the Pope wants a new law requiring the faithful to receive Holy Communion at least once a year."

"The Pope loves making laws," Cardinal Colonna said, breaking his silence at the meeting. "Before he became Pope Innocent III, Lotario di Segni, as we all know, was an avid student of the law at the University of Bologna, and it seems he hasn't lost his appetite for legalism."

"Would that he had more of an appetite to address a much greater danger than the failure of the faithful to go to Communion," said Uzielli leaning back in his chair as he wagged his finger at the other cardinals. "I refer to the festering disease of wandering pious beggars who preach the heresy of absolute poverty. They embody the true danger that faces the Church. Personally, I failed to comprehend how he could give them his blessing, and how he can be so blind to the threat that they pose to the Church in these troubled times."

"Great leaders must take risks, especially if they believe God is visiting us here on earth," replied Cardinal Cecnio Savelli, who had sat silently listening until now. The senior cardinal at the table, Savelli had white, thinning hair and a narrow face lightly lined with wrinkles that testified to his maturity and experience. A natural diplomat and wise from many years in the Church, he was greatly respected by the others. "Those who have freely taken upon themselves the radical poverty of the Gospels," he continued, "and who bring joy to everyday people, so burdened in life during these troubled times," he added as he paused to smile, "are authentic signs of God's presence among us."

"I agree with Your Eminence," replied Ugolino, nodding with deference to the senior cardinal among them, while Uzielli picked up a document pretending to read it so he would not have to comment on what he saw as Savelli's senility. "Take the case of our own zealous Italian Francesco of Assisi," Ugolino continued, "and the apostolic priest Dominic de Guzman of Caleruega, Spain. They are both taking the Gospels and the Church to the common people, instead of them coming to the Church. Let us be patient like the Pope and test their fidelity to the Church before denouncing them as protesting heretics. By blessing the work of Francesco, I believe the Pope has given us a pattern to follow."

"Spoken like the loyal nephew that you are," Uzielli said sarcastically, "Ugolino di Segni of the house of Segnis. Nephews here in the Eternal City tend to walk in the footsteps of their uncles. At the age of twenty-nine, your Uncle Lotario, who was made a cardinal by his uncle Clement III, then made you one. Ah, if only I had been blessed with an uncle who was. . . ." Uzielli left his sentence unfinished as, with a red-flushed face, he began rearranging the documents on the table in front of him, suppressing his anger at himself for allowing his secret personal feelings to surface.

"Peace, peace, my brothers," smiled old cardinal Savelli. "Our God, who works in strange and in gracious ways, has gifted us with this great reformer Pope, Innocent III. Let us proceed with his Spirit-inspired desire to convene a general council, for God knows that Holy Mother Church urgently needs one."

"Cardinal Savelli is right: Our Pope is a great reformer, a scholar, and a genius of administration," replied Ugolino, "and, personally, my hope is that, God willing, he'll be with us for many long years. He's only fifty-three, and I pray he may live as long as his predecessor Celestine III."

"My God, he lived into his nineties!" Uzielli moaned to himself. Quickly recovering his composure, he reflected that cardinals even in their seventies had been elected Pope. Then he said aloud, "Yes, indeed, Ugolino. May God grant long life to His Holiness, good Pope Innocent III."

*O*n December 31, the Seventh Day of Christmas in 1214, Francesco finally arrived at the city of Arles on the banks of the Rhone River, halfway between Montpellier and Marseilles. The invisible rope that previously had led him like a halter down the coast of Spain to Murcia had just as strongly pulled him homeward along the Spanish coast into France. As he passed Barcelona, it had not allowed him to visit again with his wise and holy friend Samuel. Mindful of the ominous warning of the French inquisitor monk at Narbonne that he never return there again, he made a wide detour to the west before joining up again with the main highway near Montpellier.

It was in Arles that Francesco learned the final act in the tragedy of the Children's Crusade. When the great mass of children had reached the port of Marseilles—just east of Arles—the sea, of course, did not miraculously part before them so they could walk to the Holy Land. As they crowded in the thousands upon the docks, praying for a message from God, some local ship captains offered them free passage to the Holy Land. Instead, those ruthless captains transported the young crusaders to North Africa, where they sold them to Arab slave traders— at a great profit, it was said, because Arabs prefer youthful slaves with pale skin. Francesco wept in grief when he heard the fate of the children crusaders, easily imagining the horrible destiny of those teenage boys and girls.

As he walked the twisting narrow streets of Arles, his tears were in stark contrast to the merriment of townspeople celebrating the great festival of the Twelve Days of Christmas when work and war were suspended from Christmas to Epiphany. As he approached the great Romanesque Cathedral of St. Trophime, some monks wearing habits he had never seen before were coming up the street toward him. Billowing clouds of thick white smoke created by the first monk wildly swinging a golden censor led the procession of chanting monks. In the middle of the line, four hooded monks were carrying a portable tent formed by a golden silk canopy supported on poles. Walking beneath the canopy was a monk holding high an ornate vessel with golden needlelike sunrays extending outward from a small circle of glass. People along the street were dropping to their knees as the monk holding the golden vessel would turn to the right and the left in a gesture of blessing. However, no sooner would the procession pass the kneeling people than many would jump to their feet and begin uttering curses at the monks. Francesco scratched his head in confusion, having never seen such a contradiction of adoration followed by anger. As the procession neared the place where he stood, Francesco could make out the monks' chanting:

Sanctus, Sanctus, Holy, Holy, Holy.

Sacred is the skin that heals the limp;

Holy is the relic that raises up the dead.

Holy, Holy, Sanctus, Sanctus, Sanctus.

Blessed be the short that it makes longer.

Blessed be the thin that it makes thicker.

Blessed be the sagging it makes stronger.

O holy relic of the Christ's Circumcision.

Francesco had heard about the miraculous holy relic of the foreskin of Jesus that had been cut off at his circumcision. He'd heard it said that seven different cathedrals in Europe had claimed to have the original relic. So he wondered if this, indeed, was the true foreskin. Seeing a smiling shopkeeper in the doorway of his shop, Francesco asked, "Sir, to what order do these monks belong?"

"Monks, my ass!" he said, slapping Francesco on the back. "These lads are Goliards. Oh, they've been tonsured like clerics, but they're only wandering students who delight in mocking the clergy, the Church, the Pope and, as you see in this scene before you, enjoy making fun of the gullible folks' fascination with relics. I'd kiss their relic," he said, "if, indeed, it could make the short longer," bursting into loud laughter as he patted his crotch.

Along with the shopkeeper, Francesco did not kneel as the procession passed them. That caused one of the Goliards to wink at him and stick out his tongue, wiggling it in a suggestive sexual gesture.

"Those vagabond Goliards are what you might call clerical troubadours or tonsured minstrels," said the shopkeeper, "and many—including me—love their anticlerical humor. There are also many folks on this street today—as you've witnessed—who are not so delighted to be hoodwinked by their fake relic."

"Why are they called Goliards?" asked Francesco.

"Some say it's because they claim their phony order was founded by a Bishop Golias, but most say he's only a myth, an imaginary saint—of which I'll bet there are many. What's not mythical are their humorous spoofs on the Pope and the Church, which, if you ask me, needs to lighten up, stop being so pompous, and laugh at itself. Those Goliards

are great theater, and if you really want a good laugh, stranger, be sure not to miss tomorrow's Feast of the Ass at the cathedral."

Curious about this holy day festival, Francesco decided, as he walked away from the shopkeeper, to remain one more day in Arles. He smiled, recalling the holy clown-like Sufi *sha'ir* he and his friend Ali had visited in Cartagena. The dozens of strings of beads Rashid wore around his neck were reminiscent of the Goliards' pious procession with the fake relic of Jesus' foreskin. Rashid's beads poked fun at Muslim piety, yet they were also parable playthings which taught that God had a thousand names. He fondly recalled Ali's words: "For true holiness, play is even more important than prayer." Numerous times since leaving Murcia he had recalled something Ali said or some experience they had shared, and he wished Ali could be with him for this Festival of the Ass.

On the next day, January 1, the feast of the Circumcision of Christ, curiosity led Francesco, as if by the nose, to the Cathedral of St. Trophime. The large square in front of the cathedral was already crowded with festively clothed people filled with anticipation. The first sound of drums and trumpets coming from one of the streets leading to the cathedral caused a surge of excitement to race through the crowd. Then, with one great voice the crowd roared its delight as Goliard monks appeared, leading a donkey dressed like a bishop.

"Heehaw, Asshop, Heehaw, Asshop," the monks chanted as they escorted up the cathedral steps the donkey with a miter tied atop its head.

"Heehaw, Asshop, Heehaw, Asshop," the crowd shouted back, now pressing forward toward the cathedral doors. Behind the Goliards, to Francesco's shock, came a procession of tonsured priests attired as women and dancing as wildly as clowns. They were preceded by a Goliard monk swinging a censor that poured out stinking black smoke that smelled like the burning leather soles of old shoes. As the Goliards were about to lead the donkey inside the cathedral, a group of armed soldiers appeared from within and blocked their passage. At the appearance of the soldiers, the crowd began loudly booing and shouting obscenities at them.

"His Grace, the Lord Bishop of Arles," shouted the captain of the guard, "has forbidden this shameful, irreligious display of the Festival of the Ass! He has strictly forbidden any chanting or antics performed by the Goliards inside the cathedral and will discipline any tonsured

clerics or priests who participate in it as minstrels or buffoons. Any tonsured clerics who disobey these orders of His Grace, the Lord Bishop, shall have their clerical privileges stripped from them. Now, for the rest of you, unless you wish to experience equally severe consequences, I would advise you to go home and return to this cathedral in two hours to attend this holy day's Solemn High Mass, at which His Lordship the Bishop will preside."

After a volley of shouts and curses at the guards, the people in the crowd dispersed to their homes or to other outdoor festivals of the feast day. Francesco, however, chose to enter the cathedral to pray while waiting to attend the Solemn High Mass. Finding a quiet place, he sat on the floor with his back against one of the massive stone pillars and reflected, "Heehaw, Bishop Ass! That's disrespectful, but I do like the sound of it: Brother Ass, heehaw. So it'll no longer be holy Francesco, but heehaw Francesco!" Then he patted his leg, saying, "Good Brother Ass, you've carried me to Spain and back; now carry me safely home to Assisi." From that day onward he enjoyed referring to his body as Brother Ass.

As he departed from Arles, Francesco traveled the coastal road past Marseilles and Toulon until he reached St. Raphael, about halfway between Toulon and Nice. He rejoiced that he would soon be back in Italy again, home in his beloved Assisi. As he approached the edge of the village of St. Raphael, he saw a line of ragged, hungry beggars huddled together, shivering in the January cold as they waited their turn at the door of a dilapidated hut where, it appeared, bread was being handed out.

"Blessed is she who gives bread to the hungry," Francesco cried out as he passed by the poor hut, "for heaven's gate will open instantly to her."

"I certainly hope so," replied a man's voice—and when Francesco looked over, he saw that the figure dressed as poorly as the beggars was indeed a man—"for otherwise those gates won't open for me either."

The voice caused Francesco's feet to stall on the road, for there was something about it that stirred up a faint memory: When and where had he heard that voice before? He crossed the road to identify the voice's owner, and as he approached the doorway, the beggars began shoving him and yelling, "Get to the back of the line. Don't try to crowd in front of us; we're just as hungry as you are!" At that, a

broad-shouldered man in a shabby tunic stepped out of the doorway to see what was causing the commotion. Francesco gasped in disbelief and exclaimed, "Jacques Coeur!"

"Francesco of Assisi!" he replied, equally surprised. "Where did you come from?

Later into that night Francesco sat with Jacques in front of the small fire inside his hut and listened to his tale of how his life had radically changed that night over a year ago when Francesco visited his camp of thieves near Toulon. Jacques told Francesco how he had stolen his heart that night as they had walked under the stars. Only three days later, after wrestling with his conscience, he simply walked away from his band of thieves and began to make amends for his life of stealing and sin.

"God is great! How wondrous!" Francesco said, recalling Ali's words about how in chance encounters one is given a taste of the Divine Beloved. At the thought, like Ali, he ran his tongue along his upper lip.

"I agree. God is great! And I've never regretted that decision to reform my life. I prayed, but, oh, so poorly, I fear, that God would show to me a way to repent. I returned to church, confessed my sins to a priest, and considered going on a pilgrimage of penance to Rome. You may laugh, but I've even thought of trying to join some monastery, if they would take me—or becoming one of those self-whipping penitents. Then one Sunday at Mass I heard a priest speak of the Gospel scene at the Last Judgment where Jesus said to the sheep, 'Enter into your eternal reward, for I was hungry and you fed me.' Well, there it was, an answer to my prayers. I knew at once how to repent for my many years of thieving and other sins: I would feed the hungry by buying bread with what little money I could make as a cobbler. I had learned that trade as a child, as my father had been one. And so by day I repair the soles of other peoples' shoes, and at night I repair my own soul as I feed the poor."

"What a wonderful story, Jacques, of the strange workings of God's grace!"

"It's also a story of how God used you, Francesco, as an instrument to awaken me. I was *so lucky* that night—or should I say *so blessed*, when you walked into my life. I still pride myself on being a thief, only now I aspire to being a master thief like you. Over a year ago you told

me and my companions that you were a thief who was 'trying to steal heaven,' and I'm still trying to live by those words."

"Jacques, I discovered that God can make music out of two old sticks. So I'm honored if the Holy Spirit used this old instrument from Assisi to make the music of your homecoming song." Standing on his tiptoes, Francesco hugged him, saying, "Brother thief, I give thanks to God."

He spent that night in Jacques' hut, and the next morning as he stood at the door, about to depart, Jacques surprised him. "Only heaven knows how great a sinner I am," he said, placing his hands on Francesco's shoulders. "I was a thief who robbed others of more than their money. I've stolen peoples' security, self-respect, innocence, and even their virginity, seeking sexual pleasures by overpowering others by my charming personality or by force. I'm ashamed to tell you some of things that I've done. While I'm guilty of some appalling deeds in life, I need to ask you, Francesco: Could you ever allow me to accompany you back to Assisi and become one of your Little Brothers? Last night I dreamed I was dressed in gray, just as you are, and barefoot, which is funny for a cobbler. And I was feeding the poor, not here in St. Raphael, but in Assisi! I'd understand if it isn't possible. I've got this scar on my face that tells everyone I'm no angel; I was a criminal and. . . ."

"*Brother* Jacques, how wonderful! Yes, you can join the Little Brothers, for we are a band of sinners. In a way we're also a band of thieves, who try to steal from the poor their sadness and their fear of God. As for your scar, I've got my scars too, only they're not visible on the outside. And you don't have to return to Assisi to join our brotherhood. I gladly accept you this very moment as the first French member of the Little Brothers of Assisi." Standing again on his tiptoes, he embraced and kissed Jacques on the cheek.

That very morning Francesco and Jacques departed, both of them barefoot, and soon crossed over the border between France and Italy. As they traveled together along the crowded coastal road that led to Genoa, an even deeper bond was formed between them. As the many miles of their journey to Assisi disappeared beneath their feet, Jacques was enchanted by Francesco's tales of his adventures in Barcelona and Murcia, as well as his time in prison in Narbonne. Jacques had developed a great hunger for soul food during his penance of feeding the poor, and so he devoured Francesco's acquired insights into Jewish prayer and Islamic mysticism. While he only had an audience of one,

Francesco once again was the joyful minstrel as he sang songs in Spanish and French and vividly retold the gleeful tales of his visit to Rashid and the Goliards' procession with the relic of Christ's foreskin and the Festival of the Ass he had witnessed at Arles. Time and distance quickly passed as they traveled through the coastal towns of La Spezia and Pietasanta before turning westward into the interior of Italy. By now Francesco truly felt he was back home again. After passing through the great banking city of Florence, they continued southeast toward Umbria. With each step, Francesco's heart blazed more and more like a blacksmith's furnace in his desire to be reunited with his brothers in Assisi, as well as with Clare and Emiliano. He was childlike in his eagerness to unpack for Padre Antonio all the fabulous riches he had found during his travels to Spain. Just south of Florence, they entered the city of San Giovanni to the peeling of Mass bells from the city's main church dedicated to San Giovanni, and they stopped to hear Mass.

After Mass, Brothers Francesco and Jacques continued walking southward until they reached the broad and beautifully blue Lake Trasimeno, which seemed to extend from horizon to horizon. Francesco wanted to bathe in the lake to wash off the dust from the road, and so they both plunged into the water. When Francesco dunked himself beneath the surface, he recalled Ali's words about diving all the way to the bottom of the sea to find the Pearl of Great Price. As they stood on the shore shaking the water off their bodies like two wet dogs, Francesco shivered, but not because he felt a chill. He remembered how when he had told Ali that he didn't know how to swim and would drown if he dived to the bottom of the sea, Ali had replied, "Yes, of course, how else does one find the Pearl of Great Price?" Looking across the lake toward Assisi, he shivered again, wondering if something lay ahead that would require him to lose his life, as Jesus had said, in order to save it. Though he was tempted to visit the old hilltop fortress city of Cortona, north of the lake, the rope around his waist wouldn't let him. Instead, it tugged him southward around the lake toward Perugia. Bypassing that fortress city, which held so many unpleasant memories for him, they continued southeastward toward Assisi. As they drew closer, its powerful hilltop magic caused Francesco to begin veritably dancing his way to Portiuncula.

"Your brothers will be surprised to see you again," said Brother Jacques, who was straining to keep up with him, "after being gone for over a year."

"Yes, and I've purposefully not sent a message ahead telling them of my return. I love surprises! It will be so much fun to surprise my dear brothers Leone, Pietro, Giles, Bernardo, and all the rest, and especially *cara mia*, Sister Clare. You must come with me, Brother Jacques, to meet her, she is so wonderful and creative and so devoted to prayer. And I'm eager for her to meet you. Also while I've been away, I've come to the conclusion that upon returning to Assisi I will go immediately to my father, Pietro, and seek reconciliation with him. I've told you the story of my renunciation and his violent reaction and rejection of me. Now I'm convinced that regardless of how he may respond, if I am truly dedicated to peace, then I must try to be reunited with him. My prayers have been that he will embrace me as his prodigal but loving son."

The long journey home ended just as a giant orange sun, highlighted by a few wisps of trailing purple clouds, was straddling the western horizon. As they crested the hill overlooking Portiuncula, Francesco screamed, "My God! What have they done while I was away?" With Jacques running behind him, he raced madly down the hill toward the stone buildings whose new red tile roofs glistened in the setting sun. With tears streaming down his cheeks, confused and frustrated, he beat his fists against the walls of the new stone buildings. Then his anger overflowed, and he began kicking at some nearby wooden poles of construction scaffolding, causing roof tiles stacked on the top plank to come crashing to the ground. Close by, a group of brothers who had just joined the order became horrified at the destructive behavior of this madman in gray and shouted an alarm. One of them ran off to get Brother Elias, and other brothers came running from all direction in answer to their shouts.

"Father Francesco!" cried Brother Leone as he came running up to him from around one of the new buildings. "Thank God, you're home again!" he exclaimed as he embraced Francesco and lavished kisses on his cheek. Other older brothers likewise ran to embrace him, weeping tears of joy. The newer members, who stood in awe of this famous holy man they'd never seen before, were equally mystified by his anger.

"Brother Leone," agonized a weeping Francesco, "what happened to our simple wooden huts? Who . . . how . . . did these new stone

houses. . . ." In his great distress at finding the once-primitive huts replaced by sturdy stone buildings, he forgot about Jacques, who awkwardly stood at the edge of the crowd.

"They were donated by our friends in the nobility and by the grateful citizens of Assisi," said Brother Elias as he stepped forward, having joined the crowd around Francesco, "in response to our grave need to house our new members. Welcome home, Father Francesco!" Elias nervously pushed a strand of hair behind his ear as his eyes darted from brother to brother. "I've so prayed and hoped that upon your return you would be grateful to see all that has been done since you left. It is God's will, surely, since the money for this building was so generously given to us." With his head drooping, he continued, "Now I can see that you're angry with me! Oh, how I prayed while you were away, Father Francesco, that I might be able to fulfill the heavy responsibility you placed on me when you departed. I'm so inadequate, lacking your inspiration from God. You departed without giving any instructions, and now I've. . . ." Then he raised his hand to his eyes as if he were about to cry.

"Oh, forgive me, Brother Elias," Francesco said, eagerly embracing him. "Please pardon me, Elias, for being so rash and thoughtless in my speech. I did not intend to hurt you by criticizing your efforts to care for the needs of the brothers. It's only that I was so surprised; I mean all these stone buildings seem so . . . so . . . ah . . . contrary to our original. . . ."

"Of course, I understand, Father Francesco," Elias replied, using his sleeve to wipe away the tears that had never appeared. "But as you yourself have often told us, 'Change is good. Nothing in life remains static.' These stone quarters are really very simple, and they were necessary to shelter the constant flood of new members into the order. Many of them have joined us late in their lives, and their health does not permit the harshness of living in the mud-and-twig huts and sleeping on the hard ground. Also, we needed a library building and study rooms for our new priest members and those brothers studying to become ordained."

"Priest members. . . ?" asked a stunned Francesco.

"Yes," Elias said, again nervously readjusting a strand of hair behind his ear, "you see, since you have been away, our Blessed Lord has generously sent us some parish priests who have taken the habit and are now members of the order. They celebrate Holy Mass for us, and since

they're ordained, they can properly preach in churches. Aren't we blessed?"

"A blessing, indeed," Francesco nodded, slowly feeling himself being dragged down deeper and deeper into that mystic sea in which Ali Hasan had so gleefully suggested he would drown.

"Naturally, Father Francesco, our new priest members can't be expected to work in the fields or do manual labor like our lay brothers." The word "lay" slammed against Francesco's ear as if he had been struck by one of the large wooden planks at the construction site. He struggled to fight back an attack of dizziness as Elias continued, "Come inside, Father Francesco, and see our new library where our priest members and those preparing for the priesthood can study. We already have a great number of manuscripts, and more, which have been purchased by a generous patron, are coming soon. You must come and see the library. Soon God willing, we can look forward to having some of our brothers in the order as distinguished professors in the great universities and. . . ."

"No, Elias! Professors and priests—no! We were never intended to be anything other than simple, insignificant brothers. Scholars and priests will only be elevated above the others, causing divisions among us. God has called us not to teach in the great universities but to speak humbly to the poor, not to aspire to high places in the Church but to live in simplicity, in solidarity with the peasants and the poor. I refuse to step inside the library, for I fear that just as weapons lead to war, books lead to compromising the Gospel! Books are ladders that will only raise some of the brothers above others, and among us all must be equal. . . ." Then, suddenly remembering Jacques, he turned to him, saying, "Forgive me, Brother Jacques. Please come over here." Placing his hand affectionately on Jacques' shoulder, he said, "My brothers, meet our newest member, who I'm proud to say is truly French and truly a man of God. His name is Jacques Coeur of St. Raphael. He has been my faithful traveling companion and a dear friend since I personally received him into our Order of the Little Brothers on the last leg of my return journey."

"You two must be tired and hungry," said Brother Leone after the brothers had warmly welcomed Jacques into their midst. "Come and have some supper—and then to bed with you!"

"My beloved brother Francesco," said Pietro taking his arm. "It's so good to have you home. But before you go to eat supper, can I have a

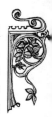

word with you?" Jacques went inside with the others as the two old friends remained outside and embraced each other with great affection. Then Pietro told Francesco that while he had been away in Spain his father had died. Francesco was stunned by a sharp jolt of pain at the news. It felt as if someone had ripped out his heart, and his great homecoming desire that he and his father could be reconciled was now dashed to a thousand pieces. Placing his arm around Francesco's shoulder, Pietro attempted to comfort his old friend, telling him that his father had lived a full life and was now at peace. As Francesco sobbed, however, he felt it was more true that because of him his father's last eighteen years had been lived in torment. Then, wiping away his tears as he made the sign of the cross upon himself, he prayed for his father's soul and vowed silently that at the first opportunity he would visit his father's grave and there would make his reconciliation with him. Then, after thanking Brother Pietro for being the one who told him of his father's death, he performed one of his mystical, magical disappearing tricks as he hid away somewhere inside of himself the sorrowful news of his father's death. Placing his arm around Pietro he told him that now they should go inside for supper and share in their brothers' joy at his return.

As they sat eating their supper surrounded by many of the brothers, Francesco the minstrel conjurer performed another amazing magic trick of finding a way to be truly joyful upon his return home. Weaving together laughter and wild stories of his adventures on the road, he cleverly hid his broken heart and his feelings of being sick to his stomach. What turned his stomach sour wasn't just the new stone living quarters, the library, and having priests in the brotherhood, it extended even to the supper meal itself, for the brothers' diet was no longer simple peasant fare. Brother Leone looked into the smiling face of his beloved friend and easily detected beneath it a grieving, brokenhearted man. As Francesco commented on how tasty the meat was, Leone knew well that for his old friend this supper meal was as much a penitential act as eating crusts of old black bread sprinkled with ashes.

"Francesco, my beloved Francesco," Clare cried with joy as she clutched the iron bars of the cloistered grating so powerfully that they almost snapped. "I feared I'd never see you again. Dearest Francesco, how I wish I could embrace you."

"The grill of your cloister," Francesco replied, his fingers intertwined with Clare's as he gripped the iron bars, "only separates bodies, not souls and hearts."

"Your eyes are red, my brother. You've been crying."

"I've just come from visiting my father's grave—he died while I was away in Spain. I had intended to go to him and attempt to be reconciled upon returning home, but sadly our reconciliation had to take place in the cemetery. Yet after my cleansing tears of sorrow for causing him pain, my heart now tells me that he and I are now at peace.

"But, Clare, that's not the only reason for my grief. You should see what they've done at Portiuncula while I've been away!"

"I know, Emiliano has painted a vivid picture for me during his frequent visits. I'm so sorry, Francesco, for I know what they've done must rip apart your soul."

"I should never have left, never, never. If only I had. . . ."

"Don't blame yourself, Francesco, for the same thing probably would have happened even if you had been here! Have you not given the gift of equality to your brothers so that none would be superior to another?" Francesco nodded his drooping head in agreement with Clare's wisdom as she continued, "So even if you had stayed here in Assisi and the majority of them had wanted to live in comfortable quarters with a sturdy roof over their heads at night, how could you have refused the will of the majority?"

"True, sadly true, Clare. But I can see that you're able to continue living in the poorest poverty. Don't some of your sisters desire more comfort and less penance and fasting?"

"Yes, some do, but more disturbing is the fact that the Pope wishes it even more than they. He keeps insisting that I change our living conditions here. I feel trapped between remaining loyal to the Church, being obedient to the Pope, and trying to be true to our great dream. Francesco, I'm so glad you're home. Please help me discover how I can be obedient to the Church without disobeying the wishes of God."

As Francesco sat in a shroud of silence, Clare did not know if he was praying or thinking, or perhaps both. Behind the iron grating of the grill in the wall of the visitor's room, she sat slowly twisting and untwisting the strands of the rope belt she wore around her waist.

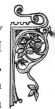

"I wrestle with the same question, my beloved Clare," he finally said. "I've prayed and searched but have found no answer! Like you, I love the Church, but it's often a painful love. When you look at me, you see a wild songbird whose wings have been clipped—even though the Pope only clipped a little of my hair in forcing me to become a tonsured cleric."

"Although your wings have been clipped, Francesco, at least, you've still got your feet—which I'm glad to see are still bare. You're free to go where you wish, while I'm caged up here in this convent. O dearest friend, what is to happen to our dream? Whatever are we to do?"

"We must be graceful acrobats, like those flip-flopping, somersaulting tumblers who perform on tightropes high above the heads of the crowd at village fairs. One moment we're an obedient brother and sister of the Church, then, flip-flop, we're an obedient son and daughter of God. We need almost angelic agility to be able to somersault from one obedience to the other without falling off the rope. And while the tension we feel is great, we must remember that great tension is needed in the rope for it to support our somersaults."

"You said *graceful* acrobats. Indeed, I will pray to the Holy Spirit, asking for the grace of an angel's nimbleness not to lose my balance."

Francesco and Clare continued to talk about grace and how God's grace develops our natural gifts so they can be used as instruments of the love and harmony of the Spirit. Francesco spoke of how they could be like fiddles or flutes that play a new song for those who have given up hope that the Church could ever be renewed, that it could again become freshly faithful to the Gospel of Christ.

"Francesco, you be the fiddle, and I'll be the flute." Clare said as she placed her two cupped hands just to the left of her mouth, holding her invisible flute. "O, may the Wind of God blow through me such a sweet song that it causes the Pope to swoon. Then he will allow me to live as I believe God wants me to live—in the peasant poverty of the Gospels."

"Dearest Clare, let us also be like the bread and wine that mysteriously becomes the loving presence of our Lord Jesus Christ. Then we will not only be a song of hope, we will feed the hungry with the bread of hope."

"I myself am hungry for that bread of hope, and I've been talking with my sisters about us going to Holy Communion once a month. It has sounded strange to many of the sisters, but after much discussion I think we've almost reached a consensus to ask a priest to come here once a month to say Mass so we can receive our Blessed Lord. Naturally, that means we'll also have to go to confession once a month so as to be worthy to receive Holy Communion."

"That's amazing, Clare! Without speaking to one another, we've both been thinking the same way. Even though to most people it may sound strange to go to Holy Communion as often as once a month, we need to feed our hunger for the Bread of Life if we are to be that bread for others."

"The remaining difficulty for us at San Damiano is that some of the sisters here are fearful about confession. As you know, penances in the past have been so severe that many people have stayed away from confessing until they are near death."

"That's true, Clare. Yet on my trip, along a road in France, I met some Irish monks on pilgrimage to Rome who told me that they frequently go to confession. They say that it helps to polish the soul, to weed one's garden of vices while they're still small plants. For them, it's more a process of spiritual direction than an exercise in inflicting penances. Perhaps it can be that way for you and your sisters."

"And for your brothers?"

"That is needed, for sure, but perhaps you and your sisters here at San Damiano may have to lead the way if we are to embrace such a change. While several have told me they believe change is good, I believe they're talking only about those changes that might make their lives more comfortable. They're rarely interested in receiving spiritual direction."

"My experience with men, which mainly comes from my brothers and father, confirms that. It tells me that men are not inclined to be spiritual or, for that matter, to seek any kind of direction. They feel that as men they're supposed to know where they're going in life and so for them seeking direction is a sign of weakness."

Francesco went on to tell Clare stories about Ali Hasan and Sufi dancing, about Samuel of Barcelona and striving to see the *Shekhinah*. He even shared with her the astonishing news of how Muslims believe the earth is round. He was amazed that her only reply was quoting the angel who appeared to Mary: "With God, all things are possible!" They were both surprised at how the afternoon had disappeared when the bell rang for the sisters to gather for vespers. Francesco promised to return to tell her more about his days in Spain and all that he had learned on his pilgrimage. As they parted, each asked the other for a blessing.

Then Francesco said, "Giddy up, Brother Ass," jokingly slapping his leg, "and get me home before supper."

The morning after visiting Clare, Francesco arose early, before dawn, to go and see the second most important person in his life, his beloved teacher and mentor Padre Antonio. He approached Antonio's hermitage shortly after dawn as the brilliant morning sun was shooting yellow arrows through the tall trees.

"Padre Antonio, you old hermit," he called out playfully, "it's your old friend and disciple Giovanni Francesco, who's returned from Spain a very rich man." He called out again, standing at the entrance to the hermit's cave and waiting, but there was no response from within. After calling a third time, he entered the darkened cave and found that it was empty except for several mice that scurried into the darkness. After sitting in that silence for a few moments, Francesco said, "Forgive me, brother mice, I am sorry for disturbing you so early in the morning. Can you tell me the whereabouts of your gentle host, Padre Antonio?" The hiding mice were as silent as the abandoned hermitage, which clearly appeared to have been uninhabited for some time. "Farewell, brother mice; I must go to the abbey to see if Padre Antonio has returned there. Perhaps Father Abbot finally sent those two sturdy brothers Antonio had been expecting to take him back to the abbey where he could be properly cared for in his blindness and old age."

Arriving at the monastery gate, he rang the bell, and when the porter monk answered the bell, he said, "Brother, I am Brother Francesco of Assisi. Is it possible for me to visit my confessor, Padre Antonio, who is a member of your abbey?"

"Peace to you, Francesco of Assisi, and welcome to the abbey," the monk replied with a slight bow. "Please follow me, and I will take you to Padre Antonio." They walked in silence to the end of a long hallway where they exited through a door that led down a path toward a group

of small buildings. Francesco followed the monk down the path as it wound around the buildings and out into a grove of trees, the site of the monastic graveyard!

"There, Brother Francesco," said the monk pointing to a grave with new grass growing on it, "lies Padre Antonio." Then, silently bowing, he departed, leaving Francesco alone at the gravesite.

"My beloved Antonio," Francesco sobbed as he fell to his knees at his old friend's grave, "how I ached to share with you the story of my pilgrimage to Spain, to tell you all the marvelous things I learned—all because of you. O saintly Antonio, because of your wisdom I've returned to Assisi a wealthy man. I shall so miss you. You were truly like a father to me. You gave me life in countless ways. . . ." He sobbed freely, soaking his tunic with his tears. "How I shall miss your humor and advice. To whom shall I now go to find guidance?" Then he sank back onto his heels and continued sobbing, asking the wind to join him in his grief as it mournfully wailed, moving through the branches of the tall trees of the cemetery, causing them to creak painfully in response.

"Moan with me, Brother Wind. Groan loudly your grief-filled prayers for this holy man who once lived as a freely as you, whose love was as strong as your greatest ocean gales and as gentle as your spring breezes."

Francesco yearned for the clouds to release their rain and join him as he tearfully poured out his heart at the grave of his old friend and teacher. He profusely thanked Antonio for his wise counsel about traveling with a poor man's heart, empty of convictions and even religious beliefs. He thanked Antonio for telling him to remember Saint Peter's words in the Acts of the Apostles that "indeed, God shows no partiality; rather, in every nation, whoever hears God and acts uprightly is acceptable to God."

"Antonio, I believe that you can still hear me, and I want you to know that I have found such men! On my journey I met men of other nations and faiths who are truly acceptable to God: a Jewish holy man from Barcelona named Samuel and my soul brother, a mystic Moor named Ali Hasan."

Francesco spent hours at the grave recounting in great detail all his adventures, even the Festival of the Ass. He told his old mentor how his journey had transformed him, making him freer to be his true self and

less concerned about the approval of others. He related how his strong emotional friendship with Ali made it easier to be more affectionate with his brothers and old friends like Emiliano and Clare. Leaning down, he kissed the earth on top of Antonio's grave and spoke of how he was now able to see that God was present in countless ways and in religions other than Christianity. While he had only glimpsed the *Shekhinah*, he saw God's glorious presence vibrantly alive in all of creation. Pausing and looking around to insure that no one was near, he then told his old mentor about the earth being round, adding that he felt sure the old hermit was so wise he already knew that.

"Oh, Father Antonio, you became a loving father to me when my own father disowned me—if only you were still alive. You of all people could help me to understand and be at peace with all the changes at Portiuncula and. . . ." Pausing mid-sentence, he held his breath, silently aware that something was moving in his heart. "But, you *are* alive! Dear Antonio, I know you are now fully alive in the risen Christ. I feel that here in my heart. You're now one with Christ, rejoicing with all the saints in heaven. I am convinced of that, regardless of what the Church might teach about the dead having to wait to enter heaven until the Last Judgment." Then he surprised himself by laughing as he said, "You see, Antonio, I'm still as heretical as always—but you're to blame! So now, from your place in heaven next to our Risen Lord and his Holy Mother, I ask you to continue to inspire me."

The peeling of the monastery bells calling the monks to vespers was carried by the wind across the rows of silent graves. "Padre, it's time for you and your brothers out here to join the others invisibly for vespers in the abbey church, and it's time for me to be on my way home before dark." He leaned over and kissed the earth on top of Antonio's grave. Slowly standing up, he traced the sign of the cross over the grave, praying, "In the name of the Father, and of the Son, and of the Holy Spirit. Saint Antonio, hermit and lover of God, pray for me, your son, Giovanni Francesco."

Chapter 20

"FATHER FRANCESCO, HAVE YOU HEARD THE SAD NEWS?" Brother Leone greeted him with this question at the door of the new refectory after Francesco had returned from Antonio's grave. Francesco thought, "Antonio's death, this new dining hall, and the food that is being served tonight are sad enough news; what now?"

"We just learned that shortly before noon today our beloved Bishop Guido died! Earlier this afternoon we had heard the cathedral bells tolling in the distance, but we didn't know until just before you returned that they were tolling for his death. We've been told that a messenger has been sent to inform His Holiness Pope Innocent III of the bishop's death, and before supper the brothers gathered in our chapel to pray for his soul."

"Brother Leone, please excuse me to the brothers; I won't be eating tonight but will be in chapel instead," Francesco said, making the sign of the cross on himself. "Eternal rest grant unto him, O Lord, for Bishop Guido was truly your humble and obedient servant." When Leone offered to accompany him, he shook his head, saying, "No, thank you, Leone. I need to pray alone—the bishop's death is a great loss to me, the second one of this day."

Twilight was casting a purple shroud over the hills of Umbria as Francesco made his way into the darkened chapel, where only a single candle flickered. He knelt before the hanging crucifix and sobbed. "O my Beloved Lord, since my return from Spain, my whole world reeks with the stench of approaching death. From the moment I arrived at my dear Portiuncula, I've had to face the reality that my brotherhood is dying, slowly but surely being smothered to death by comforts and

compromises." Touching his chest, he went on, "And my old Spoleto wound of failure has opened again and is bleeding, the scab torn off by the dissolution of another cherished dream, one far more precious than becoming a knight. Shortly thereafter I was greeted with news of my father's death, having too late come to realize my need to reconcile with him. Then today when I went to share with Padre Antonio the joyful news of how rich was my journey to Spain, I found him long dead and in the grave. Now, once again that dark angel of death has visited me and stolen another dear friend and guide, Bishop Guido, who guided me in how to speak to the Pope and has always supported me. No more crosses, my Lord! I plead with you; do not demand of me any more poverty, for I am gravely fearful of what you shall next ask of me." Emotionally and spiritually spent, he sank into silence and allowed his lungs to continue his prayer as he breathed his sorrow in and out.

"O God, have mercy on the soul of Bishop Guido," he began again aloud. "As a bishop he had to carry the heavy cross of the many duties and decisions for which he alone was responsible. He was a holy man, unlike so many bishops today who live like nobles in great splendor. I know he tried to live as simply as the poorest of his flock. All of us are sinners, bishops and popes included, but I pray, O merciful God, that you may be blinded to his sins by his many good deeds, especially his protective support of me and my Little Brothers. I pray that you grant unto him a place of reward in heaven, seated next to my beloved Antonio."

That night Francesco's prayers about the deaths of his father and his two old friends mirrored his Lord's agony in the Garden of Gethsemane. For a second time Francesco begged that he might be spared the bitter chalice that held the death of his dream for his community, and his prayer ended just as Jesus' did, "But your will be done."

The following afternoon, along with a great number of his brothers, Francesco entered the Cathedral of San Rufino to pay his respects to Bishop Guido, whose body was lying in state on a raised black-cloth-draped catafalque platform in the cathedral's center aisle. Guido looked serene and at peace in his white miter and priestly vestments, his body flanked by six towering, flickering orange candles in massive silver candlesticks. Long lines of mourners passed by praying and paying their final respects. Most of them reached out to touch his funeral bier and then make the sign of the cross upon themselves. The

sick, diseased, crippled, and afflicted were especially eager to touch his body, for the people of Assisi were convinced that their dead bishop was a saint. While the black-vested canon priests of the cathedral prayed the Office of the Dead, Francesco and his brothers knelt in prayer off to one side of the cathedral. At the conclusion of the Office of Dead, the brothers, along with all the people and clergy, departed, while Francesco remained behind kneeling in prayer, salted by his tears.

In the dark shadows of the cathedral, not far from where Francesco was praying, stood two priests who had remained to keep vigil over the bishop's body until the cathedral was locked for the night. Though they could not see Francesco, he recognized one of the voices in the hushed conversation as belonging to Dom Tomas, who had long been Bishop Guido's secretary.

"You've heard," Dom Tomas said, "that all of us priests are to gather here at the cathedral next week along with a delegation of laymen from Assisi to vote on Bishop Guido's successor. Who could replace such a good and holy man? I only wish we could properly mourn his death for months without having to select his replacement."

"I agree, Tomas," the other priest replied. "The rush is because of the approaching Lateran Council, isn't it? Every diocese in the world will send its bishop, and Assisi should have a new bishop to send to the council."

"I know that's the reason, but I still regret we're not allowed to mourn the death of such a great man in a proper way."

"Who among our priests do you think will be elected our next bishop?"

"Not you or me," Tomas said, chuckling softly, "that's for sure. I'd like to see us choose Dom Alessandro Farnese. He's a good pastor, intelligent and well-liked by clergy and people alike. He'd make a fitting successor to Bishop Guido since the two of them thought along much the same lines when it came to theology, the Church, and the care of the poor. From all I hear, he's the most popular choice."

"And what about our chancellor, Monsignor Paulo Carafa?"

"Most priests find him too heavy-handed, and they don't trust him."

"I agree, but he is a brilliant canon lawyer."

"True, yet many are convinced that Paulo is an agent of the papal curia. As the bishop's secretary, I know he receives more messages from

Rome than what would be normal for the business of our little diocese. And then there's that other issue . . . ," and his voice softened to a mere whisper, and Francesco couldn't hear any more of the conversation.

When his prayers were finished, Francesco stood up, made the sign of the cross, and departed silently and invisibly through the shadows to the front door. As he stepped outside, his heart exploded. "Emiliano! My beloved *caro mio*, Emiliano." He ran with tears streaming down his cheeks and threw his arms around his old childhood friend. Unseen by him until now, Emiliano had also attended the Office of the Dead for Bishop Guido and afterwards had waited for Francesco outside the cathedral. The two old friends were now welded together in a long-awaited embrace. When Emiliano pulled himself away from Francesco's tight hold, it was only to invite Francesco to his home to have supper with him and his son Francesco. When Francesco declined, saying that he needed to eat with his brothers at Portiuncula, the powerful grip became Emiliano's. He took Francesco's arm as if in a vice and good-naturedly marched him off toward his home. As the two friends walked through the same twilight streets of Assisi where as young men they had played football together, Emiliano was able to drain much of his friend's sorrow by telling him of the recent successes of the Third Order of Laymen.

More delicious than the rare wine that Emiliano uncorked that night was his news about the wonderful fruitfulness of the lay members of the Third Order. While they had encountered some opposition in Assisi, they were true instruments of peace in the surrounding cities and countryside. Although their refusal to bear any arms and their resolve to daily live out the Gospel without compromise had angered many, it had also attracted significant numbers to their ranks. Late into the night they talked about the Third Order, and then at Emiliano's insistence they also delved into the new insights around prayer and the spiritual life that Francesco had gained during his travels to Spain. Francesco found his friend's great hunger to learn how to pray and his passion for sanctity a healing balm for his recent disappointments and sorrows. He rejoiced in God's generosity, for it seemed that the old friends were now closer than they ever had been.

"Go now, and do your work!" Cardinal Uzielli yelled angrily as Canaletto quickly closed the door to the cardinal's private study. In his many years as majordomo, Canaletto had never seen Uzielli so angry.

"I'm glad these are not the olden days," Canaletto mumbled to himself as he hurried down the hallway, "when they used to kill messengers who delivered bad news! I tried to sweeten it a bit with a little honey of the latest gossip in Rome, but to no avail. Even those recent reports from my agents about the exploits of Cardinal Montino failed to soften Uzielli's rage." Canaletto recalled the time when they first learned from the servant at Montino's household how, very late at night, Montino would dress as a layman and secretly sneak out of the back door—how Uzielli had chewed on that piece of backstairs gossip as if it was a piece of choice veal. He had instructed him to bribe Montino's servant to follow the cardinal and find out where he went and whom he met disguised as a layman. "Then, when I told him another newest juicy tidbit that came from Cardinal Sacchoni's servant, he spit it out as if he had bitten into a sour olive, saying, 'Fool, everyone in Rome knows that!'"

Reaching the stairway, Canaletto continued mumbling to himself as he descended the stairs to the main floor, "I saved the best for last, and it was worth it just to watch his face. Even though he values my skills and my stealth, Uzielli treats me like a minion, like some underling. So I wasn't sorry to see him feel a little of the same kind of pain that he inflicts on the rest of us. But in a job like mine, you have to be crafty and careful in how you play your hand—lest you lose your hand, or your head! His Eminence's nerves are on edge—with much work to do in preparing for that council—and my morsel of household gossip must have pushed him over the edge. I've not seen him so furious in years. Knowing how he likes to take out his anger on those servants who simply happen to be close by at the time of his rage, I must be careful to stay out of his way until he calms down. But now I must be busy," he snickered, "for His Scarlet Eminence ordered me to go and do my work; while some might find that work disagreeable, for me it is a delight."

Several hours later Canaletto was in the kitchen overseeing arrangements for the lavish dinner banquet the cardinal was hosting

that night. A half-dozen cooks were preparing the various banquet dishes, while other servants were busily polishing candlesticks and ironing table linens.

"You sent for me, Signore Canaletto Majordomo Magnifico?" Sebastiano said, grinning as with youthful agility he made a sweeping bow to Canaletto.

"Ah, at last you present yourself! I sent for you over two hours ago. Where have you been?"

"I came as quickly as possible, with the wings of Mercury on my feet, Signore Majordomo," he said with a wide dipping sweep of his right hand. "Pray, tell me, how I may be of service to you, my Lord?"

"His Eminence Cardinal Uzielli has instructed me to send you on a special mission," Canaletto smirked.

"Well, Canaletto the Cardinal's Cat: Tell me, to what destination does His Eminence now wish to send me? I feel the wings of Mercury itching to take flight."

Canaletto paused and briefly glanced around the busy, noisy kitchen to insure that all the servants were, as usual, eavesdropping. Then with pontifical flair, he exclaimed, "Sebastiano, you are to go to hell!"

Sebastiano's body bolted backward; he stumbled against a kitchen table as if he had been struck by an assassin's poisoned arrow.

"And, Judas Sebastiano," Canaletto shrieked as he let loose a second speeding arrow, "you are to go to hell this very moment!" The kitchen now had become as silent as the catacombs; the servants and cooks stood opened-mouthed at the scene unfolding before them.

"No! I'll go and explain to His Eminence, and he'll. . . ."

"Cardinal Uzielli does not want to see you—now, or ever again! He has instructed me that you are to depart from his house this very hour. I am personally to make sure that you leave," Canaletto said, again taking careful aim, "just as you came here! Now, my fallen angel, out to the stables!" Confident that this well-staged confrontation had properly burned a searing impression of his dictatorial authority on the startled servants in the kitchen, Canaletto removed a firebrand from a stove as he marched Sebastiano out the kitchen door toward the stables.

Upon reaching the stables, Sebastiano saw that a pile of dry wood had been prepared. "Just as you came, Sebastiano! Now, take off those expensive tailored clothes you were given by the cardinal as a sign of his affection and a mark of your prestige among the other servants. Don't

 just stand there! Take them off, all of them, and those finely crafted leather shoes as well, and toss them on that pile of dry wood."

After Sebastiano had undressed and tossed his clothing onto the stack of wood, Canaletto set fire to the wood. As the flames hungrily devoured his beautiful clothing, Sebastiano was forced to stand naked before the grinning majordomo, whose eyes danced with the obvious delight he was taking in Sebastiano's shame. Canaletto stood with his hands on his hips, his eyes slowly poring up and down over the naked, humiliated outcast, prolonging the delicious pleasures of his revenge. "Now you know," he thought to himself as he visually tortured Sebastiano, "how it feels to be humiliated. Now you know something of how I felt that night you so callously mocked me when you came upon me in the kitchen secretly boiling my black hair dye of leeks and walnut shells."

Pointing to the fire, Canaletto said, "As your clothing is disappearing in smoke, so will all Uzielli's memories of you, my dear conceited, arrogant Sebastiano." Then Canaletto slipped another arrow into his bow and declared, "Tonight at the banquet your duties will be assumed by a new, younger and more handsome lad, whom I've been grooming to replace you as the cardinal's personal table waiter and valet. Soon, poof, like smoke, you'll be ancient history. Now, go back to where you came from, *peasant.*" Canaletto spit this last word out as if it was soaked in acid. "I am to inform you that His Eminence orders you to leave Rome and never return. You're not to seek employment in the household of any other prelate or noble prince using your, how shall we say, *personal talents*. If you should attempt to become even a common houseservant or groundskeeper, know that you will be found floating upside down in the Tiber River."

"Please, Canaletto, I. . . ."

"Silence! Be grateful to God that for betraying the cardinal as you did, he has not ordered you to be mutilated or put to death! His Eminence is a most generous man to have let you off so easily; so count your blessings—and be on your way."

"But what will I do? I have no trade, no skill. . . ."

"Perhaps you can find some fat pig farmer's daughter to marry and spend the rest of your life herding her father's pigs. Yet, to show you my compassion, I will not send you away from here looking like Adam without his fig leaf. Do you see that old, discarded stable boy's tunic on the peg over there? Put it on, peasant, and be on your way to Hades!"

As a mortified Sebastiano quickly slipped on the ragged, dirty, flea-infested tunic, he begged, "Please, Canaletto, how will I eat or live? I have no money."

"You're a clever boy, Sebastiano. You'll think of something. Become a beggar! You're already showing some skill at it. Perhaps you could be a street thief and steal your food, or . . . ," grinning from ear to ear, he said, "use your talents to become a flesh peddler and sell yourself." Laughing with the satisfaction of an archer who has skillfully hit the center of the target, he added, "Regardless, count yourself lucky, very lucky, that you weren't castrated, beaten within an inch of your life, and thrown bruised and bloodied into the gutter." Then, extending his arm and pointing toward the gate, he declared, "Now, go!"

As the utterly disgraced Sebastiano walked barefoot, robed in his threadbare tunic, down the lane to the gate, he could feel upon him the eyes of all the servants inside the great house. As he reached the gateway, he turned for one last look at Cardinal Uzielli's grand palazzo. As he did, Canaletto took aim and released his last poisoned arrow: "Ah, Sebastiano, one final thing. Don't come sneaking back here to the gardens looking for comfort from your *amoretto,* your secret lover! I've already dispatched him far away to Sicily as an indentured field hand on an estate owned by His Eminence. Now, Judas Sebastiano, go to hell!"

The shaft of Canaletto's final arrow plunged straight through Sebastiano's soul and out the other side as he turned and limped shamefully down the street. To the men and women he passed on the street he was as invisible as every other ragged, barefoot beggar in a city with hundreds of homeless vagabonds. Also invisible to their eyes were the multiple arrow shafts protruding from him. Yet to the seeing eye, he was a living statue of his namesake, the popular Saint Sebastiano the martyr, who was commonly pictured wearing only a loincloth, shot through with arrows after being executed by a military squad of Roman archers.

*F*ollowing the burial of his friend Bishop Guido, Francesco had gone north to Monte La Verna to be in solitude. His solitude wasn't calm and quiet, however, because a noisy intruder kept interrupting his prayer. Death kept reminding him of his entombed father and friends Antonio and Guido as well as the dissolution of his dream for the Brotherhood of Poor Men, which he diagnosed as being sick unto

death. While once creation had been his second Gospel, communicating to him God's grace and presence and beauty, now it seemed only to speak to him of death and dying things. Even as he prayed, he was assaulted by the presence of a barren white skeleton of a dead pine tree just outside his hermitage. Remembering Antonio's advice to deal with his prayer distractions by entertaining them like visitors, he began singing to the dead tree:

> O Brother Pine, once so vibrantly alive,
>
> you are now a skeleton of bony branches
>
> waiting for Brother Wind to drop you
>
> onto Sister Earth who will embrace you
>
> in her arms of dark rot and rich decay.

He felt the urge to embrace the dead pine tree as he moaned aloud, "How I wish I could have so fully embraced my dear father, Pietro, and my spiritual fathers, Padre Antonio and Bishop Guido, before they were placed in Sister Earth's dark arms. Whitened Pine, are you also a sign of the impending death of my spiritual child, my beloved Brotherhood?"

As if attracted by Francesco's singing, a goldfinch flew down and landed on the ground near the entrance of his hermitage. When Francesco reached out his hand, the small bird fluttered up and perched on his finger. *"Bon jour, amie de coeur,"* he greeted it in courtly French, "'Love of my heart, at long last you've come to trust me.' While I am fasting, it is not proper for you to do so, so dine on these bread crumbs I have for you." As the goldfinch ate the crumbs out of the palm of his hand, he thought, "Day after day I have sat here quietly waiting with crumbs of bread in my hand, as each morning she would come a bit closer. Lord, do we come to you as this small bird has slowly come to trust me? Do you, my gracious Leige Lord, befriend and tame us as I have tamed this goldfinch? As she had to overcome her fear that I would harm her, so I must overcome my fear of you." Meanwhile, a few other small goldfinches fluttered to the ground but remained at a safe distance from him. Slowly moving his left hand while trying not to frighten the bird eating in his right hand, he tossed some crumbs to the other birds. *"Bon jour,* little ones of God, you who are so precious to my God that not one of you falls to earth without heaven mourning."

As careful as he was, the act of throwing crumbs to the other birds startled the little goldfinch that had been eating out of his hand, causing her to flutter a few feet away. *"Amie de coeur:* Do not fear. I will not harm you." He softly hummed a little tune, trying to lure her back, and within a few minutes she flew back and again perched on his finger. "Why should I fear the Lord?" he thought. "In the same way I will not harm this little bird, how can my Lord harm me, even when he visits through his angel of death?" Just as Francesco was finding confirmation to his belief in a God of infinitely tender love, he inwardly flip-flopped, somersaulting back into his old indelibly imprinted childhood image of an angry, punishing, parental God. Rising to the forefront in his mind was the specter of Christ as the Imperial Judge presiding over the fate of the living and the dead. The panorama of nature before him was replaced by images of frightening apocalyptic scenes he had seen carved over the doorways of French cathedrals, depictions of sinners cringing before Christ at the Last Judgment. Those images evoked in him loud echoes of hell-fire preachers describing in vivid, gory detail the hideous punishments of the damned after the Final Judgment. What drove the jagged stake of terror into his heart was the teaching that on Judgment Day an angry, unsympathetic Christ Judge would publicly expose his most secret and hidden sins. The searing embarrassment and shame of that intimate revelation before family members and friends was a terror more feared than the fires of hell.

"Oh, little yellow bird, you've chosen to become a friend of one of the strangest men in all of Christendom. You've perched on the hand of a man who in reality is two men inside one body. There's one Francesco who believes in a gracious and merciful God whose love and capacity for forgiveness is as limitless as that ocean I saw on my journey to Spain. This God is the wellspring of endless joy and gratitude, who so deeply wishes to be loved and known that he crowded all creation with his glory and presence."

The goldfinch stopped pecking in the palm of his hand and tilted her head upwards. "Ah, then there's another Francesco, the one whose hand you felt trembling just now when he became a victim of his beliefs in a punishing, vindictive God. That vengeful Father God of an eye-for-an-eye punishment evokes the soul-shattering fear and guilt that can only be appeased by the most torturous of penances. I have so tried to placate my Leige Lord's fury and win his forgiveness by my

many penances—scourging my body with a horsewhip till it bled and was covered with welts, fasting until I fainted, and spending long nights sleeping on hard stones for my bed. How I long, Sister Goldfinch, that this second man inside me, who was shaped from my early childhood, would cease haunting me with fear and guilt."

"*Amie de coeur,* little one, you have nothing to fear, for you have not sinned as I have. *Bon ami,* now almost thirty-three years old, Brother Ass, my body, has begun objecting to my private prayers of penance. He's heehawing with aches and pains, begging me to stop. But I ask you, *bon ami,* is it possible for a sinner like me to have done enough penance in my life to have gained mercy and forgiveness? I hope so, for I so dread being stripped naked, my sins exposed to all the world at the end of time."

Francesco felt his body wrench, as once again his old wounds of Perugia and Chambery began oozing pain. "Perhaps, *bon ami,* my little yellow bird, you are giving me an answer not by word or song, but simply by being who you are, a goldfinch! It is said that you make your nest in thorn bushes, eating thistles and even the thorns themselves. Thus, you are revered as the holy bird of the passion of Christ, who went to his death wearing a crown of thorns. Some even say you are a feathered prophet who foretells the coming passion of Christ's friends, announcing they will soon share in the crown of thorns. Until this moment, I had forgotten that old belief." Then, having satisfied its hunger, the small yellow bird sprang off Francesco's finger and flew away. As it disappeared into the trees, Francesco wondered if the goldfinch prophecy was true. And if so, he wondered what sharing in Christ's crucifixion and crown of thorns he might experience.

*M*eanwhile, far south, across the mountains and beyond Lake Trasimeno, six horsemen galloped into Assisi's cathedral piazza of San Rufino. Four were members of the papal guard escorting the two other riders, who were Vatican clerics. As the taller of the two clerics dismounted, he gave his riding cloak to one of the guards, revealing the purple cassock that identified him as a member of the papal household. Then, accompanied by his black-cassocked companion cleric, he went to the door of the episcopal palace, which also housed the Chancery of the Diocese of Assisi. He knocked loudly on the door, which was marked by a wreath of black ribbons.

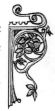

"I am Monsignor Cappellari," the purple-robed cleric authoritatively announced to the servant who opened the door, "the personal secretary to Cardinal Uzielli. I must see your chancellor, Monsignor Paulo Carafa, at once. Kindly see to the needs of my priest scribe here, and attend as well to my military escort and their horses."

The small, quiet chancery of sleepy Assisi was unprepared for the purple Roman storm that swept with speed and pomp down its hallway. The priests in the rooms along the hall had been busy making arrangements for the next day's election of their new bishop and were not prepared for a visitor from the Vatican. The door to the chancellor's office closed behind Monsignor Cappellari, who visited with Monsignor Carafa alone for an hour, while his scribe secretary sat waiting in the hallway. The priests of the chancery and the servants of Bishop Guido's house found themselves caught like flies in a web of mystery being spun by this important visitor. Some whispered a suggestion that the business that had brought him was connected to Francesco and the Little Brothers and to Clare and the Sisters of San Damiano. There was also speculation that it had to do with recent rumors of secret cells of Albigensian heretics in that part of Umbria.

Inside the chancellor's office a stunned Carafa listened in delighted disbelief to his messenger from Rome. "His Holiness Pope Innocent III has named you to be the new Bishop of Assisi," said Monsignor Cappellari. "The usual procedure of Rome approving the peoples' selection of their bishop has been set aside. You, Monsignor, like others soon to follow you, will be *episcopi apostolicae sedis gratia,* bishops by the grace of the apostolic see! The Vicar of Christ has this power as the supreme head of the Church and as temporal leader of the Papal States, to which this city and diocese of Assisi belongs."

Paulo Carafa was speechless, torn between sheer delight at becoming a bishop and feelings of apprehension as to how his fellow priests of Assisi and the people would respond to this unusual intervention by Rome in the affairs of the local Church of Assisi.

"If you accept, there is to be no delay in your consecration as bishop," continued Monsignor Cappellari. "His Eminence Cardinal Uzielli feels that your presence among the bishops attending the forthcoming Lateran Council is expedient. The voting on some of the ballots may be close, and. . . ."

"Monsignor, I am honored by this unexpected. . . ."

"Reward, Monsignor? Is that the word you are searching for?"

"Well, I mean to be so chosen by His Holiness. . . ."

"You have been raised to the episcopal rank by the grace of your patron, Cardinal Uzielli, who personally petitioned the Pope to choose you as the most ideally suited and qualified candidate to become the next Bishop of Assisi. As you are aware, the apostolic custom of the Church is that the Pope only confirms as bishop the priest chosen by a vote of the clergy and people, or the candidate selected by a king or prince. Your case, however, was not a complete break with tradition, since you are a native priest of this diocese as well as its chancellor."

"I am familiar with that apostolic tradition," replied Carafa. Wishing to display his knowledge, he added, "I am also aware of the writings of the Church Fathers that state, 'A bishop must be chosen from the church over which he is to govern and be elected by all the people, and if anyone is forced upon them as a bishop from outside, they are not bound to submit to his authority.' Since I was not chosen by my fellow priests, naturally I am very concerned about how they will respond to this decision from Rome."

"*Bishop* Carafa, that's why *I'm* here!" he replied. "I'm to insure that they fully comply with this decision of the Holy See. My instructions are that you are to call an immediate meeting of all the canon priests and clergy of the cathedral, along with all the available clergy of your diocese. At that meeting I shall read to them the papal decree of your selection as their bishop; then they will be free to state any objections or concerns. And these," he said with a smile, "will all be duly recorded by my scribe secretary and taken back with us to Rome."

"We are fortunate that all the priests are already gathered here in Assisi to attend the election of the new bishop scheduled for tomorrow."

"Excellent, at that gathering I shall save them the time of voting and will announce that the Vicar of Christ has chosen you!"

"I know that after your long ride you must be in need of some refreshment, but before I attend to that, may I ask you why Cardinal Uzielli specifically selected me to be bishop?"

"As his private secretary," Cappellari said, walking over to the tall window that looked upon Piazza San Rufino, "I, of course, am aware of your correspondence to His Eminence, and the valuable information you have provided him. Naturally, Cardinal Uzielli desires that you continue to be his watchdog here in Assisi, his ears and eyes, particularly to monitor the lives and teachings of the highly suspect communities of men and women founded by Francesco Bernadone. The Holy Office and His Eminence need you to root out the enemies of Holy Mother Church."

"Please inform His Eminence," Carafa said, "that I accept the most generous gift of the office of bishop. Assure him of my loyalty to His Holiness and my obedient service to Cardinal Uzielli."

"That is precisely what His Eminence Cardinal Uzielli expected!" Cappellari said with a slender smile as he turned away from the window. "Now, if we might have some dinner."

"Father Francesco, Father Francesco," Brother Leone called out joyfully upon Francesco's return to Portiuncula from Mount La Verna, "glorious news! The word has just arrived from Rome that Pope Innocent has invited you—yes, you, Father Francesco—to come to Rome to attend the upcoming Lateran Council." Embracing Francesco with excitement, Leone bubbled over, "Yes, yes, it's true! Can you believe it? Along with all the lord bishops and abbots and superiors of various religious orders, the Holy Father has requested that as the founder of our order you are to attend and represent us at the council! We're all so thrilled by this great honor!"

"Rome," sighed Francesco, "yes, yes, an honor indeed, Brother Leone. But this old founder feels more like a flounder, a fish out of water even here in Assisi. Whatever shall I feel like when I'm in Rome with all those princely prelates and brilliant theologians?"

"The news we hear is that over a thousand are to attend: bishops, cardinal princes of the church," Brother Leone said, eagerly racing right past Francesco's objection, "patriarchs from Eastern Churches, noble princes from the crowned heads of all Christendom, distinguished scholars, and laymen. It will be the greatest and most ecumenical of all the councils."

"Could I go with you, Father Francesco? It would be the opportunity of a lifetime!"

"Yes, I would love to have an old friend like you accompany me. But, please, Brother Leone, it's *Brother* Francesco."

"Excuse me, in my excitement I forgot. But, thank you, I'd truly be honored to go with you and once again see the Eternal City and the Pope."

"Then it's decided! You, Brother Leone, my old friend from the very beginning and truly my brother, shall be my companion at the council. Now, since you and I are only simple men, perhaps we had best take along with us someone well-versed in Latin and a scholar. So what do think if we also ask Brother Pietro to accompany us?"

It was not unusual for the citizens of Rome to see lamps burning brightly in the papal study at three o'clock in the morning. On this predawn summer morning in 1215 the Pope was dictating letters to two secretaries at the same time as he paced back and forth in his study. Energetic Innocent III was renowned for his extraordinary capacity for work; it required two shifts of papal secretaries to take dictation. Some of these clerical scribes would work from dawn till dusk, and others were on call at all hours of the night. The Pope seemed to need little sleep—or perhaps he abstained from it—and he often rose from his bed at midnight to begin working. Since he had become Pope in 1198, he had already dispatched more than five thousands letters dealing with a wide range of religious and social issues, the most important of which he had personally dictated. While only fifty-four years old, he possessed enormous talent and intelligence. Now, fifteen years into this new century, he was the most powerful man in the Western World.

On this predawn morning he paced back and forth in front of a huge map of the world that covered an entire wall of his study. "It was wise," he thought to himself as he waited for his secretaries to complete several sentences he had dictated, "for me to have firmly established the title of the Pope as Vicar of Christ instead of Vicar of Peter, which most previous popes have used. As the Vicar of Christ, I can more freely institute my choice of who will be bishops to succeed the apostles. The title also gives me the authority to bring to their knees those recalcitrant bishops who might otherwise be tempted to think of themselves as my equal. Moreover, as Vicar of Christ, I have full power over kings and emperors. Christ was both high priest and king of kings, and as his vicar, naturally, I share in both offices."

Noticing one of his secretaries yawning, his pen having paused to rest on the page, the Pope ceased his reflection and immediately returned to his rapid dictation. When the two secretaries were again busily writing, he again turned around to look at the great map on the wall behind him. To the far right were the vast empty spaces of Russia, which his agents had reported were being overrun by Mongolian tribes led by the great khan called Genghis. Pope Innocent reached up with his finger and traced the path of the rapid moving cavalry of Mongols

that had annihilated the powerful Tartars. As he studied the map, it came alive for him. He envisioned Genghis Khan's golden-yellow banners marked with a blue-gray wolf flapping in the wind, leading the advancing barbarian hordes at a pace that was said to exceed a hundred miles a day! "Unbelievable, such speed," he thought, "and our agents report that their cavalry is followed by an army of more than one hundred thousand fighting men shouting, 'Take no prisoners!' These barbarians will not stop when they reach the frontier of Christendom," he thought as he moved his finger along the map to the location of Poland and Hungary, "unless their forces are occupied elsewhere. Fortunately, the reports say that the great khan has struck first at the Muslims of Central Asia, and our spies say they will likely sweep southward toward the Caspian Sea, attacking Islam."

As the Pope stood lost in thought in front of the giant floor-to-ceiling map, the two weary secretaries relaxed, grateful for a brief pause. "Perhaps the great Genghis Khan," he pondered, "is an answer to our prayer, for if he can keep the armies of Islam engaged on their eastern front, then we may be victorious in recapturing the Holy Land. Otherwise, if he turns west, I will have to mount a crusade against those Mongol heathens to save Poland and. . . ." His thoughts trailed off as he began slowly moving his finger westward across Germany, France and the Low Countries. "I have enough troubles in these lands," he thought, stabbing his finger on the kingdoms of France and Germany, "with those festering pockets of heresy and anti-clericalism. Presently they are disorganized and often war against one another, but if they ever became united! Mother of God, what a threat that would be to the Church! So this new council that I have called to reform the abuses in the Church is of critical importance. We must enact the sternest laws possible to reform the corruption in the Church, laws that absolutely bind priests to their clerical celibacy. The council must also renew the practice of the sacraments and stamp out the horrible abuse of fake relics and all the other stupid superstitions that so readily pass for Christian faith."

Turning around, he saw a secretary nodding off, and so in a loud, urgent voice he said, "This letter is addressed to His Lordship Jacques Duese, Bishop of Montbeliard. My Lord Bishop, we write to you in regard to the issue of your failure to observe *visitatio liminum apostolorum,* your canonically prescribed periodic personal visit to Rome. As you know, it is required by law that every bishop must meet personally with the Pope within the defined time period. Since you have failed. . . ."

*A*s the opening of the Fourth Lateran Council approached, the population of Rome began swelling with bishops, abbots, and nobility from all over Europe pouring into the Eternal City. While this council's scope, vision, and composition was historic, as with every general council the bishops quickly formed themselves into three groups. The first group was composed of the conservative, traditionalist bishops who wanted to see nothing change in the Church. Their champion was Cardinal Uzielli, who had formed an alliance with the two archconservative Cardinals, Ghislieri and Ferretti. The second group was made up of progressive bishops led by Cardinals Ugolino and Montino. These leaders were eager to correct the corruption in the Church and to respond in creative ways to the new era in history they saw unfolding. Supporting them from behind the scenes was the aged Cardinal Cecnio Savelli. Although Savelli had remained silent through most of the preparatory meetings for the council, making it difficult to know precisely where he stood on the key issues, his influence at the Council was not to be underestimated. The third group consisted mostly of indifferent bishops who might be swayed either way and were more than content to leave Rome to the Romans. For these bishops and abbots the Church didn't extend beyond the boundaries of their own diocese or abbey, and they believed that the less the papal curia and its humming beehive of clerics was involved in their small plot of the vineyard of the Church the better. These bishops and prelates were unconcerned about the particulars of the council's new legislation as long as any new laws enacted did not affect them personally.

Cardinal Ugolino invited Francesco and his two traveling companions to lodge with him while they attended the Lateran Council. Francesco insisted on sleeping in the servants' quarters, to which Ugolino graciously agreed. He was most eager to have the liberal and renewal-conscious bishops attending the council personally meet Francesco of Assisi and Dom Dominic de Guzman of Caleruega in Spain. He also prearranged for a private meeting between these two reformers who had never met each other.

In the evenings before the council officially began, Ugolino held gatherings in his home for specially invited bishops and cardinals. Among them was Cardinal Savelli, who made it a point to visit with

Francesco and Dominic. He told these young preachers that he saw in them a hope to bring back to the faith those now called heretics who had left the Church solely because of its corruption and the abuses of its clergy. Like Montino and Ugolino he hoped that the labors of these two holy apostolic preachers wedded to reforms to be enacted by the council would bring home the lost sheep.

"*F*ood, so much and so delicious," Brother Leone exclaimed one night as they sat in the servants dining room. "I've never sat at such a wonderful table. Ah, how these Romans love to eat and drink."

"Think of it, Francesco," chimed in Pietro. "If the servants eat like this, what must the meals at the cardinals' table be like?"

"While he may provide a lavish table for his guests," Francesco replied, "my heart tells me that at his private meals he eats very simply." He picked up the napkin next to his plate and unfolded it, causing Leone to smile, for he had never before seen Francesco use any such refinement of the wealthy, as common people simply used their sleeves to wipe their mouths. "Even if he is a Cardinal Prince of the Church, I sense in him a man who strives to live the Gospel. Why else, brothers, would he invite the likes of us to find shelter under his roof?" As he chuckled, he began heaping bread, meat, and pasta into his napkin.

"A late-night snack, brother?" asked a servant who was sitting across the table from him.

"Yes, one grows hungry after the sun sets," Francesco said with a laugh as he proceeded to reach over and take his companions' napkins, filling both of them with food as well. As everyone looked on in disbelief, Francesco added, "We natives of Assisi are notorious in Umbria for the size of our midnight snacks."

Brother Leone couldn't wait till the meal was finally over and they had departed from the servants' dinning area so he could ask, "Father Francesco, how could you, of all people, grow so hungry after sunset that you would need to eat such a large snack?"

"The poor of Rome, good Brother Leone!" he answered with a wink. "Not just after the sun sets, they're hungry day and night—and for far more than a snack. This food I collected tonight that's fit for a prince is also fit for them."

Night after night, Francesco collected all the leftover food and table scraps at Cardinal Ugolino's palazzo to give it away to the poor and homeless of Rome. He began with scraps of bread and leftover meat

wrapped up in napkins but soon abandoned the napkins for large cloth bags and baskets. Then he began nightly to collect food from the back kitchen doors of the other prelates and the noble princes of the Eternal City. Rome at night was a dangerous place, and so Leone and Pietro anxiously objected, but to no effect. The poor and homeless Francesco visited each night were the outcasts of the city who begged by day and slept by night in the abandoned ruins of old Roman monuments or in the darkened alleyways cluttered with rotting food, human waste, and garbage. The citizens of Rome considered those whom he fed to be the city's real garbage.

*I*n November of 1215 the first session of Fourth Lateran Council opened with a grand procession into the giant Basilica of St. Giovanni Lateran led by nobles representing every Christian kingdom of Europe and the East and the other distinguished laymen who had been invited. Behind them were the superiors of religious orders, priors, and lord abbots, followed by more than four hundred bishops and seventy-one archbishops, all of whom, one-by-one, took their seats on either side of the main aisle. When these were all in their places, the members of the College of Cardinals entered the assembly. As they passed down the long aisle, various cardinals would nod to this or that bishop. Just inside the doors of the Basilica in one of the last seats was the most newly consecrated bishop, Bishop Carafa of Assisi. As Cardinal Pietro Uzielli walked past him, he turned and nodded toward him with a smile.

When all these dignitaries were in their places on either side of the basilica, trumpets sounded, and all eyes turned toward the front doors as the massive choir intoned the Gloria. Just as the choir completed the phrase "glory to God in the highest," the Vicar of Christ, Pope Innocent III, began to process with great nobility down the aisle lined with rows of hundreds of bishops, archbishops, and cardinals in their white miters and copes. The Pope's massive golden cope was decorated with countless jewels, and on his head he wore the magnificent triple-crowned papal tiara adorned with the most stunning precious stones. This was the first time that Francesco had seen him wearing this three-crown tiara, which symbolized that its wearer was the prince-ruler of the Church Militant, the Church Suffering and the Church Triumphant. The three crowns also signified his absolute authority as teacher, ruler, and sanctifier, and that he was the father of princes and

kings, the ruler, of the world, and the vicar of Christ our Savior on earth. Innocent wore the papal tiara as no Pope before him, with complete confidence that he was, indeed, all of those things it symbolized.

Upon reaching the papal throne at the opposite end of the Basilica, the Pope turned to face the members of this great council and led them in making the sign of the cross and praying the Credo. The choir then intoned the ancient hymn to the Holy Spirit calling down the creative wind and fire of God to renew the earth. Many who were present also hoped the ever fresh and creative Spirit would renew the hearts of the bishops and inspire wise decisions at this universal council representing the entire Church.

"Come, Holy Spirit," Francesco inwardly prayed as he sang the Latin hymn. "O passionate Spirit of God, if you could only come now as you once did on that first Pentecost." He could imagine hundreds upon hundreds of leaping tongues of fire descending in a holy firestorm from the ceiling of the Basilica. "Rest, Fire of Heaven, upon the heads of these successors to the apostles. May your fiery tongues set ablaze those white miters on their heads so they will feel the urgency of the reform needed to heal the Bride of Christ." As he continued singing the words of the hymn, he sighed, "Loving Holy Spirit, sweep down on Portiuncula as well, for she also needs a reformation calling all there to return to and embrace living the Gospel without compromise."

Despite their ardent common prayer, there were many present that day who for religious and political reasons weren't at all eager for the Spirit of God to respond to their invitation to visit them with the Pentecostal chaos of radical change and newness. These resistors to change felt that history was on their side: Roman tradition was fireproof. They knew that centuries of the Vatican bureaucratic machinery wouldn't be overturned by one ecumenical council—or a dozen of them. As to the concern of Pope Innocent and a few cardinals and bishops about the grave danger presented by those Gothic heretics north of the Alps, with their pious ideas about returning to the Gospels—well, the Church had dealt with the likes of them before. The way to respond to them wasn't by instituting reforms for the clergy and throughout the Church. After all, wasn't she the Bride of Christ? How could she be guilty of corruption and sin? No, the best way to deal with these budding heretics in France and Germany was with another kind of fire! Burn enough of them at the stake, and their followers would

disappear like the early morning fog is burned by the heat of the rising sun.

"God help us," sighed Pope Innocent as the hymn to the Holy Spirit ended. With a great rustling of vestments and bobbing of white miters, the bishops all sat down.

Chapter 21

"An entirely new era in the history of the world is dawning," Pope Innocent began the Fourth Lateran Council in a clear, strong voice filled with regal confidence. "Profound and rapid changes are spreading across all of Christendom. A true cultural and social transformation is taking place as the old feudal system collapses and a new social order arises. . . ." Seated behind the last row of bishops on one side of the basilica, Francesco of Assisi nodded as he thought, "The Holy Father speaks very much like my own father, Pietro: 'Indeed, a new class of rich merchants is arising, gone forever is the old, stable order with its three classes of the Church, nobility, and peasants.'"

"Today," the Pope continued, "society is stirred by a spiritual agitation, and the changing conditions of life are but part of a broader and deeper movement of history. These stirrings are having and will continue to have repercussions in the spiritual and sacramental life of the Church."

"'Spiritual agitation,'" thought Cardinal Uzielli as he nervously fingered his large jeweled episcopal ring. "Heresy is a better word! Those agitating for change and newness in the Church are slithering vipers that must be stamped out by every means at hand."

"'Spiritual agitation,'" reflected Cardinal Savelli, whose white hair blended perfectly with his white miter. "Like the turbulence of new wine, the agitation caused by the Spirit's finger is delightfully stirring up the sluggish stew in the pot of Peter. Indeed, as the Pope says, there will be 'repercussions' if the spiritual ferment created by visionaries like Francesco of Assisi and Dominic of Spain and their dynamic religious orders of men and women is allowed to brew." Then the old cardinal

 looked across the nave of the Basilica of San Giovanni, over the top of the rippling waves of white miters. He glanced up toward the ceiling at a large crack that was still visible, even after being plastered over and painted. "That crack was created by an earthquake at the end of the ninth century," Savelli thought smiling. "I wonder if these bishops gathered here today can feel in the events of these times the tremor of an approaching earthquake that will do more than create a large crack or two in the Church. It may well be an earthquake of such magnitude as to split the Church right down the center!" Savelli lowered his gaze from the crack in the ceiling to the bishops and dignitaries seated in tiers across the aisle. There behind the last row of bishops his eyes came to rest on the poor man of Assisi, Francesco Bernadone. The old cardinal smiled again as he reflected on the words of Isaiah, "'See, I am doing something new—remember not the past!' Forgetting the past," he sighed, "will be most difficult for these bishops because the past is the bastion of their claim to power."

"All of society," the Pope continued speaking, "including the Church, has passed from a relatively stable and static state toward a greatly dynamic, expansive, and creative stage. We must be wise stewards, insuring that the new wine of the Spirit is poured not into old wine skins, but into fresh new skins. While still reverencing the old, we must embrace the new."

"'The new wine of the Spirit,'" thought Cardinal Ugolino. "Only with the greatest of caution does one add highly volatile new wine to the old. Yet while it may be unpredictably explosive, unless we do mix the new vintages of such people of vision as Francesco of Assisi and Dominic de Guzman into the old wine skin of the Church, alas that old wine will soon become vinegar!"

"'We must embrace the new,'" Cardinal Montino reflected on the Pope's words. "Yes, and we must embrace it not with suspicion as if it was a viper or an enemy but without hesitation, as one would embrace a lover. My brother cardinal, the crafty, ever-suspicious Uzielli, sees all those who point out the corruption in the Church and live with the radical zeal of the first Pentecost as poisonous vipers that must be destroyed. Uzielli does more than 'reverence the old,' he has canonized it as so sacred as to be untouchable."

Pope Innocent concluded his opening address to the bishops:

"Fathers of the Council, while our vision for the Church is to create new, innovative wineskins to hold the message of salvation, in these

limited weeks of our sessions, we must respond to the grave crisis that has brought us to this Fourth Lateran Council. As Shepherds of Christ inspired by the Holy Spirit, we must enact new and harsh laws to bring the faithful—under the pain of mortal sin—back to the sacraments! We must also decree the sternest possible laws to correct the numerous clerical abuses, especially with regard to the law of celibacy. Moreover, God calls us not to be timid shepherds but to suppress—with brutal force, if necessary—the growing number of renegade heretical groups who spread false and pernicious doctrines that threaten the orthodoxy of the True Faith. Finally, holy urgency for the welfare of the souls of our faithful requires that we rigorously strengthen existing laws to insure their isolation from those noxious Jews and Muslims living in our midst. May the Holy Spirit then guide us with zealous diligence and fraternal consensus to accomplish these much-needed reforms as we now begin this Fourth Lateran Council, in the name of the Father, and the Son and the Holy Spirit."

As the sessions of the council began, even though his old gray tunic was freshly laundered, Francesco felt out of place amidst all the golden splendor of the bishops, the richly, elaborately robed nobility, and the Roman pomp and ceremony of the council. Despite that feeling, he faithfully attended each of the sessions, grateful for the presence of Pietro at his side translating the ecclesiastical Latin spoken by the bishops in their debates over the council's decrees.

Among the seventy new canon laws the council passed was one that required all believers, under pain of mortal sin, to make an oral confession to a priest and receive Holy Communion at least once a year during the Easter season. They also declared as divinely inspired the Greek concept of transubstantiation to define the Holy Eucharist. While Francesco affirmed a more frequent reception of Holy Communion, he failed to understand the need for the new doctrine of transubstantiation.

The bishops also codified the existing laws concerning all Jewish and Muslim nonbelievers living among Christians, decreeing that they must wear identifiable clothing or symbols. When Pietro translated the Latin of this decree, Francesco felt a bad taste in his mouth. He rejected this law as contrary to the will of God—and, indeed, wicked. His heart ached for the new friends he had made on his pilgrimage to Spain, Ali Hasan and Samuel of Barcelona, and all so-called nonbelievers. "Even if they do not believe that Jesus is the Son of God," he thought, "my

friends love the one God and show compassion and kindness to others—even to strangers. So how could they be called nonbelievers?" He recalled Samuel's words about ignorance being the source of war, fear, anger, violence, and prejudice. "Ignorance is the source of this new misguided and foul canon law," he thought, "and great will be the evils spawned by this decision of the apostles' successors. They have forgotten the teaching of the first bishop, St. Peter, that anyone from any nation who is upright, just, and compassionate is acceptable to God!"

The council bishops also condemned as heretics the Waldensians and the Cathars, along with certain teachings of Joachim of Fiore, the Italian mystic who before he died in 1202 called for the Church to be purified and prophesied a soon-approaching age of the Holy Spirit, in which the hierarchy would be replaced by a new order of "Men of the Spirit." Near the end of the council the Pope once again called Christendom to mount a new crusade to liberate the Holy Land. In the presence of all the bishops he boldly declared that he himself would take up the cross and lead the armies on this new crusade.

"How zealous is the Holy Father!" thought Francesco, "His promise to take up the cross himself challenges me to join him on his new crusade. This time, nothing will stop me from going to the Holy Land."

The Great Council, as it was being called, concluded in only two weeks, yet it seemed to Francesco more like two long, penitential months of sitting on those hard benches enduring endless boring hours of debate among the bishops. "Brother Ass," he said, patting his buttocks as he stood up on the last day to leave the basilica, "this council has been a greater penance for me than wielding on myself the discipline of the whip. Surely I've done enough penance to wipe away a hundred years in purgatory." While he was disappointed with many of the new laws enacted at the council, he was grateful for the occasion to meet the Spanish priest Dominic, whose dedication to true poverty and preaching the Gospel caused him to feel a real spiritual kinship.

After the council's solemn closing, many of those attending immediately departed for home while others lingered, reluctant to leave behind the many pleasures of Rome. On his last evening in Rome Francesco observed his nightly custom of visiting the kitchen doors of prelates and nobles to fill the large bags he would take to the unholy bowels of the Eternal City. As he walked the streets generously sharing his food, from out of the shadows of the alleys came children, women, the blind, the lame and stumbling old men whose skin was pulled taut over their bony bodies. Knowing personally the taste of hunger for hope as well as for bread, after emptying his bag, Francesco began to nourish their hearts by singing to them in Italian and French. In the dancing circle of yellow light cast from a single wall-mounted flaming torch that illuminated a dreary, dank back alley, the troubadour of Assisi performed for a crowd of Rome's destitute and homeless. Those gathered around the edge of the circle of light were enthralled by the songs of this barefoot minstrel beggar. His music as well as his feats as a tumbler-magician stole away their sadness and conjured up laughter and joy.

"Again! Do it again! Do it again!" chanted the dirty, ragged children in the crowd after he had strained himself to do one of his old acrobatic tricks of turning handsprings and finally landing on only one hand with his feet spread wide apart in the air.

"Splendidly performed! You're as good as ever," a man's voice declared from out of the darkness of an alleyway behind the crowd, "if, indeed, you're the same man I saw performing that tumbling with such childlike abandon some six years ago."

Francesco strained to see into the darkness, "You are correct, my unseen friend, for I was in Rome about that time. This is only my second visit."

"Back then, just as you are tonight, you were so joyfully happy," replied the voice that remained hidden in the dark shadows. "And because on both occasions you've been dressed as a barefoot beggar, it was not hard to recognize you."

The small gathering began drifting off, sensing the end of the evening's entertainment, as Francesco stepped out of the circle of the torchlight toward the entrance to a pitch-black, narrow lane between two buildings. He caught a glimpse of the figure that had spoken to him as it now withdrew even deeper into the darkness. Francesco wondered if he might be a leper afraid to show his disfigured self.

"Stranger," Francesco called, speaking into the darkness, "that first time when I was here in Rome, where did you and I meet?"

"We didn't. I only saw you briefly from across a room, but that was an experience I've never forgotten."

"You're being very mysterious. I'm intrigued; where in Rome did you first see me?"

"I would prefer not to say."

"I respect your wish. However, you surely would not have spoken to me tonight unless you wanted to make contact. This old heart of mine can see into the darkness where you're hiding, and it sees no ordinary beggar who's hungry for bread. So my heart is asking me, 'What is it that this invisible beggar hungers for?'"

"The impossible!"

"Ah, but with God all things are possible," Francesco said, stepping into the shadows. "So said the angel to Mary the Mother of God, and I've personally found it to be true. So take courage, my friend; tell me, what is this impossible thing for which you hunger?"

At Francesco's invitation a gaunt young man in an old tunic stepped out of the murky shadows. By the light of the street torch Francesco saw that his face was not that of an ugly, disfigured leper. To the contrary, he was very handsome, even if somewhat haggard and stained by the dirt and grime of sleeping in Rome's gutters.

"Believe me, Francesco of Assisi," the man said, "it's impossible because I am a sinner. Oh, I'm aware that holy Rome and all the world is full of sinners, but I'm no ordinary sinner. My sin is so terrible that what I hunger for is unattainable."

"How do you know my name?"

"That day when I first saw you, your name was on every lip. And you made such an impression that I could never forget you."

"Stranger, you say you're no ordinary sinner, yet who among us is an ordinary sinner? In our own unique ways we each fail to love God. Yet sins are not tattoos; they can be removed. If you went to confession and were absolved, then what seems impossible can become achievable."

"I can't; it's too dangerous. I can't take the risk of confessing to a priest—even if they are bound to total secrecy—for it could mean my life. But you, Father Francesco, will you hear my confession?"

"I'm not a priest! The Lateran Council, which just met, decreed that laymen like myself can no longer grant absolution or say Holy Mass, but only ordained priests."

"Then I'll go to hell with my sins, " he said, slinking back into the darkness. Trying one more time to reach out from his edge of despair, he said, "I guess the Church has the right to say who can or cannot perform the ritual of confession, but it can't prevent you from listening to another man's sins, can it?"

Francesco nodded, saying, "I can't argue with your theology. I'm willing to listen to your confession, but. . . ."

"You're a holy man, and everyone says that God hears the prayers of the saints. Once I've confessed, surely you would pray asking God to forgive me, wouldn't you? You were right earlier; what I hunger for is peace of heart. So please feed my hunger to know that my sins are forgiven."

Francesco swallowed as he thought, "This man's soul hangs by a thin thread, and I'm convinced that this evening's encounter has not happened by chance. As Ali Hasan liked to say, it is in just such chance meetings that we're given a taste of the Beloved. So, despite how the new canon laws of the council may interpret confession, this man has asked me to pray for his pardon, and surely I can do that. Our Lord said, 'feed the hungry,' and this man's hunger is for peace in his soul. O God, make this sinner named Francesco an instrument of your peace and reconciliation so that another sinner imprisoned by guilt and shame may be set free."

"Before you agree," the man said as Francesco was about to respond, "you must know what kind of sins you will hear. . . ." Pausing, he swallowed and said, "For I'm a male prostitute!"

"Among the sons of God," Francesco answered, "no matter how grievous or how many one's sins may be, every prodigal is welcomed home with open arms and great love. I fear, however, that this street is too public; so let me suggest that we walk over to the bridge on the Tiber where we can have some privacy."

When they stood alone along the empty embankment of the Tiber River, the man began, "My name is Sebastiano. I was the personal valet of Cardinal Uzielli until. . . . You'll have to be patient, Father Francesco. You see, I've never gone to confession before, so I don't know what ritual words I'm supposed to use."

Francesco reassured him, "When you stand with a contrite heart before God, no ritual words are required—only that you open the spigot of your heart and let it drain out." So, as the flowing melody of the Tiber River wound its way through Rome, Sebastiano knelt before Francesco, and out of his heart drained a torrent of deeds and misdeeds, indignities, guilt, pain, and remorse. When his heart was finally emptied, he bowed his head to his knees and gave out a great sigh, for it felt like seven massive marble blocks had been lifted from his shoulders.

"O ever-generous God, whose mercy flows as endlessly as this river, whose compassion is as eternal as this Eternal City, forgive your son, Sebastiano, who is truly sorry for his sins." With his hands resting on the young man's shoulders, Francesco continued his prayer, "Each time he slipped and fell, O God, you instantly raised him up by your unconditional forgiveness, for as the Divine Lover, your loving mercy is infinite." Then, placing his hands on top of Sebastiano's head, Francesco said, "That you may know with confidence, Sebastiano, that God has granted you full pardon, I repeat to you the words of Christ, 'Your sins are forgiven, go now in peace.'"

Sebastiano grabbed Francesco's hand and kissed it again and again as he wept tears of gratitude and liberation.

"As we part, I say to you," Francesco uttered softly as he raised Sebastiano up to his feet, "what Jesus said to his righteous host when the tarnished woman whose sexual sins he had forgiven washed his feet with her tears and dried them with her hair: 'Her many sins have been forgiven because she has loved much.' God says that to you, Sebastiano. And, as Jesus said to that woman, 'Your faith has saved you. Now, go in peace.'"

"But, Father Francesco, I don't want to go. You've accomplished only half of the impossible reality for which I hungered. I want to become one of your companions."

"You want to become a. . . ."

"I know it's impossible—I mean, after all the horrible things I've done, having sold my body and all . . . but I had to at least tell you, even. . . ."

"Sebastiano, your former sins do not prevent you from joining me and my band of companions who are called the Little Brothers. As for being a prostitute, we've all sold ourselves for something we desired, even if it wasn't for money. I am your brother prostitute, for I've shamefully sold myself by the compromises I've made in my life. Your former way of life isn't the issue. Becoming a Little Brother requires a call from God to give away all your possessions to the poor and to live a life of gospel poverty."

"I've heard no voice from heaven, but something has been hounding me ever since I first saw you in the papal antechamber those many years ago. Don't misunderstand me: I think I fell in love with you on that day. Or maybe I fell in love with love and with that kind of

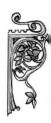

ecstatic joy you exuded. Being thrown penniless out of the cardinal's house into the gutter woke me up, and I realized I've been looking for love in the wrong places. I know this sounds sacrilegious, but when I was having sex with strangers, I began to pray. And my prayer was that God would give me a truly great love in my life. Tonight it became clear how and where I would find that love—as a Little Brother of Assisi, living a life of joy and meaning as do you, Father Francesco. Now I've opened my heart, even if. . . ." On and on Sebastiano rapidly talked. It reminded Francesco of how as a young man he himself had talked with his father. So he let Sebastiano's stream of hopes and fears, dreams and apprehensions flow out of him until he ran dry.

"I accept you, Sebastiano," Francesco said, his voice overflowing with affection. "Henceforth, you shall be known as Brother Sebastiano of the Little Brothers of Assisi. And tomorrow you can accompany me back to Assisi. Now, Brother, the hour is late, come and spend the night with me and two other brothers where we are staying in the servants' quarters of Cardinal Ugolino's residence."

"No, I can't! It will mean my death if I'm recognized anywhere in 'holy' Rome. That's why I lived back there hidden in the slums, where those who live and work in the great houses of the prelates and the wealthy of Rome would never see me. You can't trust anyone, especially those who work in the palazzi of the prelates. I'll sleep tonight under that bridge over there, and tomorrow on your way out of Rome I will meet you and your two brothers about a mile up the road to Spoleto at the shrine of St. Christopher."

"Yes, I do recall that shrine. My brothers and I will meet you there and will be happy to have you join us as we travel homeward. Now, Brother Sebastiano, may God protect you from all evil this night and tomorrow as you sneak out of Rome."

"Father Francesco, before you leave, I have one more thing I want to ask you. It may sound unbelievable, but you're not the only one I've recognized in the slums of Rome. On numerous occasions I am convinced that I've seen His Eminence Cardinal Montino handing out food to the poor and hungry. He wears a long, hooded cloak and is dressed as a common layman! Out of fear of being recognized, I never got close, but I'm sure it was he, for on numerous occasions I'd served him dinner as Cardinal Uzielli's personal valet. Do you think I'm mistaken?"

"I do not believe that your eyes deceived you, Brother Sebastiano, for Cardinal Montino has the eyes of a lover. He loves God and imitates his mysterious Beloved, who often hides his identity when he gifts us."

As Francesco, Pietro, and Leone were meeting Sebastiano at the roadside shrine of St. Christopher, a mile back in Rome a violent storm was exploding in the papal study of the Lateran Palace, where the Pope was standing in front of his great map of the world. That map was a highly detailed, full-color reproduction of the *Mappamundi*, depicting a large round flat world surrounded by an outer ring of water, which according to Scripture represented the one great ocean upon which the earth rested. The rest of the wall beyond the map's outer ring of water was filled with various symbolic biblical creatures, angels, sea dragons, and monsters. In the center of the circular map was the Holy City of Jerusalem, next to the Mediterranean, "the sea of the middle of the earth." The top of the map was east, and at the very top Adam and Eve were pictured enclosed in the Garden of Eden, which was walled in by high mountains and from which four rivers flowed: the Ganges, Nile, Tigris, and Euphrates. The earth was covered with scores of buildings representing all the significant cathedrals in Christendom and all the cities mentioned in the Bible. And, of course, each country, river, and lake from the Bible was also indicated. The earth itself was divided into three parts: Asia to the right, Europe to the left, with Africa at the bottom. England, pictured as a long, narrow island, along with other scattered islands were located at the far left of the circle, with a narrow body of water separating them from the mainland.

As if one of those hideous monsters painted on the *Mappamundi* had suddenly come to life and spouted fire, Pope Innocent angrily shouted, "How dare those English bastards!" The Pope's hands noticeably shook with rage as he read the scroll Cardinal Uzielli had handed him. "By all the saints in heaven, what gall those barbarians have to challenge so blatantly our authority, throwing this Anglo-Saxon gauntlet in the face of Rome."

"I agree, your Holiness," Uzielli replied. "It is a most dangerous precedent for the Church and all of Christendom, and that is why I, along with my colleagues," he added, gesturing toward the other three cardinals, "came immediately to your study as soon our courier arrived from England."

"This Magna Carta that King John has signed," and here the Pope read aloud from the scroll, "'limits the absolute power of the King of England.' My God, this charter threatens the authority of every king by granting rights to the barons and even to their freemen! How utterly audacious of those English barbarians! It was only yesterday that they stopped painting their faces blue and going off to battle stark naked. Now they've gone stark mad!"

"Your Holiness, we . . ." began Uzielli as the Pope turned around to face the giant map on the wall of his study and began pounding his fist on the spot where England was pictured.

"This charter," the Pope said, interrupting Uzielli as he turned around and again began reading from the report, "'insures that no man shall be held in prison for any length of time without granting him a trial in which the verdict will be determined by a jury of his peers.' By *his peers* —my God, is this not a revolt?" The cardinals made no reply to his question as he angrily stomped back and forth in front of the great map on the study wall.

"'All taxes of the Crown,'" the Pope continued reading as he paced, "'shall be collected only by legal means and not by force.' And this document goes on to say that 'it guarantees justice to all free men in the Kingdom.'"

"Your Holiness," said Uzielli, "our agents report that King John was forced to sign that *carta*. They say John twice refused to sign this rebellious document, and only after his barons had raised an army and surrounded him, demanding his signature, did he cease resisting. And finally on June 12 he signed the 'Great Charter' at a place in England they call Runnymede." The Pope whirled around and began thumping his index finger on the island of England in an unspoken question that Cardinal Ugolino proceeded to answer, "It's near Egham, Your Holiness, I understand in a meadow on the south bank of the Thames, west of London."

Seated beside an unoccupied secretary's table was Cardinal Savelli, as usual, keeping his thoughts to himself. "Innocent is a man of contradictions. On one hand he's such a great visionary, and on the other he behaves like an absolute monarch, with no patience for those who threaten his authority or think differently than he does."

"I, Pope Innocent III, the Vicar of Christ declare this so-called Great Charter null and void!" the Pope shouted as his fist hammered at that small dot of Egham as if he was driving a nail into the map. "And

I release King John of England from all obligations to observe any of these sixty-three articles."

"Your Holiness," replied a hesitant Cardinal Ugolino anxiously wringing his hands, "will not history perhaps misperceive such an act as a sign that the Church is an enemy to liberty, even if you. . . ."

"I don't give a damn, Ugolino! I am an enemy of anyone who dares to violate a solemn contract. King John entered into an agreement to be a vassal of the Pope, *my* vassal, and handed over his crown to the papacy in order to have his excommunication lifted! If those barons had wanted relief from King John's heavily enforced taxation and all their other complaints, they first should have come to me, their Liege Lord, to appeal for justice! I, Pope Innocent III, am the feudal Lord of England, Ireland, and all the lands of the English Crown. In their lust for freedom those crude English barons have insulted the Holy See. Furthermore, as every good lawyer knows, by forcing their king to sign under duress they've automatically nullified all the outrageous articles of this rebellious charter. I declare the Magna Carta null and void!"

"Your Holiness," Uzielli replied with delight, "I shall see that your papal declaration nullifying the so-called Magna Carta of June 12, 1215, is dispatched at once to England by our swiftest courier. I applaud this strong stand Your Holiness has taken against libertine laws, especially in these times when heretics boldly claim they need not obey the Pope, their king, or anyone except God! Once the seeds of rebellion granting equality of persons and challenging the rightful authority of the Pope or a king are sown upon the winds," he said, pausing for effect, "horrible beyond imagination will be the resulting apocalyptic harvest of evil."

"I agree with you, Cardinal Uzielli," the Pope replied, his back still turned away from the cardinals as he continued to study the map.

"Thank you, Your Holiness, I applaud your grasp of the gravity of this situation," he replied, "for even now just such ominously evil seeds are also being cast upon the winds in Umbria by Francesco of Assisi. Like the Magna Carta of England, he grants equality to all the members of his order and insists that none shall be superior over the others, that they must all be equal in all things! Our newly consecrated, zealously orthodox Bishop Carafa of Assisi reports that Francesco frequently encourages the common rabble to live in 'the glorious freedom of the children of God.' He lives in the illusion that Italy has been miraculously transported back to the Garden of Eden up there to the top of your map, where it is surrounded by a great wall of mountains."

"Your Holiness, I am sure," Cardinal Ugolino interrupted, "that Brother Francesco, as a faithful son of the Church, uses those words of Holy Scripture within the context of. . . ."

"And his woman disciple, Sister Clare," Uzielli asserted, unwilling to have anyone snag away from him the bone he was chewing on, "has gone even further. It is reported that in her convent all the policies, even daily matters of her community, are decided by the common consent of all the sisters! Holy Father, we have our own seditious Runnymede right here on our doorstep in Assisi, and unless. . . ."

"Yes, yes, Your Eminence," mumbled the Pope as he nodded his head, but his attention wasn't on what Uzielli was saying. He was riveted on his great map of the world as he pondered the consequences of this English Great Charter. "England is far away," he thought, "and my papal decision making the charter null and void will not prevent this new infection from spreading. No one can end a plague by a decree, even if he is the Pope." Slowly he used his finger to trace a line across the map from England to France and then to Germany. "This disease of the common people," he thought, "demanding equality and a voice in how they shall be governed is even now festering in the mouths of heretics in these northern countries. I may be the Vicar of Christ, but I cannot halt this pestilence that some day will surely rob kings and emperors of their power, and perhaps even popes! Uzielli is right. It does appear that Francesco of Assisi is infected by this new sickness of freedom and equality that marks our age." Then, running his finger reflectively across his lips, he thought, "But perhaps he can show us how it can work for the good of the kingdom of God instead of destroying the Church and society."

*F*rancesco, Leone, and Pietro were all eager to return to Portiuncula and be with the brothers again. While they had been away only a little more than a month, it seemed much longer. The long trek back home to Assisi from Rome was shortened, however, by the presence of Sebastiano, whose youthful enthusiasm delighted Francesco. He saw Sebastiano as a sign of hope for his community of the Little Brothers.

"Father Francesco, I'm new to this life and only a beginner in prayer, so would you teach me how to pray?" asked Sebastiano.

"Brother Sebastiano," he smiled, even though his ears stung at being called 'Father,' "when it comes to prayer, we're all beginners like you. Yet if we only open our eyes as we walk this dusty road toward Spoleto and see that great presence in the faces of the other travelers on the road, in the trees, flowers, and those white puffy clouds drifting overhead—even in the dust beneath our bare feet—then we're praying."

"What great presence?" asked Sebastiano.

"What our Jewish friends call the *Shekhinah*," Francesco answered, making a broad sweeping arc with his hand, "the invisible presence, the glory, the radiance of God that fills all of creation." Then he stopped, stood still, and spread his arms out wide as he inhaled deeply before beaming a luminous smile. "She's everywhere, Sebastiano, as a wise and holy old Jew told me in Barcelona! It is her invisible breath that causes the glowing embers of lovers' hearts to burst into roaring flames. She is the comforting presence of God that scoops up into her warm wings the weary, lost, and homeless."

"She?" Sebastiano asked, eagerly looking around.

"Yes, my beloved Sebastiano, for the sons and daughters of Abraham, God's *Shekhinah* is feminine! Isn't it wondrous that the Father's glory is a Mother?"

The four brothers walked on in silence, reflecting on the numerous ways in which they had personally experienced the *Shekhinah*. Although they didn't say it aloud, Francesco's old friends Pietro and Leone and his newest friend Sebastiano knew they had encountered the *Shekhinah* in Francesco's warm, loving brown eyes. The glorious mystery of God shone out of them with the shimmering sheen of the sun. For his part, Francesco was far away, thinking about saintly Samuel of Barcelona and his beloved friend Ali Hasan. His heart pained him as he worried about those decrees of the Lateran Council that would force all nonbelievers to wear some shameful sign or identifying dress, making these men he loved easier targets for hate and violence.

*U*pon arriving at Portiuncula, Francesco was surprised to find it almost as crowded as Rome, except not with bishops and nobles. As the four brothers crested the hill, Francesco's heart felt crushed at the sight of the great swollen lake of gray habits encircling the small church of Saint Mary of the Angels. Grasping his heart, he moaned, "Dear

God, what am I do? The number of brothers increases every day. How will I manage to feed and care for so many men?"

As he returned to daily life at Portiuncula, he found that while the task of feeding, clothing, and housing this large army of brothers was colossal, far more difficult was the predicament of how to reconcile the three divisions that had sprung up among the brothers. The largest group favored abandoning the original harsh rule of his unconditional Gospel poverty, finding little spiritual value in living a life of poverty harsher than that of peasants. These men looked to Brother Elias as their leader, as he was eager to introduce a more relaxed rule of life that would attract more followers. The second group was composed of most of his original followers along with the more idealistic new members who were eager to follow Francesco in his radical poverty and penitential life. The third group was composed of those who had joined partly because they were attracted by Francesco's radical poverty, but they were also anticlerical. Their idea of poverty included being poor of the Church, the sacraments, and especially the priestly clergy. Francesco suspected that prior to joining the Little Brothers many of these men may have belonged to splinter groups of Cathars and Waldensians in northern Italy. What frightened him most about this third group was the belief they expressed in a mandatory poverty for bishops and monks. If priests and prelates didn't voluntarily give away their wealth to the needy, these radical brothers proposed that it be taken from them at sword point, if necessary, and given to the poor.

Feeling overwhelmed by the divisions in the brotherhood and the mountain of practical details he faced in administering his mushrooming order, Francesco frequently sought to escape to another mountain, Mount Subasio. There were many caves in a densely wooded area up the mountain, just east of Assisi. One of them, which Francesco named L'Eremo, became the hermitage to which he often retreated seeking guidance in prayer and solitude.

One day, during a lengthy period of solitude there, he heard the voice of Brother Leone coming up the mountain shouting, "The Pope has died, the Pope has died!" Francesco had faintly heard the tolling of bells from the churches of Assisi but did not know for whom they tolled.

"Pope Innocent has died," Leone wept as he came running up to his hermitage. "Our good friend and benefactor has gone to heaven."

"How is that possible? He was only fifty-five. . . ."

"True—and tragic. News has reached Assisi that on July 16, while visiting in Perugia busily working on the details of organizing his new great crusade, he was struck down by a fever and died just a few days later. Imagine, it was only eight short months ago that we saw him in Rome at the closing of the great Lateran Council, and now death has taken him. What a loss to the Church—and to our order as well—as he was our patron and protector. I'm sorry to interrupt your retreat, Father Francesco, but Brother Elias insisted that I come at once and inform you."

"You did what was right, Brother Leone, as did Brother Elias. I will return at once with you to Portiuncula to join the brothers in praying for the soul of the Pope. Far more than ordinary men like us, and especially when death comes like a thief in the night, dead popes need our prayers."

As the two of them hurried back to Portiuncula, Francesco was wrapped in worry. And so he prayed, "O Gracious God, what do you now have in store for the Church and especially for our brotherhood? How precarious is our continued existence, depending on the choice of the cardinal to be elected as the next Pope. I have so much faith in men like Cardinals Ugolino and Montino. But help us, O God, if the cardinals choose Pietro Uzielli as the next Pope, for surely that will mean the end of the Little Brothers."

Only a week or so later, the bells of the Cathedral of San Rufino began jubilantly peeling, a sign everyone interpreted as an indication that the College of Cardinals had elected a new Pope. Portiuncula hummed with excitement and speculation as the brothers waited for a messenger to come from Assisi with word of who had been elected the new Vicar of Christ.

"We have a Pope! We have a Pope!" the messenger shouted. "Only two days after the death of Innocent III, the cardinals achieved the necessary two-thirds majority. The new Pope has taken the name Honorius III, and. . . ."

"Tell us quickly," pleaded Francesco. "Which cardinal was elected Pope? Do you know his name?"

"Yes, his former name was Cardinal Cecnio Savelli. We hear he's an old man, very quiet—holy, but reserved. Everyone is surprised, since so little is known about him."

"Allah akbar!" Francesco shouted enthusiastically, forgetting the brothers who stood around him. "God is great," he quickly added,

having seen the shock in the eyes of his brothers at his praising the new Pope in Arabic. "Let us give thanks, brothers, for God has indeed blessed us with a good and holy man as our new Pope! I had the privilege of meeting Cardinal Savelli when I was in Rome for the Lateran Council. Yes, he may be elderly in terms of age, but his ideas are very youthful, for he's a man who gives his ear to the Holy Spirit. Our friend Cardinal Ugolino arranged for me and the Spanish priest Dominic, who is a mendicant like us, to meet privately with Cardinal Savelli. He asked us many questions and encouraged both of us to remain faithful to our visions, telling us how he shared the dreams for the reform of the Church initiated by Pope Innocent III. Brothers, our prayers have been answered—let us all sing a joyful *Te Deum* in thanksgiving."

The next year, 1217, the feast of Pentecost, which fell on May 5, was chosen as the date for the general assembly of all the brothers to initiate the First General Chapter of the Little Brothers of Assisi. As thousands of brothers from all over Italy gathered at Portiuncula, Francesco told Bernardo that he felt like the prophet Moses in the desert facing the vast multitudes of the Israelites at the Exodus.

"How can I feed all these thousands of followers?" he said. "I am no Moses, no miracle worker who can call down from the skies daily showers of manna. I'm certainly not the Lord Jesus, who was able to multiply a few loaves of bread and a couple of fish to feed the five thousand." Though Bernardo tried to comfort him, Francesco felt overwhelmed by the urgency of having to feed and care for his thousands of followers without placing a great burden on the people of Assisi and the surrounding villages. He turned over to Brother Elias the problem of rescuing the gathering of this First General Chapter from total disaster and fled to the far edge of the Portiuncula encampment to pray.

"O God, have mercy on me, and let this bitter cup pass," he cried out as he knelt in prayer. "I'm only a simple man and have no skills to organize and provide for the necessities of such a vast multitude. I'm no Moses who can divide and subdivide, who can appoint seventy-two wise elders and sub-elders to manage the multitude. O God, rescue me!"

Although Brother Elias's personality was such that most brothers found him a difficult man to love, he indeed had a genius for detail,

organization, and delegating work, and his leadership was just what was needed at this moment in time. Under his efficient direction, the first General Chapter proceeded smoothly, and much communal work was accomplished. On the final day the brothers voted to send some of their number to preach the Gospel outside of Italy. Those who volunteered were to be divided into pairs and travel to France, England, Spain, Tunis in Africa, and Syria.

At the conclusion of the chapter Francesco shocked everyone when he resigned as the leader of the Little Brothers. "I am totally unfit to lead you," he said as he stood before them with tears running down his face. "God did not give me the brains to organize and make plans for tomorrow. If I have to administrate, I'm a fool, a clumsy clown; and when it comes to delegating, I'm a disastrous dunce. Now, my beloved friends, from among our brothers you must elect one who will be your new leader."

While Elias simply smiled, many pleaded with Francesco to withdraw his resignation. However, after many failed efforts to get him to change his mind, they held an election. When all the votes were counted, Francesco was relieved to hear that they had elected the capable Brother Pietro Catanii, his old and dear friend from the very beginning. At the news, Brother Elias was deeply disappointed. Embarrassed that he wasn't chosen as the brothers' new leader, Elias immediately volunteered to go on mission to faraway Syria.

In the turmoil of Elias's declaration, Francesco surprised the gathering with an announcement of his own.

"The faith of the people of France has grown cold!" announced Francesco. "And since French blood is in my veins, I am volunteering to go there to help rekindle the great fire of love for God among the French people. I know the language and so does Brother Jacques Coeur. So I ask that, if he's willing, he be assigned as my companion." Brother Pietro approved, though he knew that there were many who would have loved to accompany Francesco, such as Brothers Leone, Giles, Bernardo, and a number of the newer brothers.

Having nothing to pack, Francesco and Jacques departed the very next day, taking the road out of Portiuncula that led north toward Florence and then beyond to France. Away from the thorny bramble bush of management and division within the order and once again walking the open road with his old traveling companion, Francesco's heart gushed over with joy. However, the day after arriving in Florence, his joy was quickly stolen from him. As they were preparing to leave the city, a messenger arrived from Cardinal Ugolino, who was visiting Florence at the time. The message he delivered was brief: "Father Francesco, you must come and see me at once. It is most urgent."

Francesco hurried to meet his patron, Cardinal Ugolino, worried about what new problems might be brewing in Rome. "Father Francesco, my dear friend," the cardinal began when they were together in private. "What is this I hear that you are going away on a mission to France? You are needed in Assisi far more than in France. Your presence with your brothers at Portiuncula is absolutely essential to insure that your holy work will not be led astray by some of the more . . . ah . . . radical elements among your new members. And the others need your inspiration. Now, please, you must turn around and go back to Assisi at once."

"Your Eminence, I know that as a bishop and shepherd God speaks to me through you, but, alas, these ears cannot bear to hear your message. How can I return to Assisi? Look at me: I'm a poor man— poor in the skills required to manage all the daily problems, poor in the talent to resolve conflicts, poor in balancing the day-to-day details of organizing and administrating such a large community. I never dreamed. . . ."

"The large numbers are a sign, Francesco, that so many good men and women are eager to dare to live the life of the Gospels. I believe it is an obvious sign of God's blessing upon you and your vision. Indeed, you never dreamed or designed it, but the Spirit of God did. And that creative Spirit has used you as an instrument to stir up the spiritual imaginations not just of a handful, but of thousands. Yes, thousands— and I assure you, this is only the beginning!"

Francesco slumped forward in his chair, on the verge of tears, with his head sunk in his hands. "Oh, how I had so hoped," he thought, "that I could escape from Assisi by going to France, perhaps to be martyred there trying to reconcile the heretical Albigensians. Even in the brief time I've been away, my heart has been made joyful again by traveling, meeting new people, being a wandering minstrel beggar— being free."

"You must know that I speak not just for myself, Francesco," said the cardinal. "I know for a fact that His Holiness Pope Honorius, if he knew you were leaving Italy, would want you back at Assisi. The hope you enkindled in him during the Fourth Lateran Council burns even

brighter today. So, in the name of Pope Honorius, your Holy Father, Christ's Vicar on Earth, I beg you to return."

"But, Your Eminence, if I return, whatever will I do? I'm no leader; I possess not even minimum skills to administer. Moreover, they've elected a new leader, the brilliant and talented Brother Pietro. He doesn't need to have my old shadow hanging over him. Nor am I a great preacher versed in theological knowledge or skills of oratory. If I return, what will I do?"

"Pray, Francesco, and God will tell you what to do."

For some reason, at that moment Francesco remembered Ali Hasan. He swallowed deeply and became a Muslim, "one who surrenders to the wishes of God," and bowed to the wishes of Cardinal Ugolino. He said that he would return to Assisi.

*T*he next morning Francesco and Jacques began walking back to Assisi. Several times Francesco sat down, telling Jacques that he just wanted to look around and drink in the beauty of the countryside. Jacques was quite sure that his real reason was the need to rest, for he looked exhausted. Jacques had already noticed that the day before they arrived in Florence Francesco seemed more tired than usual. When Jacques asked him about it, Francesco confessed that their walking over the past days seemed to drain his strength. He said he feared that his old Perugian marsh sickness was returning. Their journey from Florence back to Assisi took almost twice as long because of his need to stop frequently and rest. Jacques had heard Francesco's painful story of his shameful return from Spoleto, and he wondered if Francesco's great reluctance to return home now in similar circumstances was also draining on him. "I can understand it if it's more than marsh fever that's making Francesco weary," he thought one day as they sat resting alongside the road. "If I were him, I'd be embarrassed to face the brothers so soon after leaving on our missionary trip to France. It can't help but be a painful encore of his return from Spoleto to Assisi after he had gone off to war for the Pope, even if the voices he heard this time belong to a cardinal."

Francesco was similarly deep in thought: "I should be skilled at looking stupid, yet here I am devastated at once again returning to Assisi a failure. It makes little difference that a cardinal speaking in the name of the Pope has asked me to turn around with my tail between my legs and go home—to me it feels the same as Spoleto. My old

marsh fever makes me fatigued, but I'm also sick and tired of the whole mess I created back at Portiuncula. O God, I feel lost, and my poverty weighs too heavily on me. Help me!"

As the mountain fortress city of Perugia appeared in the distance, Francesco proposed to Jacques that they go up into the city to pray at the tomb in the basilica where Pope Innocent III was buried. The two men knelt at the tomb as Francesco poured out his gratitude to the once powerful pontiff, whose heart had so longed for reform of the Church and who had blessed and protected the infant community of the Little Brothers. As he prayed, he felt a strange mixture of sensations. The pain of his old wound of imprisonment in Perugia so many years ago blended with his pain at the death of Innocent and the deaths of the other significant parental figures in his life—his mother, father, Bishop Guido, and Padre Antonio—creating a profound sense of his own dissolution and death. Yet he sensed something more than the draining of his life dream and his life energy; there was also a strange sense of peace. Then he saw in his mind's eye an image of the crucifix from the little chapel of San Damiano, and he rested in a prayer of communion with his dying Lord.

*F*rancesco's early return surprised his brothers at Portiuncula, and while they covered his embarrassment with their great joy at his return, he didn't stay long. Kneeling in front of Brother Pietro, he begged him for permission to go on retreat to his beloved L'Eremo on Mount Subasio. Cardinal Ugolino had told him that when he returned all he needed to do was pray. So he prayed and prayed, fasted and did penance in the solitude of his cave hermitage. Two weeks later he reappeared at Portiuncula beaming with joy at the noon meal, telling the gathered brothers he was hungry enough to eat a horse.

"Father Francesco, it's a taste of heaven to see you again," said young Brother Sebastiano, rushing to embrace Francesco before he could sit down at the table. "Whenever you are with us, it's like having the sun break through the clouds on a dreary, cloudy day."

Francesco grinned broadly at his enthusiastic and affectionate welcome. Francesco had finally surrendered trying to prevent the brothers from addressing him as "Father," especially the younger ones like Sebastiano. While he was only thirty-six years old, his body felt more like sixty-six, an age old enough to be a grandfather, no less a

father. He also looked far older than his actual age, since his spartan life and harsh penances were collecting heavy taxes on his body.

"The sun always shrines gloriously on me," he replied, sitting down, "whenever I see your smiling face, Brother Sebastiano. What a joy you and all the rest of you are to this old man," he said as he spread out his arms to include the other young brothers nearby. "You are a great treasure; I am so glad that you've cast your lot with this old clown of God and the rest of us wandering beggars." Francesco slid over on his bench, making room for Sebastiano and asked, "Now, tell me, Brother, how's your new life as a Little Brother of Assisi?"

"I love it! But I need help, Father Francesco, as do several of my friends among the newer brothers. We have lots of questions about how one can truly live the Gospel, and we feel we have so much to learn about how to pray. If you could. . . ."

"Brother Sebastiano," inserted Brother Bernardo, who was seated across the table, "don't pester Father Francesco. He's too busy to talk with you young brothers. I'll find one of the older brothers to instruct you in prayer. Father Francesco is only here briefly for a visit from his solitude. His solitary praying is essential, for his powerful prayer stirs up the wind of the Holy Spirit that fills to the full each of our sails, as well as inspiring all the brothers out on missions."

"Thank you, Brother Bernardo, for your concern for my solitude and your appreciation of its value," Francesco said with a broad smile, "but I'm not too busy to speak to these young men about the things that delight my heart. Besides, Brother Sebastiano isn't a pest; he's an answer to a prayer."

"Me, an answer to a prayer?" asked a stunned Sebastiano, as he and a surprised Bernardo wondered what intentions Francesco had been praying for.

Late that afternoon Francesco sat on a grassy mound under a canopy of tree branches in front of a semicircle of fifteen or so younger brothers, along with a few old friends from the beginning days. That group gathered in the woods could have been a great multitude if all the brothers who wanted to hear him speak had been allowed to attend. Francesco had carefully limited the numbers present at any one time, for he in no way wanted to appear as some sort of great master of prayer or some peasant pope speaking with great authority on weighty matters of God and how to live the Gospels.

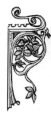

"Father Francesco, we've all heard," Sebastiano began, "that you practice bodily penances and believe in their great spiritual value. Could you say something to us about penance?"

"Let me respond with a question, Sebastiano. Do you complain about the weather—how hot or how cold it is?"

"Yes, doesn't everyone?"

"Well, don't! Now, your next question?"

"You are always so joyful, Father Francesco," said another young brother. "How can I always be joyful like you?"

"Be always grateful—whatever happens."

"How often shall we fast?" asked a brother who was new to the order but middle-aged.

"*How often* isn't as important as *how* to fast. When you fast, do so with all the joy of a bridegroom on his wedding night."

After a brief ripple of laughter at that paradoxical example of happiness, one of the younger men asked, "We know you are dedicated to poverty, Father Francesco, but what is the greatest poverty?"

"Never to have discovered the kingdom of God within yourself—and outside yourself," he said, spreading his arms out wide to encompass all the beauty of creation that surrounded them.

With wit and wisdom he responded to the questions of the young brothers in answers as brief and simple as strands of straw. When one of them finally asked about prayer, he didn't answer. He simply closed his eyes and seemed to sink into a silence somewhere deep inside himself. The brothers seated around him at first were restless, wondering if he had suddenly drifted off or become lost in some deep thought. Slowly, however, one by one, his listeners found themselves being drawn into his prayerful silence until they also were completely absorbed in peaceful stillness. After about half an hour Francesco began humming, ever so softly at first, then louder, bringing them up out of the deep well of holy silence, until all of them had opened their eyes and were engaged in a communion of smiles.

Leone turned to Pietro and said, "We've just had our own Sermon on the Mount. And, typical of Francesco, it wasn't on a great mountain, but only on a little mound."

As everyone followed Francesco when he began walking away from the grassy mound, Sebastiano stopped the community leader, asking, "Brother Pietro, may I walk with you? I want to ask you about a most unusual experience I had as we were seated back there in silence with

Father Francesco. When we began sitting in silence, my head was crowded with an endless parade of thoughts, but slowly my mind became still, as if his silence was somehow flowing directly into me. Beyond stillness, my heart seemed to vibrate gently with the same light and love as I imagine his heart does. It felt as if I had crossed some threshold into a new place of . . . of . . . awareness. Brother Pietro, did I imagine all that, or did it really happen?"

"You didn't imagine it, Brother Sebastiano! Over the years, many of us original brothers have spoken to each other about feeling a kind of direct communion with his peace, his holiness. I myself have had that experience! When I've asked Francesco about it, he told me it was caused by the enormous power of deep prayer, the ability of sacred silence to resonate in the hearts of those united with God. We know that he is a finely tuned instrument of that communion, and personally I feel that being such a simple instrument may be the highest expression of teaching and preaching."

Sebastiano reflected, "I now understand why Father Francesco said that my request for him to teach us how to live the Gospel and deepen our prayer was an answer to his prayer. Watching his face today, it was clear that while he feels a failure at organization, he nonetheless can profoundly inspire and influence others. Those who exercise authority have great power, but that power pales before the kind of holy influence that can shape lives and hearts."

Several days later, Brothers Leone and Francesco went off to preach at the nearby village of Bettona. Arriving on the Feast of Saint Mark, they found the altars in the churches draped in funeral black and the streets clogged with great processions of citizens waving large crosses wrapped in black cloth to commemorate those who had died trying to rescue the Holy Land. Over the loud lamentations for those crusaders who had died, many in the crowd shrieked even more loudly for the deaths of all Saracens, proclaiming that all the infidels must be expelled from land of our Lord. Leone agreed with Francesco that this was not the day to preach about the peace of Christ to the people of Bettona, and they turned around to go home.

"Leone, those demonstrations back there mourning people who have lost their lives in the Crusades made me long to pin on myself the Cross of the Crusades," Francesco said as they walked toward Assisi, "not as a warrior but as a pilgrim of peace. By going to the Holy Land,

perhaps in some small way I can help fulfill the pledge of our great and dear departed friend Innocent III."

"Father Francesco, you are an old friend—and you are getting older! You can't go to the Holy Land," Leone said, sadly placing his arm around Francesco's shoulder. "I know your heart longs to go there, but you've been so fatigued recently by the return of your old marsh fever. And even if you were well enough for such a difficult journey, it would be far too dangerous—not to mention the fact that the Pope would order you home as soon as he learned of it."

"I'm feeling better each day, Leone. Did I not walk all the way to Bettona with more vigor than did you, old friend? My heart is shouting—can't you hear it screaming, 'Go on the crusade.' I must obey my heart. As for such a journey being dangerous, I'll take along as a companion my own Saint Christopher—Brother Jacques! He's strong as an ox, and as a converted highwayman he knows all the dangers of the road. He's more than able to protect me. I know, Leone, that you would like to accompany me, as you did when we went to Rome for the Lateran Council, but I need you here to tell the brothers where I've gone. After I've left, you can first tell our servant brother Pietro, who is now our leader, and some of our old friends. But promise me, Leone, not to say a word until after I've been gone long enough to be aboard a ship for the Holy Land. I do not want to be forced to return home a failure for a third time. I have enough wounds already from my fiasco in Spoleto and my mission to France. So, please, Leone, let this be our secret."

"I'm opposed to it, but I promise to keep your secret until you are well gone. But please consider, Father Francesco, that you are not a well man, and Brother Jacques can't prevent you from getting seasick—or do you plan to walk on the water to the Holy Land?"

"I confess, old friend, that what I fear most in going off on a crusade isn't losing my life to the Saracens, it's losing my stomach to the tossing waves. Yet seasickness, plague, or whatever may come, I'm determined to take up the cross and go to the Holy Land."

The day before he and Jacques were to sneak away from Portiuncula in the dark of night, Francesco went to say farewell to Sister Clare. As he shared the secret of his plans, Clare wept with anguish at the thought that he might never return from his crusade. Promising to keep his secret, she also promised that even if he did not return she would remain faithful to their mutual dreams. Leaving San

Damiano, he walked up the hill to Assisi, proceeding directly to the wine shop of Emiliano Giacosa. Francesco gasped in disbelief as he entered the Giacosa wine shop, thinking he was having a mystical vision as he was welcomed by an image of Emiliano as youthfully muscular and handsome as he was twenty years ago!

"Emiliano, what kind of black magic have you practiced," gasped Francesco, "to be able to turn time backward so many years?"

"Father Francesco, I'm not Emiliano! I'm Francesco Giovanni, his eighteen-year-old son. Don't you recognize me?"

"Of course; how silly of me, Francesco. Forgive me. It seems these old eyes are failing me, but they're not completely to blame. You so resemble your father at your age."

"Yes he does, dearest Francesco," Emiliano replied as he came from the back of the wine shop. "Each time I look at my son, it's like looking in a magical mirror that causes time to flow backward. But you, my old and dear friend, how wondrous it is to see you again here in our wine shop. As we did so often long ago, shall the two of us go down to our secret Giacosa rendezvous in the wine cellar and talk late into the night over cups of good wine?"

"*Caro mio,* how my heart would enjoy that, but today my time is as slim as a Lenten meal. Still, I had to come and see you, for I want to share a secret with you." Emiliano led him back to a quiet place in the rear of his wine shop. There the two sat on stools, and Francesco told his childhood friend that at midnight he was secretly leaving to go to Ancona to board a ship that would take him on a crusade to the Holy Land. Emiliano was shocked and also saddened—not so much because he might never see his friend again due to the danger of his journey, but because it was impossible for him to leave his business behind and accompany Francesco on his adventure. When Emiliano asked him how a man of absolute poverty planned to pay for his passage to the Holy Land, Francesco replied, "Old friend, I haven't even thought about that detail, but I don't need to, for God will provide! Now, tell me the latest news of our Third Order of the Lay Brothers and Sisters of Penance."

"By the grace of God our members daily increase, as does their influence for peace and good here in Umbria. I will tell you more, but first allow me to be a proper host and go down to the cellar to fetch a couple of cups and a bottle of the finest Giacosa wine."

Upon his return, along with the bottle of wine, Emiliano placed a fat leather bag on the table.

"There, *caro mio,* is the money you'll need for your passage to the Holy Land! Don't refuse it, for it is my way of being your companion on the crusade."

"Emiliano, I can't take your hard-earned money. God will provide for my needs once I reach the seaport."

"God couldn't wait! The coins in that leather bag are from God, only they come to you through my hands. The giver of the gift remains the same."

Just then young Francesco Giovanni stepped in and said, "Father, I couldn't help overhearing. I wasn't eavesdropping; when you returned from the cellar, you were speaking louder. Please, Father, I'd love to go off on the crusade. Will you give me permission to accompany Father Francesco to the Holy Land? I'm eighteen now and strong enough to protect him. And as his companion, I would learn so much from him. Please."

"No, my son, your father needs you here," Emiliano said, "and after the death of your mother and sister I couldn't bear losing you as well. I share your desire, but it isn't possible—even though I couldn't think of anything better for you than to become an intimate friend of my dearest friend in life."

Then Emiliano said that he and his son would promise not to say a word about Francesco's secret departure on the condition that Francesco would solemnly promise to return to Assisi and be the godfather of his godson's son. Answering the question that filled Francesco's eyes, Emiliano told him that young Francesco wasn't married yet but soon would be. It was only a matter of time, for he was one of most handsome and desirable bachelors in all of Assisi. At the door of the wine shop, Francesco gave young Francesco a hug and whispered his hope that he would find a good, Godly, and ravishingly beautiful woman for his wife. Then the two old friends held each other in a long, fervent farewell embrace that they sealed with a kiss. As Francesco went off skipping down the street, humming a tune, Emiliano put his arm around his son's shoulders, saying, "Francesco, may you be as fortunate as your father to have formed a profound friendship with someone as wonderful as Francesco of Assisi."

SEVERAL DAYS LATER, BROTHERS JACQUES AND FRANCESCO boarded a ship in Ancona, an Italian harbor northeast of Assisi. The ship was bound for the port of Acre in the Holy Land, and from there it was scheduled to sail westward down the coast to the crusaders' encampment at Damietta, near the mouth of the Nile River.

"At last, Brother Jacques," Francesco said as the crew hoisted the anchor and the wind and the tide began to move the vessel out of the harbor. "I'm drunk with joy to be finally on my way to the Holy Land." He began dancing a little jig on the deck and chanting a refrain:

I've dreamed of this moment ever since my youth.

Thank God, this time I've heard no voices in the night,

no cardinal or pope telling me to return home.

Now at last I'm on my way to the Holy Land.

"I'll bet the rest of the brothers back home were surprised when Brother Leone told them where we've gone," laughed Jacques.

"Brother Bernardo is the only one who won't be surprised. Before we left, I also told him about my plans. I knew that he would have wanted to accompany me—as he was at my side in the early years—though he can't travel any longer. For a couple of years now he's been suffering from back pains, and you've seen how stooped over he's become. He did promise to shadow me with his prayers and to speak to no one of our departure."

"When they learn where we've gone, Francesco, more than one brother will be jealous of me. I'm honored that you chose me to be your companion-bodyguard. But I have to warn you, my friend, that I'm not St. Christopher."

"God is my bodyguard, Brother Jacques, but I confess I feel safer with you at my side. God's presence in the world requires human bodies and, sometimes, especially strong ones like yours to protect the weak."

Once their ship was outside the harbor of Ancona, the wind filled its sails and began its passage southward down along the Italian coast. The captain kept his vessel close to the coast where the winds and tides would make the passage easier and allow them to reach a port more readily should a storm arise. They sailed past the coastal cities of Pescara and Termoli and then around the peninsula of Promontorio del Gargano. Francesco was grateful to God that the Adriatic Sea had remained calm so that he didn't have to deal with being seasick. What did make him ill, however, was the conversation of his shipboard companions. The vessel was crowded with crusaders, their servants and men-at-arms, along with pilgrims, prostitutes, and other unsavory characters. While the first Crusades had attracted brave and holy kings like Richard the Lion Hearted and Saint Louis of France and devout noblemen who had taken up the cross for religious reasons, those going off to fight on this Crusade were mostly the dregs of the nobility and knighthood.

"Where's your sword, beggar?" A voice came from behind Francesco as he stood by the rail softly singing in French. He felt a heavy hand clamp down on his shoulder as the voice continued, "Or do you intend to slaughter the infidels with your lice?"

"I carry no weapon," Francesco said with a smile as he turned around to face an Italian knight with a large, ugly scar above his right eye.

"Not even a skinny dagger hidden under your moth-eaten tunic? If that's true, you're a fool as well as a barefoot beggar. Those infidels will cut you up into ribbons."

"I'm a pilgrim bound for the Holy Land, and I go as our Savior instructed us to travel—in peace."

"The Saracens, however, come in war!" the knight replied. "They always have and they always will, converting everyone in their path by the sword."

"Sir knight, have not we Christians done the same?"

Gubbio

Perugia

Ancona

Bertonna

Assisi

Spello

Pescara

Adriatic Sea

Termoli

Promontorio
Del Gargano

The Sea Voyage
to Brindisi-Acre

Brindisi

to Acre

"As far as conversion to the True Faith and especially with regard to this crusade, I know that *Deus vult*—God wills it!" Then, squeezing his hand tighter on Francesco's shoulder, he said, "I can see that you're no ordinary pilgrim: You're barefoot and poor as dirt. I'd wager you're one of those damn heretical Waldensians."

Looking toward his fellow knight, he said, "Hey, Camillo, come over here. I happened upon this beggar singing in French, and when I asked him some questions, he began condemning the Church. Do you think he might be one of those Poor Men of Lyons?"

"Why hesitate, Angelo, kill him and let God decide!" Camillo replied with a smirk. "Do you remember when you and I went off as Italian mercenaries on that crusade against the French heretics what the Abbot of Citeaux said at the siege of Beziers?"

"You mean when we'd surrounded the city, demanding that the citizens turn over to us all those inside the walls whose names were on our list of heretics, and they only ridiculed us with insults?"

"Yes, and when we were given the order to storm the ramparts and take the city and we asked how we would know the true Catholics from heretics, the abbot said, 'Slay everyone inside the city, for God will recognize his own and the rest will go to hell!'" At that, they both laughed roundly.

"Find a better place for your heavy hand, friend knight," Jacques said as he approached the knight who was gripping Francesco's shoulder. Unseen by the two men, Jacques had come up behind them and placed a vice-like grip hand on each of their shoulders. While his voice was calm, it was saturated with all the savage power of his old days as a ruthless bandit chief. "Let go of my friend, or both of you may continue your pilgrimage to the Holy Land alongside those fish down there beneath this rail."

"But in our heavy chain mail, we'd drown," Camillo whimpered.

"Nothing to worry about if that happened, my good knight. God would recognize you as one of his own—or you'd go to hell. Now be on your way before I lose my patience," Jacques said releasing his grip, "and be grateful that I'm now a man of peace. But don't test my conversion too far."

Without a word the two men turned and walked to the far end of the ship. Francesco shook his head at Jacques, saying, "We're messengers of peace, Jacques, and even if you didn't do them any physical harm your words were most threatening. Yet I confess, my St.

Christopher, that I was relieved when you appeared and rescued me from those two. Thank you, dear friend, even if I know you would never have actually thrown them overboard."

"Maybe! You see, Francesco, I'm not completely converted!" Jacques replied with a laugh. "Or should I say I'm not yet fully tamed? Before we left Assisi, a group of the younger brothers took me aside and asked me if the stories about how you tamed a ferocious wolf at Gubbio were true. Repeating what I've heard you say many times, I told them, 'Well, with God, all things are possible.' But while I didn't know about Gubbio, I do know as Gospel truth that once you tamed a fierce wolf named Jacques de Coeur." Then, laughing loudly, he gave Francesco a big embrace.

Upon reaching the port of Brindisi at the far southern tip of Italy, the ship took on fresh water, fruit, and food and then set sail across the Mediterranean for the port of Acre on the northern coast of the Holy Land. Once again, they were blessed with a smooth, storm-free passage all the way to the crusader fortress city of Acre. Two days later, after taking new passengers and supplies on board, they departed for Damietta at the mouth of the Nile in Egypt. While Francesco did not make immediate contact with them, a group of new passengers aroused his curiosity, for under their full-body armor and the swords girded at their waist, they wore black wool monk's habits.

As the ship was slowly pulling out into the open sea, a black-robed Greek Orthodox monk appeared on the sea wall of Acre and began shouting curses at them: "You diabolic agents of the Roman Pope, you're all bound for the fires of hell! You papist knights, soldiers of Satan, you're sailing straight to your damnation. God has damned all of you crusaders since your bloodbath of Holy Constantinople, in which your wicked brother crusaders drew their swords not against infidels but against fellow believers. They violated widows, wives, and even holy virgins vowed to Christ; they desecrated churches, melted down holy golden vessels for plunder, carried off precious relics, and defaced ancient holy icons. Their blood is on your hands and their guilt stains your souls." Though he yelled all the louder, his voice grew fainter as they sailed out toward the open sea, "You're damned, all of you, damned for your murder, incest, fornication, adultery, and sodomy. . . ." As the monk's figure faded in the distance, all those on board the ship made a sign of the cross upon themselves, for any curse was potent, but one

made by a priest or monk, even a demented Orthodox monk, was especially feared.

Francesco wondered about the monk condemning them for immorality and evil others had committed years ago on the Fourth Crusade. Yet the monk's curse implied that one must bear responsibility for others' past sins. Just a short time later he wondered if, indeed, those sins were only in the past as he overhead a group of knights talking on the ship. Their conversation shattered any lingering romantic image he had of knighthood. They told stories about tournaments in which knights dressed up as women, making a mockery of themselves. They loudly joked about finding whores once they reached Damietta and their eagerness to engage in hand-to-hand combat with the infidels—to bathe in Saracen blood and plunder the infidels' wives and homes.

As Francesco walked away and the sour acid of disappointment welled up in his heart, he spotted one of those monk-like knights who had come aboard at Acre. Curious whether at least some part of knighthood could be redeemed, he introduced himself. "I'm Brother Francesco from Assisi; I belong to the Order of the Poor Little Brothers of Assisi."

"And I am Sir Hugh de Coucy of the Poor Fellow Soldiers of Jesus Christ, also known as the Poor Knights of the Temple of Solomon, or, simply, the Knights Templar."

"Sir Hugh, you wear a monk's habit under your armor. I've never seen that before. It intrigues me why you call yourselves 'poor' knights."

"A long story, Brother Francesco, but let me give you a brief version. Our order began more than a hundred years ago, founded by the saintly abbot Bernard of Clairvaux. Its purpose was to protect pilgrims, such as you, traveling to and in the Holy Land, and to create spiritual warriors who would be vowed to poverty in the midst of the luxury and pomp of knighthood. Our rule is modeled on the Rule of St. Benedict, and all our members are called to engage in a Holy War by waging penitential attacks on themselves! We struggle more for the vitality of our souls than we do to regain Jerusalem, and so any military victories are secondary to winning our humility and conquering ourselves through spiritual discipline. For us poor knights, the real enemy is sin!"

"As a rule, knights are wealthy, since they come from rich or noble families," said Francesco, "so how can you call yourselves 'poor' knights?"

"Yes, but Christ-like poverty is not only one of our vows, it's one of our highest aspirations. Our poverty was depicted on the first seal of the Knights Templar, which showed two monk-knights riding on the same horse! While it may be humorous, it's also a very graphic symbolic image of the nonpossession required of all Knights Templar. We also desire to be 'poor' when it comes to expressing any joy over our victories in war, to refraining from boasting or in any way celebrating personal triumphs as champions on the field of honor. There are words in our code of honor that I repeat daily: 'How blessed to die a martyr in battle.' And we wage that battle on two fronts: one against our adversaries of the flesh, and the other against the enemies of the faith."

As Hugh described the principles and high ideals of the Knights Templar, Francesco felt an enkindling wind sweep across the dying embers of his dream of the knighthood. As the flames of desire began to leap up, he thought, "Had I known of the Poor Fellow Soldiers of Jesus Christ before I pledged myself to my Liege Lord as a servant of peace, I might well have become a Knight Templar."

After they had sailed some distance down the coast from Acre, Hugh pointed westward toward the coast. "Over there," he said, "across that mountain range is Nazareth and the Sea of Galilee, where more than thirty years ago in 1187 the Knights Templar suffered great defeat and infamy at the hands of the Saracens. Outside the walls of Tiberias a large troop of mounted Muslim troops engaged about ninety brave Templars who did not flee the battle and so were slaughtered. A short while later, those barbarians paraded past Tiberias, exhibiting on their lances the heads of the slain Templars."

"How gruesome," Francesco said.

"Then a great horde of those accursed soldiers of the devil led by the great Sultan Saladin besieged Saphori, near Nazareth, the village of our Blessed Lord. After much deliberation, our barons and lords ordered their troops to retreat and march toward Tiberius. The Bishop of Acre led the army, holding aloft a golden, jewel-studded reliquary containing a large piece of the True Cross. Our troops were greatly emboldened by the sight of that most holy relic of all Christendom. However, in the intense midday heat, the knights found themselves surrounded by the cavalry of the sultan in an unsuitable position atop

a rocky plateau not far from the lake of Tiberias. That night the Saracens built a wall of dry brush and wood around the crusaders' camp. At the first light of day they set fire to the wall of kindling and began firing their arrows through the blinding smoke and intense flames into the confused ranks of the Christian warriors. In the chaos the infidels attacked, intent on butchering the crusaders."

"Did the relic of the Holy Cross save the knights?"

"No! And only the devil knows why it didn't. Those who survived said the battlefield was as ghastly as hell itself. The Muslims chopped off heads, limbs, and even the genitals of those noble knights, and their evil magicians crept among our dead, removing the eyeballs of vigorous young knights. It is said that the infidels believe that a young man's eyes hold a healing elixir."

"Unbelievable! Such brutality. . . ."

"There's more: The Saracens slayed the Bishop of Acre on the slopes of that plateau and captured the relic of the True Cross. When the soldiers of Christ saw this, they knew that all was lost and surrendered. Stripped of their armor and clothing, they were roped together by the neck and led away like common farm animals."

"And the relic of the True Cross?"

"The story is told that Sultan Saladin offered to spare all the Knights Templar who would spit upon the Holy Cross of our Salvation and convert to Islam. A few cowards did, but the rest of the captured brave knights refused, and the sultan ordered them beheaded. It is reported that accompanying the sultan were some of their holy men, called Sufis, who asked him for the honor of assisting in the beheading. Inexperienced, they hacked away at those gallant martyrs of Christ, while the sultan praised Allah as Christian heads rolled. Reports tell how carts rumbled through Damascus piled high with knight's heads, as if they were watermelons."

"Sufis? I can't believe they would do such a thing. Are all these atrocities true?"

"So I've been told. While that event took place thirty years ago, we Templars believe they are gospel truth. And there have been many other reports of similar brutality."

"And the True Cross?"

"Alas, some say the heathen swine buried that holy relic at the threshold of one of their mosques so that all those coming to pray there could stomp their feet on it."

"Forgive me, kind knight, I must go and sit down, for I feel very sick to my stomach—and it's not from seasickness."

When the ship docked in the crowded harbor of Damietta, most of the passengers departed for the Christian forces' tent city, which overflowed with crusaders, whores, and merchants from various parts of the world selling all sorts of luxuries and every known vice under the heavens. Encamped on this west bank of the Nile were John of Brienne, who was King of Jerusalem, and his crusaders, along with the bishops of Nicosia and Bethlehem and the patriarch of Jerusalem. The senior prelate among them was the arrogant Cardinal Pelagius, the personal legate of Pope Honorius III, who exercised papal authority over the crusade. Pelagius considered himself a military genius and was obsessed with capturing Cairo, defeating Sultan Malik, and ultimately wiping the scourge of Islam off the face of the earth. He constantly badgered King John to march his crusaders the short distance of only a several leagues from Damietta up the Nile to capture Cairo. King John, however, felt it more important militarily to maintain control of the mouth of the Nile at Damietta so he could exercise a stranglehold over all supplies going up and down the river to Cairo.

A couple of nights after Francesco arrived in Damietta there was an eclipse of the moon, which the crusaders interpreted as an omen that they would defeat the Muslims. For Jesus had foretold of signs in the heavens, in the sun, moon and stars, that would precede the end of the world. King John reminded his troops of a similar eclipse that predicted the victory of Alexander the Great in his battle against the Emperor Darius. Spurred on by what they believed to be a lunar portent, the crusaders engaged in a fiercely fought bloody battle with the troops of the Sultan Malik Al-Kamil. The fighting only subsided when days of heavy rainstorms flooded the camps of the Christians. When the flooding subsided, an unknown oriental plague broke out, causing large numbers of crusaders to suffer painful black blotches, which ravaged the flesh of their legs and bodies and resulted in numerous deaths. Because of this pestilence the Christians were forced to suspend any fighting with the Saracens for three months. Those who recovered or who had never fallen victim to the plague became bored and turned all the more to whoring, gambling, and drinking, which in turn led to arguing and fighting within their ranks. The Sultan Al-Kamil used this

Mediterranean Sea

Mt. Carmel

The Holy Land

Acre

Sea of Galilee

Tiberius

Nazareth

The Crusader Siege
of Damietta

Caesarea

Jerusalem

Bethlehem

Damietta

Cairo

Nile River

lull to move the majority of his troops from Cairo to within a three leagues of the camp of King John.

Inactivity in the crusaders' camp increasingly bred the disease of discontent among the majority of the common soldiers, who were tried of sitting around doing nothing other than fighting the flies and the heat. The sultan was so close, they argued, why should they wait for their leaders to make up their minds about what to do? They felt they could simply strike out across that short distance of desert, attack the sultan, and scoop up the plunder. So while King John's barons sat in their lavish tents playing chess and strategic war games, debating the various merits of engaging the infidels in battle, a large horde of troops took matters into their own hands. They rushed out of camp leaderless, ready to engage their infidel enemies as they shouted rallying cries of "Saint George, patron of crusaders, grant us victory" or "Saint Michael the Archangel, guide our swords to slay the infidels" or "Santa Maria, protect us from all harm." At the spear point of this rushing undisciplined army ran a pious cleric holding aloft a giant cross, and he was followed by a soldier carrying a tall pole on which was mounted a jewel-covered golden hand whose index finger pointed skyward.

At the outcry over the departure of these soldiers from camp, Jacques and Francesco joined several others who had climbed atop a military siege platform. From there they watched the waves of yelling men riding on a sea of white flags emblazoned with red crosses, all flowing outward across the yellow desert sands. The crusaders' raised sword blades and spears glistened from the light of the blinding hot sun, which also flashed like lightning off the golden hand on the tall pole.

"It's a precious relic of the hand of one of the Holy Innocents," the man standing next to Francesco replied in answer to his question about the meaning of the image on the pole. "May those first holy child martyrs, who were slaughtered by the wicked King Herod, now protect our men."

At that moment Francesco let out a loud gasp at the sight of pitch-black clouds tumbling over the rim of the far-distant yellow sand dunes. In a flash those seeming clouds formed themselves into long lines of warriors mounted on horses flanked by helmeted troops that snaked all along the rim of the dunes. Against the background of the blazing blue desert sky billowed countless green flags bearing the white crescent-moon symbol of Islam and its accompanying black infidel words scrawled in the devil's script. Upon seeing the raging wall of screaming foot soldiers brandishing their shimmering swords and spears and waving their crusader flags, the Saracens turned and retreated, disappearing from sight beyond the dunes. In loud cries of victorious glee the Christian troops broke any semblance of order and began wildly racing after their retreating enemies while shouts of encouragement and rejoicing surged from the camp behind them.

The Saracens, however, had only feigned a frightened retreat, and behind the cover of the dunes had swung around the flanks of the pursuing crusader foot soldiers, enveloping them in a tight web. Then, with a thunderous roar of "*Allah akbar,*" the Saracens rode down like the wind upon the confused, disorganized multitude below. Their slashing scimitars mowed down the Christians like wheat before the sickles of harvesters, quickly turning the sea of yellow desert sand into a blood-red lake strewn with severed limbs and heads and hacked, bleeding bodies. The massacre of that day would have been total had it not been for the Knights Templar and a few brave nobles who valiantly rode out of camp to rescue those who survived the first wave of the Saracens' charge.

Sickened to the point of nausea by the gore and butchery that day, Francesco, who once dreamed of being a crusader knight, turned away from the grisly battlefield, vowing he would personally go to petition Sultan Al-Kamil for peace.

His spur-of-the-moment vow to be an envoy of peace was severely tested as he and Jacques spent hours trying to convince King John and his nobles that it was the only sensible resolution to the bloody conflict. The king reluctantly agreed, over the strong objections of Cardinal Pelagius, and the two were given permission to go to the Saracen camp of the sultan.

Just as they were stepping out of the guarded entrance of the white-tented crusader encampment, the sentry screamed, "Look out! To your left, down near your foot—a viper!"

Francesco bolted backward, startled at the sight of the deadly snake so close to his foot. Yet as the soldier swiftly raised his sword, Francesco screamed, "Stop! Don't kill that snake!" raising his arms in front of the guard.

"That's a viper, you barefoot fool!" the sentry yelled. "They're more evil than hell itself—sneaky, deadly poisonous. If you had. . . ."

"Brother crusader," Francesco replied, "snakes are not evil! God created nothing evil. Snakes strike out to defend themselves when they feel threatened; otherwise, they mean us no harm unless we frighten them." Then, leaning down toward the coiling viper, he said, "Bless you, Brother Snake. Don't be afraid; no one is going to harm you. Now, little brother, you had best start wiggling away from here back out into the desert."

As the snake slithered away and Francesco and Jacques left the crusader encampment to cross the desert toward the Saracen camp, they could hear the crusader sentry saying to his companion, "If you ask me, either he's as witless as an idiot not to want to kill that snake—or in league with the great serpent, Satan!"

"I'm not sure who is more dangerous," Jacques said as he shifted the white flag of truce they had been required to carry from his right shoulder to his left, "that viper back there or the Saracen soldiers who may kill us rather than taking us to the sultan. Then, even if we're able to speak with the sultan and he allows us to return safely, I wonder if those crusaders back there will keep us from reentering our camp, being suspicious that we've become traitors and spies for the sultan. Neither side trusts the other, and they're especially distrustful of anyone who can easily pass between the two battle lines." As they walked through the blood-soaked sand at the site of the recent battle they both had witnessed, Jacques pointed to the desert floor and said, "Our blood may soon be added to that of those poor lads who died out here."

"God is with us!" Francesco replied. "And even if we die, as the Knights Templar say, 'how blessed to die a martyr in battle'! I might amend that and say, 'far more blessed to die a martyr of peace.' Ah, Jacques, once you relished danger and surely quoted the old saying that it's better to meet death by the sword than to die in your sleep on a bed of straw."

Francesco prayerfully fingered his peasants' breviary—his worn, knotted Pater Noster cord—as they crossed over a tall dune, leaving behind the security of the crusader battle lines. He prayed that God

would grant them success on this mission of peace. Then he shuddered, feeling his old Perugian wound reawakening as he recalled the horrible fate of those innocent children crusaders who were taken captive and then sold into slavery. "O God, let not that despicable fate befall Brother Jacques and me." Soon a city of tents arose out of the endless wasteland of yellow sand dunes. It appeared to be rippling in waves as the intense heat rose up off the desert floor.

"*Allah akbar*," yelled Francesco when they were within shouting range of the sentries at the Saracen camp.

"Look!" shouted a guard, "Is the desert heat playing tricks on my eyes, or do you also see two unarmed beggars carrying a white flag approaching us? The shorter one speaks Arabic, yet clearly he's no Arab."

"It's a trick!" said the other black-helmeted guard. Cupping his hands around his mouth, he shouted, "You two infidels out there, stop right where you are! Turn around and go back to your fellow unbelievers or you'll go straight to hell, for we have orders to kill on sight all. . . ."

"I am Francesco of Assisi. My companion Jacques and I are unarmed. We come in the peace of Allah."

"You must be mad! The sun has baked your brain for you even to dare to approach this camp," the first sentry shouted. "Halt! Or we'll fill both of you with arrows."

"We're not mad! We're holy beggars of the One God whom both you and we worship and love. As beggars, my companion and I implore you in the name of Allah to allow us to enter your camp, for we come on a holy mission to speak of peace directly to Sultan Al-Kamil."

"Peace? In the name of the Prophet, who among the swarming horde of those devouring crusader locusts ravaging our land wants peace?"

"Allah wants peace! *Salaam aleikum*, brothers. Know that we are servants of *salaam*."

As he watched the Saracen sentries lower their weapons, Jacques thought, "Amazing! To believe in miracles and then boldly act as if they will happen—this can only work for holy fools and innocents." The guards not only allowed him and Francesco to enter their camp but escorted them directly to the large majestic red and golden silk tent of the sultan. In the desert breeze blowing a measure of coolness off the Nile, long, thin, green pennants fluttered from the gold-capped tops of

the tent poles. The guards spoke in subdued voices with an officer of the sultan's court, who then went inside the tent. Francesco and Jacques waited and waited, until finally the official approached them.

"The great Sultan Al-Kamil has consented," the official said to them, "to grant you a most unusual audience—unusual because you are both Christians and, therefore, enemies. Al-Kamil the Great has granted this exception because our sentries reported that upon arriving you extended an Arabic greeting of peace, praising Allah."

"We come not as his enemies but as friends; we come in peace," Francesco replied with a bow, "and we are most grateful to the sultan. *Allah akbar.*"

"As the personal guests of the sultan, our desert tradition dictates that no harm shall come to either of you while you are within his tent or in our camp. But be advised: The time of the great Al-Kamil is precious, for he is occupied with many problems concerning the siege of Damietta. Do not burden him too long. Now, extend your arms out wide so we may search both of you to insure that you come in peace and have not come to assassinate him with daggers hidden under your robes."

"*Salaam aleikum.*" Francesco greeted the sultan with a deep bow as they entered the luxurious domed tent made of scarlet silk and edged in elaborate golden designs intertwined with intricate Arabic lettering. Large plush Persian carpets with richly woven floral designs covered the floor of the tent, giving the feel of walking in a field of soft flowers. Francesco was well aware that the tent and its furnishings were worth a king's ransom.

"*Salaam aleikum* to you. Be seated," the sultan said, motioning toward two cushions on the carpet in front of him.

Francesco and Jacques sat on the cushions about six arms lengths away from the place where the sultan sat on a throne of several large ornate cushions. Behind him was a semicircle of his white-turbaned chief advisors, and on either side stood two massive, muscular bodyguards holding large curved scimitars across their chests. As Francesco eyed the towering guards and the members of the sultan's court, he felt like Daniel in the lion's den. But with a prayer that his old personal charm was as powerful as ever, he smiled broadly.

Even though several of his ministers surrounded him, the presence of Al-Kamil seemed to fill the entire tent. He wore a white turban, in the center of which was an immense purple jewel mounted in a gold setting that highlighted the features of his face. His hawk-like nose, pitch black beard, and piercing brown eyes produced a countenance that was simultaneously serene and lion-like. Draped around his seated figure was a cloak of white silk interwoven with gold threads.

"You're either very brave," said the bejeweled sultan, "or very foolish to have dared to approach our encampment. A single arrow from one of my skilled archers could have dispatched both of you to your heaven."

"Allah the Compassionate is merciful to children and the mad," Francesco answered with a slight bow of his head to the sultan, "and if death had been my fate, to die for my God would have been a grace for me."

"For which of your three gods would you have died so readily?"

"Like you, my Lord, we only worship one God—but a God of three persons."

"One, two, three," counted the sultan on his bejeweled fingers, "three gods, as I count. We worship only one God, Allah! But on matters of theology let us not wrangle like camel merchants. Now, my barefoot visitor, you've not come to convert me, have you? As my guest, I promise I'll not attempt to force you to embrace the Way of the Prophet if you do not attempt to use the sword of scriptures to convert me to Christ."

"No one should be forced to change his heart by another's words or swords."

"Wisely said. Yet, sadly, both of our religions use the sword. However, you've aroused my curiosity. Why would two Christians risk their lives in the middle of a war to come and speak with me, whom they must consider an infidel and an enemy?"

"This savage, bloody war—or any war—is only brothers killing brothers. Whatever the cost, we had to at least attempt to be instruments of holy peace."

"Holy peace? Do you not believe," he asked, pointing a long bejeweled finger at Francesco, "that this war of your crusader brothers is a holy war as the Pope has declared it?"

"I believe that all war is unholy and that there can be no holy wars."

"Again, wisely spoken. My humble understanding of the teachings of the great Prophet Muhammad is that he was opposed to war, and only reluctantly endorsed it in defense of one's country or to protect

our faith. While some Muslims may believe otherwise, personally, I agree that there are no holy wars!"

"I'm glad to hear you say that, Sultan, for we are all sons of Abraham, brothers and lovers of the same God. I believe we must try to forge a peace, a *pax*, a *salaam*, between our two sides." Francesco breathed a prayer of gratitude for Ali Hasan as he continued speaking with insight about the teachings of Islam and the many spiritual truths they shared in common.

"Francesco of Assisi, I am impressed by your knowledge of the Qur'an and apparent fondness for Islam. Yes, we are all lovers of the same God—only many of us are what the Prophet Jesus called 'lukewarm,' is that not right? Now if someone truly loved the All Holy One—I mean with blazing ardor—would not the lover and beloved be fused as one?" Francesco nodded in agreement, not sure where the sultan was leading him. "Lovers always seek to be one with their beloved, and the greater the love the greater the identification. Do you not agree?"

"Yes, Sultan, you have spoken wisely."

"And in you, Francesco, I sense a great likeness to the mind and heart of the Prophet Jesus, and I see in you a mystical mirror of your Jesus Christ. Yet among our Islamic mystics there are some who reflect an identification that is more than a likeness in speech and attitudes to the teachings of the Prophet Muhammad." Turning to the right, he said, "Al-Junaid, come before us." At this request, from behind the rows of richly attired officials surrounding the sultan stepped a man Francesco instantly identified as a Sufi, since he wore a rough brown cloak and a white turban. The man bowed profoundly before the sultan and then sat down on the carpet to his left.

"By the grace of the Prophet and the will of Allah," Al-Kamil said, "as the ruler of my people and commander of their armies, I attempt to be a devout Muslim, and so I constantly keep a holy man at my side. It has been my practice to balance the advice of my political and military advisers with that of my mystical adviser." Then he grinned, showing his pearl-white teeth, which contrasted with his pitch-black beard and mustache. "Now, my Christian lover of God, a question: In your faith are there holy men who have totally identified themselves with the one whom they call the only Son of God?"

"Yes, my lord sultan. We have many great saints who have not only lived holy lives faithful to the teachings of the Gospel but who have

even given their lives out of love for Christ. What greater identification is possible?"

"Al-Junaid," the sultan said, directing his gaze toward the seated Sufi, "while the Qur'an requires that we observe complete modesty regarding our bodies, as your sultan I ask in the name of Allah the Revealer that you remove the upper half of your tunic." The Sufi stood and obeyed instantly, dropping his brown cloak onto the carpet and then lowering the upper half of his tunic. As he did, he revealed a series of pinkish slash wounds with purplish scabs on his chest and arms that appeared to have been made by a sword.

"Al-Junaid is no ordinary Sufi holy man," the sultan said, gesturing toward the wounds on his body. "He is a passionate lover of both Allah and the Prophet Muhammad. Look at him, Francesco, and see that in his own body he bears the same wounds that were inflicted upon the Prophet Muhammad by his Arab enemies in Mecca who were militantly opposed to his teachings about the one God Allah. But Al-Junaid is not unique; there are more than a hundred of our Islamic mystics who bear the same painful wounds of the Prophet in their bodies. Some of these holy men even experience bleeding from their wounds. . . . I know what you are thinking, but, no, they are not self-inflicted!"

"How did they come by these wounds?"

"Our holy men are dedicated to the truth and never speak falsely. They have reported that after long and profound times of fasting and prayer, or in moments of great ecstasy, these wounds of the Prophet mysteriously appear on their bodies. No sane man seeks pain, and these men are not demented, so your question is a good one. While we've translated into Arabic all the great Greek medical manuscripts, none of them speaks of this holy affliction. So as for how this happens—only Allah knows!"

"Lovers seek to bear the sufferings of their beloved," answered Francesco. "Perhaps when a love is great enough, it is possible for someone to be united not only in soul but also physically with the beloved. But such love or ecstasy would have to be. . . ."

"You are wondering why I provided this demonstration of Islamic passion and love? While I love God," the sultan said as he nodded to Al-Junaid, indicating that he could clothe his body again, "and am devoted to the Prophet, the only wounds inflicted upon me have been by the crusaders. For the peace of Allah I am willing to be wounded,

willing to risk having my name and honor slashed in the process of being tricked by King John into a false truce, only to have his army slaughter my people. You say you came to me pursuing peace, I also seek peace, an end to this senseless slaughter of war. Yet, the Qur'an says that when we are invaded, as we are now by the crusaders, we are bound to go to war to defend our land and our faith."

The sultan and Francesco spoke at great length of their desire for peace and their mutual hopes for a just resolution to the present conflict.

"I am convinced," Sultan Al-Kamil finally said, "that Allah the Generous has given me a wondrous gift in you, my gray-robed Sufi, Francesco. I seek a truce to the madness of this war, especially in the blockage of the Nile at Damietta, which is causing enormous hardships on my people in Cairo. Will you return as my personal messenger to King John, offering him and his crusaders a resolution to this conflict and an end to the hostilities so that we can all go home? If you concur, then my advisors will assist me in preparing a list of our conditions and the concessions we are willing to make to King John if he accepts my offer of peace." When Francesco agreed without hesitation to being the sultan's personal emissary of peace to King John, Al-Kamil said, "A tent and refreshments will be provided for you and your companion while my council and I decide upon our conditions for peace. When we are finished, you will be called back. For now, go in the peace of Allah. And Francesco. . . ."

"Yes, my lord?"

"Pray!"

Because of the complexity of the situation and several previous failed attempts at a truce, the sultan and his advisors took a good deal of time planning and praying over their peace offer. Meanwhile, back in the crusaders' camp, a host of explanations abounded as to why Francesco and Jacques had failed to return after several days. Some maintained that the two had been insane in the first place to go unarmed into the nest of the infidel vipers and were killed on sight. Others believed they had been taken captive as hostages or as slaves, since the Arabs were notorious for trying to make a profit from their prisoners. Cardinal Pelagius, who found the barefoot poverty and unlettered simplicity of Francesco to be repugnant, pointed out that he had displayed esteem for the teaching of the infidels. The cardinal suggested that instead of converting the enemy, Francesco himself had been converted to Islam! When the other two bishops and their clerics  affirmed Cardinal Pelagius' judgment, an order was issued by King John that should Francesco or his companion return to their camp they were to be arrested immediately. If they refused arrest, the guards were instructed to kill them on the spot as Saracen spies.

"*F*rancesco, thank you for your patience," the sultan said as Francesco and Jacques again sat before him in his scarlet silken tent. "I've been told that you possess a remarkable memory, and so my scribe will slowly read the terms of our truce proposal to you so that you may commit them to memory. While I will also give you a written copy for King John, I desire that you be my lips to speak my personal longing and passion for peace to those Christians who lust for war. When the scribe had finished reading the scroll, the sultan said, "If all Christians were men like you, Francesco, I would seriously be tempted to become one. Now, go with my blessing and a pledge of complete safety from all harm until you've reached the crusader encampment, and may Allah protect you. *Salaam aleikum!*"

"*I* am not a spy," Francesco said adamantly as he stood before King John, his barons and the bishops. Attempting to speak with the conviction and authority he had once heard in the voice of Innocent III, Francesco continued, "I am a loyal Christian, a servant of Holy Mother Church and of the peace proclaimed by my Liege, Jesus Christ. I pray that you can lay aside your suspicions of treachery and listen, for I bring good news of peace."

The priests present objected that whatever he might say would be lies, since he was an agent of the prince of lies, Satan. To support this charge they gleefully retold the guard's story about the viper that Francesco had blessed, calling it his brother, and how he had prevented the sentry from killing it. They embellished the story, saying that when he addressed the viper as his brother, the serpent stood straight up on its tail and bowed its head toward Francesco. Dismissing this story as fantasy, Francesco faithfully repeated word-by-word the terms of Sultan al-Kamil's detailed offer of peace to King John and the nobles of his court. He concluded by summarizing the sultan's message relating his solemn promise that if the crusaders would lift the siege of Damietta, all Christian prisoners in his custody would be released, and all lands the Christians may have lost in the war would be restored, other than

two militarily important castles in Egypt, for which he would pay the Christians an annual fee they considered fair. Finally, this truce would last for twenty years, at which time it could be renewed.

"Lies, all lies!" snarled Cardinal Pelagius, leaping to his feet. "This barefoot fool and snake charmer has been cleverly deceived by that cunning infidel who is an agent of Satan, the Great Deceiver. Only fools and children would believe that you can trust the word of an infidel. They all speak with the venomous tongues of serpents. It's a trap, Your Majesty, and when it is sprung it will open up the gaping jaws of hell itself, swallowing up all God's holy crusaders. Be not swayed or deceived, King John, for like the recent foolish attack on the infidels, this apparently generous offer of peace by the sultan of Satan is only an ambush. We must not pursue peace but only a holy war! We must march on Cairo at once and exterminate this apocalyptic plague of Islam from the earth, beginning here at Damietta with the slaughter of every infidel man, woman, and child in the city."

*S*ultan Al-Kamil's peace proposal was rejected by King John, and by November of 1220 the crusaders had captured Damietta in obedience to the orders of Cardinal Pelagius. As the crusaders went about slaughtering the city's inhabitants, Brothers Francesco and Jacques worked in the stench of rotting corpses, tending to the dying and wounded on both sides. Then, under the relentless urging of Cardinal Pelagius, King John marched his army southward into Egypt to capture Cairo, which the cardinal referred to as the head of the serpent.

"Brother Jacques," said a weary and disheartened Francesco, "this is not the Holy Land but a hellish land. Let us depart from this evil place and attempt to make our way back up to Jerusalem. And before we return to Assisi, I would love to visit Bethlehem, for I have a great devotion to the Infant Jesus and the sacred manger."

As if God had wrapped them in a cloud of divine protection, Francesco and Jacques were able to travel from Egypt to the various holy sites where Jesus was born, suffered, and died. But instead of being inspired as pilgrims to the Holy Land, Francesco was bitterly disappointed. After years of the wars and atrocities by crusaders and Muslims, the land seemed plundered of its sacredness. A sad and disillusioned Francesco now longed to return home to Assisi, and so they traveled north from Jerusalem up to Acre.

As Francesco and Jacques were preparing to board a ship bound for Venice, a ship from Damietta sailed into the harbor bearing terrible news about King John. The crowded docks came to a standstill as everyone waited for details from the disembarking crew. Then as fire that leaps faster than a fleeing deer across the dry stubble of a harvested wheat field, so the news spread across Acre that King John of Jerusalem had been disastrously defeated. Enticed by the promise of oriental booty in Cairo, John's crusaders had boldly and foolishly camped just outside that fabled city of Egypt on a narrow island in middle of the Nile. Angered by the crusaders' rejection of his peace proposal, in the middle of the night the sultan ordered the Nile to be dammed just below the crusader camp. As the crusaders slept, the island was inundated by the rising river, and by the time they awoke they found that their barges had floated away, leaving them trapped. While the sultan could have allowed them all to drown, he exercised restraint and ordered the flooding stopped, permitting the waterlogged Cardinal Pelagius and King John, now red-faced by their stupidity, to sue for peace. While he graciously allowed the humiliated Pelagius and the soaked crusader army to depart, the sultan kept King John as a hostage to insure that they would not return.

*I*n the late winter of 1221 Francesco arrived back at Portiuncula in the midst of a light snowfall. The joy of his return was immediately soured, as the first news he was told was that his old and beloved comrade Pietro had died while he was away on the crusade. A pestilence had swept through the community, and he along with a number of other brothers had died from it within days. Brother Elias, who had returned from Syria before the pestilence struck, had now been elected by the brothers to replace Pietro as leader of the order. Francesco walked in tears to the new cemetery of the brothers outside of Portiuncula to pray at the grave of his dear companion.

"*Caro mio* Pietro, a white shroud lays over your grave, symbolic of your new tunic, the white robe of the saints in heaven that you and these other brothers resting here now wear. May you, Pietro, and all of you my sleeping brothers be cradled in the arms of the Mother of God and rest in peace." As he concluded his prayer, he broke down sobbing. In the midst of the light snow, he looked upward, saying, "Brother Clouds, you have joined me in my sorrow, weeping your white tears that fall like soft apple blossoms upon the graves of these precious

men." Then, wiping his tears away with the sleeve of his tunic, he said, "Pietro, death seems to shadow me everywhere. Again I've come home a failure, disappointed that my desire to be an instrument of peace in the Holy Land died on the banks of the Nile River. I returned with half my heart grieving because of all the unspeakable horrors I've seen done in the name of Christ by so-called Christian crusaders. Now your death has filled the other half of my heart with grief. Moreover, my sorrow overflows, for back there in Portiuncula I smelled another kind of pestilence. It was not just the stench of that passing disease from which you died but a more enduring pestilence of compromise that will destroy the beautiful dream that you and I, Bernardo and Giles nursed into life." Again, he lapsed into endless sobbing, his tears melting tiny holes in the snow at his bare feet.

Instead of returning to the brothers at Portiuncula, he walked through the falling snow that was blanketing the winter gray landscape along the path to San Damiano to see Clare. She listened tearfully as he shared his grief at the death of Pietro and the other brothers taken by the pestilence and then poured out the tragedy of his pilgrimage of peace to the Holy Land.

"Clare," he wept, "upon my return from Egypt, before I went to the cemetery, Leone briefly reported that my community of brothers continues to be divided into hostile opposing camps over how they should live poverty. There's no peace in the Holy Land and no peace in Portiuncula."

"I'm so sorry, my dearest Francesco. Know that I share your wound," Clare replied, "for it's a daily struggle here to remain faithful to what God called us to do. Leone may not have told you, but we've also heard that Rome wants you to compose a new rule, and we both know that means you'll be forced to make more compromises."

"Leone was kind to spare me that news after I learned of Pietro's death. But I'm not surprised, and I can guess who whispered in Rome's ear about the need for a new, more lenient rule. I get so angry. . . ." Then he caught himself and, sighing, said, "Clare, how can I write a rule for others when I can't even rule myself?"

"I know how you feel—I mean about being angry," Clare said with a sigh of her own. "Bishop Carafa of Assisi has formally ordered that I relax some of my personal disciplines. He has forbidden me from sleeping on the bare floor, as you do, ordering that I sleep on a straw

mattress. He also insisted that I must eat 'something' each day. Fortunately, he didn't say how much of 'something.'"

"How can he do that? What makes him think he can legislate how you sleep and what you eat or don't eat? Does he think he's the Pope or God? Damn it! He wants to dictate how you can love God. He may be able to have you cloistered, but he can't cloister your conscience."

Nodding her head in agreement, Clare again stretched her fingers as far as they could go through the bars of the iron grating to grip Francesco's fingers with affection.

"Why does it seem that there are so few men in the Church like Bishop Guido and so many like Carafa, Matteo, Uzielli and . . . forgive me, Clare, but my heart is not just sad—it's mad. I'm becoming so angry at what I see, hear, and find in the Church. In the Holy Land, the sultan was a good man eager for peace, and there could have been a twenty-year peace truce between Christians and Muslims if it wasn't for the papal legate Cardinal Pelagius! He saw himself as a clerical Alexander the Great—another Julius Caesar, and . . . , forgive me, Clare, for what I'm about to say, but there are times when I think that Peter of Waldo was right to leave the Church."

"Don't despair," Clare said. "If there is to be the kind of great reform that good Pope Innocent so wanted, then it must come from inside, from those like ourselves who are willing to endure the cost of living our dream."

Forever the tumbler, Francesco turned his negative thoughts upside down. "You're right, Clare," and he said with a smile, "I'm staking my hopes on our new Third Order of Brothers and Sisters of Penance, who as laypeople are more free to live our original dream in a way that best fits their lives in the world.

"I know that our visiting time is limited—and that you excel in keeping all the rules of your convent, including the time allowed for visiting—but I have one more thing I want to talk about with you, Clare. Lately I've been pondering in my heart a growing desire to imitate our Lord Jesus Christ more perfectly."

"Francesco, what more can you do than you've already done to imitate him—except to be crucified? That brings me to a gift I have for you—that is if your poverty will allow you to accept it. Some days ago a man from Assisi came to our door asking to see me. He offered me a small, handheld wooden cross of the crucified Lord that he himself had painted. I told him that here at San Damiano we already had the only

painted crucifix we needed, the beautiful one that spoke to you. The man pleaded with me to allow him to leave it, since he was on his way to Florence and couldn't take it with him."

"A painter from Assisi, Clare? Do you remember his name?"

"Yes, Jacobi of Florence, the man whom good Bishop Guido had commissioned to paint the frescos on the walls of the Cathedral of San Rufino."

"I met him, Clare, in the cathedral the afternoon I preached to the people in the piazza, and we spoke for some time about his fresco. Did he say why he couldn't take the crucifix with him?"

"I could tell that he was very frightened, and he said that he had to flee from Assisi that very day. Then, as if he had a sudden idea, he asked if I would hide the crucifix until you returned from the crusades and then give it to you."

"Why did he have to run away?"

"When I asked, he said that Bishop Carafa had ordered him out the city before sunset that day. The bishop had also given his name to members of Assisi's Fraternity of Father Matteo Parini, saying he was under suspicion of witchcraft and heresy for his unorthodox painting in the cathedral."

"How could Bishop Carafa threaten him with heresy and witchcraft for his painting?"

"Francesco," Clare smiled as she extended her fingers through the iron grill and squeezed his index finger, "it's so easy today to charge someone with the suspicion of heresy and imprison him without actually proving him guilty of it. And the very accusation puts the fear of God into people."

"I don't understand, Clare, how his paintings of our Lord could be judged unorthodox."

"Do you remember his beautiful fresco of Christ entering Jerusalem on Palm Sunday? Well it seems that he returned to the cathedral and repainted it. He added a figure in the front of the crowd welcoming Jesus into the Holy City—and that figure is an unmistakable likeness of you, barefoot, in a gray tunic, and with a halo!" Then, giggling, she continued telling him how Bishop Carafa had thrown a fit upon seeing it and demanded that Jacobi paint you out of the fresco at once. They say he literally screamed at Jacobi about how for more than two hundred years now only the Pope and no one but the Pope could create saints—not the common people as they once

did, and certainly not a painter! When Jacobi refused to alter the fresco, Carafa cancelled his commission and accused him of heresy for depicting you as a saint, ordering him out of Assisi before sunset. The bishop required that a priest be present as Jacobi gathered his belongings, and the cleric saw the painted crucifix Jacobi had done for his personal devotion. The priest was horrified and told Bishop Carafa that the painting was radically unorthodox and violated the established canons of art. He said it was bewitching and could only have been created with a hand guided by Satan himself. The bishop ordered that it be destroyed, but Jacobi was able to escape with it among his meager possessions. I brought his crucifix here for our meeting and have it in this black bag. It is, indeed, most unusual. Would you like to see it?"

When Francesco eagerly agreed, Clare removed the crucifix and held it up for him to see. "Ah, look, Clare, it moves! It's alive! The figure of our crucified Lord's body has such depth and realism. Jacobi has creatively added a third dimension, giving the image a sense of perspective. It makes it seem like you're actually standing at the foot of the cross looking at the agony of our Lord's crucifixion. Yes, of course, I would love to have it—it would be a great inspiration for my prayer."

"My only concern, Francesco, is that it's too dangerous for you to have in your possession. If the Parinians learn that you have it—and they will since their spies are everywhere, even in our communities— they will use it as an excuse to attack you. Remember that Bishop Carafa ordered it destroyed!"

"I'll hide it until I can take it to my hermitage at Mount La Verna where it will surely be an inspiration for my prayer."

"I can see how meaningful it will be in your prayer life, Francesco, but I can't stress enough how careful you must be lest this cross cause you any more pain and rejection than you've already been exposed to.

"While you're still admired in Assisi, you're also judged as being too radical in your ideas by many who have been swayed by the preaching of Bishop Carafa. I hear that daily there is a swelling in the number of Assisi's citizens who pride themselves as defenders of the faith by becoming members of the Fraternity of the Parinians, which Bishop Carafa publicly and heartily endorses because of its allegiance to Rome. Another reason you've fallen from favor in Assisi paradoxically has to do with the huge number of your followers, a number we hear is now somewhere between three and five thousand!"

"Yes, Clare, you should see poor Portiuncula. It now looks like a gray army is encamped out there."

"That's exactly why you're in trouble with the commune and the people of Assisi. When you were only a small handful of men whose simple poverty had been blessed by Pope Innocent, the townspeople were proud to have such a famous holy man from their city, one of their own who was a friend of the Pope. But now, we hear in the convent that when the people of Assisi look over their city walls out toward Portiuncula, what they see is a swarming plague of hungry locusts threatening to devour Assisi and the surrounding countryside. Pious locusts true, but still thousands of hungry parasites that consume what they do not plant, devour what they do not labor to produce! Just as our Blessed Lord was rejected by those of his own village, so you, my beloved friend, now seem to have been graced to follow him."

"Dearest Clare, I'm a monster who's given birth to a catastrophe. How I wish I had never. . . ."

"Francesco," Clare said softly, her fingers straining through the iron grill to grip his fingers more tightly, "have faith that your vision has come from God. Do not despair, for I firmly believe that out of what you now see as a catastrophe will arise a great blessing for all Christendom. One day Assisi will regard you as their most beloved of sons and will bask in the honor that your barefoot brothers have gone forth from here as gray flocks of songbirds singing the joyful good news—not like swarms of hungry locust devouring the countryside but as carriers of seeds of joy and abundant life.

"Now, our time is almost over," she said as she returned the painted crucifix to the black bag, "and I will leave this for you at the porter's entrance. But before we say farewell, I have a bit of good news. A woman who comes from the city weekly and generously brings us gifts of fruit, food, and gossip told sister porter that the young priest at San Rufino, Dom Tomas, the former secretary of old Bishop Guido, has left."

"Left the priesthood?"

"No, Francesco, he's left the diocese of Assisi. The servants at the bishop's house told stories of how he and Bishop Carafa frequently argued, sometimes very loudly, over Carafa's new, rigid directives for the diocese. Because of their radical differences, Carafa didn't object when Tomas asked to leave the diocese. The people, however, were sad to see him depart because he was a kind and loving priest."

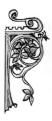

"Where did he go?"

"He went to Portiuncula and became a priest member in your order of Little Brothers!"

"Really? That must have happened while I was away. I know that Elias has accepted several priests, which has been difficult for me. I only wanted a humble band of brothers who would be as lowly as peasants, and priests like to live on top of pedestals. Having priests like Tomas, however, might change my thinking. I'm glad he has joined us; from what I know of him he'll not perch on some priestly pedestal reigning over others but will become a lowly brother—and, I believe, a holy one at that. Thanks, Clare, for that bit of good news. It will help to lighten my journey home through the snow."

Two years later, in the autumn of 1223, a forty-one-year-old Francesco traveled with three other brothers from Assisi three days south to the Rieti Valley. This beautiful valley was about halfway to Rome; on his preaching trips he occasionally used it as a place of retreat. He had named his favorite spot in the valley *Fonte Colombo*, "pool of the doves," because of the white doves that came to drink at the pool near his hermitage. This particular visit, however, was not for the solace of solitude but to fulfill an order from Pope Honorius that he rewrite the Rule of the Little Brothers. He had personally chosen Brothers Leone, Jacques, and Sebastiano to accompany him as moral support in the midst of his struggle to accept the compromises demanded by Rome—and influenced by Brother Elias—for him to relax the original rule. Like the feeling of a surgeon cutting off his hand was the pain of removing one of his precious first rules: "When the brothers go out on the road, they are to carry nothing with them." His skin crawled with the fleas of defeat as he next altered his original cardinal requirement of becoming a Little Brother: giving away all of one's money to the poor. It was amended to read: "If he cannot do this, then his goodwill shall be enough." He felt sure that Elias was behind that concession, seeing it as a way to increase the number of new members. Perhaps even more painful was the clause he had to include in the rule about brothers being able to own books. For Francesco such a dispensation was soul-wrenching, for he feared books far more than the vipers of Egypt. Yet Elias, as well as Rome, had insisted upon it because among the ranks of the brotherhood there were now priests who needed books to pray the Divine Office. Francesco, however,

wasn't fooled: He knew that prayer books were only the camel's nose inside the tent. Finally, bitter bile rose up from his stomach filling his mouth as he conceded that, in addition to two habits, each brother could have a *caparone,* a large cape—and a pair of sandals! As he reread his completed new rule he felt like Judas. Yet while he had been forced to make life more lenient for others, he himself continued to go barefoot, had only one tattered tunic and no books, not even a prayer book.

"Ah, Leone, God is a better dispenser of penance than I ever was," he said the day the courier from Rome departed with his new revised rule. "Making all those compromises was more penitential than rolling naked in the freezing snow or fasting for forty days. I felt like a tailor making alterations on a garment for a longtime customer who had doubled his original weight. 'Signore Tailor, this gown you make for me is now far too tight. Widen it here, open up the sides, make it more slack in the back and add more cloth until it's comfortable.' Oh, Leone, in pleasing the Pope again, I fear I've betrayed my Lord Jesus."

The brothers were aware that since his return from the crusade Francesco suffered from frequent bouts of sickness and fatigue, as well as increased difficulty with his eyesight. With the hope that a few weeks of rest there would restore Francesco, they proposed remaining at Fonte Colombo. November slipped into December, and as Christmas approached he surprised the brothers by spontaneously proposing that they celebrate Christmas in nearby Greccio rather than returning to Assisi. He told them he felt the Spirit wanted him to proclaim the Gospel of the birth of Christ to the people of that small village. The four brothers arrived in Greccio a couple of days before Christmas, where as zestfully and enthusiastically as ever he preached to the crowds about Jesus being born in a manger in Bethlehem.

On Christmas Eve morning he told his companions, "When I preach about the wonderful birth of our Savior and describe the simple village of Bethlehem that I visited in the Holy Land, the people are politely and piously attentive, but even my weakened eyes can see that they're bored and disinterested. They've heard that wondrous story too often for it to excite their souls to explore all the mysteries it contains. But this morning before dawn I was lying awake, and I had a marvelous idea: Tonight, let the people of Greccio visit Bethlehem!"

"Father Francesco," asked Sebastiano playfully, "do you intend to magically transport all of the village of Greccio to Bethlehem in the Holy Land?"

"No, my beloved Sebastiano, I will magically transport Bethlehem to Greccio!" As the others looked at him with eyebrows raised, he continued, "Tonight, even though we are sinners, we shall work a miracle and raise the lifeless Gospel of Bethlehem out of its tomb of repetition."

"You say *we*, Father Francesco, how can we work such a miracle?" asked Leone.

"We shall use the magic of reality!" Francesco replied, as like a sorcerer he began mysteriously undulating his hands in spirals before them. A few hours before Midnight Mass in the village church we'll invite all the people to come to an old abandoned stable I saw on the edge of the village. We'll borrow some real live animals to put in the stable—a couple of sheep, a donkey, and perhaps even a cow. Then we'll ask for volunteers from the village to play the parts of the shepherds; you, old, white-haired Leone, will be one of the Magi, and we'll find two villagers to be the other two kings. The children will gladly play the roles of angels, and you, Sebastiano, shall be the archangel who announces the glad tidings, since you're as handsome as an angel."

"You of all people, Father Francesco, know that I'm no angel, but I'll try."

"Brother Jacques, you will make a marvelous strapping figure of a Saint Joseph. And if one of you can find me a large white veil, I will play the part of Mary the Mother of God, even though I'm much better suited to playing the part of a donkey. Now, we'll need an infant. . . ."

"I saw a large wooden doll in the village woodcarver's shop," Sebastiano said. "I'll go and ask if he'll let us use it as the Christ Child."

As Francesco enthusiastically gave instructions to collect what was needed and how to improvise the costumes, Leone smiled to himself as he thought, "The real miracle in all of this is the resurrection of the old Francesco! He looks years younger, and the color has returned to his face." As they busily cleaned up the old stable and excitedly visited amongst each other, Brother Leone referred to what was about to happen that night as the Bethlehem Miracle Play.

That night the villagers gathered around the entrance to the old stable, now filled with live animals and with some of their neighbors

dressed as shepherds, Magi, and angels. As the people settled into their places in anticipation of the play, Francesco spoke to them by the glow of several flickering torches: "Soon Mary, Joseph, and the Christ Child will enter the stable behind me, for on this holy night the Word will be made flesh right here in Greccio. Yes, in your very village you are about to witness what should happen every day in each of our lives: God being made flesh in our flesh—in our own bodies and lives. For until that happens, the kingdom of God proclaimed by our Blessed Savior cannot come! Now, let the play begin."

Then Francesco said a prayer as he slipped the white veil over his head, and with Jacques at his side as Saint Joseph he placed the wooden infant wrapped in a white cloth into the straw of the manger. Kneeling down before it, he exclaimed, "Come, let us adore him, Christ the Lord." Then Sebastiano led the children angels in singing an old folk ring-dance song adapted into a Christmas carol, and with hands linked they danced in a ring around the infant figure in the manger. What began as make-believe, in the shimmering torchlight took on a mysterious reality. Even the wooden doll in the manger seemed to become a live infant who at any moment would cry to be fed.

After the enactment of the birth in the stable and attending Midnight Mass in the village church, the people of Greccio continued their celebration throughout Christmas day with feasting and folk songs. It was a Christmas like none before. The villagers spoke of how deeply moved they had been by the real-live enactment of the story of Bethlehem, which they found so much more powerful than simply reading the Gospel from the pulpit. Each year after that they continued staging a Bethlehem play, with villagers playing the various parts, and soon moved it to the front steps of the village church. And the woodcarver of Greccio who had loaned the wooden doll that served as the Christ Child began carving small wooden figures of Bethlehem and constructing small stables. The villagers would use these figures in their homes as prayer shrines for the Twelve Days of Christmas.

*I*n late January when Francesco returned to Portiuncula, he returned to chaos. The divisions created by differences over what degree of poverty they should observe had reached a boiling point, with some factions even refusing to speak to one another. When Francesco tried to address his family-community about the Gospel of peace, about its call to acceptance, love, and harmony, he found himself

preaching to the deaf. When his usually effective charismatic presence and words failed, he decided to reach into his quiver to use his sharpest arrow—prayer—and he announced that he was departing for Mount La Verna.

"La Verna is much too far away," Brother Elias told him with great solicitude. "Your health is so fragile, and that would be too difficult a journey for you to undertake. What if you should become ill along the way and die? Oh no, Father Francesco, I couldn't allow that. Your presence is needed here at Portiuncula. The new novices, our wealthy benefactors, and especially the pilgrims who come daily all want to see you and receive your blessing. No, La Verna is out of the question."

Francesco stood before Elias, his head hung in disappointment, as he thought, "Now, it seems, I've become some kind of living relic, which like all relics attracts streams of pilgrims and their money. Only this old relic is encased in worn-out flesh instead of in those bejeweled, golden reliquaries found in cathedrals. Elias is concerned about my health, but I fear he's more concerned about the success of the Brotherhood and its treasury."

"Why don't you take a few days away at your favorite L'Eremo?" Elias said, placing a hand on Francesco's shoulder. "I'll send a couple of the brothers to accompany you, just to watch over you—but at a prudent distance away."

"I'm going to La Verna!" Francesco replied in a voice as soft as a whisper yet as sharp-edged as a sword. "I'm going to La Verna, and I'm going alone! Thank you, Brother, for your loving concern for me and my health, but do not fear; I shall return. God is not done with me here, not yet."

That night after midnight, while everyone else was fast asleep, Francesco crept away from Portiuncula in the darkness, fearful that Elias would prevent him from going further than L'Eremo. He headed northeast for Tuscany by way of Lake Trasimeno, carrying over his shoulder a bag containing a loaf of bread and the small crucifix painted by Jacobi of Florence. He had shown it to no one since Clare had given it to him, even Leone, for fear that word of it might spread and attract the anger of Bishop Carafa and the venom of the Parinians, who now counted many citizens of Assisi among their ranks.

By mid-afternoon Francesco had to sit down and rest. It seemed to him that the road to La Verna had grown three times longer and more arduous than he remembered. His frail body was telling him in

countless tongues that after forty-two years it was wearing out. As sunset neared, as he was again forced to stop and rest, and he reflected, "Now, I truly am a Muslim. My beloved friend Ali would be proud of me, for finally I've surrendered to the reality that my beloved dream is dead! I have come to accept that more than one person at a time cannot live in the absolute poverty of the Gospels without any compromise. For a group of hundreds, if not thousands, to embrace such radical poverty is totally unfeasible. I surrender that realization of my community's failure to you, Lady Poverty, and I present you with this token of my love." As he lifted his arms toward the sky, he declared, "In my arms I carry my dead dream to be buried up on Mount La Verna."

Standing up, he sighed, "Giddyup, Brother Ass, I know you're tired and aching, but to bury the dead is a work of mercy. We've more road to cover before we can sleep tonight. Let us depart in peace and joy, for my most basic rule in life has been to 'give thanks whatever happens, pray without ceasing, and always be joyful.' So, Francesco Giovanni, you must give thanks for the death of your dream, since gratitude heals." Then he began singing as he walked:

> My soul rejoices in you, God my Savior,
>
> and gives thanks for all you've given to me:
>
> the gifts of great love in Emiliano and Clare
>
> and my dream of being your poor troubadour.
>
> And I thank you for my brothers, especially
>
> Pietro, Bernardo, Giles, and Leone,
>
> for Bishop Guido and wise, holy Padre Antonio.
>
> *Allah akbar*, great is my God,
>
> for giving me those rich early years
>
> when the brothers were only a handful,
>
> nesting poor as birds in thatched huts.
>
> My soul rejoices in the golden memories
>
> of those early, carefree times
>
> of barefoot freedom, full of hope.

His song was drowned out by his fatigue, particularly the loud voices of his complaining legs, but he refused to listen to them. "Old

La Verna

Arezzo

Pieve Sto Stefano

Cortona

Perugia

Tiber River

Lake
Trasimeno

Assisi

Spello

Mount La Verna

legs, I apologize that I've made you walk so far. I heard your voices back there at the crossroad telling me to take the northern road to La Verna, but I wanted to see beautiful Lake Trasimeno and the hilltop city of Cortona along this route. We're in no hurry, and no one is expecting us at La Verna, except God, who is as present on this road as on that peaceful bluff. I know that, brother legs, lately you've begun to prefer that I just sit and do nothing. And it's painful for me to remember how only twenty-five years ago you so delighted in running for hours playing football in the streets of Assisi, how you never tired of dancing or being stretched to your limits in acrobatic tumbling. Age takes its toll, however, Brother Ass. My physical energy is diminishing daily, as are the once-roaring fires of passion in my heart. Even composing songs seems more difficult; once they effortlessly created themselves, but now I have to labor to make them flow. My eyes, once as sharp as a hawk's, now are growing fuzzy and clouded; even the daylight has begun to hurt them. O God, please do not ask me to embrace the terrible poverty of blindness, as you required of my beloved Padre Antonio."

Pausing to rest beside Lake Trasimeno, he recalled how on his way home from Spain he and Jacques had enjoyed bathing in its waters. He was no longer the same man, he lamented. "Aging itself has become my most demanding penitential discipline. I feel not only the aches and pains of getting old, but also the sting of losing the resilient vitality of my youth." As he saw his image in the waters of Trasimeno, he said, "I'm becoming as wrinkled as an old wineskin that has been drained almost dry—an accurate image, I'm afraid, for it seems I've run out of my once-abundant juices of excitement and enthusiasm. Once they gushed up out of me like a fountain, yet soon they'll be burying me alongside my dream for the Little Poor Men of Assisi. But before they find us dead here on the banks of Trasimeno, Brother Ass, let us be on our way."

He left the lakeshore and turned northward, climbing the road leading up to Cortona. Upon reaching the top of a high ridge, he turned around to look back at the panorama of the vast lake. The serene beauty of the blue lake inspired him, and he broke into prayer:

O Holy Creator of all things beautiful and lovely,

I thank you that my poor eyes can still behold

such glories of your creation as Lake Trasimeno.

I thank you as well for your emptying me of myself

through the painful penitential renunciations of aging.

Your son Jesus said, "Blessed are the poor;"

so I rejoice in being poor of my youthful vitality,

my once bubbling enthusiasm and endless energy,

stripped of my strength and my good eyesight.

By his dying, my Lord emptied himself on the cross

so that you could raise him up to a glorious new life.

Give me a mustard seed of faith in your holy plan,

trusting that by aging we are emptied of ourselves

so that we can be filled to the full with new life.

With joy I give thanks for your gifts of my infirmities.

Blessed are those who are poor

of their youthful health, strength, and vigor.

With one last parting look at the lake, he turned and continued up the road to Cortona and then trudged up the mountainous road from Cortona to Arezzo. There he turned eastward and continued toward La Verna. Finding walking the mountain terrain more difficult than ever before, he reflected, "My Liege Lord, Jesus Christ, I feel like you must have felt as you climbed up Calvary. Besides your cross, you carried your dead dream of the fulfillment of the peaceful kingdom you came to announce. Like you, I was God's troubadour singing the song of good news that most who heard me found to be too shrill for their ears."

At long last he arrived at Mount La Verna, and after climbing up through dense pines and beech trees, he finally reached the plateau atop the giant rock outcropping. Completely exhausted, all he could do was lay down and rest. Too tired even to pray, he slept most of the next day. Needing energy on his way to La Verna, he had nibbled away all of his loaf of bread, and now he began a total fast.

He decided to begin his retreat by burying his dead dream of the Little Poor Men of Assisi. Directly behind his hermitage he dug away the pebbles and soil with his hands to make a shallow hole into which he silently laid an invisible corpus.

"Dust to dust, ashes to ashes," he said repeating the Lenten prayer of Ash Wednesday. "Nothing in this life is imperishable; even dreams

 die. With a broken heart I consign you to the earth with the prayerful hope that by my compromises I was not responsible for your death. It seems that the will of God is that death should be part of life; so I pray that I may have the strength to accept the fate of the Little Brothers as God's will." Then he covered the empty hole with gravel and dirt. Standing up, he gathered a few nearby stones that he piled on top of the grave. "The will of God is often mysterious, for your ways, O Lord, are not our ways. With Holy Mary the Mother of God I say, '*fiat*, let it be.' Now let me grieve no more over my old dream—rather, by prayer and fasting may I discover how I am now to imitate my beloved Lord."

Day after day he prayed, sitting for hours on end simply holding in front of him the graphically painted crucifix of Jacobi he had carried with him. His prayer was not of the lips but of the eyes as he stared with intense affection, contemplating the dying agony of Christ on the cross.

Late in the afternoon of the twelfth day of his complete fast, he walked, with his crucifix in his right hand, to the edge of the stone cliff, which dropped sharply down to the domed treetops below. With his toes on the very edge, he stood looking at the enormous orange globe of a sun that seemed to be hovering in the blood-red western sky, as if hesitating, reluctant to descend behind the bluish, mist-draped mountains. "Brother Sun, what are you waiting for?" The sun didn't answer and only seemed to grow larger. "This day is ending, and Sister Moon is eager to grace the night sky with her full, round, milky September face. Brother Sun, are you delaying your setting because something is supposed to happen before this day ends—something that you want to see with your giant orange eye?"

Chapter 23

THE ONLY SOUND WAS THE SILENT SIZZLING MADE BY THE great orb of the sun that inexplicably appeared to hang suspended in the sky. Not a leaf stirred anywhere in the forest; the breeze that earlier marked this September day seemed to be holding its breath. Paused in his prayer, Francesco wondered why everything seemed so still. Then, feeling the painted crucifix in his hand, he raised it up in front of his face again to gaze lovingly at the figure of his crucified Lord. "Before Brother Darkness comes to hide your pain and suffering from these old eyes of mine, my beloved Christ, I steal one final long look at you nailed in love to your cross. These past dozen days as I've prayed with my eyes glued upon your pierced body, meditating on your passion, I find that your crucifixion has become as vividly alive and real to me as if I were with you on Calvary those many years ago." Then, as tears flowed in torrents down his cheeks, he began lavishly kissing the painted Christ on the crucifix. "O my Beloved, with all my heart I yearn to share your pain, long to be pierced with the same love that you experienced for each of us, for all of creation, for the world and. . . ."

Suddenly his lips stiffened, his tongue became as rigid as a mute's, unable to speak another word. It felt like someone was pouring autumn's newly fermented wine into the old, worn wine bag of his body. This infusion of his former youthful effervescence and bubbling zest caused his recently diminished senses of hearing, touch, and especially sight to spring into a heightened teenage-like stage of awareness. The formerly stagnant green moss on the rocks now began to pulsate and squirm as if it was made up of thousands of miniature creeping creatures. Gazing out over the edge of the cliff at his feet and

down at the green crown tops of the trees below, he saw swimming in them patches of exotic shades of green he had never seen before. In his precious days praying there at La Verna, he had become accustomed to the various songs of the many birds in the surrounding trees, but now his ears rang with a chorus of hundreds of stunningly beautiful bird voices. And they were coming from all over, from up out of the leafy domes of the trees below, from plants and flowers and even from the stone outcropping beneath his feet. Francesco shook his head, attempting to clear it of what he was hearing and seeing, fearful of what had taken possession of him. Then, looking down at the painted crucifix in his hand, he screamed, "What? It's impossible!" for the figure on it had vanished. At that moment he began to hear a strange whirling sound overhead. It seemed to be harmonizing with all the birdsong surrounding him on that stone ledge of the cliff.

Looking up toward the whirling sound, he gasped in horror, for suspended over him, hanging midair, was a life-size image of the crucified Christ from Jacobi's cross. With his arms outstretched, Francesco dropped to his knees as he watched the body of the crucified Christ slowly begin lowering itself toward him. Then, not just with his ears but with every pore of his body, he heard a voice saying, "My Beloved Francesco, I've heard your prayer. Your wish is granted!" The giant orange-red orb of a sun behind the descending crucified body now began expanding larger and larger as its fiery outer rim burst into six spiraling giant wings covered with tonguelike feathers of fire. Terrified, Francesco dropped the wooden cross as he fell backwards onto the earth with his arms outstretched and his palms opened wide. The earth beneath him began rhythmically rising and falling, and he was filled with the ecstasy of anticipation as the fire-winged Christ slowly lowered itself closer and closer until it came to rest on top of his body. Then he heard a voice like rolling thunder, saying, "I love you," as a searing pain plunged through his hands, feet and entire body. He cried out with a primal scream that expressed the twin reality of unbearable pain and ecstatic joy that was exploding within him. Then everything disappeared into darkness.

It was night when he regained consciousness. Overhead, the large milky-white full moon of September was gazing down on him like a giant white eye. His hands ached with pain, and holding up his right hand, he could see by the light of the full moon that his palm was bleeding and had been pierced. Upon examination, so were his left

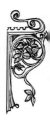

hand and both his feet. Feeling a severe pain in his right side, he glanced down to see that his tunic in the area of his chest was bloody and ripped, and it appeared from the rest of his blood-splattered tunic that he had been in some kind of fierce struggle. With great effort he raised himself up onto his knees but fell over when he attempted to stand because of the agonizing pain in the soles of his feet. With difficulty he crawled into his hermitage hut and collapsed. For the remainder of the night he was only able to snatch bits and pieces of sleep.

The next morning, resting his weight on his heels to keep pressure off the soles of his feet, he stumbled outside his hut. In the early morning sunlight he could see reddish flesh wounds in the palms of his hands and soles of his feet. In the center of the wounds were small bluish-purple knobs as hard as nail heads. Lifting up his blood-splattered tunic, he saw an ugly reddish wound about a hand-width in diameter on the right side of his chest.

"What happened to me?" he groaned. My eyes and ears heard and saw such strange things in that seizure. Did I somehow inflict these wounds upon myself?" He glanced around the terrain at the top of the plateau to see if there were pointed sticks that might have caused the gashes, but the only piece of wood he saw was the cross of Jacobi lying on the stone ledge at the edge of the cliff. When he reached down to pick it up, he again screamed in agony, for it was, indeed, bare of its original painted image! Seizing the cross, he flung it as far as he could out over the cliff and watched it disappear into the trees below him. Then he slumped down on the stone ledge, burying his head in his pierced hands, sobbing, "What happened to me? Was what I experienced real, or have I finally gone mad, raving mad, and stigmatized myself, marking myself for life like they brand criminals and slaves?" After a few moments of sitting in his grief and confusion, he prayed, "O God, help me to understand what actually happened to me here yesterday at sunset."

He began trying to recall the events of the previous day. The first thing that came to him was the feeling of being like an old cracked wine skin that had been filled with fall's newly fermented wine. "My old skin," he thought, "unable to hold that vigorous new wine, must have burst open, that potent vintage flowing out through my palms, feet and side. Is that what happened to create these wounds in my body? Or did I myself—or even someone or something else—pierce

me?" He began rocking back and forth, trying to calm himself as he moaned, "I've been wounded before in my life. My old hidden wounds of Spoleto, Perugia and Chambery. . . ." He stopped abruptly at the very sound of the word and repeated it: "Chambery! What happened last night felt just like what I experienced that night long ago when I was a mere youth in France." Slowly he repeated a name he hadn't spoken in years: "*Chateau d'eau*, the water castle. Yes, that magical sense of the full moon, and the earth moving beneath me—and the intensity of the pleasure that transported me out of myself. Only. . . ."

He paused and looked at his hands as he recalled the Fair of Chambery. "I remember vividly awakening the next morning after that night of exotic pleasure being filled with guilt and enormous fear that unless I went to confession I would be doomed to the eternal fires of hell. This morning I'm equally terrified—but not of hell. I'm frightened of the Church! I recall Saint Paul having said something about carrying in his body the marks of Jesus, but I've never seen any frescos of him with those wounds in his hands and feet. And I know of no other saint who has been branded with the wounds of Christ as it now appears that I've been. I'm already suspected of heresy, and once this. . . ." He didn't finish his sentence because his mind was too busy trying to wave away the angry swarms of fearful images about what might happen to him once his wounds become public.

"O God, be merciful to me," he moaned. "Take away these wounds of your Son. For once Bishop Carafa or Cardinal Uzielli learn about these wounds, they will surely say that I inflicted them upon myself. And those hounds from hell—the Parinians—once they hear about my wounds will accuse me of witchcraft, self-mutilation and sensationalism. I must keep them a secret, but how can I. . . ?"

"Francesco, Francesco, where are you?" He heard the voice of his old friend Leone calling from somewhere in the nearby groves of pine trees. "Father Francesco, where are you?" came the voice of Brother Jacques from further away. "Are you all right?"

Francesco stumbled to his feet and was momentarily filled with the urge to follow the cross he had thrown over the ledge by jumping to his death. When the temptation passed, he awkwardly walked back to his hermitage hut and called out, "Up here, on top of the ledge, my brothers. But there's no need to come up here. I'm perfectly well. Please don't disturb my solitude."

"We must, Father Francesco, I'm sorry," came Leone's voice as he reached the top of the ledge. "Obedience forces us to violate your solitude! Brother Elias gave us strict orders to come here to La Verna to see if you were all right, and . . ." he paused, "to bring you back home to Assisi."

"Come in peace then," Francesco moaned as he shrank as far back as possible into the darkness of his hut. Upon entering the hut, Leone was shocked to see his friend's bloody, torn tunic, and so Francesco knew it was impossible to attempt to hide his wounds. When he told the story of what had happened the previous afternoon and how fearful he was of the implications of the wounds, Leone shook his head in disbelief and wept. He promised not to speak of them to anyone, and then with a wry, thin smile he asked, "Father Francesco, do you know what feast yesterday was?"

"No, Leone. I've lost all track of time."

"It was September 14, the feast of the Exaltation of the Cross."

As Francesco was about to say how appropriate was that feast in light of what had happened to him, Brother Jacques arrived at the top of the ledge with a donkey. When he stepped into the hermitage, he gasped at the sight of Francesco's blood-splattered tunic and his hideous wounds. After Francesco told him the story about how he had received the wounds, Jacques also promised not to speak of them.

"Unknowingly, Brother Elias acted providentially when," Jacques said as he pointed outside toward the donkey, "he insisted that Leone and I take along this ass. While Elias was worried about your failing health, Father Francesco, I think he sent the two of us to find you since he was even more anxious that you would be inspired in your solitude to run off to France, Spain, or who knows where, and just disappear. And he placed both me and Leone under strict obedience to bring you back to Portiuncula, regardless of what you might say."

As Jacques cradled him in his arms, carried him out, and placed him on the donkey, Francesco smiled, thinking, "Indeed, the devil did tempt me to escape, and for once I almost regret not giving in to a temptation." They departed at once, carefully making their way down from the top of La Verna, and headed eastward toward the road that led down to Assisi. As they traveled, Francesco suffered not only from the pain of his wounds but even more from the agony of anticipating the consequences of being stigmatized with the wounds of Christ.

"I will need a new tunic," he moaned to his companions. "This one is so badly ripped and bloody that it will only draw attention to me. Let us stop in the first village that we come to find a new one."

"As you see, we're returning by way of Perugia," Jacques said. "It'll be a shorter route, and we can stop at Pieve Sto Stefano not far from here where this road meets up with the one leading south to Perugia. Quoting the new Rule to us, Elias insisted that we take money along with us; so we can use some of it buy you a new tunic."

"Not a new one, Jacques. It must be a secondhand one. And please select a tunic sized to fit someone as tall as you are, so it will hang well below my feet and the longer sleeves will hide my hands. I'll look foolish in it, but I prefer that to being gawked at by my brothers and the hordes of pious pilgrims I fear will come if the word gets out. O God, haven't you sent me enough afflictions already?"

Just outside the village of San Stefano they came upon a small stream where they stopped to rest. Jacques lifted Francesco off the donkey, set him on its bank and then went to the village to purchase a tunic. Leone remained to bathe Francesco's wounds in the stream, cleansing them ever so cautiously so as not to cause him more pain. As he lovingly cared for his old friend, he prayed silently, "Lord, I believe, help my unbelief. Is it possible that my beloved Francesco had a seizure of some sort, during which he used a sharp stick to inflict these wounds upon himself? Yet if he did, how would one explain these purplish nubs that feel like nail heads in the center of the wounds in his feet and hands? It's all a mystery to me." As he carefully dried off his old friend's hands and feet, he continued to reflect, "My beloved friend is the priest of priests! While other priests can change the bread they hold in their hands into the body of Christ and transform wine into our Savior's blood, Father Francesco somehow has changed his own body into the body of Christ. If it would not embarrass him, I would kneel before him in wonder and adoration."

Tearing off strips of Francesco's old tunic, he began making bandages out of them to bind up the wounds in his friend's feet and hands. As he was finishing, Jacques returned carrying a used tunic that at first appeared to be a grayish-brown shade but in the full sunlight was clearly brown. "I'm sorry about the color, Francesco, but you told me that you wanted a used tunic, and this was the only one I could find that fit your description." When Francesco began to mumble an

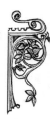

objection that it wasn't his usual gray, he bit his tongue, accepting yet another painful change in his life.

Lifting Francesco up onto the donkey, Jacques suddenly exclaimed, "Al-Junaid!" When both Leone and Francesco looked at him puzzled, he said, "In that brown tunic, Francesco, you look just like that Sufi Al-Junaid we saw in the tent of Sultan Al-Kamil in Egypt—remember the holy man with the wounds of the Prophet Muhammad?" Until that moment Francesco had not thought again about the stigmatic Sufi who had so identified himself with his beloved prophet that he mystically bore his wounds in his body. His heart throbbed in wonderment as he anguished, "Without knowing it, did I passionately wish that same experience would be mine? I don't consciously recall desiring it, but it seems I did. O God, come and help me to fathom your purpose in this bizarre experience that holds such grave dangers for me."

As the three traveled southward, the pain from Francesco's wounds lessened somewhat, but while his spirits lifted, he was still easily wearied by the journey. Late in the afternoon of the first day, they decided to stop at the well of a tiny village. Jacques lifted Francesco off his donkey and set him down to rest against the old stone wall of a mill. Leone used the occasion to express his wonder at the miracle of the stigmata, asking Francesco what kind of holiness or prayer produced such an identification with Christ. At that very moment a deformed boy of about fifteen came stumbling awkwardly up the road. His legs swung with little coordination to the left and right, seemingly independent of each other, as his frail body swayed from side to side in an attempt to maintain his balance.

"See that lad coming up the road, Leone? God has also visited upon him the stigmata of Christ. His malformed young body has been stigmatized for a lifelong Calvary, with the pain of never joyfully running with his friends while kicking a football down the road. He'll never be able to work or know the joy of falling in love with a beautiful maid—or the fulfillment of joining in marriage. For cripples like him, all the future holds is a life of begging. Surely, Leone, his wounds came not from prayer or holiness, yet because of his stigmata at birth he can become a saint. Remember that poor weeping mother we passed on the road carrying in her arms the tiny coffin that contained her dead child? Only a few village women were accompanying her to the cemetery—but no husband, who was perhaps killed by the pestilence or in some

war. She bears in her body the wounds of Christ as surely as do these hands of mine, even though her wounds are invisible to others."

Then, observing that no one was watching, he slowly extended his hands beyond his sleeves with his palms turned upward.

"Leone, forgive my long response to your question, but being transformed into the likeness of our Lord comes from love—either the great love of God or a great love for God. Yet that great love, of course, is also a great mystery. I cannot comprehend why God so loved people like this lad approaching us—or especially his own Son Jesus—to so wound them, or why, uninvited, he imposes the wounds of his Son on someone who so intensely loves him?" Leone and Jacques sat pondering silently as the misshapen lad who was staggering past them turned and smiled beautifully, wishing them a good day. Francesco returned his greeting with a smile filled with tenderness, saying, "And a good life to you, lad."

Then turning to Jacques, he said, "Ah, dear friend, if you would be so kind as to lift up old Brother Ass onto Brother Donkey. It's time that we move on." As they departed from the village, he reached out and touched Jacques' arm, adding, "You also have a stigmata, the scar of that wound that disfigures your face. And you, Leone, I'm sure you must have your hidden wounds, just as did Mary, the Mother of God. Recall how old Simeon, after foretelling in the temple that her son would be the light of revelation said to her, 'and you yourself shall be pierced by a sword.' In her quiet, hidden ways she also was stigmatic. Does not every disciple of the Lord mysteriously share in his wounds? Like those plain, unattractive village girls whose stigmata is their lack of beauty; those crippled of body and mind; those pierced by the wounds of the grinding exploitation of poverty. Since La Verna, I have come to believe that everyone united with Christ in baptism is stigmatized in either a visible or invisible way. So, Leone, my personal sharing in the passion of Christ back at La Verna isn't unique or extraordinary."

"That may be true, my holy friend," Leone thought to himself, "but few bear the wounds of Christ so transparently as you."

As they passed the fortress hilltop city of Perugia and continued down the road leading to Assisi, Francesco mused, "Those mystic wounds of the Sufi Al-Junaid were not visible until he uncovered himself, but, unfortunately, it will not be easy to keep mine hidden." Turning around, he looked back at Perugia, thinking, "Once again I'm coming home to Assisi as an invalid, this time being carried by a little donkey. Yet these new wounds won't be as simple to hide as the wounds that stigmatized me years ago in the dungeon of Perugia."

*U*pon arriving back at Portiuncula, Francesco would reply to anyone who asked, "I now wear a tunic with long sleeves to keep my hands warm. And, see, it's also long enough to cover my feet to keep them from getting cold—yes, brother, even in the summer or fall. In old age the stove of the body grows cooler, as you yourself will find out some day." Then, before the person could ask, he would add, "And I've come to prefer the color brown to our usual gray because it's more like the color of Sister Earth."

Because Francesco was exhausted by his journey and by a return of his marsh fever, Elias insisted that he now sleep on a bed with a straw mattress, contending that he was in too frail a condition to sleep on the floor. Although Francesco requested solitude so he could rest after his return from La Verna, a procession of old friends came to see him. Lying on his straw mattress with only the tips of his fingers and his toes showing from his tunic, he would warmly greet his visitors. Like a mother hen, Brother Leone was there to insure that the visits were short. One by one his dearest friends came to see him: Brother Bernardo, now bent over and aging, the old but ever-innocent Giles, and a now-aging Masseo. Next came Brother Silvestro, whom Leone leaned over to tell Francesco was now a renowned preacher in the order. Francesco smiled broadly, remembering the day on their return from their first visit to Rome when a young Silvestro had frightened away the birds as he tried to preach to them.

When Francesco greeted his next visitor with a title of respect, he was corrected. "No, Father Francesco, it isn't *Dom* any more. I'm now Friar Tomas, simply one of your brothers who has come for your blessing."

"No, Tomas, it is you as a priest who should bless me, but . . . very well." Placing his hand on Tomas' bowed head, he prayed, "O God, bless Brother Tomas with a heart fiercely on fire with love, with the humility of Sister Earth and an unquenchable passion for poverty and humble service." The blessing completed, Francesco asked, "Now, tell me, Tomas, why do you call yourself Friar?"

"It's from *frater*, Latin, as you know, for brother. That's how we're known by the people now; they call us Franciscan Friars."

Before Francesco could respond, the ever-solicitous Leone took Brother Tomas by the arm and quickly ushered him out. Francesco closed his eyes and drew in a deep breath, not so much because his eyes or his wounds pained him, but out of grief that the Little Brothers of Assisi had been renamed.

"Vanity and pride," he thought, "are the most insidious of sins because they rob God of glory. Old, fat, puffed-up self-importance is the most diabolic of the soul's enemies. Not only have I been robbed of my original dream, now I'm forced to bear the shame of having my own name imposed on my brothers. Whoever heard of artists or painters putting their names on their art works? Why did they even need a new name? What was wrong. . . ?" His penitential thorn-pricking thoughts were interrupted as he felt a large warm hand on his forehead. Opening his eyes, all his pain vanished. Emiliano leaned over and kissed him on the cheek.

"*Caro mio!* The sight of you is better than any medicine or tonic. Thank you for coming to visit me, since, as you see, I couldn't come to visit you. My well-wishers have imprisoned me in this bed to prevent me from sleeping on the bare floor, and my caring warden, Leone, keeps guard, insuring that I don't escape." Francesco wanted to hear all about the Third Order, about his godson Francesco and all the news of Assisi. However, the tapping foot of Brother Leone soon cut short Emiliano's visit. Before he left, he leaned down and placed on Francesco's forehead a kiss concentrated with the soul of his friendship.

Leone could see that Francesco was tiring, so he saw to it that Brother Elias was his final visitor of that day. Elias entered the small room gushing over with good wishes for Francesco's recovery to full health and insuring him that all was going well in the order. As he chatted, he nervously tucked a loose strand of hair behind his ear, wondering with intense curiosity why Francesco had insisted on wearing such an oversized tunic—and a brown one at that. When he departed, Francesco asked Leone to hang blankets over the window because the daylight was beginning to irritate his eyes. As Leone was attending to the windows, the door opened and Sebastiano stuck his head in, asking, "Father Francesco, may I see you?"

Over Leone's loud objections, Francesco raised his hand, delighted to see Sebastiano's beaming, youthful face, and eagerly welcomed him into the darkened hut.

"I won't be long, for I was told you needed to rest," Sebastiano said with a glance toward Leone. "But I had to tell you how good it is to have you back again among us and. . . ."

"And. . . ?"

"Father Francesco, you're like a spiritual father to me, and I need to ask you a question. I've a new friend in the community, one of the new younger brothers whose name is Brother Innocenti. . . ."

"A nice name; I like it."

"He's a poet, like you, and a beautiful person. He and I have become the best of friends, the kind I've always longed to find, a true *caro mio*. Each night after supper during recreation we walk together and talk soul to soul. Well, the other day Minister General Elias called me into his office. . . ."

"Ah, Minister *General*. . . ."

"Yes, that's his new title, which he says means the 'head servant.' Well, Elias told me that Innocenti and I had a particular friendship and that they were not allowed in the brotherhood because they were so dangerous to the spiritual life. He told me that from now on whenever I go walking in recreation I am to do so with no less than three of the brothers to insure the purity of our friendships. Father Francesco, do you think particular friendships are dangerous? How would you advise me?"

"The Minister General is very prudent," Francesco said softly as he recalled his intimate friendships with Emiliano and Ali Hasan, allowing the waves of beautiful memories to wash over him, muting the irritating voices of his wounds. Sebastiano sat patiently waiting for an answer as Brother Leone began tapping his foot impatiently waiting for the young brother to leave.

"Particular friendships are dangerous, yes. . . ." Francesco said as he again momentarily drifted off into his own thoughts: "It does not surprise me that Elias should warn him of the grave dangers of particular friendships, for he himself has one—with power. His *caro mio* is authority and control. Elias is a good man who does what he thinks is right; he's quick of wit, works hard, and is a master at managing details. But because of his humble birth, he is enamored and enthralled by his intimate contacts with powerful men of influence, like bishops, cardinals, and especially the Pope."

Brother Leone coughed diplomatically. "Ah yes, Sebastiano, as to your question about intimate friendships," Francesco said, carefully

selecting his words so as not to undermine Elias's authority in the community. "Indeed, Elias is right; they are dangerous—since God is dangerous! Yes, indeed, Sebastiano, deliciously dangerous."

Sebastiano smiled, signaling that he had decoded Francesco's message. Francesco ached to show him the wounds in his hands and feet so he would see how truly dangerous a deeply intimate, particular friendship could be, but prudence, aided by Brother Leone, intervened.

"Brother, can't you see that you're wearying poor Father Francesco. Time for you to go. Now, be off with you." Before he departed, Sebastiano leaned over and kissed Francesco on the forehead, whispering, "Thank you, *carissima.*"

*W*eeks of rest did not improve Francesco's health. He continued suffering from fatigue, and his eye afflictions grew worse. He often complained of the light and insisted that the room be kept as dark as possible during the day. At night even candlelight seemed to pain his eyes. Leone and Jacques wondered privately if his reason for keeping the hut in darkness wasn't partially to prevent any of his visitors from seeing his stigmatic wounds. Yet as his caretaker, Leone was aware of the intense burning and itching of Francesco's eyes, as well as his blurred vision. Francesco had intense headaches, which he said caused his forehead to ache as if someone had jabbed a flaming red spike into it.

With the ever-increasing parade of brothers, visitors, and pilgrims to the door of his hut, it was decided to move him to another location. At night Brother Leone and a couple of other brothers secretly transported Francesco to a small hut adjacent to the convent of San Damiano. Elias then delegated them to care for Francesco and his needs. One morning he said his need was for them to carry him up to the convent. He and Clare had a long private visit in which he told her his La Verna secret. She wept when he showed her his hands, and she grieved as she recalled her words to him at their last visit: "Francesco, what more can you do to imitate Christ except to be crucified."

When they carried him back to the hut next to the convent, he felt renewed by his visit with Clare, but within days the ravages of his sickness returned. His eye disease worsened, and his eyes now filled with acute drainage that pained him day and night. Coupled with his severe headaches, this torment forced him to embrace the most difficult

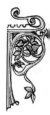

fast of his life: going without sleep both night and day. They continued to use blankets to cover the one window in his hut because he found the sunlight as searing as yellow acid to his eyes.

And so, what happened one morning came as a great surprise to Leone and the other brothers. Shortly after sunrise they heard him calling to them. "Brother Leone, and the rest of you, come quickly!" Upon entering the hut they found him sitting up in bed smiling. "Brother Filippo, I know that Brother Elias had you bring along a pen and parchment should I want to send any messages, or . . . ," he chuckled mischievously, "to record any gems of spiritual wisdom that might dribble from these old lips. So, Filippo, run and get your pen and parchment, for I've been inspired with a new song!" When Filippo returned and sat with his pen poised over a fresh piece of parchment, Francesco began singing like a lark:

> All praise to you, Brother Sun,
>
> who brings us the day, and for the gift of light.
>
> All praise to you, Sisters Moon and Stars,
>
> who brighten the heavens so precious and fair.
>
> All praise to you, Brothers Wind and Air,
>
> both fair and stormy—all the weather's moods.
>
> All praise to you, Sister Water,
>
> so lowly, useful, precious, and pure.
>
> All praise to you, Brother Fire,
>
> who brightens up the night;
>
> how beautiful and joyous are you,
>
> full of power and strength.

"Father Francesco, what title shall I give to this song?" asked Brother Filippo.

"Let's call it . . . ah . . . the Canticle of the Creatures. This morning before dawn it came playfully dancing into my mind." Then, beaming at them, Francesco added, "and being inspired again is the best tonic I've had in weeks. So, Brother Leone, as you can see, your patient—or, rather, your prisoner—is feeling better today. So, old friend, and all of you, I'm eager to know what you think of my new prayer song?"

"Prayer song?" replied Leone, "Song, yes; but prayer? You made no reference to the supernatural, the spiritual, the kingdom of heaven or even to the Lord. Your song only praises ordinary material things."

"But, Brother Leone, they are not ordinary. True, they're material, but they're matter soaked with the sacred. Must we baptize Brother Sun and Sister Moon?" Leone did not answer but only shook his head in disbelief.

"Shall I take your prayer song to Brother Elias?" asked Brother Filippo.

"Not yet, Brother. Inspirations rarely arrive dressed in their finest attire; like a wrinkled gown, they need to be ironed out. Poets need to be—or to have—tailors who embellish their works by sewing on a word here or there and smoothing out the crumpled edges. Before we show it to Elias or others, I'll have to address the concerns of my best critic, Brother Leone. So for now, let's put away the Canticle of the Creatures. I'll return to it later to do a bit of tailoring on it."

While his hideaway in the small hut next to San Damiano had given him a brief reprieve from visitors and pious pilgrims, soon the knowledge of his presence at San Damiano was discovered and quickly spread, attracting large numbers of people to his door asking to see him. This loss of his privacy, combined with the arrival of spring, caused him to request a visit to his beloved Rieti Valley, where he hoped to find some solitude and healing in the peacefulness of Fonte Colombo. Elias agreed, on the condition that Brother Leone and at least four of the friars accompany him. With a mother's gentleness Brother Jacques carried him out of the hut and placed him on the back of a small gray donkey. The two then exchanged an affectionate farewell. Jacques was not to accompany him on this journey because Elias had insisted he go to France with a friar who was carrying a message to the Bishop of Marseilles.

So, with Leone leading the donkey, and the other four friars, whom he jokingly called his four guardian angels, Francesco rode away from the hut at San Damiano. As they went past the convent, he looked at its barred windows confident that his beloved Clare was watching him. So he smiled and raised his right hand, tracing the sign of the cross on the convent, careful that only his fingers extended beyond the cuffs of his long sleeve.

The journey down to Rieti Valley was slow, as Francesco needed numerous rest stops because of his fatigue. But the closer they came to

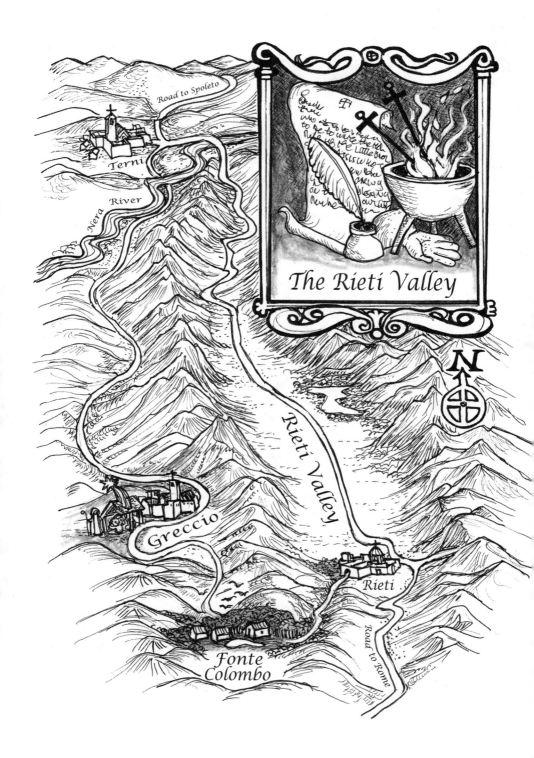

The Rieti Valley

Road to Spoleto

Terni

Nera River

Rieti Valley

N

Greccio

Rieti

Fonte Colombo

Road to Rome

Fonte Colombo, the more his spirit seemed to thrive. About a week or so after they arrived, the usually sleepy village of Rieti erupted with excitement at the arrival of Cardinal Ugolino and his large entourage on their way to Perugia. Upon learning that Francesco of Assisi was staying only a short distance way at Fonte Colombo, Ugolino, accompanied only by two companion clerics, went there to visit him. He greeted Francesco warmly, explaining that he was passing through Rieti on his journey from Rome to Perugia, where he intended to arrange for the transfer of his uncle Pope Innocent III's body so it could be properly entombed in the Basilica of St. John the Lateran in Rome. While Ugolino had been informed privately about Francesco's stigmata wounds and his enormous reluctance to display them, the cardinal discreetly didn't speak of them or request to see them. Moreover, he hadn't needed Leone's quick review of Francesco's physical condition to see that it had rapidly deteriorated since he last saw him.

"Father Francesco, I am distressed to see your weakened condition and to learn of your increasingly painful headaches and your failing eyesight. These will prematurely rob us of having you where we need you—here on earth. And we must do everything possible to see that heaven will wait for your arrival. Your physical presence is a most powerful influence and one that's so necessary if we are to make progress on the needed reforms initiated by Pope Innocent and the Council. You are the kind of blazing lamp our Savior spoke of that needs to be put on a stand so all can see its light."

Francesco tried to explain that he wasn't as sickly as he looked and that all he needed was a few weeks more of retreat in the serenity of Fonte Colombo, but Ugolino held up a gloved hand.

"More than the healing powers of nature are needed," Ugolino replied. "And your old friend, Pope Honorius, would be grieved to see you so afflicted, Brother Francesco. So for the good of Holy Mother Church and your Order of Friars, I am immediately sending one of my couriers back to Rome. He will carry my personal request to have our most distinguished physicians in the Eternal City come here at once to examine you and then treat your afflictions." As Francesco began to object, the cardinal raised his hand and asserted, "No, this is not a debatable issue! Think of this as a papal command, Father Francesco, for if His Holiness Pope Honorius knew of your condition, he would surely order it himself. Now, I regret that I cannot remain with you, but

I must be on my way to Perugia. So I leave you in Brother Leone's capable hands."

Francesco thanked him for his genuine concern and the thoughtfulness of stopping to visit him, but he gulped as he reflected on the cardinal's plan. "Seeing the distressed look on your face, I don't want you to be alarmed, Father Francesco. Fear not; these eminent physicians from the Eternal City possess the most advanced medical knowledge of the thirteenth century. I can assure you that you will be in competent hands."

A week later four Roman physicians arrived dressed in their traditional purple gowns and red gloves and accompanied by several assistants. The villagers of Rieti buzzed with curiosity and excitement, for unlike their local folk healers who treated the sick, these distinguished purple-gowned physicians from Rome were borne along in a prestigious cloud of authority. Proud of their studies in Greek and Arabic texts in the medical schools of Salerno and Bologna, the four considered themselves the high priests of their profession. They saw themselves as scholars who were not to be associated with common bonesetters and herbalists—and especially not with surgeons, whom they considered mere manual laborers or barbers, and only a notch above butchers.

When the physicians came to Fonte Colombo, they found it inappropriate for their work, and so they ordered the patient to be moved to nearby Rieti, only a two-hour walk away. Francesco refused. After asking him countless questions about his pains and afflictions, examining his eyes and probing his forehead with their red-gloved fingers in an attempt to determine the source of his severe pains, they walked a distance away to hold a hushed conference.

Upon their return, Signore Giraldi, the chief physician, gave Francesco their diagnosis that he was not suffering from the common eye afflictions caused by tumors or cataracts, but rather was beset by trachoma. "*Glaukoma*," Giraldi said pontifically, "is the Greek medical term for this disease that leads to blindness. It can cause the intense pain in the forehead that you reported, and such severe distress anywhere in the person creates a trauma throughout the entire body. The learned Greek philosopher Plato said that such pain is even experienced in the soul."

"How true, how true," thought Francesco, "my soul is racked with pain."

"Besides fatigue, fevers, cramps, and sweating," Giraldi continued as he counted them off on his red-gloved fingers, "attacks of diarrhea are often common." Seeing the unspoken question on Francesco's face, he said, "Severe pain, we scholars know, effects many of the muscles of the body, causing them to lose control. As you know, even those who are hanged suffer from loose bowels.

"Naturally, the procedure of healing your disease will be painful, so would you like for us to give you an anesthesia? Ah, I see you're unfamiliar with this Greek medical term; it means 'without feeling.' We will soak a sponge in mandragora, a mixture of pressed leaves from the wondrous mandrake plant, or with 'drowsy drops' from the East, and then hold the sponge over your nose, causing you to fall into a deep sleep." Then smiling, he summed up, "Anesthesia: without feeling."

"I can't think of anything worse," Francesco said, "than being without feeling. No, I don't want anything that would do that."

Making a slight bow, Signore Giraldi said, "Before we begin, then, Father Francesco, my distinguished colleagues and I would like to remind you that the final result of this newest medical treatment does not rest in our hands, but rather in those of Almighty God."

Francesco nodded in affirmation, for he believed that the ultimate fate of everything rests in the hands of God. As the physicians turned away from his bed to unpack their instruments for the procedure, Francesco overheard one of them say to the chief physician in hushed tones, "Giraldi, I'm glad that you added that final caveat. We all know what happened to the physician who failed to cure the cataracts of near-blind King John of Bohemia." Giraldi nodded and whispered in response, "They had him sewed up in a sack and thrown into the Oden River."

Even as blurred as his vision was, Francesco could see out of the corner of his eye that one of physicians' assistants was tending a fire in a small coal brassier just outside the door. As Signore Giraldi and another physician put on heavy leather gloves and went outside to the brassier, the two other physicians came and held Francesco's arms firmly on the bed. Leone, Filippo, and the three other brothers knelt by his bed praying for the success of this newest of medical treatments. Francesco braced himself, praying for God's help with whatever pain might come, but his prayer froze on his lips when he saw Giraldi and his colleague enter the hut carrying glowing, red-hot iron rods. As they stood poised over him with their raised fiery instruments, his lips broke free of ice:

All praise to you, Brother Fire,

who warms the night and lightens the darkness.

All praise to you who purifies souls and . . .

and please, Brother Fire, be gentle.

He screamed loudly as the red-hot iron rods pierced his temples just above his eyes, and then he passed out. Brothers Filippo and Niccolo ran out of the hut with their hands over their mouths, and Brother Leone wailed in agony as he and the other two brothers slumped over, burying their heads in their hands. The two physicians raised and lowered their rods again and again, cauterizing the hidden disease lurking in Francesco's forehead. As the stench of burning flesh filled the small hut, the physicians again went outside and returned with thinner but equally red-hot rods. Two of the physicians proceeded to grip Francesco's head firmly in their red-gloved hands, and the other two pierced his earlobes with the thin red-hot needles. Then the four doctors stepped back, allowing their two assistants to come to Francesco's bedside with a large bowl, which Signore Giraldi explained to Leone contained old wine that had been mixed with the sterile whites of two just-broken eggs. After bathing his forehead and ears in the solution, the assistants wrapped Francesco's forehead in dressings covered with ointment.

"You see, Friar Leone, the old wine in the mixture that we've used," instructed Signore Giraldi, "is strong in alcohol, which Arabian science has proven will help to heal the cauterized wounds in Francesco's temples and ears. We are leaving some of the jars of ointment we've used, as well as some of the old-wine-and-egg solution for your use with the patient. Upon our return to Rome, we shall send a detailed report of our medical treatment to his Eminence Cardinal Ugolino and another copy to His Holiness Pope Honorius III, who was most solicitous that Francesco of Assisi be given the finest medical treatment available today."

"Will this new treatment cure his eyes?" asked a red-eyed, tearful Leone.

"Ah, *cure* is an interesting word," said Giraldi with a deep sigh. "Yes, if it is God's will. However, if the procedure is not successful, then notify us and we will return and repeat the operation, since one treatment sometimes is not sufficient. Naturally, we pray for a complete cure, for the patient is so beloved by both His Eminence Cardinal Ugolino and His Holiness Pope Honorius. Friar Leone," he concluded with a slight bow, "we are your humble servants. Good day."

Leone stood alone over his unconscious friend and groaned, "Dear Francesco, your imitation of our Lord and Savior is now complete. Along with the wounds in your hands and feet, you now bear the scars of his crown of thorns, which you'll likewise carry to your grave." Tilting his head back and looking up to the heavens, he cried out, "Enough, Lord! Do you hear me? Enough! Leave this poor man alone."

When Francesco regained consciousness, the first question he asked Leone and the other four friars around his bed was, "Brother Leone, did you thank Signore Giraldi and the other physicians? How gracious it was for such eminent physicians to come all this way up here from Rome to treat a humble beggar like me."

His recovery from having his forehead cauterized was quicker than they expected. The burned punctures in his forehead had already formed scabs when a messenger arrived from Assisi. Elias had sent him to inform Leone that Francesco must be returned at once to Portiuncula, where they could better assist his recovery. When Leone told him the message, Francesco grinned, thinking, "Ah, Brother Fox wants me back home because he's worried that I might die down here in the Rieti Valley and that my dead body will be pilfered away in the dark of the night by clerics from the closest relic-hungry city. Ah, like birds of prey, they've already begun circling overhead, patiently waiting."

"You're smiling, Father Francesco!" Leone said, "You must be eager to be back home in Portiuncula, near Assisi and all your friends."

Leone had the four friars construct a makeshift saddle out of blankets tied around the belly of the donkey to make Francesco's return ride more comfortable, and they departed the next day from Fonte Colombo on the road to Terni. Francesco asked Leone to obtain a large hat with a broad brim that he could wear low on his head to hide the festering scabs on his forehead. As they passed the village of Greccio, a crowd of villagers came out to gift the friars with bags of bread, fruit, and vegetables and to ask Francesco for his blessing. They fondly spoke of their beautiful memories of the Christmas when he created a living Bethlehem in their village, and they tearfully waved farewell to him as he rode out of sight down the road.

A couple of hours later the brothers arrived at the Nera River crossing. They were disappointed to discover a different ferryman than the one who had numerous times transported them across the river asking no toll other than their blessing.

"Bartering days are over," said the fat man, his dark, hairy arms folded across his chest. "These are new times; money is now the exchange for business—not vegetables or fruit! And know that I'll charge extra for the donkey."

The brothers knotted together in discussion about what to do, for they had already spent all the money Elias had given them. As Francesco sat waiting on the donkey, he thought, "Ah, my dear father, Pietro Bernadone, you were right! That new age you predicted when I was a youth has come. This common ferryman now wants the delicious, sensual feel of cold, hard coins in his palms, and without that sensation he's not disposed to showing any kindness to strangers. This new world is peopled by buyers and sellers, and woe to those without money." Then he whispered a tiny prayer to Lady Poverty, and a reply came to him at once.

"Signore," he said, addressing the ferryman as if he were a physician, merchant, or prince—not in an attempt to flatter him but simply because he spoke to everyone in a way that acknowledged the person's inherent dignity as a child of God, "would you like to be a saint?"

"You don't look like the Pope to me, you donkey-riding friar in a hat that's too big for you—if, indeed, a friar ye be! Me thinks that you and your companions look like the friars I've seen before in these parts. I know that you practice poverty, but I practice business," he added as he tapped his head, "cause I ain't dumb. Since saints go to heaven and sinners go to hell, and since I don't want to go to hell, tell me, friar: What's your offer?"

"I can make you Saint Christopher! As he carried the Christ Child on his shoulders across this river, you can carry the six of us and Brother Donkey. I assure you, God will richly bless and reward you."

"Clever! But ye ain't the Christ Child."

"Our Lord said, 'Whatever you do to the least of my brothers, you do unto me.' So, Signore, because we are the least, you *will* be ferrying Jesus Christ across this river."

As they boarded the flatboat ferry and the ferryman pushed off to the other side, Francesco whispered a quick prayer of gratitude to his generous Lady Poverty for her inspiration in convincing the ferryman to transport them without charge.

Several hours later, near sunset, as they reached the edge of Terni, they saw a large, dark cloud of swallows spiraling down the chimney of a house.

"An omen of death," moaned Brother Niccolo, "or, at least, great misfortune, whenever you see swallows do that—so the people in my village believe."

"I also saw a dead pigeon back there on the road," Filippo said, "but I didn't mention it because that's also a warning of approaching death."

"Did you spit on it?" asked Niccolo laughing. "In my village they used to say that if you spit on a dead bird in the road you won't get it for supper."

"Enough talk about death and misfortune," snapped Leone. "Let's find a place where we can rest for the night."

The six of them slept that night outside of Terni, not far from the church shrine of the tomb of Saint Valentine, who was martyred there three hundred years after the birth of Christ. As Francesco was falling asleep, he remembered the story of how the saint's heart was removed and taken as a relic to Venice, the city of romance. He wondered, "If they bury my heart separate from my body, where would I like to have it placed?" He reflected on how throughout his life he had left his heart in many places, like San Damiano, Saint Mary of the Angels, La Verna, and also in people like Emiliano, Clare, Ali Hasan, Jacques and even young Sebastiano. Before he received an answer to his question, he was wrapped in the arms of sleep.

Early the next day, just after sunrise, they headed for Spoleto, and at midday they paused to rest and break bread. Several small yellow goldfinches fluttered to the ground not far from Francesco, and he tossed them a handful of small pieces of his bread. As they cautiously approached and began eating the crumbs, they reminded him of the small goldfinch who had eaten out of his hand at La Verna. That memory caused him to sigh as he thought, "Ah, the yellow-feathered

prophets. Brother Niccolo recalling the folk belief about the swallows being an omen of death is like my recollection about goldfinches at La Verna. Since they nest in thorn bushes and eat sharp thistles, the common belief is that they also foretell death. And some pious folk even say they prophesy a person's impending participation in the passion of Christ's crown of thorns." He recalled asking himself on that day how he might experience the passion of Christ. Now he knew how the little yellow bird's prophecy had proved true.

They resumed their journey, but not for long. Francesco was weakened by bouts of diarrhea, which accompanied his eye disease, making it necessary for his brothers to lift him off the donkey so he could rest flat on the earth. As he lay there, he reflected on sharing in Christ's passion and on how physical penance had been so much a part of his pursuit of holiness. He recalled how in his youthful enthusiasm he had sadly often been extreme in his self-mortification and had not accepted Padre Antonio's wisdom about moderation. Antonio had quoted St. Paul's words about one's body being a temple of the Holy Spirit, saying that just as you would never desecrate a church or shrine, so you should never abuse your body.

"Today," he thought to himself, "as fatigue, disease, and pain force me to lay here, I understand Antonio's wisdom. Giving away your possessions is but the beginning of becoming unselfish. The goal is being selfless, and the penances I inflicted on myself only made me more self-conscious. I fasted, I rolled in the snow, I used the whip to lash myself. It was always I, I, I. In subtle ways I took personal pride— and even gloried—in the extent to which I could endure pain. Now I must embrace penances in which I can no longer find glory—like diarrhea! I now understand that we do not need to inflict harsh penances upon ourselves, that life itself, and especially old age, gives us all we need to become truly selfless and poor in spirit if we can receive what comes in a spirit of gratitude—and even joy."

He squeezed the sides of his forehead with his fingers, hoping it would relieve some of the pain. "God has generously sent me all the disciplines I have needed, but I only saw them as this or that trouble, disappointment, heartache, or shameful failure. Yet each of them held the power to cleanse me of *me*, if only I could have understood how God brings us to holiness. Asceticism can be a sickness if it draws attention to oneself; likewise, sickness can be an asceticism that does the same. So now in my old age I try to keep my pains and sufferings

hidden from others and have only spoken about them confidentially to a few friends, like kindly Leone. I tell him so I won't be tempted to become some silent, suffering, heroic martyr. In sharing them when I do, I'm acknowledging my poverty and my weak humanity rather than polishing my halo."

"Father Francesco," Leone said softly, "do you feel rested enough to resume our journey?"

"Yes, old friend, and I'm glad you called me out of that deep well of reflection into which I had sunk. We'd better be on our way before Minister General Elias sends a couple of brothers out to find out what's delaying us." Then Filippo and Niccolo lifted him up and gently placed him on the donkey, and they again began moving northward.

*A*s they passed through the small hamlets and villages along the way, the poor folk from the area began coming out to the road in large numbers, for news that holy Francesco of Assisi was coming had quickly traveled ahead of them. Francesco, an embarrassed prisoner on the back of his donkey, was unable to run away from their beggar-like pleas for him to bless them. Some even held up their sick infants for him to cure. Brother Filippo had to wrestle away one man who had pulled out a knife and was attempting to cut off a large piece of Francesco's habit as a relic. The friars struggled to prevent him from being knocked off the donkey by the crowd's overly zealous attempts to touch him. This chaotic scene frightened Leone, and he recalled Brother Niccolo's omen of misfortune at the swallows diving down a chimney. Recently Leone himself had felt an intuition of impending disaster, and he feared that Francesco might die before they got him home to Assisi.

As they approached the ancient Roman walled city of Spoleto, which was perched on the eastern mountainside of the narrow, steep gorge, Leone's sixth sense gave birth to a sense of dread. For the road directly ahead of them was blocked by mounted knights and a troop of foot soldiers attired in the colors of the Duke of Spoleto.

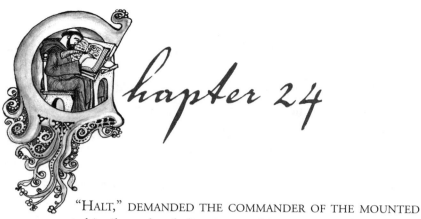 Chapter 24

"HALT," DEMANDED THE COMMANDER OF THE MOUNTED troop, his silver-plated chest armor shimmering in the sunlight. "State your name and the reason for your entry into Spoleto." Sensing Leone's inner tension, Francesco urged him not to be anxious, for since they had heard of no war between Assisi and Spoleto they had nothing to fear. "Besides," he said, "we are unarmed," to which Leone added "and clerics."

"I am Friar Leone of the Little Brothers of Assisi, and my companions are also members of our order. We are clerics of the Church, and this man on the. . . ."

"You on the donkey," snapped the officer, pointing a gloved hand at Francesco, "with that hat that's hiding your identity: Who are you?"

"Signore, I am Francesco of Assisi, we come in. . . ."

"Guards, surround the man on the donkey," he ordered, and instantly a dozen solders quickly sprang forward and surrounded Francesco. "By the authority of His Lordship Duke Marcello Guinicelli of Spoleto," he said, "you and your companions are to be detained right where you now stand." Turning in his saddle to the man mounted next to him, he commanded, "Ride with all speed to His Grace and inform him that we have successfully apprehended Francesco of Assisi and are holding him and five of his friars!"

As Leone's mind filled with the ominous image of those swallows driving down the chimney at Terni, Francesco sat peacefully in his makeshift saddle of folded blankets. While on the outside he was waiting patiently, his mind was quickly calculating the possible consequences for himself and his friends if the Duke of Spoleto was a member of the secret fraternity of the Parinians. "Even if they imprison

me to try me for heresy," he said to himself, "I will insist they release Leone and the other four. I thought I was going home to die peacefully, but it appears that Spoleto has once again reversed the tides against me."

Then, smiling, he addressed the officer in charge of the knights, "My companions and I were only passing through Spoleto on our way to Assisi. We've committed no crime or offense against the duchy of Spoleto, and. . . ." He was interrupted by the sound of the hoofs of several knights' horses galloping down the narrow streets from the fortress on the hilltop. The wind flapped the large flag bearing the duke's coat of arms on the colors of Spoleto that was carried by a mounted squire. Riding around the military roadblock, they came to an abrupt stop directly in front of Francesco. A tall man with aristocratic features framed by jet black hair and a pointed black beard, and wearing a scarlet riding cloak and a purple felt cap with a white-plumed feather, slipped easily to the ground from his pure black stallion. He looked up at the officer of the guard, who pointed his glove hand toward Francesco, now encircled by a dozen soldiers.

"Ten thousand apologies, Francesco of Assisi," said the tall man in the red cloak as he made a profound bow, "if my knights have in any way inconvenienced you. I am Duke Marcello Guinicelli, and I ordered my guards to stop and question all travelers coming up this road from Terni since word arrived here that you, holy Francesco, were coming this way." Then, dropping to his knees on the ground in front of the donkey, he pleaded, "I kneel before you as a beggar. For weeks now, my little eight-year old daughter Maria has laid deadly sick in a coma. Her mother and I have exhausted the finest available medical treatments and have brought in the most skilled physicians in all of Italy. . . ." As he paused to inhale deeply, fighting back the tears that were welling up in his eyes, Francesco nodded in understanding, for he himself had recently been treated with the finest medical treatment by the most skilled of physicians. "Everyone says that you are a living saint," the duke continued, "so I beg you: Please come and cure her. I will reward you generously if you can awaken her from this sleep of death."

So, accompanied by his brothers, Francesco was taken into the walled city of Spoleto and escorted to the fortress at the top of the mountain. On their way they passed the Cathedral of Santa Maria Assunta with its large mosaic over the main entrance depicting an enthroned Christ flanked by the Holy Virgin Mother Mary on one side and St. Giovanni the Beloved on the other. As Francesco rode past the  cathedral, he looked up and prayed, "Santa Maria, intercede on behalf of this sick child, and may you, my holy patron Saint Giovanni, be an instrument to lift the sleeping darkness that holds her prisoner."

Upon arriving in the piazza of the Duke's palazzo, Francesco surprised him by requesting that they bring the child outside instead of him going inside to her sick bed, for he was anxious that his inability to walk easily because of the stigmata in his feet would only draw attention to his wounds. The Duke readily agreed, and within moments he returned with his wife carrying their comatose little daughter wrapped in blankets. As they carefully placed her in Francesco's open arms, he began gently rocking her and softly humming the tune of an old Umbrian lullaby. A large number of the household servants were now gathered around as Francesco began improvising lyrics to the tune of the old lullaby:

Little Maria of God, awaken from the grip

of the demons of the night and of the plague.

Holy Mother Mary, who cradled your Child

in Bethlehem and protected him from harm,

cradle innocent little Maria, your namesake;

ask your son to banish her sickness

and bless her back into vibrant, joyful life.

Little Maria of God, awaken from your sleep,

healed of body and mind to run and play again.

San Giovanni, beloved friend of our Holy Savior,

who escaped the poison in a chalice given to you,

ask your Beloved to free this beautiful child

from the poison of her present affliction

and restore her to the fullness of health and life.

Sleep in healing slumber, Maria, to awaken to life,

Sleep in healing slumber, sleep, sleep so as to. . . .

Francesco bent down over her so that his large-brimmed hat covered her face, and he kissed her tenderly. Raising his head, he traced the sign of the cross over her and then handed her, still unconscious,

back to her parents. With tears flowing down his cheeks, her father thanked Francesco profusely for attempting to heal her, trying to give him a bag of gold coins as a token of his gratitude. Francesco refused, saying, "Thank you, Signore Marcello, but as you see, I've done nothing. Have faith in God's endless compassion, for faith moves mountains and opens eyes." Then, he gently nudged his knees into the donkey's flanks for it to begin moving forward. The heartbroken parents turned and carried their lifeless daughter back up the steps to the palazzo. As Leone took the donkey's halter to lead it out of the small piazza, a loud piercing scream brought him to a stone-still stop.

"She's opening her eyes!" screamed the *signora*, a cry quickly echoed by the servants gathered around the doorway. "She's opening her eyes! She's awake!"

"Holy Mother of God," shouted the duke, who turned and came running down the stone steps toward Francesco, weeping with joy. "It's a miracle! Francesco of Assisi has worked a miracle and has healed my little Maria!"

"I've worked no miracle! Your faith, Signore Marcello, and that of your wife have healed little Maria. That lullaby I sang was a cradle prayer sung to Santa Maria and to San Giovanni: It was they, and not I, who were the instruments of God's healing for your little Maria. I provided only this old bag of bones as a cradle in which to rock her as the two saints pressed God for her healing. And let us not neglect those good physicians, for perhaps their treatments finally achieved their curative effects, and I was simply present when that glorious hour arrived. Regardless, Signore Marcello, thank God and our Blessed Lord's Mother and San Giovanni—not me."

Francesco was firm that they not accept the duke's almost insistent invitation for all of them to spend the night in his home, saying that they couldn't delay a single hour more their return to Assisi. He said it had already taken them far too long and that by this time Minister General Elias must be gravely concerned. So, with lavish expressions of gratitude the duke bid them farewell as they rode down narrow streets from the hilltop palazzo toward the cathedral. As they departed, Francesco leaned over and whispered to Leone walking beside the donkey, "Old friend, let's get out of town as quickly as possible before the report of what has happened up there spreads across Spoleto."

Exhausted by the experience, Francesco requested that they sleep overnight just north of the city under the three great arches of the old towering Roman aqueduct that spanned the forested gorge. When they arrived, they found others preparing to sleep under the abandoned aqueduct: beggars and the very poor. As they lay side by side, Francesco nudged Leone and whispered, "These are our kind of folks, right, old friend? Instead of sleeping in some fine marble palazzo, this is the place for the likes of us to sleep, eh?"

He rolled over and sighed a brief prayer of gratitude for God's mysterious ways. Here outside of Spoleto, where once he had tasted the bitter acid of shame and sadness, God had wondrously used him as an instrument to bring joy where there was sadness, hope where there was despair. That night he saw clearly how the invisible stigmata of Spoleto he'd borne for years had been one of life's prime penances that gracefully and surely had shrunk his inflated self-importance. "If we can accept those times," he thought, "when we're not in control and are impotent to guide our destiny, we are emptied of our self far more effectively than any flagellant's whip or prolonged fast."

Then he gently patted his hip, adding, "Brother Ass, forgive me for my abuse. What I'd never consider doing to some animal I've done to you many times over the years—so, please forgive me."

"Filippo," Francesco announced at sunrise, "please get your pen, for in the early hours before dawn I've once again been visited by the muses—or the Holy Spirit." As the brothers yawned and stretched after a night's sleep, he continued, "You were right as usual, wise Leone. My Canticle of the Creatures did need to be tailored; so I've added a few strips of new fabric. Brother Filippo, if you have your pen and ink ready, I've changed the beginning of each stanza. Listen, Leone, and tell me what you think. Then he began singing:

> Most loving and generous Lord God,
>
> we praise you for all your wondrous creatures,
>
> especially Brother Sun, who is rising at this moment,
>
> for he is strong and bright and gives light to all.

He continued singing the successive stanzas of his canticle, beginning each new one with, "Praise to you, O Lord," until he came to the one for Brother Fire. As he sang that stanza, his imagination was

immersed in the solid wall of brilliantly reddish-orange flames that had filled his mind the moment the physicians were inserting their red-hot irons into his forehead.

"Much better, Father Francesco!" Leone said, rubbing his back after a rough night's sleep, amazed how at times Francesco was able to arise from sleep as energetic as he had once been as a young man. He knew from experience, however, that this zestful outburst likely would be short-lived, and by midday he would again be exhausted. "You have expressed praise for all creatures; only now you're praising God for them. It's more. . . ."

"Orthodox? And not so pagan?"

"Well, some of us can't grasp how God can be both up in heaven and also in the wind and the water, the moon and the sun. Maybe someday I'll be able to do that, but for now I like what you've added."

"It's still rough and needs some refinement, don't you think, Filippo?" asked Francesco. "When we get back home to Assisi, I'll have Sebastiano's friend, Brother Innocenti, who is a poet, improve its rhythm."

"Perhaps, Father Francesco, but I like your poetry just as it is. As you were singing it just now, I was wondering if it shouldn't be called the Canticle of Brother Sun, since most songs are named for their opening words."

Francesco smiled, telling them that he didn't care what name they gave it and that he would continue revising it as they rode northward toward Foligno. Leone's prediction about Francesco's stamina proved to be true. By midday he had to rest and was helped off the donkey so he could lie down on the grassy earth. As they laid him down, he said, "Ah, Sister Earth, all praise to you, for you are like a mother who sustains us with food and nourishment—and now gives me rest on your soft green bosom."

He closed his eyes, attempting to nap, as the brothers sat off at a distance quietly visiting while the donkey grazed nearby. "Soon enough, Sister Earth," he reflected, "I'll be resting not on your bosom but in your womb. In my bones I can feel old death approaching—closer each day as it becomes harder for me to travel." His reflection turned into a prayer: "O God, hear me. I'm sick and, oh, so tired. Please speed my journey home—and I don't mean to Assisi. Don't take me before I reach Portiuncula, however, for I need to say farewell to my old, dear friends and to ask pardon from those whom I've offended."

Francesco napped briefly and restlessly. He was beset by a series of disjointed dreams of being in Egypt on the crusade, working in the orchards in Spain, and having disagreements with his father in their family cloth shop. He was awakened abruptly by a scene in his dream when his father shouted that he would never be a man. "Brother Leone," he said raising his head, "the day is passing swiftly. Let us be on our way again."

After mounting him back on the donkey, they continued up the road to Foligno in the green, fertile plane of the Umbrian valley between the Topina River, Mount Aguzzo, and Mount Subasio, not more than a good six hour walk from Assisi. As they passed alongside the walls of Foligno, they saw a group of children playing. Upon noticing the brothers, they stopped their game, and the biggest boy among them shouted, "Look at the funny old man in the too-big hat and baggy clothes riding on that swayback old donkey." This caused the other dirty-faced urchins to begin hopping up and down, chanting, "Funny old man, funny old man in the too-big hat, the too-big hat."

"Don't be so disrespectful," scolded Leone, shaking his finger at them. "Didn't your parents teach you to respect your elders, especially if they're holy clerics of the Church?"

"No, no Leone," laughed Francesco. "Don't rebuke the children. They're right—I am a funny-looking old man. It pleases me that even in my dilapidated state I can still bring a bit of joy into the lives of these children whose parents clearly are the poorest of the poor." At that moment he recalled what Ali Hasan had said to him, "For true holiness, play is more important than prayer," and without a word he swung himself around and hopped off the donkey, landing on his feet.

"If you think my poor donkey is swaybacked," he said to the children, "watch me walk!" Then, exaggerating his unwieldy walk caused by the painful stigmata wounds in his feet, he comically hunched over and waddled over to the children.

"Funny old man, funny old swaybacked man," they chimed with delight as he circled around them.

Then, playfully billowing out his oversized tunic to embellish its large size, he sang, "This silly, skinny old man in the much too big tunic and a hat big enough for two heads has come to entertain you. Behold, before you stands Francesco, the traveling buffoon, the brown-robed clown, minstrel, tumbler, and magician all rolled into one."

"Do some magic tricks for us!" they cried.

"I can't. See, I lost my hands while on the crusades," he joked as he slid his hands up inside his long sleeves. "They were eaten for supper by a camel who stuck his head in my tent. But I still have a mouth—so be seated, ladies and gentlemen, and I'll tell you a story."

Leone and the other friars stood back in amazement as he squatted, sitting on the ground while the children gathered around him in a circle. The brothers knew how much pain all this must have been causing him, but he showed no sign that he was in any way suffering. After three or four long stories, Leone coughed loudly and nodded his head northward up the road toward Mount Subasio. When Francesco acknowledged his signal, he began to lead the donkey over to where Francesco was sitting.

"Ah, my young friends," Francesco said, "look at the sun! While I've been talking, good Brother Sun has rolled so far across the sky that it's now time for my companions and me to be on our way again. Even Brother Donkey wants to go home. So I bid all of you farewell—until we meet again." Then, after getting up with great difficulty, he stood still with his eyes closed, trying to let a brief spell of dizziness pass, as everything seemed to be whirling around.

"You said you were a magician," said the older boy who had first taunted him, "but you haven't shown us any magic yet."

"No hands, young sir. Remember the camel that ate them on the crusades?"

"But they've returned! I saw your fingertips as you were telling us those stories!" Then the lad tossed him a crudely carved wooden top with which they had been playing. "Here, catch this, traveling minstrel magician, and make it disappear!"

As the top came sailing through the air Francesco caught it deftly in his right hand and, raising up his arm, allowed it to disappear up his sleeve, saying, "It's disappeared forever in the enchanted land of magic!"

"Bring it back! Bring it back again," chanted the children. "Please bring it back."

With as deep a bow as his throbbing head would allow him to make, he bent over and then let the round top fall down his sleeve into the palm of his hand. Gripping it, he tossed it back to the young lad.

"My top is bleeding!" the boy said in astonishment as the other children crowded around him, gawking at the bleeding toy top. "It's all red with blood!"

"Magic!" said Francesco with a wave of his hand as two brothers lifted him back up on the donkey and began leading him again on their journey northward. Behind them, the cluster of the children were all talking at once about the funny old magician in the baggy tunic who had entertained them and worked the magic of making their wooden top bleed real blood.

*L*ater, as they rode past the town of Spello, Francesco recalled the old, hunchback beggar Tommaso, who had come from there. "May you rest in peace, Signore Strapazzate, and may eternal light shine on you. Many in Assisi are convinced that I've replaced you as Signore Vova Strapazzate, a crazy beggarman with scrambled brains. You were, indeed, one of the children of providence, a seer whom heaven had inspired—at least in my life."

"Shall we stop here at Spello to spend the night, Father Francesco?" asked Leone. "You look very tired. If you had the strength, I would suggest that we go on; we can't be more than three hours away from Assisi. However, by that time it will be dark. So I leave the decision to you."

"Let's not stop here in Spello," he said looking around at the faces of the other friars, whom he could see were eager to be back home again and sleeping in their own beds. "But I think we should ask Brother Donkey, since of all of us he's surely the most tired from having to carry this old bag of bones for so many hours." Leaning down close to the donkey's head, he listened, nodded and then raised up again, saying to the brothers, "He says he's eager to sleep in his own manger, and I know Brother Ass is as well. So, forward. Besides, I'm impatient to see old friends, including Brother Jacques, who by now must be back from France." He inhaled deeply several times, suppressing the pain and fatigue he felt saturating his entire body. While he longed to stop and rest his aching body, it was more desirable to arrive at Assisi at nighttime when the cover of darkness would allow them to return unseen. If it appeared they might reach Portiuncula earlier than Leone had calculated, he would ask for a rest stop to insure that they didn't get back until everyone was asleep.

Three hours after passing Spello, Francesco was relieved when he finally saw the dark shapes of the walls and towers of Assisi against the moonlit sky. Skirting the walls of the city, they made their way through the olive groves below the black silhouette of San Damiano's chapel. As

he rode past San Damiano, he raised his right hand with his palm up and blew a kiss across his fingertips upward to his *cara mia*, Sister Clare, whom he felt certain at that late hour of the night would be laying prostrate in prayer on the chapel's stone pavement.

"Ah, Brother Ass," he said as the friars gently laid him in his bed at Portiuncula, "it's good to be in our manger at long last. Now, try to get some rest before our next journey."

As Leone and his companions on the trip to Fonte Colombo left Francesco's hut, Friar Niccolo whispered to Friar Filippo, "My God, after all he's been through on this trip, where on earth do you think he intends to go next?"

Leone, who overheard Niccolo, sighed inwardly and thought, "On the great journey."

*T*he next morning Portiuncula hummed like a beehive with the news that Francesco had returned from Rieti. As quickly as water leaks from an old worm-eaten rain barrel, rumors spread among the brothers about Francesco's distressing procedure, the ugly scars on his forehead, and the unsuccessful treatment by the Roman physicians to cure his painful eye disease.

"Damn! Damn them!" shouted an enraged Jacques upon entering Francesco's hut and seeing the hideous scars on his forehead. He kicked a three-legged wooden stool with such force that it sailed across the room and crashed loudly against the opposite wall. Kneeling beside Francesco's bed, he sobbed like a child at the horrible punctures in his friend's forehead, "Those damn butchers! If I had been there, they wouldn't have done that to him!"

Smiling, Francesco tapped Jacques on his hand, saying, "Oh, Jacques, Jacques, Jacques, I also wish you could have been with me. How wonderful to see you again."

"Thank you, Francesco; it's wonderful to see you too. I've yearned for this day of your return."

"It's been such a long trek back from Fonte Colombo, Jacques, I don't even know what day it is!"

"It's September 8, the feast of the Nativity of the Virgin Mary," answered Leone, who was changing the dressings on his stigmata wounds.

"September 8 already? Today is one of my favorite feasts," Francesco said with a smile. "Santa Maria and Lady Poverty have both

been important holy women in my life. My private name for this holy day is Marymas, a kind of autumn preface to Christmas. Today is traditionally the last day of summer. How I wish it could also be the final day of my life. Holy Mother of God, help me to die a good death."

"A fitting prayer, "Jacques said, "especially on this day dedicated to Mary. It sounds just like the new prayer I heard the peasants praying when I was back in France. Instead of saying the Lord's Prayer on their Pater Noster cords, they're praying a new prayer, which they call the Hail Mary."

"Really? They're replacing the ageless prayer that was given us by our Lord?" replied Francesco. "But I'm intrigued about this new prayer. Who composed it and how does it go?"

"I was told it's the new prayer for the successful recapture of the Holy Land. Some said it took shape in Carthusian monasteries, while others claim the words just miraculously appeared. The first two parts are taken directly from the Gospels, beginning with the angel's greeting to Mary, 'Hail Mary, full of grace, the Lord is with you,' followed by Elizabeth's greeting, 'Blessed are you among women, and blessed is the fruit of your womb, Jesus.' In some places the prayer ends there; elsewhere the people have added, 'Holy Mary, Mother God, pray for us now and at the hour of our death.'"

"I like it!" Francesco beamed. "Pray for us at the hour of our death. For *me* this surely is 'the hour,' at least I pray that it is. You know how the peasants traditionally observe this feast day by beginning their fall planting. Ah, if only I would die today so they could sow this old seed in the earth."

"Francesco, don't talk like that!" fussed Leone. "You're only forty-four years old! That's not old for a man these days. Soon you'll be up again and your old merry self!"

"Leone!" he said, playfully imitating a mother's reprimanding tone. "Don't be naughty—remember that lying is a sin! With these wounds from La Verna, not to mention these new ones from Colombo, how on earth can I ever be my old self again?" Tapping his forehead, he added, "And, please, Brothers Jacques and Leone, promise to protect me from any more visits by physicians from hell—even if they say they come from Rome or Perugia!"

"I promise," Jacques said. "I'll not let them touch you again."

"For a sick man who claims he's dying," Leone said, "you're surely in a spirited mood this morning."

"The next thing," Jacques added, "you'll be telling us is that today is the day you'll fly away to God, for folklore says that on this holy feast of Mary the swallows from north of the Alps fly away to the sunny south."

Francesco extended his arms and began flapping them like wings as he said, "Jacques, you old thief. You've just stolen my great finale, but . . ." his arms fell down along the sides of his bed as he moaned, "how quickly I find myself drained of all energy. I might awaken like this morning, feeling better, only to. . . ." His reflection was interrupted by a knock on the door.

Francesco's door opened and closed numerous times that day, as his comrades came to visit him—Brothers Bernardo, Giles, and others still alive from his original band of companions as well as new brothers like Sebastiano and Tomas. As one would exit, another one would enter, all of them sobbing openly without shame at the sight of his pierced, scar-enflamed forehead and his sickly, pale appearance. Summoning up all his energy, Francesco tried to console those who had come to comfort him. When Leone saw his condition worsening, he closed the door to all further visitors. The following days witnessed a radical deterioration in his health. He suffered from increasing physical pain, high fever, and bouts of diarrhea.

Five days after Francesco's return from Colombo, Brother Elias returned from visiting his home city of Cortona and hurried at once to visit him.

"Father Francesco," he said upon entering the sparse hut, "why are you laying there on the hard, bare earth? Rushing over to him, he knelt on the bare earth beside Francesco, tucking a loose strand of hair behind his ear. "While in Cortona a messenger informed me that your sickness had grown worse." Startled at the sight of the ugly scars on his forehead, he swallowed hard and said, "We must get you a proper bed with a straw mattress."

"Thank you, but after all my years of sleeping on the earth I find the bare floor more comfortable than I would a fancy straw mattress on a wooden frame. Thank you, Elias, for visiting me directly upon your return, but I'm sure that as the Minister General you must have much more urgent problems demanding your attention than this one sick old brother." He intentionally avoided using the popular new title "friar,"

feeling that it implied a state elevated above ordinary people. In the early days of the order he had purposely added the adjective "*minores*"—the lowest—to the term "brother," emphasizing that they were people of no importance.

"Father Francesco, I'm sorry that your medical treatments were not only painful but also, it seems, unsuccessful. His Eminence Cardinal Ugolino, His Holiness, and I had so prayed they would be effective." Francesco smiled inwardly at how Elias had linked himself to the two most significant men in all of Italy.

"Perhaps," Elias continued, "the treatment takes time to accomplish its desired cure. We shall pray for its speedy healing effects.

"Now, I have some good news. After learning of your sad condition while I was in Cortona, I sent a messenger to Perugia, requesting the famous physician Signore Giorgio Trissino to come here and treat you. He is renowned for his ability to heal diseases such as yours and is the most highly acclaimed physician in all of Umbria. On my way here a courier from Perugia caught up with me and related the good news that Signore Trissino said he should be here in a week or so to treat you."

As Leone used a soft cloth to daub the sweat beads on his old friend's forehead, Francesco thought, "Elias, I hope I'm dead and buried long before another doctor uses the latest medical science to inflict any more of the tortures of hell upon me."

As Elias watched the loving way old Leone cared for Francesco, he thought, "I see death written plainly on Francesco's face. He's gaunt, and the stench of sickness almost oozes out of him. Yet we must do everything we can to keep him alive."

As Leone went outside to rinse out his cloth, Elias mused, "Francesco's already frail body has become a blotched, wrinkled-skin reliquary holding the living relic of a saint. At all costs, I must protect that relic while it is alive—and even more importantly when his soul has left it." Seeing that Francesco was slipping off into sleep, Elias said a brief prayer over him, asking God's healing, and then departed.

As he walked toward his room, Elias reflected on how each village along his way back from Cortona was teeming with rumors about the impending death of Francesco of Assisi. What disturbed him more, however, was the other rumor whispered to him by a couple of village priests who were aware that he was the Minister General of the Order of Friars. They confided to him reports from reliable sources that groups from Perugia, Sienna, and even Florence were plotting to steal

Francesco's dead body. Each city was eager to posses the holy relic of the most famous saint of their century. One priest told him he'd heard that agents from Perugia were already secretly in or near Assisi waiting for him to die.

"I must send word, " he said aloud, "to the commune of Assisi, explaining how it is critical for our city to possess the holy relic of the entire body of Francesco. It must not be stolen, especially by Perugia!" In his head he began composing a letter he would send to the wealthy merchants of Assisi. He would remind them that for both financial and religious reasons Assisi should retain what surely would become the most important relic of this age. "I'll also remind them," he thought, "that such a relic will attract hundreds of thousands of pilgrims to Assisi. As businessmen, they'll be able to gauge the resulting financial benefits. Then, having baited the hook, I'll ask them to supply, at no cost to our order, a sufficiently large guard of armed soldiers to protect Portiuncula both day and night from any nefarious body robbers.

"Now, I must begin at once," he thought to himself, his quick mind jumping to the next important project, "to design the most magnificent basilica in all of Italy, one fitting to enshrine Francesco's body, for surely he'll wish to be buried here at Portiuncula. The finest architects must be found to refine my designs and the greatest artists of this age commissioned to do the frescos of his life. It is fitting to create a grand masterpiece that will display the spiritual greatness of our holy order and its founder to the entire world."

September 14, the feast of the Exaltation of the Cross, was the second anniversary of Francesco's receiving the stigmata on Mount La Verna. While he had so hoped those wounds might disappear, now two years later they were as acute and visible as ever, and they even continued to bleed at various times. Moreover, to his great disappointment, the anniversary of his mystical physical fusion with the crucified Christ came and went, leaving him still alive. His sickness tormented him like a cruel minstrel tumbler, as it flip-flopped him from sweltering fevers one day to icy chills the next, from relatively pain-free days to days with intense headaches. Throughout this time Leone attempted to guard his patient vigilantly from visitors, making rare exceptions for those he knew would revive his dying friend, like Emiliano Giacosa.

"*Caro mio* Francesco," Emiliano said as he knelt teary-eyed next to his bed. "Forgive me for coming to see you uninvited, but rumors that you are sick unto death are on the lips of all in Assisi. I just had to come."

"Thank you for doing so, *caro mio*. Just to see your face is better than any tonic. Forgive me for not sending word to you to come and visit me after I returned from Fonte Colombo, but I haven't been myself these past days. Pain is a thief, Emiliano, that robs the mind of the powers of thinking properly. I should have thought of you and your needs. . . ." Reaching out, he gripped Emiliano's hand. "Forgive me. It's so good to see you again. What a wondrous blessing from my generous Lord."

Mindful that the human hourglass, Brother Leone, was keeping track of the time, Emiliano quickly told Francesco that while he had been away from Assisi down at Fonte Colombo there had been two marriages. After his son, young Francesco Giovanni, had married, Emiliano found himself more and more lonely. Then, by the grace of God, he met and courted a woman some fifteen years younger than him. They soon fell in love and were recently married, during the time when Francesco was away in Rieti.

"As God said to Adam," Francesco replied with a smile, "'it's not good for man to be alone.'" Gripping his friend's hand tightly, Francesco expressed his great joy at the news. He was about to ask Emiliano about the Third Order when he was restrained by a loud cough from the brother hourglass.

"The time has gone so quickly," Emiliano said, turning to Leone. "Please give me the gift of just a small bit more time for Francesco to see and bless someone. I promise. . . ."

"Leone," Francesco said in the most authoritative voice he could muster in his weakened condition, "Open the door!"

Into the hut walked a living image of a handsome, strong Emiliano in his early twenties, and on his arm was a strikingly beautiful young woman. At the sight of the two young lovers, Francesco's face flashed with the brilliance of the sun coming out from behind thick, gray clouds. With one eye on Leone, Emiliano quickly condensed the story of how young Francesco and his bride were married shortly after Easter. He then asked Francesco to bless their marriage. As the two young people knelt by his bed, with tears trickling down his gaunt cheeks, Francesco called down upon them every possible blessing of heaven.

When he finished, Leone opened the door and stood impatiently beside it.

"One more favor, *caro mio*," begged Emiliano. "Francesco's wife Maria is with child. So please, I plead, bless both her and her child. Your holy blessing is more powerful than a hundred relics of St. Margaret, the patron of childbirth. So Francesco rested his hand upon her belly, now beginning to swell, and tried to send through his wounded palm all the graces of Christ's cross and resurrection. Then, leaning down, a sobbing Emiliano wrapped an affectionate embrace as best he could around the bedridden Francesco, bidding farewell to his oldest and dearest friend for what he knew in his heart would be the last time he would see him alive.

"Too long, too much! They've worn you out," lamented Leone as he shut the door emphatically after Emiliano and the young couple had departed.

"No, dearest Leone, they renewed rather than exhausted me! You know that young Francesco is my godson—and, ah, that young couple was so filled with hope and excitement about their dreams for the future that they made me want to live! Yes, Leone, at least for the moment, instead of praying to escape this vale of tears, I long to live! Oh, how I ache to live long enough to see their child." Then he fell silent before adding, "How silly of this old man. With these blurry eyes, I can barely see you standing over there by the door! I'll be completely blind by the time their child is born." Rolling over on his side away from Leone, he began softly sobbing.

The next day he felt sicker than usual, perhaps partially because he was fully aware that he had seen his old friend Emiliano for the last time in this life. He knew that Brother Death was sitting just outside his hut, measuring the time he had left with that unique hourglass filled with the blackest of ebony sands. Surely, he felt, Death's grim hourglass soon would completely empty itself into the bottom globe. In that awareness, he begged Leone to have him carried on a wooden stretcher up to San Damiano for a last visit with his beloved *cara mia* Clare. Reluctantly, Leone agreed, and twice the brothers attempted to carry him to her convent, but the swaying movement of the stretcher made him so nauseous that both times he had to return prematurely.

On September 24—five days before Michaelmas, the autumn holy day feast of Saint Michael the Archangel—the renowned purple-robed, red-gloved physician Signore Giorgio Trissino from Perugia finally

arrived at Portiuncula. He profusely apologized to Elias for his delay, explaining that his presence had been required at the sickbed of the pestilence-stricken Archbishop of Perugia. Accompanied by a couple of friars, Elias took him immediately to see Francesco. Setting his large black satchel on the floor, he proceeded to ask Francesco countless questions, peering closely into his diseased eyes and probing around the scars of his previous medical treatment at Colombo. Just as Signore Trissino was about to pronounce his diagnosis, he noticed blood trickling down from Francesco's sleeve. Without asking, he jerked back the sleeve, gasping at the sight of the bleeding wound in Francesco's hand. Then he swiftly reached across and pulled up the other sleeve, exposing the second wounded hand.

Elias was horrified and mystified at the sight of the stigmata, and Trissino demanded to know the source of the wounds. When Francesco remained silent, the physician announced, "*Dementia praecox*, premature insanity! Clearly these are self-inflicted injuries induced by frenzy . . . or. . . ." Then his voice became inaudible.

Brother Elias recovered his composure enough to take charge, asking the doctor for his diagnosis and proposed cure for Francesco's afflictions. Signore Trissino inhaled deeply, raising himself up to his full height, and pointing a red-gloved hand at Francesco he said pontifically, "*Retentic semenis!*" After a brief pause he continued, "Allow me to translate that medical term into laymen's language. The patient, as a sworn celibate, suffers from 'withholding the semen,' which expert physicians have determined poisons a man's blood because of an imbalance of humors. Perhaps the greatest physician of all time, Hippocrates, suggests a remedy for this condition. He discovered that bleeding the patient, along with giving him other purgatives, greatly reduces the kinds of fever that afflict him." Pointing his red-gloved finger toward Francesco's hands, he added, "And manics—the mentally disturbed—upon seeing their blood flowing out from their bodies, are known to grow calm and remain tranquil for days.

"Now, before we proceed with the cure of bleeding him, we should address the other affliction of prolonged intense headaches from which the patient suffers. While I see that he has received . . . ahem," after clearing his throat sarcastically, he continued, "the Roman treatment, I propose an infallible cure for his headaches: applying *hirudo medicinalis* to his forehead for several hours." Bending over, he removed a large blue jar from his leather bag, saying, "I prudently brought along a jar

of them. My preference, of course, would be to apply *hirudo troctina*, but in these times of war with the Muslims it is impossible to obtain those large Algerian leeches, which are found only in Africa. However, the hungry European *hirudo* leeches contained in this jar will be greatly beneficial in hastening his healing."

Placing the blue jar on the floor, he took his black bag and removed a special knife to bleed Francesco, saying, "Now, if a couple of you good friars would securely hold down the arms of the patient as I. . . ."

At that moment the door to the hut flew open, almost breaking off its hinges. Brother Jacques stormed into the hut, shouting, "Physician, do not even lay a finger on that poor man!" The sight of Jacques' large physical stature and the intensity of his anger, which caused his long facial scar to flame bright red, so frightened Signore Trissino that he dropped his bloodletting knife. As the purple-robed physician drew back in fear of the large onrushing friar, he accidentally knocked over the jar marked *hirudo medicinalis*, spilling a slimly glob of wiggling black leeches onto the floor.

"Get out of here!" shouted Jacques. "All of you, except Brother Leone." Shaking his fist, he added, "And that includes you, Brother Elias, and those two friars you brought with you. Don't force me to send any of you to the local bonesetter to reset the bones I'll break in your body if you don't leave this very moment!" Signore Trissino needed no second invitation; grabbing his knife off the floor, he threw it into his bag and hurried toward the door. Nervously stroking a strand of hair behind his ear, Elias snapped, "How dare you order me to do anything: I am the Minister General! And it was I who invited this distinguished physician, Signore Trissino, to come here, acting with the authority of the Pope Honorius and Cardinal Ugo. . . ."

"Out! Get out of here, Elias!" Jacques shouted. "I don't give a damn who you are. Nor do I care what any Pope or cardinal says. Let this holy man die in peace—not by torturing him to death with tools from hell. Out! Out! Out!" He continued screaming, as Elias, fearing for his safety, fled directly behind the physician, followed closely by the two frightened friars who had accompanied him.

"Thank you, Brother Moses," smiled Francesco. "Once again you've rescued me."

"Dearest old friend," Jacques said, bending over him, "I was happy to. But what happened to my old name, Jacques?"

"Ah, my old friend, I called you that because just now you appeared as I imagine Moses must have looked when he angrily smashed the two stone tablets on Mount Sinai upon finding the Jews worshipping the golden calf. Thank you for your holy anger, which was so intense it scared away that Perugian physician—and even Elias. I know that both of them wish to prolong my life, but I wish it would end this very day."

Meanwhile, after profusely thanking and apologizing to Signore Trissino for what had happened in Francesco's hut, Elias sent him on his way back to Perugia with the assurance that his services would be richly compensated for by Pope Honorius and Cardinal Ugolino. As the purpled-robed physician departed mumbling, Elias stood shaking in anger. He thought, "My God, I've got a revolt on my hands. I already have to deal with those frantically zealous brothers who have been misled by the heretical teachings of Joachim of Fiore about the approaching new age of the Holy Spirit. They believe that Francesco has been chosen by God to usher in this Pentecostal age and are insisting that we make a radical return to his primitive idea of absolute poverty. Some are even threatening to form their own brotherhood based on the first rule. And now, Friars Jacques, Leone, and other intimates of Francesco in the order have defied my authority and want to control all access to him. Jacques even threatened to break my bones! God in heaven, I'm losing control!"

*F*rancesco continued to linger on the edge of Death's cliff, aching to be released from his long personal passion experience. For Francesco, the month of September seemed to have been composed of one Good Friday after another as he hung on his cross of suffering, waiting to die. The days of the week and even the time of day often became muddled to him, and on the next to last day of September he asked Leone what day it was. Learning it was the great feast of Saint Michael the Archangel, he pleaded with Leone for a holy day favor of having Brother Sebastiano and his friend Brother Innocenti come to his bedside to sing for him his Canticle of the Creatures.

Late in the afternoon after Leone had finished changing Francesco's dressings, Brothers Sebastiano and Innocenti arrived with another friar who was skilled at playing the lute. Together they sang Innocenti's poetic revision of Francesco's song, now called the Canticle of the Sun. Their singing was a salve that lessened his pains. It caused him to reflect: "Once I sang a song of love and farewell over the graves of my

mother and father, and now these young friars are singing over mine, even if I'm not yet laid to rest." When they had finished, Sebastiano begged for a little time alone with Francesco. Innocenti and the other friar went back to their duties, and Leone and Jacques stepped outside to give Francesco and Sebastiano privacy.

"Oh, Father Francesco, I'll so miss you," moaned Sebastiano, "but I can't ask God to keep you here, for you've suffered so long. I love you," he said, leaning over to kiss Francesco. "You've given me what I have so hungered for—a great love—and you've taught me how to make real love in my life."

"And you, Sebastiano, have given me far more than I ever gave you," Francesco returned, affectionately squeezing the young friar's hand. "Ah, if only I were your age again," he said so softly that Sebastiano could hardly hear him, "I'd do it differently."

"Do what differently?" Sebastiano asked, gently laying his head on Francesco's chest, his eyes welling up with tears.

"Instead of running after God," Francesco replied, resting his bandaged hand on the young friar's shoulder, "I'd let God run after me!" Then he softly chuckled as he added, "Which is what my Beloved did anyway—only in my pride I thought it was I, Francesco of Assisi, who was doing the pursuing. Instead of surrendering and allowing God to transform me, I vainly saw myself as a spiritual athlete competing to win the glorious crown of holiness by enduring the harshest imaginable penances."

"I fear I'm draining you, Father Francesco. But I yearn to be a saint like you, and so I must ask: What other possible path could you have taken?"

"You're not tiring me, Sebastiano. I need to talk about what I've been thinking about while laying here on the precipice of death. In you, Sebastiano, I find the future hope of the Little Brothers. So listen and remember. What is the path? Love! Love passionately and unconditionally. Love God and your neighbor more than yourself. Also, if I were to start again I would have loved my body, not hated and tortured it—even if that is what the spiritual masters have said is the way to release the spirit they saw shackled inside our sin-seeking bodies. As human fathers in our society believe the best way to produce a real man out of a boy is by a relentless discipline of the whip or the hand, so spiritual masters have taught that a harsh physical discipline is necessary for the maturity of the soul. Indeed, I grew up believing that

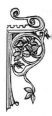

only by severe fasting, privations, and inflicting bodily discipline could one's sensual appetites be curbed, unruly emotions harnessed and the demons of flesh be kept at bay."

"Father Francesco, some friars quote you saying that penance is mandatory if we are to make payment for our sins. And many pride themselves in imitating your penances. As you know only too well, I would need to live at least two lifetimes to be able to do enough penance for all my sins of the flesh."

"Ah, my young friend, our misdeeds are indeed like red wine spilled on a white tablecloth, but I'm convinced that every truly passionate act of unselfish love removes the stain of a past sin. I believe that if you love passionately and unselfishly—if you open yourself to the one who loved us passionately to the point of death on the cross and let him love in, through, and with you—then all the penalties of your past mistakes will disappear! As for some friars quoting my teachings on penance, oh, how I wish that my words of yesterday might be forgotten—for as we mature, so do our beliefs. I once judged sin mainly to be surrendering to a temptation of the devil, but now at the end of my life I realize that much of what I thought of as sinful was merely human weakness that caused me to love poorly, conditionally, and halfheartedly—by placing my own selfish needs and pleasures before the needs of others."

"Francesco?" inserted Leone, sticking his head inside the door and giving Sebastiano a grim look.

Mustering all his strength to speak resolutely, Francesco said, "Please, dear Leone, just a moment more. He's not tiring me." Leone frowned as he closed the door. Then, speaking again in a soft voice, Francesco returned to Sebastiano. "My voice is growing faint, yet I've more to say. So lean your ear closer. One last thing you must know and remember concerns the new relaxed regulations about your vow of poverty, the ones I was forced to include in our new Rule of the Little Brothers. Ah, Sebastiano, you know about love, that lovers don't make rules about how much or when they love, don't you? Great lovers simply strive to love as intensely as they can and to love more today than they did yesterday." As his voice grew fainter, his grip on the young friar's shoulder grew tighter. "It's exactly the same with poverty. To you, my young brother, who embodies my legacy and hope for the Little Brothers, I say: Forget about the rule! Instead, in this regard

imitate me: Fall madly, passionately, profoundly in love with Lady Poverty. Let your love for her be unbounded, and then. . . .”

"Brother Sebastiano, out, out!" Leone exclaimed, storming into the hut, his patience having been fully exhausted. "Poor Father Francesco needs to die in peace instead of preaching himself to death."

Sebastiano raised his head up off of Francesco's chest and kissed him. Then, asking for Francesco's blessing, he knelt beside his bed as Francesco placed his hand on top of his young friend's head and wordlessly blessed him. As Sebastiano stood up to leave, Francesco smiled weakly and whispered, "*Arrivederci, caro mio*, and remember—love!" Sebastiano departed sobbing.

*T*he next day as the vesper bells were ringing, concluding the last day of September, Francesco silently bemoaned that yet another day had slowly dragged by without his having died. "Perhaps tomorrow," he prayed silently, "God will find me worthy to come home." On the first of October his breathing became more labored, and he requested to see Brother Elias. When the Minister arrived, he saw clearly that Francesco was on his deathbed and was most solicitous.

"Brother Elias, in your responsible hands are the needs of all the brothers, and I need to tell you one of my needs," he said, pausing to gasp for breath. "You need to know that regardless of what others may say," he stammered before again pausing, "it is my final request not to be buried here at my beloved Portiuncula!"

Externally, Elias's face was composed and revealed nothing of the turmoil that had just erupted beneath the surface. Inwardly grimacing in great pain, Elias thought, "Not buried at Portiuncula! What about my plans to build a majestic basilica to enshrine his tomb here—one that will excel any church or shrine in Italy?" Not to be deterred, Elias smiled as his swiftly calculating mind began mentally relocating his imaginary magnificent church over at San Damiano as an extension onto the little chapel there. Leaning closer, he asked, "Pray tell us, Father Francesco, where do you desire to be buried? Tell us where, and I promise that we shall lay you to rest at that place."

"*Collis Infernus.*"

"That rocky hillside outside the western walls of Assisi?" gasped Elias. "The gully where they execute and bury criminals?"

"Good, you know the place. Then it's settled. That's where I want you to bury me."

"But, Father Francesco, it's a rocky outcropping, only a deep gully—and totally unsuited as a building site for a. . . ."

"I like the idea of being buried there," Francesco answered, ignoring Elias's allusion to its undesirability as a building site, "alongside outcasts, prisoners, gypsies—near the spot where the garbage of Assisi is dumped."

"Perhaps," replied Elias, quickly readjusting a loose strand of hair behind his ear, "we should discuss. . . ." At that moment Leone tapped Elias on the shoulder and shook his head, indicating that he should terminate his visit. Nodding to Leone, Elias told Francesco that he would see that his burial request was recorded in writing. Then, asking God to bless Francesco, he departed.

Jacques and Elias sat watching the slow and painfully difficult wrestling match between Bony Death and Francesco's frail body. When news spread among the brothers that Death was about to be proclaimed the winner in this Herculean contest, several of his old friends came to visit him for the last time to say farewell. His face beamed with joy as he opened his eyes to see his old companion Bernardo, stooped and using a cane, along with Brothers Rufino, Giles, and Silvestro all standing at his bedside. He rallied as they recalled the fond memories of their adventures of going to Rome to see the Pope and how wonderful were their early days of living in thatched huts when life was so joyfully simple. Tears filled his eyes as they spoke of those from the old days who were either too sick to visit him or who had already joined beloved Pietro Catanii in death. Finally, after Leone indicated that it was time for them to leave, managing a smile, he bid them *arrivederci*. To which Bernardo replied, "Yes, Francesco, until we meet again in paradise."

"No more visitors, Jacques!" Leone said. "Guard the door to make sure that they were the last." Then, like a mother hen fussing over her chicks, he asked, "Francesco, it's almost sunset. Would you like some warm soup?"

Answering that he didn't, he began to reflect on Bernardo's parting words about them meeting again in paradise. His kind farewell had actually awakened Francesco's old anxieties about being a sinner who did not deserve heaven. "We may meet again, dear Bernardo," Francesco thought, "but it will be when you're on your way to heaven, briefly passing through purgatory, where I'll be a longtime penitent. In

fact, I'll be lucky even to reach purgatory, since doubters and heretics go to hell, not paradise."

Worn out by his visitors, he closed his eyes and fell asleep almost at once. When he awakened a short while later, he could faintly make out the shadowy shapes of Leone and Jacques keeping vigil in the darkness. He closed his eyes again, pondering how his bedridden inactivity and the absence of the stimuli of daily life had gifted him with a reflective state much like meditation, allowing his mind to turn deeply inward. "My fitful sleep and half-sleep," he mused, "act like a great paddle agitating the depths of the bottomless well of my memory, magnifying the creative dreamlike state that often happens in the predawn twilight before fully awakening."

Then, the great paddle spun around and around, and out of the darkness he was visited by guests unseen and unheard by Brothers Leone and Jacques, who were keeping vigil in the darkness beside him.

"GIOVANNI FRANCESCO!" IT WAS A VOICE HE INSTANTLY recognized, yet he was amazed to open his eyes and find his beloved Padre Antonio bending over him, holding his black cat Nicoletto in his arms. "Take heart, son, you're almost home. Do not be afraid or anxious about your past sins; everyone is awaiting your arrival—right, Nicoletto? Ah, Giovanni Francesco, you look surprised to see me! Don't be—nor should you be surprised to see the others who've come to visit you."

Then, to Francesco's amazement, the crucifix of San Damiano appeared behind Antonio—the one that had spoken to him so many years ago. He watched the crucifix growing larger and larger until it filled the entire hut and the various figures painted around the crucified Christ on the cross became as large as life. To the left of Christ's body, directly below his extended arm, stood the Virgin Mother and St. John the beloved disciple. As Francesco gazed at the figures, unbelievably, they both stepped out of the painting! When they walked to his bed, to his bewilderment, he recognized the woman as his own mother, Pica, and the man as his father, Pietro.

"O my beloved Giovanni," his mother said, kissing his bandaged left hand, "my dearest son the priest, I'm so proud of you." As he began protesting that he wasn't a priest, his father reached down and took his right hand, speaking as pontifically as ever, "Francesco, my son, I'm also proud of you. You hide your wounds like a real hero, not bleating about them like some sickly sheep. All these years you've endured the sufferings of life without whimpering. Whenever the goddess Fortuna's wheel would stop on this or that misfortune, you didn't whine for sympathy. My beloved Francesco, you're a real man!" Leaning over, he

 kissed him on the cheek, saying, "I love you." As Francesco's head swam with delight, his parents were instantly transported back onto the cross again, causing him to wonder, "Was I dreaming or hallucinating?" Then he heard Nicoletto's soft purring and looked up to see Padre Antonio again standing in front of the towering crucifix at the foot of his bed.

"Giovanni Francesco, I know you're anxious, but don't be afraid."

"I'm not afraid, Padre—I'm terrified! I'm dying, and on the verge of standing before Christ the Judge. I've sinned and I've doubted some of the dogmas and teachings of the Church, like the earth being flat. Many of my beliefs are surely heresy: that all of creation is saturated with God's presence, that there are saints in other religions and that even their holy books are inspired by the Holy Spirit, and. . . ."

"Giovanni, do not be anxious. *Vidi et scio,* as the ancients said, 'I've seen and I know'—and, soon, so shall you. Forget your fears about doubting the dogmas of the Church! When you finally stand before the Lord, I assure you that you'll not be asked if you've believed in this or that dogma or in a single article of the Apostles' Creed. You'll be asked only this: In your brief years on this small, round planet, have you loved God with all your heart and soul and generously responded to the pleas of the hungry, homeless, and suffering?"

"Padre Antonio is correct," said another voice he recognized. As he looked up, he was stunned to see kindly Bishop Guido at his bedside. Holding his golden crozier in his right hand, he had on the very same ceremonial cope he was wearing on that day in Piazza Maria Maggiore when he had wrapped it around Francesco's naked body.

"You're no heretic! Indeed, the creed of your heart may not be orthodox by the standards of today's Church, but it's true and it's visionary. My heart told me as soon as I met you that you were an enfleshment of God's words to the prophet Joel: 'I will pour out my spirit upon all the people; your old men shall dream dreams . . .'" and, ah, Francesco, did you ever cause this old man to dream! Joel goes on to say, 'and your young men shall see visions.' Indeed, you saw a great vision. I knew that you were no heretic, but rather, that you would lead us beyond the present frontiers of our faith and far more deeply into the mystery of God."

"*Parvulus eos ducebit*—A child will lead them,' do you recall that?" affirmed Antonio.

"As for orthodoxy," Guido continued, placing both hands on his crozier and leaning forward on it, "*Vox populi, vox Dei*, 'the voice of the people is the voice of God.' You gave voice to the cry of the *minores*, the lowly ones longing for a God of love and joy and for their freedom as the children of God. The Spirit speaks to the Church through the voice of the people as well as in the hierarchy and the Pope. Your entire life became a prophetic *vox populi* as you dared to live out the Good News you heard being proclaimed in your heart by the Spirit. So do not. . . ."

"Francesco . . . Francesco, forgive me for disturbing you." Opening his eyes, the only figures Francesco saw beside his bed were Jacques holding a flickering oil lamp next to Leone, who had fresh bandages in his hands. "Don't be perplexed," Leone said as he began to lift the bottom of Francesco's tunic over his feet. "We only want to change your bandages since they're all bloody and must be uncomfortable."

"Dearest Leone, you're not bothering me. I was a bit confused when I woke up. I must have been dreaming. But, please, go ahead and tend to old, dying Brother Ass."

His bandages changed, Francesco dozed off into a state of semi-conscious sleep that seemed to last for several hours as he hung on his cross of pain and fever somewhere between heaven and earth. He could feel either Jacques or Leone wiping away the sweat from his forehead with a damp cloth. He also became aware of someone trying to pry open his mouth. "It must be my Holy Viaticum," he thought, "my last Holy Communion to safeguard me on my journey from this world." He recalled the ritual words he knew that priests said when giving Holy Communion to a soldier before going to the battlefield: "Receive, brother, the Viaticum of our Lord Jesus Christ. May he preserve you from the malignant enemy and bring you to everlasting life." Relieved at the thought of receiving Holy Viaticum, he started to open his mouth and also half opened one eye to see if he recognized the priest giving him his last Holy Communion.

As he did, he gulped, as if swallowing a walnut, and quickly closed his mouth. For bending over him, he saw the old hunchback beggar Strapazzate!

"Prince of paupers, open your mouth," said Strapazzate. The hunchback was wearing his usual ragged tunic, which now, however, glistened with tiny sparkling lights, as if stars had been sewn into it. "Open wide so I can place an *obolos* on your tongue. Alas, blessed beggar Bernadone, there's no bridge across that dark, poisonous River Styx, which serpentine-like coils itself nine times through the underworld. The only way across is by ferryboat, and grisly old Charon in his dark, tattered sailor's cloak demands an *obolos* of each dead shade as a fee for the ferry ride across the Styx. Whether Pope or pauper, none will old, greedy Charon carry for free."

"Perhaps I could offer him a blessing."

"Not according to what I've heard. As I slept nightly on the cobblestone alleys of Assisi, I could hear 'em talking way down there, far, far below me. You need good ears, keen ears, to hear the voices. You need at least three pairs of good ears. Beneath the cobblestones where I'd be sleeping, way down under lots of layers of one old Assisi after another, under the dust of broken pottery and the crumbled stones of ancient buildings, I could hear 'em."

"Hear who?"

"The ancient ones who once lived here in Assisi long ago in Roman times. I heard 'em chatting away from one grave to another, a'speakin' about being buried with a coin, an *obolos*, for Charon in their mouth."

"Tommaso of Spello, you always were kind to me. But no, thank you. All I need upon my tongue to cross the river of death is the Body of my Lord Jesus Christ. Indeed, as a lad I heard about Charon and the myth. . . ."

"Myth!" exclaimed Strapazzate with eyes as large as white dinner plates. "Kind Signore Bernadone, to whom painted wooden crucifixes speak, how do we know what is myth and what is dogma? Does not today's dogma often become tomorrow's myth?" Then, as in the old days, Strapazzate began spinning around. He wobbled a bit as he stopped, and, after straightening himself, he leaned over close to Francesco's face and said, "Son of Pietro Bernadone, remember that once you've crossed the Styx you will follow the road to the court of judgment, from whose Judge nothing—nothing—is concealed. Yet fear not: You'll not be sentenced to join the wicked stranded on the other

side of the great river of fire, for you've been compassionate to the poor, to outcasts and to misfits judged to have scrambled brains. Giovanni Francesco, you shall enter the Elysian Fields, the paradise of the blessed. So, rejoice! As Horace, the lute-tongued Roman poet of the age of Augustus, said, '*O noctes cenaeque deum.*'"

"Strapazzate you amaze me—and confuse me, for my Latin is weak."

"'O nights and feasts of the gods!' Tonight will be such a feast of the gods, a feast far more sumptuous than any ancient banquet, a feast from which you as a slender-bodied youth will depart stuffed like a Christmas goose. Twelve hundred years ago old Quintus Horatius spoke of you: 'We rarely find anyone who can say he has lived a happy life, and who, content with life, can retire from the world like a satisfied guest from a banquet.' Famed as a man of fasting, your whole life has been a sumptuous feast. So now open your mouth, for you'll need this when. . . ."

"Francesco, open your mouth for a small sip of wine. I saw you gulping as if something was caught in your throat," Leone said as he gently raised Francesco's head, placing a cup to his lips.

"Thank you, Leone. I suspect it was only a bit of phlegm." A quick glance about the room confirmed that old Strapazzate was nowhere to be seen. Yet the old hunchback's words about crossing the Styx reminded Francesco that he had left his brothers no instructions about his death, nor had he requested the Last Rites yet. So he asked Leone to send at once for Brother Elias so he could tell him how he wanted to die.

"Naked?" asked a shocked Elias when Francesco told him he wanted them to remove his tunic and place him naked on the earthen floor of the hut so he could die in absolute poverty.

"Yes, Brother Elias, that's what the cross of San Damiano told me to do."

"The cross spoke to you?" asked a confused Elias. "But it's way over in the chapel of San Damiano!"

"The fever," Leone whispered in Elias's ear.

"Right after I sent word for you to come here," Francesco said, "the cross of San Damiano reappeared before me. As I was contemplating it, the white loincloth around Christ's waist undid itself and dropped to the floor, leaving him stark naked."

"But, Father Francesco, your asking to die naked is . . . ah . . . impossible!" stammered Elias. "When that holy hour comes, I, along with your close friends and a group of friars will be here praying the prayers for the dying! The sight of your naked body . . . with . . . ah . . . for all to see. . . ."

"I assure you, Brother Elias," Francesco replied, lightly tapping Elias's hand with the tip of his index finger, "that you and the brothers will not in any way find the sight of my naked body to be an occasion of sin." Then, managing to chuckle slightly, he added, "If anything, it will be so revolting as to be penitential for all of you. Now, tell me, Minister General, do I have your permission?"

Elias gulped, feeling trapped, for it was unacceptable to deny a dying man his last wish, but this wish was outrageous. He reluctantly agreed, departing quickly lest Francesco be inspired to make another bizarre request. As he walked away from the hut, he nodded acknowledgment to the armed guards sent by the commune, reassured by their presence that Francesco's body wouldn't be spirited away by agents from Perugia or some other relic-greedy city. While his saintly dead body was secure, Elias now worried that once Rome learned Francesco had chosen to die stark naked with his entire body exposed before those present at his death, his reputation for holiness would be thrown into even greater dispute than it already was.

"His wish to die naked as a newborn babe," Elias reflected, "in addition to his other request of being buried alongside outcasts and criminals and the city's garbage, places in great jeopardy my hopes of seeing our order's prestige enhanced by his canonization." Stopping, he looked back at Francesco's hut and reflected, "Perhaps I can prevent Leone and Jacques from undressing him as he's dying. Surely, in the midst of taking his last breath, he'll be almost unconscious, and we could prevent him from such an unchaste act. If he is still conscious, and those two friends insist on disrobing him, I'll just have to require everyone present to vow secrecy—for whoever heard of any saint wanting to die naked!"

"What day of the week is it?" Francesco asked when awakened by the sound of church bells ringing.

"Saturday, the third of October," replied Leone.

"Saturday already," he sighed. "I had so hoped I'd be given the grace to die yesterday on a Friday, like my beloved Lord. Yet how vain of me to desire such a thing. Clearly I'm not worthy to share such an honor, for here it is Saturday and I'm still alive, hanging on my cross. Do you think, Leone, I can last until next Friday?"

"If it's God's will," Leone replied, wiping the sweat off Francesco's brow as he thought, "O God, don't let him linger any longer in this pain. I'll miss him more than I would my right arm, but suffering as he is, I can't ask that he live a day longer."

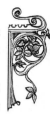

Several hours, or perhaps only a brief snip of sleep, later, he knew not which, Francesco awakened to a cracking sound. Upon opening his eyes, he saw that the giant cross of San Damiano had again filled the room. He could see that the sound was coming from an area where the paint was peeling off around a figure on the right side of the crucifix as it began stepping out of the cross. While the figure was a woman, as it came closer it changed into white-haired, old Samuel of Barcelona.

"Ready for your exodus?" asked Samuel as he came over and sat down on the side of Francesco's bed. "You know, there are as many of them as there are stars in the night sky, which God once numbered for Abraham and his sons. Like the children of Israel coming out of Egypt, I was led on my exodus to the Promised Land by the cloud of glory, just as you will soon be escorted by the *Shekhinah* cloud. That cloud of the Presence leads us ever onward, yet it is always just out of reach until we arrive at our final destination. That *Shekhinah* cloud now hovers over this place of your suffering, pain and sickness; for God is truly here, closer now than ever before in your life, as near as your fingertips."

"Samuel, that's comforting, even if I can't see it. I've often thought of you and our talks at your home, and I've often meditated on the *Shekhinah*. Thank you for coming, but you're one man I never thought I'd see stepping out of a crucifix."

"Ah, there are many doorways from the Promised Land that open unto this land! I'm sorry to say that to this old Jew you look like you're suffering from more than just a pestilence or sickness. What pains you?"

"A broken heart, Samuel. Broken by all the compromises I've made with Rome, the concessions that have watered down the once hearty wine of the Rule of our Little Brothers. I thought I had buried that sorrow at La Verna, but as I now lay dying it is an open wound that breaks my heart."

"Francesco, do you remember Rabbi Solomon Ibn-Garibrol, the one I talked about on that Saturday in Barcelona? Do you recall how I

 quoted to you his words about the servants of God being those who walk clear-eyed on the straight path, turning neither to the right or left, till they come to the court of the King's palace? Francesco, you yourself have, indeed, walked straight as an arrow, turning neither left nor right. And now you've come to the open gates of the King's court."

"Does the King mend broken hearts?" he asked, patting his chest. "For such is this heart of mine."

"Let me tell you a story," Samuel said, leaning closer. "Once upon a time, as our holy rabbis say, the great masters of the soul had access to a complicated set of keys that opened the lock of the heart, inside which dwells the All Holy One, blessed be he. As their deaths approached, each rabbi shared with his favorite disciple the secret of that intricate set of keys to the lock of the heart. Years grew into centuries, and there was a great famine of spiritual masters—and, sadly, also of truth-seeking disciples. So when the last spiritual master died, there was no one left to whom he could pass on the secret of the keys."

"You mean," Francesco asked, spellbound by the story, "the secret keys were lost forever? Making it impossible to open the door to find God?"

"Yes! No longer having those mystical keys, the only way now to find the way to God is to smash the lock!"

As he pronounced the word *lock*, old Samuel's face instantly began twisting and transforming itself as if it were made of soft clay and a sculptor was reshaping it from within his body. His physical stature underwent a contortion as well; his body became shorter, slimmer and even older. Francesco stared in utter amazement at the figure that stood before him: old Samuel of Barcelona had metamorphosed almost instantly into someone he hadn't seen since his youth—old Claude de Lune, the master lute maker he had met at the Chambery Fair.

"Francesco, the Troubadour of Assisi, who once asked me for a lute with a soul," said Claude smiling at him with eyes that sparkled as radiantly as they had on the day he had met Francesco so many years ago. "As you see, I've brought the precious stringless lute you so admired when you were a lad."

Francesco nodded, smiling as he gazed at the ancient instrument in Claude's hands. He remembered how he had not only admired that wondrous lute but had been mystified at how a lute that lacked strings, a bridge and pegs could produce music.

"Do you remember, Francesco, that day in Chambery when I told you about the three classes of musicians, the rarest of all being those hermits and troubadours of the heart who make their music for trees and flowers, birds and wild beasts? I told you that those able to forget themselves and become the melody itself are able to create the same melody that moves the sun and the stars. Francesco, you've become the master musician, one of the few able to play this rarest of all lutes."

"I haven't played a lute in twenty years! I left behind the one you made for me when I dispossessed myself. So I'm in no way qualified to. . . ."

"Ah, Francesco, even as a sapling of a lad, old Claude of the Moonlight saw in you a passionate genius of the soul who could someday play this lute of ecstasy." Holding out the old lute to him, he added, "Troubadour Francesco, don't shake your head in disagreement. For like the wood I used to make your lute, you also have been struck by lightning from heaven. It has pierced your hands and feet—and your soul—with the fire of ecstasy."

Then Claude leaned over and, placing the lute on top of Francesco's chest, began lovingly stroking it as he gently pressed it downward. Francesco could feel the lute slowly sinking beneath his tunic and into his body. "Now my passionate lightning-struck troubadour," he said, "you're ready for the greatest of all of your performances, your farewell death concert, playing on the lute of your body the music that moves the sun and the stars." As Francesco opened his mouth to speak, the old Frenchman faded back onto the cross, changing again into the figure of the woman standing next to the red-cloaked soldier. As Claude disappeared, Francesco felt himself disappearing into fibrous clouds of blinding gray fog, his high fever returning to bathe his body in sweat. As he slept, Brothers Jacques and Leone took turns replacing damp cloths on Francesco's forehead as the afternoon hours slowly crept by one by one. Occasionally Francesco would awaken to see Jacques and Leone at his bedside, and at other times to find only the gigantic cross of San Damiano filling the hut.

Partially opening his eyes late in the afternoon, the crucifix once again filled the room. Gazing at it, he began to detect a slight movement among the three figures who stood under on the extended left arm of Christ. The soldier in the short battle tunic wearing a red Roman military cloak appeared to be squirming, as if struggling to emerge from the painting. Then, with a slight popping sound, this centurion, known as Longinus, the soldier who smote Christ with his

spear, stepped out and onto the floor. To Francesco's amazement, Longinus suddenly turned into Signore della Casa, the knight for whom Francesco had been a squire when he went off so naïvely to fight for Pope Innocent III against the German Emperor Otto.

"Francesco of Assisi," said della Casa walking toward the bed, "like your other visitors I've come to you from the other side of death. Indeed, the death omens observed by those young squires came true, at least for me. I never returned home from that battle in Apulia. But I have no regrets. I died honorably on the field of battle, and it was more adventuresome than dying of old age—bored and useless in a bed."

"Signore della Casa, it's so good to see you again."

"And to you, Francesco. Do you remember that night on our way to Spoleto when just the two of us sat by a campfire and you spoke of your desire to become a knight champion? Do you recall how I told you that a champion is the last one to leave the *campus*, the field, and so becomes the victor. Well, you're still here on the field of combat! While others have retreated, escaping in concessions, you've personally stood your ground, striving to live a Christ-like poverty without compromise. Even though you're lying down, you're dying as a champion, the last one on the campus of combat." Then, raising his sword, he exclaimed, "I salute you!" touching the tip of his sword to his forehead.

"Signore della Casa, you're kind to say that, but I'm no victor. I've failed at the task I undertook; I was too innocent and naïve. And I'm dying not a champion but as a loser, defeated by the powerful forces of the world."

"Francesco, it is your eyes that have failed, not you! Do you recall that night outside Spoleto when I said your fellow squires were afraid to die because they had never lived! If one strives to live life fully with all one's heart and soul, as you've done, risking the pain of living with such great intensity, why should one fear dying?"

"Yes, I do remember, and I also remember something else you told me that night which has engraved itself in my memory. You said that when champions die their spirit glows like a dazzling sunset that spans centuries. When you suggested that, I recalled a French champion I once saw, a heroic young woman of Montelimar who refused to compromise her beliefs in the face of the very fires of hell. The roaring blaze of the martyrdom-sunset of her life has been a light spanning seas

and land, following me all these years. It even seems to shimmer in this hut."

"Francesco, *en garde*," della Casa said, as he touched the tip of his sword to Francesco's heart, "be alert, comrade, for the contest is about to begin! So, *en garde!*" As he bowed graciously and reentered the cross of San Damiano, Francesco struggled to unravel his words, "the contest is about to begin." His statement was puzzling to Francesco, for to him it seemed that it was at last concluding.

"Several times this afternoon we thought the time had come." Leone's voice awakened Francesco, but he didn't open his eyes. "We thought God had taken him home; his breathing had become so weak that Brother Jacques had to place his ear to Father Francesco's chest to see if he was still alive. We were about to send for you, and then he would revive and moan."

"Surely, Brother Leone, his end is at hand!" Francesco recognized the voice of Elias. "Even if he's unconscious, it's time to give him the Last Rites and have him anointed. We should begin prayers for the dying, don't you think?" Francesco could faintly hear Leone agreeing. Then he heard Elias again: "I will summon his old friends and a few select friars. . . ."

"If I'm dying," he surprised them by opening his eyes as he spoke, "I want Sebastiano to be here—and Dom . . . ah . . . Brother . . . Tomas. He can administer the Last Rites to me."

"Wonderful, Father Francesco, you're conscious!" said Elias. "We know how terrible your suffering has been these past days, and good Brother Leone here believes that today you may finally be escorted by the angels to God. . . ."

"Or be ferried across the river Styx. Well, at least I've got my *obolos*. . . ." he replied, eyeing Elias and noticing Leone's bewildered look.

"Yes, yes, of course," Elias replied, "but if I can make a request of you, Father Francesco. For the sake of propriety and holy modesty, I've brought you a new habit in which to die and be buried." Francesco softly mumbled something, and Elias bent his head down, tilting his good ear close to Francesco's mouth, saying, "I couldn't hear you, Father Francesco."

"Naked!" he shouted, causing Elias to leap back. "I've told you I wanted to die naked, laying on the bare earth. I'm on my deathbed, and I'm not about to compromise again—modesty be damned!" Elias

departed at once, and as he opened the door to leave he heard Francesco say, "Jacques, my trusted friend, I place my dying wish in your large, strong hands. Please see to it that I go back to God the same way that I came from God out of my mother's womb—with nothing."

Death's stranglehold on Francesco again stole his consciousness, and he found himself feeling his way through a pitch-black cave. From his left he heard a familiar voice, saying, "Signore della Casa was right." The darkness vanished, and he saw Padre Antonio at his bedside, "I've returned, drawn back to help you banish the evil spirits that are haunting you about being a failure in life. Do you remember the first time we met, when I came upon you as you were pouring out your anguish in having to choose what to do with your life: to become a knight or a priest, a merchant or a troubadour, a husband or a minstrel?"

"Of course, Padre. It was one of the most significant days in my life."

"Francesco, you've become all of them! You're a knight champion, who has not fled the battleground of uncompromising poverty. You have been a passionate troubadour of the glad tidings, living an endless canticle of joy and passionate love. You've become a merchant-peddler of God's kingdom, cleverly dispensing to one and all—prelate or pauper, peasant or prince—the Gospel's precious way through the eye of the needle. With song, story, and intoxicating joy, you marketed the mystical merchandize of the way of Christ, whose purchase price was not gold but the cost of passionately loving with all your heart, soul, mind, and body. Like a wise merchant, you never cheapened your merchandize by offering it on sale at half price—it was all or nothing! Did you not also become a husband by wedding yourself to your beloved Lady Poverty in the nuptials of nothingness, for better or worse, in health or in sickness, unto death? And always you were a traveling minstrel-magician, who made sadness and gloom disappear and happiness appear out of thin air. Yes, Francesco, and there was one last occupation: Do you recall how your parish priest thought you had a vocation to be a priest? Well, he was right, for. . . ."

"Have mercy on me, O God. According to your mercy blot out my iniquity. . . ." At the sound of the friars gathered around his bed chanting Psalm 50, Antonio disappeared. "Wash me completely of my guilt," they chanted mournfully. "Cleanse me of my sin . . . for my sin is always before me. Against you only have I sinned; I have done what

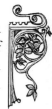

is evil in your sight. . . ." Instead of comforting him, these guilt-soaked prayers only pried off the scab of his childhood wound of the fear of hell, which began bleeding guilt and shame. The chanting voices faded away, and Francesco discovered that he had shrunk to the size of a child again and once more was in his mother's kitchen as she opened wide the door to the stove, saying, "Giovanni, do you see the flames? The fires of hell are just as terrible, my beloved Giovanni, only, unlike these flames in my stove, they never ever stop burning. Giovanni, never sin, never sin. . . ." Then she vanished, and Francesco was swallowed up in great thundering storm clouds that rained down jagged lightening bolts of fierce anguish that struck his body, piercing it again and again.

Feeling someone touching his tunic, Francesco opened his eyes to see Padre Antonio lifting up the cuffs of his sleeves, exposing his stigmata. "Padre Francesco, let's return to what I was saying about you being a priest. Even before you were given these wounds that fully consecrated your body into the body of Christ, you were a priest according to the order of Melchizedek. Since that day at San Damiano your entire life has been one endless Holy Mass, a seamless consecration of yourself into the body and. . . ." placing his finger on the bleeding wound in Francesco's right hand, Antonio continued, ". . . the blood of Christ. Inspired by the Holy Spirit, you remained a layman, even if old Rome tried her best to make you a cleric by tonsuring you. You rejected being a member of that elite clerical caste that sets itself above the common people."

"I felt unworthy to be ordained a priest."

"Good! That allowed you to explore your baptismal ordination, when you were anointed with holy chrism as a priestly prophet in Christ. You became a living mirror by which anyone could see himself or herself as being priestly." Then, leaning over, he kissed Francesco on the forehead above his scars, saying, "May the love of God protect you now, for as we pray in the Night Hour of compline, 'Be vigilant; your enemy the devil, like a roaring lion, goes about seeking someone to devour. Resist; be steadfast in your faith.'"

"Father Francesco," said Leone, his voice causing Antonio to disappear before Francesco could ask him why he had quoted that compline prayer. "The friars have finished the Prayers for the Dying; do you care for a sip of warm soup?"

"Old friend, what time is it?"

"Almost sunset now. You've been drifting in and out of sleep."

"I hear the sound of many voices outside my hut. Who's out there?"

"A great multitude of the friars has gathered there to pray for you."

"Thank heaven. This old sinner needs all the prayers he can get." Mustering all his strength, he said, "Jacques, please lift this old sack of bones up in your strong arms and carry me to the door of the hut so I may bid farewell to the brothers gathered out there." Jacques dutifully slid his arms under Francesco's frail body and lifted him up as Leone carefully adjusted the sleeves of his tunic to cover his hands. A hush fell over the vast multitude of friars kneeling around the hut as Leone opened the door and Jacques carried him just outside the hut.

"Brothers," Francesco said to them, "please forgive me for all my mistakes and if in any way I may have offended any one of you. Pardon my failures to guide you and my clumsy attempts to compose for you a holy rule of life." Scanning the crowd, he continued, "If good Brother Elias is out there among you, I ask his forgiveness for my outbursts of anger and for the great distress I've caused him by my stubbornness. Brothers, be humble and docile; do not imitate me in my mulishness. I know there are divisions among you concerning how you should live out your poverty, but I pray the Spirit of unity, who is also the Spirit of diversity, will inspire you to live out your poverty in a rich variety of ways—so remain united." Then, pausing to gather his strength, he implored, "Brothers, forgive me for my sins of uncharitable, judgmental and impatient thoughts about some of you."

Coughing, he gasped for breath for a moment and then said to his friend who had cradled him in his arms. "Jacques, lift me higher and turn me toward my beloved Assisi." Jacques' strong arms easily raised Francesco up higher, and he turned him toward Assisi, whose roof tiles now glistened crimson in the light of the approaching golden orange sunset. Taking a deep breath, he prayed: "Beautiful Assisi of Umbria, city of my birth, blessed be you for ages upon ages to come. Noble Assisi, the self-rule of your commune has given to each of your citizens the dignity to be a king or queen: Blessed be you among those who love freedom. Holy Assisi, whose many churches are beehives buzzing with prayer and filled with the sacred honey of peace, may you become the City of Peace." He concluded his blessing by tracing the sign of the cross over the city, saying, "May God's blessing rest upon you, Assisi, now and forever. Amen."

As Jacques carried him from the fresh autumn afternoon air back inside the hut, Francesco was overwhelmed by the stench of sickness in

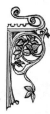

which he could easily sniff out the scent of death. "Brother Death is close now, Leone. I can smell him. It won't be long now," Francesco said as they laid him on his straw mattress. "Soon I'll no longer be such a pest to the two of you. I can't ever thank you enough for all the days and weeks you've cared for me, cleansing me after my attacks of diarrhea, cleaning and bandaging my wounds. Alas, it was I who should have been your servant rather than you being mine. But please, beloved Jacques, whether or not I'm awake when good Brother Death comes to the door, remember my last wish and strip me of my tunic, laying me naked on the bare earth floor."

Jacques nodded in acknowledgment. Exhausted by his blessing of the friars and Assisi, he quickly sank into a deep sleep. Once again he found himself walking through murky clouds of thick blinding fog. Then, to his surprise, he came face to face with a man wearing a simple white flowing robe whom he instantly recognized.

"Your Holiness! Pope Innocent!" he quickly exclaimed, kneeling down before the pontiff.

"Stand up, your holiness Francesco," Innocent replied as he lifted Francesco to his feet. "And it's no longer Innocent; now they simply call me Lothario. They say it's my eternal name recorded at my baptism in the Book of Life. It appears that papal coronations come and go, but baptisms are forever. But I rather like Lothario: my mother chose that name for me."

"Oh, I'm sorry to hear that in heaven you're called by your baptismal name. I was baptized Giovanni, but I really like the name Francesco."

"They said that in your case there'd be an exception to the rule."

"I'm glad to hear that, Your Holiness . . . I mean, Lothario. But why have you, of all the holy ones, come to visit me?"

"I've come because when I first met you I failed to properly comprehend that you were far more than a reformer, even a holy one. You were a mystic!"

"Oh no, that's impossible! Unlike Saint Paul on the road to Damascus or the great prophet Moses, I've not seen God face to face. Nor have I ever experienced that blissful union of which other saints speak. I've only experienced. . . ."

"Pain, confusion, and stressful tribulations, like the great one you're facing now, Francesco?"

"Yes, even if briefly at San Damiano I felt the joy of an intense loving union with God that was quickly followed by doubt and. . . ."

"Ridicule, suspicion of madness, and the rejection of your family and friends? While your joyful, intimate feelings of union were a great blessing, your primary mysticism was a union of the cross. Your experience of intimacy with God on Mount La Verna was a mystical sharing in the passion of the Crucified One, whose suffering is shared by so many poor, rejected, and disempowered ones of this world. In your compassion for them you were mystically united with the suffering Christ. You also share with the mystics of other religions that deep intimacy with God. You ask how I know? *Vidi et scio*: I've seen and I know. Truly, Almighty God has an almighty appetite to be intimately united with his beloved ones and creatively and lovingly fashions mystical experiences for each according to his or her culture, historical period, and religious beliefs. The ways of God are far beyond us, but union with the death and rising of Christ is not restricted only to Christians!

"You are so intelligent and learned, a philosopher and theologian, while I've not been schooled beyond the simple needs of a merchant's son."

"On the contrary, Francesco, you've been schooled in the greatest of all universities: the school of living the Gospels. I regret that I was not more of a mystic, which I now realize all men and women are called to be, even if the spiritual masters of this thirteenth century believe it's a gift given only to a few spiritual elites. If only I had desired it with the same passion as you have."

"I didn't seek to be a mystic; I only tried as best I could to love Christ passionately."

"To love passionately makes one a mystic, Francesco. As one who has loved greatly, you know that with lovers what wounds one also pierces the other. So my Godly-wounded Francesco of Assisi, soon you'll become a saint in heaven and will enjoy full mystical union with God. Shortly you'll become a canonized saint, but in the process you'll paradoxically lose some of your prophetic ability to be a challenging inspiration to personal, joyful holiness. So be prepared for that day when they elevate you up on a pedestal and encircle your head with a halo."

"The tonsure was painful enough—a halo would be even worse."

"I couldn't agree more. Halos lead to legends, and legends replace reality. The human scourge of disappointments, failures, childhood traumas, sins, leeches, and even diarrhea is eclipsed by sweet stories and pious sayings—for saints must never, never be human. Since saints, like guardian angels, have their work cut out for them, after some Pope gives you a halo, then, who knows what group or profession will have you as their patron saint? If I were Pope now, I'd make you the patron saint of mystics."

Innocent III disappeared as quickly as a delicate candle flame in a strong wind. To his surprise, Francesco found himself back on his bed in his hut, facing the mammoth cross of San Damiano.

As he pondered the significance of the cross in his life, he again heard that cracking, peeling sound of something pulling itself out of the paint of the crucifix. To his astonishment he saw the small angel painted at the extended right hand of Christ begin to emerge like a butterfly out of a cocoon as it crawled out of the cross, unfolding its wings. As it flew toward him, he was awed by how gorgeous was the angel's face and how it was clothed in shimmering light that seemed to drape itself around the angel's body like silken cloth. Its multicolored wings glowed with an iridescent brilliance of the sun. Surprisingly, however, the intensity of the sunlight did not irritate his eyes but, rather, made them feel soothingly cool. As this luminous angel drew closer to him, like a dam breaking, he felt all his pain draining out of his body.

"Francesco of God," the angel said in a voice as smooth as olive oil and four times more melodic than the sound of lute strings being caressed by a master troubadour, "the Lord is with you. Do not be afraid, for you have found favor with God." The stench of death was gone, and the smell of the soiled straw of his bed was now replaced with the pungent fragrance of a hundred lilies filling the hut.

Francesco's head was swimming in ecstasy as all of his senses felt drunk with a beauty that was too intense to absorb. Most of all, his soul throbbed with the greatest of joy at the affirming message of the angel. "Your holiness is brighter than the sun," the angel continued as it held a hand over its eyes. "Pope Innocent was infallibly correct. By your ceaseless passionate love of God you have rightly earned the title of patron saint of mystics. Lament not your failures, Francesco, nor

 bemoan your human failings. Rather, be proud of your steadfast faithfulness by which you have become a champion!" Extending an arm toward the crucifix, the angel proceeded to say, "Yes, a champion, like Christ nailed in glory on his cross. And since you have suffered with him, you shall share in his great divine glory. Even now that divinity radiates like the sun from within you." In the blink of an eye the angel flew over to the cross and removed the large golden halo that had been painted behind Christ's head, instantly returning to Francesco's bedside.

"The ancient Romans created the halo, this luminous circle of light, to encircle the heads of their gods and, later, those who shared in the glory of the gods. I now place this halo around your head, for from this day onward you shall be known as Saint Francesco of Assisi. Everywhere in Christendom there will be statues and holy images of you that shall be venerated by the people. You shall be the most popular of all the saints and will be honored even by non-Christians. Francesco, great is your glory: cities shall be named after you—and so will sons and daughters, as numerous as the stars of heaven. Does that not make your heart explode with pride?" Before Francesco could answer, he was distracted by a chorus of voices faintly murmuring, "Holy Mary, Mother of God, pray for us at the hour of our death." Squinting across the room, he made out several vapor-like kneeling figures fingering their prayer cords, repeating over and over, "Mother of God, pray for us now and at the hour of our death." He was barely able to discern some of the faces of those kneeling: his mother and father; Bishop Guido; old Filippo Villani, his father's merchant friend; Pietro Catanii and a few other brothers who had died.

"Saint Francesco, look," bellowed the angel trying to regain Francesco's attention as it pointed toward the far wall of the hut, which then instantly vanished, opening a clear view of Assisi atop Mount Subasio. At the far western end of the city was a magnificent stone basilica with a tall, impressive, square bell tower and a stunning rose window in its façade. "Son of Pietro Bernadone, take great pride in what is before your eyes, for that is the future Basilica of San Francesco, built to enshrine your saintly tomb. Its inside walls will be covered with beautiful, glowing frescos of scenes from your life. They will be painted in the new, realistic style you yourself once imagined by a great Florentine genius named Giotto di Bondone, who is to be born forty

years from this very year of your death. Millions upon millions of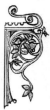
pilgrims. . . ."

Behind the angel's strong, melodious voice, the praying voices
continued like the murmuring of waves washing upon the shore: "Holy
Mary, Mother of God, pray for us now and at. . . ."

"No!" Francesco screamed as he reached behind his head and seized
the golden halo placed there by the angel and flung it with all the
strength of an Olympian discus thrower through the mysterious
opening in the wall, directly at the basilica. As the disc-like halo struck
its target, the mammoth yellow stone basilica shattered like a great
terra-cotta clay pot, crumbling to the earth in billowing clouds of
brownish-yellow dust.

"Be gone, Lucifer!" Francesco shouted. "Glory and praise belong to
God and to God alone. I want no glowing haloes, basilicas, frescoes, or
statues in my image." His tirade turned to prayer: "O God, come to my
assistance. O Lord, make haste to help me. As I lay here weakened by
sickness and the ravages of dying, I need you to shield me from the
diabolically poisonous serpent of vanity and pride that has come
creeping into my bed."

"The prayers of the saints and your faith has rescued you."
Francesco heaved an enormous sigh of relief upon hearing Padre
Antonio's voice. Opening his eyes, he found his mentor beside his bed
fingering a knotted prayer cord.

"Congratulations, Knight Francesco!" said Signore della Casa, who
now was standing next to Antonio. "You were indeed *en garde* and so
survived the threat of being lured off the *campus* of combat by the
craftiest of all enemies."

"No, my friends, I fear I did badly. Like a dry sponge I was soaking
up all those words I so longed to hear, eager to. . . ."

"Francesco," Antonio interrupted, "Signore della Casa is right, for
you were not dealing with an ordinary adversary. While our night
prayer of compline warns us that the devil goes about like a roaring
lion, as Saint Paul says, and as you just found out, Satan masquerades
as an angel of light. I feared he would come, knowing that he'd be eager
to hook a big fish like you."

"I'm no big. . . ."

"The old anchorites of the Egyptian desert said that the demons
take far greater glee in the fall of a great saint than they do in the defeat
of ten thousand lesser lights. And, Francesco, you are. . . ."

*O*nce again rolling waves of dense fog filled the hut, engulfing Antonio and Signore della Casa. Francesco was now no longer in bed but walking alone through the impenetrable fog. "I agree with what your Pope said." Francesco at once recognized the Moorish voice of his dear friend Ali Hasan. Invisible giant hands parted the heavy curtain of fog and out of it walked the barefoot brown-robed Sufi with his arms opened wide for an embrace. As the two friends approached each other, Francesco gasped in pain as if an iron spike had been driven through his heart. To his horror he saw that Ali's hands and feet also bore the stigmata.

"'What wounds one lover pierces the other,' as Pope Innocent put it," Ali said, "and in the mystery of Allah's will, my beloved Francesco, I have been allowed to share your wounds. Allah has gifted me—as you were gifted—to become a *shahid*, a witness, a martyr to our faith."

"But, Ali, you're a peaceful Sufi. You were opposed to war and killing. How, then, did you become a warrior and die for your faith in battle?"

"One need not die in battle to become a *shahid*—dying in any Godly action, like building a mosque or traveling on the *Hajj* pilgrimage to the Kaaba in Mecca, can make one a martyr. Indeed, it was on just such a pilgrimage that I met my martyrdom. After I left you on that road from Cartagena, I went off to fulfill my Muslim duty to go to Mecca. As I crossed over the straits to Morocco, I joined up with a small band of brother pilgrims also bound for the Holy City. Having heard reports of ferocious fighting between the troops of the Sultan and King John's crusaders at the mouth of the Nile, we decided to stay far away from the Christian crusaders. We took a southern traders' route across the desert. However, as we were entering a small village south of Cairo to fill our water bags, we were surprised by a band of crusader knights who had circled east of Cairo exploring the possibilities of making a surprise attack upon Sultan Al-Kamil from the rear. The ten of us were dressed in the traditional white robes worn by pilgrims on a *Hajj* to Mecca and had already entered the state of *Ihram*, which prohibits all sexual relations, fighting and even arguing with others. The mounted crusaders at once fell upon us with their swords, but because our Ihram vow we made no attempt to defend ourselves as they savagely hacked us to death. As blood and limbs began flying everywhere, I cried out, 'In the name of the prophet Jesus, whom you

call the Christ, who commanded that we are to love our enemies, stop this butchery of unarmed men.'"

"That infidel," shouted one of the knights, "dares to blaspheme the holy name of our Savior Jesus Christ! If that bastard heathen believes enough in Jesus Christ to quote him, I say let him also share in his crucifixion!" Seizing me, they dragged me over to a grain barn in the village, and finding some large iron spikes they nailed my hands and feet to the wooden door of the barn. One of the knights drove his spear into my heart, and as I bled to death under the blistering desert sun the crusaders proceeded to slaughter every man, woman, and child in that small village."

"Oh, my beloved Ali, I know how excruciating is the pain of being pierced by nails, and. . . ."

"Francesco, I didn't come here to speak of my martyrdom. I came to escort you to your place of honor next to the throne of God, the highest place in paradise that is reserved for the *shahid*, the martyrs of all religions."

"But I am no martyr! I haven't died witnessing to my faith."

"Francesco, in Islam a woman who, trusting in the mercy of Allah, dies in childbirth is honored as a *shahid*. You've been in labor now for over twenty years trying to give birth to a dream of God. Soon, very soon, you'll die, still giving birth to that dream, and then your spirit will be released to fly away from Assisi in all directions—across mountains, oceans and . . ." breaking into a great smile, Ali concluded, "and even all around the earth!"

"Oh, Ali, if only what you say could be true." Francesco said as he found himself once again lying on his straw mat, with Ali kneeling beside his bed, his arm draped across his chest. "I've been such a failure at poverty, at prayer and even, it seems, at dying, for I've been lingering here for weeks on the edge of my grave. You said, 'very soon.' Oh, how I hope that you are right."

"I am. *Vidi et scio.* So rejoice, my beloved troubadour and soul companion, for when you do die it will be not only in total poverty— as you so ardently desire—but also singing!"

"Singing, Ali?"

"Do you remember how I told you our Muslim scholars had translated the great Greek philosophers and astronomers into Arabic? Well, when I was a student at the university in Salamanca I studied some of the writings of Plato. I recall his words about swans: 'When

they perceive that they are about to die they then sing with splendorous beauty, rejoicing that they are going to the God they serve.'"

"Oh, Ali, how dearly would I love to sing at my final moment here on earth—to sing more lustily than ever before in life. God, please give me the voice and the passion when that moment finally arrives."

"That moment is upon you, Francesco! Tonight, there's a new moon. Just after sunset the new silver crescent moon of October will appear in the pale blue-green western sky. We followers of the Prophet are moon people. Our calendars and spirituality are divinely ordained to follow the phases of the moon. A new moon signals the fixed times for pilgrimage to Mecca as well as the beginning and end of the fasting of the holy month of Ramadan—and the crescent moon appears even on our flags."

"But why would a new moon signal the time of my death?"

"Because the first sighting of the crescent new moon in the evening sky signals the end of the great fast of Ramadan, and the beginning of a great feast of feasts. Dearest comrade, your fast has gone on far too long, and I don't mean simply from food. For years now you've fasted from success, good health, peace of heart, the affirmation of others and the comforting assurance of God's pardon. Now, sooner than three small grains of sand can funnel through the narrow neck of an hourglass, you'll be transported from fasting to feasting." Leaning over, he kissed Francesco. "Having loved with such passion, you will be carried away into the heart of the Divine Beloved."

At that moment Ali was engulfed by swirling clouds of luminous silver-gray mist. Francesco struggled to fill his lungs with air so he could sing. As he found himself back on his straw bed, he saw that the hut was crowded with praying friars, including Elias. "Jacques," he whispered weakly, raising his head slightly, "It's time! It's time! Be quick: Strip me of my tunic, for Brother Death is now about to open the door of this hut. Thanks be to God!" Jacques and Leone lovingly untied his rope belt, raising his tunic up over his head and then sliding his arms out of the sleeves. Francesco then pointed to his bandages, gasping weakly, "Naked, naked." When Leone had finished quickly unwrapping them, Francesco made one last request, "Please, Leone, open the door so all my brothers and sisters in creation can attend my death."

Jacques gently lifted him up off the straw mattress and placed his naked body on the bare earthen floor as those friars privileged to be present knelt down around him. As Leone opened the door wide to the amber sunset of this October 3, 1226, the giant orange orb of Brother Sun seemed to be floating on a shimmering golden river of light that flowed into the hut.

The friars kneeling around Francesco could see his lips moving and strained to hear his last words. Elias turned and whispered to Leone, "Can you hear what he's saying?"

"He isn't saying anything!" Leone said, turning to Elias with a smile and tears streaming down his cheeks. "He's singing!"

At the moment of his death, the troubadour of Assisi went off singing into eternity, and from the leafy branches of the trees arching over the hut there came an explosion of full-throated, melodic songs, as hundreds of his beloved larks joined their voices to his silent passionate song.

The next day, October 4, 1226, the dead body of Francesco, now attired in a new habit and sandals, was carried to his funeral Mass of the Dead. Then, in what seemed like an endless procession of his friars, his body was transported on a litter from Portiuncula to San Damiano so as to pass by Sister Clare and her cloistered sisters. From her grilled convent window a tearful Sister Clare blew a kiss to her beloved Francesco, whispering, "*Arrivederci!* 'Till we meet again!" In that moment she felt a moist kiss on her right cheek: It seemed to have flown to her on the autumn wind. As she nodded to Elias, the pallbearer friars lifted up his funeral bier. They began carrying his body through the silver-leafed olive groves, while, high above, the walls of Assisi were lined with hundreds of silent mourners. The path and their procession ended on the western rocky slopes of *collis infernus*, where the friars buried Francesco as he had requested: beside convicted criminals, outcasts and gypsies, outside the walls of his beloved Assisi.

Epilogus

cta est fibula—the play is over! Allow me to introduce myself to you who have gathered around this traveling medieval stage of actors and minstrels, saints, villains, and an odd, colorful assortment of clerical scoundrels and religious rascals. I am the *magister bibendi*, the master of drinking and revelry presiding over this Festival of Francesco of Assisi. While unseen, I am the one who has now and then spoken to you from offstage during this mystery passion play. So now that I've been properly introduced, it's on with the *epilogus* of the magnificent tale of Francis of Assisi. (As you can see, I've begun to use the English version of his name—the one with which you are so familiar.)

In ancient times "*Acta est fibula*" was said at the end of a drama, and the great Augustus borrowed that expression on his deathbed. The play is over: saintly Francis of Assisi is lying in his grave—enjoying the opportunity to rub elbows with the real *minores* of his day, prisoners and outcasts. There are, however, those who maintain that ever zealous Brother Elias had him temporarily buried inside Assisi's church of San Giorgio. Regardless, as with all great dramas, this tale isn't over when it's over, for stories of great heroes like Francis have long tails.

In the following year, 1227, aged Pope Honorius III died, and the cardinals elected as his successor a man who by now you know quite well, Cardinal Ugolino di Segni, nephew of Pope Innocent III. As Pope he took the name of Gregory IX, and in 1228, only two years after Francesco's death, Gregory canonized him as a saint of the Catholic Church. Before the Pope himself died in 1241 he continued to support both the new religious orders of the Franciscans and Dominicans and also established the papal inquisition, placing it under the direction of the Dominicans.

In 1230, four years after Francis's death, Minister General Elias solemnly placed Francis's body inside a magnificent basilica, one of the first of Italy's great Gothic cathedrals. As the chief designer of this basilica, Elias had showed great skill as an engineer and architect, especially considering the difficult problems of constructing it on the

steep slopes of the rocky gully of Convict's Hill outside the western gate of Assisi. He entombed Francis's body in a 200-pound stone sarcophagus that he had surrounded with a welded iron grill of about the same weight, placing a large stone and a great slab of granite on top of the grill to insure that no relic robbers would steal the body.

Saint Clare of Assisi remained the leader of her community of poor women until her death in 1253, when she also died a champion. In her life of prayer and poverty, she inspired many to similarly holy lives. Even her blood sisters, Agnes and Beatris, and her mother Signora Ortholona Scifi joined Clare at San Damiano. Throughout the twenty-seven years after Francis's death, with resolve and fortitude, Clare remained faithful to their mutual dream, even in the face of all the pressure of popes and bishops to compromise her rule. A mere two years after her death in 1255 she was canonized a saint. Saint Clare added the dimension of the feminine spirit to Francis's ideas of poverty, deep prayer, and passionate love of God. While forced by the Church to live a cloistered, hidden life, she saturated it with prayer, joyful sacrifice, and a transformative love. Prevented by a clerical prohibition from preaching or performing public works of mercy, she lived deeply and authentically, becoming a model of sanctity for women whom the circumstances of life prevent from an active social involvement. Saints Francis and Clare are now wedded for life as shining examples for following one's destiny and for intensely passionate living and loving.

The brotherhood of the friars absorbed the spirit of Francis the revolutionary, and within a hundred years after his death experienced its own religious revolts. By 1256, thirty short years after Francis's death, the Friars Minor had radically moved away from a primarily lay brotherhood to become a religious order of educated clerics involved in organized pastoral care, preaching, and hearing confessions. Some of the friars saw this as a betrayal of Francis's dream and splintered off into small groups, living in a way truer to Francis's original vision. Called the *fraticelli*, the little friars, or the spirituals, they renounced the rule's relaxing of absolute poverty that had been embraced by the majority of friars, and some of them even renounced the Church. While enamored by the poor, they had become so extreme by 1317 that they were condemned as heretics, with some being burned at the stake. They disappeared from history.

In time, a growing number of friars sought to reform their order by returning to being wandering, poor preachers. They became known as Observant Friars, while those who chose not to join that reform movement were called Conventual Friars. The tension between these groups soon grew so intense that it became necessary for Pope Leo X to split them into two separate congregations in 1517. While his body was

long since buried, the passionate spirit of the revolutionary Francis was very much alive. It continued to inspire splinter groups within the Observant Reform Friars to break away, seeking to live a more authentic life of poverty. The largest of these radical groups was called the Capuchins, and in 1536 the Pope made them the third branch of the Franciscans. Today the three independent congregations known as the Friars Minor are commonly called Franciscans.

The Spirit of Francis of Assisi couldn't be contained within the Friars Minor any more than it could be buried under tons of stone and an iron grill. It soared up out of Assisi, across Italy, across Europe and beyond, sailing with Columbus and the other explorers to the new world. In 1610 the first seat of government in what is now the United States was established in present-day New Mexico by a Spanish expedition from Mexico. They named it *La Villa Real de la Santa Fe de San Francisco de Asís.* The Royal City of the Holy Faith of Saint Francis of Assisi, known today as Santa Fe. In 1769 a Spanish ship sailing from San Diego northward up the Pacific coast came upon an ideal spot for a settlement and named it after Francis's little chapel at Portiuncula, *Nuestra Señora La Reina dellos Angeles de Portiuncúla,* Our Lady the Queen of the Angels of Portiuncula, known today simply as Los Angeles. The same Spanish ship, San Carlos, continued sailing northward up the coast, where they discovered a wonderful bay they named *San Francisco.*

Before we conclude, one final word about the Poor Knights Templar, whom Francis so admired. In 1311, the Council of Vienna responding to enormous pressure from King Philip IV of France, condemned the knights as heretics and guilty of homosexuality. Philip swayed the bishops to condemn them as heretics in order to seize the Knights Templar's enormous wealth—a paradoxical twist of fate for the poor monk knights.

*S*o, friends, while it seems we've finally come to the end of this play, we really haven't, for Francis of Assisi was no saintly shooting star briefly flashing across the stage of the thirteenth century. Rather, he was a polar guiding star for a lay mysticism for past ages and for ages to come. Francis and Clare are twin seeds of a passionate spirituality that were planted in the soil of Umbria seven centuries ago but may only now be breaking through the soil of society to bloom in their full radiance. Francis is not simply the patron saint of birdbaths and the blessing of pets, and certainly not just a saint of the Middle Ages. He is a mystical prophet for our day, pointing out to all who dare to imitate him a way to fulfill the first and great commandment with great passion.

EDWARD HAYS is the author of many best-selling books on contemporary spirituality, including *Prayers for the Domestic Church, Secular Sanctity, The Old Hermit's Almanac, Pray Always, Psalms for Zero Gravity,* and *Prayers for a Planetary Pilgrim.* His artwork graces the covers of many of his books and is also featured in a line of liturgical prints, posters, and cards.

A Catholic priest in the Archdiocese of Kansas City, Kansas, since 1958, Hays has also served as director of Shantivanam, a contemplative center in the Midwest, and as a chaplain at the Kansas State Penitentiary in Lansing. He spent an extended period on pilgrimage to the Near East, the Holy Land, and India. Today, Hays is retired from the active ministry but continues to write and paint in Leavenworth, Kansas.

More from Edward Hays...

SAINT FRANCIS—
THE PASSIONATE TROUBADOUR

Signed Edition Print:
(accompanied by a certificate of authenticity)
400 of both size prints,
pencil signed and numbered by Edward Hays
Full size: 16"x 20" $50.00 / P501
Household size: 10" x 13" $35.00 / P503

Unsigned Edition Print:
Full size: 16"x 20" $24.00 / P502
Household size: 10"x 13" $16.00 / P504

Greeting Card:
5 cards and envelopes for $5.00 / SF501

Prayer Cards:
pack of 25 for $4.50 / HC501
Prayer Card back side text: an adaptation of
Greeting Card text

PRAYERS FOR THE DOMESTIC CHURCH
ISBN: 0-939516-11-X / 215 pages / $16.95

This visionary prayer book will help you reclaim the
ancient and Christian heritage of making your home a
Domestic Church, a center for recognizing and celebrating God's presence in your family. A gallery of more
than 120 original blessings and ritual prayers for a full
range of family and personal life, for holidays, holy days,
meals, and daily personal prayer. leatherette cover

PRAYERS FOR A PLANETARY PILGRIM
ISBN: 0-939516-10-1 / 292 pages / $16.95

Freshly creative morning and evening prayers for each of
the four seasons, as well as rituals and contemporary
psalms for sacred seasons, seasons of personal change
(aging, work, divorce, women's changes...), psalms of
solidarity and social justice, and a wide variety of occasions. Part II is a comprehensive handbook of instruction and exercises for the pilgrim path of prayer.
leatherette cover